"Caleb Crain has written a novel of surpassing intelligence and unexpected beauty about a young American's year in ⸻Commu⸻ nd about how we find, and construct the story ⸻ His ⸻ nent is to make the unfolding of Jacob Putnam ⸻ resonate with the unfolding of Czechs' new historical freedoms, so these separate arcs seem of a piece. His precision of description, whether of architecture or emotional weather, is enviable; his dialogue both playful and profound. It is rare to read a book of this length and feel that every sentence mattered, rarer still to finish a novel of such intellectual depth and be so moved."

—Amy Waldman, author of *The Submission*

"Youth and innocence—remember them? Caleb Crain's *Necessary Errors* stabs the heart with the story of Jacob Putnam's sentimental education in Prague, and reminds us that to be young is to live abroad in a fallen empire where the talk goes on all night, the dumplings are sliced thick, and blue jeans are rare and too expensive. Pick this novel up and you won't forget it."

—Benjamin Anastas, author of *Too Good to Be True*

"As someone who is often unduly nostalgic about having been in her twenties during the 1990s (though not for as good a reason as having been in Prague during the aftermath of the Velvet Revolution), this novel triggered something like a sense memory. Caleb Crain is remarkable at capturing that time in life when ambition and longing are at once all-consuming and all over the map. I winced in self-recognition more than once—and marveled at the author's insights more often than that."

—Meghan Daum, author of *Life Would Be Perfect If I Lived in That House*

"Caleb Crain describes a young man's and a country's first tastes of freedom with a lucid and matter-of-fact intelligence. *Necessary Errors* offers an invaluable record of Prague at the beginning of the 1990s in a style that places it among the great novels of Americans abroad. It's *The Ambassadors* for the generation that came of age with the downfall of the Soviet Union."

—Marco Roth, author of *The Scientists*

"I don't know that I've ever read a novel that gets down, the way this one does, how it felt to be an American and a gay man at the end of the Cold War—so exiled from the country you grew up in that you go abroad to make a new world. Caleb Crain's *Necessary Errors* is an adventure of the head and heart. His hero, Jacob, turns to the cafés, bedrooms, and libraries of newly free Eastern Europe, an American in search of a European bildungsroman, in search of love and possibility both."

—Alexander Chee, author of *Edinburgh*

Necessary Errors

a novel

CALEB CRAIN

PENGUIN BOOKS

PENGUIN BOOKS
Published by the Penguin Group
Penguin Group (USA) Inc., 375 Hudson Street,
New York, New York 10014, USA

USA | Canada | UK | Ireland | Australia | New Zealand | India | South Africa | China
Penguin Books Ltd, Registered Offices: 80 Strand, London WC2R 0RL, England
For more information about the Penguin Group visit penguin.com

First published in Penguin Books 2013

The author thanks Elaine Blair, Jonathan Bolton, Leo Carey, Benjamin Kunkel, Lorin Stein, and
Peter Terzian for their insights into an early draft. He thanks Sarah Chalfant and Jacqueline Ko
at the Wylie Agency and Allison Lorentzen, Patrick Nolan, Lindsay Prevette, and the rest of the
team at Penguin for shepherding the book into print.

Library of Congress Cataloging-in-Publication Data

Crain, Caleb.
    Necessary errors : a novel / Caleb Crain.
      pages cm
    ISBN 978-0-14-312241-8
    I. Title.
    PS3603.R359N43 2013
    813'.6—dc23
    2013006551
                    FICC 9/13

Printed in the United States of America
10 9 8 7 6 5 4 3 2 1

Set in Adobe Garamond
Designed by Elke Sigal

PUBLISHER'S NOTE
This is a work of fiction. Names, characters, places, and incidents either are the product of the
author's imagination or are used fictitiously, and any resemblance to actual persons, living or
dead, businesses, companies, events, or locales is entirely coincidental.

To Peter

NECESSARY ERRORS

Staré Město

This epoch of unexpected happiness and drunkenness lasted only two short years; the madness was so excessive and so general that it would be impossible for me to give any idea of it, except by this historical and penetrating reflection: the people had been bored for a hundred years.

—Stendhal

It was October, and the leaves of the oaks around the language school had turned gold and were batting light into its tall windows. A young Irish woman was seated alone in the teacher's lounge. She had made herself a cup of tea on the range in the corner, and she was opening a tangerine on a paper napkin, with hungry carelessness.

One of the American teachers walked in. "Are you always the first one here?" he asked.

"It's quite far, the trip from the Dům. I like to collect myself." Her hair was disorderly and thick, and had all the colors between blond and red that you might find on a peach. When she wasn't wearing her glasses, she didn't always meet a person's gaze.

The American sat down opposite her. He was younger than she was.

"Would you like some?" she asked doubtfully, offering the tangerine. "I wouldn't offer if poxy Thom and all of them were here, but seeing how it's only you . . ." She neatly turned off a cluster of three of the fruit's plump wedges and put them on the corner of the napkin closest to him.

"You eat it. You need the vitamins."

"My mother sent them to me," she continued. "You can't find tangerines in bloody Prague. But you'll spoil it if you don't take some now I've offered it to you specially."

He ate one of the wedges. "Thanks," he said. He took out his keys.

"I quite like having a cabinet with a key of my own, don't you?" she said. "I feel as if I'm an established person."

"It's very grown-up."

"Well, it may not be such a new experience for you." She had abruptly dropped the color from her voice. "As a Harv. No doubt you had *lockers* and such."

"I've never had a serious job before."

"Your man Rafe"—it was spelled *Ralph*, but *Rafe* was how everyone pronounced it, even though he was American—"your man Rafe started teaching here with us but then they asked him over the castle."

"What does he do there? No one will tell me."

"Don't you think it's peculiar that there are so many of you? Harvs, I mean. You're like rabbits or something. You're all Agency, aren't you. That's what they call it, you know."

"Agency?"

"Didn't you know? I imagine you're not one of them then, Jacob."

"How do *you* know what they call it?"

"From the telly."

She gathered the tangerine rind in her napkin, as if she were folding up a tiny picnic, and dropped it in the can beneath the sink. After she rinsed her hands, she sniffed the backs of her fingers quickly. "Are you coming to Mel and Rafe's on Saturday?" she asked.

"I don't think I was invited."

"Melinda's going to invite you this afternoon. She told me last night."

He hesitated. "I was thinking of going to a bar."

"Oh?"

"A gay bar," he added.

"Oh? I had no idea—not that you would care if I did. It's not the sort of thing a person would expect, to look at you."

He glanced at the door. "No one else knows."

"Oh, I'm good with secrets. A proper crypt." She watched him pinch the corners of the workbooks in front of him, to square the stack. "Shall we have a smoke on it?"

"Would you like a Marlboro?"

"Ehm, do you happen to have the light ones again today?" He flashed the pack. "Do you fancy Thom, then?" she asked, as they stood up.

"He seems awfully straight."

"He's such a New Lad. Too much of a lad for me. *I* don't fancy him, though he's a fine specimen, really."

"Are you telling lies about me again, Annie?" said Thom, coming into the lounge just as they were leaving it. He was a Scot with straight, tow hair and a Roman nose. "I heard the word 'lad,' used *disparagingly* I thought."

"Oh, bugger off," Annie answered out of habit. Then she added, "I mean . . ."

"Off for a smoke? Mind if I join you?"

The headmistress allowed them to smoke in what had been the shower, back in the First Republic, when the building had served as a day school for girls. There were square, cream-colored tiles on the walls and floor. Every few feet a pipe curved out of the wall, and then up and over, like an upside-down candleholder. Far above were windows, which someone kept surprisingly clean, and light came down from them as from a clerestory.

Thom hung his red jacket and his satchel on one of the hooks once intended for the girls' towels. Jacob offered his cigarettes. "Do you mind?" Thom asked as he took one. "It's a pleasant change from a Sparta."

"And are *you* going to come to Mel and Rafe's?" Annie asked.

"I think I will do, yes. Shall I see you there?"

She nodded as she inhaled. "You aren't going to be gallivanting about with loose Czech women."

"Not on Saturday night, no. And you, Jacob?"

"I'm supposed to meet a friend."

"You could meet your friend another night, Jacob," Annie interposed.

"Well, I'll see."

Later in the day, over a quick cigarette between classes, Annie told him that she hoped he was careful. "You know, poxy rubbers and all."

A dead pig was hanging, face down, beside the door to Jacob's apartment. Blood drained into a plastic bucket from the hollow where its guts had been taken out. One stream ran in a wet line down from the pig's fore chest and around its neck, where it met another falling through and out of its snout and mouth. The animal's skin was thick and pearly. Blue-and-white twine, tied around its hind trotters, suspended it from the balustrade at the top of the stairwell. The Stehlíks, who owned the building, lived up there; the pig must have come from their cottage in the country. Jacob pulled his eyes away and went inside.

He rented rooms that Mrs. Stehlík's parents had once lived in: a bath, a kitchen, and a bedroom. Sometimes Alžběta, the Stehlíks' grown daughter, who went by the name Běta, knocked and used the bath. The bedroom had been a living room until recently; in fact, Jacob slept on a couch, or rather, on three of its orange foam panels, which he laid end to end on the floor at night like dominoes, and covered with his zipped-open nylon sleeping bag in order to keep off the chill that sometimes rose through the floor. The furniture was plywood, painted white, and the curtains, like the couch, were orange. Along one of the bedroom walls ran a low, built-in sideboard, its shelves backed with speckled mirrors, where the Stehlíks must have displayed crystal and china while the grandparents were alive. Jacob kept a few books there: a guide to Prague, a Czech-French dictionary (all the city's bookstores had sold out of Czech-English ones), and Pléiades of Rousseau and Stendhal from the 1930s, which he had found while looking for the dictionary. There were too few books to obscure the mirror. On the floor at night he faced away from it so he wouldn't have to see himself not sleeping.

A window in the bedroom faced west onto a small lawn, a sidewalk, and a jagged concrete wall that protected the house from the noise and dirt of a highway. A window in the kitchen faced east onto a courtyard where Mrs. Stehlíková hung the laundry on Wednesdays and where Běta beat the family's rugs on weekends, stagily coughing, waving, and blinking to entertain herself. Someone had put a woven red tablecloth in the kitchen, to brighten the room, and Jacob was slowly ruining it with a candle that he lit at his dinners to cheer himself up. He hadn't thought to put down a plate to catch the wax until too late.

He had only himself for company. Sometimes he had the feeling, which one may have if one lives alone, that time had paused for him, though perhaps in this apartment only, as if, canoeing along Time, he had turned into a still inlet. The rooms were the same from day to day, uninterrupted. Was the feeling a safe or a dangerous one? He would turn on the hot water tap in the kitchen just to hear the soft boom as a large purple flower of gas ignited and then focused in the tall white metal heater near the ceiling. There was a similar heater in the bathroom, larger and even more ebullient in its ignitions. If he was at home when the sun set, he would sit on the floor in a corner of the bedroom, his back against the couch's front, eyes closed, a glass of water folded between his hands in his lap, and let the light warm his face and arms. He always got up just before the light was going to pass, so he would not have the feeling of its leaving him.

The sight of the pig had taken away his appetite, but there would be no food in the apartment unless he went to the stores before they closed, so he picked up his small backpack and headed out.

In the hallway, he met Běta, who was just returning from the stores, her mesh bag in hand.

—I go for food, he said in his simple Czech.

"You do not want . . . ," she began in English, and rolled her eyes toward the hanging cadaver. "How do you say?"

"Pork?" Jacob supplied. —Maybe later, he added in Czech. —But it's pretty.

—Pretty? She blinked and stepped back from it, her frizzy black hair aquiver. —It's large, she declared, —and dreadful.

"Who has to butcher it?" he asked in English, with a little sawing gesture, which she watched with horror.

—Mother and I. She smiled at him fixedly as if the injustice of it were the best part.

—That is dreadful, really.

She shrugged. "You want to help, perhaps?" she asked, in English again.

"Oh no, no. You'd better go ahead and start without me."

She echoed the sentence, to teach herself the phrase, then answered him: "Okay." In her voice he could hear her pride in knowing the American word.

In the shadow of the ugly sheltering wall it was cold, and Jacob was sorry he hadn't put on his sweatshirt under his raincoat. He didn't have his real winter clothes yet; his mother was going to mail them soon. Three houses down, a border collie ran to the fence as he approached and began to bark industriously. ZLÝ PES, read a little tin sign in black and white. Evil dog, was the literal translation. Jacob could see in the collie's eyes that if the fence hadn't been there it would have let him pass quietly. The fence was a kind of permission to bark, maybe even an obligation. As soon as Jacob stepped past the yard, the collie fell silent and trotted back to its doormat on the front steps, where it curled up to save its warmth.

None of the laws liberalizing commerce had yet gone into effect, so the stores were still run on the old system and bore their old, plain names: foodstuffs; meat; fruits and vegetables; frozen goods. As if to emphasize their plainness, the words appeared on the signs in lower-case. The stores were lodged in an L-shaped, two-story mall of rough cement. Jacob pushed through a delicate chrome turnstile to enter the largest one, which was on the ground floor. There were only three aisles, and most of the shelves were empty. In the back, however, there was a great mound of bottled beer, without any labels on the brown glass; only the metal caps told you the brand was Staropramen, which Jacob liked. It was absurdly cheap, but it was absurdly cheap in pubs and bars, too, so Jacob never bought any here. There were no spare shopping baskets, because it was the end of the day and the store was crowded, so Jacob cradled in the crook of his left arm the groceries he found: a rectangular paper sack of rice, a jar of half-pickled red cabbage, a brick of butter in foil, and milk in a clear plastic bag with blue stenciling. With tongs he put into a small white paper sack five *rohlíky*, Czech croissants, slightly pasty in flavor. They were straight, like swollen fingers, because at some point, under socialism, the traditional curve had been eliminated as frivolous. He approached a board where sour brown bread was stacked. He wanted a quarter loaf, which he risked picking up with a bare hand. Last, at an unplugged refrigerator cabinet against the wall, he picked up a white paper sack of eggs. The sack was the same kind as for *rohlíky*, but with six eggs already inside, the top neatly crimped shut. He balanced it on the bag of milk, reasoning that the milk might provide cushioning, like a waterbed.

The cashier wrote out his total on a scrap of paper as she pronounced it, because she knew he didn't understand numbers yet, and then fished the correct change out of his open palm. She sighed as she did it. He felt childish and trusting. There was no greed here, it sometimes seemed. There must be, of course, but sometimes it did seem that there wasn't. Upstairs, afterward, he bought some sausage to fry, and in the vegetables-and-fruits store across the street he found some onions and salad greens.

In his apartment he made himself a plate of scrambled eggs, two slices of sausage, and salad. He lit his candle and read a chapter of *La Chartreuse de Parme*. After night fell, he looked up to see that his reflection in the dark window looked like a Dutch painting: young man, candle, fork on empty plate, book. Of course it wasn't Dutch; there was no wife and no wealth. Only the illusion of time held in place. He stood up and drew the heavy orange curtains.

According to the pages on Eastern Europe that he had torn from a guide to gay life abroad purchased in Boston—burying the rest of the book at the bottom of a garbage bag full of food scraps soon after, so that no one would inadvertently come upon its advertisements for massage parlors and bath houses—there were two gay bars in Prague, and the one not described as "rough" was to be found in a street one block long near the foot of Wenceslas Square. After his last class on Friday, he made pancakes and ate them with a can of *borůvky*, which he had spotted in the window of a store near school, and which he thought were blueberries, since they looked and tasted like them. (They were bilberries, he discovered years later, when he had a better dictionary.) He showered, brushed the blue off his teeth, and slipped his Penguin *Typee*, a book he had brought with him from Boston intact, into the pocket of his raincoat. It was a long tram ride to the subway.

The tram was nearly empty. Most residents of the outlying neighborhood where he lived stayed home on a Friday night. He looked out the window idly. The tram ran through a manufacturing district, and for a mile or so there was nothing to see but low, gray, cement-covered walls and long sheets of corrugated metal, ineffectually undermined by weeds. Intermittently, a wall gave way to a fence, and then a gate, through whose iron bars one could see the tall front of a factory. STANDARDS AND QUALITY FOR EVERYONE EVERYWHERE, read a slogan over the door of one of the factories. Further on, the tram ran past a housing development—a group of dirty white concrete high-rises, called *paneláky*.

Since he was alone in the car, Jacob slid open a window. It was a warm night. A breeze touched him haphazardly, like someone unfolding a shirt near his bare skin. Then the breeze whipped him gently in the face; he shut his eyes. When he opened them again he took out his paperback but paused on his bookmark, a postcard from a man he had fallen in love with back in America, unhappily. He knew the words on it by heart, of course: Daniel wrote that he had taken a job at a men's magazine, which he described ironically, and foresaw that Jacob would soon have a tall, dark, Slavic lover. In a black-and-white photo on the other side, a shirtless model with a ponytail sneered angrily at the camera and seemed to be in motion toward it; the picture was blurry. Jacob had tried to convince himself he liked the image, because Daniel must have liked it, or must have thought Jacob would, or should, like it. In the time they had spent together, much of what Daniel had shared with him had taken the form of lessons. Jacob had been a poor pupil. Politics had made a path of resistance obvious. Just as he hadn't believed Daniel's claim that Thatcher and Reagan had brought freedom to the West as well as the East, he had declined to believe his theories of love, though he had been made to feel their power in his own case.

And now he didn't believe this postcard. Czech men were neither tall nor dark, for the most part, and the name that Daniel had imagined for Jacob's future lover was a Russian-sounding one, which a Czech man his age, born during the Prague Spring, would be unlikely to bear. He had traveled a long way in order to know more about something than Daniel did, Jacob observed of himself, mock-tragically. He tucked the card into a later chapter and tried to read a few pages of Melville.

At Můstek, the city's central subway station, which already, after just a month and a half, he knew well, he alighted, and the round dimples in the brass wall panels, which arched up in parallel rows like the recessed squares in the ceiling of Hadrian's Pantheon, seemed to focus on him. He rose to the street level on an escalator that debouched beside a small pastry shop, now dark, curtains drawn in each of its four glass sides. He felt the sense of difference, the uneasy alertness, that comes over a person on the hunt. He would not be able to explain himself if Melinda, Thom, or Rafe were to see him now. Or even Annie. He felt painfully aware of the few people who glanced at him, as if a part of him was trying to keep a record of their faces, in case he had to answer to them later.

He found the street easily. The far end—it was no more than an alley, really—was boarded shut, and only the windows of one pub were lit, so once he had read this pub's name off its windows and passed by it, he could have no pretext for walking here other than his real one. Therefore he had to keep walking; he had to turn out of the street when, having doubled back, he reached the end of it; he didn't stop until he came to Národní třída, a broad avenue a few minutes away.

There he rested his eyes on the books in a publisher's display window and tried to think. He hadn't seen any sign of the gay bar he was looking for, which was called T-Club. If you were to visit the street today, you wouldn't find any sign of it, either; an establishment with the same name has opened in another part of town, but the particular club that Jacob was in search of that night has long since vanished, and the boards at the end of the block have been removed, to reveal a gated pocket park, with wrought iron benches, banks of flowers, and a long rectangle of water where children float toy ships with paper sails. Of course Jacob didn't know at the time what the boards hid; he wondered if the bar that he wanted lay behind them, shuttered. He had to try again. The guide had given a street number. He would walk to that number and look slowly and carefully. He promised himself to look longer than felt comfortable.

When he retraced his steps, he found, to his surprise, that the street number corresponded to the pub with the well-lit windows. As he stood before it, awkwardly, he could see men drinking, talking, and smoking inside, a few in blue work suits, most in street clothes. They were middle-aged, for the most part, many of them bearded. They had none of the self-watchfulness that Jacob associated with homosexuality. The name painted on the window was wrong, but perhaps the name had changed. Perhaps gay life in Prague was going to be different than he expected—more ordinary—plain, even. He stepped up onto the threshold.

No one turned, but the bartender shot him a look of dismay. Jacob saw his mistake. He was not in a gay place; Daniel had taught him that much about the gay world. He was in a straight place near a gay place, and partly out of courtesy, partly as a defense, the men here, he realized, kept up a pretense of blindness, which the bartender was afraid Jacob would break by asking a foolish question; with his look he was warning Jacob not to. It was no different here, Jacob decided. It was like home.

He stepped backward silently into the street, and saw, as he did, his vision sharpened by fear and anger, a flight of stairs overlooked before. They led down and to the left. No sign indicated that they led to T-Club, but Jacob followed them anyway, underground.

At the bottom of the stairs was a floor-to-ceiling metal grille, painted black, into which a yellowish artificial vine had been artlessly wound. On the other side of the grille, leaning against the counter of a coat-check closet, was an attendant, a short, powerfully built man in his fifties, with a white pompadour and deeply lined, cigarette-gray skin, dressed, rather formally, in a fine white shirt and black slacks. He nodded when Jacob said good evening. Beyond him, around a corner, which obscured it, was the bar. Jacob could hear the tinny sound of European disco played on small speakers.

Since the attendant did not offer to open the grille, Jacob tugged at it. It seemed to be locked. There was no knob to turn. —Please, Jacob said in Czech, tracing a small circle in the air with an index finger, to signify unlocking.

"Místo není." The man shook his head. There isn't room. "Keine raum," the man added, in German, pronouncing the words as if he were addressing a child. He tapped a paper sign taped to the grille, on which was written a word Jacob did not know, no doubt an advisement that the bar was full.

—Later? Jacob asked in Czech.

For an answer, the man tilted his head back slightly and then looked away. The tilt might have been a variation on a shrug, an indication that the attendant didn't know the answer to Jacob's question, but his manner was so heavy with scorn that the gesture might equally have been a comment on the kind and number of questions it was his lot to endure. Jacob held both possibilities in mind and continued to study the man. He knew no other way to make sense of signals he didn't understand. He knew as yet only a few words of the language, and he had to make sense of such signals often, keeping, as a conversation progressed, a larger and larger hand of possibilities, like a player losing at a card game, until at last he was given a hint—drew a card that decided possibilities—and found himself free to set a number of them down.

A couple of men in their thirties pattered quietly down the stairs. They greeted the attendant, just as quietly, and he unlocked the grille with a large, old-fashioned key, admitted them, and, before Jacob had understood what was happening, locked the grille again behind them. There was no small talk as he checked their coats; they weren't, in other words, the attendant's friends.

It was a puzzle. Perhaps the attendant thought Jacob was too young for a gay bar and was protecting him. Or perhaps he thought Jacob, as a foreigner, might have come to the wrong place. Of course the sight of the two men just admitted, whose aspect was not ambiguous, would have cleared up Jacob's misapprehensions, if he had been suffering from any. —Please, Jacob said in Czech, approaching the grille again, and gesturing along the path the men had just taken. —There's room now?

The attendant answered rapidly and angrily, flicking a hand after the two men, as in dismissal. Jacob didn't understand, and he expected that the man would yell at him in German if he asked him to repeat himself. He watched the attendant walk away, to the far end of the short corridor that was his province, and light a cigarette.

He couldn't tell whether pressing his case had bettered or worsened it, but the attendant didn't seem to object to his continuing to wait, so he took out his paperback. His eyes passed hollowly over the words.

At last there were shoes on the stairs again—louder this time, a clatter—and three young Czechs rushed down. The tallest, who had a comically long face and thin, sandy curls, seemed to be telling his companions a joke, which he himself laughed loudest at. "Dobrý večer," he saluted the attendant. There was something arch about the formality with which he spoke the greeting, and Jacob felt at once that he liked the young man. He drifted away from the wall he'd been leaning against, with the intention of slipping in behind the trio as soon as the attendant opened the grille. "Ahoj," the tall, curly-haired man said to Jacob out of the corner of his mouth—now his voice was feline, and the greeting, sounding very much like the sailor's hello in English, was a familiar one—to intimate that he had noticed Jacob's approach.

The attendant had noticed it, too, and because Jacob didn't want to take advantage of the young men's entrée unless he was sure of their permission, and because he was put momentarily at a loss by the touch of proposal in the young man's voice, he hesitated, and the attendant slammed the grille in his face with a clang.

"Hey," Jacob said in English, startled into his own language.

"Are you American?" the tall young man asked through the grille. He had heavy-lidded, drowsy-looking eyes, but the rest of him seemed to be constantly in motion—turning, stretching, adjusting.

"Yes."

"Come and talk to us," he offered.

"I'd like to," Jacob answered. It seemed superfluous to say that he wasn't certain of getting in.

The three young men checked their coats, the tall one spinning, as they did, a long commentary that seemed to touch on every detail of the transaction, even down to the numbers on their claim checks (Jacob did know the general sound of numbers; he just couldn't tell them apart yet), which must have been funny or lucky, because the other men laughed when the tall one called the numbers out, but Jacob could detect nothing in the way of an appeal to the attendant on his behalf, and soon the three turned the corner, out of sight, the tall one acknowledging Jacob's predicament by no more than a wistful half wave, his hand at waist level behind him.

Jacob paced back and forth, then looked up the stairs that led to the street, deliberating. Unexpectedly, at this moment, the attendant whistled at him, as if he were a horse or a dog, unlocked the grille, and said, in English, "Please."

He quickly stepped inside. The attendant extended his hand for his coat, smiling with a perfect falsity, and Jacob surrendered it. Sometimes Jacob had a hateful capacity to go along. He paid the two crowns and took his claim check. The attendant had no shyness about meeting his gaze. Jacob wondered what he would have to do later on, to get his coat back.

The interior reminded Jacob of a small boxing hall that he had once visited in Somerville. In the center was a square for dancing, tiled in a much-scuffed black linoleum, heavier than that covering the rest of the floor, and set off by four thin, white-painted, steel-and-concrete columns, which looked alarmingly functional, as if they held up the basement's roof. Plastic tables and chairs cluttered the immediate periphery of the dancing area; farther out, on each side, the floor was raised a foot, as if to ensure a view of the dancers, in arcades palisaded by still more steel-and-concrete columns. In the far corner of the right-hand arcade was the DJ's table. The microphone was so heavily amplified that the DJ's voice, which the DJ seemed to want to pass off as a bass, extinguished the music when he spoke. The Czechs in the room laughed at some of his patter, but the amplification blurred his consonants and Jacob had no idea what he was saying. The bar proper was tended by a young man about thirty with a pink face, large glasses with lenses too smudged to show his eyes, receding flaxen hair, and a black polyester tie. He sold

Jacob a beer with wordless courtesy. The price was no higher than in any downtown bar—just a couple of crowns more than in a neighborhood pub. In this detail, at least, socialism was still intact.

The tall young Czech who had spoken to Jacob outside the grille was sitting at a table near the dancing area, holding forth to his two friends and a few others. He eyed Jacob from time to time as he spoke, without beckoning to him. After a few sips, Jacob threaded his way toward him through the crowd, which gently, unanxiously parted for him, at light touches, in the way of gay crowds around the world. As Jacob approached, he noticed that the young man was wearing a short-sleeved polo shirt in a knit cotton finer than any you could purchase on this side of the fallen Iron Curtain, somewhat nicer, in fact, than the paisley shirt he himself was wearing. It surprised him that he had already learned to make such distinctions.

"Hello, sir," the Czech said in schoolbook English, which, his smile suggested, he knew to be overpolite. Outside, Jacob had judged him to be his own age, but now he saw that he was a few years younger, nervous, about nineteen. "Please take a seat."

"Thank you."

"I am Ota. Is short for Otakar. 'Short for' is right?"

"Yes," Jacob assured him. "I'm Jacob."

"Ah, 'Jacob.'" To Jacob's embarrassment, he repeated the name slowly, holding on to the English pronunciation, and then, on a further repetition, exaggerating it, as if to teach himself not to substitute for it the Czech form of the name, which sounded like "*Yah*-koop." The boys on either side, who looked the same age as Ota, followed the interaction with shining eyes.

"The man at the door," Jacob began.

"Ivan," a boy in a blue cap supplied. So more than one of them spoke English.

"Ivan? Ivan. Why didn't he want to let me in?"

The question made Ota merry, and when he translated it for his friends, they laughed too. "But you are from capitalist country," Ota said. "Surely you understand."

"Was I supposed to pay him?"

"No, no, do not pay him," Ota said darkly. He brought his drink, a liqueur on ice, to his face, and his large, deft hand held it there for a moment as one finger slid the red plastic stirrer away from his eyes so that he could safely sip. "Is not in gay bar in America?"

"No," Jacob said. "At least I don't think so."

Ota shifted in his chair and trilled out a quick aside to his friends, who again laughed. "Tell me, Jacob, are you gay?"

"All right, smart ass."

"Smart ass," Ota echoed, and then, leaning over to the boy in the blue cap and nodding at him in order to solicit his confirmation, translated the words individually: "Inteligentní prdel."

"But why did he keep me out? Does he not like Americans?"

"Well, he likes Germans," Ota answered, before translating the exchange for his friends, who appreciated it. Jacob glanced around and saw that there were indeed several men who looked German or Scandinavian in the room, in suits with their ties loosened, and that he seemed to be the only American.

"Is Ivan gay?"

"Definitely not. Horror, Jacob, horror."

"Well, it seems wrong," Jacob concluded.

Ota laid two fingers on Jacob's forearm and made a moue as he summoned up the English for what he wanted to say. "In Czech, the name short for Jakub is Kuba."

"Cuba?" Jacob interrupted.

"Yes," Ota nodded, "and you are truly Kuba, because you are pretty, New Worldly, warm, and still Communist." As he finished his speech he drew back abruptly, as if he had lit a small firecracker, and when he translated it for his friends, or rather, when he gave them the witticism in the original, for it was clearly the English version that was the translation, they obliged him by laughing. Although Jacob knew he had been flirted with, he couldn't find the part of the joke that was at his expense—the part that made it funny—other than, obscurely, the implication that in his resentment of Ivan there was a resistance to political change.

"I don't understand. Why am I warm?"

"*Teplý*; warm," Ota glossed. "Like T-Club."

Jacob shook his head.

"T for *teplý*. Maybe I have wrong word. Not hot, not cold," he explained, wavering a hand in midair.

"Yes, that's warm."

"In Czech, warm is gay. Not in English?"

"No," Jacob answered. "I thought T-Club had to do with tea, as in *čaj*."

"Pro-o-o-oč?" Ota purred, at the prospect of a piece of Western gay lore he did not yet know. "Why? Is tea gay in America?"

"Kind of."

"You must explain. I know, that it is hard work, translation, but is rewarding."

For the next hour Ota bantered with Jacob, sometimes in Czech but mostly in English, which he continuously interpreted for his audience, shifting as continuously in his chair, so that each comment flew into the face of one of the boys, each comment to a different boy in an unpredictable sequence, fixing them with his attention and binding them together, through him, in a radiant pattern. As he shifted, too, he seemed to take glances at Jacob from every conceivable angle.

The youngest Czechs in the bar, including the ones Jacob was sitting with, chattered freely, but among the rest, conversation was rare, and they stood apart from one another. Jacob wondered how acquaintances happened among these men, if they ever did, or whether they all knew one another already. Perhaps a shift of attitude had come with the Velvet Revolution, and the grown men were not yet accustomed to it.

"Do you think it's easier to be gay here since last year?" Jacob asked.

"Since last year?"

"Since November."

"Ah. We hope, that it is easier. Yes, it is easier. Everything is easier." Ota seemed to gain momentum as he answered. "But, you know, this is state socialist bar. State socialist gay bar." He seemed anxious to be just to the old regime. He did not translate what he said into Czech, however, and his hold on his audience momentarily slackened.

"I'm going for a walk," Jacob said, rising.

"A walk?" Ota repeated.

"A tour," Jacob explained.

"Ah. 'As you like it.'" He waved Jacob up and out of his chair, graciously.

From the bar, where he bought another beer from the polite, silent bartender, Jacob surveyed the crowd. There was only one really handsome man in the room. He was standing behind Jacob and to his left, near the door. Tall and fine-featured, the man looked a few years older than Jacob—twenty-six or twenty-seven, like Daniel. His smile seemed measured, and his eyes pensive, as if he weren't entirely at ease. A courtier whom the republicans had forgotten to purge, and who was thinking through his next few steps. When he caught Jacob looking at him, he looked quickly away, but a delicate amusement slowly surfaced in his face, as if despite himself, and for a moment Jacob thought he saw in his eyes a wish for Jacob to approach him—in this climate Jacob figured he had an almost exotic appeal, and he meant to take advantage of it—before a subtle flutter passed over the man's features, like the blades of an iris swiveling shut inside a camera's lens, and whatever it was that Jacob had seen was gone, or at least obscured.

Pretending to want a better view of the dance floor, Jacob walked to an empty spot just past the man and stood there for a minute, taking nervous gulps of his beer. The man's shoes were Czech, with thin, flat soles and a rubbery leather whose dye seemed to have worn off at the toes, but he wore a Western-made sweater, cream-colored, with a neat steel zipper.

"Ahoj," Jacob said, nodding.

The man nodded back.

—Are you Czech? Jacob asked, stupidly but in Czech.

—Yes, the man said. —And you, you're not Czech? He enunciated with a gentle precision.

—No, Jacob admitted.

The man play-acted surprise, and Jacob play-acted a bashful pride at having seemed so convincingly Czech as to have necessitated an explicit denial. They introduced themselves; the man's name was Luboš.

—Why are you here? Luboš asked.

—I'm teaching English.

Luboš asked a further question, which Jacob couldn't understand. Seeing Jacob's difficulty, he repeated it, first in fluent German, which Jacob understood no better, and then in halting French.

—You speak French? Jacob asked in that language, with alacrity.

The question seemed to alarm Luboš, who leaned over and whispered his answer—"Je déteste le français"—in an accent so faulty that Jacob thought at first that he had said that he hated the French people, not their tongue.

English was no use, either, because Luboš knew only a few words, but in each of the failed attempts there had been a clue, and by now Jacob had pieced together the man's objection: Jacob could teach English anywhere, and his answer had therefore failed to explain why he had chosen Czechoslovakia.

Jacob held up an index finger while he sorted through the Czech words he knew. —I want to write, he answered at last. It wasn't what he would have said in English, but it was something he knew how to say.

—Like Havel.

—Yes, Jacob said. In English he would have said "I guess" or "Sure," but he didn't know how to in Czech.

—And that's why you're here. To write plays and to be president.

—Novels, Jacob specified.

—Ah, novels, the man said. His smile faded into a look of mild concern, as if he had just remembered something, and his eyes drifted to a plane beyond Jacob, who nervously checked over his shoulder for a rival, and felt ashamed of himself for doing so. He was afraid he must seem young to the man, that the man was indulging him, as Daniel had, and that he would therefore, like Daniel, turn inconsequently away when he was ready to find pleasure for himself.

—You're very handsome, Jacob said, somewhat desperately.

The compliment brought the man's eyes back into focus. —And what do you do in America? Are you a student?

—No, I work.

—Do you write?

—No, I work in an office. And you?

For a moment it seemed the man was not going to answer. —I work for my friend, he said at last, quietly, and with a small nod of his head indicated a man standing behind him.

In most of the men in a gay bar there is a greater responsiveness than is usual in the world outside, and though most of them make it a piece of strategy to restrain their response, and though the elements composing it are more often subtle than not—a shift of weight, an extra blink of the eyes, an effort not to look at something that naturally draws attention—its presence is palpable; the room vibrates with it. It was therefore exceptional that the man indicated by Luboš gave no sign that he was aware that Jacob and Luboš were discussing him. Jacob did not at first appreciate this absence fully; he merely took it as an opportunity to study the man, angular but otherwise nondescript, clean-shaven, about fifty. He was not Czech. Many of the Czechs in the bar wore one or two items of Western clothing, and though the items were, in themselves, cheap, at least to an American eye, in context they nonetheless served as badges of something higher, a wish for color or fineness. This man, however, was dressed entirely in such items, and so there was nothing for them to contrast with, and they appeared merely to be what they were, shoddy clothes, without a brand, loosely sewn together from fabric that wouldn't have seemed out of place on office furniture. You couldn't find such clothes in a mall; you could only buy them on a certain kind of city street, where stores go regularly in and out of business.

The man's presence in the room was like a spot cut out of a map.

—Who is he? Jacob asked.

"Businessman," said Luboš quietly, in English. Jacob wanted to take Luboš away, immediately. He didn't want to see the man, any more than the man wanted to be seen, because he compromised the picture that Jacob was composing, even if he was no more than an employer. —He's French, Luboš added, speaking in Czech again.

Jacob had finished his beer, but he pretended there were still a few drops left and raised his bottle again. For some reason neither he nor Luboš seemed to be able to say anything further. As Jacob watched, Luboš's face relaxed into a fine indifference, as if he were already wishing Jacob farewell. Jacob studied hungrily the features that went into this diplomatic attitude, but he could not think of a way to open them again.

"Dance?" Jacob asked in English.

—I can't, Luboš answered. —I must stay here, because my friend does not speak Czech.

This sounded final, at least for the evening. —Do you have a telephone?

—No.

—I am staying with a family, and they have a telephone, Jacob volunteered. He took the number out of his wallet and copied it over on a slip of paper borrowed from the bartender.

—I will call, Luboš said. Jacob had no idea whether he would.

"You are leaving," Ota inferred, when Jacob appeared at his table. "And now you know Luboš. Is problem."

"Is the problem Luboš or my meeting him?"

Ota smiled, showing his teeth. "No, no. Forget it. It is good to meet you." He held Jacob's hand in both of his when they shook. "I will see you here again."

The attendant, Ivan, surrendered Jacob's raincoat easily. At the top of the stairs, the street looked almost exactly as it had when Jacob had arrived. It was slightly darker; the pub that he had mistaken for T-Club was now closed. It was as if the aboveground world didn't believe in the one he had just been visiting. He walked around the corner to wait for a night tram.

It was with the feeling of having swum several lengths of a pool underwater and at last emerged into air that Jacob knocked at Mel and Rafe's apartment the next evening. "Jacob, darling, welcome," Melinda greeted him at the door. She was wearing a black velvet gown, which showed her off—an English beauty with black hair, slender features, bad posture, and a classic complexion, three drops of red wine in a glass of whole milk. "Are we shaking hands, then?" she continued, and kissed him.

"I'm underdressed."

"Oh no, darling. My mother posted this off to me, on account of the revolution, she said, and I don't foresee any occasions more formal, so I thought I should improve the opportunity. It was *her* mother's, as it happens."

"It's gorgeous."

"This is my favorite part of it," interjected Rafe, advancing, and he traced the V of the dress as it exposed the pale, spine-dimpled skin of her back, lightly brushed by the loose tresses of her hair.

Rafe had a boyish face, which he disguised with boxy glasses and flyaway hair. "You and Annie are the first ones here." He beckoned Jacob into the small, yellow apartment. "I'm amazed we don't have Kaspar yet. He usually shows up at three in the afternoon when he knows something's on." Kaspar was an East German dissident, or had been until recently, when those categories collapsed. Mel and Rafe seemed sometimes to have adopted him, though he was a decade their senior. "To take a bath," Rafe explained. "We have a lovely bathtub. Have you seen it before?" The tub was at the end of their narrow kitchen, and Jacob discovered Annie sitting at a small table in front of it. They waved at each other; then Jacob leaned over and gave her a kiss, which seemed to give her a mild startle. "It's not very private," Rafe continued, "especially if this isn't your house."

"Kaspar is without any shame," Melinda said. "It's quite refreshing. I'll be keeping myself demurely in the other room, a novel in hand, and he'll call to me, while soaking, and demand that I brew him tea."

"Well, not *demand*," Rafe qualified.

"No, he doesn't demand, does he. Plead in his engaging, Kaspar-like way, would I mind, could I possibly allow myself to be troubled to make him some tea, which I must then do, of course, eyes schoolgirlishly averted."

"It's very sexy, her schoolgirl thing," Rafe said. "Staropramen, slivovitz, or some wine from Slovenia that happens to be quite good?"

"His informants put him on to it," Melinda explained.

"I'll try the wine," said Jacob. The kitchen's top shelf was devoted to empty bottles, no two alike, and their number was a kind of boast of well-being, of openness to experiment.

An empty cup and saucer were in front of Annie, and she was staring at them while Mel and Rafe were speaking. When Jacob sat down across from her and asked what she had been up to, she seemed to shake something out of her eyes, or to dust something off of herself, a mood perhaps. "I did the wash this morning. We have machines in the Dům, you know. It's quite convenient."

"My landlords let me use theirs, but I'm not sure they're happy about it. I think the mother and daughter keep it a secret from Mr. Stehlík."

She nodded in the way of a person not closely listening. "It's very considerately managed, the Dům. It's a great luxury for there to be a machine that one has an undisputed right to. I'm very slow about the wash, as a result. I savor it, really. I spend the whole morning."

"And that was your day."

"I felt a little melancholy, so I came by early, and Melinda had me on her hands instead of Kaspar. We had a good chat." She straightened herself in her chair and met Jacob's gaze.

"You don't have to say, if you don't want."

"Oh, it's quite tiresome, really," she said. She claimed that it wasn't worth going into. She had come to Prague looking for adventure, and she'd found a great deal of that, as much as she wanted, anyway. "But one would like a spot of romance as well. Did you find any, last night? Romance, I mean."

Had she forgotten it was a secret? "No, no, it was dull." He had in fact been looking forward to telling her about Luboš. He had hoped that she would be able to hear the pattern in what, at moments, seemed to him no more than an arbitrary sequence of facts.

"Were you on the prowl last night, Jacob?" Melinda asked. "Do tell."

"I went to check out a local pub," Jacob said. "Nothing to report, I'm afraid."

"Too bad!" Melinda exclaimed, shaking a small fist in a light mockery of frustration.

"Are you a free agent, Jacob, or did you leave someone behind in Massachusetts?" Rafe asked.

Jacob wondered why Rafe had said "someone" but saw no way of finding out. "No one who would have me," he answered.

"The best sort of freedom, then—vengeful."

"That's right. Fuck 'em," said Jacob, pretending to belong to the party of boys versus girls, and clinked his glass against Rafe's.

"Such fine sentiments," Annie observed.

"Come see my cimbalom," Rafe suggested, now in a parody of refinement, rising up on the balls of his feet and putting his fingertips together.

"Your what?"

Rafe led him into the living room, where, on top of a bureau, there lay a musical instrument. It resembled the insides of a piano, but smaller and with the metal strings crossing into each other from both sides, like the lacing of a shoe. The case was a finely tooled blond wood. Lying idly across the strings were two wool-wrapped mallets, looking like caterpillars on sticks. Rafe picked them up and tapped out a scale. From the pattern of the blows Jacob saw that one would have to memorize the tuning; it wasn't simple. The sound was gentler than a harp—softer at the onset of a tone—and because it lacked the machinery of keys, it was less regular and more personal than a piano.

"It's beautiful," Jacob said. "Where'd you get it?"

There was a buzz. "Oh, the door," Rafe excused himself.

Jacob took up the mallets and tried to pick out thirds, fifths, octaves. He didn't even have a radio in his apartment. Sometimes, at night, a tram that he was riding in would set up vibrations in its rails and wires as it scraped slowly around a curve, and he would leave off reading in order to listen. The sound in the tram's wires resembled that made by drawing a wet finger along the rim of a wine glass.

It was Kaspar who had arrived. He was a short, bearish man with soft chestnut hair and a disorganized beard, and he was wearing a drooping, broad-striped sweater at least a size too large. Between kissing Melinda and shaking Rafe's hand, he nodded at Jacob from across the room, as if to signal that he should stay where he was. After the silent communication, Jacob was shy about sounding the instrument.

"Are you able to play?" Kaspar asked, once he had made his way to Jacob.

"This is Jacob," Rafe put in.

"Oh yes, I know," said Kaspar. "The writer." His eyes were glossy with delight.

"I haven't really written anything yet."

Kaspar turned to Rafe. "You told me he had written a novel."

"It'll never be published, though," Jacob explained, before Rafe could answer.

"That is not what matters," Kaspar said. His eyes weren't aligned, Jacob saw; one of them wandered, though each seemed to be studying him from its distinct angle. "It is the spirit of what you are doing." He seemed on the verge of tears as he spoke, and Jacob sensed that Kaspar was offering an idea that had given him solace.

A Westerner hardly deserved the benefit of it. "I'm an American," Jacob protested. "There's no one I can blame for holding me back." He was reluctant to contradict the man any more sharply; he seemed so fragile.

"It is still the spirit that matters," Kaspar insisted.

"If I believed that, I might never actually do anything. I might never get around to being the person I thought I was."

A flicker of mischief came into the East German's eyes. "Yes, those are the conditions we lived under."

It was a bribe offered not from an intention to corrupt but from a wish to be pleasant to a new friend. The man's skin hung loosely at his wrists and under his cheekbones, Jacob saw, as if he had recently lost more weight than he could afford to. He was like a monk who, in a misplaced spirit of penance, was offering to sell short his and his brothers' labors. "Really, I don't have your excuse."

"Is it only an excuse?"

Rafe interrupted: "I feel obliged to warn you, Jacob, that Kaspar was anti-Communist only until the Berlin Wall was breached, and then switched sides."

Kaspar glanced at Rafe. "I sound so contrary, in your story of me," he said. "In reality I had no choice. So many horrible people were becoming anti-Communist that day. It was an opportunity for them. They were my—what is the word? In Czech they are called *korouhvičky*."

"Weathervanes," Rafe supplied.

"They were my weathervanes," Kaspar continued. "If they were willing to betray Communism, there was something in the idea after all."

"So he's not going to agree that it's harder to be a writer under Communism than capitalism," Jacob said, addressing Rafe.

"No, he's probably not," Rafe answered.

"I am not an optimist," Kaspar said, "except about spirit."

Jacob was embarrassed for Kaspar. The avowal reminded him of people he knew from school with high but vague ambitions, who after graduation had moved to bad neighborhoods and taken jobs supposedly beneath them, in order not to be reminded of the larger competition they hadn't wished to enter.

"Are you a writer?" Jacob asked politely.

"Ah, no, only a translator."

"And a smuggler, eh?" Rafe boasted on Kaspar's behalf. "Countless Czech manuscripts reached their German publishers through Kaspar."

"I worked in a hospital," Kaspar explained, "In such a place it is easier to judge whether a person may be trusted."

"What do you do now?" Jacob asked.

"Why, I teach with you in the language school."

"He teaches German," Rafe said.

Jacob noticed that he still had the cimbalom mallets in his hands. He addressed Rafe: "You were going to say where you got this."

"The director of the symphony asked me to take it home for a while," Rafe said.

"The symphony?" Jacob echoed, but Rafe drifted away to answer the door again.

Kaspar intercepted Jacob's look of puzzlement. "Rafe, for example, is a person often trusted."

The room was filling up. Thom had arrived with a fellow Scot named Michael and with Henry, a wiry Englishman with wide set eyes and curly hair, who had lived in Prague since before the change. Henry was responsible for bringing the Scots to Prague. He had met them while studying philosophy in Edinburgh, and after arriving in Prague he had sent back word of teaching opportunities. Jacob recognized several other teachers from the school as well, and Annie was emerging, with the tentative, cautious steps of a cat, from the kitchen where they had left her.

"Did Rafe help you with the smuggling?" Jacob asked.

"Oh no. He wasn't working here then."

Having fetched a beer, Thom came over. "Have you brought me a ham by any chance, Mr. Putnam?"

"I haven't seen the thing for a couple of days, actually."

"Jacob's landlords hung an entire pig beside his door," Thom explained to the group. "Trying to send him a message, we think."

"'Go home, Yank'?" Michael proposed. He was a big man who wore a black fisherman's cap to hide his thinning hair and was never serious.

"It's quite impressive," Thom said, "an entire pig, especially now, when there are no potatoes in the shops. I recommend you stay on good terms with your landlords."

"I thought it was just my local store that didn't have potatoes," Jacob said.

Henry explained: "The farmers are holding back anything that will keep until January, when the market prices take effect." Like Kaspar and Rafe, he spoke Czech fluently and learned such things easily.

"Is that so, professor," Thom said.

"But hops and barley fall under a different law," Henry continued, "so you needn't worry about your Staropramen."

"As if my supply of Staropramen were the limit of my interest in the

Czechoslovak economy. I thank you for that." He took a drink for punctuation.

"Drunken sod," Michael commented. All the Scots looked up to Henry, and they only allowed so much raillery of him.

"What's that?" Thom replied. "I thought I heard the sound of a pot addressing a kettle."

Thom offered around his Sparty, and Jacob took one because he was out of Marlboros. Annie, too, stepped up at the sight of the distribution. Her presence didn't disrupt the coarse, boyish back-and-forth; she highlighted it, rather, by objecting to the men's vulgarities with an imperfectly disguised pleasure and by saying, several times, that she expected no better from them. For his part Jacob loved the coarseness, because it meant they did not suspect him; he was one of them, so long as he, too, was insulted freely. He didn't want them to watch themselves around him; he wanted to belong.

Later, Jacob and Annie found a corner. "Your new friend seems very taken with you," she began.

"Who's that?" he asked, startled.

"Kaspar."

For a moment, he had thought that the details of his visit to T-Club had got out somehow. "Oh, Kaspar. Did you know he taught at the school?"

"Oh yes. He made a comment the other day to the headmistress about my accent. He doesn't even teach English, mind you. Said I was likely to mislead the students. And Thom's accent, as well."

"Oh dear."

"As if our ways of speaking were inferior. That they are different I don't deny. But some people would think it an advantage to the students to be exposed to them."

"He couldn't have meant it. He seems to have a thing for the underdog."

"If the underdog is a Harv with running hot water and a full larder. His beady little eyes lit up when Rafe said he knew you from university."

"We didn't actually know each other. We more or less have to take each other's word for it that we were both there."

"No, you published some poem in the school paper, and Rafe read it."

"Oh, god."

"It's quite sweet, really, that he remembers it." She took a moment to survey the party as it was taking place around them. "Mind you, I don't say I dislike Kaspar."

"You just said he had beady little eyes!"

"Did I? He's quite kind at times. When one's out of sorts."

The air was misty with cigarette smoke, now, and there was a pleasant din—all talk and laughter, because Mel and Rafe had no stereo. "I'm sorry you felt down," Jacob ventured.

"I daresay you haven't noticed, and why would you, really, but all the women from the West either brought a man with them or found one immediately they got here. It's different for the men, of course."

"That's such an impersonal way of looking at it."

"But I think I'm right. Not that I mind enormously, but I had to think it through. Now did you really meet no one last night? I don't want to hear if it's *too* sordid. Because I had a friend in Berlin . . ." She left the sentence unfinished.

On Wednesday, late in the afternoon, Běta knocked on Jacob's door. He had lain down for a nap after work and when he answered was not fully awake. "Shower?" he asked her, offering the use of it with a gesture.

"No, no," she shook her curls. "You have telephone. Upstairs. Come, come. Father is not home yet."

As she nervously glanced behind, as if afraid her father might suddenly appear, he followed her up into the Stehlíks' apartment, with its brown-and-green-patterned wallpaper and its red-and-gold-patterned carpets. Mrs. Stehlíková, in the kitchen, silently out-whistled a long drag on a cigarette when she saw him, then grinned and nodded, blinking like her daughter, in welcome. On the stove behind her were two simmering pots, a stew for her family, she explained, and an even larger one for their two dogs, who greeted Jacob by nosing at his crotch.

"Come, come," Běta beckoned. In the living room, she handed him the phone's persimmon-colored receiver and then retreated.

"Hello?" Jacob said into the phone, the base of which, brown with white keys, sat on a tea tray. He perched on the edge of an easy chair of fake green leather.

"Halló? Kubo?"

"Ota?" Jacob asked, though he hadn't given Ota his number.

—No, replied the speaker, in Czech. —Luboš here. Am I speaking with Jacob?

"Yes, sorry," Jacob answered, in English. "I didn't recognize your voice." He was upset with himself at the misstep. He had thought of Ota because it was Ota who had explained the nickname Kuba to him. Of course he had been hoping for Luboš.

—Please? asked Luboš, not having understood.

—Nothing, nothing, Jacob assured him hurriedly. It was much harder to communicate on the phone than in person, Jacob realized. There was an awkward pause. Jacob's eyes were caught by two African-style wooden masks on the opposite wall, one smiling, another frowning, like Tragedy and Comedy. He nervously pressed his fingers between adjacent revolutions of the phone cord's cool spiral.

—Want to meet? Luboš asked, speaking as simply as possible.

Yes, said Jacob. —When?

—Tomorrow, at eighteen hours. At Můstek.

—Underground?

—No. In the street. Under the clock, across from the Automat.

—Yes, Jacob said again, knowing the large, ugly clock that Luboš had in mind. It sat on the roof of a glass building at the foot of Wenceslas Square, where the word DISCO, in a sans-serif font, appeared in the windows of the top floor, one letter per pane.

He and Luboš fell silent again. Having succeeded in their negotiation, it was now a comfortable silence, maybe even a confident one. There was a thrill in arranging a date while in a room that spoke so much of family, even if the family wasn't his. On the near wall hung a medieval Slavic icon, or a replica of one, a madonna's face painted in oil and set in a costume and landscape of silver, like one of those old sideshow attractions where a cousin pokes her head through a hole in a signboard so that her face appears over the body of a circus strongman, or under the top hat of a lion tamer cracking a whip, another cousin's face figuring as the lion.

—I look forward, said Luboš.

—I, too. A great deal. The energy that ordinarily went into complicating or refining one's speech instead had to be devoted to simplifying it. It wasn't possible to mislead each other, Jacob decided, when it took so much effort merely to reach across the space between them.

Jacob left the Můstek subway station and walked up Wenceslas Square, away from where Luboš would be waiting, in order to buy a Western newsweekly he liked at one of the few stands that sold it. The sun had not gone down, but it could not be seen. So neutral was the twilight, in fact, that instead of fading from behind the leaden clouds above, it seemed to be settling out of the air one walked through, as if it were a kind of dust. It sharpened the outlines and details of the buildings but dissolved what little color they had into a uniform gray. Jacob couldn't have said why he was going out of his way. As he had traveled toward Můstek, his wish to buy the magazine had grown more and more urgent, until, upon arrival, he had had no choice, even though he was late and the detour would make him later. Only when he had it in hand did he feel armed. He waved it, rolled in a fist, at Luboš when he sighted him. Running across the granite bricks, he wondered if Luboš had seen him. There were so many eyes carved in Prague's façades, belonging to cary-atids, masks, reliefs of politicians, and the figures of ideals, that one was never free of the sense of being observed.

They greeted each other in Czech. Jacob searched Luboš's face for a sign of what would happen between them tonight, a hint of what footing they stood on. It was not a soft or a warm face, though it was not unkind. The suggestion in it of toughness excited Jacob. As he looked into the face, he saw by the change in its shading that the mild and even twilight was, even as he watched, at last lapsing, and leaving exposed, as a tide might leave rocks and shells, the sharp and fragmented lights cast by street lamps and shop signs. After they had stared at each other hesitat-ingly for a few moments, not touching, Luboš proposed that they walk down Národní třída to Café Slavia, which overlooked the Vltava, and Jacob agreed. They walked slowly and with uneven steps, not yet ad-justed to each other's gaits. They soon gave up on French and German. Luboš asked simple questions in Czech, and Jacob acted out words he didn't know, which Luboš supplied as soon as he could identify them. When Jacob turned the same questions back on Luboš, Luboš then drew on this fresh vocabulary, as in a card game where you may take from another player's discards. By this means, as they walked, Jacob made the commonplace revelations of a first date: that his parents had divorced when he was a child, that he had only come out a year and a half ago, that he did not have a boyfriend. For all the struggle required to communicate—though whether it was despite the struggle or because of it he could not have said—Jacob found that his own sense of his meanings burned clear and bright in his mind, unshadowed by the misstatements he threw off on his way to them. The misunderstandings were too numerous to stop for; they were only temporary. Luboš, however, was more cautious; when Jacob asked about his parents, for example, he answered only that he did have parents, he was fairly sure, and his smile stopped Jacob from asking more. He had always known he was gay.

Just before they reached the river, they stepped to the right through two sets of glass double doors into Slavia. It was crowded and indifferent to them, but Luboš found a welcome by sharing a word with the cashier in a low and confidential tone. He then led Jacob down the long L of the café, past a fragile-looking upright piano jammed into its elbow, to a table littered with previous visitors' plates and cups but otherwise abandoned. He had walked to it as if he had known it would be there. Through the wide windows that faced the embankment, they could see the violet, dying sky across the river, too weak now to cast any illumination. The café was lit by brass sconces of a timeless ugliness. The chairs were heavy and upholstered in a pinkish fabric. It was an ugliness that Jacob was beginning to recognize. There wasn't anything like it in the West. The taste of the 1970s had been here an elaboration of that of the 1950s rather than a rebellion against it—the gaudiness and shapelessness had been made somehow to serve propriety instead of challenging it. Yet the mood of the people in the room seemed to defy the decor, or at least ignore it.

—Your dissidents came here, Luboš said.

"Is it a gay place?" Jacob asked, in English. Too late he wondered if the question might seem disrespectful.

—No, Luboš answered. Jacob tried to take his hand, but he pulled away. —Not here, Kuba. Here is not yet America.

Jacob didn't take the refusal seriously, and after Luboš ordered a glass of white wine, and Jacob a Becherovka, a liqueur with a medicinal taste, like peppermint tea left to steep too long, he slid a foot forward under the table so that it lay just beside one of Luboš's. In Boston, Daniel had informed Jacob that muscles were the currency of gay life, and that one worked to have them in order to be attractive to the men one wanted because they had them. Jacob, not having them but wanting Daniel anyway, had thus been a kind of poor relation. In Prague, however, no one seemed to have muscles of the American kind, and Jacob foresaw for himself a field of romantic opportunity that Daniel's economics had priced out of his reach. He could see no reason for someone like Luboš, who liked him—Daniel, too, had liked him; that hadn't been the problem—to stickle and resist him. If there was any resistance, he was going to push until he found out the reason for it.

—Kuba, I called you three times, Luboš said.

—Three?

—Perhaps, boys are always calling you.

Jacob took his French-Czech dictionary from his jacket pocket and pointed out the word for message.

Luboš shook his head. —The man, with whom I spoke, wasn't so polite. He said, that it's not your phone.

Jacob wanted to say that the Stehlíks had assured him that he was free to use the phone whenever he wanted, but he couldn't figure out how to say it; his sentence broke down.

—Did you want to see me? Luboš asked. He seemed to be playing on Jacob's anxiety, which must have been evident in his face.

—Yes, yes. He wanted to say that he liked Luboš, but it required some concentration, because in the transition from English grammar to Czech, the subject and object of the sentence switched places: —You are pleasing to me.

The words sounded childlike.

—And French is not pleasing to you, Jacob continued, changing the subject to one suggested by his dictionary.

Luboš seemed to want to take this up but hesitated. Instead, more in pantomime than in words, he suggested they order a plate of *chlebíčky*, which Jacob knew to be small, stale slices of bread spread with lard and topped with diced vegetables and meats. It was already too late to find a table open at a proper restaurant, where, still governed by socialist principles, most waiters turned away guests who arrived after the first seating.

It seemed grand to Jacob that he was sitting in a café in Prague with his Czech lover, forgoing dinner for the sake of whatever it was that was between them. He could smoke a few cigarettes to kill his hunger, if the *chlebíčky* didn't accomplish that.

"Or we can buy *párky* later," Jacob said, in English, thinking out loud. A *párek* was a fat roasted pink sausage, sold on the streets at all hours.

—And *párky* are pleasing to you, Kuba?

Jacob was happy to play the straight man. —A great deal, he said.

Upon the arrival of the waiter, Luboš asked him only to refill their drinks.

Jacob had arrived in Prague with a project. He couldn't see that he was carrying it; to see that would have required standing a little farther outside himself than he was able to. He would have said it was a mood, if anyone had asked, or maybe a spirit, if he was writing in the privacy of his journal. But he wouldn't have understood that it took the shape of a story he wanted to live out. It was a common enough project for an earnest, idealistic young person who was comfortable with only one pleasure, reading, and who had graduated from college in the year of the protest in Tiananmen Square, the breaching of the Berlin Wall, and the Velvet Revolution, so that his first personal experience of adult freedom—which he knew didn't count for much in the grand scheme of things but which he felt with great intensity—seemed echoed by the wider world. Although he knew that he was hearing not echoes but emanations from distant sources, he wasn't above thinking they might have a special resonance for him—that he might be receptive to them in a way others couldn't be. He had a sense that everything in his life up to that point was prelude, which might safely be skipped by anyone who came late to the story, and the recent date of his discovery that he loved men strengthened this feeling; he thought that nothing finally attached him to the world that had formed him, and that this separation was what he had instead of a skill or a legacy; this was his special advantage. Without knowing it, he was looking for people who were heroic, so he could join them. It had to be without knowing it that he set out on this quest, because he did know that it was too late. Try as he might to acquire a memory of the revolution, he would find only souvenirs. He was on guard, paradoxically, against many of the same sentiments that drew him; nostalgia would be a kind of infidelity to the change whose essence he was trying to come close to. To break through the commemorative trinkets and partygoer's clichés, it was vital that he learn Czech, from a Czech lover if possible. Even if it was too late to take part in the great change that had happened here, he anxiously hoped that it might not be so far gone that it could not be, in subtle traces it had left behind, witnessed.

In the West, gays had woken up to politics later than other groups had, and it occurred to Jacob that he might not have arrived too late for the liberation of Eastern Europe's gay people. He hadn't settled in advance on the story he hoped to hear, but he did expect to recognize it if he came across it, and so when Luboš agreed to go home with him and began, during the tram ride, to tell a little more of his personal story, he listened with a certain partiality, an effort at recognition.

The effort was frustrated. Luboš's story seemed to have no politics at all. In fact he seemed to have failed in a few instances to appreciate the freedoms that history had dropped in his lap. Luboš told him, for example, that the French businessman, the one whom Jacob had studied in T-Club, had recently taken him to Alsace for a couple of months so he could learn French, in order to improve communication between the two of them. (They were business partners, it turned out; Jacob had been mistaken in thinking the Frenchman was Luboš's employer.) Luboš had hated the language classes and had stopped going to them. He had also taken his time about telling his partner that he had quit—had hidden in coffee shops, where he could read none of the newspapers, and in clothing stores, where he could afford none of the clothes, utterly bored—and they had had a vehement argument after the inevitable discovery, and Luboš had come back to Prague much sooner than planned. The two men had remained partners, however. Georges—his name was Georges Collin—did speak German, though with difficulty, and he wanted a foot in the Czech door very badly. It was not yet legal for a foreigner to run a business like Collin's in his own name, and he did not think he could afford to wait for the law to change. There were many small but crucial tasks, such as renting an office or installing a telephone, that a Czech could navigate more adeptly than a foreigner, and, as in every business, a web of local negotiations was necessary, for which Georges wanted a native whose judgment of character he felt he could trust.

It was only the language barrier, Jacob felt, that brought Luboš to the immodesty of declaring himself trustworthy and a good judge of character. He said it without boasting, with a trace of self-deprecation even, as if he were admitting that he wasn't clever. He had none of the loud manner that Jacob had found in the few gay businessmen he had met in America—which Jacob hadn't minded so much, because it had seemed to imply a permission to josh with them as if they were circus animals rather than wild ones. Instead he had a quiet competence, a kind of security in himself. He was like an adult explaining his work to a child. He seemed more fully grown up than anyone Jacob had ever met.

And yet for no apparent reason he had passed up a chance to learn French, and now, for the sake of a tumble, he was stepping out of the tram at the foot of Jacob's street.

The neighbor's collie did not bark at them; it was in for the night. As they walked, Jacob let the back of his hand brush the back of Luboš's, and the touch of warmth felt electric in the cold air. When he unlocked the gate to the yard, he nodded to Luboš to precede him, as if he were a gallant and Luboš a damsel, and that was as much of a sign as it seemed safe to give.

—But it is pretty here, Luboš said, once they were safely inside.

For a moment Jacob saw the rooms as a stranger might. His eye picked out as incongruous the few items genuinely his, as if they were the litter he was responsible for at a campground deep in a forest. It aroused him, for some reason, to be reminded that he lived this way. If he decided one afternoon never to come back he wouldn't lose much.

He opened the refrigerator, and they both took beers. They hadn't even kissed yet. They were like teenagers alone for the first time after an arranged marriage.

—Here you write your novels? Luboš asked, pointing at the kitchen table and seating himself at it.

"In there, actually," Jacob replied, in English, and pointed into the bedroom at a little round white table, which Luboš couldn't see from where he was sitting. Jacob pulled the table to the couch for a desk whenever he made an attempt. "But I haven't written anything since I got here."

Luboš nodded. —Kuba . . . , he began.

"Yes?" Jacob answered.

—Nothing, Luboš said.

"I'll light the candle," Jacob offered, and proceeded to, instead of trying to translate the suggestion.

—It's nice, Luboš said. —Kuba . . .

—Yes, Jacob answered, this time in Czech in case his talking in English had made Luboš diffident.

—No, nothing, Luboš said again.

—There is a problem? Jacob asked.

—Yes, Luboš said, looking away. —I have AIDS.

It took a few repetitions before Jacob was sure he had understood the word. He leaned over Luboš and embraced him—awkwardly, because Luboš didn't rise from his chair—then kneeled at the floor beside him and asked, in tears, how it had happened and how long he had known. Luboš, who had hardened a little at Jacob's tears, said the news was recent. He spoke with a slight smile.

It was strange and unlucky, Jacob thought. While the Iron Curtain had stood, it had kept the disease out of Eastern Europe almost entirely. There were still very few cases. Jacob wanted to punish himself for having thought that when he left America he would leave the disease behind, too, at least for a while, but he shouldn't tell the story as if it were about himself. It was awful for Luboš. This was in the days before the new therapies; almost no one lived more than ten years after a diagnosis. The only chance to live even that long was to have the best doctors, the ones with connections to researchers, and there wouldn't be any in Czechoslovakia. Luboš probably didn't even realize that the marketplace sorted fates in the illness, that it apportioned survival by taking a kind of measure of a patient's resourcefulness.

—And you don't? Luboš asked. —It is common in America, isn't it?

—No, I don't. It's not that common. Do your friends know? Jacob asked. —Your parents?

—No, no, Luboš answered. He waved a hand, as if to say that Jacob was making too much of a fuss.

—I'm sorry, Jacob said, apologizing for his state.

—Please, Luboš said. —But I thought everyone in America . . .

—I'm too young, Jacob explained. He held Luboš's hand and cried for a little while. This was as dangerous a world as the one he had left, and somehow he hadn't thought it would be. He accused himself, somewhat bitterly, of having come to Czechoslovakia to join in a victory lap he hadn't earned, and told himself that Luboš's Frenchman, who had no doubt given it to him, must have wanted something similar. —Your health now? Jacob asked.

—It's good. He looked at Jacob with concern. —Kuba . . .

—Yes?

Luboš made an effort to find words in English. "I not know words. In Czech, *kecám*. I make joke."

"I don't understand," Jacob said.

"*Srandu*. Fun. Not true."

"A joke? You don't have AIDS?"

"No. I'm sorry."

Was Luboš only pretending in order to calm him down? But Luboš repeated the disavowal and insisted that he had meant to play a joke and hadn't expected Jacob to have such a strong reaction.

—Truly? Jacob asked.

—Truly.

He felt an absurdly powerful relief. —I am happy, he said, and embraced Luboš again, a little less clumsily now, because, he realized, he no longer thought him fragile.

"But I don't want, tonight. Sleep only. You understand?"

Jacob nodded.

—You don't make such jokes in America? Luboš asked, uncertainly.

—No, Jacob answered. It occurred to him that he was entitled to feel angry, but he felt only puzzled. He drank quietly from his beer and cast his thoughts back, as one does when one has been fooled, to see whether in his excitement he had revealed more than he would have liked to.

"I'm sort of a weeper, aren't I," he said out loud in English, more to himself than to Luboš.

—Pardon?

"And you're sort of an asshole."

Luboš smiled. —You were very sad, he said. —It was good of you to be so sad.

Jacob saw that he had been expected to respond differently. When he and Luboš lay down for the night, they kissed quietly for a while, and in the end, because Jacob very much wanted to, they did make love, safely, as Jacob had learned to do in Boston, where the few men that he had gone to bed with had all followed the rules without prompting.

In the morning, he didn't want to look at Luboš. In those days, he often felt shy with the other person after spending the night, whether it was with a man or a woman. It was a reaction he had no control over, like the kick of a gun. He stiffly offered to share his *rohlíky*, butter, and strawberry jam. He hated himself for his reserve, but he didn't know how to soften it. He tried to disguise it by telling Luboš to feel free to take a shower, but then he spoiled the invitation by adding that he had to shower himself and had to be at the school in an hour, so Luboš did not accept.

—I am glad, that we met, Luboš said at the door.

At least Jacob thought that's what he said; he wasn't sure he understood the last word, but he didn't ask about it, because he was looking forward to being alone. In the daylight Luboš's face seemed older, uneven. Jacob didn't understand why he had been drawn to it. He knew, however, that he would be drawn to it again when this mood wore off. He tried to keep that in mind. —I, too, he answered. There was something that his struggle with himself was distracting him from. There was a nuance he was missing. He tried to force his attention. He remembered that he had no way of contacting Luboš. —Telephone? he asked.

This time Luboš supplied a number. It belonged to a friend, he said, with whom they could leave messages. There seemed to be nothing else to say. They embraced quickly, for a leave-taking, and the smell of Luboš, rising off his body as they touched, first disgusted Jacob, then melted him, the second response succeeding the first almost instantly, disorientingly. This was the body he had been lying next to, the aroma reminded him, with whom he had taken a simple pleasure. He had somehow forgotten it upon waking up.

"I just had the most disturbing experience," Annie said in a hushed voice, about a week later, as Jacob sat down at her table in a café in Staroměstské náměstí, or Old Town Square. It was midafternoon, and the square, which they had a good view of through the café's windows, was nearly empty. It was too cold for tourists. Not long ago, a gold-colored statue of an East German car on legs had seemed to stride into the square, in the corner marked by the Staré Město horologe, but the statue had recently been taken down. *What's Your Hurry?* had been the name of it. There no longer seemed to be any hurry at all, only gray bricks and a few wanderers, leaning into the wind as they walked.

Jacob looked around for clues.

"You're welcome to the rest of my cake," she said, misunderstanding his glances.

"No thanks. What happened?"

"Do you see your man there, by the bar?"

"My man?"

"Not literally yours, Jacob, at least not to my knowledge. The sharp one. Don't look now. Youngish, dark hair, wool sweater, a bit naff. Don't look I said."

"Yes."

"Well, I'm sitting here, with my *čokoladový dort* and my *sodovku*, writing a letter to my mother, quite innocent and respectable, and he comes over to my table. Uninvited, but quite nicely put together, I thought at first. I could tell he was an American. He asks for a cigarette and says he's in Prague for a few days, what should he see? I don't know, I tell him. The bridge, the castle."

"Sounds innocuous."

"But he becomes very inquisitive when he hears that I teach here. Asks how much am I paid. Is that polite in America? He starts naming figures, in dollars. I explain that my salary is set by Czech law and that it's in crowns. And he points to my chocolate cake and says, 'Can you afford that?'"

"Was he joking?"

"I don't think so. I ask what he does for a living, and I believe the word he used was 'I-banker.' 'Can you afford *that?*' I say. And he gets quite hot under the collar. Tells me he came to Czechoslovakia to get away from that kind of 'self-hatred,' that was his word. He wanted to visit a place where they welcomed free enterprise and were grateful for it. I said, I work for the state and wouldn't know anything about that. And he becomes quite threatening, with this booming voice—you're too re-fined to boom, Jacob, but I find that Americans often have a talent for it—'*You will.*' And he stalks off like a little tin soldier."

"He's cute, though," Jacob observed.

"He isn't. He's nondescript, really."

"I think he knows we're talking about him."

"Does he? It's of no concern to me."

Jacob was out of things to read in English, and Annie had offered to show him a lending library that the British, during the Communist era, had set up in a corner of the Clementinum, a former Jesuit compound that now belonged to Charles University. To hide from the wind, they took a back route, down an alley that felt like a tunnel, past a Renaissance church with boarded-up windows, crumbling in on itself like an abandoned tenement in a slum, past a wine bar they all liked, and then, beside a store selling accordions and flutes, which seemed never to be open, through a passageway and into a further maze of alleys.

"I had a date on Thursday," Jacob volunteered, when they were close to a wall and safe from the wind.

"Did you."

This hardly signaled that she wanted to hear more, but Jacob wanted to try to put the experience into words. He told her about going to Café Slavia. She knew and liked the café, she said; she liked all cafés, really. He was less successful at conveying the tender awkwardness he had felt when alone with Luboš. Moreover, when he related Luboš's joke, she looked alarmed.

"That's peculiar," she said.

He found that he wanted to defend Luboš. "I think the Czechs have a darker sense of humor." Maybe the dictatorship they had been living under had accustomed them to playing with a larger part of the self as if it were false.

"It's possible," she said, mildly.

The British library was up a flight of stairs in the northeast corner of one of the Clementinum courtyards. Inside, it looked like a library that a New England prep school might have built for itself in the 1970s—comfortable chairs of artificial leather, a beech-wood card catalog, and, along the walls, like carefully trimmed rosebushes, a hedge of waist-high bookshelves, a branch of which jutted into the room every few yards, like the tongue of a capital E.

They browsed independently. Annie found a novel that her mother had recommended, by Elizabeth Bowen, and Jacob picked out a little blue Oxford World's Classic of a Renaissance travel narrative, by an Englishman who claimed to have visited the land of Prester John on his way back from China.

"Because we're at the edge of the world?" Annie asked in a whisper, as they compared their choices at a table in the back of the room.

"I guess." In fact the library's schoolroom look had made him feel guilty, and he had chosen the book in a spirit of self-improvement. Over the next two weeks, even though he would find little in it that interested him, beyond a few outlandishly fictional cannibals, he would dutifully read all the way to the end. He wasn't, after all, writing anything.

"Have you fallen for this Luboš, then?" she asked, fussing with a corner of her book's cellophane wrapper, which had come untucked.

"We just met."

"You fancy him, in any case." She didn't raise her eyes to his. "I hope you'll keep your wits about you."

"I'm not a romantic. I'm gay, remember."

"You are a romantic," she answered, and then added, quickly, "I am, too; it's all right."

"I don't think that the other thing is here yet. I think that's why he thought he could joke about it."

"But that doesn't mean he's on the level." She looked up and saw that she'd hurt his feelings for Luboš. "I haven't even met him. Don't listen to me."

"There's something very sweet about him."

"Oh, well, 'sweet.' Perhaps you aren't very far gone, then." The fluorescent lights and the Formica tabletop between them seemed to put them in a context incongruously childish. "You should tell Melinda, you know," she said abruptly. "It's absurd of you not to. There's nothing she likes better than a secret she's justified in keeping from Rafe."

"I probably will, before too long."

"You'll have to, if I go, or you won't have anyone to talk to."

"What do you mean, if you go?"

"I thought I told you. I know I did. I find it quite lonely here. And gray, you know, all the time. I'm thinking of going back to Berlin."

"You can't go."

"Well, I can, Jacob. Why don't you come with me? There's a real scene there. You'd be shut of all this poxy Czech mysteriousness."

It was as if she had ventilated the room with a draft of the cold air outside. Suddenly he saw how easy it would be to go elsewhere.

"You could teach English, as you do here," Annie continued. "We aren't undesirables."

"I'll think about it," he said, but he found later that he was reluctant to.

Annie didn't leave, not immediately. On the contrary, she grew closer to the circle of expatriates that held her and Jacob, and that circle drew tighter. They all began to feel for it. At the nucleus were the Scots—Thom, Michael, and a few others—who formed the habit, after school let out, of stopping in at a nearby pub for a drink. Sometimes they also ordered the classic Czech dinner of pork cutlets, dumplings, and boiled cabbage; sometimes they didn't bother with dinner; more than once they stayed until eleven, when the pub closed. Henry offered to join them if they were willing to meet downtown; he neither worked nor lived near the language school. Annie also urged them to move, because it made her nervous to drink so close to where she worked. As a group, they were conspicuously not Czech, even if they were no louder and no more drunk than anyone else. She hoped, too, that the clientele downtown might be a touch more genteel and put the lads on their mettle, a bit. No one else hoped this, or expected it, and it was mostly on account of their respect for Henry that the Scots did eventually move. They began to rendezvous with him three or four nights a week at the Automat, a buffet-style diner with steam tables at the foot of Wenceslas Square, which belonged to the cheapest class of eatery that the government certified, and to progress from there to a pub nearby. Annie joined them regularly at the new pub, though not at the Automat, whose food she could not bring herself to eat, and in her wake came a few other women who taught at the school, and Jacob, too, once he sensed that there would be enough women present to camouflage any lapses he might have from perfect masculinity. Rafe rarely came, but sometimes Melinda did. They had the sense that she was on loan to them, and her dresses and coats seemed to confirm the impression that she was finer than the settings they had chosen, and so, for the sake of balance and a kind of politeness, she was always particularly foul-mouthed in her banter, to show that her enjoyment was genuine—that she, at least, did not think she was slumming.

Their first downtown pub was U medvídků, where the waiters made no attempt to speak to them in anything but an abrupt, efficient Czech, and delivered beers with a promptness and mild irony that suggested that they recognized the Scots, Irish, and English to be representatives of a fellow pub-going culture. Their circle was so numerous that they usually had a table to themselves. There was sawdust on the floor, but the cutlets and gulash were excellent, as everyone agreed who wasn't, like the Scots, economizing on meals in order to have as many crowns as possible for beer. The little bears that the pub was named for were painted on a sign hanging over its front door, and Jacob soon thought of them fondly, like characters in a fairy tale that he was having the good fortune to live out. The evenings were a holiday from his project of understanding the Czechs and of eavesdropping on the after echoes of their revolution, and some nights he seemed to forget about his project altogether for a while. Their time together was wonderfully insular; it sometimes felt to Jacob as if the world beyond their table, beyond the ring of his friends, did not exist.

He would probably have forgotten about his project for good if it weren't for the problem of love. All the Scots were beautiful, especially Thom, with his square jaw and his blond hair flopping into his eyes, but Jacob was through with the mistake of falling for straight men. In America he had revealed his crushes to three straight men in a row, all of whom had been generous enough to let him get to know them anyway, and he had been able to see for himself the unlikelihood of reciprocity in such cases. He wasn't alone in not knowing what to do about love. With the exception of Mel and Rafe, almost no one in the circle had a lover, not for long anyway. It sometimes felt as if, in compensation, they were all falling in love with one another, as a group.

One night, for the sake of variety, they shifted their drinking place north, to a pub that specialized in Slavic cuisine. The food was good, but the waiters, to judge by their reluctance to serve it, seemed not to trust expatriates to appreciate it. The beer arrived infrequently, and only in large amounts, forcing all the drinkers into a single rhythm, as if they were on an assembly line. Between deliveries, the waiters sat at a table of their own, in a corner, drinking and smoking; they rose from it of their own accord only to place folded cards, on which the word REZERVOVÁNO was printed in red, on tables abandoned by diners, to prevent any new patrons from sitting at them. Once, when Henry asked for a light, a waiter made a point of fetching an unopened box of matches from the kitchen and depositing it on the table with an aggrieved "Prosím," instead of striking one from the box visible in the pocket of his white shirt. In revenge, Henry quietly taught Jacob a Czech word for waiter that was approximately as offensive, he said, as "bastard" or "son of a bitch" in English. "One sees, at times, why such a specialized profanity would have developed," he added. The word could have gotten them thrown out if spoken too loudly, and it was tacit that Henry trusted Jacob not to use it—and not to disclose it to the Scots.

The next night Jacob stayed home because he needed to rest, and the following day he didn't teach. When he arrived at the Slavic-cuisine pub that evening, he was full of longing. He was losing his acclimation to spending days and nights alone, and an interval away now left him with a burden of news that he wanted to communicate. For example, there were no longer onions in his local grocery store, and he had seen a few of his neighbors cluster quietly around the trunk of a Škoda full of unwashed potatoes. But his friends weren't at the restaurant. When he entered, a waiter turned his head to glance at him, inhaling on his cigarette as he did. Seeing that Jacob was at a loss, he remained seated. The long, empty tables were covered in coarse white linen, sterile and unwelcoming, as in a surgery tent before a battle. Jacob's friends had forgotten about him. They must have decided to try yet another pub. He felt hurt that Annie hadn't gotten a message to him somehow; he thought that, since she hadn't, someone ought to have stayed behind to intercept him. He knew objectively that the first was impossible—he hadn't been to the school, after all, and Annie didn't have the Stehlíks' phone number—and the second unreasonable, because no one knew that he planned to show up. But the prospect of a night alone, when he had been looking forward to seeing his friends, seemed unbearable.

He walked south, hesitantly at first but then determinedly. Through the windows of the Automat, he saw that the servers were shutting down the buffet, wheeling away trays of food, leaving behind only clear steaming water in steel troughs beneath. He nerved himself for a second disappointment; he was going to try U medvídků again, in case they had gone back there. It reassured him to see the bears. His friends weren't in the first room, but it was loud with arguments and endearments, and the light was soft. It was the sort of place they ought to be found in, Jacob thought. And in the second room he did find them, so deeply taken with one another that none of them looked up until he was nearly upon them, at which point they all rose with cries and greetings and embraced him. Thom had a back-up beer—the house beer at U medvídků was Budvar, and he was very fond of it—which he donated to Jacob as a welcome. "It'll give me a chance to order yet another from the bugger when he comes back," Thom said. "He thinks I'm a champion, and I don't want to disappoint him."

Every few days, Jacob saw Luboš, and from time to time they went to bed together, but Luboš did not lend himself to it, not fully. Jacob understood that he seemed to Luboš too young, too unsure of himself. Once, when he had learned the word, and more to show it off than for any other reason, Jacob referred to himself and Luboš as a couple. —But officially we are not, Luboš said, solemnly. There were no promises. Each was at liberty. Jacob made a point, therefore, of going back to T-Club. He didn't meet anyone else he wanted to sleep with; every so often, in fact, he found Luboš there, who always handled the unexpected encounters graciously and usually let Jacob take him home.

"Why do you stand here, there is nothing to see. You will sit with us." When Luboš was absent from T-Club, it was Ota who captured Jacob, though he took him no further than his table. "I have all the pretty men."

Each time Jacob saw him, Ota seemed more preppy. To the polo shirt he added a lavender wool sweater, which he wore draped over his shoulders like a lady's mink. A thin Czech leather belt, bluish where it was meant to be black, was in time replaced by a woven one, striped like a rep tie and fastened with a shiny brass clasp. Yet his complexion, never good, did not improve. There was always a patch of red spots breaking out where his sideburns would have been, if his whiskers were not so blond and delicate, or in the cadaverous hollows of his cheeks.

He quizzed Jacob on the words to American pop songs as they were being played, because he liked to be able to sing along, and he took showy note of any new man in the bar who was reasonably attractive.

"He is for you, this one, in the blue shirt. He will not say no to American cow."

"Beef, you mean."

"No, what is word, for baby beef."

"Veal?"

"That drinks milk only, not even eats grass. This one will not refuse. But I am forgetting. You are, how do you say it, occupied."

"You make me sound like a table in a restaurant."

"Is that not the word? And I am the waiter. 'May I help you, sir?' Do you love Luboš? Is that right? Or do I say, Are you in love Luboš?"

"In love with."

"Ah yes. Then are you *in* love *with* him." Jacob didn't answer. *"Ale stydíš se, Kubo.* You are shy."

"What about you, Ota?"

"I? I love you, of course, Kuba, but I am too slow. Luboš has run off with you, like a rabbit. Not rabbit. Like fox." And he translated for his entourage.

One of the boys, Milo, a blond with even bangs and a large, Roman nose, changed the subject by asking, in Czech, which state Jacob was from.

—I live in Texas, Jacob began, pointing a finger over his shoulder, as if the past were literally behind him, because he didn't know how to form the past tense. —And then in Massachusetts.

"Stop this," Ota interrupted, and mocked Jacob's gesture, which had in fact become a crutch. "Já jsem bydlel," he instructed. "Já jsem bydlel, ty jseš bydlel, on bydlel."

It was easier to speak of the past in Czech than Jacob had expected. —I lived in Texas and then in Massachusetts, he said to Milo, more correctly.

—Were you a cowboy? Milo asked, with an amusement gentler than Ota's. He asked as if he hoped Jacob would pretend.

—No, Jacob said, sorry to disappoint him.

—That's too bad, Milo replied, and glanced under the table. —I like those big boots.

Ota again interrupted: "'*Ty velké boty,*' *prosím tě, kluku.* Ah, this reminds me. Do you hear?" He pointed at the speakers. "What does it mean, 'things on your chest'?"

"A burden, a secret. Like the boy with the fox under his shirt."

"And the fox eats the boy in the chest, I remember, and he says nothing. Do you have tape recorder?"

"No, but I can borrow one from the language school, since I'm the teacher."

"Ah, teacher, then will you borrow it? And I will give to you the cassette of my favorite band, Depeche Mode, and you will write all the words of all the songs on a paper, that yes? And you will give to me the paper."

He handed Jacob a cassette, which he must have been palming since before Jacob sat down next to him. "Jééé," commented Milo, admiringly, when he leaned forward and saw that it was a copy of *Violator*, the band's new album. The group seemed to have an intense following among Prague's youth; Jacob had seen their name spray-painted on the side of a *panelák*—the first apolitical graffiti he had spotted.

"You may listen a week, two weeks, a month—as you like it," Ota added. Listening was to be Jacob's reward for service. Jacob accepted the commission.

On the nights Jacob stayed home and transcribed the lyrics, he felt a homesick pride: gay teenagers around the world learned his mother tongue by memorizing pop songs.

But then he didn't see Ota for a little while. The fault lay with Ivan, T-Club's doorman. For several weeks, after Jacob's first visit, Ivan had admitted Jacob as soon as Jacob presented himself, but then, mysteriously, he reverted to a policy of making Jacob wait. Did he want a bribe? Jacob had no intention of giving him one; it would have been wrong, and for someone being paid a state salary in crowns, too costly.

Jacob was now sometimes made to wait ten minutes and sometimes an hour and a half. He and the doorman both understood that there was nowhere else he could go. He tried the city's one other gay bar, where he danced for a few hours with a group of gypsies, some in half drag, but it was, as the guidebook had warned, rougher; there was little talking, which was what Jacob most wanted; it was much farther away; and he had been made to wait there, too, by a doorman who looked as if he would hit Jacob if he questioned him about it. Ivan would never hit, Jacob felt certain. Nonetheless, as soon as Jacob appeared at T-Club, he was at Ivan's mercy.

He asked Luboš to take him to the movies, and they met at a theater in Malá Strana, the Lesser Town, for a Saturday matinee. An American thriller was playing with Czech subtitles. In the small, cobbled courtyard in front of the theater, while they stood reading the poster, an usher, a boy in his teens, approached and asked if they wanted to see the movie without paying; when his grandmotherly colleague was distracted, he let them in through a side exit, and Luboš handed him a small tip. Since seating in the theater was assigned, the boy had to make a show of directing them to their seats, which he did as formally as if he had not just belied his uniform. The movie itself was not likely to be as entertaining, but when the lights dimmed, Luboš allowed Jacob to hold his hand. —Don't be afraid, he said to Jacob half jokingly. —I'm here.

Jacob gave himself to the movie's artificial terrors, and afterward, in the cold air outside, the sun just setting, he felt refreshed and at ease. They crossed the river on the Charles Bridge, against the flow of tourists; Luboš had chosen a restaurant on the east bank. They walked through Staroměstské náměstí and then down Celetná—all the way to náměstí Republiky, the Square of the Republic, where, to Jacob's surprise, Luboš led him into the Municipal House, a salmon-colored palace, fronted by a grand canopied entrance of tarnished iron, with bronze atlantes bearing geometric lamps, and above the atlantes, a half-moon mosaic of allegorical women, nude and clothed. There was a restaurant just inside, to the right, which looked as if it were reserved for visiting dignitaries. But Luboš was speaking to the maître d'; they had a reservation.

The dining hall held perhaps fifty tables, wrapped in white linen, the silver placed with an almost military correctness. All but a few were empty. The light of the chandeliers was brightened by their gilding and by reflection in the yellow and white of the walls, which framed, on high, murals of the city of Prague. In one, a woman extended her arms to the viewer, as if in welcome.

Luboš and Jacob followed a waiter down a few steps to a table on the main floor. —Kuba, in this building, they declared the republic.

—In November?

—In 1918. The First Republic.

—Where did they declare the current republic?

—Perhaps in Wenceslas?

—You weren't there?

—I was there a little. I'm not so engagé.

As the twilight failed, the white curtains became more opaque, more solid. It was still just possible to see through them, but one saw not the street but the scaffolding outside the windows. The overall effect was thus of a stage set of a restaurant interior that was becoming more plausible as the lighting was adjusted.

—Kuba, I have a question, Luboš began. He often said this by way of introduction, to help Jacob distinguish an actual question from the uncertainty sometimes audible in his voice as to whether Jacob understood what he was saying. He was smiling unevenly, like a diplomat obliged to raise an awkward subject for the sake of the country he represented. —How did you earn money in America?

—I told you. I worked in an office.

—You did not sell yourself?

—Sell oneself? Jacob echoed the phrase, to ask for clarification. It was a reflexive verb, and sometimes they had unexpected meanings.

—Your body. Your sex. You know what it is, prostitution?

He saw, this time, that Luboš was playing a game of some kind.

—Many people do it. And you are pretty and manly.

—No, I never did. He decided not to try to hide his puzzlement. —Why are you asking?

—I had the impression, that it is normal with you in America.

Jacob could not tell at what level the joke was being played. Was this a misapprehension caused by years of Communist propaganda, or a joke at the expense of the propaganda? Was Luboš mocking the misconceptions that straights have of gays? Or perhaps it was a poke at Jacob's innocence, which Jacob knew he still had not really shed.

—Never? Luboš asked once more. He still wore a diplomat's smile, as if the question weren't his, or were asked for a purpose other than that of eliciting an answer, but in his tone of voice there was a conflicting note, which Jacob would have called sorrow, if that didn't seem discordant, and in the repetition of the question there was insistence, as if Luboš needed to have something settled, though perhaps he wasn't sure he was ready for it to be.

It occurred to Jacob that a pause might be mistaken for complicity.

—No, never, he said.

—Well, then, Luboš said, as if winding up a conversation. He seemed to see further doubts in Jacob's eyes and added, —I did not really think it of you specially. I was kidding.

—You kid a lot.

—An awful lot, you're right. Don't become angry.

—No, no, Jacob assured him. Luboš seemed afraid that he might have hurt Jacob. Jacob realized he hadn't washed his hands, and they felt hot and prickly; his palms were white, with red mottling. —I'm going to . . . , he began, and he rubbed his hands in pantomime.

In the restroom he paid fifty hellers to the attendant, even though he wasn't going to use a urinal; it was simpler than trying to explain. Recently someone had taught him an obscene word for the women who worked in restrooms, who looked grandmotherly but were usually quite stern. A word for them and a word for waiters—perhaps there was an obscenity for everyone who was placed by work in the way of the public. He washed his face, too, and decided not to let the conversation return to Luboš's question.

The beauty of the dining hall struck him, when he reentered it, like a kind of heat that he could feel on the skin of his face.

Because he knew it by heart, he decided to discuss one of Emily Dickinson's poems in his first meeting with the school's most advanced class, which he had recently been asked to teach as a substitute, every other Thursday. He wasn't sure how advanced the students would be. Běta was one of them—she had enjoyed his momentary disorientation when she had told him, upon crossing his path in the stairwell at home, that she looked forward to seeing him Thursday afternoon—but that gave him little indication, because it was hard to say how much English she knew. He always tried to speak Czech to her, for the sake of practice, and she, after one or two ironic sallies into English, usually gave her ground and retreated into Czech, as if it were somehow immodest for her to continue in Jacob's language when he wasn't speaking it.

He found her sitting in the back row, sharing her textbooks with a bald man who had forgotten his. Neither she nor Jacob betrayed to the other students that he lived in her parents' house; she gave her name with the others, neutrally, when he asked the students to introduce themselves.

After reviewing an exercise set by the regular teacher, he wrote the poem on the blackboard, his hands shaking, as they always did before strangers. He then asked them to say what they thought the pronouns referred to, taking them one by one.

> That it will never come again
> Is what makes life so sweet.
> Believing what we don't believe
> Does not exhilarate.
>
> That if it be, it be at best
> An ablative estate—
> This instigates an appetite
> Precisely opposite.

When he called on Běta, she said, "Já?"—me?—and pointed at herself, wide-eyed. But she was able to say when "it" was life, and when afterlife, and what it is we don't believe. Slowly the class unriddled the poem, which Jacob liked because the ambivalence in it was so fine, and the ambiguities so few. It was odd, too, in being composed almost purely of ideas; it had so little in it of the sweet world whose loss concerned it, except perhaps in its sound, which was like a nursery rhyme's.

After class, he found Annie at the top of the stairs, trying to shift her cassette player and manila folders into her knapsack before they slipped from her hands.

"May I?" he asked.

"Oh, that's grand, thanks. In these shoes I need a free hand for the banister." A tall, south-facing window—a modern rectangle of Gothic narrowness—lit the stairwell with thin cold light, which burned into a filament a straw-colored plait that fell over her eyes. "Do you keep to the curricular schedule, Jacob? I don't see how I'm going to catch up. Today I had them pronounce words that end in B and G and so on, because not one of them could say 'dog.' They say 'doc,' have you noticed?"

Thom was waiting for them in the lounge. "Annie, my love, you don't happen to have any of those apricot pastries left on your hands, by any chance?"

"Did you try the little shop across the way?"

"I did, but the schoolgirls have eaten them all up."

"You have to go quite early," Annie told him. "What will you offer in exchange, then? I've only four left."

"Only four! I can offer a Sparta."

"Mmm. They're rather rough on the back of the throat, I find. I always feel afterward as if I'm coming down with something."

Jacob donated a Marlboro light instead, which liberated two pastries, one for him and one for Thom.

"Is it true what Michael says, that he's going back to Edinburgh because you've found a Czech girlfriend and now he has to drink alone?"

"Michael's going back to sign on, is what he must have meant to say, before Thatcher and her lot do away with the dole altogether and he misses his chance."

"I had no idea you were such a conservative," Annie said.

"I think a working man has a right to know his tax monies are not ill-spent."

"What's her name, then?"

"Jana." He said it shyly.

"A proper Czech name. She sounds quite nice."

"She is that, yes."

"She would have to be, to put up with such a lot as you. Is she impressionable?"

"Quite her own person, rather."

"Will we be meeting her?"

"In time. She doesn't speak much English yet."

"And I don't suppose you're speaking Czech to her. How do you communicate?"

"It's always possible," Jacob put in.

"It is, yes," Thom reflected.

Annie carefully wrapped the last pastry in the white sack she had bought them in. "Did either of you men of the world know that there's now a paper shortage? Your man in the shop, there, was reluctant to give me this sack. I had to plead with him for it. That's why I bought so many. It was *šest* or nothing."

"What will you do," Jacob asked, "if she falls in love with you?"

"I think we're getting a bit ahead of ourselves," Thom protested.

"Sorry," said Jacob.

"Of course she will, though," said Annie. "You're such a lad, Thom, not to think of that."

President Bush was coming to Prague for the first anniversary of the Velvet Revolution, and Jacob invited Luboš to be his date for the celebration in Wenceslas Square. They met under the clock of the disco, as was now their custom. The president was not scheduled to speak until two, but at noon the streets were already full. It was a national holiday, and the crowd was merry. A man in a Mao suit was selling a card game called Marxeso, which was played like Concentration; the object was to turn over matching pairs of twentieth-century dictators, who were Communist except for Hitler, Mussolini, Hirohito, Khomeini, and Saddam Hussein. Girls in peasant dresses were selling cheaply printed copies of the United States Constitution in Czech. The week before, Jacob had tried to teach his students the difference between a Republican and a Democrat, but the difference did not tell here; Bush was being welcomed in a general and symbolic capacity.

Jacob offered to treat Luboš to pizza at a new, Western-style place near the Můstek subway entrance. It was a restaurant where you stood to eat. A waitress came quickly once they found an end free at one of the high tables.

—Was it like this here last year? Jacob asked.

—No, people were afraid then, Luboš said. —The police were beating people. Today it is like a game.

—So you *were* here.

—A little, he said, as he had before.

The dough was chewy, and the tomato sauce heavily sweetened. Soon they were climbing uphill toward a blue-painted stage that had been erected at the top of the square. Government loudspeakers, mounted in the façades of the buildings like fleurons of gunmetal, had been turned on again for the occasion, and one or two of them crackled meaninglessly because of a short circuit, already out of repair after just a year's disuse.

Luboš seemed to be studying the paving stones.

—You're silent, Jacob accused.

—I'm nervous. He glanced around them before explaining: He and Collin had a third partner, another Czech, who had recently gone missing, just as they were about to sign a lease and hand floor plans over to a builder. Luboš had been asked to apply for extensions on all the permissions and licenses that the business required, a task in some ways more difficult than applying for them in the first place.

—Where is he? Jacob asked.

—We do not know. Please tell no one.

—Whom would I tell?

They stood together awkwardly, leaning against a building a few numbers up from the Hotel Evropa. From time to time Jacob tried to stand on the ledge of a sort of false plinth in the building's façade, as if he wanted a better view, but in fact as a pretext for putting a hand on Luboš's shoulder.

—What will you do, when you return? Luboš asked.

—That's far off, Jacob answered lightly.

—Not so far, I think. Will you return to the office, where you worked?

—No. In fact Jacob dreaded the burden of earning a living. To be here was something more than a holiday; it was a kind of rift in the net, so new that it was not yet clear how it would be rewoven into the systems of money and responsibility. —I want to write, Jacob added.

—Ah yes. Does it pay?

—No, not now.

A brass band's rendition of John Philip Sousa issued from speakers above their heads, too loudly at first. Then came George M. Cohan. The embassy must have provided a mix tape. —I too do not know, what I will do, Luboš said, in the Czech he kept simple for Jacob's sake. —Especially if Collin's business does not succeed.

—You could translate.

—I am a terrible translator, even of German. I am only good enough for this, to help a businessman from abroad. Forgive me. Do not worry; I am not going to cry over it.

He looked fixedly at Jacob as if daring him to look away. He seemed to be appealing to Jacob for once as an equal, and it filled Jacob with lust. He wanted to pin Luboš to the building they were leaning against. —Do you really need this other man? Jacob asked. In Czech, "the other" is literally "the second," so Jacob specified, perhaps unnecessarily: —This third man.

—His name is on all the forms. His name and mine. The Frenchman's name is nowhere. And we need him even aside from this. All is in great disorder.

"Je to bordel," Jacob said in sympathy. *Bordel* was a mildly vulgar word, which Běta used to describe anything it was her duty to clean up. A mess, as in a brothel.

—You speak Czech so prettily now, Luboš said. —Like a cabdriver.

At two o'clock, a few Czech officials seated themselves in folding chairs on stage. Two wore ill-fitting suits, and a third a patterned sweater. It was still a rare thing to see formal clothes of any kind on the streets of Prague. There were almost none for sale in the stores. As a sort of a joke, Jacob sometimes wore a beige knit tie, which he'd thrown into his knapsack in Boston at the last minute, but he almost never saw a tie on other men. The absence was a relief. No one's clothes signaled that they lived better or higher than you, or that their style was more current. The men on stage, for example, were probably government ministers, but they dressed like clerks in a discount shoe store. A Thoreauvian intellectual might live a little to one side, under such an arrangement, without looking any shabbier than the rest of society. The peculiarity of his ambition would not be visible.

Another official came to the microphone and announced that President Bush had been unpreventably delayed and would appear as soon as he was able to. After a few minutes, the seated officials exchanged glances, rose, and filed sheepishly off stage. The crowd seemed to pardon them; it was, after all, a very cold day.

The people in the square fell into the long patience customary in those awaiting a ceremony rather than an entertainment. The music gave them a sense of progress. During the silence after each song, they listened intently, and then, as the next song started, relaxed again into chatter and into fidgeting for warmth. At intervals one of the officials repeated the announcement of the president's delay and the assurance that he was en route. It pleased Jacob to think of himself as hidden in the crowd—not recognizably American.

—Your president is as punctual as you.

—I didn't vote for him.

—You were, perhaps, too young.

—Punishably young, Jacob joked.

—I'm not afraid, Luboš returned. —The socialist republics are enlightened about youth. You are old enough here to cast your vote as you wish, in that respect at least.

It was not until four that the Czech officials returned to the stage. This time they remained standing, their hands clasped before them, as if so instructed, while men from the American Secret Service, much more sharply tailored, took the corners of the stage and studied the crowd. Havel's foreign minister next emerged, followed, at last, by the American president and his entourage. After an introduction, the president read in his plaintive, nasal voice from a short script, pausing for the interpreter at the end of each clause with a practiced air, as if he himself found the resonance of the phrases reassuring and even enjoyed their echo in another language. He said only platitudes, yet Jacob felt nonetheless a prickling on the back of his neck at the old words in their Yankee cadences, and a pride in thinking that his was the country invited to represent democracy, not France or Britain. Later, when he learned a little history, he realized that the Czechs and Slovaks couldn't have invited the leaders of those countries; in 1938, Daladier and Chamberlain had betrayed Czechoslovakia to Hitler. At the time, though, he only understood America's presence in Bush's person vaguely, and not altogether inaccurately, as a recognition of something like its purity of spirit.

In their mere politeness, the president's words left the crowd with nothing to discuss, and when the stage was cleared, people fell thoughtlessly into streets and arcades that would take them away from the square. Jacob felt a little giddy. He was at the right distance from his country, he thought. This was where he wanted to see it from. Even the insipidity of Bush's speech pleased him; it reflected America's stability and confidence, and it suggested that it was safe to stay away. There weren't going to be any turns in the story that he'd want to be on hand for. In the general dispersal, he and Luboš drifted north and soon found themselves in view of the chief train station, named for Woodrow

Wilson. There was a park in front, which Jacob hadn't noticed before. At this time of year the flowerbeds were empty, but on the northern side of the park there were crudely trimmed shrubs and a thin shelter of trees.

—Kuba, what are you looking for? Luboš asked.

—I want to see the statue.

He was already ten paces ahead of Luboš. He could tell it wasn't really a nice park. At the edges of the sidewalk, wind had collected cigarette butts and wrinkled wads of the wax paper that fries and mayonnaise were served in. It occurred to Jacob that he didn't often see litter in downtown Prague. This trash came from the train station, probably. In a minute he would let Luboš lead him away, but first he wanted to take a closer look at the statue, which seemed to represent a soldier in a flowing coat standing beside—yes, how strange—standing beside another man, and embracing him.

—It is unsuitable here, Luboš said, awkwardly, upon catching up.

There was no plaque. Jacob walked around the statue, to see it from all angles. The soldier's rifle, hanging from a shoulder strap, fell between the men, separating them like the mythic sword that lovers are always sleeping on either side of, and the soldier's left leg strode forward, decisively, as if to signal that the embrace would not slow his march. The stride turned the soldier's cock and balls chastely away from his admirer, who seemed to be rushing toward him with a desperate hunger.

—Do you know, what it is? Jacob asked.

—It is for the liberation from the Germans.

Now Jacob saw the Soviet star on the breast of the soldier's uniform. The Russian, who was taller, had to bend his head deeply to place his kiss, which was sheltered by the men's arms. The Czech's face, too, was almost entirely obscured. Jacob wondered if it were possible to enjoy the statue the way tourists did when they bought Soviet Army overcoats and badges on Charles Bridge—as a trophy of sorts, and as kitsch. But he decided that the passion it represented was too bodily; there could be no room in his understanding of it for irony, except at the expense of the aspect that most interested him. An image had been widely circulated, the year before, of Honecker and Brezhnev kissing; Jacob saw that one could make that kind of joke about this statue. He didn't want to, yet he was not ready to see himself in the statue, either.

—Are they lovers? Jacob asked.

—I don't know, Luboš said. —It is not good to be here.

—Why not?

—Because of men from the train station. Men and boys.

Jacob shrugged. —Such people aren't dangerous. Is the statue pleasing to you?

—No, Luboš answered. The sun had set, and it was hard to read anything in his expression besides his diplomatic smile. —Let's go.

They walked together silently toward náměstí Republiky. Neither of them had a coat warm enough for the night. —Shall we have dinner? Jacob asked.

—I must home, Luboš said.

—May I come, too?

—No.

Jacob wanted to embrace him as in the sculpture but didn't dare. When they were alone Luboš was tender and put hands on him so gently. Outside, their tenderness was hidden, though they carried it with them nonetheless, like a ballpoint pen of Jacob's that had once slipped through a hole in his coat pocket into the lining, so that it was always near to hand, though he never retrieved it.

—But where do you live? It felt like a breach of an unspoken contract for Jacob to ask.

—Far from the center, was all that Luboš would say. —Don't be angry, Kuba. We'll see each other soon.

There was a going-away party for Michael the next evening at a bar in Malá Strana. The street door of the bar was unmarked, like a speakeasy's, but it opened and closed too often for Jacob to mistake it. Inside, a long, narrow room was crowded with tables of loud, oblivious, uninterruptible drinkers, none of whom Jacob recognized, but a staircase in back led down to a warren of further rooms, with pale yellow walls and a bar of their own, and here Jacob found everyone packed into a corner where they did not quite fit, their cigarettes open on the table before them for one another's taking.

"I'm going to Berlin after all," said Annie, when he sat down beside her. Her eyes were bright with the news. "If such as Michael can feck off to where he likes, when he likes, so can I, you know."

"Oh, no, don't go, Annie."

"I'm not off for good *just* yet. I'm going week after next to have a look around. Thom is covering for me at the school. Why don't you find someone to cover for you as well, and we can go and interview together?" She added, confidentially, "It's a *real* city, so far as your interests are concerned. If you know what I mean."

The last few months would turn out to have been a detour, if he followed her. Leaving would be a kind of revenge on what had frustrated him here. At his age it was in his power to start over as often as he liked, and he wouldn't have that power forever.

"Would you miss your friend, is that it?" Annie asked.

"I'm not expecting anything from him."

"That's not quite what I asked."

"He's probably sleeping with someone else."

"You think he's cheating on you?"

"He's probably cheating when he's with me, if there are any rules to break, but I don't think there are. Evidently that's how it's supposed to be with homosexuals."

"Homosexuals—where?" interrupted Melinda, turning to them.

"Hush," said Annie.

"Here, actually," Jacob volunteered.

"Darling, how lovely. I'd been hoping, but I didn't want to pry and you're not so obvious. But *how* is it supposed to be with homosexuals, exactly? I missed that part, in my eavesdropping."

"No one is allowed to limit anyone's options."

"Man is dog to man, is that it? I've heard tell of that. It sounds very exciting to an outsider, but it might be a lot of rot, you know. The sort of thing men say when it's convenient."

"But it's men on both sides, or rather all sides, in this case."

"That doesn't mean you have to believe them any more than we do."

"Well, it's what I was told," Jacob said. "By a Thatcherite in Boston," he added.

"Yes, I hear you have them in America, too, now. I'm so sorry. And is it catching in Prague as well, is that what you're finding?"

"I guess so. The free market. Or maybe it's just that he likes the other guy better." But he pictured Collin as he said this, and added, "But I don't believe it."

"Nor I. Is any of this for general consumption, by the way?"

"No. If you don't mind."

"I shan't tell Rafe, then. He wouldn't mind at all, but he has no discretion."

"We're going to Berlin together," Annie put in.

"Not you, too, Jacob? But you can't, not just as I've found you out. It would be like having to wrap the Christmas presents up again and put them back under the tree."

"One earns actual cash in Berlin, Mel," Annie explained.

"Your mother sends you the loveliest packages of fruit and chocolates. I don't see what you need hard currency for."

"But she doesn't send nice Marlboros, like the ones Jacob has."

"Now that would be a mother indeed. Where does Jacob get them, I wonder."

"All the Harvs have a few extra dollars here and there," Annie observed. "From their government no doubt. For the work they do for the Agency."

"I buy them with the money from my plane ticket home," Jacob said. "I cashed it in."

"Was that wise?" Melinda asked, laying one of her white hands on his forearm. "Perhaps I needn't worry too hard about your leaving us after all."

"Excuse me, excuse me." Thom clambered over them as he made his way out of the corner. "Are you going to have a *pivo*, Jacob, or are you going to piss away your evening in mere talk?"

Jacob followed him to the bar.

"I must admit I'll be sorry to see the wanker go," Thom confessed, as he pulled a twenty-crown note out of his wallet.

"But you'll have your apartment back."

"Ah no, Michael's been sleeping on Henry's sofa, not mine. I'm at the Dům with Annie, and they don't allow us guests. But I'll wager Henry is pleased, come to think of it. One for you. Does Annie need another? That makes an order of five, then. *Pět, prosím.* A great relief, because I dread to say the number four. Can you say it, Jacob? A diabolical word. They laugh at me quite brutally but I hear that even Havel can't pronounce that consonant in the middle of it."

Next to them, Rafe and Kaspar were discussing something in German, but they switched into English when Jacob tried to listen.

"I was saying to Kaspar," Rafe explained, leaning toward Jacob's ear, "there was a report this morning at the ministry, from somebody at the WHO, that the death rate is climbing across Eastern Europe. A very slight but steady uptick."

"Chernobyl?" Jacob suggested.

"No, that's good, that's very good, but the curves are the wrong shape. It's not *anything*, apparently, or not anything you could do anything about—not malnutrition or an obvious problem like that. It's accidents. People having their strokes or heart attacks a little sooner than they ordinarily would, that sort of thing."

"And I say, it is capitalism," Kaspar said.

"It's exciting, capitalism," Rafe continued. "Makes the ticker go a little faster." He was speaking in the ironic, amoral, speculative tone of voice that at Harvard had been the specialty of the boys from the better prep schools.

"They don't even have capitalism here yet," Jacob demurred.

"I know!" Rafe rejoined. "Think what'll happen when they do."

"You are in a strange place," Kaspar said, thinking aloud.

"Who—us?" Rafe asked.

"Yes. You bring capitalism here without bringing it with you."

"I don't follow," Rafe objected.

Kaspar spoke softly, perhaps a dissident's habit, and Rafe and Jacob had to cock their ears toward him to hear. "You none of you have money, and forgive me, you will not make money, not you. You do not have such souls. I am speaking of all of you here, in this group, not you or you especially. This is a lovely thing about you. But it means you are dangerous. You are—what is the word—tempting, perhaps."

"Seductive," Rafe supplied.

"Yes, like a charming woman, or a charming boy." He paused to chuckle over his evenhandedness. "You do not even seem to care about money, but you bring the anxiety with you, the anxiety you do not show."

"The anxiety about money," Rafe said.

"Yes, but it is a larger anxiety, too. It is an anxiety about place, about your place. We do not have it here. It was taken from us, you may say. We are not accustomed to it."

"We're like missionaries," Jacob offered, thinking he saw Kaspar's point.

"Yes, you do not know you are bringing it. You think you are bringing something else."

"Like missionaries with smallpox," Rafe joked.

"No, it is psychological, after all," Kaspar insisted. "It is that you believe that you would never take anything from us. And we *feel* that in you, we know that it is true, and so we cannot resist you."

"Wow," Rafe said, raising his eyebrows. "How about that? That's quite a compliment."

"Well, no," Jacob objected. "I think he's saying the people of Eastern Europe should mince us up for the try-pots before it's too late."

"Oh, it is too late," Kaspar assured them. "Since Kerensky, I think, it is too late."

"Of course it could be that missionaries make nothing happen," Rafe added, as an afterthought. "It could be that they arrive early but don't actually do anything to further the imperialist cause."

"I hope that's it," Jacob said. "I would rather not believe we're making straight the way for McDonald's."

He finished his beer and ordered another; he wanted to catch up with his friends. A fine haze hung in the low room; at one table, four young Czechs played cards with a studied intensity, in poorly made, neatly ironed shirts, as conscious of their serious poses as college students in a film of the French New Wave. "Putnam!" shouted Michael, his cap turned backward, summoning Jacob to the pool table to make a fourth in a game with Henry and Thom. They played loudly and badly. When it was three games to one, Jacob and Thom losing, the four of them realized at the same time that they had to take a restroom break, and they all filed into the small lavatory together. There was only one toilet and one urinal. Michael, who came third, unbuttoned his fly and began to pee at once into the sink.

"Keep an eye on the door, there," Michael told Jacob. "We don't want any Czechs seeing this."

"We don't want to frighten them with your impressive manhood, is that it," said Thom, from the urinal, which was adjacent. "Or is it your appalling disregard for personal hygiene?"

"We don't want them to get the idea they needn't wait in queues. It would be the collapse of all social order in Czechoslovakia."

His dick was unself-consciously exposed. Jacob leaned against the door to keep it shut.

"Bloody poof, showing yourself like that," Thom continued. "Have you no shame?"

"Keep your hands to yourself, now, and don't worry your pretty head. It all goes to the same place in the end."

"As the vicar said to the schoolgirl."

"I don't know as I've heard that one."

"Me neither, as it happens."

"You're a stupid git, you know."

"And I'll miss you, too, once you're gone," Thom answered, and flushed for punctuation.

Henry said only, "I think I'll take a pass on washing me hands."

On Thursday night, there was a sharp knock at the door just as Jacob was putting away the last of his groceries. Though he imagined it would be Běta at the door, it was her father, Vladimír. He was a tall, good-looking man with gray hair as thick as a metal-bristled brush and dark lips that outlined his mouth. He kept his eyes fixed on Jacob's when he spoke, as if he were administering a test of character, challenging Jacob to return his gaze as steadily as he gave it. He insisted on speaking in English.

"Good evening, Mr. Jacob." It sounded as if he had rehearsed, in order to be sure of himself in Jacob's language. Though the form of address sounded humorous in English, it would have been correct in Czech, and perhaps a little more than correct. Such a form acknowledged the intimacy of people who had dealings with each other but established a certain air of respect between them. Jacob returned the civilities, and Mr. Stehlík then asked, "It is good here?"

Since Mr. Stehlík made no gesture as he spoke and did not glance away, it took Jacob a moment to understand that he was referring to the apartment Jacob was renting. "It's great; it's perfect," Jacob replied.

"That is good." Only now did Mr. Stehlík glance around him at the kitchen they were standing in, as if it would not have been proper for him to notice Jacob's use and enjoyment of the premises until he had been given this reassurance. Jacob was suddenly conscious of the spatter on the stove from at least a month of pancakes. He should be a better housekeeper, he told himself; he was paying a low rent, a favor that the Stehlíks had granted to the school.

"Please, you have telephone," Mr. Stehlík announced.

"Telephone? Upstairs?" Jacob answered, excitedly. He knew that Mr. Stehlík thought phone calls were expensive and should be brief, and it surprised him that Mr. Stehlík was so unhurried.

"Your friend Mr. Luboš say, that tomorrow he cannot."

Nothing in Mr. Stehlík's body language suggested a readiness to move from the spot, but Jacob asked, nonetheless, "Can I talk to him?"

"No. He call in the morning."

"Oh." Mr. Stehlík lacked the past tense, as Jacob had in Czech until recently. Luboš was not on the phone upstairs, and he was not going to meet Jacob under the clock tomorrow night for dinner. Probably Mr. Stehlík had made no effort to fetch Jacob when the call came through. Jacob wondered when Luboš had called; if Mr. Stehlík had not yet left the house, Jacob too had probably still been at home. It was as if Mr. Stehlík had robbed him of Luboš.

"Did he say anything else?"

"Please, I do not understand. Repeat?"

"Do you mind if I call him back?" Jacob asked, aware that in his anger he was speaking more colloquially and less intelligibly. But the finger he pointed toward the ceiling conveyed his wish.

"Mr. Jacob, can you telephone outside? There is telephone at the pub."

"Oh," Jacob said. He made a perfunctory smile to disguise his disappointment.

"Telephone upstairs is of me and of neighbor." These lines, too, sounded carefully prepared, as if they were the real burden of the visit. "It is for business, but neighbor telephones all the time. Day and night. Is difficult."

"I understand. Of course." Jacob was not on the phone more than thirty minutes a month, but he was in reach and the neighbor wasn't. Wishing not to lose all rights to the phone, he asked if he might still receive short messages, like the one just left by Luboš.

"Yes, yes," said Mr. Stehlík, but Jacob doubted that he meant it. "And your family, when call from America, yes."

"Thank you," Jacob answered.

"Please," he replied, and exited.

Jacob opened the refrigerator and stared into it vacantly, with the false purposefulness that lingers for a few moments when a person of a solitary nature is released from the company of a strong personality. If Mr. Stehlík were to return, Jacob would seem to be planning for dinner. Slowly he came to see the refrigerator's dull tin shelves for himself rather than through eyes loaned to Mr. Stehlík, and when he returned to himself, he found that he was admiring the row of jams and preserves he had collected in the past few months from stores all over the city: strawberry, gooseberry, apricot, currant, and lingonberry. It was nice to have a different one every time he made pancakes. But he wouldn't make pancakes again tonight, he decided.

Though it was tomorrow night's date that was canceled, somehow the news left him feeling cut off from the world tonight, too; the evening ahead seemed long. He decided to try to call Luboš. The pub with the pay phone was across a concrete plaza from the mall of stores, in the direction from which he had just come.

The neighbor's collie barked furiously. Jacob took a lunging sidestep toward it, because he felt a viciousness in himself tonight, as fierce as the dog's, and the animal paused for a moment, frightened into silence. But Jacob kept walking, and the dog realized that the challenge was empty—that the fence remained between them—and renewed his barking with even more force.

At the pub, Jacob was told there was no phone. —Outside, a man advised him, and when Jacob walked back outside, he saw that he had walked right past the phone booth, a frail, slender structure with an orange-painted frame and sixteen panes of glass, most of them cracked. A narrow margin of grass had grown up around it, a little wildly, where the municipal lawnmower had evidently not been able to reach. The grass had died with the coming of the cold weather, at about the height of a child.

The apparatus inside was intact and took Jacob's coin. The call went through; he heard the doubled buzzing that signaled that the phone was ringing in the house of Luboš's friend. It rang for a long time. As he waited, he remembered a time when he was a boy and had called his best friend repeatedly, as an experiment, asking each time if his friend had picked up the phone on the ring or between rings, until the two of them determined that there was no connection between the ringing sound heard by the caller and the actual rings of the phone called.

—Please, a voice answered, a standard but to Jacob's ears somewhat officious way to answer the phone in Czech.

—Good evening. Is Luboš there?

—Who's calling?

—Jacob.

—One moment.

There was scuffling and scratching as the receiver was set down. In a short while the voice returned, now speaking English: "He is away. May I take message?"

—I will call later, Jacob answered, insisting on Czech.

"Do you have telephone?"

—No longer, Jacob said. —I will call again.

The booth's glass gave some shelter from the wind, and Jacob lingered there after replacing the receiver. And suddenly it was all too much for him. He felt sad and misplaced, with the abrupt, overwhelming, dizzying sadness that comes over people in countries not their own, which has none of the richness of feeling that usually comes with sadness but is rather a kind of exhaustion. It hardly mattered about Luboš, he felt. It wasn't really Luboš that he missed; it was still Daniel, as it had been before, as perhaps it would always be. As he thought of Daniel, the feelings and circumstances of Boston returned to him with unexpected intensity. He didn't enjoy remembering them, but they seemed more powerful than he was, and more real than his surroundings. They seemed to establish a context for themselves in the night around him more solid than the rickety booth that he was, rather pointlessly, still standing in. He felt lightheaded, as if he were a little drunk. And like a drunk he became maudlin. That a person like Daniel had taken him up, however briefly, was the only remarkable thing that had ever happened to him. It was stupid of him to be here, so far away.

He would call Daniel. He took his calling card out of his wallet, put another crown in the phone, and dialed his American telephone company's access number for Czechoslovakia. Since the machine had a rotary dial, he had to say aloud to the operator both his calling card number and Daniel's number, which he still knew by heart. The phone rang, and his throat tightened, as it always did when he called Daniel, for fear of saying the wrong thing. It would be lunchtime there. He would have to disguise the impulse of the call, he thought hurriedly, because if Daniel knew it, he would express disappointment. But he wanted to confess his impulse and to have Daniel be kind to him for once.

Daniel's machine answered. Jacob left a plain message, in the hope that Daniel might be home, hear his voice, and pick up, but he didn't pick up. Jacob finished speaking and was left alone again. The night was putting a chill on him. The same sorrow began to well up in him, but he choked it off, became angry at Daniel for having once more failed him. The familiarity of the anger was a consolation; it was enough of one, at any rate, to carry him back to his rooms, where he was able to make a dinner—some fried sausage, a spoonful of red cabbage from a jar, a peeled carrot, and two toasted and buttered slices of brown caraway-seed bread—and recover some of his strength.

Until bedtime he read Stendhal. He had put it aside when he began to try to learn Czech in earnest, because it was too much of an effort to read a book in one foreign language at the end of a day spent learning another, but now, beside the medieval travelogue he had forced himself to choose at the Clementinum, it seemed the lesser of two evils, and the effort it required helped to abstract him.

He fell asleep with difficulty and awoke a few hours later into an unpleasant and complete alertness. His sleeping mind had somehow stumbled onto the thought that it was possible for him to die here. He wasn't thinking of any specific threat; it was almost a mathematical sort of realization—the longer he stayed, the higher the odds of dying here— but he wanted to die at home. It frightened him a little to discover he had such a strong opinion about where he wanted to die, and since he was alone, he decided there would be no embarrassment—he wouldn't be burdening any witnesses with it; there was no Daniel present to construe it as an appeal—in letting himself cry openly.

After a few minutes of this he began to feel better. He got up to wash his face and pour himself a glass of water. Because the feelings in the last few hours had been so potent and their shifts so sudden, it occurred to him to write a short story about them. After all, his development as a writer was the justification he gave himself for staying abroad, and he'd written almost nothing so far. He took a pen and paper and made some notes. He decided to imagine that he had reached Daniel on the telephone. Perhaps the Daniel of the story would feel a little guilty, would worry that his hardness of heart had set Jacob wandering. No, that was implausible; Daniel was beyond guilt. After Jacob had spent the night with him, Daniel had told the story to his boyfriend as an amusement rather than as a confession. Jacob yawned; the anxiety that had awoken him was receding. Perhaps the Daniel of the story could be different, though, more like the Daniel who sometimes surprised him. He had so many thoughts about Daniel, and it had been so long since he had allowed himself to think them. His emotions hadn't really been engaged here in Prague, only distracted, he said to himself; it had not actually been life. As he set down his pen and returned to bed, he decided he would go with Annie to Berlin.

It was late morning when they settled into their train compartment, and they collapsed at once into the pleasant, premature fatigue that follows a successful morning departure, especially one achieved with only minutes to spare—by the time they had reached the train station, they had been cheerfully shouting at each other to hurry—and that serves as a kind of blanket to protect the traveler from the strangeness and emptiness that follow.

They had the compartment to themselves. Once outside Prague, they saw that a light frost lay on the ground, not on the exposed clay of the railroad embankment itself but on the grasses that rolled away from it. The modernity of the city had stopped abruptly at its border; the train was carrying them through pastures, farmlands, and occasionally a village—a few boxy white stucco houses and a rusty car in the crook of a hill's elbow. The steady, muffled clatter of the train reassured and calmed them. "Kontroll bíjety," a boyish conductor announced, in European pidgin, as he slid open their compartment door on its rattling casters and propped it open, somewhat rakishly, with one foot.

"Prosím," Annie said, surrendering her ticket, and asked Jacob, aside, "Do they think we're German now?"

"I do not think, that you are German," the conductor interposed.

"Sorry, I had no idea you spoke English. How rude of me."

"Not at all, madam." He tipped his hat and was gone.

They decided to eat the lunches they had packed, though it was still a little early. Annie had brought a thermos of coffee, hot, and another of milk, cold, and an extra cup for Jacob. She also had oranges, a salad of cucumber and tomatoes, and a tin of sardines. Jacob, who abstained from the sardines, had brought a soft cheese, a salami that Běta had recommended one day when their paths crossed at the butcher's, and half a loaf of bread, as well as a knife to cut them with, wrapped for safety in his towel, since the knife didn't fold. For dessert he had brought two small plastic pots of *smetanový krém*, a sort of sweetened crème fraîche.

"We'd have had to eat soon anyway," Jacob rationalized, "because the *krém* wouldn't have stayed cold."

"You know it's for children, Jacob. I mean, with ladybirds and butterflies and such like on the packages."

They dozed; they read. At the border the train stopped for half an hour while two teams of border guards, first larkish Czechs and then impassive Germans, inspected passports. As the train drifted into motion again, Jacob sat up to see if the landscape would change, and it did: now all the roofs of the little houses were red, as if by regulation. The trees were more neatly trimmed and even, in places, pollarded. Cars, when he saw them, were brightly polished. By a subtle change, the hills, which were steeper, and the villages, which were even more ingeniously placed, now looked strangely familiar to Jacob, who recalled that his great-grandfather had immigrated to Texas from Germany and that his grandmother knew German because it had been spoken in her childhood home. He wondered if it was here that he ought to have come in the first place.

Annie interrupted his reverie. "Is your heart set on Berlin, then?"

"I thought yours was."

She leaned toward the window for a better view, tugging the gray green curtain out of her way with a quick hand, and her face was lit up by a reflection from a field of uncut straw. "It's just that it's something of a challenge to go back to a place sometimes. I wish you would come tonight after all." They had discussed this. She had a plan to meet some of her old friends, and Jacob had decided to explore Berlin's gay nightlife. "Instead of foraging."

"Foraging?"

"Pillaging. Whatever it is that you do. But you need to make up your mind too, I suppose."

"You could come with me."

"No, I would have to face them eventually if I moved here. I'll go by myself. I only asked the ones I want to see."

They fell silent. Annie slipped off her shoes and pulled her feet up beside her on the banquette. The train slowed but did not stop for a small station house in yellow stone with a mansard roof and bricked-up windows.

"You know, in some ways I find it's much better in Prague than it was for me in Berlin. It's more steady, with the group that we have."

"We don't *have* to move."

When they alighted at Berlin Lichtenberg, they quarreled, because Annie wanted to board an elevated train just pulling in upstairs, and Jacob, feeling cautious, insisted on standing in front of the grand transit map of the city posted beside the ticket booth and puzzling out their route. According to the map, more than one elevated train passed through the station, as well as an underground train. But that was as much as Jacob could figure out. Before leaving Prague, he had memorized the name of the stop nearest the tourist bureau where they hoped to reserve inexpensive rooms, and he couldn't find it anywhere on the map.

"I don't understand."

"How peculiar," Annie agreed, after he had asked her to help him search and she too had failed.

They felt rising in them the slow panic that hunger for dinner brings in travelers who don't yet know where they are going to sleep. A German man, as if sensing their anxiety, came forward offering "Zimmer, zimmer," but they waved him away. It was a gray, cheerless station; the floors were dusty and the paint was peeling off the walls. Jacob marched them outside, over Annie's protests, in search of a street sign so that he could locate them on a map of the two Berlins that he had bought in Prague. The burden of their luggage aggravated their sense of unease and vulnerability. The street name they found wasn't listed in the index of Jacob's map.

"I'm not going any farther, Jacob. Shall we go back inside and ask at the ticket window?"

The ticket seller took money from them and pointed to the track where Annie had wanted to board the elevated in the first place.

"I told you."

"I thought people would speak English here," Jacob said.

"Oh, they do, in Berlin. But this is East Berlin, and very much so, in my opinion."

Inside the elevated train, a new transit map explained the mystery: Before unification, the transit systems of East and West Berlin had intersected at only one station. Only that station had appeared on the maps of both cities; there had been no need to remind riders of the existence of places they could not visit. In the new map, the two webs now touched along one filament, hesitantly, and Jacob was able to see both the station where they had boarded and the one near the tourist bureau. He saw, too, that the map that he'd bought in Prague had been no help because it didn't really show both cities; it showed only as much of East Berlin as was unavoidably included by a rectangle large enough to contain all of West Berlin. It was merely an old map of West Berlin that had been opportunistically relabeled.

The eastern city lay below, in white, cold, massive buildings that turned away from them like the spokes of a great turbine as the elevated train took a curve. The architecture looked as grand and sober as cemetery marble.

"There's no one about, is there," Annie remarked. "But then it's midday in winter. You know, we could have stayed in East Berlin. It would have been less dear."

"Absolutely not."

"You sometimes give the impression that you don't much care for socialism, Jacob."

The western city now wheeled toward them, and they saw that it was crawling with traffic and spotted with advertising. The quiet in the car around them became fragile, like an egg to be cracked.

"Gah, it's wonderful," said Annie.

They descended into the hum of the city in a sort of intoxication.

That night found Jacob sitting in a Kreuzberg café, reading.

"With his book he is like Alice," said a man nearby. He spoke in English so Jacob would take notice.

"Alice didn't have a book," Jacob protested, and shut John Mandeville.

"No, didn't she? In the underground?" The man and a friend of his laughed.

"But you know where you are, don't you," said a third man. He was lanky, with pale skin, a large nose, and fine, sandy hair. Like the others, he was in his thirties. "Don't listen to these silly old queens."

"What have you called us? You are too bad."

"He is for me. I spoke to him the first."

"But he doesn't want you," the sandy-haired man again intervened. "Am I right?"

"He's not the one I would choose," Jacob answered. At this the two silly ones laughed even more.

When it was late enough, the sandy-haired man, who said his name was Markus, left the café with Jacob and took him to a club in the top floor of a factory building, a loft space with cement floors and ceiling-high, many-paned windows. The room was dark, loud, full, and hot, and the lights of the city glittered outside, a low-hanging constellation that Jacob already felt he was coming to know.

"This is the great place to come now, if you are gay," Markus said. "You see I am showing you the sights." He seemed to be making fun of his own generosity. He was careful not to make any claim on Jacob, not to expect any return for his courtesy.

Jacob looked over the other men in the club with open hunger and curiosity. It seemed a place to be unabashed. He didn't know if he wanted Markus or one of the others.

"How is it you speak such pretty German?"

"I speak absurd German. You're not even pretending to speak German to me."

"But your pronunciation is beautiful."

"And how about your English."

"I spent a year in America. And I am an actor. It is my job to learn accents."

"I would never learn German if I moved here. Everyone speaks perfect English."

The conversation was only a pretext for studying each other's eyes. Jacob felt lightheaded. He had decided an hour ago that he couldn't afford to spend any more deutschmarks on beer, but Markus had continued to buy beers for both of them. There was a lovely sense of being cut off, unrecognized. In Boston some of the clubs had tried to offer this impersonality but hadn't managed it.

Overhead lights flickered on and off. "It is closing soon," Markus explained. "Now is what I call tiger time. The great beasts pad about, eyeing one another, trying to make up their minds at last."

To Jacob it seemed as if Markus had given voice to the small indifference that still kept them apart, and it made him want to end it. He pulled Markus toward him and they began to kiss. There was no clumsiness, as there was with Luboš.

"Let's go to my place," Markus suggested. Jacob became aware that they were standing in the center of the room and that the lights were on steadily now, but he saw in Markus's expression that his suggestion came not from embarrassment but eagerness.

The sun came in heavily through the curtainless windows and woke Jacob. Markus was stepping into trousers. "Forgive me, I must go to work."

"Oh, of course."

"Would you like tea? Lemon? Honey?"

"Sure," Jacob answered. Markus was unbuttoning a shirt in order to put it on. "What is this?" Jacob asked, lightly touching a painted circle under Markus's skin in the small of his back.

"It's a mantra. Do you know what that is? It's a saying that you repeat during meditation."

Jacob had known the word but didn't mind being given a lesson. "How does it go?"

Markus uttered the syllables.

"And what does it mean?"

" 'The lotus rises from the swamp,' " Markus said quickly, as if he would rather not have said it.

"I'm sorry. Is it a secret?"

Markus laughed. "No, no."

The sun washed the wood of the floors almost white. Jacob pulled sheets around him for cover; the apartment was only a few stories up from the street and the mattress was higher than Jacob was used to, as if atop a pedestal, because it had been placed above a sort of bureau-wardrobe in order to economize floor space. Beside a desk stood a small bookcase of plays in German and English, and Jacob began to read the titles. It was a real home. It was as if Jacob had been given a passkey to the inside of life in Berlin, as if he had been accepted into a kind of freemasonry.

"Here you are." Markus carefully handed up a tea tray. When Jacob took it, in his unsteady hands, the cup rattled loudly in the saucer until he set it on the bed beside him. "You may stay as long as you like; the door will lock by itself behind you. There is a towel in the shower, and here is my phone number."

"I don't have a phone number myself, or I would give it to you."

"You are traveling."

"Maybe I can see you again before I go back?"

"Excellent," Markus answered, but he did not suggest a plan, as if he feared Jacob, as his guest, might be speaking only out of politeness. "And please, here is for a taxi. Czech crowns do not go very far, and I have brought you to a different part of town from where I found you."

Jacob scarcely remembered having told Markus that he was living in Prague. "No, please, that's not necessary," Jacob said weakly. In fact he had no idea where he was, and with the money in sight, he felt a little greed for it and didn't see why he shouldn't take it.

Markus saw his hesitation. "Yes, take it; don't be ridiculous."

They said good-bye, not tenderly, but as if their parting might break into another round of activity. Left alone, Jacob climbed back into bed and dozed, enjoying his nakedness, which was novel to him, because he never slept naked in his own bed. He remembered the tea. Annie would have a good idea where he was, but he shouldn't keep her waiting. He took a leisurely shower.

Before leaving, he stepped into the living room, because he hadn't seen it yet. Its formality reminded him that he hadn't been invited into it, so he looked no more than hurriedly at the leather armchair, Bokhara rug, glass coffee table. In a painting, placed on a wall the sun wouldn't hit, was a tangle of reds and oranges. It called forth no response in Jacob; he felt only that he shouldn't be looking at it, that he was loitering. A neighbor would look through a window and think a thief had got into the apartment.

When the taxi came, it was a German car that in America would have been considered a luxury model. It was clean, and no barrier separated the front and back seats. The young driver asked if Jacob would like to hear music; a Mendelssohn song without words was playing softly on the radio. When Jacob agreed, the driver turned it up. Jacob felt that he had slipped somehow into an atmosphere of solidity and consideration that he couldn't have purchased in Prague and that he couldn't have afforded even if it were for sale there—that he probably couldn't have afforded even in America—yet he and the atmosphere seemed to recognize each other. He fell into it comfortably; he somehow felt it was due him. He knew he would step out of it when the taxi put him down at the door of the hostel. In America it was the privilege of a life he had decided he didn't want, of deferments and compromises, but he hadn't quite faced up to the idea of going without it always, and he had been hoping to leave the question behind when he left America, along with the question he faced in bars. Markus made his living as an actor. No, Jacob corrected himself, he hadn't said that; he had only said he was an actor. Jacob didn't know for certain that it was to a theater that Markus had had to go so punctually on a Friday morning.

After the morning sun, the upstairs hallway of the hostel seemed dim and its air stale, like an invalid's room. Jacob's footfalls were involuntarily quieted by the carpet. He didn't think Annie would still be asleep, and he knocked on her door, which he came to before his own.

"Hello? Who's there?" he heard her ask from within, in a timid voice. He would have pictured an old woman if he hadn't known her.

"It's me. It's Jacob."

He heard the deadbolt thrown, and the doorknob turned, but she didn't unlatch the small chain at eye level until she saw him. "Jeez, you frightened me. I didn't know who it was."

"Who did you think?"

She wandered back into the small room, searching among her unpacked clothes and makeup and open, facedown books and the washed-out containers from their train-board lunch for the ashtray where she had set her cigarette. "I had no idea, really. You weren't in when I knocked a short while ago, so I didn't think it could be you."

"I'm just getting in."

"So I gather." She bounced gently down on the bed beside her suitcase and squinted at him through the smoke. "Are you all right?"

"I'm fine."

"Yes, I can see that you are, now."

He wanted to tell her about it, but she wanted breakfast first. They found a place on the next street and ordered eggs and tea. He narrated his adventure while they ate.

"How much is it in crowns, do you think?" Annie asked when the bill came.

Jacob had to figure it into dollars first, before he could answer. It was about three days' salary.

"It's on me," he volunteered. "I happen to have the deutschmarks."

"You'll need them soon enough. Aren't you going to buy a pair of blue jeans?"

"They aren't my deutschmarks. Markus gave them to me for cab fare, and I didn't use them all."

"Well, I won't stop you if you want to disembarrass yourself of them."

"There's only change left," Jacob assured her, and showed it to her in his palm.

She hadn't finished her tea, and they were both reluctant to start the business part of their day, asking for work in language schools, so they sat a little longer.

"Are you still seeing your Czech friend?" Annie asked, to make conversation.

"He stood me up the other day."

"Oh?" She clinked a spoon idly in her cup. "Perhaps he's a little afraid of you."

"No, no."

"You needn't become alarmed. I'm not saying he's afraid of anything you might do."

"I know what you mean," he said, more quietly, thinking she meant he was an outsider, who would eventually leave. "You haven't told me anything about *your* evening," he continued, to change the subject.

"Oh, haven't I?" she said. "It was fine, as you Americans say. 'Fine.'"

"That's good," Jacob responded, but he was not so inattentive as to believe her. "Where should we go first?" he asked. "There are a couple of language schools over on the Ku'damm."

"Oh, are there?" she echoed, uncertainly. Jacob had noticed the addresses on billboards the night before, on his way to Kreuzberg. They hadn't otherwise prepared at all. In Prague Jacob hadn't needed to. On his third day in the city, frustrated by a broken pay phone on the street, he had stepped into an office building to ask where he could find a phone that worked. The building's porter had listened to him ask his question in English and in French, and had then directed him by gestures to the third floor, where, instead of a pay phone, Jacob had found the municipal office for foreign language instruction. The porter had thought Jacob had known where he was. Within an hour, he had signed a contract for a year's employment.

"I don't know as I'm up for it, Jacob, I'm sorry," Annie said.

"We have to try, at least," he insisted, thinking with confidence how easy it had been in Prague. "Today's our only weekday. The worst they can do is say no, and if they do we'll just ask which of their competitors has low standards and might take us."

"It isn't that." She looked as if she were going to cry. "Oh, I'm a right eejit."

Now she was crying but working to stop herself. "What is an eejit, anyway," he asked. "Is it like a git?"

"You know, an eejit. A person who does a thing everyone knows he shouldn't do, but everyone knows he will do, anyway." In the act of explaining, her composure began to come back to her.

"Like an idiot."

"It's not as cold as that." He waited; she drank a little of her tea. "So I went to the bar, to meet my friends," she continued. "And there was this man, whom I used to be with. I didn't think he'd be there, or I wouldn't have gone. An awfully fine man. He was on the stuff, we all were, a little, when I was here before. Which made it rather carefree."

"And you had some last night."

"What do you take me for, Jacob? I may be an eejit, but I'm not bloody stupid."

"I'm sorry, I didn't mean—"

"I know you didn't," she said. "But that's just it, as it happens. If I came back, I'm not sure that I wouldn't, in the end. Which would spoil it. The memory isn't all bad, you see. But it's the having left that keeps it from being all bad, if you understand what I'm saying."

She seemed fragile and brave. "Let's not move to Berlin, then," he said. "It was you who brought me here."

"I didn't see my way, then."

"It's okay," he said. But he wondered if he really could give up what he had caught a glimpse of.

"You haven't fallen in love, have you."

"No, no," he said. "I wanted to see, is all."

He continued for a while to assure her that he didn't want to stay, but in the end they decided he might as well take a look at the language schools. There was no harm in his exploration.

The interviewers were concerned that he couldn't speak German. They were disappointed that he had no training. They doubted that they could help him obtain a work permit.

"There'll be something for you, if you want it," Annie said, gamely. "Are you willing to wait tables and such like? I could ask my friends. They're bound to know of something."

"How can I wait tables in English? No, don't ask them yet." He didn't think she much wanted to see her friends again so soon, and he was hoping that Markus would have a suggestion. He and Markus had arranged a date for Saturday night.

It was a relief to fall into tourism and shopping until then. A ruined, red-brick church tower seemed to be the center of the city. The high streets were pulled closer to it as they approached, as if by a kind of magnetism. The plaza where the tower stood was ringed by glassy stores, some of a great height, which seemed to have encouraged one another, with glances and nudges, to come as close as they dared to the old ogre, still standing despite an ugly hole in her head, and then, because the ogre didn't topple but continued monotonously to stand, they had lost interest in her and had begun to amuse themselves instead with one another, with gossip and barter.

Jacob and Annie didn't go inside the tower because there was an admission fee. "When you live here, you just piss money away," Annie observed. "But it isn't the same if you're going back to Prague." As Friday turned into Saturday, it became clear that they couldn't really afford anything. Everything was an extravagance, if calculated in crowns, and the business of filling their time with leisure—the purchases of a snack, a bus ticket, a postcard—took on an unreal character, as if they were paying a visit at great expense to selves no longer their own, to selves that they would not really be able to return to until they had given up on Prague for good, whenever that was. To make these selves speak from exile they had to spill money recklessly, like Odysseus pouring blood into a hole in the ground in the underworld. Whenever they stopped spending, they seemed to be walking in a fairy city where they were invisible, or looking through a grandparent's pair of eyeglasses, too strong, at a world strenuously sharp and distant.

To save the cost of the ticket, they didn't enter Checkpoint Charlie but merely walked along the Wall, until Brandenburg Gate. The souvenirs that were sold on blankets here were for the most part the same ones sold in Prague: *matryoshky*, badges, and Russian military coats and hats. In the discount clothing stores, where Jacob could almost afford the jeans, they recognized the other customers as having also come from the East: the men's long whiskers and the coarse henna in the women's hair gave them away. A small band of Slavic men brushed past Jacob as he was waiting for a changing room, and he had to look after them to make sure that the tallest wasn't Luboš, as for a moment he had seemed to be.

"That's bad luck," Annie said, when he told her.

He didn't buy the jeans.

He and Annie had spent Friday night together, but Markus had warned Jacob that the bar that he wanted to take him to strictly refused to admit women.

"That hardly sounds European," Annie commented, "but on the other hand there is something very German about it, isn't there."

"Markus said there must be some men who couldn't be themselves if there were women in the bar."

"Well, it isn't as if one would want to go to such a place. I'm going to have that lovely escarole soup again, at the place near the hostel."

And Jacob, it turned out, was to have no dinner at all. Another man was drinking with Markus when Jacob arrived, a tall man with a wounded look named Ernst. The two Germans had already eaten their dinner elsewhere. Markus suggested vaguely that if Jacob were hungry, the bar they were in might serve hamburgers, but he seemed not to notice when Jacob failed to follow the suggestion up. Ernst made no effort to speak English, though he seemed to understand it. To Jacob's surprise, he also gave no sign that he intended to leave. In fact, when he wasn't glaring at Jacob, he refused to look at him, as if Jacob were the interloper, not he. At a loss, Jacob prattled vacantly about his search for blue jeans. From time to time he looked into Markus's eyes, in search of the welcome he had been looking forward to, but it was either veiled or absent.

At last Ernst left the table for the men's room, and Markus explained the situation. An hour before Jacob arrived, Ernst had revealed that he was in love with Markus. It would perhaps be better if Markus saw Jacob another time.

"But I'm leaving tomorrow," Jacob said. "I don't know if I'm coming back. I wasn't able to find a job."

"That's a pity," Markus said formally. And then, as if he did take pity on Jacob, lust flared up in his eyes for a moment, though it was quickly banked. He didn't offer to help. There wasn't time to go into such a subject before Ernst returned to the table.

"Why did you make a date with both of us?" Jacob asked. He almost felt sorry for Markus as he asked the question, as if Markus had trapped himself accidentally in a social obligation. Perhaps Jacob could think of a way to get him out of it.

"I had not foreseen that Ernst would tell me such news. You and I have just met. You must be reasonable."

It was when he was told to be reasonable that Jacob realized he had been betrayed. "I don't believe you," he said, though he wasn't sure exactly what he didn't believe.

"Would you like money for a cab?" The offer was almost surreptitious, because Ernst was in sight again.

"No." Jacob made an effort to smile at Ernst, so as not to lose face. Let Ernst be the sullen one. A part of Jacob admired Markus for having arranged to be the only one of the three free of the worry that he might be left on the shelf. Maybe that was what he didn't believe: that Markus had come into such an arrangement accidentally.

He drank the rest of his deutschmarks in another bar and cried childishly as he walked back to the hostel. He felt as if he were being taught a lesson. In the morning he woke up looking forward to Prague. In the train he told Annie the story of his displacement lightheartedly, sensing, as he told it, that his enjoyment of her sympathy was already greater than the wound he had received.

To Jacob, as the train descended into the valley that held Prague, the sky seemed to be upholstered in gray silk. Or perhaps, he thought, his head against the glass of the window, it was a coat of very fine mail. The sky was one of the things he was up against in Prague. It was one of the city's weapons.

Moving to Berlin would have been like choosing the easy essay question on a final exam, the one the professor puts there for the students who would otherwise flounder. Jacob wasn't supposed to be one of those students. The story in Berlin was evident: communism had ceased to struggle, and capitalism hadn't, and now the still-living beast was swallowing the dead one in dazed, erratic gulps, like a boa constrictor nearly demoralized by the size of the meal it had embarked on. It was harder to know what was happening in Prague, because it wasn't being swallowed. Capitalism still hadn't arrived; communism hadn't yet altogether departed. In Prague, therefore, it had to have been a third force that set the story in motion. Or a third system, since those two weren't simply forces.

Annie interrupted his thoughts: "I don't suppose we need tell them *why* we changed our minds."

"They won't need a reason, so long as we're coming back."

"We'll just tell them how boundlessly attractive they are." The train was curving slowly around a bend in the Vltava. The river was black and dull, like deeply tarnished silver. "I *am* glad it didn't work out for you with your man in Berlin," she added. "It is selfish of me, but I am."

"It was an adventure," he said neutrally. He was beginning to regret the episode. A picture of Luboš came into his mind, and he felt a pang. He told himself he hadn't lost anything. It would be unfair to reproach himself for having slept with someone else; Luboš had all but said that he had other lovers. But he still felt that he had cheated, somehow. It was in trying to sort out this sense of betrayal that he began to have an inkling of the mission he had set for himself in Prague. He had to feel his way toward it at first. It was like trying to find something set down absentmindedly in the dark. When he did put a conscious hand on it, it seemed so ridiculous that he nearly drew his hand back. It seemed youthful and foolish. But perhaps it had only become ridiculous because he had abandoned it. Perhaps his abandonment, however temporary or optative, had damaged it. He had carried it without seeing it, before, and now he not only saw it but also the crack in it. He wasn't sure he could take it up again earnestly; he wasn't sure he could work himself back into it—see it again from the inside, now that he had seen the outside. To find the spirit of change—was that it?—after the change had happened. It was like a plan to look for a kind of bird that was known to have already flown south. And what's more, he had thought love would bring him this discovery. It didn't make much sense.

But then, abruptly, he found himself inside the idea again—and on the train, too, and looking out the window at the gray sky and black water. He would find it, if he didn't give up. The shadow at least was still here. He would have to find a way to be patient.

When Jacob returned to his rooms, he found no note in Běta's loopy script waiting on the kitchen table; Luboš had not called. He wound up his Russian-manufacture alarm clock—to set it ticking seemed an emblem of his return to life here—and curled up childishly on the sofa under a red fireproof blanket, which he had bought downtown for a hundred and fifty crowns a few weeks before the Berlin trip, at a department store named for the month of May. But the comforts failed him. That night, from the pay phone near the pub, he called the number Luboš had given him but learned nothing from the man who answered. When Friday came, he went to T-Club.

Ivan must have recognized Jacob's unwillingness to struggle, because he admitted him after only half an hour.

"I forgot your cassette," Jacob said, as he sat down next to Ota.

"Is okay, my friend." Tonight Ota was wearing a lime-green Oxford shirt, which called out what was sallow in his features. " 'Some day,' as the Americans say instead of good-bye."

"Is that what they say?"

"That is what they say to me. But perhaps they do not say it to everyone." He pulled an elbow behind his head with one hand, so the other could scratch between his shoulder blades. There were shadows under his eyes.

"It's as if I never went away," Jacob said, looking over the crowd. "I wonder if it will always be this way."

"Oh yes, everyone is always here," Ota agreed, inattentively.

"Not everyone. I don't see your friend Milo."

"Do you like Milo?" he asked, and then he shrugged. "He is a good boy, and so I do not know where he is tonight." He let his head loll to one side, like a puppet whose string has been dropped. "And where were you, that you went away?"

"Berlin. I was thinking of moving there, but I'm not going to."

"Ah, Deutschland. And why did you not like it?"

"I don't know. The people there are kind of hard."

"They are the hardest people in the world, and Americans are the softest, and between the two there is equal danger."

"It sounds as if someone has been breaking your heart."

"You are always breaking my heart, Kuba, but do not joke about it tonight."

A song ended, and a few of Ota's acolytes came in from the dance floor, like Fagin's children returning from the streets. They gave Jacob nods of recognition. One pushed toward Ota a rum and cola he had brought him from the bar.

"Do you know if Luboš is coming tonight?" Jacob asked.

"And how would I know this, Kuba?" The faces of his acolytes were so cautious that Jacob couldn't tell whether they were following the exchange. "Luboš, Luboš," Ota complained.

"I haven't spoken to him for a few weeks," Jacob said, and blushed as if he were admitting to an embarrassing desire.

"There is mystery with him, yes?" Ota answered. "You are always beginning to know him, only."

"He is always virgin again," risked one of the boys.

"Shut up," ordered Ota. "Kuba is also always virgin." He stroked Jacob's hand once, and only once, protectively, and then laughed the moment away.

A couple of beers later, Jacob's eye paused on an unassuming suit, and then he recognized the dry features of the man wearing it. Collin was talking to a man younger than he was, but not so much younger as to belong without effort to the bar's circulation of glances and poses.

Collin had been standing there long enough to fall into the stillness and economy of gesture of a hunter in a blind. Jacob had probably looked at him a number of times without seeing him.

"Ah, not him, Kuba," Ota advised, as Jacob rose.

"But he might know," Jacob answered, and confident with alcohol and the lateness of the hour, he made his way toward Collin, across the bar.

—Pardon me, Jacob said in French. Since neither man acknowledged him, he repeated himself. —Pardon me.

Collin nodded, and his companion turned his eyes on Jacob.

—No one has introduced us, but I believe you know a friend of mine, Jacob said.

—I wasn't aware of it, Collin answered. He gave no encouragement to proceed.

—I had the impression that you knew Luboš.

—Yes, I know him. He didn't bother to meet Jacob's eye, though his companion watched Jacob steadily. Jacob realized that because his French, however stiff, was better than his Czech, he was able to feel the chill in Collin's manner more sharply than he could feel it with someone like Ivan the doorman.

—I have not heard any news of Luboš lately, Jacob continued, feeling he had nothing to lose, and then, wanting to provoke Collin, he added: —Is he in France again?

—No, Collin answered. He showed no surprise at Jacob's knowledge, and no curiosity about it, just as he had shown none when Jacob had begun by addressing him in French.

—Do you know how I might get in touch with him?

—I'm afraid I can't help you. You will excuse me, there is a matter I was discussing with my colleague.

They waited for Jacob to leave.

"I don't understand," Jacob admitted when he returned to Ota's table.

"Cough on him, as we say," Ota advised. "He is not a suitable person."

Jacob tried Luboš's number one more time the next afternoon.

"Moment," said the man who picked up. "Message."

Jacob didn't know whether he was going to be given a message or asked to leave one. The line was silent for almost a full minute. Finally he tried to speak again and was again interrupted.

"Moment, moment," the man said sternly. Then, more gently and more slowly, "Tomorrow, Sunday, fourteen hours. Under clock. Yes?"

Jacob repeated the details back, the phone trembling against his ear.

The hour was at the center of a bright, cold afternoon. Jacob arrived early. Across the plaza, in front of the glass-walled pastry shop, four Czech teenagers were singing in English. A small crowd ringed them, composed of as many Czechs as tourists; there were few tourists now that the days had grown short. Jacob's coat had at last come, and he was wearing it—seal-gray, polyester, with lumpy padding, still musty from the closet in central Massachusetts where it had been stored.

He was looking in the window of a bookstore—a strict one, where you were allowed to walk through the aisles in one direction only—and wondering if he had time to see whether they had a Czech-English dictionary in stock yet, when he heard Luboš salute him.

He was the most handsome man in sight, as always. —But you are early, Luboš noted.

—And you, 'late but nevertheless,' Jacob answered. It was one of the mottoes of last November's revolution.

—I am not late, Kuba. I am precise, as a good Czech. He looked Jacob over frankly, as if for him, too, the interval had dissolved a resistance he hadn't known consciously how to overcome. In his smile Jacob saw a chipped front tooth. It gave Jacob a pang to think that he hadn't noticed it earlier and never would have, if they hadn't managed this reunion.

—You have something . . . , Jacob said, tapping his own tooth.

—That happened when I was a child. He covered his mouth with a hand, as if to press it shut. Then he smiled again, abandoning the effort. —At least I am not a vampire, he added. This was a reference to Jacob's eyeteeth. Their first night together, he had discovered that Jacob felt both bashful and proud of the teeth's prominence.

—I am happy, that we are seeing each other, Jacob said, because he was bursting with it and felt that he had to say so.

—I too. I missed you. In Czech, missing had to be said in the third-person singular, like raining, and so Luboš didn't seem to reveal as much by the confession as he would have in English. But it touched Jacob anyway. He again had the sense that a barrier between them had fallen. He hoped it was that he no longer seemed so young to Luboš. He stepped on Luboš's foot because he couldn't think of another way to touch him in the open square.

On Národní třída, a gallery was exhibiting the hand-drawn typography of a Czech illustrator, and Jacob proposed seeing it.

—He is the author of a children's book, that everyone read, said Luboš.

—I didn't know that, Jacob admitted. —I liked the poster, simply.

They passed the singers. They also passed under a wrought iron balcony. Melinda had recently pointed it out to Jacob as the place where Havel had stood a year ago when he declared the republic. As they walked, Jacob leaned shoulder to shoulder against Luboš, who, Jacob remembered, either did not know where Havel had stood or had pretended not to. It would be rude to insist on knowing which was the case.

—It is for Juliet, Jacob said, pointing at the balcony. There was something fanciful in its metalwork vines.

—Yes, Romeo, Luboš answered, while he also answered Jacob's pressure against his shoulder. Perhaps Melinda was misinformed. The balcony seemed to keep a kind of watch over them as it receded.

—You know, I looked for you, Jacob said.

—I know, Collin told me of it.

Jacob took alarm. —Did I make trouble?

—How could you make trouble, Kuba?

—I can, Jacob insisted, but in fact he was relieved to hear that his conversation with Collin hadn't led to anything.

—I don't believe.

—I went to Berlin for a weekend, Jacob said, to introduce his proof.

—And you were not a good boy?

—No.

—How so?

—With an actor. Are you angry?

—Very.

—I apologize, Jacob said, flushing.

Luboš hesitated, as if he needed a moment to verify that he wasn't in earnest and that Jacob was. —I'm only talking nonsense, Kuba. We're not playing a tragedy.

Jacob inspected Luboš's face, sideways, not sure whether to believe him.

—With an actor, Luboš echoed. —But you really are very bad. They will have to keep an eye on you.

—Who will? Jacob asked, delightedly.

—They.

—But they don't exist anymore.

—So think you. Even when you are guilty, it is innocently.

—Oh no, Jacob protested. —You have to leave me something, on which I can stand.

—You are a rascal then. Is that enough for you?

—That's excellent.

Glass cases along three walls of a gray room told the artist's story. Upon leaving art school in the 1960s, when the relenting of Communist orthodoxy that followed Stalin's death seemed finally, a decade late, to be reaching Prague, he had taken a job as a designer and illustrator. He lettered children's books with a playful, almost flowery script, painted ironic brooches of rubies and garnets as vignettes for a discreet edition of Diderot's *Indiscreet Jewels*, and designed the jackets for a daring series of pocket-size novellas, several of whose authors were later to become dissidents.

—You understand, after 1968 this was not possible, said Luboš. The artist had never done anything openly political. But after Czechoslovakia's style of socialism was "normalized" by Russian tanks, the artist took the precaution of working exclusively in the children's division of his publishing house. In a tamer but still uneven hand, he wrote out the words in innocuous books of Slavic folklore—tales of tricksters and princesses—and in fantasies of elves and goblins by Western writers deemed safe for import. He illustrated an edition of *Candide* with somber images borrowed from the darker of these fantasies, but a censor thought he saw analogies, and the book was never published. On the gallery wall hung one of the unused drawings; the lines forming the face of the naïf hero seemed like scrawls that converged only by chance, and the hatching over his breast resembled a crossing out. After the setback, the artist retreated further. By the start of the 1980s, he had limited himself to illustrating picture books of typical Czech families living through the small adventures of daily life. He drew and lettered them with an abandonment of control and disregard for finesse that suggested that he, too, was somehow a child, as unformed as the children he wrote for. The blots and unevennesses suggested a child's intensity of effort. At this point, he decided to risk writing a picture book of his own, adding to the domestic formula only a fluffy dog of an absurdist size and dirtiness.

—Every child in Czechoslovakia loves this dog, Luboš explained.

It had wild eyes and a somehow reassuring shapelessness. —And you? Jacob asked.

—I am too old, said Luboš, with a touch of reproach at having been made to say it. —But it is very sympathetic.

Made bolder by success, the artist applied his new childlike style to illustrations of *Tristram Shandy* in the late 1980s, taking as his own the wriggling lines that Sterne had drawn to represent the path of his stories. In a dramatic irony, at this moment of return to an adult audience, the artist's struggle was overtaken by the revolution and he became free to address whomever he wanted.

Luboš was silent as they took in the exhibit, except when they came to a book translated from English, such as an illustration from the 1970s of Lewis Carroll's Alice, pictured emerging with the Fawn from the wood where things have no name. Then he asked whether Jacob had read it as a child. He was more absorbed than Jacob had expected him to be.

—Do you like the exhibit? Jacob asked.

His studied neutrality returned to his eyes. —I don't know. It is a little sad, I think.

—Sad, that he could not draw freely? Jacob suggested.

—That is true, but it is also sad that his innocence was genuine, I think.

—But it became knowledge. In the limited vocabulary they shared, Jacob found himself speaking so generally he hardly understood what he was saying.

—A childlike knowledge, which is a kind of promise. But you misunderstand me. It is sad because it will no longer serve.

—Why not?

Luboš shrugged. —And do you like it? he returned the question.

—I do, Jacob said. He felt the artist had found a way to save force by indirection. To keep alive an impulse in danger of being smothered.

—It is like you, Luboš said, thinking aloud.

—No! Jacob replied, more sharply than he intended.

—Yes, it is like you. It is a kind of innocence and a promise . . . He turned away from Jacob with embarrassment, as if he knew it was impolite to turn a person into a symbol.

Jacob thought he saw Luboš deciding that he was too young and fragile. But he was not as innocent as his wish to follow history to Prague, if that wish was in fact an innocent one. —On the poster the artist calls this his first and last exhibit, as if this were the only moment for it. Until now his innocence was not understandable and after now it will not be possible.

—But no, don't say that, Luboš answered, in a lower voice. —For I have decided I want to have you in your silly innocence.

Later that afternoon, in Jacob's apartment, was the only time with Luboš when Jacob felt that nothing was reserved.

"Have a little faith, won't you," Annie said.

"Kafka's house is over there," Jacob protested.

"But it's around the *corner* from Kafka's house. It's this street, I'm sure of it."

"Who's meeting us?" Jacob asked.

"Hans," answered Henry. "Someone I know from work."

"Bit of a soldier of fortune, isn't he," said Thom.

"He does seem to have got around."

"Is all that true, then?" Thom continued. "About his being in the trenches in Beirut when Mossad attacked, the bodies falling to the right and to the left of him and so forth?"

"Where's he from?" Jacob asked.

"He's Danish," Henry explained. "One of the last great believers. He went to Moscow and the Russians sent him here."

Annie stopped and raised one hand. "Do you hear anything?"

"Could that be it," suggested Thom. The large white door of a wedding-cake-like apartment building was propped open by a sign painted with the word JAZZ and a red arrow.

The four of them climbed a spiral staircase that rose behind and around the cylindrical cage of an unmoving elevator.

"And you didn't believe me," Annie said at the third story, where the burble of talk and clinking glasses met them.

"What do you mean, the Russians sent him here?" Jacob asked.

"They gave him a position at the international students' center on Vinohradská, the one that looks like an unpleasantly large spider," Henry replied. "The one Parliament voted last week to shut down. A web of the KGB, they called it, in an allusion to the architecture. As it was, in fact."

"Is Hans KGB, then?" Thom asked. "He seems to want to give that impression."

"If he were, I don't think they would have left him here," Henry said softly. "But don't say I said so."

"Och, it's so full of espionage, Prague, to hear you talk," Annie commented. "Bags I the entrance fees." She rummaged in her purse for bills.

Trumpets and other horns sounded through two tall, hot rooms, set in an L along two sides of the building. The band sat on risers in one end; in front of them and continuing around the corner of the L were staggered a double row of long gray linoleum tables with metal legs, such as might be set up in a school gym in America on election day. So loud was the music in the band's room that Jacob and his friends felt it fluttering against the skin of their faces. They turned the corner into the L's farther leg, where it was possible to talk, and Henry waved to a stout blond-pink man with curly hair, who had to be Hans.

"Henry, my fellow!" the man said. Henry submitted to a hearty embrace. "I am drinking sekt. I hope you will join me."

"What's sekt?" Jacob asked. Even in this room one had to speak at a certain volume.

"Ah, the American," Hans commented.

—If you please, four glasses and another bottle, Henry asked a waiter in Czech, matching the rhythm of his request to that of the waiter, who was hurriedly collecting empties at their table's far end.

Brass and jabber were flooding the room and rising around the gatherings of drinkers and rendering each gathering an island. Scattered among the tables were a few young Westerners like themselves, unshaven but freshly showered, who had probably chanced upon the club thanks to the placard in the street. But for the most part, the rooms were full of Czechs—some intent upon the music, others flowering with the beer into an openheartedness rarely shown in public. They seemed even happier than the Czechs who drank at U medvídků, and Jacob realized that the music had brought them. Middle-aged rather than young, they regarded one another with the familiar boldness of those who have grown up together.

"Are you pleased about Denmark, then?" Henry asked. The Danish team had defeated Spain the night before.

Hans was loud and precise in his satisfaction. Under this cover, Annie leaned in to ask, "Have you seen your man since we came back? What's his name again?"

"Luboš. Yes. It went well."

"And what do you make of this fascist government?" Hans asked, addressing the group generally.

"Do you mean the coupon plan?" Henry asked.

"It's plunder, of course," Hans said, answering his own question. "I am surprised that they have waited so many months."

Hans's eagerness to put forward his opinion reminded Jacob of Daniel. Hans's features were rounder; his skin, paler and thicker. "You think it's a bad idea?" Jacob ventured, despite not knowing what the coupon plan was. Under the sweetness of the sekt there was a metallic tang, which was a sort of provocation.

"Of course. It's lottery capitalism, without disguise." His tone was contemptuous.

"Well, they haven't passed the law yet," Henry said, by way of con-ciliation.

There was a silence until Thom asked, "What is this coupon plan, then? I seem to have overlooked it in my careful study of the Czech press."

"Yes, I'd like to know as well," Annie seconded. "We're quite be-nighted, aren't we," she added, in solidarity.

Jacob looked to Henry, in the hope that Henry would save him from having to admit he had no idea what it was, either. Somehow the presence of Hans involved Jacob's pride.

"It is an organized plan to steal the nation's assets," Hans pro-nounced, and there was a further silence.

Then Henry mildly—almost apologetically—explained that the coupon plan was a scheme for privatization. Small businesses were to be auctioned starting in January, but since there wasn't enough private capital among Czechs and Slovaks to buy large businesses, they couldn't be sold off the same way. The plan was to give every citizen vouchers, also called coupons, which could be used to bid on shares of large industries such as the national carmaker and the national brewery. Because the vouchers could be traded, it was hoped that they would instantly create a sort of meta–stock market. Critics worried that the common people would not know which companies were of any value and might be tricked into surrendering their vouchers too cheaply or end up with shares in dud companies.

"The danger is what you call insider trading," said Hans, "an evil that you have under such excellent control in the West."

Henry laughed politely.

"But you can't want the state to keep the large industries," Jacob protested, thinking he saw a flaw in Hans's position.

"I can want that, as it happens. Socialism is not yet illegal in this country, whatever the case in yours. The working classes built the heavy industries with their labor, and they have the right to own them."

"But they will own them, it sounds," said Annie. "I don't suppose *we* will be granted any vouchers? As workers here?"

"I'm afraid not," Henry answered.

"No, I didn't think so," Annie said.

"The workers will not own them under such a system," Hans corrected. "There is no better means for workers' ownership than the state, led by the Communist Party."

At this, Henry involuntarily glanced around; fortunately, however, no Czechs were in earshot. It was as if the expatriates had on their hands a drunk who had started to reminisce about a heartbreak, and they felt the responsibility of preventing him from starting a fight to console himself. Oblivious, and with a show of magnanimity, Hans topped up everyone's glass. Annie tried to refuse but didn't pull her glass away quickly enough. "If you insist," she yielded.

"But where are the insiders to do the insider trading?" Jacob asked. He felt in him the combativeness that Daniel had used to arouse. "I mean, there aren't any anymore, right? After the revolution." Daniel was beautiful and Hans was not, so Jacob was hitting back lazily, a little wildly.

"Are you joking?" Hans asked. "Havel's castle is full of lackeys and opportunists."

"How do you know that?" Jacob challenged.

"There's also the possibility that the Communists themselves will act as insiders," Henry suggested. "State Security did quite a bit of industrial espionage."

"Are you on about spies again?" Annie asked, drawing a Sparta out of her purse.

"We must hope that they, at least, will keep faith with their ideals and their training," Hans said stiffly.

"Are *you* joking?" Jacob asked.

There was a flash of anger in Hans's eyes, and it immediately shamed Jacob. Hans was on the losing side; he would soon be unemployed. It was unkind to embarrass him. It was even a betrayal of sorts, because he was Henry's friend.

"I didn't mean—," Jacob began.

Hans smiled falsely. "It is understandable that an American should have trouble with, how should I say it, the idea of ideals. In your country they are hardly a force in public affairs."

"Oh no, they are," Jacob said.

"Then you shall tell me the name of the ideal that inspired your country to overthrow Allende, who was democratically elected, and to replace him with Pinochet, a torturer and a murderer. Do you know to what I am referring?"

"Yes, Chile," Jacob was able to answer, but only because he had once read a novel about the coup. He felt a chill in his stomach and drank more of the sekt, to calm himself. "But it happened without our knowledge."

"Ah, the American people and their knowledge. Indeed, they were so upset that a few years later their government gave money to death squads in El Salvador, and your military supervised torture in El Salvador's prisons."

Was this true? It seemed suspicious to Jacob that he had never heard the question argued before in this way, as if America were culpable rather than inadvertently complicit. He reproached himself for never having cared to find out the facts. It was surprising how tender he was about his country's honor; he had always thought of himself as merely a critic, but his mouth was now dry with apprehensiveness. "Many Americans voted against Reagan because of El Salvador," he said, somewhat tentatively.

The Dane sighed. From the heat of conflict, Hans's face was lightly flushed, and in its corners, where prickly white sideburns gave way to finer curls, Jacob saw that he might have found Hans desirable, under other circumstances. Seeing that Jacob had finished his glass, Hans poured him another. It occurred to Jacob that this wasn't the first refill, or even the second. "And Nicaragua?" Hans continued. "Are you going to defend your country's actions in Nicaragua as well?" Hans's manner was a little bit that of an older brother.

"I'm not defending any of it," Jacob said. It was as a critic that he should answer Hans, he saw. "I'm saying that America does have ideals, and Iran-Contra is a perfect example, because when it was exposed, it was a national scandal. There were hearings in Congress. It was on the front page of every newspaper."

"But Oliver North is not in jail," Hans answered, with a quickness that suggested he had met the argument before, "and Mr. Bush, when he visited several weeks ago, to accept tribute from the so-called liberated Czechoslovakia, seemed still to be your president."

"He isn't my president."

"Oh yes, he is."

"You say that as if I had voted for him. You don't know anything about me."

"It is true, I don't."

The table fell silent. "I don't want any more sekt," Jacob declared, rising to his feet. The periphery of his vision darkened for a moment as he stood, and he had to wait for the blood to return to his head. "I'm going to get something else to drink," he told his friends, meaning something nonalcoholic, and walked off toward the bar in the other room.

His thinking mind, as he walked, repeated the stages of the argument and struggled to improve his position, looking for new defenses and new points of attack—America's benevolence to Western Europe and the Third World, the death in Stalin's Russia of millions by starvation and gulag. But his deeper mind had fallen still. His eyes seemed not to see the faces he passed but to take impressions, the way children lay a blank white sheet of paper over an old headstone and raise its contours with a bar of charcoal. The still images his eyes took were not charcoal gray, however; they were gold, as if the boldness of the drums and horns was tinting what he saw. He was a stranger here. He wasn't known to any of these people. A girl with a bandanna tied across her forehead as a headdress glanced down bashfully under his stare, and then up again to see if he was still looking. All these people were so happy in not knowing him.

He asked the bartender for a glass of tonic water, but the bartender merely looked at him. Jacob repeated himself, more loudly, but the man backed away and turned to another customer. Jacob started to accuse him of ill treatment but then realized that he'd been speaking in English. Of course the man hadn't understood.

In Czech he succeeded in purchasing the tonic. He turned to face the band as he sipped it. He seemed to be standing at the best vantage point for seeing and hearing—at the focus of the room. The faces of the musicians shone with sweat; their shirts were damp on the chests and under the arms. The metal of their instruments seemed to concentrate the room's light, the gold, angry light that seemed to have more substance and presence than Jacob himself did. Their music was a kind of sorrowful shouting. It was American and not American, white and black. But it made no connection between these worlds, Jacob decided. He had drunk in Hans's bitterness; his thoughts were saturated with it. The powerless tried to reach across with their art, he reasoned, but it was in the failure of the attempt that the powerful found their pleasure, which the powerless misunderstood as sympathy. The better the art, the more poignant the failure. The only one who really suffered under the illusion was the artist.

Jacob took one more sip of his sour tonic, and threw up—a sudden and horribly comic expulsion. For a moment, he leaned over the vomit on the floor in front of him, as if he were going to try to wipe it up with the handkerchief he always carried in his back pocket. But to his relief he had to acknowledge that there was too much of it. (What had he been eating? he of course wondered.) He was going to have to let someone else clean up his mess. He ran to the men's room and locked himself in a stall.

There he felt abruptly clear-headed. He sat on the closed toilet seat and stared at the metal panels around him. The gold that had been coating his sight had subsided; now the air seemed dusty blue. He tried to reassure himself with the thought that throwing up was a silly and trivial offense. Young people often did it after drinking too much. He hadn't thought that he ever would, but evidently it had been his turn to. That's all it was.

"Jacob?" Thom called, after about a quarter of an hour. "Are you in here?"

"I don't know."

"I needn't tell anyone, if you don't like."

"You might as well. I'm going to stay in here forever."

"Is it as bad as that?"

"I threw up in front of everyone. In the middle of the other room."

"Was that you, then? You had a cross-eyed look when you left the table."

"I'm going to wait here until everyone else in the club has gone home."

Thom was too considerate to laugh. "How are you feeling?"

"Oh, much better now."

"I always feel much improved after a good retch, myself. Nasty stuff, that sekt. Should have warned you about it."

"It shouldn't be mixed with politics," Jacob said, speaking through his hands.

"That Hans is rather full of himself, isn't he. I know he's Henry's friend, but I didn't appreciate his tone."

"Oh, he's all right. He just wanted a debate."

"I thought he became a bit personal."

"Only because I took it that way."

A couple of strangers came into the men's room. Jacob waited silently inside his stall, and Thom waited silently outside it, until they left.

"How shall we proceed, then?" Thom asked.

"The Czechs will yell at me if they see me."

"I expect they've already forgotten about it, but we could keep them from seeing you, if you like."

"Could you get my coat and hat? I can't go back in there."

"Do you want to go home?"

"No, no, I'm fine. I just can't go back in there."

"I'll fetch your coat, and then we'll walk you out, all of us in a ring, if that's agreeable. The way they do for heads of state, when they pass through a crowd that might have snipers."

"That would be—that would be great. You're a prince."

It was a little too much to say, Jacob sensed, as soon as he spoke. From inside his metal box, he couldn't see Thom's face.

Left alone, Jacob inspected his clothes for spatter. He was clean. Gingerly he rose, let himself out of the stall, washed his hands and face, and drank from the tap. To feel a nation's guilt was as spurious and grandiose as to take credit for its triumph. Yet both the guilt and the triumph were real, and the emotions were powerful. In the detachment of his half sobriety, somewhat like an invalid, Jacob handled the feelings as if they were dry pages that he could inspect or shuffle or fold up, as he chose.

"Are you all right, Jacob?" Annie asked, when his friends met him outside the men's room in a group, as Thom had promised. Hans had stayed behind. "We were so concerned about you."

"Go, go, go," Jacob said, slipping into their midst and crouching so as not to be seen. He was already cheerful enough to make a game of it.

In the morning, Jacob lay for a while in bed in a state of dry alertness, looking up toward the blank plaster of his ceiling, until he heard four gentle knocks on his apartment door.

He shuffled into last night's pants. "You have telephone," Běta said, speaking softly and pantomiming a phone call, as if she weren't sure her English would get through at such an hour. Perhaps she had heard him come in late the night before. "Is brother," she added.

"Brother?" Jacob asked. He didn't have one.

She shrugged. "Yes, brother." She continued in an even softer voice: "He say—excuse me, he say-s—to Father, that is your brother." He could tell from her smile that she was ahead of him, but he could not figure the puzzle out. "Family—telephone—okay," she hinted. "Father allow. Father allow-s."

"Oh," Jacob said, at last following.

She held up a finger to her lips. "Is American brother. Not Czech brother. I know, because I have spoke—have spoken—to him, also." Being in on Jacob's secret seemed to have given her confidence in her English.

"Thank you," Jacob said, as they mounted the stairs. He tried to imagine who it was.

"Not at all," she answered.

Beneath the African-style carvings of Tragedy and Comedy, Mr. Stehlík was sunk in his sofa, distrustfully eyeing a document propped on his knees. "So you have brother. I do not know this. I think, that you have only sister."

"I do have a sister." That much was true.

"Your brother says, that telephone is important," Mr. Stehlík continued, waving Jacob toward the phone, with an exaggerated deference. "Please." He took an ashtray and a handful of papers with him to the kitchen.

Jacob didn't dare sit down. "Hello?" he said wonderingly into the phone.

"Jacob? This is your brother Carl."

Carl was one of the straight men whom Jacob had fallen for the year before, in Somerville. They had met at a dinner party thrown by a man who was having a nervous breakdown, of which the dinner party had been in several ways a symptom, and the spirit with which they had gotten through that evening—a shared recognition of the irrationality, an unspoken agreement to treat it as lightly and tactfully as possible— had been continued in their friendship, where it had made it relatively easy for them to finesse Jacob's brief, awkward confession of romantic interest. By the time Jacob had been disabused, the two had become a little more than friends—they were conspirators, confidants. There was always melody in Carl's voice, and hearing it now—it rose on Jacob's name, then fell from even higher during the pronouncement that followed, as if it were a serious revelation, only to curl up in a chuckle at the end, over Carl's own name, as if that were the biggest joke of all—Jacob thought that he had fallen for its music more than anything else.

"It's so good to hear from you," Jacob said. Then, confused by the delay in the transatlantic line, they both spoke at once:

"I apologize for the—"

"Are you coming to vis—"

They waited for the echoes to subside.

"You go first," Jacob said.

"It's hard to reach you, man. Is that your landlord? Is he listening now?"

"Yes. Not to you."

"Okay, well, that guy, he's got a serious pole up his ass."

"It really is very good to hear from you."

"He's like, 'Telephone busy. Is family? Only family!' I'm sorry if I get you in trouble, but I had to get through." Carl gave Mr. Stehlík a Russian accent when he imitated him, rather than a Czech one—gluey and sonorous, rather than spare and flat. The wrongness of it gave Jacob a flash of homesickness. He felt a nostalgia for not knowing the difference.

"Are you coming to visit?"

"I'd like to, but that's not why I'm calling, I'm afraid." He stopped. "I'm afraid I've got bad news."

"What?"

"Your friend Meredith?" Carl paused, but then he evidently decided to get it over with. "She died. She killed herself, actually."

"She—"

"Matthew called me, because I had your number. He wasn't up to telling you. I'm sorry."

Jacob said nothing for a little while.

"How're you doing?" Carl asked.

"Fine. Is Matthew all right?"

"He's all right. I mean, he sounds really broken up. But he's all right. They stopped going out a while ago. She was going out with another guy." Carl gave the man's name.

"I don't know him," Jacob said. He didn't at that moment feel as if he knew Meredith, either, but he found that he was crying. Out of the corner of his eye, he saw Běta poke her head into the living room for a nervous look, and then bow out apologetically.

"I'm sorry," Carl repeated. "I wish I had known her better and could talk about her with you. I did meet her that one time, at your house for dinner."

"That was the last time I saw her, too," Jacob realized.

"She was a poet, I think you said."

"I can't talk about her right now."

A suicide makes a fault in a novel, as suicides make a fault in life, and only the shadow of Meredith's story falls on this one, as if in leaving a movie theater she had walked across the path of the projector.

Jacob asked for details. Carl told him about a hotel room and an overdose, and then a second hotel room and a rope.

"Why didn't anyone lock her up?"

"I don't know. Sometimes it isn't so easy, you know."

"It should be." He held on to his anger long enough to end the phone call. The stubborn little motherfucker, he thought.

—My friend died, he told the Stehlíks, in their kitchen. The dogs padded over to where he stood and sniffed him. —Herself to herself.

—Self-murder, Běta supplied the word. —Jesus Mary.

—She was your girlfriend? Mr. Stehlík asked.

—She was, several years ago. It was a little more than the truth, and much more than he had meant to say.

—It is a great pity, Běta said, with none of her usual tentativeness. —It is a mess. It always is, in such a case.

Mrs. Stehlíková wrung her hands, classically. —If you will want to smoke a cigarette, it doesn't matter when, you will come to see me.

—Yes, if you will want anything . . . , Mr. Stehlík offered.

Jacob thanked them.

—To sit with us, Mrs. Stehlíková continued. —Or if you will want to borrow one of the dogs for company.

—Yes, take Aja, but not Bardo, Běta elaborated. —Bardo is tiresome. The boxer and poodle looked up intelligently at the sound of their names. —Yes, you, Běta told the poodle.

—Oh, he's not so tiresome, Jacob said. —I have to teach today, he added, and they excused him.

It was a relief to fall into the routine of teaching. He walked his students through dialogues about having a watch fixed and having a ticket refunded. He found himself thinking not of Meredith but of Luboš, with an urgency that surprised him. They had a date for Saturday night, but Jacob wanted to see him sooner. No one answered, though, when he called Luboš's number from the faculty lounge between classes.

The only other person in the lounge was Kaspar, who poured a thermos of soup into a bowl, and as he took a spoonful of it, slurped a little. "Forgive me," he said, with his quiet smile.

"Of course. Is it good?"

"Very. My landlady cooked it. Would you like to try?"

"No, no. Thanks, though."

"In Czech, it is called *boršč*. Do you know it?"

"Borsht. I didn't know the Czechs made it."

"They do not make it. It is Jewish soup."

"I hadn't thought of it that way. Don't get it on your clothes. It doesn't come out."

"Are you Jewish, Jacob?"

"No."

"I thought, because of your name. Do not take offense."

"I wouldn't take offense at that."

"That is good. Some people do."

The trees outside the lounge window were bare for winter, and past their forked trunks the sky was chalky gray like cigarette ash, and so bright that it was a little painful to look into.

"Are *you* Jewish, Kaspar?" Jacob asked, to make conversation.

"I am not, but I think I am sorry for that. It interests me very much."

"Do you talk to your landlady about it?"

"I do. She is a very kind woman."

"I think it's going to rain," Jacob said, inconsequently. Then, more inconsequently: "I heard this morning that a friend of mine committed suicide."

"Suicide? I am very sorry, Jacob," Kaspar answered.

"Please don't stop eating," Jacob said. In just a quarter of an hour they both had to teach again.

"Was he unhappy?"

"She. She was unhappy when I knew her. But I thought maybe she was getting happier."

"Sometimes it is a mercy."

"No it isn't," Jacob said sharply.

"Are you a Catholic?"

"I'm not anything. But it's just death. It isn't a mercy."

"Perhaps I have the wrong word."

"No, you had the right word," Jacob answered, unwilling to hear anything less than an explicit retraction.

"You feel very strongly for her."

"I guess."

"You were in love?"

"We had a lot in common."

"Ah, she was a writer."

Jacob didn't answer.

"That will be hard for you," Kaspar added, thoughtfully.

"We were both pessimists," Jacob tried to explain.

"Pessimists?"

"We both thought it was going to be hard."

"But I thought that you did not believe in the difficulty of writing. You told me so that evening at Melinda's party."

"We didn't think *writing* was going to be hard."

"No? Do you think they want you to make art?"

"Who's they?" Jacob asked, sickening at the realization that the topic was drifting from Meredith to himself. "They don't care one way or the other. They aren't why it's hard."

There was an awkward silence. "In any case there are many reasons why it's hard," Kaspar said, blinking heavily in distress at having crossed someone in pain. "I should not have argued with you. Please forgive me."

"No, it's all right. You don't have anything to apologize for."

"I wish that you would forgive me anyway."

"Of course I do. Of course I do."

Kaspar resumed his soup. It looked like blood, though of course neither of them felt like saying so aloud.

By the time Jacob had finished teaching, later that afternoon, the gray of the sky had darkened further and there was a quick, erratic wind. Libeň, the district that contained the language school, stood on a hill, and at the foot of it, in the dusty square where Jacob customarily changed trams, he saw that people were passing in and out of a subway station that had been under construction since before his arrival in the city. If the station had been open that morning, Jacob hadn't noticed it; he didn't think it had been. Běta had told him when he moved in that the authorities planned to extend the northeast arm of the subway four stations closer to her family's home. She had also told him not to expect it to be ready during his stay, because the government had all but shut down its merely municipal functions. But the station appeared to be open now; it seemed to be the first day of service.

Jacob decided to take it into town. He didn't expect to find his friends. He didn't know where they were going to be that night—probably at home in bed early, recovering from the night before. But there was no one at his apartment. Perhaps he could buy flowers of some sort for Meredith. He could throw them into the river for her. She would have made a face of scorn at that: "Oh," she would have said, with brittle disgust.

The station had a décor like the older ones it joined—stone polished to the point of reflection, panels of yellow-tinted metal. No placards had yet been hung to warn of fines or to point directions, but Jacob had a November stamp in his transport pass, and he knew he would be able to tell which was the downtown track. He estimated, as he walked past the glass booth that housed the station supervisors and downstairs to the platform, that the subway extension would cut a quarter of an hour from his trip to Wenceslas Square. Moscow was said to have paid for the old stations. It meant something for these to open despite the revolution.

An old woman in a blue apron hurried out of the supervisors' booth in pursuit of him. She was yelling. On the landing halfway down to the trains, she caught him by the wrist and yanked as if she were going to drag him by force back upstairs.

—I don't understand, Jacob said. —The station isn't open? he asked. He could see that it was. People in ordinary clothes with no special demeanor were standing on the platform below.

—The other side, the other side, the woman yelled.

He looked around but didn't see any barrier that he had crossed. —I'm sorry, he said. —I don't understand. With his free hand he gently tried to peel back her grip, which was upsetting to him.

She clenched harder and yanked his arm again, startling him. —No! No! You must up! She was addressing him with the familiar second-person pronoun. It was her privilege as a woman with white hair to treat anyone as a child.

—Up? Jacob repeated. —The station isn't open?

—Yes, but you must down by the other side. Come, up!

The banister bisecting the staircase, he realized, was meant to separate upward from downward foot traffic. He had been walking down the up staircase, as yet unlabeled.

—I didn't know, Jacob apologized. —There are no signs.

—That doesn't matter. Come!

—I'm almost down already. When I return, I'll remember. On the next trip. When I return, you'll have a sign.

—No! No! You may not go this way! Now she was pulling on his arm with a two-handed grip. —Up! Up!

—I won't! Let go!

—You must! You must do it normally!

—Leave me! Jacob said, shaking his arm as roughly as she was shaking it, a little frenzied by her touch.

—You Russians, the woman said.

—I'm not Russian, Jacob answered, pulling off her hands with his by force, one at a time, and walking down the rest of the stairs to a train that was just coasting up to the platform.

The train carried him smoothly into the dark. He felt the looks of his fellow passengers settle on his sneakers, as they always did on the subway, where the seats faced one another across the aisle. He closed his eyes. He wanted things. He refused to stop wanting them. Maybe he even wanted to write a story about Meredith.

He ate a pizza in the stand-up restaurant at the foot of Wenceslas Square where he and Luboš had eaten the day of Bush's speech. He stood at the counter in the front of the restaurant, which looked through plate glass into the street, and while his back was turned to the view, it began to snow. An unexplained calm in several faces prompted him to look over his shoulder and discover it. It was the first snow he had seen in Prague. He paid quickly and stepped out into the square.

From the stately shoulders of the National Museum, and from the sword raised by the saint before it, the long square swept down. The flakes continued at millions of separated points the suppressed gray light of the sky, and by attracting the eye to middle distances that an ordinary view collapsed, they gave the square a depth that Jacob had not appreciated before. They sped down toward the paving bricks and into them, like ghosts into walls, along curves that were neatly interrupted by the flakes' vanishing. He thought it was unfair to Meredith that he had the luck to stare up into the beauty of the square and enjoy his sorrow for her.

He turned away. He remembered a flower shop in Malé náměstí, the Little Square. The narrow, crooked street that ran to it was nearly empty of tourists, but for a more perfect solitude he took advantage of a recent discovery and opened a person-size door cut into the carriage-size door of an apartment building, and stepped into a private passage, which wound through the interior of the block in loose parallel to the public street outside. Afraid to call attention to himself, he didn't click on the passage lights. He could see well enough by the twilight that sifted down from the first-landing windows of the irregularly placed staircases that lined the passage. He heard only his own footfalls. When, at the end of the corridor, he emerged, he found that the snow was falling more heavily. He hadn't worn his winter coat or brought a hat, and his hair was soon matted with it.

—Do you have roses?

—But it is winter, see? You see what we have.

There was nothing better than red-dyed carnations, so he took them. He considered the First of May Bridge, the one near Café Slavia, which cut across Střelecký island, because it would be more or less solitary, but then he decided that with such ugly flowers he couldn't choose anything less than the most beautiful bridge, the Charles, even if it was so beautiful as to be a cliché.

On the bridge itself, standing in what was now sleet, he was miserably cold and wet, and it was difficult to compose himself and find the feeling that he had meant to put into the gesture. It helped to face the river, so he leaned over the thick stone ledge and looked upstream toward the long shining weir, which cut the water into planes. Beneath him, where the river flowed quietly around the piers of the bridge, the water was black, and when he dropped his first flower, it felt more like an experiment than a tribute. The carnation turned gray as it fell, and after it hit the water, it dipped and rose once or twice on the surface like a person turning on a bed to get comfortable, before the current carried it under the bridge, out of sight. As he dropped the rest, singly, he had an incongruous memory, which he could not shut out. It was a story that an older gay man, a professor of French literature, had told him in a taxi in the spring. Though sick, the professor had agreed to come with Jacob's friends from a dinner party to a bar. In the taxi he had changed his mind about his strength and decided to go home, but not before telling Jacob—who had confided his hopeless crush on . . . he couldn't remember now for sure, but it must have been on Carl—a story from the 1970s, of asking a straight friend to undress and lie on the floor, while he, the professor, not then a professor, sat above him on a chair and dropped twelve dozen roses onto his chest, one by one. "This is how beautiful you are to me, that's what I was telling him," the professor recalled. "At first he laughed and thought I was ridiculous, but I didn't say anything, and after the hundredth rose or so, I could see that he saw that I meant it, and then I could see that he was hard, and I kept dropping the roses."

Jacob flattened and folded up the wrapping paper that had carried the flowers. He wished they had been roses.

Returned to his apartment, Jacob changed into a dry T-shirt and underwear, and ate some bread and jam. He left the cushions he used for bedding on the couch, because he thought he would be warmer there than on the floor. But he woke up cold nonetheless after what seemed only a few minutes of dozing. He carefully doubled his red blanket so that it would be twice as thick but still cover all of him and tried again. Instead of drifting back over the events of the day, however, his mind fell into a rut, like a heavy lawnmower yanking after it the child who is supposed to be pushing it. First he had to sound out all the letters in the Czech word for "bookstore," which is a long one, over and over. The task gradually changed into a nonsensical conversation in English about buying a bus ticket, and this too he seemed to rehearse, as if he were preparing in his mind to teach it as a lesson at the language school. He could only stop himself from repeating it by making an effort to come awake. When he did, he recognized in the repetitions the stamp of fever.

As an experiment, he swallowed. The back of his throat pained him. He waited for a while in the almost-dark, hoping the symptoms would subside. The heavy curtains no more than dimmed the light from the street lamps outside, and under the covers he felt a certain security in the room. Those were his books on the shelf, after all. On the floor the lime carpeting was bland and familiar. There was the wardrobe where he hung his shirts. There was the small, circular, white-painted table he used as a desk. He felt that the room was on his side and that it was safe to wait here. He closed his eyes. But the fever continued to force his mind to run through drills.

In the medicine cabinet, he found a thermometer left behind by Běta's grandparents, wider and easier to read than the kind he had grown up with. The back of it was a solid forest green. It reminded him of a pen he had owned as a child, a souvenir from a French town, given to him as a gift, which had had a window where a skiff sailed from one side of a bay to another as you turned it upside down and then right side up again. On his way back to the couch, he fetched from the wardrobe his down sleeping bag, which he hadn't used since buying the red blanket. Under this layer and the others he took his temperature. It was in Celsius, which he couldn't interpret, but he didn't think it looked high and so fell once more into an uneasy doze, the glass wand resting in his hand.

Upon waking this time, he draped the red blanket around him and went to sit at the kitchen table. While retaking his temperature, he put water on to boil for tea and wrote nonsense in one of his notebooks with colored pencils. The words looked grand in their variety. I'm going mad, he thought in a spirit of adventure. To translate the measurement, he wrote beneath the words, in orange, the equation $212 - 32 = 100 - 0$, and then by longhand arithmetic found that he was slightly more than 103 degrees Fahrenheit, a number that scared him.

—Good evening, what is it? Běta asked civilly after his knocking woke her.

—It is not well with me. He handed her the thermometer to read.

—That is high enough, she agreed.

She brought him into the living room and went to tell her parents. Through their half-open bedroom door, he heard their unguarded murmurs together. In a minute, they filed in quietly in their robes—like a king and queen in Shakespeare, Jacob thought.

—I am sorry—, Jacob began.

—Psh, Mrs. Stehlíková stopped him. —Does it hurt?

—In the throat, he answered.

Mrs. Stehlíková said something, but too rapidly for him to understand. He had the sense of play-acting that one has when calling attention to an illness that hasn't taken away the ability to walk or think.

Běta translated: "Mother say, that when she has pain in throat, she smokes a cigarette. But she is joking, of course."

After conferring with her father, Běta tried several telephone numbers without success. Then she proposed something; Mr. Stehlík answered with subdued exasperation. Her next call got through. Unable to follow what was happening, but feeling cared for, Jacob sank a little into his fever.

"How are you?" Běta asked in English, when the call was over.

"So-so."

Father and daughter repeated the expression, which seemed to amuse them. "That is, between?" Mr. Stehlík asked.

"A little less than between," Jacob clarified.

"There is hospital here," Běta said, pointing on a map to a clinic just beyond their post office, "but is closed. I call friend, who is doctor; he is not at home. But there is doctor at night hospital, and I speak to him. He say you must come. But is here." She pointed to a boxed red cross halfway to the language school. She waited for Jacob to understand the implication.

The Stehlíks did not own a car. "Taxi?" he asked.

"Taxis are asleep. By night tram. But I will go with you." She gave him a moment for the idea to sink in, and then repeated, "By night tram!" in a commiserating exclamation.

After midnight, night trams ran less than once an hour. "No, I'll just go to sleep. I'll be better tomorrow."

"You may not. Temperature is too high. Doctor say, that you must to him. He is nervous."

"Ježišmarja," Jacob permitted himself. The women laughed.

—At least he is speaking Czech well, Mr. Stehlík observed, in that language.

"I go to dress," Jacob said, falling into what he thought of as a Czech pattern of English.

—The next tram will come at two forty, Běta said, consulting the laminated schedule they kept by the phone. —I will come for you at two twenty-five.

—Thus, agreed Jacob.

In his rooms he dressed properly, pocketed his passport and long-term residence permit, and laid on the couch to wait out the interval.

—It is unbelievable, he complained to Běta, ungratefully, when she came to fetch him.

—It is unbelievable, she agreed with a shrug. —And nevertheless . . .

They had to walk to the head of the street to cross the highway, because of the concrete wall that shielded the neighborhood from it. The night tram's line ran through a field on the far side, a large empty field adjacent to a factory that built engines and industrial machinery. It was lit by street lamps, which looked out of place because there was no street. There were only the tram tracks and high dead grasses, and here and there curving wet furrows where the wheels of a backhoe or a truck had bitten through the raw soil. At the bottom of a gully a dozen unused concrete sewer pipes were stacked in a shoddy pyramid. To power the tram, a web of electrical wires curved through the air, below the lamps but high above the ground.

Until the tram came, Jacob didn't say anything. He was angry at his bad luck, and he was making a show of his frailty and his need to conserve his strength.

—I'm going to die, he said when they were safely aboard. They were the only passengers. In Czech his sentence consisted of a single word, compact and strange. He repeated it for the pleasure of the sound. —I'm going to die . . . on a night tram.

—It is a special fate, for an American, Běta observed.

He groaned, because he really did feel miserable.

—But don't speak that way. Truly you aren't going to die.

—Truly?

—It isn't possible. On a tram? It is nonsense.

She closed a window for him. She was right. The tram was even more simple and solid than his bedroom, and its progress suggested that nothing aboard it could be final. The wires sang as the tram rounded the corner at the top of the field. It edged past a checkerboard of motley vegetable patches, now dry and silver.

—But I am going to die, he insisted. —We're all going to.

—But not on a night tram, Běta answered with a touch of impatience.

By the time they reached the hospital, Jacob was too exhausted and feverish to see continuously, and he found later that he had no clear memory of how they got into it from the tram. But he was able to remember the emergency room, paneled in dark wood like the tailor's department at a men's clothing store, each of its curtained chambers like a changing room. In the center was a great table, as in the kitchen of an old hotel. Jacob sat on the table, while a sullen doctor in a white coat attended him. The doctor seemed displeased that he had been woken; directed by a nod from Běta, Jacob saw in the nearest chamber the rumpled sheets and pillow where the doctor had been lying. He spoke brusquely to Běta and not at all to Jacob.

"Angína," the doctor diagnosed.

—I don't understand, Jacob said. —But Běta will remember the word.

—You need antibiotics. Do you understand that?

Jacob nodded. The doctor said a little more to Běta and then left them alone. Běta signaled for Jacob to put on his coat again; they were going home.

—Antibiotics? Jacob asked.

They knocked at the pharmacy attached to the hospital for a quarter of an hour, but no one answered. Jacob wondered, as they waited, whether the doctor's rudeness had covered embarrassment.

When they reached home again, empty-handed, Běta gave him her family's supply of Paralen, which she said was like aspirin, and he agreed to leave his door unlocked, so she and her mother could check on him in the morning without waking him. She told him that according to her dictionary the English word for what he had was "quinsy."

The antibiotics, which Běta fetched from a local pharmacy the next morning, seemed weak; they moderated the illness but did not defeat it. Jacob, however, found it easy to accommodate himself. In the mornings he was cool and lucid, for the most part, though he became dizzy if he stood up quickly. When he could, he took advantage of his morning strength by making a soup or a soda bread—something large and simple, which would keep. Then, as a treat, he lay on the couch and read Stendhal. Somehow he was always able to resume the story of Fabrice without confusion, though he could not call it to mind until he picked the book up. It was as if the French language were a separate room from the one he inhabited when he spoke Czech or English, and the story of Fabrice were going on in that room only. To be present in the room without reserve he needed a silence like the one his illness afforded. He had never had one like it in America.

At some point in the afternoon a small task would find him impatient, and then another would fluster him, and for a remedy he would run a hot bath. After stepping into it, he would carefully dry his fingers and read Stendhal there for half an hour more, prolonging the day's span of clarity by means of the water and the novel. It usually held until dinner, during which he would begin to feel disoriented. At night he sweated himself to sleep, the fever breaking at some unconscious hour early in the next day.

He wondered once or twice if it was conversion sickness, but he didn't torment himself with the idea, because he had never done anything not allowed, not even with Luboš, and because the illness felt too familiar. He was fairly sure that the Czech quinsy translated as the American strep throat, in his case, anyway. He had suffered from strep so often as a child that he recognized it as an old companion.

The illness made an interlude, not unlike his first weeks of solitude in the apartment. When he telephoned the school, the head of the English department, a clever and matronly woman, assured him generously that he would not be expected at work for at least two weeks, then grew alarmed and cautious when he admitted that the doctor hadn't issued a certificate of illness during his middle-of-the-night visit to the emergency room, and finally generous once more upon hearing that Běta would take him to the neighborhood clinic first thing Monday for the proper documentation, called a *neschopenka*. "It is a crime to stay home without one," the head of the department sighed into the phone. "It is the old system, still. We have not got trust here. And there is a control, a special police, who visit to see that you are at home as you say. You must ask Běta to go to the shops for you, in case they should come."

Běta did shop for him, though no police officer ever visited. The first errand he set Běta, however, was a telephone call to Luboš's number, saying that he was too ill to keep their Saturday date. As soon as he sent her off, he regretted it, because he realized that in his condition he could probably have won a limited permission to use the phone socially himself, and he was afraid Luboš might perceive an attempt to establish distance in his deputizing of the call.

He had a great deal of time to think about Luboš during his enforced holiday, so much time and so little shaped by physical effort that his thoughts took on an abstract and idealist cast. He was growing proud of the relationship, he felt, and he wondered if the pride was false or naïve. By its nature a relationship was not an accomplishment. It was just a connection that happened to exist, for as long as it did exist. To a confidant, if there had been one, he might have excused the pride by referring to the communication that Luboš and he were establishing between cultures.

What really pleased him was less grand and more peculiar. It was that he had felt no wish to back away after his reunion with Luboš, perhaps because of Luboš's belief in his innocence, or whatever quality it was that they were agreeing to call by that name, which had nothing to do with sexual fidelity or appetite. He felt sure that Luboš had the quality, too.

It was an end to shame, he thought with exaltation. (He was sipping tea and sitting in the kitchen's morning sun, as he thought this. The illness, during its abatements, seemed to make him more susceptible to such accesses.) It was odd that, directed by Daniel's scorn, he had spent so much time trying not to be taken as an innocent. It was hard to know what the quality in question meant to Luboš, exactly. It might be no more than an echo of Christianity or of Communism. The innocent belonged to the communion, in both cases. They were happy in it; they had no wishes apart from it; their hungers were satisfied. No, that wasn't right, Jacob corrected himself. It was not the innocent but the believers, or maybe just the saved. . . .

He listed in his journal things he wished he knew about Meredith. Where she was buried. Whether she had been worried about money. Whether her parents had ever spoken to her again. Once, when Běta was unpacking with care the eggs, onions, lentils, carrots, and milk that she had bought for him, and laying the items gently on the kitchen table for his approval, he remembered almost unwillingly the violent way Meredith had used to take her Peters edition of the *Well-Tempered Clavier* out of her satchel, as if she scorned to have any concern for the book as a thing, and the similar violence—or rather, a precision so dry it sounded like violence—with which she played from it, throwing down the notes dismissively as if none of them deserved to be part of the piece of music they together suggested, as if the time spent playing them were a waste she couldn't keep herself from.

—I also had a friend who committed self-murder, Běta offered, seeming to read his thoughts.

—I'm sorry, Jacob answered.

—It was very sad! Běta said, nodding and smiling as if the emotion caused by such an event were a joke the two of them shared.

—Did she say why? In a note?

—No. Did your friend?

—I think, that no, said Jacob.

Běta thoughtfully twisted her mesh bag into a ball. —My friend was a dissident. The parents did not want me to see her, because of it. But I saw her.

—Were you a dissident?

—Me? She pointed to herself and widened her eyes, as if he had suggested that she knew how to repair a car engine. —No, no. She was much smarter than I. But she was my friend, and I saw her. But she wouldn't get out of bed. It was very hard. She was an orphan—do you know that word?

—Yes. It seems that your friend was depressed.

—Yes, and now it is we who are depressed, we who were not dissidents. Is 'fair'!

The word *férový* is formed by adding to the English word *fair* the standard Czech suffix for adjectives, and Běta's use of it seemed to Jacob to make a humorous reference to the changing standards of judgment.

On Wednesday morning Luboš visited as a surprise. He was brought to Jacob's door by Běta. "Your friend is here," she said, in the formal tone of voice she used in the presence of others, "but I tell him, that you are ill."

—I am only here to see you with my own eyes, Luboš quickly reassured Jacob in Czech. —It is for you to say whether I stay for a few moments. Are you well enough?

—You will stay all day, if you have it free, Jacob insisted. For a moment he feared that the enthusiasm of his welcome would betray him to Běta, but she seemed to see in it no more than a conventional exaggeration, a signal to her that for the moment he didn't need her protection.

After Běta withdrew, Luboš and Jacob at first remained stiff with each other, as if unsure of their privacy. Or perhaps Luboš still felt unsure of his welcome. To Jacob the mere presence of Luboš, by violating the apartment's quietness and isolation, meant sexual possibility. It was a good morning, Jacob thought to himself; he was strong enough. He wanted to seat Luboš in the sun that was flooding the kitchen and kiss him slowly.

The sun reminded him that he had no photographs of Luboš. —Can I take your picture? he asked.

—Oh, Kuba.

—So that I will remember you when I'm back in America.

—It's a kind of cruelty, then, and not so much a flattery.

—A flattery, too. I wouldn't want to remember if you weren't so beautiful.

He stood Luboš in the kitchen, with its white kitchen walls and table, so that the illumination would be general. He was aware that he wanted a picture of Luboš in order to show it off in a future he couldn't yet imagine, and he thought confusedly that it was better to take the photograph now, before they had sex, if that was in fact what they were about to do, in case the gun kicked again and the attraction he wanted to capture was compromised. But he didn't think the gun would kick; his lust felt heavy with momentum.

Through the viewfinder of his Minolta, he saw that the staging of the photograph was setting Luboš even further into himself—the diplomat advancing, the animal retreating.

—But do not seem that way, Jacob said. —Be here with me.

There was a flash of near anger in Luboš's features, the best state of their rough beauty, and Jacob photographed it. He took another as the interruption subsided.

—Is there a problem? Jacob asked.

—There is nothing.

—I want to embrace you.

—Well, then.

After a while, Luboš interrupted. —Your neighbors, Kuba, he said, meaning the open window rather than anyone in particular.

Jacob didn't think the window was the problem. —It is one to me if you are with anyone else.

—Don't be so worldly, Luboš replied. —It's not what I like about you.

—I want, for it to be free between us. It's only for happiness between us.

—Happiness is so serious, in your conversation.

—I'm American, Jacob shrugged.

Luboš lifted the Minolta from around Jacob's neck. —And now I a picture of you, which only you will see.

—What do you mean? You'll be able to see it in two weeks. There's a shop in Národní.

Luboš smoothed the cowlick on Jacob's forehead. —Perhaps in two weeks, then. Say *sýr*. I imagine, that no one else takes your picture.

—It doesn't occur to anyone else.

—Thus let it remain.

They made out a little more, but then Jacob felt dizzy and had to lie down. Luboš brought him a glass of water and sat on the floor beside him.

—How is your business? Jacob asked.

—Collin says, that we are too slow.

—There are others in the same business?

—There will be many.

—And what is it, the business? Luboš would forgive Jacob's inability to remember.

—A kind of trade.

—Import and export, Jacob said, and he rolled over grumpily.

—You do not like Collin, Luboš observed.

—No.

—I too do not.

—Why not? Jacob asked, still facing away, studying the coarse threads of the fabric covering the sofa cushions.

—Do you know, what a *neschopenka* is?

—Yes, Jacob answered, turning back because he was curious. —I had to get one.

—The other partner, the third partner as you call him, is a doctor. He gives *neschopenky* for money. Do you understand? The police are looking for him.

—I understand.

—It's difficult to explain.

—But I understand. It's not so difficult.

—They're not good people, Kuba, he said, as if he were still not sure whether he had put it simply enough.

—Let them drop.

Luboš shrugged. —It's a question of possibilities. A kind of sullenness came over his features as he said this, and then the old smile covered it.

For Jacob, watching, it was as if he finally discerned the music that a noise had been interfering with—as if the music overcame the noise just long enough for him to pick out the tune. —You're afraid, that I will leave, he said. —It isn't that you don't care for me.

—Oh, you aren't leaving soon.

—And so you can't break with them, he persisted.

Luboš paused before replying. —They and I, we know each other a longer time, he said, more quietly.

It was a new kind of check to Jacob; it was like a problem in economics. However shabby Collin was as a person, he had given himself; he had gone so far as to risk incrimination. Jacob, in comparison, had offered no more than a provisional promise to stay in the country. Luboš had been able to see the limitation before he could. It was perhaps the freedom to put off meaning it that had attracted Luboš to Jacob. Luboš had probably never ventured before into caring for a person who played with so little at stake.

—But if I stayed . . . , Jacob began. —America isn't necessary for me. I only want to be a writer.

—In fact you don't understand, Luboš said.

But Jacob thought he did. He thought that they were both sorry about what was dividing them, and that they could be together in their sorrow over it, at least. They lay down on the basis of the somewhat willful misunderstanding.

Jacob was summoned one morning to the Stehlíks' telephone. "Were you planning to teach the lesson on the subjunctive to your advanced students?" Melinda asked. "As your substitute I need to know."

"Does English have a subjunctive?" Jacob replied.

"Well, if you don't know, darling, I don't see how you can expect any of us to. The BBC or whoever it is that manufactures these delightful workbooks seems to be under the impression that there is such a thing, but the language is really in your countrymen's custody at this stage, I feel, so shall we say it's a skip?"

"Why are you asking me this, Melinda? You know I never plan more than ten minutes before class starts."

"I'm trying to outfox your landlord. The one who keeps the flaming sword beside the telephone. Am I overdoing it?"

"He's not paying any attention."

"Oh, sorry. How embarrassing. How are you, then, dear?"

"Still a bit weak-minded in the afternoons and evenings. But it only hurts when I swallow. The side effect is I don't have any desire to smoke, which is lucky, because I can't leave the house to buy cigarettes."

"Shall we arrange a shipment?"

"Prague smokes for me, is my current feeling."

"It does that, doesn't it."

"Luboš visited yesterday," Jacob volunteered.

"Luboš? . . . Oh, Luboš! Well done. Under their very noses. You *are* improving."

"It wasn't acrobatic or anything."

"But I'm so pleased to hear that it can be when you're in the pink."

"Oh dear."

"Darling, I'm just taking the tiniest fraction of the piss out of you."

"I'm so misunderstood."

"And an invalid, too. I'm calling in fact to say how sorry I am that Rafe and I won't be there today."

"Here? Why? I mean, I'd love to have you."

"Oh, you don't know yet, do you. And that's because I was supposed to verify that you are agreeable. That you were agreeable? That may be the subjunctive, come to trouble us. Please say that you are agreeable. For Thanksgiving."

"How did you know it was Thanksgiving?"

"You forget that Rafe is an American. When he told Annie, she had the idea of going over to cook you a Thanksgiving dinner, while you lie in your sickbed."

"With a turkey?"

"Well, no, a chicken. I don't believe there are turkeys in Prague."

"They have them in the basement of Kotva, the department store in náměstí Republiky. I asked."

"Do they? Annie will be crushed. She thinks she's tapped every resource."

"I won't tell her."

"Perhaps you shouldn't. It's meant to be something of a coup de théâtre. They descend with a trussed fowl and sundry victuals. You know—something out of Dickens."

"Who else is coming?"

"Thom, Kaspar, perhaps Henry. Rafe has to go to the institute.

There are so many Americans there now they decided to have something. And so I have to go, too, as the ostensible girlfriend. I'd *much* rather pay *you* a visit, I assure you. And I will do, very soon."

"You must tell us to go, if at any point we seem to be tiring you," Annie said by way of preface. "We've brought a whole feast, you see," she explained, bobbing, almost dancing with pleasure in her achievement. Dislodged by the long trip, her blond hair was straying away from her face in all directions like a lion's. "You wouldn't have thought it of me, would you, that I could manage such a thing. It isn't a turkey, mind, but we *can* 'stuff' it for you, if you like. You see I'm very well informed about your 'Thanksgiving.'"

"Very," Jacob agreed.

"It sounds disgusting, in my opinion, 'stuffing,'" she continued. "I'd never heard of it before Rafe told me. To put your fingers inside a raw bird. It's the sort of thing they did on the frontier, isn't it. To extend the meat."

"No one's ever done that sort of thing in Ireland?" Thom put in.

"I suppose they might have done," she granted. "Meat pasties and such. I'm *prepared* to stuff, is what I mean to say." From her bag she unpacked dry bread, sausage, carrots, apples, and at last a plastic-wrapped chicken.

"And I brought beer," Henry said, as he stocked the refrigerator with bottles, "which I don't suppose you'll be well enough to drink, come to think of it."

"You'll drink them."

"But it's Thom who has the pièce de résistance," Henry added.

From his backpack Thom took a burlap bag. "Brambory," he announced.

"Where did you get them?" Jacob marveled.

"They're just potatoes." Annie objected. "I don't think a potato ought to upstage a *chicken*."

"It's a fine chicken you've brought, Annie," Thom reassured her.

"But potatoes," Kaspar almost whispered. "You can't buy them anywhere."

"I bought them from one of my students," Thom explained. "Little wanker asked to be paid in pounds—pounds or Tuzex, he said. Had to ask him what a Tuzex was."

Jacob didn't know either. "It's a kind of artificial currency," Henry explained, "for buying luxury goods in special shops. It was a way of distributing regime perks, really."

"Whiskey and perfume and fur coats and such like," Thom clarified.

"It doesn't make sense any more," Henry continued, "or it won't in a few months, when Klaus finishes liberalizing the crown. But there used to be limits on how much Tuzex and Western currency a person could buy in a year, and people hoarded them."

Jacob nodded. No doubt that was Collin's ambition—to run the equivalent of a Tuzex shop in post-Communist Czechoslovakia.

"I told Thom I know a recipe for gratin," Henry said. "I couldn't find Gruyère. But I did find *a* cheese, and I have a bag of milk, in case you're short."

"I don't know what to say," Jacob said, accepting the bag from Henry. "It all sounds so lovely." The milk lapped and quivered inside its plastic. "There are more chairs in the bedroom. I'm sorry I forgot to bring them in here."

"You're to rest while we work," Annie ordered.

Jacob sat at the kitchen table and closed his eyes for a moment. When he opened them, he found Kaspar seated across from him. "I have brought only poems," Kaspar said. "A small book that I am translating."

"From Czech?"

"From Czech into German. The fellow was a journalist in the First Republic, and in Paris he fell in love with the surrealists. You will look at it later. I shall put it on the bookshelf in your bedroom for you now."

The international gay guide was not there but safely hidden in a drawer under T-shirts. "Thank you. I don't know if my Czech is good enough."

Kaspar merely smiled. Jacob closed his eyes again. He listened blindly to Henry offering and uncapping beers, Annie clattering through pots and pans for a roasting tray, and Thom washing off his pocket knife so he could peel potatoes with it.

"Are you all right there?" Thom asked. "Shall Annie make you some tea?"

"Shall I?" She opened a cabinet. "Is this your usual?"

"The yellow one," Jacob specified. "You have to light the burner with matches."

"I had better turn it off until I find them then, hadn't I, or we'll all be gassed. But you're meant to just sit there," she insisted, stopping him as he moved to rise.

"Here." Henry supplied a light. "Kaspar told us what happened to your friend. I was very sorry to hear it."

"It's kind of awful but I'm fine," Jacob said as blandly as possible.

"It's a rotten thing to do," said Annie. "It's a disappointment, when someone does that."

"That's one way of putting it," Jacob replied.

"Well, I don't know the circumstances."

"Not that it keeps you from commenting," Thom said.

"I'm not hurting Jacob's feelings. Am I, Jacob? You must say, if you'd rather not talk about it."

"I don't mind."

"It's supposed to be better to talk about such things," Annie said in her own defense.

"But it's so ugly," Jacob said.

His friends paused, in case he was going to say more. The kettle began to whistle, and Annie poured it.

"Are you angry?" she suggested. "That would be quite natural."

"It doesn't seem fair to talk about it. It's not as if she can answer back." Because he hadn't put that aspect of Meredith's silence into words before, he was suddenly aware he might cry.

"I imagine that part is natural, too," Henry observed, in a tentative tone.

"It's nice that you're all here." His emotion embarrassed himself and them, and there was another pause. It was as if they were a family, communicating by silences as well as speech. It was Thanksgiving, after all, Jacob thought, though the holiday couldn't resonate for the others as it did for him.

"Does this look right?" Annie asked after she had washed and dried the chicken, and set it in the roasting pan.

"It looks as if it favored the left side, in life," said Henry. "As if it might have had a limp."

"Oh, it does, doesn't it," Annie agreed. "Like a tennis player, with one arm bigger than the other."

"All the chickens are perfect in America," Henry said.

"Are they?" She gave Jacob a worried glance.

"They're given antibiotics," Henry explained.

"But you don't mind, do you, Jacob?" she asked.

"I don't think so. Let me see."

"*Is* it the left side?" Annie asked. "Oh, I see. I was imagining it upside down."

"I'm fairly sure the head of the bird went here, when it had one," Henry suggested.

Now that his attention was called to it, Jacob saw that the bird's right leg was slender, from what looked like a disease rather than an injury. It was a little sad to think of the animal alive. "They don't seem to have decent antibiotics for humans here," he said, "so I don't suppose they can manage them for chickens."

"Have you ever given thought to vegetarianism?" Kaspar asked.

"Not *now*, Kaspar," Annie warned.

"It's only a question. I'm not a vegetarian myself."

"Perhaps I'll pop outside for a fag while you lot confer about the lifestyle of the bird here," said Thom.

"I'm going to lie down for a while myself," Jacob announced. "Is that all right?"

"Of course," Annie said. "It's your apartment."

He woke to the sound of his friends murmuring in the next room. He heard the oven yawn creakily as someone checked on the roasting chicken. "But I don't under*stand* that," he heard Annie's voice say, rising above the others to protest something. Through the part in the curtains of his bedroom window, he saw a knotty mantle of clouds, darker than the gray of the cement highway barrier, bringing a premature dusk. All day he had wondered if it would rain—he had developed a shut-in's fascination with the weather. He tensed his legs under the covers to stretch them, and then let them lie loose and indolent. It was a luxury to think of his friends assembled in the next room.

"Good morning!" Thom greeted Jacob when he at last returned to the kitchen.

"I felt like Prince Myshkin in there," Jacob said, "lying faint and grateful on my sofa while society swirls about."

"Were we too loud for you?" Annie asked.

"No, not at all."

"You do not have consumption?" Kaspar asked.

"Did Myshkin have that? Or was it his friend? Anyway, no." Jacob found the question irritating. Kaspar seemed to miss the petting he got when he was in Mel and Rafe's keeping, and in their absence put himself forward the way a nervous child does, by hunting for an error to atone for or a tragedy to regret. "They told me I have quinsy," Jacob continued, "another nineteenth-century disease."

"That's what you have, isn't it, Kaspar," Annie said.

"Quinsy?" Jacob asked.

"No, the other," Annie clarified, "but that isn't the proper name for it."

Jacob now wished he hadn't joked.

"It's rather a personal matter . . . ," Thom cautioned.

"It is no secret," Kaspar said, with a gesture of his hand brushing Thom's scruples away, like crumbs from the tablecloth. "The head of the German department, too, has TB, and we were talking about it just last week."

"Dr. Černý? I didn't know," said Annie.

"He was encouraging me to be stronger. He does not like it that I am so often away from work."

"Hardly fair of him," Thom noted.

"And I will tell you something, but you must promise not to say it to others. I said my case was in the bones of my legs. And then he showed me. But you must promise to tell no one."

"We promise."

"He removed it," Kaspar said, tapping his own nose.

"Removed his nose?" Annie asked.

"I don't understand," Jacob said.

"His case was in his nose."

"Isn't it real, then?" Thom said.

"It was to encourage me!" Kaspar repeated. For him the department head's motive was the best part of the story.

"You oughtn't to have told us that," Annie said sternly.

"You aren't telling the truth, are you?" asked Jacob, who thought that at least one of them would have noticed the prosthesis, if there had been one. "Right there in the teacher's lounge, he took off his nose?"

"He is an old Communist," Kaspar explained. "No one else is competent to run the department. But he can no longer threaten, and the school does not yet have money to lure. How to get us to obey? That is his problem."

"He could appeal to your good nature," said Annie. When Annie and Jacob had come back from Berlin, the headmistress had scolded her for arranging a substitute on her own rather than through the office.

"But he does not know how. He tries by—," he gestured instead of saying it again.

"So it's once again the problem of socialism with a human face, as it were," said Henry.

"But when there is no longer socialism, and the face is wounded. And when, as Jacob says, the antibiotics are rather mediocre."

"So you do think capitalism will be an improvement, after all," said Jacob.

"Oh no. Under capitalism no one will take any trouble to persuade another, only to buy him."

"You miss socialism, then?" Henry asked.

"I missed socialism even when we had it."

"But it was socialism that caused the damage," Jacob said. "The poor antibiotics and so on."

"But the *idea* of socialism didn't," Kaspar answered, humorously, so as to suggest that the quixotism of his defense wasn't lost on him. "The powerful will find a new kind of force. The one you are accustomed to, probably. But for the moment there is this clumsiness. It is an interlude."

"It must be awful, not to have a nose," Annie said.

"It would be a pity if there were nothing about the coming changes you approved of," Henry commented, "when you worked so hard against the last government."

"But I did not work against the government," he protested, with the innocence that Jacob imagined he put on when asking Melinda for tea while in her bathtub.

"You worked as a dissident."

"But that is not the same, except perhaps to your friend Hans. I worked to continue certain possibilities, and it happened that the government did not like them."

"No, Hans wouldn't understand that distinction," Henry said.

"I think that Havel is a good man. He is in earnest. It is only that my place has changed. I am through the looking glass."

The room had grown dark while they were talking, and when Annie lit the candle on the kitchen table, the flame created a scene different from the one it created when Jacob was alone—a scene of conversation.

While the roast stood and the gratin cooled, Thom dropped into boiling water two long white cylinders of Czech dumpling, which he had mixed earlier from a box. After a few minutes, he fished the cylinders out and cut slices by garroting each cylinder several times with thread.

"So that's how it's done," Jacob commented.

"Jana taught me," Thom said, with a certain pride.

"It *is* clever," said Annie. The exposed, perfectly white flesh of the slices steamed lightly. Thom set two on each plate while Henry carved the chicken. There was barely room for the friends around Jacob's small kitchen table; Henry had to eat with his plate on his lap and his beer on the floor. They were gathered in a corner of the apartment as they were gathered in a corner of the city, as if to make of their shared mood a haven, and the emptiness outside their circle seemed like a protection. What if they were to stay here together forever, Jacob wondered, apart from their families and their pasts, improvising the rest of their lives? He had told Luboš that he couldn't stay, but he had spoken then as if the decision were someone else's, as if his presence weren't his own property. He could choose to give it away if he wanted to. If he continued to want to so badly . . .

"I completely forgot to tell you," said Annie, "that Thom and I checked out one of the school's tape players, for you, in case you were wanting to hear some music. We teachers can take them home, you know."

"Oh, I've already got one checked out."

She looked crestfallen.

"But did you bring any tapes?"

"Thom did. And I thought I was so clever. When you told me about that fellow loaning you a tape, I ought to have known you would have a way to play it."

"What tape might that be?" Thom asked.

"Depeche Mode," Jacob answered. "It wasn't my choice."

"I was going to propose an exchange but in that case I think I'll offer a simple loan," he said, handing Jacob a cassette he had been keeping in his shirt pocket. "I think you said you liked this band."

"I liked their last album. I don't know this one."

"A friend just sent it from Edinburgh."

"I wouldn't think you'd like them," Jacob said, opening the cassette to read the insert. "They're even faggier than Depeche Mode."

Annie gave him an admonishing look.

"That may be, but they're proper socialists," Thom replied, and winked at Kaspar.

"Oh, all that God and Marx stuff," Jacob said, remembering the lyrics.

"That is something that is worse, I hear," Kaspar said.

"What?" asked Annie.

"The life of gays."

It took Jacob a moment to realize that it was his own description of the band on Thom's cassette tape that had introduced the topic.

"I have friends," Kaspar continued, with a vague gesture that implied he was not free to be precise about their identity, "and they tell me that many of the young men now—." He hesitated. "Perhaps it is not delicate."

"Oh, if you don't want to tell us," said Annie. "We *are* eating, and I'd rather not hear a story like the last one."

"Is it that bad?" Jacob asked.

"It is not so bad, in that way," Kaspar hazarded.

"Please tell us. I'm curious now. You're tough enough," Jacob said to Annie.

"Whatever I am, I am not 'tough,' thank you."

"Don't be mad."

"I'm not 'mad,' either," she muttered. She studied her plate.

Kaspar delayed a moment more, as if trying to find the most polite way to put it. Just before he spoke, Jacob realized that he knew what Kaspar was going to say. "They sell themselves."

How ugly he is, thought Jacob. What a piglike face he has.

"What do you mean?"

"For deutschmarks."

"You tell such *stories,*" Annie said, looking up and staring at Kaspar fixedly, as if she were making an effort not to glance at Jacob.

"My friends worry," Kaspar said. "They see it, they say. They are older."

It's just his tendency to exaggerate, Jacob said to himself. But it was difficult for him to contradict Kaspar without exposing himself. "That seems unlike the Czechs," he risked.

"How unlike them?" Kaspar countered, happy for a debate. "Or rather, how is it more unlike them than unlike any other nation?"

"They're so proud," said Jacob.

"Yes, they are, it is true," Kaspar conceded.

"There are women who sell themselves at the western border crossings," Henry said. "To the truckers. No one is sure what to do about it. None of the dissidents wants to take a moral position on anything sexual."

"Why not?" Jacob asked. He didn't really want to hear any more, but he didn't want to seem to have been thrown.

"I don't think they're comfortable with the idea, philosophically," Henry answered. "They're rather famous for respecting their marriage vows more in spirit than by the letter. Havel in particular."

"You wouldn't know it to look at him, would you," Thom said. "With that little moustache."

"It's the use you put it to," Henry answered cheerfully.

They insisted on washing all the dishes, pots, and pans before they left. Jacob thanked them until he felt silly doing it. Once in bed, he fell asleep after only a few paragraphs of Stendhal, and in the middle of the night, he woke to the sound of rain, an old habit, a legacy of childhood, pointless now that he no longer had a bicycle or a dog that he needed to be sure were inside and dry. He recognized, however, by the clarity with which he remembered the bicycle and dog and by the dryness of his sheets, that his nights of fever were finally behind him.

Although Jacob didn't believe Kaspar's rumor, he found the next day that he wanted to see T-Club again with his own eyes. The wish seemed to him a little ridiculous, like a miser's compulsion to open his strongbox to reassure himself of his treasure.

It was a Friday night. Ivan gave Jacob a half nod to signal that he had seen Jacob arrive, and it raised Jacob's hopes. But then he seemed to put Jacob entirely out of mind. Since the improvement in Jacob's Czech, Ivan no longer yelled at Jacob in German. He had adopted the simpler tactic of affecting not to hear him. Between the arrivals of more-favored guests, the doorman stood lost in thought, his arms folded over his belly, his ass resting against the half door of the wardrobe, oblivious to Jacob's occasional questions and to the bar's disco. His eyes were sunk deep out of sight, as if he had somehow retracted the living part of himself, like a hermit crab drawn into its shell. He didn't pare his nails, comb his hair, or count his money; there was no sign that it cost him anything to keep Jacob waiting.

Jacob was too agitated to read. He tried to settle himself into a patience that matched the doorman's but could only manage it for a few minutes at a time and always lapsed into watching Ivan for a sign. The black vertical bars of the entrance grille and the smooth, dark concrete of the floor made him think of a jail, and then the artificial vines made him think of a zoo. A cheap zoo. It was absurd to want so badly to get into such a place.

—Please, Jacob said. —Please.

Ivan met the appeal with a look of disgust and admitted him. Jacob had waited more than an hour. He told himself he didn't care what a doorman thought of his willingness to beg.

Once inside, his eyes adjusted slowly. That night, the dance floor was striped with blue and purple lights, which flashed in a lazy rhythm independent of the music, and a few teenagers danced among them industriously, knifing and swaying in high-waisted pants and pajama-like shirts. At the surrounding tables, darker, sat men in their twenties in faded denim jackets, and in the outer belt, near Jacob, stood older men in still quieter clothes—the Czechs pale-skinned, the Germans pink. Jacob ordered a beer from the balding waiter with large glasses, the kind one, whose name was Pavel. Ota had introduced Jacob to him a month ago, explaining that everyone in the bar forgave Pavel for not being gay. The affection implied by the comment had seemed to embarrass the waiter at the time. Pavel did not now show that he remembered the introduction, but he exchanged Jacob's money for a beer with his usual air of gawky good intention. —Thanks, Jacob said.

—There is no cause for it, the waiter answered.

There was nothing new. The loners held themselves with the same shuffling alertness. Those with friends still kept their chatter loud for the benefit of those who might want to overhear, still directed one another's stares by nudges, and occasionally gave a girlish scream.

One came from Ota. He was at his usual table in the rear, wearing a thin wool sweater. It was robin's egg blue, with a black-and-tan argyle pattern covering the chest but not the arms. His curls were waxed with gel and teased higher than usual. As Jacob approached, he saw that Ota was not wearing a T-shirt and that the scratch of the sweater had raised the skin of his neck and cheeks to an irritable and prickly red. The fabric held him so tightly that the outlines of his collarbones and almost his ribs were visible as he turned his head to greet Jacob.

"My prince has come," Ota said. His audience laughed. "Is that correct?"

"The English is correct," Jacob answered.

—But you are not my prince, Ota sighed in Czech, taking one of Jacob's hands in both of his. —It is really a pity.

—You are laughing at me.

—But through tears, Kuba.

Ota named for Jacob the young men at his table. Two were familiar; two, new. One of the new ones, who had the dark coloring of a gypsy, gave Jacob a smile of hungry interest. His hair was long, worn in the early Beatles bowl cut that was becoming fashionable. There was also an older man, a German in a loosened tie. He had a small, prim moustache.

Ota said that the German was a distinguished guest. —But here we have the American ambassador to the Czechoslovak Federal Republic, Ota continued, by way of introducing Jacob. —Shirley Templová! As you see, she is no longer blonde, unfortunately. But she is *woman*, now.

—I thank you, Jacob said, bowing slightly.

—In fact he is named Kuba, Ota amended. —Like Fidel, who is not a blond either.

"Ahoj," Jacob saluted the group. The one young man was watching so closely that Jacob felt shy. The German, on the other hand, did not seem to recognize the greeting; either he understood no Czech or he had no interest in Jacob and did not care if he showed it. —But you are a blond, Jacob returned to Ota, because he guessed that Ota was vain on this point tonight.

—Is it not pretty? Ota asked. The gel drew his curls into such tight circlets that his scalp showed clearly beneath them. The curls seemed to lie on his head like something separate, like a necklace laid in a mass on a dresser. They were an empty, pure color, like clean, dry sand.

—Very much so, Jacob agreed.

"Another *hit* song from the United States," the DJ announced, interrupting all conversations, in a singsong English he must have learned from recordings. He continued in singsong Czech, a strange thing to hear. He spoke too quickly for Jacob to follow, but what he said made Ota and his friends laugh.

"Sakra," Ota swore.

—What did he say? asked Jacob.

"Nothing, nothing," Ota answered in English, as if to insist on the language barrier. "It was something in Czech."

—I know that, but what did he say?

—Look at how he is staring at us, Ota remarked of the acolyte across the table who seemed interested in Jacob.

—What? this young man responded.

—What? Ota mocked him. —I am quite good to you, he told the young man.

It seemed to please the young man to be told this, and his eyes shifted between Ota and Jacob.

—What did the DJ say? Jacob repeated.

—But do not be dull. It was a silliness. He said that the song was from America, and that we all want to have many ties of international brotherhood.

—As formerly with Russia?

—He did not say that, but as you wish.

—But wasn't it a joke?

—No, it wasn't. And for that reason we laughed. Be very pretty, Kuba, and buy me one whiskey. Here you have money.

—Keep your money, I will buy it, Jacob offered.

—Are you sure? It costs twenty-seven crowns.

—That is expensive, Jacob admitted, and took Ota's money after all.

—So I thought.

The German, seeing the money passed, added money of his own to the table, and indicated by pantomime that he, too, wanted a whiskey and that he would pay for both his and Ota's. —Is it possible to pay with deutschmarks here? Jacob asked, hesitating to pick up the German bills.

—Of course, Ota said. —Here as everywhere.

The press of men at the bar was thick, but Jacob was approached by Pavel before he got far into it. It seemed crass to pay with foreign currency, but Pavel showed no surprise. To confirm the order, Pavel told him the name of the American whiskey the bar served. Before he could return, Ota appeared at Jacob's elbow.

—The whiskeys are coming, Jacob assured him.

"I will wait with you," Ota said in English. "I have question. I have *a* question, excuse me. Do you like George?"

"George?"

"Jiří. The pretty one. The dark one."

"Oh. He's very handsome."

"Do you want him? He is wishing for you, but you must say now."

"Why now?"

"You must," Ota said with simple impatience. "He is, how to say, like a fruit."

"Ripe."

"Yes, he is ripe."

"I don't know," Jacob said, deliberating.

"As you like it," Ota answered. The indifference in his voice seemed unfeigned; it was only as a favor to the young man that he had asked.

"I wasn't really looking, tonight," Jacob continued, though Ota was hardly listening. There was an attraction, and Jacob was young enough that it was little trouble to make up the difference between his wishes and an opportunity. But he wasn't sure.

Ota circled back to his table, and Jacob continued to worry the question alone. It was a relief when Pavel brought the whiskeys.

The negotiations with himself turned out to be pointless. At Ota's table, he found the young man kissing the German, who bent over the seated youth from behind and slipped a hand between the buttons of his shirt. When the kiss ended, the youth's eyes followed the German's departing lips with a false look of adoration and then passed to the whiskeys that Jacob was setting on the table before him. Ota took one. The youth took the other, and the German did not resent the appropriation. Perhaps the German had all along intended to buy it for the boy.

"Schuss," said the boy, raising his glass to Ota. He made no effort to meet Jacob's eyes.

The German took out his pocketbook and gestured to Jacob to buy a whiskey to replace the one the boy was drinking.

"Get it yourself," Jacob said in English.

Ota intercepted the cash and passed it to another of his followers. Jacob sat glaring. It was only his vanity, at first, that was injured. The German was so plain, dry, and small. The German had a complacency of manner—was that the attraction? To Jacob it was even more disgusting than his looks. The man seemed to consider it natural that the youth had chosen him. He seemed in fact ignorant that any other choice had been possible; he was as perfectly indifferent to Jacob as Ivan had been half an hour before.

The boy sent to the bar by Ota, a blond—his name was Milo, Jacob remembered—returned with the German's new whiskey. The German stroked the boy's hand as he took it. The boy flinched and a few drops spilled in the transfer; the German took no notice. And in trying to understand this interaction, Jacob assembled a new picture of what he was looking at. You fucking idiot, he said to himself.

—Ota, may I talk with you?

—Gladly.

—We two apart, Jacob specified.

—With you, of course.

They took a table at the edge of the room, where the shadows seemed to make an arcade. The men who were seated nearby, the sort who came to T-Club primarily to drink, did them the courtesy of pretending not to take an interest.

It was difficult to begin. Jacob felt he had been treated like a child. Ota sat expectantly forward and seemed to be trying to shade with heavy lids the brightness of his eyes. —You must pardon, Jacob said, more gently than he intended. —I do not know how to ask fittingly.

—That isn't a bother, Ota replied. His eyes stayed on Jacob's, while the rest of him shifted in the unaccustomed chair, and then his eyes too wavered.

—Are you a whore, Ota? Jacob asked. He hadn't been able to think of a politer word.

Ota set down his whiskey and covered his face with his hands. The spindly fingers came together like slats of wood fitted to one another and made a blind. Jacob looked down into his drink.

"You must understand," Ota said, choosing to speak in English; perhaps it felt less real to him. "It is a good time to know languages."

"I see." Jacob felt blood rising into his face.

"If you say hello, if you smile."

"I see."

"Ach, Kuba. You look, you seem to say—." His voice cracked like a boy's, and he started gasping. "When you first come, I think so many things. I think, we shall be friends, Jacob and I."

"I'm sorry," said Jacob, alarmed.

"No, no. Is all right." He stopped himself. "It will not be. That is all." He pushed at his eyes with his thin fingers. "It is only that I think that it will go one way, and it goes all the time another."

—But why this, Ota? he asked in Czech. —Why did you—?

—You do not understand. It is so much money. It is only money, but there is so much. We are only boys, Kuba.

Jacob nodded. He found that he wanted to hear that it was out of Ota's power.

—My father, he does not make so much in one month. He does not speak to me, he is shit, and in one hour, I . . . He hates me anyway. So then why not?

While making this speech, Ota sank back gradually in his chair, until he regarded Jacob from a posture of sullen challenge. In the course of a few sentences Jacob seemed to have changed in Ota's eyes from a fairy prince into a disapproving father.

—But don't be angry, Ota continued, as if what he saw in Jacob were changing again.

It occurred to Jacob that his hand on Ota's might console him, but he could not bring himself to place it there. —I'm not angry, Jacob said. —I'm only sorry.

They remained in place, and Ota's grief and protests rose and fell for a while, like a patient whose painkiller is slow to take effect. It began to seem to be a performance.

—Now you will never like me, Ota murmured. He seemed to be both in earnest and play-acting.

—Ota, Ota, Jacob said. Ota didn't seem to recognize that he had given anything up.

—But tell me, Jacob resumed. —You also arrange?

—That is only for friends, Ota said quickly.

—I understand, Jacob said, but he no longer knew whether he believed him. —And tell me, Jacob continued. —Because now I must know everything.

—And I will tell you everything.

—Why did Ivan keep me out?

—He wanted, for you to pay him.

—But I didn't pay, and nevertheless then for a while he let me in.

—I don't know. You never spent any dollars, and you were with us so often, maybe he thought, that you were trying to earn some. But you never paid him for that, either.

—I confused him.

Ota shrugged. —He is an old Communist. He only understands money. Then, as if recalled by the mention of Ivan to the thought of what he owed to this world, he added: —But he's not so bad. It's his system.

—Not that, Jacob said. —Don't tell me, that he's not so bad.

—As you wish, Ota said. With his handkerchief he began to repair his appearance. —I am feeble, he reproached himself.

—I still have your cassette, Jacob said.

—It's not a hurry.

—I must return it. It's already a month.

—Bring it to T-Club the next time.

—No, elsewhere, Jacob said. —Of this place I have had enough.

Ota laughed. —I too, I too.

They made an appointment to meet at two the next afternoon in a Wenceslas snack bar, which, Jacob discovered when he got home, was described in his gay travel guide as a good spot to pick up hustlers. The next day Jacob waited there an hour. Under glass in a long case were two plates of *topinky*—appetizer toasts—stale and yellow. Jacob ordered a coffee but it was too sour to drink, even with sugar. Ota did not show up, and Jacob never saw him again.

He allowed himself a certain blankness in his thoughts. Ota had only spoken about himself, after all. Nonetheless, on Sunday morning, while a low fog was haunting the streets, Jacob walked to the phone booth beside the pub to call Luboš.

He took off one glove to dial the number and then with his bare hand touched one of the booth's few uncracked panes of glass and watched a mist appear between his fingers. The spots of mist weakened and erased themselves when he took his hand away.

For once Luboš himself answered. —I want to talk with you, at least, Jacob said.

There was a pause. —Ota told me, that now you know.

—Yes, Jacob answered. In fact, until that moment, he hadn't been sure about Luboš. The telephone made it possible for him to hide the fact of the revelation.

—A rendezvous at Můstek? Luboš proposed.

—Yes, Jacob agreed.

Between their conversation and their appointment, the fog did not lift. Night, however, fell, and when Jacob emerged from the Můstek subway station, the fog was making halos around the lamps of Wenceslas Square, fine, white dandelions of light, and the bright stones of the pavement, closer to him than any of the buildings and therefore, in the cloudy air, less obscure, seemed to give by their reflection an upward glow, like footlights. Jacob knew before he could see his features that Luboš was the dark figure standing just past the bookshop, in front of a bank that never seemed to open. He was wearing a tan windbreaker; he was shivering and his hands were in the pockets of his jeans for warmth. Before he could take them out, Jacob kissed him.

—Tonight it can't be seen, Jacob assured him.

—By good fortune, Luboš said, in reproach. He pretended to look around them for observers, but the gesture had an air of courtesy, of keeping up an old form. —To Slavia? Luboš suggested.

They walked past the sweetshop with glass walls, the balcony where Havel had declared the republic, and the gallery where the two of them had seen the exhibit of children's book illustrations. Then they walked down Národní třída as so often before. They walked past an antiques store where Jacob had once bought magic lantern slides of St. Vitus Cathedral and past the former offices of the Cuban cultural center, indefinitely shuttered. It had now been more than a year since the change, but everything was still in its old place. In a row there were a pharmacy, a stationer, an optician, and a travel agency, each labeled as such in the governmental lower case. A couple of months ago, on a street just parallel to this one, behind these smoke-gray Haussmann-like buildings, Jacob had been photographed for his residency permit in offices that had until very recently housed the secret police.

—A year later, and all is the same, Jacob said. —It is like a race where they fire the gun but no one moves.

—And yet we do move, as Galileo says, Luboš answered.

The National Theater came into view, amiable and glittering, like a woman with sloping shoulders and a bejewelled gown. Inside the building, Jacob had been told, the motto THE NATION TO ITSELF was inscribed in Czech on the proscenium arch. The theater was something the nation had given itself, in other words. It was a Victorian idea of independence. It was the idea behind choosing a playwright for president. Jacob couldn't decide if it was modest or grandiose.

In the Slavia, their table this time faced the theater rather than the river, and Jacob let his eye wander up and down its columns, which were both decorative and terribly earnest, until he couldn't see them any more for familiarity.

—What are you giving yourself? Luboš asked, to bring Jacob's attention to the menu. His tone was almost businesslike, as if he were concerned to move their interaction forward, and Jacob wondered if it was a tone he used with clients.

—What is it? Luboš asked, when Jacob didn't answer.

It shamed Jacob that Luboš was able to notice his momentary sulk. —I am deciding, he said, in half apology. Since Luboš had been willing to meet, Jacob ought to be able to spare him childishness. After all, Jacob had believed from the start that Luboš was sleeping with Collin, and he had known for just as long that Collin employed him, and if he had never put those two facts into any intimacy with each other before, why should it now make a difference that he could no longer think of them apart?

He looked through the menu for the name of a drink that he recognized. —I'm giving myself a soda water, he said.

He had mistaken how far Luboš was from him. But Luboš couldn't have mistaken the distance. Jacob could imagine himself being seduced, being given money, and then deciding not to feel bad about it. Like the cab fare that Markus had given him in Berlin. But he couldn't imagine setting out to be seduced for that purpose. Or maybe he could. But he couldn't imagine going to bed with a person he wouldn't also go to bed with for nothing. He didn't care about money that way, he decided. But almost as soon as he consoled himself as to his principles, he wondered if he was underestimating Ota and Luboš, or overestimating himself: Perhaps it was only that he had never been made so to care for money.

Luboš ordered for both of them. He was all surface with the waiter, his face was a set of patterns, and he did not come back to himself after the waiter left. It was the manner that Daniel had had when he had shut Jacob out after their first night together, and that Markus had had when he had shut him out in Berlin.

"Do you know, what is a *masáž*," Luboš asked.

—A brothel? Jacob answered. Literally it meant a massage, of course.

Luboš seemed for a moment to hate Jacob for having put it so bluntly. —In this case, yes.

The waiter returned, and shifted their drinks from his tray to their table. —The business is of this sort, Luboš continued. —Or rather, it used to be.

—No longer?

—The third partner is said to be in Africa. He is indicted. Do you know that word?

—It was in something that I read about the life of Havel.

—Thus, said Luboš. —And thus there will be nothing. He shrugged, as if he had been telling ordinary news. —And now you know.

—Yes.

A silence fell, and together they looked absentmindedly at the other customers of the café—the young Czechs from the art schools, who were wearing their scarves indoors and gesturing ironically; the tourists who had opened themselves from layers of sweaters and coats like flowers opening from calyces and were bent studiously over postcards; the lovers. Jacob was annoyed to discover that he had forgotten his cigarettes.

—Kuba . . . , Luboš began. He looked as if he were troubled by a duty of some kind.

—Yes?

—I did not know how to tell you, Kuba.

—It isn't a bother, said Jacob.

—But it is a bother, he insisted.

—Well, so, you didn't tell me, did you.

To Jacob's surprise, Luboš could not meet his gaze and was watching his own fingers gathered around the small glass of liqueur that he had ordered for himself. —I didn't even want to try with you. Even at the beginning. I tried to frighten you off. Do you remember?

Jacob recalled the embraces and the tears of their first night together. —I thought it was a joke, Jacob said.

—It was. I didn't think, that you would be gentle with me.

—I was a fool, Jacob said. He did not want any more compliments on his ignorance.

—You don't understand. I don't mean that night, though I didn't expect gentleness then, either. I mean, that I didn't think, that you would be gentle with me now. I didn't think you would understand me now.

—Now, Jacob echoed.

—But I found that I wanted you even so. And here he shrugged again, this time with a kind of despair. —Even if you judged me.

—I wouldn't judge you, Jacob protested. —I was in love.

—But no longer, Luboš pointed out.

Jacob found that he couldn't contradict this. He sensed that Luboš didn't blame him. It was after all a country full of people who expected to become hateful as they learned to do things for money.

—'In love' is not said, Luboš continued, coolly. —We say *zamilovaný*.

Jacob repeated the word. Its structure suggested that love was a state that one could be put under or put into, like a spell. Like Merlin inside his rock.

The moment was receding. In teaching the word, Luboš had taken a step into abstraction.

—Stay with me, Jacob said. —It isn't fair.

—Without the being in love, Kuba? It was for that that I wanted you.

—If you left this business . . .

—You have a kind of freedom, Luboš said. He addressed Jacob as if one of them were onstage and the other in the audience. —We're not yet rich that way.

He seemed to be praising Jacob for being able to escape him. He laid a couple of bills on the table between them, to cover the cost of his drink, and they said good-bye. Jacob tried to stay at the table for a little while alone, but the cheer of the café began to seem incongruous.

Vyšehrad

"Ah, there are so many things monsieur must want to say: difficult things!"

"Everything I want to say is difficult. But you give lessons?"

—Henry James

Jacob thought about going home. He still had some American change, which he kept in an empty matchbox in his sock drawer, and one night, after he had finished his pancakes and jam, he took the coins out, spread them on the kitchen table, and admired the burnt sienna patina of one of the pennies, which in the candlelight was iridescent with violet and green where people's touch had salted it. The portrait of Lincoln was ugly and noble, and Jacob took off his glasses to look more closely. On the other side, an erratic line of shrubbery was engraved beside the Lincoln monument's steps. The idealism seemed to be in Lincoln rather than in the coin's design, which was homely. It was so homely, in fact, that there was a kind of democratic grandeur to it. It was the most beautiful currency in the world. Jacob was on the verge of tears.

It was money that would be the problem if he returned to America. Since childhood he had wanted to be a writer—to make art out of words—and he didn't know how to make a living at it. The office job he had left had involved writing. The company had been housed in a brick building, originally a factory, partitioned into narrow corridors and large suites and fitted with teal carpeting and glass doors with chrome handles. The doors had been held shut by discreet magnetic devices in the floor and ceiling, silent in operation, which receptionists could release by pressing buttons under their white linoleum desks. Jacob had been seated in a room at the back of his company's suite, beside a heavy-breathing photocopier that took up half the room and dried the air so thoroughly that it gave him nosebleeds. He had taken the job in the hope of striking a compromise between art and commerce. He hadn't been asked to lie in the writing he did there, exactly. Is it corrupt to persuade people to buy what they don't need? Sometimes Jacob had been able to tell that the people in question were poor. Once he went so far as to lock himself into the suite's small, exposed-brick men's room—one of the few rooms in the building that locked with an old-fashioned bolt—in order to talk himself out of quitting. It took an hour. The work came to feel like using the best part of himself falsely. At the time he told his friends that it felt like prostitution. He wouldn't say that now, probably; still, he was not eager to go back to the job, or to any job like it.

It was easier to stay abroad. Jacob's workload as a teacher was light, and in the hangover-Communist economy, it was no hardship to live on the salary. He didn't want anything expensive, such as a car or a television, and even if he had wanted such a thing, there weren't any in the stores. He would have liked a bicycle, but he could wait. The only thing he really missed was Western toothpaste—he had also missed Western soap until he had figured out that the children's soap in Czechoslovakia was just as mild—but friends visited Berlin and Vienna often enough to keep him supplied. All he needed to accommodate himself to the idea of staying was a plan for escape. At his request, his parents had mailed him application forms for graduate school in America, and he now filled them out. For an essay, he made up something he didn't quite believe concerning Melville, whom he did like. Once he sent the applications off, he was able to feel that he had in reserve a way of going back that would put off his dilemma. Armed with that feeling, he was free to stay indefinitely.

Money, then, was accounted for, but it would have been hard to say what, if anything, he meant to do about romance. The possibility of sex was still so new in his life that it seemed plausible he could simply set it aside—not hide his nature from himself but refrain from doing anything about it, much as he was planning to refrain, for as long as he remained abroad, from any serious professional ambition. According to one way that he found of looking at it, he had tried to tell a story about himself and a lover, and it hadn't ended well, but rather than feel it as a story with an unhappy ending, he preferred to think he had made an error in the telling. He had gone about it the wrong way. He had been naïve, and from now on he would be sophisticated. He wasn't ever again going to make the mistake of confusing a person with an idea. Ideas were ideas, and people were just people. He now understood that he was in a relationship with Prague, and if he had been hurt, it was Prague that had hurt him. The funny thing was that the hurting made him want to stay. It was a kind of attention that Prague had paid to him. He had to prove he could stand up to it—that he could make a success of whatever materials came into his hands. He was used to thinking of success as taking the form of knowledge, and through Luboš he had been given a difficult piece of knowledge, and the difficulty suggested value, though Jacob wasn't sure the value would hold up anywhere else in the world. The fear that it might not was another reason to stay, actually. It was as if he held a large sum in a currency that could only be exchanged at a steep discount. Moreover, he couldn't bear the idea that anything connected to his being gay might cause him to lose his nerve—might cut short his experience. His friends here were straight, and none of them were leaving.

When he returned to work at the language school, he kept to himself for a week or so. His friends seemed to think he was still recuperating, and he let them think so. Many of them were making plans to go home for the holidays.

In mid-December, a mild weekend came, and he looked on his city map to see if there was any green within walking distance of his apartment. He thought he saw the symbols of a park and a pond to the south. He found a brake of pines and birches there; a foot path led in from the road. The day was warm enough for him to unbutton his coat. It was the first melt of the season, and leaves that had frozen green were now relaxing into their deaths, and where the sun had burned off the snow it was beginning to fade the grass beneath. He came out into a meadow beside a car-repair garage. Flimsy-sided trucks were parked in it, and on folding tables there were wire cages of hens and rabbits in dozens of varieties. It was a fair. The people were from the country, and the animals were for sale. There was the dusty smell of straw and the sharp smell of chicken dung. Dachshund puppies in a nest of newspapers let Jacob stroke them, rather equanimically for puppies, and at the foot of the meadow he found a man selling what seemed to be guinea pigs and hamsters. Jacob didn't recognize the words on the cage labels. Though he had his camera, he felt too timid to take pictures; he wanted to be present and natural more than he wanted documentation. He pointed, and the man put a tiny sparrow-colored hamster into his cupped hands.

—How big will it be? asked Jacob.

The man measured about two inches of air between his thumb and forefinger. It cost only twenty crowns. Jacob returned the animal for a moment, shook the cigarettes out of a pack he was carrying, dropping them loose into a coat pocket, and then coaxed the hamster into the empty box. The box fit into his shirt pocket, and next to his chest it was likely to stay warm.

—I have a new friend, he told Běta after knocking at her door.

—He's rather small, he continued, taking the cigarette pack out of his shirt pocket.

The dogs were curious. —Bardo! Aja! Běta reprimanded. —These dogs. She pulled the door close and leaned only her head out. Jacob flipped open the box top and she peered in. —Oh, he's so itty bitty, she said excitedly.

—How do you say . . . ? Jacob asked.

"Křeček," Běta instructed. —It isn't a mouse, is it.

—No, not a mouse.

"Tak, křeček," she repeated. —Boy or girl?

—I don't know, Jacob answered. —But his name is Václav. You don't know, by chance, where I can purchase a house for him?

—But I have one, Běta answered. —I will lend it to you.

An hour later, Václav was living in a small glass cage, which Jacob furnished with a couple of empty plastic film canisters and shredded pages of the American political weekly that Daniel sometimes wrote for. Jacob set down water in a shallow porcelain salt dish, which the Stehlíks had left in the apartment but which he was too American ever to use for salt. Václav began to gnaw on a section of carrot as long as he was, cramming full first one cheek and then the other, and Jacob sat by, watching his progress contentedly, one hand resting in the cage so the creature would begin to find his smell familiar.

Jacob squinted through a window at the dashboard. "It's a Ford," said Melinda, after leaning over to open the passenger's-side door, which was where Jacob expected the driver's-side door to be. "Your countrymen's handiwork." She picked up workbooks, her purse, a roll of toilet paper, and some candy wrappers from the seat beside her and dumped them in back. The car lurched slightly as she did, her foot having slipped off the clutch. "Oh Jesus. Sorry about that."

"Do I get in here, on the wrong side?"

"The 'wrong' side may be putting it rather strongly, don't you think?" She leaned forward and wrapped her arms around the steering wheel and gave herself a sort of underbite as if she were holding in a wish to tease him further. "I know it isn't as chic as a Trabant, but at least it isn't a bloody Škoda."

"Are they bad? I've never been in one."

"Oh, not so bad, I suppose. But Rafe says the automobile part of the business is inextricable from the tractor part, and we mustn't invest."

"I'll tell my broker."

"Let's see, the motor *is* still running, I believe. No it isn't, is it." She restarted the car.

"This is so exciting." He shivered as the warmth of the vehicle began to reach him through his coat.

"I am glad. I forget that it's an adventure to go for a drive when you haven't done for a while." She looked behind her as they edged out from the curb. "We ought to go for a proper one some day. There must be a castle you haven't seen yet."

"I'll hold you to that." They drove uphill behind a slow, fat bus, composed of two carriages joined in the middle by accordion-like pleats of black rubber. They watched its rear bob up and down in a leisurely way.

"I believe he's obliged to change lanes ahead," Melinda narrated. "Yes." The car growled as she forced it around the shifting bus. "That's the bus you'll take, though you may have to change to a tram."

Jacob added, "Where'd you get the car, anyway?"

"It's me mum's. She says she'd rather it were here than in London, because she saves on the insurance. Of course that's only what she says. I fancy her real concern is to ensure that I'm bringing an asset of value to the marriage. The nonmarriage. What have you. To give me leverage, you understand. That's an American word, isn't it—'leverage'? At least it feels American. Every daughter comes with a cow, that sort of thing."

"How'd you get it here?"

"I drove it. Fifteen bloody hours. But if ever I decide to pack it in with Československo, all I need do is drive away. That is pleasant to think of, some days. If Rafe were to take up with that tart who answers the phones at the defense ministry, as he threatens to, for example."

"Does he really?"

"Yes but no. His taste in women is far too nice. But he likes to pretend that he could be vulgar. Like all men." A light was changing ahead; she slowed the car by downshifting. "Say, that's a rather self-flattering thing to have said, isn't it. About his taste. Giving myself back-handed compliments, now."

"But if the shoe fits . . ."

"I don't know where I am this afternoon."

"Literally?"

"No, I do know that we turn here. I'm quite good with maps, for a girl. As even Rafe will attest."

They turned into a lane that ran through an empty block. Perhaps the expanse had been intended for a lawn; there didn't seem to be any grass on it, however. There was just a thin crust of ice—the kind of dirty shellac that forms when a covering of snow melts by day and re-freezes by night—pulling away from orange, sandy soil. At the end of the lane they turned right, into a parking lot in front of a nondescript concrete building from the 1950s.

When Jacob got out, his legs felt heavy and he stomped his feet. The view of the sky was unobstructed on all sides, and the evenly quilted, colorless blanket of cloud above them glowed softly with the light that it was holding back. Melinda didn't put on her coat until she got out of the car, and even then she didn't fasten its clasps. Her nonchalance was an ornament to her beauty, and her fingers whitened with cold as she put her purse on the hood—on the "bonnet," as she called it—and fussed in it to make sure of a document she thought they might need. Admiring her, Jacob felt something like pride in her fine looks. There was no one feature that you would single out; the delicacy was in all of them and in the play and balance between them. The pleasure of having her as his friend went to his head a little. If he had been straight, he might have worried about falling in love.

"It's always gray here, isn't it," he said. "That's what they don't tell you."

"Oh goodness, you sound like Annie." She held up a folded letter. "I have my original introduction to the institute here. It says nothing about you, of course, but I find that it's often of service to have a piece of paper of some kind, even if it isn't strictly speaking pertinent."

She was passing on to Jacob an English class that she had been teaching privately. The students were research chemists. Without meaning to, she had spontaneously privatized the lessons a month and a half before, by threatening to quit; the chemists had coaxed her to stay by offering to pay her in cash out of their own pockets.

In the lobby the floor was black marble, and there was an abstract brass sculpture, loopy and gobby, which, it occurred to Jacob, may have referred to the different shapes that electrons' orbits are supposed to have: *s*, *p*, *d*, *f.* A small, thin man with flat blond hair rose from a banquette to greet them.

"Hello," the man said, careful to give the English *o* the color that it didn't have in Czech. "This is your friend?"

"My replacement, superior in every way. Ivan, Jacob. Jacob, Ivan."

"We are hearing many good things about you," Ivan continued. "We are very excited for your lessons."

"I hope I don't disappoint you *too* badly."

"Pardon?" For a moment the man was at a loss. "Ah, you are joking, I see." He laughed politely.

"He's an *excellent* teacher," Melinda interposed, and then, sotto voce, appearing to mumble to herself as she looked again into her purse, instructed Jacob: "No irony *quite* yet, darling." Then, in a clearer voice: "Say, Ivan, I do have this letter still, if you think it will be of use."

"Letter?" He glanced at it to puzzle out her meaning. "Oh, it will not be necessary. It is now a private arrangement." He named the sum that the chemists were willing to pay for an hour's lesson. Melinda had told Jacob the number in advance. It seemed almost too generous: if Jacob taught the chemists once a week, they would be paying him almost a third of what he earned at school. But Melinda had assured him that this was now the going rate for private English lessons.

"Brilliant," Melinda said. "I shall abandon you to their mercies now, Jacob. Take good care of him, Ivan."

"So soon?" Jacob asked. He meant for the question to sound humorous.

"Don't worry, they're awfully chatty," she reassured him. "They'll scarcely even let you teach them." They embraced, and she was gone.

"Please," Ivan said, and escorted Jacob down a hall. They walked past several signs forbidding visitors, past the entrance to what seemed to be a cafeteria, and through a set of double doors into a large conference room.

A gaudy, mildly asymmetric chandelier of chrome and glass, which would not have looked out of place at the top of a Christmas tree in an American shopping mall, hung over a long oval table of dark-stained maple. The bulbs of the chandelier were reflected dully in the table's polish, and as Ivan led Jacob to the front of the room, this irregular constellation slid along the surface as if following him. The eyes of the institute's chemists also followed. The chemists were sitting in deep, leather-cushioned chairs, winged with side headrests like the chairs of astronauts in movies. Ivan, who looked about thirty, seemed to be one of the youngest in the group. The oldest, in their seventies at least, wore white lab coats and were sitting together at the table's far end; they politely suspended a conversation as Jacob entered. Thick curtains blocked the daylight from a row of tall windows. Behind Jacob there were carefully washed blackboards.

"This is a nice room," Jacob said, trying to make the best of its heaviness.

"It was the director's, but we have no director now," said a tiny old man. His hair, dyed black, was neatly parted and combed, and the frames of his glasses were made of black plastic and steel. As he spoke, in a high and for a Czech unusually musical voice, with an almost German accent, he gestured with his liver-spotted hands. "Now it is the people's."

"Not the people's," corrected a man in his forties a few seats to the right of Jacob. He was wearing a suit that actually seemed to fit him, but he slouched in his chair and as he spoke scowled at his notebook like a teenager, as perhaps the effort of speaking English made him feel that he was.

"The people's of chemistry!" the old man revised, and there were chuckles around the room, and whispers of surreptitious translation.

Ivan posed a grammatical question: "Is it correct to say 'the people's of chemistry'? Or should it be 'the people of chemistry's'?"

Jacob repeated the two phrases aloud. "Neither, actually," he decided, and the chemists laughed as if this were a great joke. "I'd get around it by saying, 'It belongs to the people of chemistry.' Or, 'It's the scientists' rather than the administrators'.'"

"The administrators," the man in the nice suit echoed, still scowling, as if Jacob had just taught him the name of his enemies.

"This room is too fine for science," said a plump old woman. She spoke very slowly, summoning up each word with a separate breath. The room was obliged to wait for her, and Jacob felt the pity that one feels when an older person tests a group's patience without meaning to. The many lines in her face were soft and hesitant, like her voice. "We will ruin it," she continued, "with our dirty fingers." When she reached the last word, she smiled with relief at having finished and with pleasure at her own joke.

"What did they keep in the cabinets?" asked another chemist, swiveling in his chair with childish speed to point at a wall of them at the back of the room. The abstract quality of speech in a foreign language seemed to be making them giddy.

"Bones!" cried the tiny old man.

"The bones of the people of chemistry," said the man in the nice suit.

"The bones," the tiny old man resumed, in a further refinement, "of former administrators!"

Jacob asked the chemists to introduce themselves. They gave their first names, listening to one another attentively, while he jotted down a seating chart. The tiny old man was named Bohumil; the plump old woman, Zdenka; and the man in the suit, Pavel. Some spoke English brokenly; others, fluently, even expressively. Pavel, for example, spoke it as easily as he wore his suit, but with a certain brusqueness, as if his ease with such surfaces was an accomplishment he had until recently been holding back and he still suspected that he could be attacked for it. Whenever he spoke, in the hour that followed, his scowl caused Jacob to worry that he was losing patience with the lesson, but Pavel never said anything to confirm this interpretation.

Jacob chose a lesson he had recently given to one of his intermediate classes, about the way word order changes when a question is embedded in another sentence. The chemists listened to a taped dialogue; they read from photocopied pages that Jacob passed around. As an exercise, they were then to take turns acting out a simple dialogue in pairs. One person was to ask his partner about an item, and then the partner was to ask why he was asking.

Jacob had learned the language teacher's trick of selecting prompt words with an unexpected relevance. "The potatoes," he prompted Ivan, who, proud of his role as Jacob's escort, had seated himself beside Jacob.

"Frank, do you have the potatoes?" Ivan asked, anglicizing his neighbor's name.

František, an older man, considered. "Why are you asking," he began, and looked to Jacob, who nodded in encouragement, "me," and waited for a second nod, "if I have the potatoes?"

"Great," Jacob said.

"Because I cannot buy them in the store," Ivan answered.

"The data," Jacob said, hoping it was a word that the chemists used in their workaday conversations.

"Pavel, do you have the data?" asked a woman who, though young and pretty, wore a white lab coat as otherwise only the older chemists did.

"Why are you asking if I have the data?" Pavel returned, and he gave the line a hint of petulance, as if he really were a well-dressed man bickering with an attractive woman.

"Because the instruments are not accurate," the woman said. The group hadn't been expecting an extra line of dialogue from her, and they laughed.

"Pardon me," said Pavel. "Can you say, please, what is the difference between 'accurate' and another word, 'precise'?"

"What the difference is," Jacob corrected, to stall for time.

"Ah yes. It is a question inside a sentence. Then, can you say what the difference is?"

Jacob felt the chemists' eyes studying him. "Precise. Accurate," he repeated, but he couldn't hear the answer in his own voice, as he sometimes could. "Is there a difference?" he asked himself aloud.

"A colleague told me, that there was a difference," Pavel said. He sounded anxious, as if he were afraid that Jacob might call his question foolish.

The room fell silent. Jacob wondered if it was a test. It occurred to him that since the chemists were paying him out of their own pockets, they had a right to find out if he knew what he was talking about. This might be the first time any of them had tried to exercise such a right.

"The colleague and I were discussing a number," Pavel continued, all the while frowning. He did not look willing to release Jacob from the question. "I said that the number was accurate. He said, 'Yes, of course, but is it precise?'"

Jacob saw the answer now, and in his relief also saw his questioner more clearly. Pavel's hands were trembling. His question was a sort of public confession. He had been left at a disadvantage in a contest with another man, and he had carried the memory of the conversation with him for a long time afterward, the way a child carries a parent's incautious remark if it senses that the parent will be reluctant to explain. He was not trying to test Jacob. He was hoping that Jacob would be able to pull the sting.

Jacob came up with an example. "Suppose that my temperature is thirty-nine point two." He wrote the number on the blackboard. "If my thermometer says forty-one"—he wrote that number on the blackboard and then crossed it out—"it's not accurate. If it says thirty-nine,"—he wrote a 39 beneath the crossed-out 41—"then it's accurate but not precise." He then added a decimal point and a 2 after the 39, and circled the full number. "But a reading of thirty-nine point two is accurate *and* precise. Thirty-nine point two five would be even more precise. And so on."

Pavel nodded. There was a buzzing at either side of him as the words for temperature and thermometer were translated and as the scientists reminded one another that American numerals had periods where Czech numerals had commas.

Ivan raised his hand. "And if the thermometer says forty-one point seven eight, it is precise but not accurate?"

A few moments ago they had doubted Jacob; now he was in danger of becoming their oracle. "No," Jacob pronounced. "I would know what you meant if you said that, but no. A precise measurement is always an accurate one."

Pavel fell back into his astronaut's chair. "I am accurate when I say that the words 'precise' and 'accurate' are the same. But I am more precise when I say, that they are different."

The pretty young woman beside Pavel held her head for a few

moments in perplexity. She dropped her hands into her lap when she understood. —That's it, she congratulated him in Czech.

"Let's get back to the exercise," Jacob said, and they allowed him to return their attention to word order in interrogative relative clauses.

Jacob proposed dialogues about eggs, a car, and privatization coupons. When he proposed tickets, however, Bohumil, the tiny old man, whose turn it was, asked, "May I choose another word?"

Jacob allowed him to.

"Zdenka," Bohumil said, turning to the plump old woman, who happened to be sitting beside him, "ask me about the girlfriend."

The old woman blinked calmly and sat up straight in her chair. Jacob was afraid that in her preoccupation with the mechanics of the grammar she might not have noticed Bohumil's introduction of the premise for a joke.

"*A* girlfriend," Jacob corrected, but the correction came too late for Bohumil to respond without interrupting Zdenka.

"O Bohumil, do you have," began Zdenka, in her labored way, "*your* girlfriend?" She had tried at the last minute to avoid Bohumil's mistake.

"A girlfriend," Jacob corrected again.

"O Bohumil," she began over again, "do you have *a* girlfriend?"

"Good!" said Jacob.

"Why are you asking me if I have a girlfriend?" Bohumil quickly replied.

"Good," Jacob praised him, to be evenhanded.

Bohumil continued: "Who told you?" Some of the chemists chuckled.

"Because," Zdenka answered, with the fingers of her right hand stretched out in anticipation, "she left keys."

"Her keys," Jacob supplied. Evidently Bohumil knew who he was joking with.

"Because she left her keys," repeated Zdenka, at her own indomitable pace. "Is it now to me?"

"It can be your turn, sure."

"Is it my turn?" she corrected herself, before proceeding. "O Bohumil, ask me about a boyfriend."

"Zdenka, do you have a boyfriend?" Bohumil turned to her as he asked the question and looked at her over his glasses for added effect.

"Why are you asking," Zdenka responded, not returning his gaze but sitting erect in her chair, with grandmotherly innocence, her eyes fixed on a spot in the ceiling, "me if I have a boyfriend?" She took an extra breath. "I, too, have a girlfriend!"

Over the outburst of further laughter and of commentary in Czech, Bohumil asked Jacob, "How do you say, *osvobodit, osvobozená?*"

"Liberate. Liberated."

"My wife is a liberated woman," Bohumil said proudly.

"Aha," said Jacob.

"And she is young and pretty," Zdenka concluded, beaming with her triumph, "my girlfriend."

"It's like vaudeville in here," Jacob observed.

"Czech vaudeville," said Bohumil. "Do you know Voskovec and Werich?"

"No," Jacob admitted.

"Ah, you would like them, I think. They were First Republic." He folded his hands thoughtfully. "Like us," he added, pointing to himself and Zdenka.

"Will you tell us something about yourself?" Ivan asked, a little plaintively. "Since how long are you here?"

"How long have you been here," Jacob corrected, though he saw that teaching had become a lost cause. "Since August."

"And are you a teacher in America?"

"I don't know what I am in America." There was a murmur as the remark was translated.

"We, neither," Pavel put in, in his deeper voice. "We do not know what we are, in the new Czechoslovakia."

"I thought you were chemists."

"We are chemists now," said Pavel. "But the future . . . ?" He spread his hands.

"We are researchers," one of them volunteered. "It is not business."

The room fell silent for a few moments. They had come to the lesson to distract themselves from the uncertainty in their lives, but the uncertainty was present here, too.

"And how long do you stay?" Bohumil asked, politely.

"I'm not sure."

"Until we learn English," Bohumil decided for him, to the group's approval.

When Jacob's homeward tram paused at the metalworks, he noticed new graffiti on the corrugated siding that hid the factory from the street. He looked into his French-Czech dictionary for the words he didn't know: they turned out to be the words for "Christmas" and "oranges." Last week oranges had appeared in the *ovoce a zelenina* near the Stehlíks' for the first time since his arrival, shrink-wrapped in groups of four on white Styrofoam trays. The label had said they were from Syria. He had bought a package and had eaten the fruit eagerly. Two days later, he had returned and bought more. He had felt confident about his greed for them, as if he were setting the Czechs an example. He tried to assemble the words in the graffiti into a translation. Until now, all the political graffiti that he had seen had been left over from the November revolution. It had referred to Havel and to Civic Forum, the movement that had put Havel in the castle, and there hadn't been much. Graffiti was one of the things he had come too late for.

OUR CHRISTMAS PRESENT: ORANGES FOR SIXTY CROWNS, the line of graffiti read. THANKS, MR. KLAUS! When Jacob had bought his oranges, he hadn't noticed the price, and it took him a moment to understand that the line was ironic. Klaus was the finance minister, and he was beginning to let things cost their true price. Their free price. Had Communists painted the graffiti? The only thing the oranges had put into Jacob's head when he ate them was the hope that there might soon be bananas, which he could hardly remember the taste of. He pictured Communist strategists sitting around a table—a table like the one where he had just been teaching the chemists English—conspiring. Capitalism— the presence of oranges, at any price—was still fragile here. There had to be sacrifices, Jacob thought. The high prices were temporary, and in time economic growth would reward everyone. Of course it wasn't Jacob who was making the sacrifices. He found himself wondering where the oranges used to come from. Maybe Cuba had sent them, at Warsaw Pact prices. There couldn't have been very many, in that case. He would give Václav some when he got back. A part of him thought: There may be Czech children who can't afford to eat oranges for lunch this winter, and here I am planning to feed one to a hamster. Only a corner of a segment, though. It was the first time Jacob had been away from him for so long—for seven hours, he counted. He had left the cardboard tube of a toilet paper roll in his cage in case he wanted something to gnaw on or climb.

By the time Jacob reached his apartment, the sun had set. The light above the oven was the only one he had left on. The salt dish for Václav's water had spilled, and Václav wasn't visible. On end in a corner, the toilet paper tube came within a few inches of the cage's rim. Jacob looked down it and saw nothing. The hamster must have scaled the roll and hopped out. Jacob went still and held his breath.

After a few minutes, he heard Václav under the wardrobe in the bedroom, chewing. He got on his hands and knees and tried to tempt him with a bit of dry *rohlík*, but the animal was timid, so Jacob poked a broom handle under the wardrobe and then grabbed him as he ran out. He worried that Václav might have eaten poison, and he sat talking with him for a while afterward, admonishingly. He tried to share the promised orange, but the hamster was too rattled to eat.

—Václav escaped, but I caught him, Jacob told Běta, when she knocked soon after. —With my own hands.

—Clever thing.

—Who? I or he?

—Both? Excuse me, please, but I must count the windows. She covered her face with one hand and shook her head beneath it. —Is here the census. Do you understand? With a notebook and many questions. It is horrible.

—Did you tell him I'm here?

—You? No.

—But you have to.

—I think, that no.

—But yes. A census must count everyone. Even Americans. Please ask him.

—You're so eager, she marveled. —But first I have to count the windows.

After Jacob's kitchen and bedroom, Běta opened a door beside his wardrobe—unlocked but never tried by Jacob—into unused rooms that continued the ground floor. "Ježišmarja," she said, looking down in dismay. She stepped carefully in, among a sofa that matched the one that

Jacob slept on, a table-mounted sewing machine with a cast-iron foot treadle, two veneer-and-plywood wardrobes, a pillar of linoleum tiles whose pattern matched those in the Stehlíks' upstairs kitchen, skis, ski boots, a green woman's bicycle with flat tires, a tea set whose cups were stacked crazily, black plastic bags stuffed with cloth of some kind, rolls of carpet, a disconnected water heater, and, leaning against a wall, in a glassless frame, a poster of a shirtless man holding a baby against his chest. Though uninvited, Jacob followed Běta in. —This is frightful, she commented. —Our shame!

She proceeded into another room, and then, turning a corner, yet another, both as cluttered as the first.

—Why aren't the rooms open? Jacob asked.

—When the grandparents lived here, it was not so.

—If I had a friend . . . , Jacob began.

—You must ask Father, Běta cut him off. They had walked a C-shape and now were coming out into the stairwell, through a door opposite the entrance to Jacob's apartment. —On the ground floor, six windows.

—And seven doors.

—Doors don't interest him.

Jacob walked back into his apartment. In his bedroom he shut the door to the unused rooms. He would no longer be able to feel that the room he slept in was the last one at the far, snug end of a cave. He already had the sense of sharing the space. Sharing it with Carl, he hoped. He would be able to show him everything. Carl wouldn't even know how to validate his ticket on the tram—how to slip it into the metal device, the size of a fist, that was mounted on a pole in the center of the car and how to pull so that a distinctive pattern was punched into the ticket's numbered, tic-tac-toe-like grid. Now that Jacob had a pass, he rarely used the tickets. But sometimes he bought a handful to get him through the first few days of the month, before he got the new month's sticker. They were more satisfying, somehow, in their triviality and multiplicity, and because of the ritual of punching them. He used them as bookmarks and forgot to throw them away. The only time he had been checked on a tram, the *revizor* had patiently held half a dozen up to the light before finding the one ticket punched in a pattern that corresponded to the car and the day that they were in.

—You are right, Běta conceded, upon returning. Her face was pink from having gone up and down the stairs.

—Excellent!

In her manner she played up the impression that she begrudged him the official recognition. —First name, sir?

He spelled it out for her. "Jay," he called.

"Yuh," she echoed.

"Ay."

"Ah."

"See."

"Tsuh."

And so on. She took down his family name, year of birth, and country of origin.

—This is good, Jacob said. —Now I will be Czech!

—I think, that no.

—But yes!

"Yah-tsop Poot-nahm," Běta intoned as she rose from her chair, pronouncing his name in strict accordance with the laws of Czech phonics, —*you will never be Czech!*

"What if I were your *half* brother," Carl suggested, as they planned by phone for his arrival.

"But we're the same age."

"I look older, I think."

"She had a very dramatic life, our mother," Jacob objected.

"Or father. In that case the age thing wouldn't be as much of a problem."

"Be serious."

"I could be your stepbrother."

"He only heard you on the phone a couple of times. And Běta won't care."

"So we're just friends. We're having the conversation where you tell me we're just friends."

"As I recall we already had that conversation. I'll say you're willing to pay as much as I'm paying. Eight hundred crowns a month."

"What is that, thirty dollars? My god. We're robbing them."

"You'll have your own room and your own window. But you'll share my bathroom and kitchen."

"My own window!"

"It's the equivalent of a week's salary," Jacob said, with some asperity. "It's not free."

Annie's mother bought her a ticket home for the holidays. The day before she flew, she and Jacob took the tram to his place after work. At Palmovka, where they had to transfer, she insisted on stopping in at a *cukrárna*. "You don't mind, do you? I stop in almost every day, and I'd like to wish them a happy Christmas."

In the store window, behind smudged glass and in front of a half curtain of polyester lace, lay white trays of cookies, rectangular-sliced cakes, and pastries. A motherly woman in a hairnet served behind the counter, placing on a cardboard square the sweets that each customer ordered. "A co dál?" she prompted, as soon as a customer made an indication. "A co dál?" And what further? When a customer said that that was all, the woman tore a length of light gray paper off a roll and wrapped the cardboard and the sweets in it, twisting shut two corners on top. Two pretty teenage girls, also in hairnets, assisted her, one at the cash register, the other ferrying new trays to the counter from a room in back.

"I'm partial to the amber biscuits there, the ones on the tray to the right. I don't know what's in them. Butter, I suppose."

"They look dry."

"Do you think so? I quite fancy them."

When they arrived at the head of the line, the woman greeted Annie warmly.

"Dobrý den!" Annie replied, girlishly. She pointed at the cookies she wanted and asked for three, please, in Czech. —And I want . . . , she continued, still in Czech, but then broke off. "How do you say it, Jacob? My friend will say it for me. *Moment*," she pleaded. "*Va*-something, isn't it?"

"What do you want to say?"

"Happy Christmas."

"Slečna vám přeje veselé vánoce a štastný nový rok," Jacob supplied.

"You can't be serious," Annie said.

"I said for New Year's, too."

The woman returned the wishes directly to Annie.

"Tomorrow I'm going home," Annie explained. "Domů."

The woman smiled regretfully.

"Oh, do tell her though that I'm coming back."

Jacob ordered some meringue cookies for himself.

"They aren't her daughters," Annie commented as they walked to the eastbound tram stop. "I asked."

A tram came quickly, its bell trilling as it stopped for them. They took seats in the back. It was thought rude to put a bag on a seat, even if a tram was mostly empty, so they put theirs between their feet and held their wrapped cookies in their laps.

The tram pulled away, along the white gray of the road and under the dark gray of the sky. Lower clouds were moving across a field of upper ones, like fingerprints on the glass of a window being raised. The tram passed into the factory district, and Jacob found himself trying to look at the ugly roadside walls of metal and cement through Annie's eyes. Soon he would be trying to look at them through Carl's.

"Ehm," she began, "is he very small then?"

"You can close your hand around him. Or I can."

"You have quite large hands, don't you. Mine are dainty. Ladylike, you see. So he isn't at all like a rat."

"Not at all."

"No tail, for instance. I'm quite fond of animals generally, mind. But not a rat."

They were passing a factory of timepieces, and Jacob pointed out a triangular mosaic of oversize clock faces on its façade, underneath the company name in stocky lettering.

"I think I'd rather you didn't hand him to me or anything," she pursued. "Is that all right?"

"Of course."

"I did want to see you. I haven't seen so much of you lately."

"I stopped seeing Luboš."

"Oh? I thought perhaps you might have done." When he didn't say more, she asked, "Are you looking forward to the arrival of your friend?"

"He's just a friend."

"Oh, a friend," she echoed.

"He's straight."

"I didn't say he wasn't. Will I like him? Is he going to shake my hand in a hearty manner?"

"Hail fellow well met."

"Yes, that's what you call it. Making 'deals' and such like."

"No, he isn't like that. You'll like him."

"I expect I will. I expect one likes your friends."

"Look," Jacob said. They were passing the one entrance to the locomotive factory where you could catch a glimpse of it through the gates. A wet road twisted downhill into a huddle of soot-stained buildings, and three chimneys handed milky smoke into the lowest layer of cloud. After the monotony of the walls that hid the factory, the view was startling, as if one had hiked over a mountain ridge and discovered a city in the next valley. The tram didn't stop, and so the sight was taken away as quickly as it had been given.

"It isn't any wonder you fell sick with that next door to you."

"It's like looking at the nineteen thirties," Jacob said.

"A spot of nineteen thirties in a landscape of nineteen forties."

They found Václav safely imprisoned. He hid when their shadows fell on him, but Jacob put his hand into the cage with some seed, and the animal emerged and began to stuff the food into the pockets of his mouth.

"It's not like you," Annie said.

"The hamster?"

"How will you take him back to the States? Not like you not to plan for that, I mean."

"He can fit in a cigarette pack. But it's a long way off."

"He's quite lovely." She bent over, her hands folded between her legs, to study him. "An absurd name. I think I will just put my hand in and try to touch him, perhaps, if you don't mind. You don't think he'll bite, do you?"

"I don't think so."

"He doesn't seem the sort."

She held her hand beside the creature and talked to it in a high voice as if it were a kitten. It let her stroke its back a few times, then made a few rabbitlike hops to the protection of its pile of shredded paper.

"It has a lovely soft coat," she said, holding the hand that had touched it in her other hand. "You won't mind if I wash my hands, though? You won't be offended?"

They brewed tea. Though it was only late afternoon, the light was beginning to fail, and Jacob turned on the small chandelier over his kitchen table.

"I can't stand that everyone is leaving," he said. Melinda was driving Rafe to London, where he was to meet her mother. Thom was returning to Edinburgh by a series of trains and the ferry. Henry was taking a bus to Spain to see a three-year-old daughter whom none of them had known that he had, as well as the ex-girlfriend who had borne her, with whom he was still on friendly terms.

"We'll be back soon enough," Annie assured him.

"The Stehlíks have invited me upstairs for the day itself. Which is the eve, here."

"Your friend isn't coming until after, I take it."

"No."

"It will be different when he does come. One is quite cozy at the Dům, with Thom just down the hall. Though I see less of him now he has Jana. He is useless, really, as a cook, but he is willing to do the washing up."

"I guess it will be different." There was a kind of attention exchanged between people when they lived together, and he expected that with Carl there would be a lightness to it, and even a tenderness. The conversation would draw Jacob out of himself. "I'm not in love with him."

"Of course not," Annie said, thinking in her case of Thom.

"The most I ever said to myself was that I wished I had a lover *like* him."

Because their memory of the sun was fresh, the light from the bulbs of the chandelier seemed faint and dim, and in such a light it seemed safe to talk. "Sometimes," Jacob volunteered, "when I'm here alone, it's as if there isn't anything in my head at all."

"Yes?" she said. She had been warming her hands around her cup, and now she pressed them against her cheeks. "Do you know that sounds a bit peculiar."

"I just lie in bed and watch the sun move across the blanket. Not impatiently."

"You'd like to be a writer as well, wouldn't you?"

"As well?"

"Henry fancies himself a writer, but I don't know as he does any writing."

"What about you?" Jacob asked.

"I mean to, but the days go by, don't they. Your saying so made me think of it."

"I keep thinking I'll write something about my friend."

"Which friend would that be?"

"The one who . . ."

"Oh yes. Would you like to come to Dublin with me, by the way? It'll be a fine time."

"What would I do with Václav?"

"We get along quite well, my mother and I. I know it's usual for people to row with their mothers, but she and I never do. She's a very tolerant person."

"I'm fine. Don't worry about me."

"I'm not worried. It is an offer, if you like."

Her concern embarrassed him, and he wondered what had prompted him to mention his moments of idleness. They weren't a source of anxiety; they were somehow pure. Maybe he was afraid of losing them. He decided to try to write something while his friends were away. That would be a good use of the time, he thought. In the event, however, he didn't write a word.

In the new year, Carl arrived. Ruzyně airport was on the other side of the city from Jacob's apartment, at the end of a long and tedious journey by tram, subway, and bus. Though Jacob himself had arrived in the country by train, he had been to the airport once before, to pick up a package of books and clothes that his mother had sent by freight mail. On that trip, he had waited in line for his package in a basement office, where half a dozen women had sat talking and eating their lunches amid ringing telephones. From time to time, one of the women silenced the phone at her desk by sightlessly lifting the receiver an inch from its cradle and then replacing it. After a while someone asked Jacob what he wanted and then told him that his package was probably in an adjacent garage where packages were sorted into heaps according to day of arrival.

This journey promised to be more pleasant. Melinda had offered to play chauffeur, for one thing. And unlike the international freight office, the passenger terminal was a part of the country's public face, and as a matter of national pride, it was likely to be efficient and maybe even relatively cheerful.

They were able to park by the curb just outside the terminal, a low, glass-fronted box from the 1960s. The city's name stood in widely spaced metal letters atop the overhanging roof. Arrivals were at the far end of the building, and they walked the hundred yards or so of its length inside, to spare themselves the winter wind.

"Is he tall?"

"No."

"Short?"

"No. My height."

"Any distinguishing features?"

"He had little round glasses the last time I saw him."

"So he looks just like you. Does he wear plaid shirts in vivid colors, as well?"

"I thought you liked my shirts."

"I adore them. *Nezlob se, prosím tě.*"

"What does that mean, exactly?" It was something Luboš used to say.

" 'Don't be angry.' "

"I thought there might be more to it."

"It's quite useful. You say it instead of apologizing. Is he a looker?"

"A looker," Jacob echoed.

"I thought there was a chance he might be, given, you know."

"We're just friends."

"Annie did tell me. I mean because you were taken with him at first. Annie did tell me that as well?"

"He has the kind of face you take an interest in."

"Even more dangerous."

"Why are you asking?"

"Oh, I don't know. So as to be able to help, should you have trouble spotting him in these massive crowds," she said lightly. Beside them at the rope barrier, only a few other people stood waiting.

Between the rope and the translucent white doors that hid customs ran a long expanse of tiled floor. Half an hour after Carl's flight landed, people began to file down it. Most were young and carried backpacks.

"There he is," Jacob told Melinda. "In the dark blue pea coat."

Carl recognized Jacob and flashed a hello with an open palm. He was walking toward them slowly, weighed down by a red polyester backpack that projected a foot above his head. His mouth had set with the effort of travel, but it began to soften as he approached. His eyes took on the self-consciousness of someone who is delaying a greeting. Jacob found himself aware that he and Melinda probably had the same look of anticipation, which could be mistaken for guardedness. Carl would see Jacob thinner than he remembered him, because of Jacob's illness, and he would see, standing beside him, a beautiful young Englishwoman whose white scarf called out the faintly purple blood that colored her lips.

In fact, when Jacob turned to check, he saw that Melinda had unwound the scarf. The hollow at the base of her neck where her collarbones met was pale and delicate. She caught his eye on her and without comment returned her gaze to Carl.

"How are you, man?" Carl said, almost singing the words, as he always did when he spoke.

They embraced. "I'm so glad you're here," said Jacob. He introduced Melinda.

She gave Carl her hand, and as he took it, the two of them both smiled at her formality. Because Jacob knew both of them well, without their knowing each other, the reserve between them seemed like an illusion to him. He had the sense that he was watching friends perform a play.

"Pleasure," said Melinda.

"Likewise," he answered.

"Melinda's giving us a ride in her car," Jacob explained.

"Awesome. I'm ready to go."

The wind, cold and astringent, seemed to have swept the sky clear. They squinted against the sun and against dust kicked up from a narrow traffic island in front of the terminal, where an orange soil had been laid down but not seeded, and they hugged their coats to themselves instead of fastening them.

"How was your flight?" Jacob asked, once Melinda had started the engine.

"The best part was the end. You exit the plane on one of those little staircases. It's like you're Nixon in China. You're the president."

"Did you kiss the ground?" Melinda asked, studying him in her rearview mirror.

"I don't know if Czechoslovakia and I know each other that well yet."

"I suppose it's the pope as does that, isn't it."

"He's Polish, right?" Carl asked.

"Mmm," said Melinda.

"Hey, don't make fun of me yet. I just got here." He laughed at himself and leaned back in his seat. "I'm in the unreal stage," he narrated. "This is Prague. I can't believe I'm in *Prague*."

"The little mother with claws," Jacob said.

"What's that?"

"That's what Kafka called it."

"Nice," said Carl. The road took them past close-nestled suburban houses in gray and white stucco, the sort the Czechs call villas. A few residents had put up signs in German advertising rooms for rent. "Is this it?" Carl asked. "Is this the little mother herself?"

"I don't know a more scenic route, sorry," Melinda said. "Unless Jacob can find one in the map. Which is in the pocket in the door, I believe," she prompted.

"No, no, please," Carl said. "I just didn't know if we were in the city proper. Thank you for the ride, by the way. It's most excellent."

"There are a number of us who will do anything for Mr. Putnam, you will find."

"What if I want to take it personally?" Carl asked.

"I'm sorry?" Melinda replied.

"What if I want to think you're doing it for me?"

She didn't meet his eyes in the mirror. "It was for you, more or less, that I *cleaned* my car, seeing as how you are a stranger to me," she said, after a pause. "Jacob can tell you how it looks ordinarily."

"Where are we?" Jacob asked.

"On that map we're on Leninova, but the names have changed around here."

"Oh, I see."

"It used to be that from the airport you took Leninova all the way to the Square of the October Revolution, and then turned right onto the Slovak National Uprising. Which had a certain ring to it."

"Is this the October Revolution up ahead?"

"Yes. And now it's called Victory Square. See? I suppose it was a victory for someone. I believe the Slovak National Uprising has now become a saint of some kind. That's the new dispensation."

"It seems to me you should still be able to turn right on a Slovak national uprising," Jacob hazarded.

"Not in Prague, darling. Perhaps in Bratislava."

They took a steep curve that doubled back on itself as it descended and then they began to follow the river.

"Where's the castle?" Carl asked. "I thought there was supposed to be a castle."

"We were heading toward it, but it's behind us now," Jacob explained. "On the left here, at the top of this hill, is where Stalin's monument used to be."

"Is that something they just knocked down?"

"No. It wasn't finished until after Stalin died, and they knocked it down half a dozen years later. But everyone still remembers it."

"The memory is a sort of national scar," Melinda elaborated. "The architect is said to have hanged himself, I believe. There's to be a party there tomorrow night, by the way, according to Henry. A happening of some kind."

The steep front of the hill, which had been the statue's giant pedestal, seemed to be frowning across the river. Their car turned away from it at the entrance, where it could be scaled by terraces and stairways, and they were soon embraced by the solid stone palaces of the Old Town.

"Maybe I should tell you now," said Jacob. "I'm not out here, the same way." He felt Carl and Melinda exchange glances.

"I, for example, know," Melinda volunteered, "but it is one of the secrets I keep from my boyfriend."

"Aha," said Carl.

"You really haven't told him?" Jacob asked.

"You asked me not to."

"I know, but I didn't know you would actually do it."

"We take such matters very seriously, as you see," Melinda continued, addressing Carl.

"I'll keep my mouth shut."

"It's transitional," Jacob added, in his own defense. "How is everyone in Boston?"

"They're all right. Don't let me forget, I brought you a program from Meredith's thing."

"How's Louis?"

"His father hospitalized him finally. Against his will."

"God."

"Yeah. But he was pretty crazy. There's a whole story. I had to pretend I was going to meet him. I was the bait. I'll tell you about it some time." The context raised by Jacob's questions and Carl's answers was too weak to hold them. The threads of it fell on the two of them but then slipped off. The buildings began to absorb Carl's attention. "This is a really beautiful city, isn't it."

"It is."

"I mean, people say that it is, and you hear about it, but it's so . . ."

"Yes?" Melinda asked.

"I don't know. Monumental."

She apologized: "In fact we've skirted the impressive area."

"It makes it hard to leave," Jacob warned. "It attaches you."

"I can see how that would happen."

"The claws, as it were."

The Stehlíks had furnished Carl's room with a real bed, large enough for a couple. It was nicer than Jacob's provision for sleeping, which still involved the nightly disassembly of his sofa, and Běta apologized but did not explain. Jacob suspected that the largesse was unintentional—that Mr. Stehlík didn't want to give Carl a grown-up's bed any more than he had wanted to give Jacob one, but that it was easier to let Carl sleep in it than to find somewhere else for it to go. The suspicion seemed corroborated by the continued presence in Carl's room of the two locked wardrobes, which Běta apologized for almost as soon as she met Carl. "I cannot move," she told him, shaking with silent laughter at her inability.

"No problem," Carl assured her. "This is great," he added, surveying the room with appreciation.

"But yes, it is problem, but you are kind."

"She's a sweetheart," Carl said, once he and Jacob were left alone.

Jacob agreed. Běta's parents were not on hand, because Mr. Stehlík's employer had moved him to a post in Warsaw just before Christmas, and he and his wife had driven there a few days earlier, for the first in an indefinite series of long stays. The circumstance had complicated the negotiations for the extra room; Jacob sensed that Mr. Stehlík would have liked to be able to look his new tenant over before admitting him. But Jacob sensed, too, that Mr. Stehlík knew that a large house was safer when it had people in it. "Mr. Jacob, you will be responsible," he had required of Jacob in yielding.

While Jacob cooked lentil soup and Irish soda bread, his own favorite of the few meals he knew how to prepare, and one of the most elaborate, he and Carl talked. By walking through Jacob's rooms with his American eyes, Carl desanctified them. He broke their strangeness and their quiet, but Jacob felt content to lose his hours of solitude when he heard Carl tease him for having let melted candlewax ruin the folkloric integrity of the tablecloth, admire the cement wall out their bedroom windows, and confess, as he paused in the kitchen after a shower, wrapped in a towel, that the whoosh of the gas water heater in the bathroom had terrified him. "Are there any numbers, do you know, for the annual deaths in Czechoslovakia from fires caused by water heaters? That thing is dangerous, man."

"I kind of enjoy it. It wakes me up in the morning."

"You have short hair already."

During the exchange, Jacob kept his eyes on the soup. He wanted Carl to feel that he could trust him. But Carl must have noticed the effort; the intimacy was never repeated.

They ate dinner with the hamster's cage in the center of the table.

"He won't think he's going to be an hors d'oeuvre?"

"He was my company until you came. I don't want to displace him right away."

"Of course not." Carl's hair was still wet from his shower. "Is he eating because we're eating?"

"I put that carrot in there just now."

"Oh, I thought maybe it was sympathy eating. But it's opportunity eating. This is really good by the way."

"Thanks."

"You're so set up here. You've got Václav. You've got a pantry. You've got a fucking pantry, man."

"I love my pantry."

"As you should."

"Our pantry, now."

"That's big of you."

"I've developed Depression-era habits," Jacob boasted. "I always buy at least one extra bag of rice. At least one extra bag of sugar. There are shortages. You'll see."

"What are the boxes?"

"Dumpling powder."

"Dumpling powder. Excellent."

In Rome the statues, in Paris the paintings, and in Prague the buildings suggest that pleasure can be an education. In Rome someone like Jacob wasn't likely to distinguish sharply between the education he received in sculpture and the pleasure he took in the nudes depicted—in the beauty of the slaves and prostitutes who had modeled for the sculptors centuries before. So in Prague, Jacob wasn't sure whether he valued the city's buildings for their forms or merely as an opportunity for a kind of aestheticized history. The buildings interested him mostly as shadows cast by the way the Czechs had seen the world, or had wanted to see it, at different moments.

Their first morning together, Jacob took Carl to the foot of Wenceslas Square. They started at Bata's shoe store, with the spare, rectilinear modernism of the First Republic. At Havelská, Jacob pointed out the shadowy arcade at the foot of the building where Mel and Rafe lived, so that Carl could admire the graceful curves of its Gothic arches. Fourteenth and early fifteenth centuries. He hoped that Carl could appreciate the simple things and not just the eye-catchers. He didn't think Carl would mock his way of looking at buildings, which was part of his project of trying to come close to the revolution; Carl's irony was too gentle. But he worried that Carl's companionship might distract him from it, and so he was on the lookout for signs in Carl of a fellow seeker.

It was Jacob, however, who first strayed from art to commerce that morning. "This is new," he said. "This building was shut before."

"What is it, crystal?" Carl replied. "That's a thing, isn't it, Bohemian crystal. The sort of thing my mom would know about."

"Do you mind if we go in?"

Jacob had visited several state-run crystal shops in the past. They had been cluttered with vases and goblets that were for the most part identical except in size and occasionally color. This shop, in contrast, was set up like a Western boutique. A ginger-tinted bowl, in the shape of a turban that had been doffed intact, had been given a shelf of its own in a window. Translucent pink and green sand dollars lay in a display box widely spaced apart, as if in a museum. The sand dollars were probably ashtrays; Jacob remembered that he hated expensive ashtrays on principle; then he also remembered that he ordinarily had no interest in crystal.

"This is one of the new stores." He was speaking to Carl, but he was trying to explain his interest to himself. "Private retail only became legal a few weeks ago."

Carl nodded politely. "Isn't Mozart's opera house around here?"

"Oh, sorry. You didn't come to see this, did you?"

"I came to see everything."

"I don't remember an opera house," Jacob said once they were outside again.

" 'The site of the world premiere of *Don Giovanni*,' " Carl quoted from a guidebook he had brought with him.

Across a narrow, cobblestoned pass stood a closed church. Jacob knew from habit and a general sense of direction that their next turn should be to the left, but Carl walked right, following a map in his guidebook. He was heading toward an alley with empty storefronts—into a kind of nothingness that one found throughout Prague, that one stumbled on in corners; Jacob had learned to avoid it. He had trained himself not even to see it, for the most part. The alley led back to Můstek, where they had just been.

"There's nothing here," Jacob said. He shivered. He put up the hood of his coat, which blinkered his sight like a horse's, and focused on Carl. "It isn't here," he repeated.

"I think it has to be. Is that it?"

Carl pointed at a hoarding that Jacob must have stopped noticing some time ago. It was unlabeled, except to forbid entry.

"You're not allowed to go over there."

"Well, I can go up to it, can't I?"

"People don't."

The cobbled pass was so narrow and the hoarding so tall that from a distance they couldn't see more than a slice of white building behind the plywood, and close up, the angles made it impossible to see anything but the hoarding itself. Its brown paint had puckered where water had got underneath, and a wire fence had been built in front of and against it, as if to hold it up.

"I think this is it," Carl suggested. "Behind here." He paced the length of the hoarding, in search of a seam through which to glimpse the building. "I don't know if it's right behind. It might be behind behind."

"There are a lot of buildings that are open," Jacob said. "Quite beautiful buildings."

Carl didn't take the hint. "Do you know the opera?"

"The opera house?"

"No, the opera."

"No," Jacob confessed.

"You should listen to it sometime," Carl said softly. In Boston it had been part of Carl's chic, Jacob remembered, to like works of art that a sophisticated uncle might have been enthusiastic about. In Boston he had introduced Jacob to Astrud Gilberto and to Auden. "The list. The lover versus the father. Versus death."

"I saw the Miloš Forman movie."

"There you go." While remembering the music, Carl seemed to be seeing something other than the cold, gray street they stood in, and Jacob felt envious. "Should we climb over?" Carl asked.

"No," Jacob answered with alarm.

"If you fold your hands and make a kind of stirrup . . ."

"No. I don't want to get arrested."

"They're not going to arrest us. We're Americans. They love us."

"You say that like it's a good thing."

"It's good for *us*. That's why the Stehlíks rent to us, isn't it?"

"They get money."

"But they don't need money. Everything's paid for."

"They don't know for how long."

"It's like a cargo cult," Carl insisted. "You bring home an American and you put him on the mantelpiece for luck."

Jacob led Carl back to Melantrichova, a street so narrow that in places the buildings on either side were buttressed against each other, two or three stories above their heads. They followed the curl of the street, marshaled closely by ashlar until abruptly the stone walls fell away, and they were released into the expanse of Staroměstské náměstí. A group of tourists had already collected to admire the famous clock, but Jacob drew Carl into the openness of the square itself.

"This is where the Czech nobility was executed," he said, repeating something Rafe and Melinda had told him.

"It's like cupcakes," Carl answered.

A cold sun had lit up the yellow, pink, and green facades of the Baroque palaces that edged the square. "There's a sort of war, you know, in Prague," Jacob said, "between the simple and the pretty."

"Really?" They were walking slowly together, their steps matching now. The Týn church watched them from behind a row of low palaces, like an antlered deer, shy at their approach, waiting just inside a thicket. Their steps turned naturally toward a great bronze-and-stone monument in the northeast of the square. "Who's that?" Carl asked.

"Jan Hus."

"And he's one of the simple ones?" Carl guessed.

At the base the martyr was almost indistinct from the metal of which he was formed, and he seemed to rise from it, indignantly. His fingers were thick as if from labor, though he had been a scholar. "I think so," Jacob answered. "He was sort of a Protestant before there were Protestants." Hus stood apart from the other figures, breaking the symmetry.

"He's the sort of statue who could take you to hell."

"What do you mean?"

"Like the statue in Don Juan. Did they kill him, too?"

"They burnt him at the stake."

"Intense."

As they circled the monument, so close to it that they lost track as they walked of how much of it they had seen and how much remained undiscovered, Jacob hung back and let Carl take the lead. One of Hus's followers reached out a hand in his misery, so that the hand projected beyond the frame that the rest of the statue implied, and Carl raised one of his toward it, as if for comparison. His hand looked frail beside the statue's, with its knotty fingers.

"Hus was two centuries earlier than the nobles killed over there," Jacob felt obliged to explain. "But it all runs together in the national myth."

Carl leaned back and looked up to find Hus's line of sight. "He's staring at these pretty buildings you don't like."

"I like them," Jacob said. "There's a contrast, is all."

"Didn't you say 'war'?"

"After the Hapsburgs put down the Protestant revolt, they made Prague as beautiful as they could," Jacob said. "Crushingly beautiful."

"So beautiful that no one would ever want to leave."

"So beautiful that it seemed right that they had won. The way Louis Napoleon remade Paris."

"Like capitalism," Carl suggested. "'We'll give you so much pleasure, you'll never want to try another socioeconomic system.'"

"Something like that."

"'They came for the freedom, they stayed for the McNuggets.'"

"That's terrible," Jacob said, with delight.

"That's not mine. A friend came up with it while we were watching the Berlin Wall on TV."

"He doesn't think I was *too* much the frosty bitch on the ride home," Melinda suggested.

"God no," Jacob reassured her. "Why would he think that?"

"I was afraid in retrospect that I was too proper. Too English. I can't quite get used to him. He isn't like you, is he. You were right about that and I was wrong."

"I don't remember that we said that much about it."

"But we thought it, anyway, or at least I did. He isn't like you, and I can't decide whether to like him anyway."

"Such flattery."

"We're taught that Americans don't mind personal comments. You won't mention any of this, will you. I forget that you're flatmates. You won't gossip about me."

"The beautiful and mysterious Melinda Stone."

"Gor, is that all you can come up with? 'Mysterious'?"

He couldn't tell if she might really be offended underneath the pretending to be. They were standing at the edge of a booth, whose benches were crammed with the rest of the group, in the basement of Blatnička, a wine bar just south of Malé náměstí. The ceiling was low, and large blond-wood casks elbowed into the room from along the walls. Loud reflections of chatter hid their words.

"At first one thinks he is as enthusiastic as he seems," Melinda went on, returning to the subject of Carl, "and then one becomes aware of his irony, and you worry he's making fun of *you* for thinking he could be so eager, and then you realize, no, he really is that enthusiastic, and for some reason he feels obliged to make fun of *himself* for it. Or to make fun of his need to make fun of himself. But perhaps this is too much analysis."

Carl was sitting only a couple of yards away, across from Thom and Jana. It felt very pleasant and sly to be talking about him so near but without his knowledge.

"You've given it some thought."

"Oh I wouldn't call it thought. But what else is one to do with one's evenings in this town?" She and Rafe were always making an effort to figure out the members of the group and how they fit together. It was part of the way they presided, to the extent that anyone in the group did preside over any of the others. They tried to understand people; they tried to place them.

"What worries me is—," Jacob began.

"Yes?"

"I shouldn't say."

"Darling, you must, once you've begun so promisingly."

"What if it's something less than enthusiasm. Or if that's all it is, enthusiasm."

"I don't follow, but keep on and perhaps I'll catch you up."

"What if he's sort of a rogue?"

"Did you say a rogue?"

"What if he's just here to drink beer and get laid. If it's sort of animal on his part."

"Oh, I *would* look forward to that. And you wouldn't?"

"I don't know." He felt lightheaded; he should have kept his mouth shut.

Annie rose from her perch at the edge of a bench, and when she was at eye level, Melinda told her, "Jacob is afraid that his friend Carl is a rogue. Do you think there's any hope of that?"

"A rogue?"

"That he's here for the drink and the loose women," Melinda clarified.

"You're quite mad, Jacob. He's quite a solid person, I find, and he has very pleasant manners. Before meeting the two of you, I had no idea Americans could pay attention in such a way to other people."

"You thought we were hicks."

"Not given to listening, rather."

"I'm very taken with the eighteenth-century cast of the anxiety," Melinda said. "With the Samuel-Richardson-novel aspect of it."

"I wonder if it isn't almost treacherous to suggest such a thing of a friend his first night here?" Annie considered.

"I rather like that about Jacob," Melinda replied. "His ruthlessness. He does it so sweetly. He has ideas that he wants us to live up to."

"I don't have ideas."

"You're a romantic. You have a whole city of ideas. A republic of ideas. Like any Don Juan." Carl had told them about the search for the opera house.

"I'm not a Don Juan."

"If the women don't correspond to the ideas, there are always more women. Or men."

"But I'm not a Don Juan."

"You're the only one of *us* who's getting any."

"Really?" Jacob pointedly queried.

"On the open market, I mean. Rafe doesn't count."

"I'm not any more."

"What became of the parade of Czech youth?"

"There was only ever one Czech youth, and he was older than me. And it's over now, anyway."

"I'm sorry," Melinda said. "Poor love."

They waited a moment for the topic to dissipate.

Melinda reverted to the subject of Carl: "It is only natural in us to wish for him to have adventures, but it would be wrong in us to expect them of him. We must allow him to be himself."

"Of course I *like* him," Jacob said. "I brought him here, for god's sake."

"I find I'm quite fond of him already," Annie volunteered.

"That's settled, then," Melinda concluded, because while they had been speaking, Carl himself had stood up on the bench where he had been sitting, in order to extricate himself, and was now holding onto Jacob's shoulders for steadiness as he hopped to the floor.

"What is?" Carl asked.

"That we shall allow you to blossom untrellised," Melinda supplied.

He looked into her eyes. "Why thank you, I think."

"I forgot to ask how your Christmas was," Jacob said to Melinda.

"Rafe did splendidly. Me mum now likes him much more than she does me. This despite his dashing off to meetings every afternoon and not even pretending to pretend that his absences had anything to do with shopping for our gifts."

"Rafe is your boyfriend," Carl said, as if he were confirming the identity of a landmark.

"Yes," Melinda answered, and then seemed for a moment to lose the thread of her story.

"Rafe's coming later," Jacob said. "Did he really have to work while you were in London?"

"He didn't have to, of course. But since we were there, and since people who could answer some of his questions were there, . . ." She trailed off again.

"What questions?" Jacob persisted in asking.

"Oh darling, I have no idea. Something to do with tanks, I fancy. Or rockets. I only know as much as he murmurs in his sleep. If he's asked about it directly, he bores on for hours, so I don't ask as a rule."

"Is he a spy?" Carl asked.

"'E's a bit of a 'andful, this one, in't he?" Melinda said to Jacob, with a shrug toward Carl.

"Did I just make an ass of myself?" Carl asked.

"Not at all," she assured him, in her own voice again.

"Tell me later," Carl said to Jacob. "I mean, tell me if I made an ass of myself."

"Officially Rafe is no more than a translator," Melinda offered, "but, being Rafe, he has taken it upon himself to become indispensable to the ministry as a researcher."

"The ministry?"

"The Ministry of Defense."

"I hope I get to meet him," Carl said, diplomatically.

"You will, shortly. He's very eager to crawl up Stalin's underbelly, or wherever it is that Henry proposes to take us."

"If I was out of line—," Carl began.

"Oh, there are no secrets here, you'll find. Not with this lot." Her eyes were guarded as she smiled at him, and Jacob sensed that she was afraid, as before, that she had been too strict.

"We're very free with one another indeed, you'll find," Annie said, with a certain pride. "Very much in one another's business."

When Rafe arrived, they settled their bill, and Henry offered to lead the way to Stalin's monument. Snow had fallen while they had been drinking, but it was only a dusting, and the men's boots and the heels of the women's shoes struck the paving stones sharply through it as they walked. At the monument, they climbed several flights of stairs, lit by glare that escaped from street lamps along the embankment below. Near the top, at a utility door on the western end of a landing, they bought tickets and were admitted. Inside, they stepped onto a small rectangle of linoleum, beside a closet whose door had been left ajar for the sake of the light from the bulb inside. The linoleum measured out as much of the pedestal's interior as anyone had used until that evening. It was like a stage representation of a room, with two walls cut away, in the corner of a much larger stage that remained unlit. Beyond was loose, uneven dirt; the smell of it thickened the air. Jacob had started to unbutton his coat upon entering, and he rebuttoned it at once, because it was as cold inside as it had been outside, and seemed colder. He could not see the ceiling. In the distance, in the rear of the cavernous space, were the lights and murmur of the party. "Should we?" Jacob asked, once the group had as-sembled. Henry agreed brusquely, as if impatient even with the possi-bility that they might lose courage, and stepped out onto the dark earth, which gave back none of the little light that fell on it, except in occa-sional shining patches, which they began to notice as they made their way and which they tried to point out to one another, where a leak, a spill, or an underground spring had turned the dirt to mud.

Annie took Jacob's arm. "Do you mind?" she asked.

"Not at all."

"This would be Henry's idea of a night out. I don't suppose there's a loo."

"There is not a loo," said Jana, in the careful English she had begun to speak. She and Thom were just beside them in the dark. "I ask already."

"It's boggy here," Henry called out, from ahead.

"Perhaps we've found the loo then," said Thom.

"Must you?" said Annie.

"It's none of my doing. Not yet, mind you."

The light at the entrance fell away behind them, while that of the festivities remained at least as far ahead. In the darkness between, it took all their concentration to keep from stumbling, and they fell silent. One had to put down a foot tentatively, feel the slope of the soil beneath, and test the footing before trusting it with one's full weight. Because the soft earth muffled footfalls, the only near sounds were one's own breathing and that of one's friends and the rustle of their coats. Each of them was alone and yet they were together, Jacob felt, and if the dark had not been so frightening he might have wanted the feeling to last longer.

The lights, which the small crowd nearly obscured, were powered by black cables that ran all the way back to the door they had come in by. Henry and Thom vanished into the crowd to scout for beer.

"Who are they, darling, can you tell?" Melinda asked Rafe.

"Students and artists, it looks like," he answered. "Czechs; no Westerners."

"Are we conspicuous?" Jacob asked.

"I like to think I'm always conspicuous," Rafe said. Standing as they were in shadow, it was hard to know how to understand the note of cheeriness in Rafe's voice. There was a suggestion of effort in it, as if he were trying to set a tone. What light there was caught only in his loose hair, and his face remained dark. "Do you need a job?" he asked Carl abruptly.

"Me?"

"Yes, you."

"It's very generous of you—"

"I haven't offered yet."

Carl chuckled politely. "I may look around, but I'm only planning to stay a few months."

"That's clever of you. I don't know why none of us thought of that."

"Never say never, I suppose," Carl answered, trying to match Rafe's casual manner, but not quite managing to. The darkness and the sense of being sequestered underground seemed to have brought the group into an unintended intimacy. They felt themselves being studied by one another, even though it was impossible to see where a person's eyes were looking.

"There's plenty for everyone," Thom declared, as he and Henry returned with a round, in bottles.

"Would *you* like more work?" Rafe asked Jacob privately, after they had all toasted one another. It was another private English class, he explained, in this case a group of college students who edited a political weekly. They had been the first to print a certain rumor during the revolution. "It wasn't true, of course, but it was very bold of them all the same."

"Why did they print it if it wasn't true?"

"They thought it was. Somebody was spreading disinformation. Somebody inside the StB, apparently. Nobody can quite figure out the motive."

"And these students spread it further."

"Quite innocently," Rafe smiled. "The boys, we call them. Melinda has taught them, too, but neither of us has the time, anymore."

"Thank you." If it paid as well as the chemists', Jacob would be able to drop down to half-time at the language school.

"Nonsense. Thank *you*, for taking them off my hands." He took a swig from his beer in his loose-armed, careless way. There was an awkward pause between them, on account of having transacted business. Melinda had gone off with Jana, who had learned there was a restroom after all. "Quite a setting," Rafe commented. "The real Czech underground, as it were."

Jacob let his attention wander into the surrounding crowd. The partygoers had stationed their supply of beer in a corner of the monument—there were two words for "corner" in Czech, Jacob had recently learned;

it was usually *roh* when understood from the outside, and usually *kout* from the inside, though not always—and their talk was echoed by the two perpendicular concrete walls nearby so sharply and quickly that it was beyond Jacob's skill in Czech to follow any of it. Even if he had been able to see distinctly, he didn't think he would have been able to parse the meaning of clothes and expressions as well as he could in T-Club. The partygoers were straight, after all. Or perhaps, it occurred to him, that was a false assumption. They were young; they were his age, mostly. They were excited, with the selfish happiness of people who have pulled off a stunt together, and that energy would be a kind of ring around them, he knew, that would lock him out, at first, if he tried to test it, but if he were able to break into it somehow, if he were able to think of something to say that took their interest, the party might become a place where he could meet someone, perhaps someone who was gay but for whom gayness wasn't the beginning and end of himself, who had first suspected it of himself, as Jacob had, not so long ago, who thought of himself mostly just as someone attracted to people who were playful, inventive, and gentle.

For now, though, he was a stranger. He noticed that Henry was standing beside him and seemed to be waiting to say a word. "Have you seen the art?" Henry spoke into his ear. He pointed east, where at a distance there were a few more faint lights. "It appears to be a kind of installation."

The two of them struck out across the dark together. Henry's pale hands and the bluish whites of his eyes seemed to flutter in the air beside Jacob. The lights that they were approaching were on the ground, pointed up toward white masses, and as Jacob watched his steps, the low angle of the light, falling across the hillocky dirt, made him think of a beach at night lit by a bonfire. When they came close, the white masses resolved into shapes in papier-mâché: an oversize skull and skeleton, the bones crowded into a jumble, with the skeleton's neck at a sharp angle, as if, even in this enormous space, the remains had had to be crammed in to make them fit. A large cap and a large hammer and sickle lay on the ground before the skull's hollow eye sockets.

"Oh, it's *Stalin*," Henry chuckled. "We're meant to be in his tomb with him."

On closer examination, they saw that there were in fact several skeletons, and all of them were inside a sort of wire mesh cage. At first Jacob thought that the cage was to protect the art from its audience, but on second thought that didn't seem in keeping with the evening's spirit.

A tall, unshaven man saluted them and borrowed a Petra from Henry. "Can we ask him?" Jacob said. —Please, would you be able to explain it to us? Is it Stalin's grave?

The man shrugged, as if this was a high price for the cigarette he was fingering. —What have I to explain? Here is Mr. Stalin, here is his monument, may he rest in peace.

—If it isn't a bother . . . , Jacob persisted.

The man sighed noisily. —Well, yes, it is Stalin's grave, he told them, speaking and smoking in practiced alternation. —And something else. In the cellar of every *panelák*, every family has a locker, with such a grille, and there they keep flags and banners and such shit for the First of May and Victorious February and the Anniversary of the Great October Revolution and so on. So this is sort of the locker of the government, see, and they kept here Mr. Stalin and the rest of the line for meat, until they forgot about them.

"What's the line for meat?" Jacob asked Henry, as the man returned to his friends.

"In the statue, before they tore it down, Stalin was leading three or four workers, and the Czechs always said it looked like they were queuing up at a butcher's shop."

In the still air, the smoke from their informant's cigarette hung about them, and Henry tried to wave it away. The effort made his hands cold, and he blew on them. "He's a sharp fellow. He's the one who did the Trabant on feet in Old Town Square."

"He wasn't so friendly, though."

"Oh, did you think that was the artist? I thought that was just a wanker who wanted a fag." There were more works of art farther on, but Henry excused himself. "Enough for me, thanks."

Jacob continued his walk alone, but he found that the rest of the exhibition was not as good. Either it was so abstract as to be without resonance—triangular panes of glass suspended from wires, for example, under a title like *Viewpoints IV*—or it was morbid without the touch of humor that gave the Stalin skeleton its charm. Over the course of the year, Jacob was to find in his visits to galleries that a morbid

solemnity was typical of the less-talented emerging artists. The tone
seemed to be a reaction to the new freedom—both an exploration of it
and a way of taking refuge from it. Such artists were like Western teenagers at the stage when they are impressed with the discovery that pain
and suffering are real and may be spoken about. They were boring because of their honesty.

He turned back toward the corner where he had left his friends. He
was tired and a little drunk, and he stumbled a couple of times but didn't
fall. He realized he was growing impatient with the care that was necessary to walk safely, and when he recognized his impatience he paused.
In the dimness he closed his eyes. Beneath the murmur of the partygoers, he heard the watery emptiness of the cave that they were in. It
seemed to be spinning slowly around him. A year ago he had been in
America. Two years ago he had been straight. Tonight he was underground, with the remains of the bogey man, lit by the torches of the
children who had killed him.

"Jacob? Are you all right, darling?" Melinda asked.

He opened his eyes. "Fine," he reassured her. She was with Carl,
who also looked concerned.

"There's sod all in the way of fresh air down here," Melinda suggested.

"I'm fine," he repeated.

"And we've been smoking up what there is of it," she continued.

"That's a good idea," said Jacob, and dug his cigarettes out of his
pocket. They declined his offer to share but then watched him light up
with the attention of children outside a pastry-shop window. They declined a second offer, too, however.

"I was wondering if it might be possible to meet someone here,"
Jacob said, in an effort to make his daze seem less mysterious.

"That's the spirit," said Melinda.

"Is it very open here?" Carl asked.

"Not really."

"It *is* changing," Melinda suggested, but then she hesitated. "Isn't it?
I suppose I don't actually know."

"I can't tell," answered Jacob. "Are you getting along with ev-
erybody?" he asked Carl.

"Your friends are *so* lovely."

"Oh, good."

"Thom? He's adorable. And Annie's so sweet. She's a little sad, isn't she?"

"I *don't* think I should be hearing this," Melinda interrupted. "You will excuse me."

"I'm sorry. I'll stop."

"Absolutely not. I ought to check on Rafe in any case." She began to walk away from them.

"Be careful of the gopher holes or whatever they are," Carl called after her.

They watched her step from mound-top to mound-top, bringing her feet together after each step, like someone crossing a brook on a series of stones.

"And Melinda?" Jacob asked, when they thought she could not hear.

"She, I don't know, she draws you out. Is that it? Do you find that she does that?"

"Sometimes, yes."

"We were looking at the sculpture." He gave a sharp laugh as he nodded toward it.

"What?" asked Jacob.

"Nothing, nothing. I wasn't prepared for your friends to be so charming."

"What did you say?"

"Oh, I told her I taught English as a second language in America, and I hadn't come all this way just to do more of it. That's all. It wasn't any more than that."

Carl sometimes joked about what he called his "enlightened short-sightedness"—about his reluctance, as a matter of philosophical principle, to sacrifice the self he was now for the sake of a self that it would be prudent someday to be. It was one of the traits that had made Jacob wonder if Carl was as straight as he seemed to be, and even after Jacob came to understand that it had nothing to do with sexuality, he still loved Carl for it. It was a kind of nakedness, and it set him apart from Jacob's schoolmates, all of whom had seemed to measure their lives against an ideal career.

"It's different here," Carl continued. "Not knowing what you're doing."

"Being here is what you're doing, when you're here."

"And that's how it should be, everywhere. But here it actually seems to be possible. Maybe because the city is so beautiful? Somehow it makes me really sad."

"It is sad."

"Jet lag, probably."

"Because it can't last. It's already over, really. The revolution."

"Oh, *that*," Carl said with mock shallowness. "But I'm talking about my *feelings*."

Jacob wished he could hold Carl's hand. He had never really felt any wish stronger than this for Carl, he told himself. "I'm glad you're here," Jacob said. "None of them know what it's like not to be in America."

"What it's like to know true freedom."

"I hope you'll stay," Jacob risked.

They made their way back to the crowd.

"A crisis in supply approaches," Thom warned.

"Can I get you one?" Carl offered. Jacob accepted.

"It's bloody cold in here," Melinda complained.

"Is it?" asked Annie. "I don't seem to notice it."

"You're shivering, darling."

"Am I? Perhaps I am."

"I asked him, you know," Melinda told Jacob.

"Asked him what?"

"What he had come for. To test your speculation."

"And?"

" 'To see.' You Americans turn out to be so open-ended. I understood you all to have goals."

"We have ideas, as you say."

"Mmm," she agreed.

"What's this?" Rafe asked.

"There's an attempt to figure out Carl," Jacob answered.

"The orphan," Rafe said. "Melinda's very good with orphans."

"I don't think he's an orphan," Jacob protested.

"Kaspar isn't an orphan, either, technically," Rafe continued. "He has that father."

"I don't think many people are as lost as Kaspar," Melinda said.

"How is Kaspar?" asked Jacob, forgetting that he had ever been angry with him.

"I'm afraid he's ill. He didn't teach this week."

The friends finished their last round quickly. When they emerged from the cave, they saw that a few stars had been able to pick their way through the glare cast by the city's lamps and by the new snow, which lay on its domes, towers, and gables. The snow whitened the streets, too, except for a pair of iron rails that the night tram kept fresh and black. From the top of Stalin's hill they could look down at the city's beauty as if they, too, were dictators or kings. Annie took Jacob's arm, and they negotiated the stone steps together, slowly.

"I don't want any more romance, for a little while," Jacob volunteered.

"It isn't always necessary, is it."

"I didn't tell you," Jacob continued. "He was selling himself."

"Oh?" Annie replied, as if she might need more explanation, and then, as if on second thought she decided she didn't want any, she added, "That is dreadful. I'm so sorry."

"Don't tell Melinda."

"No? I won't, then. I don't believe she tells *us* everything."

"What do you mean?"

"Just a feeling."

As they descended to the level of the city, the city gradually slipped away from their view, closing like a fan, until, at the foot of the hill, they felt the hill's steep face menacing their backs, and a row of lamps seemed to invite them to return to the city across the empty Bridge of Svatopluk Čech. Waiting on the other side, the heavy, white palaces stood shoulder to shoulder at the river's edge, as if to form of themselves a wall.

"My god, they're all spies," Carl pretended to believe. "Every last one of them."

"Even Thom?" asked Jacob.

"He's a sly one."

By way of experiment, they had made two cups of what the Czechs called Turkish coffee. It came out weaker than the version sold in restaurants, but just as bitter. As in a restaurant, they had to pick the grounds out from between their lips and teeth between sips.

"Are you growing a beard?" Jacob asked.

"I don't know. Do I look like a slob?"

"No," Jacob assured him. It both softened and roughened his face. "It's mature."

"I'll ask Thom about his case this afternoon. We're going to that ashen wedding-cake thing at the top of Václavák."

"The National Museum. Cabinets full of rocks."

"Oh? Maybe we'll go for a drink instead, then."

"No. The building is pretty. You should go."

"You should ask Rafe when you see him," Carl said. "But I suppose he wouldn't be able to tell you if he were."

"I'd be asking him to lie." Jacob lifted Václav out of his cage and petted him. "Of course only a gay person would think of it that way," he observed.

"Maybe he wants us to think he is."

"I met someone like that here. A Danish guy."

"To impress girls."

"*You* should pretend to be one."

"That's it," Carl agreed, in jest. "That's the answer."

"Instead of growing a beard."

"Hey, respect the beard, man."

Jacob was mildly envious of the trip to the National Museum; he had to work that afternoon. Rafe was going to introduce him to the student editors whose English lessons he was taking over.

"Thom doesn't know, right?" Carl asked. "About you."

"No."

"That's criminal, you know. He's a sweetheart."

"I know."

In the quarter of Malá Strana where Jacob was to meet Rafe, the sidewalk ran level with the street so that cars could drive onto it when a tram passed. The doorways had the shape of arches, and plaster lions were flaking off the keystones of the arches, as if the Renaissance were shedding the Baroque. Into many of the arches, modern rectangular doors had been fitted, smaller than the dark, tall windows of the floor above, but here and there an old, grand door remained, oak with black iron hinges, capable of shuttering the mouth of a building definitively.

The side street that housed the newspaper's offices looked empty when Jacob turned into it, but as Jacob was hunting for the blue plaque with the building's street number (not to be confused with the red plaque that gave its district registration number), Rafe startled him by appearing at his elbow.

"Boo."

"Where were you?"

"Keeping out of the wind. There's a *pasáž* behind yon door." He rang a doorbell. "I didn't ask if you were ready. Are you ready? You'll like the boys. They're posers, but you'll like them."

"Prosím," a voice said through the intercom. Jacob was afraid that the person might have been able to hear Rafe's slight.

"Tady pan Rejf a pan Jakub," Rafe announced cheerily.

"Prosím," the voice repeated, buzzing them in.

They rode a tiny elevator with dented yellow walls to the third floor. "I'm going to bow right out," Rafe said. "Is that okay?" He had folded a tram ticket into a paper star and was shaking it nervously inside a cupped hand as if it were a die that he was about to throw.

The newspaper's office lay at the end of a corridor, behind a door with a large pane of frosted glass. The room inside smelled of cigarettes and men's sweat. Underfoot were bales of the latest issue tied in twine. Torn pages of notes, ashtrays crammed full of stubbed butts, pots of glue, and cups of oily coffee cluttered the desks, beside each of which rose a tall, steel filing cabinet, like a smokestack beside a factory. Over one of the desks hung a calendar with a photograph of a fjord, its days marked up in several inks. In design the newspaper itself, at least the examples that Jacob could see, looked almost deliberately crude. The logo seemed to have been drawn with a marker, and the columns of type were clumsily arranged.

A tall, thin young man with shadows under his eyes threaded his way toward them. "Štěpán, my man," Rafe greeted him.

The boy chuckled. Two other students caught up to him: Ondřej had sandy hair and a bad complexion. Marek had black hair and was sucking on a pencil stub meditatively, as if it were a pipe. Their eyes shone with worship of Rafe, who, after a flurry of introductions and the injunction, "Mluvte anglicky, kluci!"—speak English, boys!—slipped away. Nothing had been said about money. The three turned their attention to Jacob with an air of polite disappointment.

"Please," said Štěpán, gesturing to chairs around a table where the newspaper was being laid out. To clear a space, Marek drew toward himself white sheets of cardboard, stamped with a blue grid, onto which type had begun to be glued.

"Rafe works in castle," said Ondřej, haltingly and somewhat tentatively.

Jacob couldn't tell whether the boy wanted to be reassured about his facts or his English. "I think so," Jacob answered. "He's a translator."

"Ten má ale kliku," Ondřej replied, lapsing into Czech.

"Ale mluvte anglicky!" Jacob said, trying to assume Rafe's blustery manner. " 'He has all the luck.' "

"He has all luck," Ondřej repeated slowly. He grinned at his slowness. "There we met him. Mr. President Havel invite us. At press meeting, you know, where come the newspapers and speaks the president."

"It isn't usual, that they invite a university paper," Štěpán interposed.

"It's called a press conference."

"A press conference," Štěpán repeated. Ondřej mouthed the syllables without voicing them. Marek merely looked thoughtful, as if respect were keeping him from trying to emulate Štěpán's English and modesty were keeping him from upstaging Ondřej's.

"But they invite us only one," Ondřej admitted.

"To one. They only invited us to one."

"Tell me," ordered Štěpán, "of what political party is Rafe?"

"I don't know. Should we get started with a lesson?"

"Often we have conversation only," Štěpán replied. "Is he of the left or the right?"

Jacob was afraid that free conversation would be little use to Ondřej, who didn't seem to know the basic patterns of English, or to Marek, who didn't seem to speak at all, but he didn't want to offend them by pointing out their disadvantages, and Štěpán was studying him impatiently, in expectation of an answer.

"I imagine he's a Democrat. Most intellectuals are, in America." Daniel wasn't, and he would have hated Jacob's simplification.

"The Democrats are of the left, that yes? But why, if you are free not to be? I do not understand. The Republicans are the party of freedom, that yes? And the Democrats are like our Socialists."

"It isn't that simple," Jacob protested.

"How is it?" Štěpán asked. "I do not know."

Rafe had answered these questions, too, Jacob sensed. Štěpán, and perhaps the silent Marek, who was tapping the tin band at the end of his pencil against his teeth, were testing Rafe's responses against Jacob's, and vice versa.

"Democrats are not so left," Ondřej suggested.

"No, that's true." Appreciating Ondřej's support, Jacob failed to correct his grammar.

"You are innocent, in America," Štěpán accused. "You do not know, how the Communists are. Do you know, who Senator Joseph McCarthy was? Your government was full of Communist spies."

"I don't think so."

"But yes! They are killers. The KGB was in the CIA. You do not even know."

"Perhaps I don't know," Jacob conceded.

"Do you know what is, StB?"

"'Do you know what the StB is.' The secret police in Czechoslovakia."

"Our KGB. Would you like to see a contract? Marku, please to show Mr. Jacob the contract. We will publish next week. Can you read Czech?"

"A little."

"It is a form. You sign, when you say that you will give information to the StB. And then you are theirs. They show it, if you make trouble."

The formal, legal Czech was beyond Jacob, but he could admire the letterhead, where the insignia of State Security was crisply printed, and the length of the numbered list of conditions of cooperation. "Where'd you get it?"

None of the boys seemed to hear the question.

"They are dirt, and they make people dirt," Štěpán continued. He read the contract through for Jacob, translating as he went. "The CIA must be as strong, or you will lose."

"But we've won," Jacob replied.

"But is not certain," Marek replied, speaking for the first time, "that *they* lose. We do not have the papers of StB." He tapped the contract with his pencil stub. "We have only this, and one or two other, as for amusement."

The lesson ended awkwardly. The editors left it to Jacob to bring up the matter of payment and expressed surprise when he expected money for what they felt was no more than a mutual introduction.

The two friends were lying in their beds, reading. Carl had not yet got up to shut the door of his room for the night, and Jacob could hear him subsiding into sleep—could hear his breathing become more regular. A knock; Běta.

"Are you awake?" she asked in English, apologetically. "There is war."

"War?"

"Is Carl?" She meant: Is Carl here? "Father invites, that you watch the television. Upstairs."

They padded up behind her in their socks. It would be Kuwait, Jacob realized. The British newsmagazine he liked to read had recently declared Saddam Hussein of Iraq to be another Hitler. The magazine's editorials had compared Kuwait's plight to Czechoslovakia's in 1938, when it was betrayed by France and Britain. On the stairs, even before he knew for sure that it was indeed a war to defend Kuwait, he felt proud of his country for taking a stand. He wanted to explain the moral case to Carl, to hear it worked out in his own voice, but he was too excited to speak.

The Stehlíks were dressed for bed. Mr. Stehlík pointed heavily to the television set; Mrs. Stehlíková patted the sofa beside her, to let them know they were welcome to sit down for a few minutes.

"Your America is *at* war," Mr. Stehlík said, emphasizing the preposition, which he had just learned from the anchorpeople. In those days, one of the American cable news channels was broadcast free in Eastern Europe, as a gift to the newly liberated.

There was video of antiaircraft cannons starting and shuddering in pink-orange smoke as they fired, and there was video of a city burning at night, from a distance.

"Oh, Jesus," Carl said. "Well, are we winning? What's the score?"

Bombardment had only begun an hour or two before.

"They had to," Jacob said.

"He is a bad man," Běta agreed.

"But it's such a *show*," Carl objected.

"It's always a show," Jacob answered.

—War is never good, said Mrs. Stehlíková in Czech. She could only have been following the tones of their voices. —It is blood and death.

—Well, that is also the truth, sighed her daughter.

As if to keep themselves aware of the lateness of the hour, the Stehlíks had not turned on any of the lights in their living room. Pale blue discharge from the television spilled erratically onto the faces of the group. Together they watched out two of the news program's ten-minute cycles, and the war began to make a difference in the feeling of things. It seemed to pick out the Americans in the larger picture that Jacob kept in his mind. It seemed to daub Jacob, Carl, and Rafe each with a spot of bright paint. Somewhat irrationally, Jacob began to feel himself to be less of a guest in the Stehlíks' living room. The war seemed to prove that the larger world was a setting where America was the principal actor, and therefore, by extension, a setting where Jacob ought to feel at home. The Stehlíks lived inside that world in the same way that Jacob lived inside theirs. A part of him felt ashamed of the grand entitlement that this sense of things implied, but he did not pretend to himself that he didn't share it. He merely kept silent about it.

When Jacob and Carl returned downstairs, neither was ready to go to sleep, and they paused together in the kitchen. A radiator gurgled and plinked slowly, as the hot water drained out and it cooled down.

"Did you ever register for the draft?" Jacob asked.

"I must have. Don't you have to, to get financial aid?"

"When I was seventeen, I wrote away to the Quakers for all this literature," Jacob remembered.

"I don't think it'll last that long," Carl hazarded.

Jacob didn't want the war to take either of them away from Prague. Some of his high school friends had enlisted, and they were probably in the Middle East now, or on their way there. They were somehow protecting his fragile idleness. He realized that he had lost something of Prague already, since Luboš and since Carl's arrival. The city had begun to seem less of a mystery; it had begun to put on a mask of familiarity.

They tried to guess whether the war was justified, but they didn't know enough about it to guess intelligently. They couldn't read Czech newspapers and couldn't get any American ones. The kiosks only sold the one British newsmagazine; it was not until several weeks later that it would become possible to buy an American one.

"I hear there's oil in them there parts," Carl joked.

"The Marxists will have a field day."

"You've been away. You'd be more skeptical if you'd been listening to them gear up for it."

The dark and the stillness outside the kitchen held the two of them together; their presence to each other was more powerful than anything they might have claimed to believe. Jacob was taking brief glances at Carl's beauty, at his slimness and at the pale delicacy of his skin, and it occurred to him that Carl might be growing his beard as a sort of courtesy, so that it would be that much harder for Jacob to fall in love with him again. Carl wouldn't know that it didn't have that effect.

By instinct, the friends all dropped in at Mel and Rafe's apartment the next evening. They felt not only welcomed but comforted by the sight of Mel and Rafe's lumpy brown sofa and the linoleum-topped folding table in their kitchen. As it happened, Rafe had been asked to accompany a deputation to Brussels, leaving the next morning, and it was decided that the impromptu gathering should therefore double as a send-off party for him. Thom and Carl were given as many pitchers as they could carry, which they took to a pub in the next street to have filled.

"It steams, in the cold," Carl reported when he and Thom returned. "Its like carrying soup. It's like carrying pitchers of *life*." He and Thom set the pitchers down in a crowd on the kitchen table. "Sparta, anyone?" Carl offered.

"If there's no better," Annie hinted, but Jacob was already accepting one of the Sparty himself. He and Carl had smoked up his Marlboros, and they were economizing.

"You've gone native so quickly," Melinda complimented Carl.

"The embassy is warning Americans not to be too visible."

Henry nodded. "Terrorist reprisals." He had read about it in the Czech papers.

"But *we're* not Americans," Melinda insisted. "Certainly Jacob isn't. And now even Carl is becoming so well camouflaged."

"What about me?" Rafe demanded.

"*Cela va sans dire.* You speak *Arabic*, darling."

Bitter, gray smoke unwound in the air between the friends.

"The word on the street," Henry further informed them, "is that the terrorists won't do anything in Prague because they're grateful to the Czechs for having sold them Semtex."

There was nervous laughter. Melinda set some hard salami on a plate along with a knife to cut it with. The doorbell rang, and Thom said that it was probably Jana.

"Jana is nobody's fool," Melinda said admiringly while Thom was fetching her.

"She speaks English rather well, doesn't she," Annie concurred.

"And beautiful Czech," Rafe added.

"What takes you to Brussels?" Henry asked, politely.

"A conference on armaments."

"Negotiating them down?" Jacob wondered.

"Building them up! The Czechs have never before really had to decide for themselves how much they want. A hundred tanks? Two hundred? What about missiles?"

"Are they allowed to have missiles?"

"Sure! So long as they aren't *nukular*. Fighter jets. Armored personnel carriers."

"Do you like this kind of thing?" Jacob asked.

"Are you kidding? It gives me a big stiffy."

His confession made them feel that it would be impolite to talk about the war with absolute disapproval in front of him, but luckily none of them were sure that they did disapprove absolutely.

Jana appeared and nodded a greeting to the group. No one had been able to admire her the other night, in the dark of Stalin's tomb. Now they saw that she had the sort of fine complexion that freckles lightly even in midwinter, and that her hair was almost but not quite long and heavy enough to pull straight the loose curls in it. Thom seemed to hold his breath beside her, as if waiting for his friends to respond to her beauty.

"Pivo?" Rafe asked her. "We were deciding Czechoslovakia's military policy."

"In Prague foreigners always decide it," she answered. "Yes, please, a beer."

"In fact I only give advice," Rafe protested.

"Do you write the reports?" Carl asked.

"Not officially."

"In other words you do write them."

"That's classified. The number of tanks in Ostrava isn't, but the authorship of the reports I write is."

"How many tanks are in Ostrava?" Jana asked.

"Not enough!"

"Perhaps if there were more, it would, how do you say . . ." She made a gesture with two hands as if she were spreading something inside a basin, and she made a girlish sound effect as of something crashing.

"Collapse?" Rafe guessed.

"Sink?" she guessed. "It is so ugly and poisoned."

"Oh no. Poor Ostrava!" To the others, he explained: "It's a mining city."

For a few minutes they held themselves crowded together in a single conversation, in order to welcome Jana and in order to give Rafe a chance to show off, in acknowledgment of the fact that they were about to lose him for a little while. But then Melinda broke the configuration, by touching Jana on the forearm and offering to show her the view from the balcony, such as it was, behind the bathtub in their kitchen. As the women moved away, the others shifted, too, some to refill their drinks and others to relax on the sofa in the living room, so that in a moment only the three Americans were left together.

"How did you learn Arabic?" Carl asked.

"Oh, the usual way, I suppose." It was a vague answer; there was a touch of pettishness in it. Perhaps Rafe wished that Melinda had stayed beside him. "I took a semester in college. I figured, they have the oil."

"How do you think it'll go, in Kuwait?"

Rafe shrugged. His eyes focused on Carl and then drifted away. "It's a question of getting all our stuff there. Our stuff and our boys. They don't move quickly. But I think that enough of them got there before it started."

"So you're not worried."

"I'm not worried about Kuwait."

Unwatched by women, Rafe's manner was slack, and Carl was taking advantage of his inattention to study him, in sidelong glances. Jacob wondered if Carl was trying to figure out whether Rafe was a spy.

If Rafe were, it would have become second nature with him to sense suspicion and detection, as it was for Jacob. Was it disloyal of Carl to try to uncover one of their friends? In wartime, no less. If Rafe weren't, suspicion might hurt his feelings even more. In that way too it would resemble Jacob's secret.

"Is there room for more people on your balcony?" Jacob asked Rafe. "I've never seen it."

"There's not much to see," Rafe answered. "Be my guest."

"We keep our Hoover out here, I'm afraid," Melinda apologized, as she and Jana made room for Jacob and Carl.

"I won't trip on it."

After the kitchen, the night air was empty of flavor. They had to stand four in a row, and the cold iron of the balustrade bit their fingers as they steadied themselves by gripping it. The balcony overlooked an empty, paved courtyard, lit by a parallelogram of night sky that happened to contain a gibbous moon, low and yellow.

"It's cold," Jacob complained.

"Cold keeps you honest," Melinda answered.

"In that case I'd better go back in."

"No, stay, the two of you. Tell us whether you're afraid. I don't require honesty."

"Of bombs?" Jacob asked.

"Of anything."

"Of anything," Carl echoed. He stood nearest the door to the balcony, and Melinda stood farthest from it, and it seemed that she had chosen a piquant question to make sure it passed all the way down the chain and reached him. "We're bold," Carl decided.

"We are?" Jacob asked.

"We're on the frontier. The Wild East. You are, anyway. I'm just a tourist."

"The Wild *Center*," Melinda corrected. "No one likes to be thought of as east anymore."

"Are you English teachers?" Jana asked.

"Jacob is," Carl answered. "I don't know what I am."

"Nor I," said Melinda, "though I, too, teach."

"I don't understand what they expect us to do about this warning," Jacob said. "If we were the type who stay home, we wouldn't be in Prague."

"But that's it," Carl replied. "They don't want you here." He was evolving one of his theories. "It's the frontier, and there's too much freedom. What if you got used to it?"

"Do you think that you are more free here, than in America?" Jana asked.

"Absolutely. Here there are no expectations."

"There never are, for an exile," Melinda suggested. "It's a great privilege."

"I do not think, that I feel this freedom," Jana objected. "I feel—" She turned to Melinda for the translation of a word.

"Nerves," Melinda supplied. "Anxiety."

"I wonder if it lasts," said Jacob. "Don't you think that eventually here becomes your real here? The charmless here?"

"Now I wonder if we're discussing exile," Melinda said, "or merely adulthood."

"The trailing clouds dissipate," Jacob offered.

"Sort of," she agreed.

"Were you a pretty child?" Carl suddenly asked Melinda. "I bet you were."

She flushed. "*I* don't know. You can't ask a person that."

"You were, is what you're saying. You had a happy childhood and you miss it."

"Don't we all?" she answered. "No, I suppose that's a terrible thing to say. There are unhappy childhoods."

"But those people miss them even more, so you're not wrong."

"I'm going inside, before I embarrass myself further."

"You haven't. You couldn't," he said into the night air. Soon Jana, too, excused herself, and the two friends were left. They turned and looked frankly in at the party behind the glass.

The cold had whitened Carl's face and reddened his fingers, Jacob saw as Carl lifted a cigarette to his lips. "I can fall for her, can't I?" Carl asked. "I don't want anything to happen. I mean, I know it isn't going to."

When Jacob had first fallen in love with a boy, three years before, he had seen that it was possible simply to turn away. The boy was straight; he was never going to fall in love with Jacob; and moreover Jacob then hoped that he himself would turn out not to be gay. It would have been correct to withdraw in silence, and it would have been prudent. But in giving up the misery he would also have had to give up the joy he found in his friend's company, and so he stayed and eventually came to understand and name for himself the joy as well as the misery, though the boy never understood, never heard him name them, and perhaps never even knew the half of it. Ever since, it had been a principle with Jacob not to side with righteousness against feeling. Righteousness was a trap, he felt, and he had been lucky to get out as quick as he had. He therefore now set about being broad-minded about Carl's crush. The happiness of their circle didn't seem much threatened; as Jacob's own experience suggested, nothing comes of most wishes. Furthermore, in Rafe's absence, Carl and Melinda were careful with each other the next time they met. They weren't distant, as they might have been if they were frightened. There was nothing for anyone to notice, and no one did.

The group, meanwhile, accepted Carl completely. When he announced that he had found another hospitable pub near Wenceslas Square, the group trusted him and for variety's sake took his suggestion. In two cavelike rooms, whose low arched ceilings had been yellowed by decades of cigarette smoke, he led them to flimsy tables crammed together so tightly that you couldn't get into or out of your seat without the cooperation of the people at the next table. Whenever you rose and made your way down the aisle to the men's room, chair legs caught at you like brambles and had to be shaken off. The beer on tap was Pilsner Urquell; Carl recommended the goulash; the waiters were businesslike and did not try to pass off a tourist menu instead of the regular one. For a week the friends returned almost nightly, until their coats stank of the place and even by day their eyes were red from its haze.

At that point they decided to go back to the jazz club in Pařížská. They all wanted to show it to Carl, especially Annie, who had first discovered it. Jacob steeled himself, but when they went, no one there reminded him of his misadventure. Probably none of the staff even remembered it. Carl crowed over the jazz club, to Annie's gratification. Not only the lofty rooms and loud, careless audience delighted him but also the music, which he alone among the group was connoisseur enough to appreciate. "They've got a New Orleans sound," he tried to explain to Jacob. "A bigger sound. Do you know *anything* about jazz?"

"Nothing," Jacob confessed, shamelessly.

After three or four rounds, Annie would ask one of the men to dance, and if he refused, Melinda and Jana would in solidarity insult him, so that soon a number of the friends would find themselves together on the dance floor. Annie snapped her fingers soundlessly and stepped lightly in the pattern of a square; Melinda swayed from side to side while swiveling her bent arms; Thom always nodded solemnly. Returning to the table, flushed, the dancers were told how good they had looked by whoever had remained behind, usually Carl or Henry. "You ought to have joined us," Annie would say in reproach.

The only weak link in their chain of pleasure was communication. At the pay phone near their local *hospoda*, Jacob and Carl could make outgoing calls, but they were rarely able to receive an incoming one. Mr. Stehlík, who would have hung up on their friends, was in Poland with his wife for more than a month, but once their friends began calling regularly, thanks to Carl's more gregarious nature, Běta decided that it was unthrifty to leave the phone off the hook for the time it took to walk downstairs and find out if they were home. For a while she hollered to them from the top of the stairs, but they never heard her, so she gave that up. Instead she took messages, which were almost always incomplete, because she was too polite to tell callers when she hadn't understood. "But *where?*" Jacob would ask, his patience thinning, and Běta would translate his question into Czech for herself—"Ale kde?"—and then shrug helplessly. "I don't know. He said something—'elephant'? *Nevím, nevím. To jsem asi nerozuměla.*"

"Elephant?" Jacob would desperately echo, miming a trunk.

"Asi ne," she would skeptically reply. Maybe not, after all.

The problem preoccupied Jacob. Two lodgers had a stronger claim than one on the Stehlíks' phone. It seemed almost unjust. If only there were a way for Běta to signal to them and spare herself the stairs. All the windows in the house were doubled, and in the outer frame of the one in Carl's bedroom, Jacob had noticed a small hole in the lower left corner, which had once admitted a wire of some kind. On the top floor of the Rott hardware store in Malé náměstí, downtown, he bought string and a small brass bell. If the bell were set on the edge of the table near Carl's bed, and Carl's inner window were left ajar, and a string were threaded from the bell through the hole in Carl's outer window up the outside of the house to the Stehlíks' living room directly above, where the end of the string could be held until needed by closing it in their outer window, then Běta would be able to ring for them by opening her window and giving a tug.

—But when Father returns? Běta asked.

—But we aren't doing anything! Jacob pleaded. —The hole already exists. A tiny little hole!

She acceded. Very imperfectly it worked, though now and then Jacob and Carl failed to hear the bell, which clanked just once each time it was tumbled onto the carpet.

In Jacob's favorite class at the language school his worst student was a woman in her thirties named Milena. Her hair, prematurely white, was braided and pinned in a bun, in what looked like a folk style. She had an apologetic manner; whenever she spoke, a smile so narrowed her eyes, which were already hidden behind thick glasses, that Jacob couldn't tell whether she was looking at him. She reminded him of a bashful professor he had studied with, who had closed his eyes whenever he raised them from his lectern. She never handed in homework assignments. She took copious notes during class but seemed to remember nothing from one week to the next. If he singled her out, to make sure she had understood a point of grammar, she became flustered and indicated by pantomime that he should address someone else. After every class, in what amounted almost to a ritual, two or three students approached his desk to ask ("if you will allow") about his life in America or his accommodations in Prague. Milena was never among them.

In this she was like his best student, a Vietnamese guest worker named Phuoc, who asked to be called Philip. He knew English better than Czech, as he declared during the class's first meeting, because he had taught himself English from books as a child in Vietnam. Though his pronunciation was sometimes impenetrable, his vocabulary was immense, and Jacob quickly learned that when he failed to understand Philip, it was sometimes because Philip was using a word that Jacob didn't know. Among other things, Philip had read Shakespeare, which complicated matters. During the scheduled periods of free conversation, Philip often spoke of his fondness for English and of the difference between his life in Prague and the more austere one he had lived in Vietnam, where his wife remained. But he never approached Jacob after class to say more. Jacob had the impression that Philip refrained because he didn't want to seem to step out of his place as a guest in the Czechs' world. Philip never spoke to his fellow students, or they to him, except when the language exercises required it.

Though Philip never overcame his reticence, one day Milena did. —May I in Czech? she asked.

—Can't you in English? Jacob irritably replied, but then it occurred to him that she might have been about to tell him she was giving up.

"I try," she agreed. She clasped her hands under her chin as if gathering her thoughts there, and then her head sank over her hands with the effort of concentration. "I have two children," she said with laborious slowness. "For them I learn English. I try to teach but"—here she appealed to Jacob with open palms and a laugh at herself—"I cannot." She broke into Czech: —I wanted to ask therefore, if it is possible to arrange private hours? I would pay, of course, whatever you charge.

Now that he knew the mystery of her persistence, Jacob felt ashamed of his impatience. —Lessons for you? he asked, to make sure.

—For my children, rather.

They were nine and six, she said, a boy and a girl. Jacob objected that he had never taught children, but Milena was confident that he would be able to. He named the hourly rate that he earned from the chemists; she hesitated but said she was willing to pay it.

—It is distant, our home, she said, uncertainly. He didn't think he could object; for months she had traveled the same distance to him. So she wrote out the numbers of the three buses he would have to take and the names of the stops where he would have to transfer. Later, when he consulted his map, he saw that he would be riding beyond the edge of it. Later still, when he alighted from the second of the buses, at the foot of a long white *panelák*, into a wind that threw gravel down an empty cement walkway, he realized that the journey was too long for the fee he had proposed. But now there were children expecting lessons from him; he couldn't back out.

There were only two other passengers on the last bus he had to take, which idled for several minutes before getting under way. Against the posted rules, one of the passengers was bantering with the driver. Jacob nervously read the names of passing street signs. As of two minutes ago, he was late. He was afraid he would make himself even later by failing to pull the cord in time for his stop. Sometimes a bus driver would sail past a stop if he hadn't been alerted far enough in advance.

Jacob managed to pull the cord in time. He shouted thanks to the driver, and on the sidewalk was struck by the sight of the *panelák*'s bleached concrete walls, now distant, where a few newly washed sheets, even more brilliantly white, fluttered against the ropes that held them, on balconies that ran the length of the building and brought to mind the decks of an ocean liner. Then he turned away, into a street of villas.

A rank of bare lindens defended the houses on the right. On the left, a wire-mesh fence gave way to a brick wall, painted yellow. A door in this wall bore the number Milena had given him. He rang the bell and waited, tracing with his eyes the brown serpentine fingers of a vine that had grown up the wall and over it.

"It is, how to say, wine," Milena explained when she answered the door.

"A grapevine," Jacob corrected.

"Yes. Please, come in."

They walked past a rabbit hutch, from which small red eyes watched them, and past the snow-covered furrows and mounds of a wintering garden. At the corner of the villa, two children soundlessly appeared in a doorway as Milena opened it. —But children, he cannot enter, you must step out of his way, the mother said, in a mild tone that they seemed to consider harmless, for they watched him a few moments longer before sidling back inside. "Please," Milena resumed, gesturing that he should enter.

"Thank you."

"Thank you," echoed the girl, throwing him a glance.

"You already speak English," Jacob answered, and the girl became shy. He stepped after the children into a sort of cloakroom. The pale winter sun, with its touch of violet, came in through the sidelights of the door. A narrow staircase led up into a honey-colored darkness.

"Prokop, Anežka, Mr. Putnam," Milena announced.

"Oh, they can call me Jacob," he offered. He repeated their names, and they more quietly repeated his.

Laughing for the sake of politeness, rather than because of any joke, Milena tugged off her shoes and replaced them with slippers from a low shelf. The children were already wearing their slippers. Milena tried to

dissuade Jacob from taking off his shoes, but when he insisted, she offered him slippers, too: —Please, though they are not so pretty . . .

—Mami, in English! Anežka demanded, in Czech.

—You are right, you are right, Milena replied, also in Czech. "Please,"
she addressed Jacob, "up?" Evidently the family lived on the villa's second floor.

"Tchay-kop," Prokop said, when they reached the top of the stairs.

"Dj," Jacob corrected. The sound didn't exist in Czech.

"Dj," the boy accurately repeated. "Moment," he added, and then he
ran off, Anežka following.

Milena led Jacob into a large room that ran the east length of the
building. It seemed to combine dining and living areas. In broad
windows, full of the already darkening sky, hung pots of delicate ferns;
the windows were underlined by low shelves of books along the wain-
scoting. Jacob noticed what must have been an encyclopedia—a file of
brown spines of a nineteenth-century smokiness, with feathery, gilded
lettering. In the room's far corner, a deal table supported a television
with a chalky screen. A slump-shouldered sofa faced it; draped over the
sofa was a polyester shawl, auburn and umber. The dining table was
dressed in white linen.

"Please," said Milena, touching the place at the head of the table.
"Something to a meal?"

"Oh, you don't have to do that," Jacob said. He saw that his words
confused her. She had caught the implication of refusal, but not his
precise meaning, and she looked hurt. "Did you already make it?" he
asked, trying to save the moment. He repeated his question in Czech: —Is
it already prepared? The way he phrased it sounded almost demanding.

—Yes, yes, she assured him.

"Okay, sure, thank you," he said, though he had no appetite. It was
not yet five in the afternoon.

—It is already prepared, she repeated, and backed into a white
kitchen. He saw that there were several covered saucepans simmering on
her stove. The sight made him afraid he had just agreed to eat the family's dinner, but he could think of no way to find out now whether he
had really been meant to accept the generosity.

Prokop appeared at the threshold of the room, holding something
behind his back. His sister crouched beside him, tightly hugging a

doll—a baby-girl doll with a plastic head and a lumpy cloth body. Prokop whispered something to his mother, who nodded in response. —But can he in Czech? Prokop then asked her aloud.

—He can, Milena answered. To Jacob she explained, "Prokop wants you show . . ."

The boy held out a green metal toy. At first Jacob thought it was a railroad car. —It's a tram! Jacob said.

The boy looked disappointed. —It is an *American* tram, he insisted.

—Show, Jacob said. Without surrendering it, the boy let him look. The toy was forest green, with peach and red trim. At each end was an open balcony, with steps for mounting or alighting, and at the corners were poles to grab on to, which seemed to support the roof of the car like a temple's columns. Along the sides, windows had been cut into the tin, and rectangles of what looked like exposed camera film had been placed in the frames. Through them Jacob could see an occasional glint off a gear of the mechanism inside. The boy turned the toy as he held it out so that Jacob could see all the sides, as if it were a gem and he were displaying its facets.

—It's handsome, Jacob said in praise. A placard on the car's roof read Bay and Taylor Sts. —It's from San Francisco, he added.

—From where?

—It's a city in Western America, where there are many hills, and so they have trams.

The boy now looked warily at his own toy, as if it had kept a secret from him.

—A friend of father brought him it, Milena commented.

—Shall we start the lesson?

—But no, you must have something in the way of a meal, Milena replied. —Sit, please.

The two children sat in a row to his right. —The children just ate, Milena explained, as she set before him a plate of sliced meatloaf, boiled cabbage, and dumplings, covered in gravy. It was gray and smelled like soil after a rain. As he ate, the last of the daylight slipped away.

Anežka had set her doll, which Jacob had forgotten to ask about, in her lap, and she was making its mittenlike hands paw the air in some private game.

—And what do you have there? Jacob asked. —Or rather, whom?

The girl smiled but did not reply. The stranger was not supposed to have seen.

—But Anežka, do not be embarrassed, the mother reproached her.

—How is she named? Jacob tried again.

—Květa.

—And where is she from?

—From Pardubice.

—She's pretty.

—I thank you, Anežka formally answered.

—And will she learn English?

This was too much to reply to. Jacob worried that he might not be able to rise to the challenge. His hands felt clumsy and overlarge, and he felt oafish chewing and swallowing in front of the children. They shifted in their seats with the caution of birds reassessing a branch that the wind has nudged. The boy had brought out his cable car because it was American and Jacob was American, and the idea of a match in origins had furnished some cover, but the girl had innocently stripped the cover away when, in imitation of her brother, she had brought out her doll, which was merely precious to her. The children almost seemed too delicate to teach.

In the event, of course, as the lesson proceeded, the children's delicacy was forgotten, like the cable car, which remained on the table but went unregarded. They learned greetings, introductions, and farewells, and thus were able to turn the shock of having met Jacob into a game, reimagining themselves with different names and different ages, and as coming from different parts of the world. The effort of trying to be a symbol to the children and trying not to be one taxed Jacob's energy, and on the way home, he fell asleep on one bus after another.

As it rose and fell amid the tiles of the former shower, Annie's voice, though soft, sometimes touched a note that sang because of the geometry of the room. "The end rings false, *I* find, anyway," she was saying, of a novel she had just finished. Her books were due at the British library in the Clementinum, and she was planning another trip there. Standing, because there were no chairs in the smoking room, she had folded her arms so that her elbows rested on her stomach, and one forearm was tucked around her, like a girdle, while the other fell loosely forward, extending the hand that held her cigarette. "Emmeline, the one in love, she would have such feelings—but you ought to read it. I shan't give away the ending."

"But you didn't like it," said Jacob.

"You haven't been *listening*," she accused him, and the room trilled brightly. "It's only the end I dislike. Just a page, really. What leads up to it is quite beautiful. In that savage way, where you describe how devastated people are by each other."

"Devastated?" Jacob asked.

"So I find, yes. By men, in particular. The cunning way they have of telling you how awfully they intend to behave. She's quite good on that."

"*I'm* not awful."

Melinda interposed: "As yet you haven't had much of a chance to be, or so you've given us to understand." The echoes of her voice, warmer than Annie's, seemed to set up a chatter like running water.

"You'll see, if you read it," Annie insisted.

They fell silent. The presence of their selves seemed reinforced by the room's acoustics, while the room's isolation seemed to relieve them of the burden of display.

"Kaspar asked if I would read some pages from his translation," Melinda said, "and looked so crestfallen when I said I had no German."

"Did he? He didn't ask me," Annie complained. "Of course my German is rubbish."

"But one wants to be asked."

"Mmm."

"Is he still sick?" Jacob inquired.

"I'm afraid so," Melinda answered.

"It's quite sad. He lives in such a hole," Annie reported.

"Have you visited him?" Jacob asked.

"I brought him a few tinned things Tuesday week," Annie said. "Sardines and beets and such like."

"Did you visit, too?"

"I did," admitted Melinda.

"Should I?"

"He sets a great value on your esteem, as do we all of course," Melinda answered. "But you oughtn't to feel obliged."

"Oh no," Annie agreed.

"He does still call you the writer. 'How is Jacob the writer?' So you have that to live up to."

"Even though I haven't written anything."

"He needn't know that."

"Henry is still very keen to write," Annie put in. "He thinks that with the addition of Carl you could have a proper *community* of writers. With meetings and such. No girls allowed, of course."

"The cheek," said Melinda.

"Nobody told me," Jacob said.

Annie shrugged as she took a drag of her cigarette.

"Would you bring Kaspar something from me, if you go?" Melinda asked. "But he must promise to send back the dish once he's eaten what's in it. It's the last I have."

Three days later, Jacob found himself in a neighborhood of villas gray with coal dust between Žižkov and Vršovice, just beyond the city's great cemeteries. He was bearing a creamed chicken casserole from Melinda, still warm, and in his backpack, a can of red currants from his own pantry. At Kaspar's building, he took out a key that Melinda had lent him and let himself in through a glass front door. It fell shut behind him heavily. "Kaspar?" he said aloud, through echoes, but no one answered. The walls of the corridor were painted lime green below and skim-milk white above. Self-conscious in the building's silence, he walked past a rising staircase toward a descending one behind and beneath it and then walked down into an unlit basement with an unpainted cement floor. At the end of a row of three garbage cans, he knocked mistrustfully at a gray door that was not marked in any way. There was no answer, except for a faint stirring, as of a sleeper turning under bedclothes. He sensed the presence of a person. One shouldn't be able to detect such a thing through a shut door, but usually one is able to. After a pause, he knocked again. More silence followed. Perhaps he had the day wrong. Then a small voice said, "Haló?"

Jacob identified himself but the speaker behind the door didn't seem able to hear him. —Please, the speaker said in Czech. —It is open.

"Kaspar?" Jacob repeated, as he cautiously entered.

Beneath a shelf of detergents in jugs and faded boxes, a man was seated on the edge of an unfolded cot. He had evidently just raised himself; the sheets still held in their slow waves the hollow his body had formed in them. He was leaning on his hands, and he had the haggard, unfocused expression of someone who has been woken from deep sleep in the middle of the day, a look worsened, in his case, by his wandering left eye, over which he seemed for the moment to have lost all control. The mouth was hidden by wild beard, and the skin of the face was so loose that it seemed almost to tremble. He seemed to be smiling, but Jacob couldn't tell whether it was a smile of recognition or merely of appeasement toward a stranger whose intentions he did not know. —There is no lock, Kaspar continued, still in Czech.

—Do you want still to sleep? Jacob asked.

—No, no. He shook his head with deliberate slowness, as if he felt dizzy and were taking pains not to make himself dizzier. He straightened his sweater, which had been pulled askew while he was unconscious.

As in the hallway outside, the concrete floor was raw. There was a drain in the center of it. Papers littered a card table, which seemed to serve as Kaspar's desk. Above hung an unshaded bulb, but it had not been turned on. What light there was came instead from the street, through a small square of frosted glass high in the room's far wall. This window faced east; since it was midafternoon, the light through the window was gentle and bluish. Beneath it, brooms, mops, shovels, and a hoe leaned against the wall. A dustpan and a pink cleaning rag hung on hooks. In a corner stood a steel slop sink, stained with the dried spatter of white paint.

"Welcome," said Kaspar, now in English. He seemed to have collected himself enough to place Jacob.

"Melinda asked me to bring you this," Jacob said, holding out the casserole.

"Ah, she is too good." He indicated the card table: "Please."

"Shouldn't I put it in the refrigerator for you?"

"Didn't you see my refrigerator?" He pointed. On the sill of the high window, Jacob now noticed a jar of pickled cabbage, a crumpled foil of butter, and a milk jug. "It is nicely cool. It does not freeze." Proud of his resourcefulness, he chuckled faintly. He fit his stocking feet into a pair of sandals beside his cot and stood to clear a place for the casserole on his desk. "But I shall eat this soon. Would you like some?"

"No, I'm fine, thanks. You go ahead."

"I shall wait. For now I have the pleasure of your company. Sit, sit."

He returned to the edge of his bed and gestured toward the only other seat in the room, an aluminum folding chair.

Though he had made the comparison in a moment of anger, Jacob had not been wrong in likening Kaspar's face to an animal's. There was no cunning in it, only an earnest attention, a kind of hunger. When he had imagined this visit, Jacob had foreseen the pleasure of atoning for his insult, which, because it had remained unspoken, Kaspar had never heard, but now that he was in Kaspar's presence, he was reminded of the assumption of deeper involvement that Kaspar made, as a matter of natural right, when anyone was in conversation with him. Faced with the evidence of Kaspar's illness and poverty, Jacob feared Kaspar's familiarity not as an intrusion but because he sensed that he might later be forced, for reasons he couldn't yet name, to disappoint it.

"Perhaps I should go," Jacob said.

"As you like."

"If you need to sleep."

"I don't think I need sleep any more today. Stay, tell me of yourself."

Jacob took the chair. "I brought you something, too," he added, remembering the currants.

—This is delightful, Kaspar said in appreciation, thrown momentarily back into Czech by his reading of the label. But he resumed in English. "I shall ask my landlady to make a roll for breakfast."

"Do you really pay rent here?"

"I teach German to the porter. This is her workroom, and she has pity on me. I am a Prince Myshkin for her, as you say."

"I never said *you* were Prince Myshkin."

"She has a great respect for books and those who work with books, because she is Jewish."

At the baldness of the assertion, Jacob took in a deep breath.

"Is it not true?" Kaspar asked.

"In America no one would say it like that."

"But it is because the Jews have such a respect that I have a room. I must say it," he insisted.

"Could you live in the Dům učitelů, with Annie and Thom?"

"But I am well here! It is near to hospital. I have four blankets. And the porter cooks such nice dishes. She worries for me; she has no children." A look of contentment came over his face. "I say to her that I have translated a page on the strength of her soup, and she is pleased. Will you have tea?" Kaspar took an electric pot from a shelf of hardware and filled it at the sink. With a tiny spoon, he measured out tea leaves. "This, too, is her gift."

The porter's generosity brought to mind Melinda's, and for a few minutes the two men competed in praising her. Jacob wondered if there were anything romantic in Kaspar's gratitude. It had the strength of a child's dependence. But of course they all relied on Melinda so much, even those who relied on her merely to keep them in her mind.

"She is like a gardener," Kaspar said.

"But maybe she thinks too little of herself," Jacob suggested.

"Oh yes," Kaspar at once agreed. "She has not altogether *become* herself." He said this, too, as if it laid him under no obligation. "She has not yet found her fate."

"Is her fate with Rafe?" Jacob asked.

The German seemed taken aback. "It is not for me to say." An awkwardness hung in the air. "Perhaps I mean to say she has not found her ambition, rather than her fate," he continued. "So it is with my writer, the one I am translating."

Jacob nodded absently.

"I gave you his book," Kaspar reminded him.

Jacob had forgotten. He apologized for not yet having started to read it.

Kaspar didn't seem to have expected Jacob to. "My writer, too, was concerned rather with the fates of others," he went on. "Il lui fallait cultiver les jardins d'autrui." He spoke the French words as if with pebbles in his mouth, the way Germans do.

"What did he write?" Jacob asked.

"Poems, but I translate his letters."

"To whom?"

"Do you know the surrealists?"

"I've heard of them."

"You have heard of them as a joke," Kaspar inferred. "That is the way. A joke that is not funny. They are of course failures, for they make believe to take the side of the machine against man. To take the side of chance." He paused and shakily poured the tea. "And yet it is not so. They are not truly on that side. In truth they make a protest.

They are saying that so little humanity is left to them, it is as if all were chance. But they never admit that it is a protest. It is to be such a game, which they have already lost but they are pretending that they cannot lose."

"They mean to lose," Jacob said, to see if he understood.

"They cannot win, rather. They take the side against the human, in a spite without malice."

He was smiling and stroking one side of his beard meditatively. He looked so satisfied with the pleasure of talking that to Jacob it almost seemed indecent, and something in him wanted to object. "What did the Communists think of them?" Jacob asked.

"Ah, that is good," sighed Kaspar, acknowledging the touch. "Some are taken in, in early years. And later, in revenge, they say that surrealism is despair. But it is not despair. It is a game that only a young man can play, a young man in health, in lust as we say in German, because of the animal in him, which has not yet given up.

"My writer is the friend of these men. He is a Czech in Paris, the foreign correspondent of *Lidové noviny*. Do you know it? The great newspaper. And he falls in love with them. That is to say, he falls in love with their animals—with the instinct of their art but not the idea of it. For he himself has no wish to be modern. He is a man of the nineteenth century. And so he understands their game and disbelieves in it, while yet loving it. And therefore he can say what it is."

While Kaspar had been speaking, he had held his eyes on Jacob fixedly, and they had shone so excitedly that Jacob had once or twice wished he could look away. He hadn't looked away; he had been afraid it wouldn't have been polite to. But now, as if Kaspar had detected Jacob's discomfort, Kaspar dropped his gaze and paused. He hunched forward, bobbing slightly, and said, "Yes, yes," into the air in front of him, in the voice that he must have used when alone, when talking to himself. He seemed for a moment to forget Jacob's presence. But then he cast Jacob a glance and resumed: "I translate his love letters, written from Prague to those he knew in Paris."

"He was literally in love with them? He was gay?"

"If you like," Kaspar replied, indifferently.

"Did they know before he wrote? What did they say when they found out?"

"His letters were for them a sign of the cruelty of the world. They welcomed them, but they could not answer, in their philosophy."

"They never wrote back."

"They wrote back, but they could not answer. Perhaps I do not have the right word . . ."

"No, I understand."

"It was a thing of chance for them. And so he continued to write. The letters are very painful and very beautiful."

Jacob silently considered translating Kaspar's writer into English some day. "Are you making good progress?" Jacob asked.

"It is in its way helpful to be sick. I don't know if I could else finish the translation, it pays so little."

Jacob remembered the days he himself had spent in bed reading, but he said only, "You shouldn't be sick."

Kaspar shrugged away Jacob's concern and changed the subject: "You have a new friend, Melinda says."

"I knew him in America."

"You are close."

"Not so close."

"But he lives with you?"

"I arranged for him to stay with me."

"Is he too a writer?"

"I don't know," Jacob answered, but then he remembered what Annie had said. "Maybe he is."

"And you, do you write of your friend?"

"Carl?"

"Is that his name? But I meant the young woman."

"No," Jacob lied. In fact he made notes some evenings, after Carl was in bed, but they hadn't amounted to anything. He stared around Kaspar's room, as if in search of another topic of conversation. "Perhaps I'd better go," he ended.

"As you wish," Kaspar accepted.

Carl learned that the Canadian embassy had set up a social hour for its citizens—a bar, really—on Thursday nights. He wanted to go, and so one Thursday, the friends met at Melinda's apartment, Rafe still absent, and walked together to what Carl called the "Canadian club."

It was in a coal-dusted cement building on Národní třída, a building that for some reason lay mostly empty. Its elaborate, arched mouth led in to a *pasáž*.

"It's in here?" Jacob asked. Behind a crisscross metal barricade, fine dust had settled on the interior courtyard's pavement like a light snow.

"No, upstairs, I think," said Carl. He turned right and led them up an echoing staircase into the building proper. On the third floor, at a door through which they heard American rock music loudly played, he knocked. There was no answer, and after a polite interval, Carl himself opened the door.

A dull roar washed over them. They pushed their way into the crowd. A few desk lamps lit a bar; the rest was dim. "Oh my god," Carl said. "We could be in Cleveland."

"Do you like it, then?" asked Annie, yelling.

"It's *great,*" Carl answered.

"And so he justifies every fear you ever had of him," Melinda said to Jacob, a confidence she could only share by shouting directly in his ear.

"What's that?" Carl asked.

"I was saying how considerate of you Americans to go to such lengths to share your culture with us."

"What?"

Melinda repeated herself.

"But these are *Canadians.*"

"Canadians are *subtle,*" Jacob yelled. Melinda mimed enlightenment.

"A beer?" Thom offered, gamely, and they all nodded. Carl went with Thom to fetch them.

The drinkers around them seemed as heavy as they were loud, though it may have been the thoughtless certainty with which they held their positions against traffic that gave the impression of weight. Since there was no coatroom, many of the men were wearing their coats despite the heat of the room, and many of the women were carrying theirs folded over their arms before their bellies, adding an impression of bulk to their figures. It almost seemed to Jacob that he and his friends were the only humans in a room full of heavy machinery. His friends fell silent; to make oneself understood required so much effort.

"It's horrid," Melinda shouted in his ear after a time. "*Why* did he bring us here?"

In the general blare, the undertones of her voice were lost, and since Jacob ordinarily depended on them to gauge her seriousness, he turned to search her face. To his surprise, she looked fragile. It occurred to him that surrounded by strangers, in a room where it was all but impossible to speak, she may have felt the loss of the weapons she was accustomed to fighting with. Even her personal beauty seemed muted, perhaps because it was not a habit with her to draw on that weapon consciously. Beside her, meanwhile, Annie had withdrawn into herself and was staring blindly into the buzzing air.

"It's like an American bar," Jacob answered, inadequately.

"We do have noise in London, you know," Melinda replied. "And beer."

"Maybe he's hiding," Jacob suggested. It was awkward to think out loud at such a volume.

"There's such a thing as excess of caution."

"Do I look *so* miserable?" Annie asked. She had been trying to read their lips.

"We weren't discussing you, darling," Melinda responded.

"No? I was certain you were." It seemed to please her to be disabused. "What were you on about, then?"

At this moment, Carl and Thom returned. "Bloody poofs here," Thom swore, and Jacob froze for a second. "Drinking beer cold."

"Thomas," Melinda said, on account of his language.

"Out of their 'icebox,'" Annie contributed, "though I quite like the word 'icebox,' as it happens."

"Cheers," Henry saluted, and they matched his salute.

"Are there any Czechs here?" Jacob asked. "I thought we weren't supposed to be gathering in public."

"No Czechs," said Carl. "This place is a jihad magnet."

The friends gave up talking for drinking. Jacob found it odd to see so many expatriates from North America and to know none of them. They appeared to be the sort who never stepped out of the context they traveled with. "Who are they all?" he asked Carl, who shrugged. Carl seemed to be making a show of his interest in them.

At last Henry announced, "I think perhaps it's an early night for me." It was only the end of the first round.

"For me as well," Melinda at once concurred.

"I'm not to be left here," Annie said with alarm.

The friends quickly found themselves in the corridor outside, where it was quiet and they could talk freely.

"Don't let us drag you away," Thom said to Carl.

"It was awful, wasn't it," Carl conceded.

"Jacob did warn us that you were a bounder," Melinda continued. "What was the word. A rogue."

"Melinda," Jacob muttered.

"Can I at least walk you home?"

"Me?" asked Melinda. "It's just three streets away."

"Will no one walk me home?" Henry interjected.

"Poofters right and left," Thom observed regretfully.

"I'll walk you home, Henry," Carl made believe. "But U medvídků is just around the corner, isn't it?"

The group was relieved that Carl had thought of it. They descended to the avenue and turned into the wind, toward their old haunt. Henry and Carl led the way. When Annie stopped to fasten her coat and fell behind, Jacob dropped back to keep her company. He stamped his feet for warmth.

"I'm *coming*," she said. "Is it true that all bars are like that in America?"

"I think so. I wouldn't know as well as Carl."

"Aren't your kind like that as well?"

"I guess they are."

"I don't hold it against you. I don't even hold it against Carl, really. He seems quite taken with Henry, doesn't he," she said, nodding ahead, and added, hypothetically, "You aren't jealous."

"Carl is free to have arguments about aesthetics with people besides me."

At Na Perštýně, they turned the corner that housed the gallery where Jacob and Luboš had seen the work of the children's book illustrator. It was empty now, between shows. Jacob wondered what the next show would be. He noticed that he wasn't sentimental. In fact he was disloyal, he told himself; he was careless. He didn't point the gallery out to Annie, and he didn't say anything about the cart man selling *párky* a block further on, where the avenue ended and the raised cobblestone paving kept out cars. After all, he and Annie were going to turn before they reached the cart. "I heard that your little club is to have a meeting," Annie resumed. "The one with Henry."

"On Wednesday night."

"I suspect Henry's quite a good writer. Otherwise I shouldn't care to join, I don't think. I don't mean that I shouldn't like to read your writing, and Carl's too, if he would let me. But if it were just you and Carl, it would be your private thing, wouldn't it, living together as you do."

"Chastely."

"I have your word for it. But Henry makes it a group."

"Oh, Annie. Just come if you want to so badly."

"But Henry doesn't want it, you see. He as good as said as much."

"Did he really?"

"In so many words. It wasn't anything to do with me, he said. He would be embarrassed, because it's rather blue, what he writes."

"Blue?"

"Blue. Off. But I'm not a prude, so I'm not certain I believe him. I mean, don't you think it's no more than a piece of gentleness— something to put me off with? He is quite gentle, you know, in his way."

It was too delicate for Jacob to meddle with. He didn't want to have Annie excluded, but there seemed to have been a negotiation of some kind between her and Henry, and he hesitated to tamper with it.

Once inside the familiar warmth of U medvídků, the friends again teased Carl for having led them astray with the Canadians. "One brick of Semtex in there," Carl joked in return, "and capitalism would never come to Czechoslovakia."

"A whole brick wouldn't be necessary," said Henry. "You can cast it quite thin. That's why it does so well for letter bombs."

"And who told you all this, Henry?" Thom asked. "Your friend Hans?"

"One *sheet* of Semtex," Carl modified.

"They power the detonator with the battery from a piece of Polaroid film."

"Ingenious," said Carl.

"I find it quite morbid, rather," Annie objected.

"But I don't see that it would stop capitalism," Henry added.

"It would stop it here," Carl claimed. "The thing about capitalism is, you have to be really nice to it. Really polite." He glanced at Melinda, who was fingering a box of Petra cigarettes she had dropped on the table at her elbow, as if she were admiring the russet color of its cover. She looked up from time to time to let him catch her eye, and when she did, they could see that Carl was amusing her. She was letting him look at her a little longer and more often, Jacob thought, than she would have if Carl hadn't made a false step earlier in the evening that he still had to atone for. "Otherwise it won't roll over your country and destroy life as you know it," Carl continued. "It'll roll over someone else's."

"And why should capitalism be so sensitive to the fate of one of its nightclubs?" Melinda asked.

"It's the people inside not the nightclub itself. They would 'tell.'"

"'Tell'?"

"'You killed our infant bankers.' 'You made it hard for us to loan you money.' 'You failed to coddle the juggernaut.' And it's off to Poland, or Hungary."

"Not bloody likely the Czechs would let *that* happen," said Melinda.

"I don't know," said Carl, with comically exaggerated doubt.

"Coddle the juggernaut—I'll have to remember that one," Henry complimented Carl.

There was a bit more flourish in Carl's silly talk than usual. He seemed to be laying it out for Melinda's unacknowledged admiration, and perhaps comfort, like a coat over a puddle, to be taken for granted. It was as if the two of them had been more frightened than the others by Carl's inattention and needed to reestablish their footing without seeming to be concerned to reestablish it with each other in particular, and were therefore forced into a nervous, general jollity.

"God, what was that all about," Carl said at the end of the night, as he and Jacob walked down empty streets, which the snow fell into but never seemed to land in. In Vodičkova, beside the Lucerna *pasáž*, gated for the night, they waited for a tram.

"Don't know."

A young couple were flirting in half whispers on a stoop. A man with heavy gray hair stood beneath the enameled-steel tram sign, gripping a worn leather satchel, as rich in color as the wood of a violin, and staring dully past them down the tracks. Jacob read the time of the next tram's arrival off the placard; Prague trams always ran on schedule. "Eighteen minutes," he told Carl.

"Would it be terrible if we took a cab?" There were three of the square, black cars at the corner, where Vodičkova met Wenceslas Square, the drivers talking as they leaned against their hoods, the engines idling for warmth. Carl continued: "What is it, fifty crowns?" Drivers were a distrusted caste, Jacob had learned from his students. Or rather, only the corrupt took taxis instead of public transportation, and drivers had necessarily taken some of the poison in handling them.

"It might be as much as a hundred," Jacob said.

"So three dollars. Don't look so horrified. For me it's three dollars."

"Okay," Jacob consented.

"I'm a fucking tourist, okay?"

They negotiated a fare before they got in, and Jacob asked the driver to follow the track of the night tram that they would have taken, so that as they traveled he would be able to know where they were. The driver didn't speak to them; perhaps he found Jacob's request insulting. Carl, too, was silent, and Jacob watched the tram signs trundle past, unstopped at, with their white squares for the numbers of day trams and blue squares for the numbers of night ones. At this hour there was almost no one else on the roads, and scenes passed by so much faster than Jacob was accustomed to that he felt a vague anxiety, which he knew was groundless but couldn't quite shake, like a sense in a dream that you are forgetting something important, or that you're about to lose something. All the windows in all the buildings they passed were dark. Everyone in Prague went to bed so early, and Jacob and his friends had stayed out so late.

"What a prick I was," Carl said when they were nearly home. He had the hood of his pullover up for warmth, and it blocked Jacob's sight of him.

"You weren't a prick."

"I think I was trying not to care," he continued. "But I couldn't go through with it."

The following Wednesday, Henry arrived after dinner with a sack of beers and, unexpectedly, Thom, who apologized for adding himself: "This one said he would be so lonely on the *tramvaj*, and I took pity on him."

"You should write for us, too, man," Carl invited Thom.

"Perhaps I shall, perhaps I shall . . . I'm willing to help out with the drink, in any case."

Jacob had turned on all the lights in the kitchen, as if they had gathered for a matter of business, and a window was ajar to ventilate the smoke from their cigarettes, so it was bright and cold. For a while they chattered aimlessly. They had agreed to discuss only one story at each meeting, and no one was in a hurry to be the one to reveal himself tonight; no one wanted to seem eager to go first. When Thom asked if anyone else had seen Henry's picture of his daughter, Frieda, they urged Henry to take the snapshot out of his wallet, and he was happy to, and they saw that she shared his natural grin and deep dimples, was blond, and held up a green pail of sand. In the little girl the force of Henry's wide-set, outward-pushing eyes was softened and became beautiful. Jacob was made uneasy by the photo, though the girl looked so joyful and Henry so proud that he pretended he wasn't. Earlier in the day, when Jacob had typed out some pages about Meredith, it had stirred up a childish and willful part of him, and it bothered him now that the picture suggested that Henry wasn't wholly theirs; according to the photograph, a part of Henry belonged to a child playing on a sunny beach in northern Spain—he belonged to this girl in a way that could never be challenged. His fate wasn't free for Jacob to dispose of, even in imagination, as Thom's or Carl's were—or Annie's or Melinda's or even Rafe's—and the strange jealousy that this threw Jacob into puzzled him.

"We should, we should get started," he said.

"She's adorable," Carl crowed. "She's going to be trouble when she grows up."

"Like her da," Thom said.

Henry put away the photo, and gradually the members of the group allowed their easy talk to give way to the artificial purpose they had set for themselves. First they had to devise rules. Should they read silently, or aloud? Aloud. Would each read his own story? Yes. Who would start?

Carl raised his left palm, like a boy in a classroom. "I have a confession," he said. "Um, I didn't write anything." As usual, he seemed to be inviting his friends to laugh, but since his confession put the purpose of the evening in jeopardy, they took it seriously.

"But a writer's group was your idea," Jacob protested.

"It was Henry's idea! I only seconded the motion." He looked from

Jacob to Henry and back to Jacob again, and then pulled himself away from the table. "All right, I'm a disappointment."

"No, no," said Henry quickly. "We only want to be sure you have the same chance to make a fool of yourself that we do."

"I see that it's to be my fault," Thom volunteered. "For lowering the tone." The friends ignored his joke.

"I *tried*," Carl said. Turning to Jacob: "Didn't you hear me typing?"

"I did. So you must have something."

"It's too personal."

"Mine is rather personal as well," said Henry, as if he too were backing out.

"Mine isn't personal about me," Carl clarified. "I mean, it is, but that's not what I mind about it. It's personal about someone else."

"A woman," Henry suggested.

"I didn't say that, did I?"

"I see," said Henry.

"Do you fancy Melinda, then?" Thom said. No one spoke for a moment. "A right eejit I am tonight, as Annie would say. Trying to be clever. I had no idea."

"Well, you had *some* idea," Henry observed.

"She's a fine one, Melinda is," Thom continued, in sympathy.

"Indeed," said Henry.

"If you could keep it to yourselves," said Carl. "That could be one of our rules." The others agreed. Only in consenting to this secrecy did it occur to Jacob that he wasn't sure his own pages would make any sense to Henry or Thom unless he told them about himself, and that he wasn't ready to do so. But a few moments later, he was spared a decision, when Henry, in order to take the spotlight off Carl, volunteered to read what he had written.

"I don't mind being the goat," Henry said, unfolding a typescript. He looked up to check their faces. "I'm just to read it?" he asked, and they reassured him. "Well, then," he began.

Ezekiel

He was the architect of a malady. Of a milady, of a melody. He was a piston firing in a chamber, he was all the engine, and he saw a woman die and be reborn, and both sorts came to her through the prick that he thrust between her legs, that he tore her with. From the porch he strayed into the forest of broken glass set into the top of a wall around her, which he had always wanted to climb. A crowd of wolves were watching, janissaries whose teeth were their own lovers. Rooks flew out of a furnace and pecked the woman's eyes and the man's eyes, the wolves lapping the man's blood and the woman's blood. The man howled, too, and stones fell into a cavern like a building that was being unmade, a film in reverse. He became a fry-cook in a port city, where the thermometer stripped away even his undershirt. To his ecstasy contributed the jigsaw and the underside of her knee, the angry floodlight of a locomotive before it cut into a peach tree and savaged the stagnation of a hanging fern.

"Whoa," Carl said in the following silence.

"Whoa?" Henry prompted, gingerly.

"That's amazing," Carl continued. "I think you have to read it again, though. It's dense, man. Read it again."

It seemed to Jacob that they were all keenly aware for the first time how dangerous Carl's habitual irony might be in such a situation. But perhaps it only seemed that way to Jacob because Henry's text had dismayed him and because it was in bad faith that he himself now said, "The metaphors *are* very rich." He felt that the social context required him to settle the ambiguity in Carl's tone but he was afraid he might instead be adding to it.

"I for one would enjoy a second hearing," Thom said. He sounded earnest, and it may have been only to satisfy him that Henry proceeded to read the piece once more, this time more deliberately.

As Henry spoke the words again, Jacob found that he had as much trouble focusing his attention on them as he had had during their first reading. The images that were called up by the words distracted him. He seemed to see Henry's hands bleeding, after he heard the narrator describe the jagged-topped wall, and he wondered what in real life had the capacity to hurt Henry so sharply, the gentle Henry, who explained the mysteries of Czech politics without calling attention to his knowledge, who drew out both the radical Hans and the conservative Rafe intelligently, without provoking an argument with either, yet who, if this story was to any extent the free association that it appeared to be, evidently imagined himself amid teeth and blood and hacksaws. He was violent inside, perhaps. The story was ending again, and Jacob still had no idea what to say.

"I like the image of the unbuilding of the building," Carl said. "That's really neat."

Henry nodded, a little curtly. He turned his eyes, painfully open, toward Jacob, but Carl continued: "And the teeth of the wolves. That's intense."

Henry nodded again, beginning to make a game of his mute reactions. "Am I allowed to speak?" he asked.

"I think so," Carl decided. "If you want to say something."

"I ask as a point of information only," Henry said. "I don't have anything to say as yet."

The room fell silent. Jacob tried in vain to remember a detail to praise. "Is the man at the beginning," he asked, "the same as the one who becomes a sailor?"

"A sailor?" Henry wondered.

"A fry-cook," Carl corrected.

"In a port city," said Jacob. "That's why I thought sailor."

"Am I to answer now?" Henry asked. "It could be the same person. Or it could be different people even within the same sentence."

The friends made an effort to accept this comment. "I thought it was the same guy," Carl said. "Can I say that? I like there to be a story. I like it that you're with the woman, and then you escape, and then you're in Marseilles or wherever. The Hague."

"Not bloody Czechoslovakia at any rate," Thom said. "If I may ask another question, at the risk of bollixing everything up again: Are we to understand that the woman dies?"

Henry shrugged, to indicate that he had left it up to the reader.

"The story is kind of violent," Jacob hazarded.

"Mmm," Henry agreed. A tight smile suggested a certain pride. It occurred to Jacob that Henry might enjoy their disconcertment. It might be an effect he had sought.

"But I don't know if the source of the violence is anger," Jacob continued. He didn't know that the source wasn't anger, but he wanted there to be another explanation. He wanted to defend Henry from the evidence he had placed in the record against himself. It had been placed there as art not confession, Jacob reminded himself.

"Do you like it at all?" Henry at last asked Jacob directly.

A pause. "I do." He thought he could safely answer in the same challenging spirit. "But it isn't *for* me, is it. It's kind of a joke on a reader like me."

"How so?"

Jacob saw with relief that his point was general not personal, and he continued: "Kaspar was saying something to me about surrealism, where the surrealist pretends to take the side of the machine, to show that no human can ever really take the side of the machine. He shows it as if despite himself. He wants his intentions to be misunderstood, maybe even by himself. And there's something like that here."

"I'm not sure I follow."

"I mean that a reader like me wants a story, and you're playing the game as if there are only sentences. And I'm going to look even harder for a story because of that."

"The story is like the machine," Henry suggested.

"No, it would be clever of you to argue that, because then you could hide your tracks even deeper. But no. The story is of you and milady and the landscape. And you want to convince us there is no story."

"And why should I try that?"

"Because the story itself is the wall with the broken glass," Jacob saw, as he was speaking. "It's the story itself that cuts you and makes you bleed. I don't know if any of what I'm saying is 'true,' of course."

"Which story, then?" Henry considered. "This one, or the one you think I'm really telling?"

"This one, this one. This is the way you tell it."

"As if it cuts me up to tell it."

"And you cut it up. And yet it's an ecstasy for you."

Carl objected: "He could have written a different story."

But Jacob insisted: "Any story that he tells this way, this is the story that he tells."

"And if he tells it conventionally," Carl asked, in a skeptical tone, "only then is he free to tell something else?"

"I don't know," Jacob somewhat retreated. "Maybe. Maybe a broken story is always about a writer's relationship to story."

"I don't buy that," said Carl. "Everyone has a relationship to story."

"Then every story is about the writer's relationship to story."

"Now how does that work."

"So you, for instance, aren't showing us yours," Jacob answered Carl. "That's your relationship to story right now."

"You like to skate close to the edge, Mr. Putnam," Carl said. Jacob liked hearing it.

Henry returned to the discussion: "But if every story is about story, then every story must also be about something else, as well, something other than itself, or what are stories for?"

Thom broke his silence: "That's where milady comes in, I suspect."

"She's *the* story," Jacob declared.

"'*The* story'?" Henry echoed.

"'I love her.' 'She loves me.' 'I don't love her.' 'She doesn't love me.'"

"Is that always *the* story?" Henry asked.

"Almost always."

"And I'm against it," he said, sounding out the truth of Jacob's claim in his own voice.

"You are aware of the confinement. Of the violence."

"But you're leaving something out," Carl broke in. "Because there *is* something episodic, something unattached, even in a story kind of story. Beneath story."

"The demon," Jacob said, to his own surprise.

"The demon?" Carl repeated.

"The rogue," Jacob said, trying again.

"Oh, the rogue. But isn't he a story, too?"

"A wrecker of stories."

"But that's just more story," Carl pointed out.

"Hang on a minute," Henry broke in. "I quite like that, about the demon."

"I don't know where that came from," Jacob admitted.

"He's the one who's never caught by a story," Henry said, taking up the thread himself.

"Or he's always caught and he always escapes," Jacob suggested. "Maybe he's the one you were trying to write about."

"He might have been."

Carl interrupted by rising from the table to pour himself a glass of water. He rinsed his beer bottle first and left the water running while he set the bottle with a faint click on the floor of the pantry where they were collecting an array of empties. When he took up an empty glass and touched the tap to feel through it the temperature of the water, Jacob had the impression that he too could feel the cold of the metal on his fingertip, because he had touched it that way so many times himself.

"It's about being in love," Carl said.

Henry shrugged again, to allow the possibility.

"Who are *you* in love with, Henry?" Carl continued.

"Weren't you listening?" Thom asked. "He's in love with a woman in a castle surrounded by wolves."

"But I'm not to be walled up there," Henry himself joked. He folded up his pages. "Well, thank you for this," he said, and eyed each of them in turn. "For the interpretation."

That weekend Jacob insisted on going to Vyšehrad, the old Czech castle grounds just south of the city's downtown. He was to meet Annie and Melinda there, and at the last minute Carl accepted an invitation to come along.

At the Vyšehrad stop, there were shadows before and after the subway's posted name, where letters from its old name had long sheltered the metal beneath from dirt and weather. Once Jacob noticed the shadows, the word they formed became legible even beneath the letters of the new name; until last year, the station had honored Czechoslovakia's first Communist president.

"There they are," Carl said, of their friends.

Jacob hadn't yet got his bearings. In a moment, though, he was able to follow Carl's gaze. At the top of a flight of glassed-in stairs was Annie, a cream angora scarf knotted around her neck, a pine-green hat failing to contain her hair, and a scuffed canvas backpack, crammed full for the expedition, looped over one shoulder. Beside her, Melinda, less careful but more elegant, held in the grip of thin, bright red gloves a hat of white yarn with a pompom, a property of Annie's that she was in the habit of borrowing. She seemed to be hesitating to put it on.

They took turns exchanging kisses hello.

"Is it this way?" Jacob asked. He had unfolded his blue city map, which these days he kept flat against his handkerchief in a back pocket.

Since he had given up men he had taken up geography. He visited a new sight or a new neighborhood nearly every weekend. "Is this it?" he asked, pointing through the plate glass at a concrete landscape. "Did they pave it?"

"This is the Palace of Culture, so-called," Melinda said. "Vyšehrad is farther on. Shall we?"

They stepped out onto the ungiving white plateau, which was angry with winter sun. "We're high up," Carl noticed.

"On a cliff, I'd say," Annie commented. A highway bridge of the same white concrete stretched north from the subway station and spanned a valley of villas and bungalows. They could see no way of descending to the valley; the elevation seemed to confine them to the concrete plinth of the Palace of Culture. The palace itself was a bleak vault of pale marble and brown-tinted glass. It focused the wind, which pushed and shoved them as it blew past, buffeting the hollows of their ears with a sound like that of a luffing sail.

"*Is* there culture? Should we go inside?" Jacob asked.

"It was for party congresses, and now I believe trade shows and such like. Rafe dragged me along for a function once, I can't remember what. I can't say I recommend it."

"Rafe is returning tonight, isn't he," Annie said, reminded of the news by the mention of his name.

"Oh? Mr. Stehlík just came back to our house," Jacob said.

"That's the father?" Melinda inquired.

"He yelled at us," Carl volunteered.

"He yelled at *me*," Jacob corrected him.

They came to the end of the white cement and tumbled off the corner of it into a regular Prague street of shops and family dwellings. The wind softened, and it became easier to talk.

"What were your crimes?" asked Melinda.

As they walked, Jacob described the bell and the string he had persuaded Běta to install, and then described how Mr. Stehlík had stormed through Jacob's bedroom and into Carl's that morning; pointed a finger, crooked as if he couldn't bear to straighten it, at the bell on Carl's bedside table; and asked, "Mr. Jacob, what is it please?"

"And what did you say?"

"Je to jenom zvoneček, a díra už tam byla."

"Darling, 'zvoneček' is a bit much."

Jacob translated for Annie: "It's only a tiny little bell, and the hole was already there."

"He shouldn't have minded," Annie loyally said, "if the hole was indeed already there."

"I think your speaking Czech made it worse," Carl said.

"He didn't like it that we offered to pay him, either."

"You were offering to pay for what, exactly—indulgences?" Melinda asked. The vulgarity of their offer seemed to delight her.

"We're American," said Carl. He made it seem unsporting to resist appearing crass.

"Mr. Stehlík said he had waited ten years to get a phone," Jacob concluded.

They came to a ruined stone gate, patched on top with a red chalet roof. It marked the outer limits of the castle grounds, and though they could have walked through abreast, they walked through in single file, the women preceding. On the other side, low grassy banks sheltered the road, which felt less like a road than a path. As the road curved, a finger of sun touched them, though too lightly to bring much warmth. There didn't seem to be any groundskeepers, perhaps because it was midwinter. There was no sign of any other visitors, either.

"It's a gorilla problem," Carl ventured.

"Is that an American term?" Melinda asked.

"It's a term of my own devising," he said. "It's when an argument isn't rational because it's really about deciding who's the top gorilla."

"Jacob was challenging the man's authority," Melinda said, as she followed the line of thought.

"Jacob's mistake is to think about the problem, when he should be thinking about the gorilla."

"Then can you use the phone at all any more?" Annie asked.

"Not while Mr. Stehlík is in town, I don't think," Jacob said.

"Shame," Annie said.

They came to a second gate. This one was a sort of grand façade set across the road, with no building behind it. Set in the façade above the passageway were three relief cartouches, two of them apparently empty. "Is that all there is to it?" Melinda asked of the structure, skeptically. Beyond the gate, the sloping banks that channeled the road were taller, and in the shade of them she shivered. "Tell me again, why is it we're here?"

Wind slowly bent the bare, fine-fingered trees above them and fluttered a short-trimmed, chartreuse lawn. "It's part of my quest," Jacob answered.

"Would you take my scarf," Carl suddenly said to Melinda, irony absent from his voice.

"Oh, please," Melinda refused.

"I don't need it," he said, unwinding it.

"I'm a married woman, more or less. I can't go about borrowing men's scarves."

"My nana knitted it," Carl assured her. "Your nose is as red as a button."

"How awful," she said, covering her nose. "In that case, then."

The scarf was long and loosely woven, mostly grays and whites, but sprinkled with red and royal purple. Carl made as if to wrap it around Melinda by circling her, but she tugged it out of his hands—"I won't if it's to be my winding sheet"—and allowed it to drape her only loosely, so that the line of her neck was still visible.

"It is fetching," Annie said. "Will your nana knit me one, do you think?"

"It's dashing," Carl declared.

"Oh, well, 'dashing,' " Melinda half mocked.

Carl's throat was left open to the air, and the women noticed a pendant he wore, which Jacob had often noticed but had never asked about. "Is there a figure on it?" Melinda asked.

"Saint Christopher. The patron saint of travelers." He drew it out from beneath his shirt. It was made of a dull, light metal, a cheap alloy, and it was about the size of a nickel.

"Was it given you?"

"I picked it up in Paris. In a religious shop near the Luxembourg Garden."

"I thought you might have won it in some way," Melinda explained. While she fingered it, he stood very still.

"Like a medal," he suggested.

"Yes. Or as a love token," she said, dropping it.

The openness of the flirtation was their permission. Melinda seemed to enter into Carl's game with perfect naturalness—to catch his way of handling feelings with doubled irony. Maybe it had always been her way, too. Jacob watched her turn away and hike ahead as if she had no interest in standing close to Carl any longer than she already had, no interest in tucking back into the neck of his shirt the pendant that he was now tucking back in himself, the metal once more against his skin. Jacob was sure that nothing was going to happen between Carl and Melinda—he was as convinced of that as he was that something sweet and painful now attached them. He wouldn't have been very good at talking about his impression. If asked, he might have said he "felt bad for them," but he would have sensed, in saying this, that the formulation was wrong or at least inadequate, because in another way he felt good for them; he was glad they felt alive, as they must have felt if in fact they felt anything like what he imagined. Of course there was no need to talk about it—no need for the two of them or for anyone else—no need that couldn't be put off. It was like what he had said to Henry in their writer's group. There was such a thing as a resistance to story. There was even a pleasure in resisting it, a somewhat violent pleasure—and then there was the pleasure of having the two of them near him, the pleasure he took in their beauty, as his friends, which was like a wealth he shared in, without any responsibility for it.

They passed a simple round building of white irregular stone. A belfry just as simple, round, and white rose from the center of its roof.

"Are we here because of the radio, by any chance?" Melinda asked. "It's just that there isn't that much to see."

"The radio?"

"You hear the tune on the radio every morning, at least I do."

"I don't have a radio," Jacob said.

"Well, then, you would do, if you did have one. I believe they play it every hour on the hour."

"No radio," said Annie thoughtfully. "I quite depend on mine."

"No radio, no telephone," Melinda observed. "No mod cons whatsoever in Hloubětín, are there."

"We have a hamster," Jacob said.

"Not traditionally considered an amenity."

"But what is it they play on the radio?" Jacob asked.

" 'Vyšehrad,' darling. The little harp number."

"By Smetana."

"Well yes. It's quite pretty. You know, the plinking one. Arpeggios."
She gestured instead of trying to sing them.

"Oh, is that what it is?" said Annie.

"A sentimental favorite. And I know that Mr. Putnam has a
weakness for sentiment."

Carl reported that there were more buildings ahead.

"I didn't say there was *nothing* here," Melinda said. "It's just that
most of it was knocked down long ago."

"It's the Stalin monument of the fourteenth century," said Carl.

"Always the *bonmoty* with this one," Melinda appreciated.

They came to a sort of plaza of dead grass and frozen winter mud,
where they halted. At the far end was a dark, two-spired church and
beside it, to the right, a walled yard they knew to be a cemetery. "I believe Smetana himself is in there," Melinda hazarded. To their left, a
squat yellow building was labeled as a museum, but its grille was locked
and the lights were off. In the matter of interpretation, they were left to
their own devices. Scattered in the fields were a few pieces of statuary,
for the most part in the decorative, conservative style of monuments
from the First Republic, except for one statue close to them, which appeared strangely modern: three rounded pillars rose from the earth and
leaned loosely together. The pillars looked from a distance like concrete
but on nearer inspection they proved to be stone.

"We're asked to believe that these are from the Neolithic," Melinda
said, interpreting a plaque.

Jacob also translated. "It says the three stones were unburied in the
first decade of the twentieth century."

"And buried just two months before that, no doubt," Melinda joked.

"But what are they?" Annie asked.

"An omphalos, probably," said Jacob.

"A what, dear?" Melinda asked.

"A bellybutton of the world."

"I didn't know it had one."

"There was one in ancient Greece, I think. To mark the center."

To mark the place, Jacob continued to himself, where spirit came
into the world. A kind of scar. Was this it? he wondered. Was this as
close as he would come? He would have come sooner, if he had known

about it. He realized his heart was racing, but he was afraid his excitement would seem ridiculous if he tried to explain it to his friends.

"I don't much care for it," Annie said. "Druids and such."

"Why not?" Jacob asked.

"I can't say exactly. It's a bit doubtful, though, isn't it, worshiping trees and rocks."

"Do we know that's what they did?"

"We don't know anything, really, do we. All those years and years, and rocks are all that's left. It's depressing."

Carl and Melinda started off across the fields together, Jacob and Annie following. Ruts and footprints had been frozen into the earth, and as they stepped they could sometimes feel a ridge crumble softly underfoot.

"It's their Stonehenge and their Westminster Abbey in one, then, what with the cemetery," Melinda said, "which has all the nation's poets and the painters."

"Do you ever wonder what you'll be some day?" Carl asked. Jacob and Annie could hear him but he wasn't addressing them.

"Sometimes," Melinda gently answered. "What a thought."

"It sounds a little grand," he apologized.

"But we must all become something."

"Advise me," he appealed to her.

"I couldn't possibly."

"What about you? What are you going to become?"

She put him off at first, but after a few minutes, she let him ask the lesser question of why she had come to Prague. She had come with Rafe, of course. That didn't mean she hadn't thought for herself, but she tried to make light of the thinking she had done, in the joking way that Carl made light of things. She wasn't quite able to. She said that in going abroad one wanted adventure and one didn't want it, and that there were costs on both sides. Even this modest confession seemed to embarrass her a little. Jacob sensed that she was reluctant to put into more precise words what her expectations had been, because she didn't want to be exposed to disappointments that she had so far been able to overlook and which, in so far as she was still able to overlook them, might be thought of as not yet quite existing. It was for men to have careers, in particular American men, she joked, but she didn't seem to expect her joke to be believed, not least because there was little sign of a career in Carl. One sensed, with both of them, that neither felt that anything had been promised, but that they were waiting, nonetheless, for possibilities that they weren't yet ready to give up on. They were holding out for recognition, for the hope that the lineaments of what they were looking for would be as familiar and resonant as a person's.

"And what will I be, do you think?" Carl asked, returning to himself.

"I should think you would do well as a flâneur," Melinda suggested.

"Excellent," he answered.

They found that the church was shut indefinitely for repair. The cemetery was, too, though without explanation. They turned back to the lawns they had just crossed and wandered among the statuary for lack of anything else to see. "I think somewhere there's a path that leads to Libuše's bath house," Jacob volunteered, but his suggestion of looking for it found no takers. The statues weren't originals but concrete replicas, clumsily made. They had been cast in pieces, and the mortar joining them had discolored at a different rate than the concrete, so that a gray princess was bisected at her waist by a yellow zone, sloppy where the mortar had been smeared into crevices. Her left hand, gracefully extended, was heavy at the wrist, in a way that suggested that beauty of line had been sacrificed for stability of concrete—a narrower wrist might have been too likely to snap.

"It's for stunning carp," Melinda said, and brought her own wrist down as if administering a blow.

"Oh, it's Libuše herself," Jacob said, reading the statue's caption.

"Who's she, then?" Annie asked.

A youth with a hammer sat at her feet and was turning his head as if to follow her gaze. "She was to be queen," Melinda explained, "but the Czechs refused to be ruled by a female, so she chose this peasant as her husband, and made him king."

"You can't be serious," said Annie. "I should think she would have just chopped off their heads or what have you."

"I suppose she would have done in England," Melinda said.

"Look at his hair," Jacob said. "He's the pretty one in the couple."

Carl agreed. "She's a little vague around her . . ."

"Mmm," said Melinda. "Whereas his robes cling to him in rather a nice way."

Jacob moved on to dutifully inspect the other statues. Annie trailed him for company, and when he found a path, she agreed to explore it with him.

"Don't be long; it's cold," Melinda ordered.

The path had been kept clear by a light service vehicle of some kind, whose wheels had marked it with a double rut, and the trees on either side were saplings and scrub.

"Are you certain this is part of the gardens?" Annie asked.

"No," Jacob admitted, but there didn't seem to be any harm in continuing. He noticed cross-paths through the thin woods where people had taken short cuts. In the shelter of the woods there were islands of snow, but where the snow was crossed by footpaths, the ground had been tramped clear. He wondered if men came here to meet in the evenings. He hoped the idea wouldn't occur to Annie. Of course there was no one here now but his friends.

"I did think at first that you and Carl would make a couple," Annie said. "I suppose I hoped it for your sake. He's very fine."

"I'm glad you like him."

"I hope Melinda won't be too hard on him."

"He kind of forces her to be."

"He doesn't seem able to help himself, does he. How was it the other night? With the poetry club?"

"It isn't poetry."

"You know what I *mean*."

"It went well. But I'm not supposed to talk about it."

"I didn't ask, did I. I didn't ask anything particular. So it went well. That's lovely."

"Oh, don't—"

"I'm not, am I. I'm not. It's *your* poetry club. I don't suppose what Henry wrote was really so very 'sexual,' after all."

"I think it's more the emotions he wants to keep private."

"Oh, he has emotions, has he."

"I'm not supposed to talk about it," he repeated.

"I won't *tell*, Jacob."

The path ended at the threshold of a nondescript structure: brown-tinted Czech stucco on a stone foundation. "Is this Libuše's baths?" Jacob asked aloud. The building looked modest and utilitarian.

"It's a shed, I believe," said Annie.

Annie folded her arms. Jacob tried to look into a window, but he couldn't see anything. The woods continued behind the shed, sloping downward. He took two steps and sank into a layer of black leaves that the snow had hidden.

"Please don't, Jacob. It's a drop and then there's that highway along the Moldau."

"I'm not going to fall onto a highway," he assured her, but he returned to the path.

They began to retrace their steps. Jacob hated to give up on a search, and he became sullen.

"Are you still off men?" Annie asked.

"I'm not off them."

"I mean not looking. Not for now."

"Yes," Jacob said.

"I believe I am as well." She glanced at him. He sensed that she wanted him to ask a question, but he had noticed a scratchiness in the back of his throat and he decided to conserve his energy. "I have this feeling of sufficiency," she continued. "I have the Dům. I have my teaching. I'm quite good at teaching, you know. My students are quite fond of me, have I told you that? They pay us so little, yet I find myself saving crowns. I was telling Melinda, sometimes I feel as if I could go on for years here."

"A couple of months ago you couldn't stand it."

"But I thought then that I was the only one, you see. But we're all, nearly all—it's as if we were meant to be building something in ourselves, for now. Do you see it like that? You needn't pretend to agree with me if you don't. It's peculiar to talk about, I suppose."

"I think I'm getting sick again," he announced.

"Are you? I'm so sorry. Shall we go back?"

They returned to the clearing. For a moment they thought that Carl and Melinda had abandoned them, but then Annie spotted them standing on a sort of rampart that overlooked the river. Carl turned to face them but Melinda continued to look at the other castle, the more famous one, miles away in the distance, across the river and to the north. "Did you see the baths?" Carl asked. "They're halfway down the hill. You lean out here as far as you can and look left and you can see the corner of them. They're lame."

"Jacob's ill again," Annie told them.

His only symptom so far was a slowness in the way he was registering his impressions. When his friends spoke, it required an effort to understand their words in the same rhythm that they were speaking them; the meaning seemed to lag behind. "It's just a little fever," he said.

"Ubožátko," Melinda consoled him. Poor little one.

"Will you be able to make it home?" Carl asked.

They fell silent as they walked back toward the subway. It took a little while for Jacob to notice the silence, because he found himself counting his breaths against his steps, already slipping into the trivial self-involvement of an invalid.

"It's too bad the church wasn't open," he apologized.

"It isn't as if one could call ahead," said Melinda.

"It was lovely, Jacob," Annie insisted. "Don't trouble yourself."

On the subway platform, Annie arranged to spend the rest of the afternoon with Melinda, helping to prepare the flat for Rafe's return. At Muzeum the women changed lines, leaving the men alone.

Changing to the tram at Palmovka took more of Jacob's energy than he had expected. Fortunately he and Carl found seats. Jacob wrapped his fatigue around his shoulders like a blanket and shut his eyes. He felt the winter sun tapping his face as the tram crossed the spaces between buildings.

"Are you all right?" Carl asked.

Jacob sensed that Carl was trying to find out whether he was well enough to hear a piece of news. He nodded and opened his eyes. "What is it?" But he was already asking the question from inside the shell that belonged to the illness, the shell he had built for himself in the days he had spent alone with it, before Carl came.

"I asked her if she was interested," Carl said.

Slowly Jacob asked, "What did she say?"

"She was, I don't know, cavalier. 'How could I not be?' At first. You know, as if it was all nothing, which I suppose it is. Did you like it up there? It was pretty cold with that wind. And then she said, 'But you've broken the rules.'"

Jacob nodded. To help himself follow, he pictured Carl and Melinda in his mind's eye as they must have looked as they stood at the ledge of Vyšehrad, overlooking the Vltava River.

" 'We were supposed to go as long as we could,' she said. 'Without knowing whether the same thought was in the other's mind.'

"I said I was sorry," Carl continued, "and she said one isn't sorry for such things, and I said she was right, really I wasn't sorry, and what were we going to do. She said, 'Just this, I think.' I asked what this is, and she said it again: 'Just this.' Then you and Annie came back."

"I'm sorry," said Jacob.

"Nothing to feel sorry for." He took off his gloves and folded in the thumbs so that they could lie together flat on one of his knees. "It's sort of nice." A shine in his eyes suggested that in fact he saw it as a victory.

Carl offered to scramble some eggs for dinner, and as he assembled the ingredients, Jacob found himself beginning to worry so intensely about whether Carl was going to measure out the right proportions of salt, pepper, butter, and egg that he removed himself from the kitchen and lay down on his sofa. He closed his eyes and made an effort to let go of the numbers. He imagined them floating up into the air above him. After a time, he heard Carl call out that dinner was ready.

The eggs themselves soothed his throat while he ate them, but when he asked Carl about his face, which felt warm, Carl said it was flushed. Jacob rinsed a washcloth under the tap and took it and his thermometer to bed with him on the sofa. When he was sick he didn't like to move the sofa cushions to the floor. He realized that he was falling back into the routine that he had established when he was ill before. He assured Carl there was nothing he needed, closed his eyes, and shuddered under his blanket, the washcloth folded across his forehead, until his trunk felt warm and his forehead cool.

Following its usual rhythm, the fever broke in the early hours of the morning, and after breakfast Běta walked with him to the day clinic for a new *neschopenka* and a new course of antibiotics. Jacob ordered Carl to go out and have fun, saying that Běta would help him if he needed anything, and when he returned from the clinic, the apartment was empty. In the silence he took a deep breath. It felt to him as if he were repossessing the space, as if he were returning to the strange peacefulness of his earlier confinement. And something like his impression proved to be the case in the days following. In the hours when his head was clear, it was as if he had returned to a secret kingdom he had once known. But this time he had Václav, whom he sat with and babbled to when he was too feebleminded to read, and every evening Carl came home.

He went back to *La Chartreuse de Parme*. Fabrice was imprisoned high up in the Tour Farnèse, in a wooden cell fitted inside a stone one. Fabrice could see Clélia through a hole in the *abat-jour* of his window, and he tore pages out of books to make an alphabet, with which he signaled to her. Because of Clélia, Fabrice didn't want to escape, and it occurred to Jacob that he didn't want to escape his cell, either. He wondered if he, too, was in love. Carl, in love with Melinda, didn't seem to want to be free. "Is that a good idea?" a psychotherapist had asked Jacob two summers earlier, when he had confessed that he wanted to room with a straight man he had then been in love with. He had done it anyway and it hadn't had any terrible consequences.

Because of his relapse he saw no one in his landlord's family for almost a week. Then at noon one day, during a midwinter thaw, he saw Běta working in the courtyard with Bardo and Aja and realized that he missed talking to her. He was beginning to mend, and he thought it would be nice to feel the sun and play with the dogs. Mr. Stehlík's scolding had upset him more than he had admitted to his friends; there had been something wild in the landlord's anger, as if a restraint had snapped, and it had made Jacob aware for the first time of both the anger and the restraint. It was through Běta that he was most likely to be able to repair fences, if they could be repaired. In his coat and boots, he ventured outside.

"Ahoj," Běta saluted him. The terrier growled and circled Běta nervously; the boxer hung her head and approached Jacob with a moseying gait, her tail wagging. Běta reproached both animals, and neither listened to her, but the terrier desisted when she saw the boxer's acceptance of him. —Are you better? Běta asked.

—A little, Jacob answered. He took off a glove and let Aja snuffle his fingers.

—She smells Václav, Běta observed.

—Yes.

Běta had taken two large red nylon rucksacks, emblazoned with the name and logo of a manufacturer of skiing equipment, out of the uninhabited rooms on the ground floor, and had set them down beside the driveway, evidently to load them in the car when it returned from an errand.

—Are you going to the country? Jacob asked. —Are you going for a 'ski'?

—For a 'ski'? she asked, quizzically. Jacob had guessed she would understand the English word, but maybe she didn't. She looked around to see what he was looking at. —Ah, she said when she saw the rucksacks. She looked down at the ground as if in shame, and then up at the sky as if in comic expostulation. —Do you know, what it is? she asked. She was smiling her conspirator's smile and dropped her voice so as not to be overheard by anyone inside the house.

—I don't know, Jacob answered, also dropping his voice.

—Grandfather and Grandmother.

Involuntarily Jacob looked at the bags again. —The ones who . . . ?

—Two years ago. And here we still have them.

Jacob felt his heart race. —Ashes? he asked.

—Of course, of course, Běta answered. —Jesus Mary, if not . . .

Jacob was at a loss for words, so Běta continued. —They were so lovely, so kind. They gave us everything. And here we still have them. She shrugged.

—Are you going to . . . , Jacob asked, his vocabulary faltering. —In the country?

—Finally. She clasped her hands together in gratitude.

—Near your *chata*?

—Well, yes, thus.

—Then that's good, Jacob said, and made an effort not to look at the bags again. —I'm sorry, he said, —that I angered your father.

Běta pretended to be puzzled for a moment, as if she didn't know what he was referring to. —Tata is very nervous now, she told him. —You mustn't worry, but it is better if we . . . She made a calming gesture with her hands, leaning over at the same time, as if to block an imaginary sound with her body.

—Why is he nervous?

—Yes, why? she echoed, and looked off to one side. —Just thus, she finally said, concluding a train of thought she didn't share. —Do you know, she continued, —you will have neighbor?

—In the empty rooms?

—They are not yet empty, she corrected him. She threw back her frizzy hair, and her face became jittery with good humor again. —That is *my* task, she lamented.

—Who will it be?

—Our plumber, Honza, she said.

Honza was a short, wiry, boyish man, about forty, with a tanned, lined face. He had recently started work on a project in the empty rooms, and he crossed paths with Carl and Jacob from time to time. He always shouted at them genially, as if louder Czech were easier to understand, and he addressed them as "kluci," boys, rather than as "panové," gentlemen.

Běta was waiting for Jacob's reaction.

—The little fellow, Jacob said.

—Little Honza, Běta confirmed.

—He's sympathetic, Jacob said. —How long does he stay?

—Until he finishes the plumbing? She shrugged in embarrassment. —And now I must empty his rooms. Do you want to help me?

—I'm sick, he said, and he crossed his arms over his chest and hunched his shoulders for effect.

—But perhaps you are bored?

—I'm writing.

—That's a good one! About our family, no doubt.

—No, no. It's fiction.

—Yes, well, I understand. But be nice.

—But really! I write about something else.

—Yes, well, yes, well. It will be quite a beauty! she said, as if she were already steeling herself. —Our crazy family in a book.

In fact Jacob was trying to write about Meredith. The doctor at the clinic had given him two weeks "to start with," and though Jacob wasn't sure he could afford two weeks now that so much of his income came from private students, he had them, and he had their peace and quiet. Between chapters of Stendhal, therefore, he sat at his typewriter.

A blank sheet sat fixed in his machine so long that the platen set a curl in it. It seemed wrong to write about Meredith and wrong not to write about her. He knew he was angry with her. She had been the poet of their generation—all her friends had thought themselves lucky to have met her in her youth—and she had thrown away her talent with her life. She had also thrown away an understanding they had shared, a little prize they had conspired to give themselves, that no one their age could have deserved: the sense not merely that they were going to give their lives to writing but that somehow they already had.

What killed her, however, was another thing, a darker one, which she and Jacob had joked about together at lunch one day, while their companions at the table had sat by, puzzled.

"Its relation to writing isn't causal," Jacob had said.

"No, no," she had dismissively agreed, tapping her fork dangerously. " 'Causal'—that's vulgar. 'Contiguous'?" she had suggested.

"Perhaps the territories are contiguous," Jacob had replied.

" 'Congruent'?" she had also suggested but at once took it back. "No, no. 'Contiguous.' " Suddenly she let down her fork with a clatter. "A Venn diagram!" She covered her mouth. "A Venn diagram is needed." She always wore a bright red lipstick to lunch, as if to defy any shame or awkwardness that might be associated in some minds with the process of eating.

"What are you talking about?" a young man beside her had complained, and now, in Prague, Jacob couldn't remember for certain the specific noun whose relation to writing they had been trying to find an adjective for. It might have been "unhappiness." He had tripped over the thing beneath the word later, when he and Meredith had tried very briefly to become lovers.

Was there a connection, or wasn't there? He decided to write about visiting her grave and rebutting there the answer that her death seemed to imply. She had no doubt been buried by her family in Virginia, but for the purposes of his story, he imagined the cemetery in the Massachusetts town where he himself had grown up. He knew what that cemetery looked like. If she were buried there, her plot would be down the hill, in the contemporary area where the lawn was smoother and the headstones were thicker and more polished. He imagined himself standing before hers. Unfortunately, he couldn't bring the character based on himself to say what was on his mind, and he couldn't write intelligibly about the romantic confusion that that character and the character based on Meredith fell into. He labored at the story anyway. He invented another character, a man who also came to the grave and cried there unabashedly.

He had once read an essay about a short story in which something similar had happened. Very confusedly, he tried to make the character based on himself seduce the character who cried, but he couldn't make the seduction plausible. The whole thing refused to come to life. It was no more than a series of described gestures.

He hid the pages in the evening when he heard Carl's key in the door. "Hey," Carl would call out, and then set down his bag with a thump beside the refrigerator. Jacob would come into the kitchen, sit at the table, and listen to the sound of running water as Carl washed his hands and face. Then Carl would sit down across from him with a glass of water to report on his day. His beard was now full, and his hair, too, was growing longer. He combed drops of water out of his beard with his fingers as he spoke.

Sometimes he had fallen in with American tourists at a café and had spent the day flirting with the women and debating philosophy with the men. Often he had met Henry at his office in Josefov, the old Jewish quarter, and they had gone for lunch. Henry worked at the Czechoslovak office for visiting foreign students, which stood in relation to the international students union, where Hans worked, roughly as the government had stood until recently in relation to the party, and was therefore slightly less doomed and much more busy. Carl reported that Henry took his job seriously and always returned to his office within an hour, no matter how far their confidences and arguments took them. Carl was then left to wander on his own in the district with a head full of ideas. Once he came home with a set of cream-colored plates, bowls, teacups, and saucers, freckled with age and embellished with delicate red and silver tracery, which he had purchased in an *antikvariát* for ten dollars probably because, he said, he and Henry had been talking about whether it was possible to reconcile the need for a home with the search for beauty. He presented them as a gift for the apartment, saying that he didn't think they'd survive transport to America.

One evening, Carl told Jacob that he had dropped in on Mel and Rafe in Havelská and had drunk slivovitz with them.

"How was that?" Jacob asked.

"They send their love," Carl replied. His face still seemed a little muddied by the liqueur they had given him. "Kaspar's coming to see you tomorrow," he reported. "Melinda says he was very grateful for your visit, and apparently he's back from Berlin."

"I didn't know he had gone there."

"His father's sick. The one in the Stasi."

"I didn't know about that, either."

"That may not be exactly right. Melinda said he was in the Stasi, but Rafe said he thought he was just an informer. But Melinda said Kaspar hated him so much he couldn't just have been an informer. I guess he was a professor?"

"I bet if you were a professor, you had to cooperate."

They fell silent for a moment. Jacob noticed that Václav's water dish was empty and refilled it.

"I won't be here tomorrow," Carl said. "I told Melinda I'd go with her to the castle to see the mediocre Impressionists they have."

"Rafe doesn't mind?"

"It's just bad art. I'm always missing Kaspar. I wonder if I'll see him even once before I leave Prague."

"You'll see him."

"Not seeing him would be like going to Bern and not seeing the bear."

"He's just a person," Jacob said.

"I don't know," Carl said facetiously. "This whole 'Could you spare a little crust of eating bread?' routine, where he goes to town on Mel and Rafe's refrigerator?"

"He doesn't have a lot of money. He's very principled."

"I guess so, if he won't speak to his father."

"I thought you said he went to Berlin."

"But he wouldn't speak to him, is what Melinda said. He just saw him."

The sun had set while they had been talking, and the light that still fell into the apartment was now even and gray. "Are you hungry?" Carl asked.

Jacob shrugged.

Carl got up and looked in the refrigerator. "Can you eat another tuna-fish sandwich?"

"I'll make them." Jacob was pretty sure the olives in the can he'd opened last week were still good. He also liked to put in grated carrots, because he thought the two of them needed vitamins. Carl dragged his bag to his bedroom to unpack it.

"Did Rafe say what he was really doing in Brussels?" Jacob called out across the apartment.

"I've decided not to think about that question any more," came back the reply. "You know, with the war and everything." He laughed at his own disingenuousness.

From his bedroom window, Jacob saw Kaspar trying to ring the disconnected buzzer in the gatepost at the end of the driveway. The dogs saw him, too, and began to bark, but before Běta could come downstairs, Jacob threw on his coat and, with his boots untied, walked out the back of the house and around to the sidewalk. The weather had turned cold again, and he could feel chilly air fingering his ankles.

Under the German's scarf was another scarf, and under his coat he wore two sweaters. "Don't take off your shoes if you don't want to," Jacob said. "I don't have any slippers to offer you."

"But I am wearing socks." He glanced down to show them off as he pulled his feet out of his shoes. "Pretty white socks, from the mother of Rafe, for his exercise."

"He didn't want them?"

"He said no," Kaspar answered, marveling at his good luck and staring at Jacob steadily, almost hungrily, as if he were afraid of missing any part of Jacob's reaction. Jacob stared back out of a confused kind of politeness. They stepped into Jacob's kitchen, still awkwardly linked by the eyes. The curtains were wide open, and in the afternoon sun, Jacob noticed how much thinner Kaspar's beard was than Carl's. Among its gray and red bristles were patches of cheek as neutral and delicate as the new skin revealed when a scab falls off.

"Water? Milk?" Jacob offered. "Tea?"

"I will have milk. And perhaps later tea." His eagerness to accept had the effect of making the bestower feel almost princely.

"Please, sit down," Jacob offered.

Instead Kaspar approached Jacob and touched him on the forearm, startling him. "But first, if it is not a trouble," Kaspar said, "I would like to see, where it is that you write." He studied Jacob's face. "Oh," he continued, stepping back as if sensing he had intruded, "is it already here?" He pointed to the kitchen table he had hesitated to sit down at.

"Sometimes. But it's—." Too embarrassed to finish the sentence, Jacob stepped into the doorway of his bedroom and pointed at his Olivetti, which sat, an oversize paperweight, on top of the pages that he had managed to type about Meredith.

"You write in sitting on the floor?" Kaspar's tone suggested he was willing to believe in an athletic regimen of some kind.

"No, I usually put the typewriter on that little table."

"May I?" Kaspar asked. He walked into the bedroom and crouched down beside the machine. "But it is lovely," he admired.

The Olivetti was a subtle jade color, the finish of its metal cool to the touch, and its curves sensuous. When pressed, the pads of the keys swung down and into the machine with an easy heaviness, and the type bars struck the platen with orderly, satisfying claps. It had cost a hundred dollars in a used-typewriter store in Cambridge. An older boy, another crush of Jacob's, had had one just like it, and after Jacob had bought it, Jacob had been afraid that there was something indecent about his having a typewriter just like his friend's. It was as if he had bought a piece of clothing beyond his means and then realized that the extravagance would show if he wore it in public. Fortunately, a typewriter isn't public, for the most part. Carl was allowed to borrow it, of course.

They retreated to the kitchen, and in a somewhat businesslike manner Jacob poured Kaspar a glass of milk. Kaspar drank it greedily but methodically, sucking stray drops out of his ragged moustache between sips. Halfway through, he paused and fell still, and the hamster, whose cage was at his elbow, crept out of a nest of paper. The animal, however, made no impression on the German, who looked only at Jacob, who after a while did not know where to look. He thought of finding his camera and taking Kaspar's picture, so that Carl would be able to see what Kaspar looked like.

"It is cold," Kaspar said, at last.

"The milk?" Jacob asked.

"I wanted to say, that the day is cold, but the milk also."

"I could warm the milk up for you."

"Ah no! I am only waiting a moment, in order to make longer my enjoyment."

"Oh," said Jacob. The delay was a philosophical adjustment of some kind; Jacob was afraid it was rude to have called attention to it. "Thank you for coming all the way out here," Jacob continued.

"Not at all. It is not far. And I have brought you, I now remember, something from Melinda. Fishes."

"Fishes?"

"They are from the West." He rummaged in the knapsack at his feet and brought out a red tin of Spanish anchovies.

Because Jacob had never eaten any, the gift frightened him a little, but he made an effort to rise to the challenge. "Thank you."

"Perhaps, when we have the tea," Kaspar suggested.

"Oh, good idea."

"You seem in good health," Kaspar said, resuming his milk.

"My *neschopenka* is up on Wednesday, and I think I'll go back to work."

"And your war, also, is 'up,' as you say."

"My war?"

"In Kuwait. Since two days, I think." Seeing that the news surprised Jacob, Kaspar shrugged, to make light of it. "It changes nothing."

"Well, I guess that was the point."

"Mmm," said Kaspar, slouching over his glass.

"You have a theory."

"Not today! At least there were no bombs in Prague. Do you know, I have been in Berlin."

"I heard. To see your father. Is he all right?"

"He is going to die," Kaspar answered, with a little smile. His eyes shifted to his glass, inside which the milk had left a bluish film.

Jacob had the impression that in saying this Kaspar had wanted to make him laugh. "You say that as if—"

"A month ago I was going to die, and now he." He shrugged it off as he had shrugged off the war against Iraq. "We are a family. He is, do you know—the word in Czech is *udavač*."

Jacob nodded. When the student newspaper editors had published the StB contract, they had used the word in their caption.

"He cannot bear to be out of favor," Kaspar continued. "Even with me, now, he thinks it would be something to be in favor."

Jacob nodded, trying not to take a side in a family dispute. Kaspar's face seemed looser and paler than it had been a moment ago, as if he were drawing license for what he was saying from his own illness.

"I love him as one loves a dog or a cow," Kaspar continued. "Something you do not speak to."

"Did he say anything when you saw him?"

"Many things." Kaspar waved a hand with a flourish, to suggest rhetorical flights. His smile grew crooked and subtle. "But I am interested in *your* progress," he said, by way of closing the subject.

Jacob shrugged and held off Kaspar's attention for a few more moments: "Will you write about it?"

"About Berlin?" Kaspar hesitated. "Oh, I translate, and I comment. But I am not so a writer."

"Comment is writing."

"If you say." He seemed pleased by Jacob's solicitude, and Jacob wondered if it was his duty to invite Kaspar to join the writing group. "Have you written, in your 'holiday'?"

"I'm trying to write about my friend, but I've been having some trouble," Jacob admitted.

Kaspar's face brightened at the opportunity to be of use.

"I think it's because I'm angry at her."

"It is *about* her," Kaspar said, to be sure he understood.

"It's fiction."

"Of course, of course. And what is the nature of the trouble?"

Jacob hesitated and then said, "Maybe you could read what I have."

"May I? Then let us have the tea, and perhaps to open the fishes and to have them with little breads as I read, yes? Do you say that in English, *chlebíčky*, as the Czechs do?"

"No, but only because we don't eat them. We have crackers."

"That's right. 'Crackers.'"

Jacob put teabags into cups and a kettle of water on to boil and fetched the pages about Meredith from the bedroom. Kaspar fluttered them in his hands to get a sense of how many there were, and then took from a pocket somewhere beneath his sweaters a pair of glasses with silver frames. "If I am to think while I read, I must either smoke or eat," he said, as Jacob began to cut slices from a loaf of caraway-seed bread. Jacob put the slices on one plate and then opened the tin of anchovies on another.

"A fork, I think," Kaspar suggested.

Jacob hadn't focused on the actual eating of the anchovies. He handed Kaspar a fork and watched him spear one of the tiny pink-and-silver filets out of the oil and uncurl it on a slice of bread. Since no harm came to Kaspar after swallowing, Jacob imitated him. The flavor was mostly salt and sourness. He had been afraid he would be able to feel the prickle of the fish's bones as he chewed, but he couldn't.

"It is good, *že jo*," Kaspar said.

"It is," Jacob said, polite and unconvinced.

Kaspar began to read. Jacob took up last week's newsmagazine, which Carl had bought for him, and stared at it in his lap, pretending that he was reading also. He guessed that Kaspar wouldn't notice if he didn't eat any more anchovies, and in fact Kaspar didn't notice. The room fell silent, except for the rustle of pages and Kaspar's slow chewing. When the kettle whistled, Jacob rose and poured the water and brought the cups to the table.

For camouflage, Jacob continued to run his eyes emptily over the columns of the magazine. That was the trouble, wasn't it, he thought to himself—that he was angry with Meredith. It was interfering somehow. She had been murdered, and it was unfair to be angry at her. On the other hand, because she had done the murdering, he was right to be angry at her. She had taken away her recognition of him when she left. Was he trying to take it back? Maybe what interfered was guilt. Maybe telling her story was too much like stealing it from her. He was calling attention to himself by writing the story, after all, making himself out to be something he hadn't in fact been. While she was alive, he hadn't even been able to *say* he was in love with her. Then again there might be no moral factor at all; a part of him might just be trying to protect himself, to push Meredith and what he had shared with her away. . . . The longer he thought about it, the less able he was to tell the difference between what was his doing and what was, at least in his own mind, Meredith's. It also became hard to tell the difference between what he wanted and what he was afraid of. It was a way of thinking that didn't lend itself to storytelling. There was no knight to pick up the sword, no growling bear to slay, no princess who asked to be married. Everything was also its opposite; nothing was capable of change. Perhaps he didn't want anything to change, as if by making reluctance into a principle, he could keep Meredith alive. In that case his story was like Henry's, without his having intended it to be. In that case it was a story about not wanting to tell a story. . . .

Abruptly, in an interruption of his own thoughts, Jacob realized that in giving Kaspar the pages, he had forgotten all about the main character's attempt to seduce another man.

He watched Kaspar nervously. After finishing the last page, Kaspar picked up the others, which he had set down one by one as he read, and tapped the sheaf on the table to align it.

"At the end, where the angry man makes a pass at the other one, I think I was thinking it was a symbol," Jacob said. It was almost painful how badly Jacob wanted Kaspar to make sense of what he'd written. The schoolboy in him was impatient, too, to hear whether he had done well.

"May I?" Kaspar asked, with his pack of Petry in his fist. Jacob gave permission but didn't take one himself. "And the trouble," Kaspar continued, "you think, it is that you are angry, you say, like the angry man."

"Yes."

"Perhaps, perhaps." In automatic movements, Kaspar opened the double windows beside him a crack, and some of the bitter smoke from his cigarette flitted out. "A symbol . . . It is a symbol of what?"

"Of union," Jacob said, but the answer sounded too grand. "Of wanting to know what the crying man is feeling."

"But he doesn't want that," Kaspar said, with his crooked smile.

"Yes he does," Jacob insisted. "The man who isn't crying wants to know why he's angry at the other man."

"No, he wants to not-know," Kaspar said. "The nature of what he wants is not-knowing."

Jacob took a breath. "Because it's two men?"

"Because such a union is the thing itself. It is not the symbol of it. It cannot be a symbol."

"Why not?"

"Because there are no words for it."

Again Jacob was suspicious. "No words for love between men?"

"No, no." Kaspar seemed to brush away the misunderstanding. "For sex. There are no words."

"You can write about sex."

"But if you do, the words become the thing itself, again," Kaspar explained. "It cannot be *put* into words."

"You mean it turns into porn."

"If you will."

Jacob thought of the character he had tried to create, and of his own frustration, which he had tried to put into the character. "But he does want to know," Jacob said, "and he doesn't know."

"But he will want also to not-know. To be alive in not-knowing. To be with his friend in not-knowing."

"His friend?"

"The one in the ground."

"But he wants to be with the man. That's what he says. He doesn't want to be with her."

"He is in anguish. He is lying to himself."

"What if he's really gay?" Jacob asked.

"You have not written that story," Kaspar calmly answered.

"But what if he's really gay?" Jacob repeated.

"It will make no difference." He blinked a few times, perhaps irritated by the smoke. "He is in two," he continued. "That is what it means, to want another in order to have union. He is in two."

"You mean he wants to be with him and with her."

"No, no. He is in two in order to be with her."

"Because he shouldn't be with her? Because that's not who he is?"

"No, no." He stubbed out his cigarette abstractedly. "Listen," he suggested, "perhaps it is not you who were in two. Or not only you. Do you see?" He looked out the window as if to leave Jacob the freedom to approach the idea. The sky was gray and near as if it might snow, but it had been gray yesterday as well, and it hadn't snowed then. "She was two, and so you were two in being with her. And she killed one of them. One that was she killed the other that was she."

"You didn't know her."

"No. This is true."

"That's also the fake part of the story," Jacob said with some agitation. "About the other man. That's the part I made up. I didn't intend for it to seem real. It's the part I added, that I was conscious of adding. I didn't have a real person in mind. If anything, it's a little forced. Do you know what I mean?"

"It is possible that the sense of having made it up," Kaspar slowly replied, "is the cover under which you have hidden it from yourself."

Jacob repeated Kaspar's sentence silently. He remembered having read a similar thought once before. "Freud says something like that about dreams," Jacob said. "When you say, within a dream, that it's just a dream . . ."

"Like in Freud, yes."

"But I'm really gay."

"Are you?" joked Kaspar, because it didn't feel to either of them like a revelation.

"Yes, I am," Jacob said, a little angrily.

"But you were in love with a woman. With this woman."

"I wasn't."

"Why do you write about her?"

It seemed to Jacob that Kaspar failed to realize how selfish Jacob was. "There was a thing that we had, that we were both writers," Jacob said, "and now I don't know if I have the right to keep it any more."

"You had a calling," Kaspar said. His face took on the pleased look that Jacob so distrusted, the look he had given to the typewriter.

"Like a religious calling? I don't believe in God."

"That doesn't prevent him from calling to you." Kaspar was so confident of his better understanding that now he was making jokes at the expense of what he considered Jacob's ignorance.

"I don't believe in that," Jacob repeated.

"You had a calling, and you had the good fortune to know someone else with a calling," Kaspar said, with more diplomacy.

"That's making too much of it. We hadn't earned it. I hadn't earned it."

Kaspar shrugged. "You do not earn a calling."

Kaspar had misunderstood so much there seemed no hope of correcting him. "So does this mean I'm not gay, in your opinion?"

"I don't know if I believe in this, the question of gay or not gay."

"I do."

"And I believe in God. So."

"I think you're missing the point," Jacob said.

"Yes, perhaps," Kaspar cheerfully admitted.

"There's something else," Jacob added that evening, Václav in one crook of his folded arms, as he came to the end of his narration to Carl of Kaspar's visit. "Something he said about love."

He glanced instinctively at Carl as he said the word, because Carl had become identified in his mind as the Lover, and the identification was so conscious, though tacit, between the two of them that Jacob worried for a moment that Carl might take personally what he said next. He reminded himself that Carl was too generous for that kind of misunderstanding. It was to some extent by virtue of his generous spirit that he had become the Lover, after all, though it was also true that he looked the part, tonight especially. His shirt was half-unbuttoned, his hair was long, and his face seemed to have caught and held the white gold of the winter sun that he had spent the day walking in. He sat in his chair with a touch of swagger, managing to enjoy the white-painted plywood thing. He was sprawled across it, his legs apart, humanizing its angularity with a slouch, which the curve of his spine inverted from time to time, when he yawned, and arched himself up and over the chair's back. Faced with such physical confidence in a stranger, Jacob would have tried to convince himself that he hated it because it was unearned, but of course it wasn't hatred that he felt, and it wouldn't have had the same charm if it were earned, whatever earning it might mean. In Carl, he told himself, the confidence was like the resistance in metal that makes it possible to sharpen it, and he knew that it was being sharpened, in Carl's case; Carl was in love.

"What did the two of you decide love is?" Carl asked.

"Kaspar made it sound as if it's always a mistake. As if it isn't even possible for a healthy person to *be* in love." Jacob tried to remember how Kaspar had put it: "When you think you have to have somebody, it's because you yourself are in two."

"That's classic, though, isn't it?" Carl pulled a hand over his beard. "We're severed halves, looking for our complements."

Jacob spoke quickly because Kaspar's suggestion had irritated him and it irritated him again to repeat it: "At first I thought he was trying to say that being in two was a problem that only gay people had, or people who think they're gay, because they haven't accepted their own sexual nature and would rather find it in someone else, in another man, but now I think it has to be true for straights as well, if it's true at all."

"He knows you're gay?"

"Sort of. That was part of it. But he said it didn't matter. He didn't even seem to believe me, necessarily. What's bothering me is, if he's right, if love is a way to keep from understanding what's missing in yourself, shouldn't you always resist it? You're not supposed to go to bed with your therapist, because it's better for you to understand what you're feeling. But if that's true, why should you ever go to bed with anyone? Wouldn't it always be better not to?"

Carl listened to Jacob's idea, which Jacob was afraid must sound crazy, with more attention than Jacob was sure it deserved, Carl's two arms wrapped over and behind the back of his chair and gripping the posts on either side of it, as if to pin himself in it. He fidgeted in place. "Would you still fall in love?" he asked.

"I think so," Jacob answered. "I think that's the whole point. But not do anything about it."

"I seem to be falling into that condition," Carl said. "The *cavaliere sirvente*. Or *non sirvente*, rather."

"Who?"

"Like in Renaissance love poetry. Did you ever read any of that? I took a class in it. I was in a Shakespeare play, and I sort of went through a phase. The heart is free to ride out to the tournament of love, only because its master cannot follow."

"There is a kind of freedom to it," Jacob said carefully. He had been hoping that Carl would show him that somehow Kaspar was wrong.

Jacob's stomach growled. It was dark, and neither of them had yet suggested a plan for dinner, but Jacob didn't want the conversation to be interrupted. He took his cigarettes out of the cabinet nearest the stove and lit one to dispel his hunger. Carl accepted one, too. They could talk all night if they wanted to. They were young. For years and years still, they were going to be able to live this carelessly.

"So you're saying it's not real, in a way," Carl mused.

"*I'm* not saying it."

"Only the mistake of it is real," he said, as if he were accepting the idea.

"How was the castle?"

"There was almost nobody there. There aren't any crowd pleasers. It's all young men in pain—Oskar Kokoschka, Edvard Munch. Young men in pain in the castle. So we had it to ourselves. One white room after another. I told Melinda the castle belonged to us the way the day did." He got up and started to pace. "But it's real as long as it lasts, even if it is a mistake. And if it doesn't last . . . Even if you don't go to bed with each other, it doesn't last." Jacob could tell from Carl's scowl that Carl was looking at a picture of Melinda in his mind's eye. "Because we're *mortal*." He made the portentousness of the word into a kind of punch line.

"In the long run, no one's staying in Prague, is what you're saying."

"The difference can only be in the moment. Not in the number of moments."

"These are good lines," Jacob said.

"I'm serious, though."

They went on to debate whether to drink the beer in their pantry.

The next morning, Jacob wasn't careful in placing a carrot, and the hamster escaped from his cage again. Neither Jacob nor Carl could find him. They couldn't find Honza the plumber, either, who had recently been going in and out of their apartment during the day to use their bathroom and to shut off and turn on the water on the ground floor (the valve was in their pantry). Jacob had to teach at the Libeň language school in the morning and at the chemistry institute in the afternoon. Carl was going out, too. After consulting his French-Czech dictionary, Jacob wrote a warning in block letters—POZOR! VÁCLAV, MŮJ KŘEČEK, UTEKL—and propped it up on the kitchen table. When he went upstairs to alert Běta, whose parents were again in Poland, it occurred to him to negotiate once more for use of the washing machine, which he had abstained from ever since the conflict over the bell. She granted the privilege immediately and asked, in turn, if she and a friend could hire Jacob for private lessons. They spent so long discussing the subject matter and the kind of instruction—prepositions were at the top of Běta's list—that the tea that Jacob had drunk at breakfast finished its course through his system.

—Can I? he asked, gesturing to the Stehlíks' bathroom, which he had never used before.

—Let us hope, Běta answered.

While drying his hands, he noticed the wallpaper inside the bathroom door: line drawings of plump nude nymphs romping lewdly with shepherds. The style of the figures appeared somehow French, but maybe it was just their abandonment.

—Those sketches . . . , Jacob began, once he was in the kitchen again. He knew the word for "sketch" from museum placards but not the word for "wallpaper."

—Yes? Běta dared him.

But he was running late, and he excused himself. Fortunately, just as he and Carl were leaving, Honza finally arrived, the hair on one side of his head matted where he had slept on it.

—Václav escaped, Jacob told him.

—The rascal! Honza replied. When he smiled, one saw that his teeth were tobacco yellow and as disorderly as his hair. He assured them he would watch where he stepped. Leaving the apartment unlocked for him, they exited.

The morning sun slanted on the world, which was damp and tender, winter having left and spring not yet arrived. The light sharpened the wire mesh in the fences around the villas' small lawns and threw into relief the stones in the road's asphalt. In the field beside the tram stop, darkening grass lay limp and flat.

"What are you doing?" Jacob asked.

"Taking your picture," Carl answered, as he released the shutter. "It's time for me to take everyone's picture." Yesterday at lunch, he said, he had taken three of Henry as he sat facing the restaurant's street window, where the light had been good.

On the tram, they stood and stared with their fellow passengers at the street scenes rolling past, which they recognized but which the daylight was not yet full enough to have rendered common. There was a half consciousness to the silence, a provisional unity among the strangers—a shared respect for duty or at least a shared experience of obligation to it. At Palmovka they stepped out of the stillness into a milling crowd, more fully awake, already chatting and irritable. Carl turned to the subway, Jacob to the uphill tram.

"Jacob!" Annie greeted him, jumping up from her seat as he entered the teacher's lounge. Melinda and Thom looked up from their workbooks.

The oaks outside the window were motionless, and they were bare except for delicate, dark nibs at the joints of the finer branches. The light was steeper now as it passed through them. "It is a delight to see you," Annie continued. "How are you, then? I have any number of plans for you, I hope you don't mind." She pulled him to her in her awkward, birdlike way, patting him lightly on the back to let him know the embrace was over almost as soon as it had begun.

"You're looking well, mate," said Melinda in her fake Cockney.

"Seems steady enough on his pins," Thom commented, as if it were a binge that Jacob had recovered from.

"Ehm, tell me, Jacob, would you fancy going a journey by car?" Annie asked.

"Melinda's car?"

Melinda herself answered: "Alas, no. Rafe has need of mine to shuttle ministers, and of me as a chauffeur. To an out-of-town castle that his institute has appropriated for retreats, though he won't say precisely when these retreats are to occur."

"But you can *rent* cars now," Annie said. "It's one of the new businesses. For the weekend, you see."

"You don't have to be Czech?"

"I telephoned, and the likes of us don't seem to have occurred to them, but when I said that we had long-stay visas, she said well that's all right then."

"Where are we going?"

"Krakow? It's said to be quite beautiful. Your mates didn't bomb it during World War Two, you see."

"Okay," Jacob agreed.

"In three weeks' time, is my idea. Fancy a crisp?" She turned the mouth of a plastic bag toward him.

"What kind?"

"Prawn. Don't make a face, Jacob."

"It's too early."

"I know they're revolting, but they suit me, somehow. They could be *more* revolting, I suppose. They could be cuttlefish or some such."

"Prawn is sufficient," said Thom.

"Did I offer any to you? Perhaps I didn't hear myself if I did."

Jacob had to guess how many lessons his class had advanced in his absence. He made his guess and then skimmed through a couple of lessons more, to hedge his bets. As nine o'clock approached, the Czech teachers quietly gathered their papers, and his friends, too, rose. Melinda dawdled so that she could walk upstairs with him.

"What are you doing later?" she asked.

"I'm teaching your chemists."

"Oh, bugger them. Will you have dinner with me?"

"Sure. Shall I bring Carl?"

"Let it be just us. Pick me up at my boyfriend's flat?"

"Isn't it your flat, too?"

"I meant to sound daring. I'm trying that out."

"Oh, definitely."

"There's a new place near us, a project of the Vietnamese consulate, and it's in my opinion the best restaurant in Prague at the moment. Actual Asian cuisine. Not *vepřo-knedlo-zelo* chopped into bits and fried in soy sauce. There's a lemon-onion soup, I wish I could remember the name. It's very simple but rehabilitating. The soup, not the name of it. You can feel coal dust being flushed from your sinuses."

"Is that pleasant?"

"And there are no caraway seeds whatsoever."

"I just remembered. My hamster is loose."

"Is that a thing to say to a nice girl?"

"I mean I have to go home and catch it."

"Can't Carl?"

"I haven't asked him to."

"Shall I?"

"Will you see him this afternoon?"

"I might do."

"Then it's a date."

In addition to the British newsmagazine that he bought in Prague, Jacob read magazines forwarded by his mother from America, including a serious one that Daniel wrote for, though not the glossy one where he worked as an editor. (He sometimes caught himself referring to Daniel by his full name. It had been months since he had heard him speak in anything but the public voice of his articles.) He had got into the habit of giving them to the chemists when he was through with them.

He had more issues than usual to slide out to the center of their dark table that afternoon. They scrambled for them deftly and a little savagely, like geese darting their necks at bread crumbs. Ivan watched, over a notepad where he was pretending to review the lesson of two weeks ago, flattening his cowlick patiently; to contend for an issue himself would have been out of keeping with the dignity of his role as liaison between Jacob and the group, and he limited his response to a comment, whose tone was sardonic and semiofficial. Jacob couldn't follow his meaning, and the elderly Bohumil, observing his puzzlement, explained: "We keep a library of all that you give to us, and we are not to—what is the word—to *plunder*, I think."

In Bohumil's own hands was a cover story that Daniel had written arguing the case for gay marriage, marked with a bright pink triangle. To read, Bohumil had to look down into his thick glasses, and the old man's eyes momentarily vanished.

Across the table, Zuzana, the young brunette who hid her beauty in a lab coat, nervously studied the table of contents in the magazine she had taken, tilting it toward the well-tailored Pavel beside her, for his reaction, as if unsure whether she had made a good choice. Noticing that Bohumil had begun to read his, she addressed him. —What do you have, Bohumil? she asked, in Czech. —Show.

—And you show, too, he replied. He stood his magazine up, face out, for her inspection, and she flopped shut the cover of hers and leaned it toward him, for his.

"That is the sign, I think, of the guise," she said in English, looking to Jacob for confirmation.

Jacob didn't want to seem to understand too quickly. "The gays," he corrected, after a moment.

There was an echo as several chemists practiced the pronunciation.

"They are going to marry," Bohumil said, relishing the topic with the impunity of his age.

"To marry," Zuzana repeated, slowly smiling at Bohumil's freedom as she understood. "That is interesting."

"They're going to talk about it, anyway," Jacob said. "It's not a done deal."

They made him write "done deal" on the chalkboard. "Fait accompli," said Bohumil's wife, Zdenka, half to herself, as she figured it out, almost warbling the words on account of their French origin.

"But they *can* marry now," Ivan said, "if a gay marries a lesbian." He looked to Jacob for praise, and Jacob tried to smile. There were murmurs as the other chemists established among themselves that the word "lesbian" meant what it evidently did. Ivan's head was large, the way a child's was, Jacob noticed, and trembled slightly as if with the effort of being held up. Jacob was glad that no one had laughed but slightly embarrassed for Ivan's sake.

"It is curious," Bohumil resumed, "that they want to marry. They will lose freedom."

"This depends," his wife answered, addressing the group rather than her husband, "on this, how is the marriage."

"Touché," said Jacob.

"Ah, as in . . . ," said Bohumil, and he waved an imaginary sword. Zdenka wildly waved one, too, to second his understanding.

"Tell me," Zuzana queried Jacob, "will the people vote the question?"

"Surely," Pavel broke in, his brows knitted, "it is to the Assembly."

"But pardon me, there are two houses in the American parliament, that yes?" Ivan asked.

"It's confusing," Jacob said. He drew a diagram on the blackboard to explain that the proper word was "Congress," and that it could be used to refer either to the House of Representatives alone, or to both the House and the Senate.

"It is to the Congress," Bohumil said, pointing at Jacob's nested circles, "if it is a matter of law. But it is to the Court, I think, if it is a matter of justice. This writer," he continued, meaning Daniel, as his eyes vanished again into the refraction of his lenses, "wishes it a matter of law, though I do not understand why."

"Conservatives always prefer for Congress to decide," Jacob offered, as a hint to the mystery, "and Daniel is a sort of conservative."

"He is *for* gay marriage?" Bohumil said doubtfully. "Yet he is conservative?"

"Daniel's like that," Jacob said, retreating into the colloquial, to hide from anyone who didn't want to understand.

"You call him Daniel," Zuzana observed.

"I knew him in America."

There was a delicate pause. "It is *very* interesting," Bohumil supplied, to cover it, and leaning back in his chair he quietly summarized the issues in Czech for his wife's benefit, his neighbors leaning in to overhear his explanation and nodding as they took it in.

Ivan raised his hand, and Jacob quickly granted him the permission that no one else in the room felt the need to ask for. "You in America," Ivan said, "have two parliaments, and we in Czechoslovakia have two presidents." Again Jacob failed to understand that Ivan was joking until after he had finished speaking, Ivan's eyes were so skittish, and he kept the pitch of his voice so deliberately low.

"No one I've met seems to like Klaus," Jacob hazarded.

The chemists seemed unsure how to respond. "He is doing what is perhaps necessary," Ivan cautiously began, in his semiofficial capacity.

"As *he* says," Zuzana interrupted.

"But it is difficult for us, in the results," Ivan continued. "The prices increase, but the wages do not."

"We are nervous," Zuzana said, with a shrug.

Jacob nodded. He recalled that Běta had described her father with the same adjective, and he wondered if he had missed a nuance. "*Nervozní*," Jacob asked, using the Czech word, "what does it mean exactly?"

"*Nervozní*? It is to be—," Zuzana started to explain, and then tightened her body in demonstration.

"Is it like being angry?" Jacob persisted.

"No," Zuzana answered, shaking her head. "It is to respond too, too . . ." She circled her hands around each other, as if winding a skein.

"Perhaps sometimes it can include anger," Bohumil said, speculatively.

"It sounds like it's like it is in English," Jacob said. "I don't know why I thought it might be different."

"All was here the same for so long," said Bohumil, "that we are not accustomed to the use of so many of our nerves, and perhaps the new use makes some of us angry."

"We are afraid, perhaps," said Ivan, smiling in hopes of matching Bohumil in wit, "because the Communists were saying, for many years, that under capitalism, the poor are living in the streets. They were telling us, that the poor are asking for money, to buy food. What is the word for it, please?"

"Begging," Jacob said.

"They were telling us that the poor are begging in the American cities," Ivan continued, his boyish frame quivering with half-suppressed amusement.

"It was a propaganda," Zuzana agreed. She shook her head to assure Jacob that she hadn't believed it any more than Ivan had.

Jacob was at a loss. Pavel clasped his hands in his lap and then glanced up. A moment passed. "But in fact it is true, I think," said Pavel.

—But no, Zuzana reproved him in Czech, under the impression that he was teasing. —Why do you say that? Murmuring washed over the room, as the slower students asked to be caught up.

—I saw it, Pavel replied.

Zuzana realized he was serious. —When?

—In eighty-seven. In Chicago. They open the doors, and you are to give them coins. They carry sacks of their things with them, all together. All dirty.

"Surely not," Ivan said, in English, contradicting Pavel but looking steadily at Jacob.

"The term people use is 'the homeless,'" Jacob said, returning Ivan's gaze and then glancing away. He chalked the word on the blackboard behind him. He felt a strange pleasure in disillusioning Ivan.

A blankness fell over Zuzana's features.

"The homeless," Bohumil echoed, and then added, absentmindedly, "Where is my home?" the translated title of a Czech folk song, as if his interest went no further than the vocabulary word. He continued to flip through the magazine in his hands, signaling by the continued movement his lack of surprise at the revelation. "It is too bad," he said mildly.

Ivan kept his eyes fixed on Jacob, as if he could not now afford to let his attachment to Jacob, and to America through him, seem to falter, even momentarily. "I did not know this," he admitted.

After class Ivan cornered Jacob. "May I walk with you? You take the bus number one hundred forty-four, I think."

"I'm headed that way."

"Headed that way," Ivan repeated, self-pedagogically. As Jacob squared his books, his papers, and the school tape recorder inside his backpack, he felt the eyes of the other chemists noticing Ivan as they said good-bye. Jacob returned their good-byes bravely, as if no secret were implied by Ivan's lingering, but he, too, suspected that a secret was forthcoming. As he walked down the institute's corridor with Ivan, he became unpleasantly aware of the care with which Ivan matched the pace of his steps.

"So it is not a fiction, as I thought, that people are begging in America," Ivan said. He seemed as willing to be amused by his misplaced confidence as he had been a few minutes ago by what he had imagined to be the crudeness of Communist propaganda. "This is, how do you say, a depression."

"It's depressing," Jacob corrected.

After the Victorian-parlor heaviness of the scientists' meeting room, the parking lot and the long muddy field that approached the institute looked spare and modern. There was still snow along one edge of the pavement, in a dirt-tipped, crumpled archipelago, but a mild March wind was loosening the world, opening it, the way meltwater opens the soil and makes it crack and breathe. About one more hour of daylight remained; it would take Jacob that long to reach Rafe and Melinda's place downtown.

"Do you know, the Communists were very proud of their Czech chemists," Ivan continued. "Like athletes, we were for propaganda. But under capitalism we must pay for ourselves." As they crossed the parking lot, Ivan walked so close to Jacob that he inadvertently jostled him: "Oh, pardon me!" It was unusual for a Czech to come so near, and Jacob found himself unpleasantly conscious of Ivan's thin blond hair, boxy plastic glasses, and prominent nose.

"I don't think any of you chemists will end up homeless."

"But do you know, already I do not have a home. I have a wife and two children, and we live in the flat of my mother-in-law and father-in-law."

"I'm sorry," Jacob said weakly.

"Oh no, it is very common. It is the way, under socialism. Do you know, how many years I am waiting for a flat?"

"How many?"

"Eleven years. Since marriage. And now I have a son nine years old and a daughter four."

"That's terrible," Jacob said.

"But excuse me. I do not want to talk to you about the Czech homeless. (Oh, pardon me! Again!) I have, rather, a question. If I may."

"Sure."

"Could you tell me, how did you become an English teacher? For you know, it is a very wonderful thing now, in Prague, and I think that if I could become an English teacher, it would be a very good thing for me."

"But you're a chemist. You went to school for it, didn't you?"

"Do you think," Ivan persisted, "that my English is so good to teach it?"

" 'Is good enough to teach it.' "

Ivan repeated the correct wording. "So, perhaps, it is not so good, you are saying."

"No, no," Jacob assured him. "You speak very well."

Because the air was bright and fresh, the ground around them empty, and both of them young, it was possible to imagine that either of them could become anything he wanted. And Ivan's English was in fact quite good. Jacob found himself remembering, almost as a matter for self-reproach, that he himself had wandered into the language in- struction office of the Prague school system as if he had conjured it. That was capitalism, after all, when it was going well; your wishes seemed to rise up to meet you.

"The English book that you have, from the school. Would it be pos- sible, do you think, that I could borrow it? To learn, for myself. Also, with this book, I think that I myself could teach lessons. Do you think it is possible?"

For a moment, Jacob wondered if Ivan wanted to steal the class of chemists from him, but he suppressed the fear as uncharitable. Since he only had the one book and couldn't do without it for long, he suggested that Ivan copy it on one of the institute's photocopy machines the next time Jacob visited the institute.

"But I don't know if you should give up on chemistry," Jacob felt obliged to say. It was harder to communicate, now that it was between them that Ivan wanted the use of something Jacob controlled. "There's a demand for English teachers now, but science will be more important in the long run."

They were nearing the bus stop, and Ivan let Jacob step away from him. "But this is perhaps something, that I cannot wait for."

Jacob thought of Ota, but Ivan was a scientist, and he probably saw things more clearly than Ota did. It would be a kind of rudeness to keep warning him. He would risk seeming stingy and repressive. He reached out to shake Ivan's hand, which startled the fragile-looking man, and they parted.

In the Havelská arcade that led to Mel and Rafe's apartment, plastic lamps had long ago been drilled into the stone medieval ceiling. When Jacob arrived, their yellow light had not yet crystallized against the evening; it still offered itself only as a supplement to the dark but vivid light from the sky, which, though clear, was the color of lake water before a storm. Jacob's hand, as he raised it to Mel and Rafe's buzzer, seemed to partake of the conflicting elements; a faint gilt rested on the tops of his fingers, while his palm seemed dripping with a shadowy blue, below.

He heard footsteps and then a scratching as the lock was worked. "Would you like to come up, or are you in a rush?" Melinda asked. She had changed into a white linen blouse with a high, almost clerical collar.

"Either way," said Jacob.

"Well, you're welcome to come up." She said it a little shortly, maybe because Jacob had forced her to answer her own question. "Rafe's here," she added, as she preceded him up the narrow stairs.

She called her boyfriend's name as she nudged open the door to their apartment and as Jacob followed her in. Rafe emerged from their bedroom, grinning, unkempt. "Jacob! Feeling better?" he said. "You look better."

"Thank you."

"I mean, you look well. I've never actually seen you look worse, so you can't look better, can you. Sorry I can't join you," he said, explaining, apologetically: "Work."

"What are you working on?"

"Will you have a drink? Slivovits? Becher?"

Jacob looked to Melinda, but she gave no sign. "I don't want to put you to the trouble . . ."

"Oh, come on. Have a drink."

"Some water would be fine."

"Water? You're such a cheap date! I bet you're easy, too, aren't you?"

"The water drinkers rarely are, in my experience," Melinda interposed.

"In *your* experience," Rafe continued to goof from the kitchen, as he poured Jacob a glass from the tap. He looked into the pantry, as if he might take something stronger for himself.

Jacob drank his water half down for lack of knowing what to say. "So what are you working on?" he again asked Rafe.

"Oh, a white paper," he answered. "Now that there's only one superpower, I have to prove to the Europeans that mutually assured destruction is a game that can be safely played as a solitaire."

"Can it really? How does it work?"

"If anyone looks cross-eyed at America, we blow ourselves up!"

"Brilliant!" Jacob said, hoping to match Rafe's ironic enthusiasm.

" 'Brilliant,' yes," Rafe repeated. "You sound like Carl," he added, after a pause.

Jacob apologized: "He's practically the only person I've seen for weeks, until today."

"Oh, me too!" Rafe exclaimed. "He stops by, you know. Today he photographed me, for a keepsake. 'This was Melinda's "boyfriend," ' I imagine. He's *very* devoted to everything about Melinda. Including me."

"He's joking, though it may not be apparent," Melinda said.

"I'm not joking. He did photograph me."

"I meant your tone."

"What's my tone? I'm not jealous. No, that's not true, I *am* jealous. But jealousy is great. Jealousy is the spice of married life."

"It doesn't seem quite right for you to enjoy the spice without having committed yourself to the bread and butter," Melinda suggested.

"I get away with all sorts of things," Rafe answered. "Now you two enjoy your date."

Jacob didn't feel it was safe to go. "You know, Rafe, there's something I—," he began.

"Darling, he's taking the piss out of you," Melinda interrupted. "As it happens, I told him about you the other night."

"Doesn't mean I'm not jealous," Rafe said. "A romantic dinner on a spring night with a beautiful woman."

"Oh," was all Jacob could think to say.

"I'm an awful person and if you don't want to have dinner with me I'll understand."

"Of course I want to have dinner with you."

"It became a strategic necessity. I don't know if I can hope to make you understand, given that your longest involvement to date has been, what, two months? And even then without the bother of fidelity."

"I understand the concept."

"No, you have no idea, but here I am, berating you when I'm at fault. When you have had some experience, you'll find that *that's* typical, too. The worse one sins, the more of a moralist one becomes."

"Has there really been sinning?"

"As if I would tell! But no, there hasn't been. It's all in Rafe's head."

"All of it?"

"Except for what's in Carl's head, I suppose."

"And none in yours."

"Darling, I am like Victoria upon the discovery of her destiny: 'I will be good.'"

The restaurant, only a block away, bore no sign. It was located in a shop front, the vitrine of which was white and empty. Inside, a palisade of unfinished bamboo sheltered the diners from the sight of the street. There was a wallpaper of silver and gold ferns on a pale green ground, and there were four potted palms, each a distinct variety, spaced among the modest tables. In the center of the room, a small aquarium, so low one might trip over it, burbled and glowed. While Jacob was admiring the décor, a petite Vietnamese woman gave a slight bow of greeting and wordlessly showed them to a table.

The chairs were standard socialist-issue, as were the light fixtures above and the alloy cutlery wrapped tight in paper napkins. Even the tablecloth was a common red-and-white gingham that Jacob recognized from U medvídků. So the effect of the restaurant, as one settled into it, was not of sudden transport to Asia; it was of having been invited into a child's make-believe of such a journey, where the props of everyday life have been rearranged so as to suggest a new meaning, and then accented by a few precious objects, loaned perhaps by an indulgent aunt. Its success depended on one's own complicity. When the menu arrived, it was a mimeograph, muddily typed and reproduced in violet, as in every Prague restaurant, and it listed no Vietnamese names for the dishes, not even in transliteration, but only generic Czech descriptions. Soup with onions and with lemon, read the entry that Melinda pointed to. The prices were as low as anywhere. The whole enterprise was a gesture of goodwill, Jacob felt. It was a gift that the Vietnamese were offering to the Czechs, on the occasion of their progress beyond socialism—an unassuming gift, because it was hardly an occasion that a still-socialist nation could officially acknowledge. It might have felt wrong for Jacob as an American to intercept it, if so many of the tables around them had not stood empty.

"And how are you, then, love?" Melinda asked, after both had ordered the soup.

"Oh, I'm fine," Jacob answered. "It's a little odd, the way I drop out and then drop back in," he continued, thinking of the life he led when alone in his apartment. "I'm like a movie that goes in and out of focus."

"That sounds a little alarming."

"I didn't even know the war was over."

"Carl didn't tell you?"

"He must have forgotten to. I think mostly he just thinks about you."

"How wrong of him, and how wrong of you to tell me."

"What did you two do today?"

"I don't know what we do ever. We walk, mostly, along the embankments. And keep up our defenses with droll commentary." She sighed lightly. "You mustn't think anything is going to happen."

Jacob shrugged, to disclaim prediction of any kind.

"How did you hear of the peace, then?" she continued.

"From Kaspar. He doesn't believe I'm gay."

"No doubt you're to be Jewish, as he hopes to be."

"He hasn't mentioned that lately."

"Playing coy, I fancy."

"Playing goy."

"That's terrible, Jacob."

"Sorry."

"There's evidently a woman in the case," Melinda said. "But he's bound to finish Catholic in the end—Mother Rome always gathers in the wanderers. Don't let him sweep you up while you're vulnerable. Unless you mean to be swept up, of course."

"Vulnerable?"

"You haven't got a lover again already, have you?"

"No, but what does that have to do with it?"

"Oh, nothing, nothing. But one does worry about you, darling."

He was aware that he liked to hear that she worried. "How so?"

"I don't think Kaspar's path should be yours. He is seductive in his way, though not perhaps to the likes of me."

"I don't think he's—"

"Oh, I don't mean in that way. You do turn everything to that account, don't you."

Their soup arrived. In deep white porcelain bowls, clear, thin hoops of onion floated in an amber broth. Ribbons of something green drifted in and out of the hoops—spinach, perhaps. Seaweed seemed unlikely so far from any shore. The warmth, after he swallowed, descended slowly through his chest. He began to sweat gently. There was a taste in it of something like nutmeg.

"Do you see?" Melinda asked.

They sipped silently for a little while. "Jacob, what am I to do?" she at last broke out, in a tone that both suggested she meant it and mocked the melodrama of her own manner. "No, don't answer that. Can I trust you? Will you tell him everything? You do live together."

"Not if you don't want me to."

"Confidentially, then. What am I to do? You still shouldn't answer, I suppose." He didn't. She had called him to attention and then bidden him be silent, and her eyes rested on him in the silence, appreciating him. He sensed that it suited her to see Carl through him for a moment—to let him stand in for Carl and yet not be him, and not be capable of replacing him—to have him be, in fact, as close to her as to Carl, if not closer. He felt a flicker of pride in this ambiguous role. It was like passing a finger through a candle flame too quickly to be burned, though it wasn't altogether impossible for him to be burned. She was so beautiful. "The puzzle of it," she resumed, "one puzzle, anyway, is that the pathos seems to be all on his side, between us. He pines, yet it is everyone's understanding that he is to leave shortly. All this horrid memorial photography. It isn't clear to me that it's hard-hearted of me to resist breaking off a relationship of years for one that will only last weeks. It's hardly in my interest to, is it."

"You know the answer to that," Jacob replied.

"It's haggling," she guessed.

"I wouldn't put it so harshly."

"But it is."

"Carl doesn't believe in time," Jacob said.

"I'm not sure I follow."

"He doesn't think a relationship is more meaningful if it lasts, or less if it doesn't."

"He hasn't explained that to me. How very ideal. And also quite male, I think."

"Is it?"

"Annie wouldn't let him get away with it for a second."

"But I let it pass."

"Oh, you'd let him get away with murder. You're as bad as I am. As is Henry. And Thom, for that matter."

"I'm not that bad."

"You are. The lot of you, but you in particular. I have to watch out for you." After a pause, she added, "I'm only pretending not to understand, you know."

She stopped their waitress. "Chtěli bysme dát si, když máte, vietnamské knedlíky." The waitress nodded.

"You didn't tell me they had dumplings," Jacob said.

"Do you know this dish the Czechs serve," she asked, "'Jewish pocket'? Rafe and I had some the other night. In Josefov, no less. It's a pork cutlet folded around an egg. A sort of pork cordon bleu."

"How was it?"

"Rubbery, I'm afraid. But the name of it—what's curious is they seem to have no idea of giving offense. The joke is so old they no longer hear it as a joke. It's just the name of the dish, to them."

She didn't seem to be paying much attention to what she was saying. Her mention of Rafe had abstracted her, and she had slipped into playing the docent, which was, after all, a role that she and Rafe often played for Jacob. "I don't know why I ordered dumplings," she said, trying to recover herself. "I'm not at all hungry any more. Are you?" He shrugged. "You're always game, aren't you," she continued.

The murmurs that reached them from the other tables were in English and in French, so they had leaned in over their plates and were speaking more softly than they did in other Prague restaurants, where they had the freedom of not being understood.

"Is Rafe always game?" Jacob asked, since he knew she was thinking of him.

"He is," she answered. "He wants everything and wants to know everything. Prague is too tame for him now. Have I told you this? He wants to go farther east."

He felt a twinge of panic at the thought of her departing. "Will you go with him?"

"It's under discussion."

"When does he want to go?"

"Sooner than anyone thinks, but it isn't entirely up to him."

"Who's it up to?" he risked asking.

"It would be poor form for him to leave the ministry before his appointment there has run its course," she carefully answered.

"Some people wonder if . . ."

She let his suggestion hang unfinished while she paddled about in her soup. "The question is whether that's my story, too," she finally said, without looking up.

"Which?"

"Whether *I'm* game to go farther east," she specified. "Whether it's my life and adventures as well, or only his."

"You mean you can't decide whether you want to go?"

"No, I can't tell whether, if I did go, it would be my story. Does that make any sense? I am hopeless, I know."

"I think I see what you mean."

"And that isn't the question I ask about Carl," she confessed.

"What is?"

"I—," she began, but immediately she gave up. "Oh, it's absurd. I am too grand. I suppose I just fancy a scrum, is all." The waitress intervened, laying a platter of pale wet dumplings on the table between them. Once the waitress excused herself, Melinda continued: "Don't look so gobsmacked, my god."

"No, it isn't—I don't know the word—"

"Scrum? How mortifying. Jesus. A scrum. I don't know. Like two football squads. A tumble. Jacob, please."

"Oh. Like a scrimmage."

"What you must think of me."

"I don't think anything of you."

"That's hardly reassuring. I feel I ought to say that that isn't exactly it, lest you take me at my word. I mean, I would fancy a tumble, but I'm not so simple a personality as for that to decide the question, however much I might wish that I were. It's a question of wanting to know how the story turns out. And one can only know that about one story, ever."

"How do you think the story ends, with Carl?"

"Oh, it isn't with Carl that it ends, if I choose him. I know that. I'm not a schoolgirl."

"He's a nice guy," Jacob said, in Carl's defense.

"Is he? But that isn't why one fancies him. She crossed her arms and seemed to fold in on herself, as if she were cold. "I worry that I'm tempted to choose his story for the sake of what isn't in it rather than what is."

"Kaspar's advice is to resist any choice that feels like you have to make it, because it would be a choice not to understand."

"Ought we to be taking romantic advice from Kaspar? And risk falling in love with our landladies?"

"He would say you and Carl must be keeping something about yourselves apart from yourselves. Helping each other keep it apart."

"The present and the future," she said.

"Is that it?"

"With Carl I don't want to think about the future, and with Rafe I can't think of anything else. Will I dread it if I stay, will I lose it if I give him up."

"That's sort of how Carl gets out of it, too. The meaning of love has to be independent of the future, because we all die."

"But one rarely dies right away. And so there *are* consequences. In the meantime, as it were, which does happen to be the rest of one's life." She folded her napkin neatly and tucked it against the base of her soup bowl. "Shall we order tea?"

It came in a traditional Czech stoneware teapot, white and glossy, printed with lacy blue designs.

"If I've told you this much," Melinda said, after starting a Petra, "I feel obliged to tell you the balance of it, because I can't reasonably expect you to tell him nothing, given my own shoddy record in the secret-keeping department. It may seem as if things are progressing toward, you know, but in real life things needn't, as you also know. I've told him as much, but I think he only pretends to believe me, and that's another reason to tell *you* the balance, because I think you shall believe me. You aren't in the case, and you can see it more clearly. And the balance is—"

She paused to choose her words carefully. She was in a boat not too far from shore, and a shift in the wind had showed her that she didn't know how to sail, after all, as she had thought she did. But nothing would be worse than being rescued.

"The balance of it is that I am quite attached to Rafe. It sounds miserable to say it like that, so backhandedly, but it's nonetheless true. It's so much who one is, when one is in it, that I'm not certain it's even possible to imagine oneself outside it. It's hardly his fault if I'm reluctant to go to Kyrgyzstan, or what have you, and I don't know, as you say, that I'm not simply imagining that I would be happier with Carl, or that I would be *anything* with Carl, really. Or that I'm unhappy with Rafe, in any serious way. Perhaps I simply want to have a secret."

"A secret?"

"Not that there's anything to keep secret, mind you. A secret even from myself, in a way."

"Like Rafe and his secret."

"His secret," she repeated. She flushed; patches of blood came into her face clumsily. "You think I can't leave Rafe alone with it—is that what you're saying?"

"I don't know."

"And I've brought Carl in only so as to bind myself more tightly to Rafe. What a horrible thought. It would be impossible for me to choose Carl freely, if you're right. Or if Kaspar is right. Whoever is making this argument."

"The only free act would be to give Carl up altogether."

"Oh lord, I'd rather not be free then, not quite yet. It's like Immanuel Kant or something, isn't it, your theory. But it's not true, Jacob, though I can't say why exactly. He isn't an idea, for one thing. You've seen him. No doubt I shall give him up in the end, but not that way. No, not that way."

Carl did find Václav. The hamster seemed no worse for his spree, but the day had exhausted Jacob, so much so, in fact, that the next morning, after teaching a class in Libeň, he went back to bed, where he stayed for most of the afternoon, failing, in his waking moments, to think of a way to avoid presenting his story to the writer's group, which was to meet in the evening.

"It's your funeral," Carl said, when Jacob explained his dilemma.

Jacob walked out into the Stehlíks' backyard for a few minutes in the midafternoon, to admire the thin, hard light. He could feel the rawness of the spring, its lack of moderation.

After night fell, Henry rapped at the kitchen window, and Carl went out to fetch him. "My man," Jacob heard Carl salute him, in the corridor. "Thom couldn't make it?"

"He and Jana are having a talk." As Henry stepped through the door frame, he unhitched his knapsack from his shoulder. His curls were damp; he must have showered just before coming.

"Is everything all right?" Carl asked.

"I believe so. I believe it will be, at any rate." Henry had brought beers again, and he set them on Jacob's table. "Jacob, sir," he said, as a greeting. "It's your turn tonight?"

"I guess."

It was to Henry that Jacob would have to make a revelation. It was Henry, though, who had a vulnerable air, perhaps because he was recalling their last session. Or so it seemed, at first, to Jacob, who was conscious of the shell he himself was hiding in, his wish to seem familiar and genial. On second thought, however, Jacob decided that he was only noticing Henry's usual manner. Henry wasn't able to hide behind the lids of his eyes the way a person like Carl could; the most he could do for protection was to affect a certain blankness.

They asked one another how work was, or in Carl's case, how tourism was, without much listening to the answers. "Shall we?" Henry suggested, after each had placed a pack of cigarettes on the table before him.

"Let's do it," said Carl.

"Have you heard any of this already, in your capacity as flatmate?" Henry asked.

"Not a word."

It was strange to read the story out loud. There were things in it that Jacob had said out loud before, if only to himself, when he was first grieving over Meredith, and there were other things that he had imagined saying out loud about her but had never actually spoken. He wasn't ashamed of the words, or the feelings behind them, or the exposure he was trying to make of his feelings. What troubled him was his sense that he *wasn't* exposing them. As he was reading, he began to feel that he was revealing, instead, no more than the fact that he had made a theater of his feelings, by himself and for himself, before he had come into the presence of Henry and Carl and without any reference to them. He felt dull and heavy. He wondered if he was clever enough to improvise, and when he decided he wasn't, he began to resent his script a little. The words weren't representing anything; he himself had got in their way somehow. He and they had trapped each other, and perhaps because of his growing resentment, he wasn't able, while reading, to remember the words before he came to them in the course of reading, and he began to be startled by how many details he had included, however clumsily, and to become as apprehensive about where the story was headed as if he didn't know—it was headed toward a description of his own frustrated lust, which he still couldn't think of a way to avoid. He told himself he didn't mind what Henry or Carl might think of the description, but he knew that he did mind letting them hear how solitary he had been while writing it. That was what was shameful. They could hear the size and emptiness of the imaginary room where he had thought the words up.

The silence afterward was first broken by Carl: "I didn't see that coming." Henry took in a breath but then let it go without saying anything.

"I let Kaspar read it," Jacob said. He wanted to make it seem as if at least Kaspar had been somehow present in the room with him. "He didn't think the story ended the way it did because I was gay."

"Mmm," said Henry. "You aren't, are you?"

"Actually I am."

"Oh, I see." After a pause, Henry asked Carl, "Did you know about this?"

"I did," said Carl. "I think Thom still doesn't."

"It's how Carl and I met," Jacob announced.

"No it isn't," Carl objected. "We met because of Louis."

"I know, but Louis thought *he* was gay."

"He did?"

"For a couple of weeks. He was hoping it was that instead of what it turned out to be." To Henry, Jacob explained: "It turned out to be schizophrenia." He knew he was being glib about Louis's misfortune, but he felt rudderless, unable to stop himself without a sign from Henry, a suggestion of which way he was going to turn. "I did have hopes," Jacob continued, addressing Carl again, "which you crushed."

Henry spoke up: "There's less fuss about that sort of thing, isn't there, when both parties are men."

"It's live and let live," Jacob quickly replied. This was one of Daniel's ideas, and he liked the bragging rights that it entailed, though he didn't really have enough experience himself to know for certain that it was true.

"Because you both know how men are," Henry continued. He looked from Carl to Jacob and back to Carl again. He seemed to be deciding that he liked to be in on the secret, however belatedly. "It's sort of Bloomsbury, for the two of you to become flatmates in the end."

"It's not *that* Bloomsbury," Jacob hurried to say.

"It's sort of Prague," Carl suggested.

"The old regime falls, but no one gets laid," Jacob glossed.

"It's postrevolutionary," Carl said. "The Prague Non-orgy."

Václav heard something they couldn't and scrambled under the shredded magazine pages in his cage. The three humans sat drinking their beers. The white-plastered walls and the white-painted furniture of the apartment had become so familiar to Jacob that he rarely asked himself any more what difference it made that he was living in Prague, but it now occurred to him that he wasn't sure he could have read this story aloud in Boston. He couldn't fairly ascribe the freedom that he felt to the Czechs' and Slovaks' revolution, now that he was spending so much time among expats. The society he and his friends were making together was more or less the opposite of what was usually claimed for Europe: they owed less to tradition, they could make fewer assumptions about one another. It was a second America, in a way; they were immigrants, living on a frontier, as Carl had called it, though an economic rather than a geographic one. A conversation about writing might have been richer in Boston, but Carl and Jacob would probably have been too absorbed in their romantic lives and their careers to have time for it. And in Boston Jacob would not have known anyone like Henry: a person on a quest. Nor, come to think of it, would Jacob have been as conscious of the questing side of Carl. Prague called it out in them. Here Carl and Henry could talk for hours over lunch about the purpose of life, without embarrassment. Without too much embarrassment, anyway. Carl couldn't stop himself from kidding, but here he could have the conversation despite the kidding. What made it possible was the fact of Prague—the fact of being away from home (Henry had explained that even the Czechs sometimes worried about *nezabydlenost*, or not feeling at home, in Prague, which had been overrun, after all, by Austrians, Germans, Russians, and now Americans)—and the candor with which someone like Henry was willing to talk about his experiment. In England, Henry had had girlfriends, he had had a child, he had had a career, and he had left all of them in order to come here, learn Czech, and master the country's politics without any apparent wish to intervene in them. He had come for adventure only, and in the light of his devotion to adventure, they were able to see their own steps in that direction more distinctly. Of course Henry wasn't going to mind about Jacob. Jacob began to see why Carl made such a hero of him—why the two made such heroes of each other.

"I was cruised by a man Friday last," Henry volunteered. "While crossing Letná."

"What's Letná?" Carl asked.

"The park around Stalin's monument. Seemed quite lively. Do you know it?"

"No," Jacob half lied. He had read about it in his guide, but he hadn't tried it out.

"Mmm," Henry continued. "But all this notwithstanding, I might agree with Kaspar. I don't see that it's necessarily you in the last scene. Given the Henry James story and all."

Jacob had forgotten that the essay where he'd found the plot twist had been about James. He felt caught out, and he didn't know what to say.

"I thought for certain you had it in mind," Henry continued, evidently unsure how to proceed.

"What story is this?" Carl asked.

"A fellow visits the grave of a woman he knew," Henry related, "and it's only when he sees another man weeping at *another* woman's grave that he realizes he could have had a love affair. Should have done, that is."

"A love affair with the dead woman?" Carl asked.

"Yes, sorry. He never had one in the James story. He feels he's never really lived."

"But it's the guy weeping who's never really lived," Jacob broke out. His verdict had a prudish, disapproving sound, even to himself. "If it's the same guy weeping over the same woman."

"But it isn't, is it? Isn't that the point?" Henry asked.

"In my story or in James's? I mean, if James was gay, it wasn't with a woman that he would have not had a life."

"I'm all turned around," said Carl.

"Me too," said Henry.

They puzzled silently for a few moments. "Hang on, I'm wrong," Henry resumed, reconsidering. "It does matter whether it's you at the end, and it matters whether you're gay, because if you're gay there's no story, is there. It's like what you said about my story. Your fellow's not really *in* the story, once he turns out to be gay. *You're* not in the story, that is. But you are in it, if you're not." Henry had pressed himself back and up in his chair, stiffly, in his excitement at handling an idea, homosexuality, that still carried a slight charge of taboo. "Because in the case where you're gay, you haven't failed to live your life, at least not yet. As you say. It's regret that ties up the loose ends, that makes it a story. If you turn to the other fellow, it's a kind of non sequitur. Not that I'm one to mind a non sequitur. It becomes a different story. The story turns without conclusion to another story."

"Like a daisy chain," said Carl.

"The Henry James is a story, and yours isn't," Henry summarized. "Yours doesn't end properly. There's something left out."

It was a challenge. Henry was returning the blow that Jacob had struck when they had discussed his story, returning it not in a spirit of revenge, but as proof that he had taken it in good faith and liked Jacob well enough to hit him just as hard.

"I do know that Henry James story," Jacob confessed.

"Aha," said Henry, who seemed as pleased at the deceit as at the revelation.

"I haven't read it, but I read an essay about it once."

"That's pretty postmodern of you," Carl offered.

"I hate postmodernism." Jacob noticed that his heart was pounding again as it had at Vyšehrad. "I hate it, and I seem to have written a story about wanting to live inside a story that's already been written."

"Or about not wanting to," said Carl. "It's a little ambiguous."

From time to time Jacob worried that, surrounded now by expats, he was failing to get to know Czech language and culture. The day after the writing group's meeting, for instance, the worry overtook him. He told himself he hadn't come here to—but then he halted in his thoughts. What he was now doing was so formless he wasn't sure how to describe it. Technically, the English, Irish, and Scots were as foreign to him as the Czechs and Slovaks were, but he couldn't fool himself. He still couldn't read a newspaper in Czech.

After teaching in Libeň, he headed downtown, alone, in the stern and aimless way that he had forced himself to explore the city in the fall, when he had first arrived. He bought a copy of *Lidové noviny* at a kiosk in Palmovka and puzzled over it during his ride. He rose from the subway at Můstek and drifted north past Mel and Rafe's, along his old path, over the cobblestones of Melantrichova, with a dreamer's sense of repetition, as if he were reciting a poem that he had recited so many times that the words had lost their meaning. A prayer, maybe. He decided to get lost, though he knew that with the map in his back pocket it would be hard to. He turned left. He turned left again. He found himself in a square that for a moment he didn't recognize, but then he saw an *antikvariát* he knew. He hadn't ever entered the square from this direction, but he had been here before. He had come one evening in search of a bar that he had heard was rough. It hadn't been; none of the straight bars were. In that year, Czech drunks never did anything worse than sing and tell rambling stories. They were gentle for some reason—perhaps, Jacob speculated, because even in their cups they participated in the national mood of liberation and melancholy, the blanketing pensiveness about the old order passed away and the new one not yet come, or perhaps because they had learned, through living for decades under a regime where the smallest legal infraction could ruin a life, to get drunk quietly, and the habit hadn't yet left them. If they lived a little longer in the marketplace, experience of rivalry and inadequacy might give them more of a wish to hurt one another. But they didn't have much of one yet. Jacob had left the "rough" bar after half an hour, bored, and he kept walking now. Soon he was in a narrow street that he had never seen before, which didn't seem to lead anywhere in particular. The river must be ahead of him, he thought vaguely, but he must have been wrong in thinking so, because he didn't come to it. Through a tall door shutting behind a woman in a kerchief, he glimpsed a *pasáž*, lit at the far end by sunlight—sunlight on a pile of yellow sand—and after the woman turned a corner, he doubled back and opened the door himself.

The corridor was quiet, except for the faint echo of a bird somewhere nearby, chattering. The arched ceiling was low and of a smooth, dirty white stucco. It felt like a violation to walk down this *pasáž*, as it didn't in those around Wenceslas Square or those that branched off Melantrichova. To reach the sunny patch he had to walk quite a ways through shadow, and while he was in it, a draft touched him on the forearm and chilled him. A pocket of winter air was hiding here in the darkness from the spring. In the sunlight, when he reached it, he found a shovel set in the sand, and next to it a blue plastic tub with rope handles. Next to that, someone had spilled a heap of white cobblestones. The courtyard was being repaved. He was afraid for a moment that he might have to retrace his steps, but another corridor seemed to lead out, at an angle, toward a different street. At the edge of the courtyard, from a metal trash can whose lid had been tipped up, a sparrow was fetching a thin red string. "They won't like that," Jacob warned the bird, as he passed into shadow again. "It's not your string. It isn't normal."

Exiting into the new street, he again refrained from taking out his map. The cold air of the *pasáže* seemed to trail after him into the street, which was shaded by a tall First Republic building. He shivered. There was a pub in the ground floor, and Jacob realized he was hungry. He stepped inside.

A large room was roaring with conversation, its air dusty with cigarette smoke. No one noticed him. A sepia light fell through tinted windows. The diners and drinkers were workers, most of them in blue jumpsuits. He took a seat at one of the long dark tables, after asking permission of the men already sitting at it.

—Please, one of them said, with a gesture, and returned to a discussion with his friends.

The man's face and forearms were dark from sun. He looked about thirty. He hadn't shaved in a couple of days, and the blond stubble on his chin glittered as he talked. Around his beer glass, his fingers were thick and his fingernails oval. His eyes, however, were fine and quick, and he caught Jacob studying him. He nodded amiably.

Jacob unfolded his *Lidové noviny*. He attempted the lead story, which had eluded him on the train. Newspapers were written in a different register of Czech from the one he had learned to speak. They were full of the words for handling ideas, the equivalents of "approve," "inquiry," and "comparable," assembled on the same pattern as the English words but from Slavic roots and prefixes instead of Latin ones. So once he was able to identify "refer," it shouldn't be hard to recognize "infer" and "transfer" and "defer" . . .

—Please, a waiter whined.

—Good day, Jacob said, but he saw, as he said it, that the waiter considered Jacob's greeting a waste of his time. —What do you have in the way of ready food? Jacob added, trying to be more purposeful.

The waiter sighed dramatically. —I'll bring you a menu. He began to stalk off.

—But please, Jacob said. The waiter would bring the tourist menu, overpriced, if he wasn't stopped. —Do you have pork meat with cabbage and dumplings?

—Of course.

—Thus, one, please, and one beer.

—Thus, the waiter agreed. He seemed relieved. Evidently he hadn't wanted to fleece Jacob if he didn't have to. In blue ink he wrote the price of the dish on a slip of gray paper; he slashed once, below the number, to represent Jacob's beer; and he anchored the slip under the ashtray nearest Jacob.

—It isn't a bother, if I smoke? Jacob asked the men at his table. They had finished eating—they had stacked their plates—so Jacob thought they wouldn't mind. There were three of them. Besides the quick-eyed man, there was a heavyset one with a ragged beard and a sharp-looking one with his black hair smarmed and his sleeves rolled up.

—Not at all, answered the quick-eyed man.

Jacob nodded his thanks. Now he had more of their attention than he was comfortable with. He felt lucky that he was smoking Sparty rather than Marlboros today, though he wondered if even Sparty might seem a little precious here. The men were watching him. He tapped nervously on the little blue trireme that decorated the pack. —If you would like . . . , it occurred to him to offer, and he held out the open pack to them.

It was as if he had enchanted them, or as if he had broken an enchantment. They laughed and accepted. They were drunker than he had realized.

—Thanks many times, the quick-eyed man said. Jacob nodded again but then looked away, because the man seemed so at ease in his skin that he was hard to resist, and Jacob didn't want to gawk. He didn't want to offend them.

The workers, however, didn't seem to fear that the rapport was fragile. "Hele," the quick-eyed man hailed Jacob. —Look, where are you from? He was addressing Jacob informally; he was quite drunk.

—From America.

—That's what I told you, said the sharp-looking man, as he lightly thumped the table.

—Look, the quick-eyed man again addressed Jacob, as if the injunction would help Jacob cross the language barrier. —And in what way do you work?

Jacob couldn't help but return the man's amiable gaze. In America the return might have triggered either a suspicion that Jacob was gay or a suspicion that Jacob was mocking the man, or both, but here there was no interruption. The man and Jacob seemed able to look at each other fondly without either thinking the worse of the other, though their eyes didn't lock, because the worker's frame wobbled slightly from drink and his eyes didn't compensate for the wobble, for the same reason. —In what way? Jacob repeated, uncertain of the meaning of the question.

—Yeah, and forgive, but also, how much does it pay, if it isn't a bother?

The other two workers fell expectantly silent. —Not at all, Jacob said. They wanted to hear the good news.

To answer honestly, he would have to say that he hoped to be a writer when he returned to America, and that he didn't know how much writers were paid. But he couldn't say that; it would sound both arrogant and weak. He would have to answer as if he were still the self he had been when he left, which, now that he was invited to describe it, he saw as a discarded shell. The shell, however, had made more money than he, in the future, was likely to, and he found that he wanted to impress the men. —In America I wrote papers for business, he said. The same ignorance that prevented him from understanding the newspaper kept him from describing his work more precisely. —They paid me thirty-five dollars each hour, he added. That much, anyway, was easy to communicate.

—A thousand crowns, the man in the beard grunted.

—A thousand crowns an hour, echoed the sharp one, emphatically.

—And that is little! the quick-eyed man exclaimed.

—In truth? his friends challenged him.

—That is little, that yes? the quick-eyed man asked Jacob, for confirmation. —You aren't rich.

The part of Jacob that was still a boy from a public school, who had worked hard to get into and through Harvard—the part of him that he had just revisited, in order to answer the man's question—felt threatened. The man had asked his question so colloquially. "Nejseš bohatej," rather than "nejsi bohatý." You're one of us, his manner of speaking implied. He was recognizing something about Jacob. A part of Jacob heard it as, You're no better than us.

—No, I'm not rich, Jacob agreed. Despite himself, he couldn't keep a note of disappointment out of his voice. He had been proud of making so much money, even though he had hated the job. Even now he could see a way to be proud of America for having been able to pay him so much.

—But . . . , the man began, and then faltered. Somewhere there had been a miscommunication.

The waiter set a beer before Jacob, violently but without spilling any.

—To health, the quick-eyed man said, raising his own half-empty glass for encouragement.

—To health.

—With papers you work, the man continued. —For real work of course they pay more.

The beer was Staropramen. The sour tang was so closely associated in Jacob's mind with intoxication that the first sip alone somewhat disoriented him. Even in Prague he almost never drank in the middle of the day. It was too late to ask for a soda water, though. He would drink only half, he decided.

—More? he repeated, not quite following the man's line of argument.

—They pay more if you make houses, roads, plates. As the man said the word for plates, he gave a quarter-turn with his thumb to the stack of plates in front of him, by way of demonstration. —Cigarettes, he added, with a nod to the Sparta he was smoking. From the gestures, Jacob saw that the man thought that it was the difference in language that was keeping Jacob from understanding.

—They pay more to those, who work with their hands, the man tried again, with the manner of someone who has been reduced to saying something so obvious that he is afraid that he risks sounding impolite. Now Jacob got it. A road was more valuable than a corporate newsletter, so a construction worker like him would naturally make more than a paper-pusher like Jacob.

—But in America . . . , Jacob began. He paused. The man's eyes caught him again. Jacob kept expecting to see a taunt or a challenge in them, but they held only a concern that Jacob should understand that he hadn't meant to hurt Jacob's feelings. He believed that the world wanted nothing so much as the muscular power that Jacob could see in the line of his neck as it descended into his work suit. He believed that the world badly wanted him to work in the sun and have a little beer in his belly at midday. He was the base, and he had been obliged to remind Jacob that Jacob was the superstructure. The reminder was inadvertent, not a personal matter. It was only the man's rough-and-tumble way of being in the world.

He actually doesn't know, Jacob marveled silently. He doesn't realize

that capitalism will pay those who work with paper more than those
who work with their hands.

—When I return to America, they won't pay me that much again.
Me personally. The work was unusually well paid, in my case.

—But still, the man said, relaxing as he sensed that Jacob held
nothing against him. He turned to his friends to make sure they were
admiring the plenty that he thought was in store for them all.

—Please, the waiter said, as he laid Jacob's plate on the table.

—A good appetite, the quick-eyed man wished Jacob, and his
friends seconded the wish with nods.

With his fork Jacob cut a wedge from one of the dumpling slices and
dredged it in the grayish purple cabbage. The food tasted the same as it
did everywhere in Prague—the dumplings were as bland and dense as
the white of a bagel, the steamed cabbage was both tart and sweet, like a
jam or a relish. Jacob ate quickly because he felt embarrassed. He felt as
if he were sharing a table with someone who hasn't heard the news that
his girlfriend is going to break up with him. From time to time, as he
ate, he smiled at the man, nervously and treacherously.

"He's not my cup of tea, really, Kafka," Annie said, when Jacob met her
the following Saturday in Old Town Square, near the horologe. She said
Kaff-ka rather than *Koff-ka*. In the sun they were almost warm.

"He has to be. You're in Prague."

"He doesn't have to be, Jacob. Don't be so bloody sure of everything."

"I'm not."

"I could be more of a Rilke person, for example."

"Are you?"

"No, but I could be, for all you know."

"What do you have against Rilke?"

"The same as against Kafka, I suppose. He's always in a fret."

"But what if his life was like that?"

"I'm not obliged to read about it."

"We don't have to go to the exhibit, you know."

"Don't be a prat, Jacob. I said I would go."

"It's right in here," he said. He pointed to one of the yellow layer-
cake buildings that Jan Hus faced.

"It's just that I'm not fond of insects." As a door thudded shut behind them, they found themselves suddenly alone in a dim, silent foyer. A heavy gray drapery blocked access to the rest of the ground floor, so as to guide visitors up a flight of stairs. The steps were red-and-white marble, mottled like salami.

"There won't actually be insects," Jacob said.

"I know," she said as they ascended. "Only pictures of insects." Then, softening, she added, "I am half-mad, you do know that, don't you. I am glad you're well again. I have missed our outings."

A small round woman with boxy glasses took from them one crown fifty hellers each and then tore small tears in two chits to represent their payments.

Annie hummed to herself contentedly, hugging her large leather purse tight, as she drifted away from Jacob into the center of the gallery, which they had to themselves. It was not a large room. The walls were yellow and tricked out with baroque molding; a strip at waist height defined a dado, and at intervals, shallow pilasters interrupted the walls, as if to suggest but not insist on alcoves. In most of the pseudo-alcoves, a small lithograph was hanging. In the last one, several copies of the same book lay in a glass case, open to different pages.

"Have you read *The Metamorphosis*?" Annie asked.

"A while ago. I guess I'd have to read it in Czech if I wanted to reread it here, since he's neither British nor American."

"I told my students about your American library, by the way."

"You shouldn't have."

"And why not?"

"It's all spy novels and presidential biographies and Mark Twain in schoolboy editions."

"I don't mind a spy novel now and then, myself," Annie objected, putting herself, on principle, in the way of Jacob's dismissal.

"I think they figured that since no Czechs would dare go to a library attached to the American embassy, they might as well stock the sort of thing CIA agents like to read."

"Is it Agency to read Mark Twain, then?"

"I imagine that CIA agents like to think that it is, when they're filling out questionnaires about what to put in the embassy library."

The exhibit they had come to see was of lithographs by a German

Praguer, a friend of Kafka's, who had been commissioned to illustrate the first Czech translation of *The Metamorphosis*. In the first image, the creature sat in a chair facing a large window that fronted a street. Its back was scaled like a fish's. It was propped on edge like a turtle, and it was waving many childlike hands. The expression on its face, which seemed to end in a platypus's bill, was so ambiguous that the creature could have been welcoming the people it saw in the street or threatening them.

"Did I tell you that I told Henry?" Jacob asked.

Annie looked at him with alarm. "You told him?"

"That I'm gay," he specified.

"Oh, *that*." She returned to studying the lithograph. Jacob leaned in again, too. A cluster of human eyes stared out of the valance above the window that the creature was looking through, as if the eyes were a pattern in the fabric. "A bit morbid, isn't it?" she said. "Paranoid. And how did Henry take it?"

"Oh, he took it well. It was part of my story for this week. In our group, in our poetry corner."

"You don't actually write poetry now."

"No, but I told Carl that you call it that, and he's started calling it that, too. 'Henry's poetry corner.'"

"He *would* take it well," Annie said. "He would see the freedom, like. That would be what he sees in it." She was pleased that Jacob's report confirmed her estimation of Henry's liberality, and this pleasure seemed, by adding to her confidence, to aggravate her impatience with the exhibit. Almost dancing, she walked ahead to the next image. "Gah," she said, squinting at it, twirling with a finger a loose curl of her hair. "It's a lad thing in the end," she said, in a half whisper that was both conspiratorial and mocking. "That idea of freedom. Not that he would know what to do with a bloke."

"I think men do know, usually."

"Do they?" She looked suddenly at a loss.

"Because they're men themselves."

"I'm sure you know more about this sort of thing than I," she replied, with brittle diffidence. She had lost her confidence again.

"Annie."

"What?" she challenged and silenced him.

In the second lithograph, the creature hid under a sofa while the sister entered the room with a plate of food. Sewn into the back of a chair was another uncanny eye, singular like the Masonic eye on the back of a dollar bill. In this picture the creature's face appeared more crustacean. It was such a strange punishment, if that's what the transformation was.

"I'm thinking of not Friday week but the Friday after that, for Krakow."

"Two weeks from Friday," Jacob translated.

"Can you and Carl manage it then, do you think?"

"I think so."

"We'll have a grand time," she promised, and as she spoke, she seemed to be looking at the time they were going to have and drawing courage from it.

In the third image, the family were seated around a table. The father's eyes were closed and his head tilted back, as if he were dozing, and a Masonic eye looked out from the back of his chair, too. Did the eye represent enlightenment of some kind, or was exposure to view part of the ordeal of the son-creature? The mother was worrying a vague white cloth. The creature peered in from the next room, hunched over on all fours, or however many feet it had. Its representation was out of accord with the laws of perspective, too large and too flat—like a figure in a medieval painting that has attracted a disproportionate share of the artist's attention.

"Do you remember the way the sister brings different kinds of food," Jacob asked, "and he discovers that he likes moldy cheese and rotting vegetables?"

"It's a perfectly vile story, in my opinion."

"I wonder if it stands for homosexuality. It arises in the family, it provokes disgust. He discovers in himself new appetites. The father wants to punish him."

"Wouldn't there have to be another beetle or what have you?"

"No. If you find yourself disgusting, sex is a way of cutting yourself off, not of connecting you."

Annie seemed unconvinced. "I always thought it had something to do with money, myself," she said. "From the way he talks about his job. He sounds like a beetle even before he realizes he is one, if you know what I mean. Sort of deadlike and industrious."

"He's capitalism," Jacob said.

"Or just, losing hope, rather."

"If you have no love, that can happen."

"It isn't just gays it can happen to."

In the next picture, the markings on the creature were such that it resembled a flattened globe of the Earth, and it was ringed by its hands, like a crab on its back ringed by its claws. An old woman stood over it holding a square broom. It could also stand for incest, Jacob thought. There was so much of the sister in the story.

"Do you mind if on the way to Krakow we went—I mentioned it to Carl but he said he couldn't speak for you—I've always been curious, you see."

"What?" Jacob asked.

"If we went to—I'm not good at pronouncing it—Oss-vee—"

"Where?"

"Will you let me speak? I haven't even said the name of it yet. Oss-vee—well, Auschwitz is the name you would know it by, anyhow. If you don't want to, I understand, and I can go by myself while you and Carl go elsewhere. I can take the bus or what have you. It's right there, where we'll be, practically."

He found that the suggestion unsettled him, and though Annie moved on to the next image, he stayed where he was, because he had lost his focus and was staring at the image without seeing it. Instead of recognizing the creature, he felt, he was merely resting his eyes on the round pattern in the lithograph where it was supposed to be. A hollow pattern. For the moment the shape was like—what had been the word for the tattoo on Markus's back? A mandala. He hadn't thought of Markus in a while.

"Who is this?" Jacob asked, calling Annie back. He pointed to the woman with the broom. "I don't remember this character."

"She's the char, isn't she? The one who finds him. Such a beastly story."

"Finds him?"

"I believe he's dead in this picture."

Jacob now noticed the family clinging to the sides of the image, framing it.

In the last image, slightly larger than the others, the creature was standing on the roof of a Prague apartment building, now with a head shaped like a squirrel's and eyes like an owl's. It had the same innocent hands. Its back was dissolving in a flurry of lines, which must have been intended to represent beating wings.

"Does he fly?" Jacob asked.

"I couldn't tell you for certain but I don't believe so," Annie answered. "It's too bad Henry is such a priss about his writing group, because I'm quite well read, for someone who's not a Harv."

"You are."

"But it doesn't matter," she added, with a little savagery. "I am looking forward to Krakow." When he failed to take the subject up and instead continued to examine the creature on the roof, she asked, "Does the story really speak to you so much?"

"I don't know. It is sort of the famous Prague story."

She shrugged. "But it's become a little naff, hasn't it, with all the American backpackers buying T-shirts of him and so on."

"It's still a good story."

"No one in a Kafka story has an inside, is what I don't like. A story of his is like a silent film instead of a talking one. One complication follows another, and you never return to where you started. And all you want is to go back to the start, because everything has become steadily worse the further into the story you go. It's cruel, really."

"But life is like that."

"It isn't like that so *inexorably*."

It was strange that Markus had had such a symbol drawn on himself, Jacob thought as they walked back into the bright square. It was like defacing a product so that it couldn't be returned to the manufacturer.

Late Monday found Jacob in the northern Prague district where Prokop and Anežka lived. After the bus grumbled away, he heard sparrows bickering in the lindens that lined the children's street. The new length of the days seemed to have excited the birds, as if it gave them time that they hadn't planned for and had no idea how to fill except with frenzy. Two fell on the sidewalk almost at his feet, in what looked like combat but of course wasn't, and then skittered away, skimming just a few inches above the uneven planes of the broken cement.

At the children's house, the vine that grew along the brick wall was budding new leaves, iridescent chartreuse, which seemed to draw and hold the late-afternoon light. As he waited for Milena to answer the bell, he heard a flutter and noticed almost at eye level a small gray-brown bird with a rust-colored breast. Such quiet colors. It couldn't be a robin, because its face was red as well as its breast and because it was so small he could have cupped it in one hand. But in America it would have been a robin, and he accepted it on that understanding, which left him a little melancholy.

"Please," Milena said, beckoning him in, after a brief struggle with the lock.

The courtyard had altered with the season. In their hutch, the rabbits were bolder now, or perhaps merely warmer, and eyed passersby in the hope of food, while sitting lengthwise across the mesh at the front or pacing back and forth with the lope of run-down windup dolls. On the ground beside the hutch, there grew a few green sprouts. Over long raised beds of gray dirt, three lines of white string ran in parallel between stakes.

In the foyer, at the foot of the stairs to the family's apartment, Jacob sat on the floor to unlace his shoes. He admired a row of seedlings on the floor beside him, arrayed to catch the sun that fell through the door's sidelights. They had been planted in recycled white plastic cups, of the sort that yogurt and the children's dessert *smetanový krém* were sold in. When Milena saw him looking at them, she said, "I must . . . ," with her nervous smile, and then looked from the seedlings to the garden outside, to convey the idea that they were overdue for transplanting. "Children upstairs," she assured Jacob. "Neighbors. *One* neighbor." She raised an index finger for counting, then hid it behind her other hand as if afraid that such a simple gesture might seem crude. She meant that her children had remained upstairs to entertain a guest. Not long ago the neighbors had asked Milena if their children could participate in the lessons, too. For more than a month now, Jacob had found, upon arrival, a variable supplement of children sitting solemnly around Prokop and Anežka's dinner table, each clutching a crown or two in a small fist. Sometimes there were half a dozen additional pupils; sometimes, as today, only one.

As a consequence of the irregularity, every lesson became an introduction, as self-contained as possible: about numbers, or about moods, or about colors. Jacob tried to come up with ways of turning the lessons into games, whenever possible. The night before the long bus ride, he would search his pantry, shelves, and wardrobe for props. Today, for example, to introduce the word *who*, he had brought postcard images of celebrities, which he had bought at an Andy Warhol exhibit in Malá Strana. To introduce *how much*, he planned to ask the children to pretend to sell a few items to one another.

Such, anyway, were his plans. He held them in mind anxiously as he climbed the stairs. Children live in a world of their own, and his plans always felt to him like an interruption of it. No matter how willing the children were to cooperate, he felt himself to be driving them out of their natural track and sensed the propriety of their resistance. A part of him would rather have shared in their wildness. In the course of the hour, as they grew fatigued, they would fall back into the comfort and support of the environment that Milena wove around them, which was itself another pattern that he felt himself to be compromising. Because she fed him, he felt the pull of her support much as they did.

As he climbed the stairs, his calves trembled; he was drinking and smoking too much. He heard light footfalls and saw Prokop appear at the head of the stairs and then slouch against a wall, shyly and impatiently. Anežka hid herself behind him and then peeped out to say, "Ahoj!" her voice like a little bell. Prokop pivoted backward as if his body were a roller crushing her against the wall, and she darted away.

Jacob paused to catch his breath. "Ahoj, hello."

"Hello," replied Prokop, putting on a plummy British movie actor's voice. Below Jacob, Milena laughed doubtfully.

When Jacob reached the dining room, he saw that the guest was Ladislav, a small boy with sunken eyes and black hair. Ladislav was waiting in his seat at the table, unsure of his liberty in a strange house. Jacob greeted him, and the boy acknowledged the greeting with a nod that almost amounted to a bow.

"Please," Milena said. As ever, she insisted that Jacob place himself at the head of the table. In the middle of the table, Anežka's doll sat with her back to Prokop's trolley car. The toys had become a part of their ritual, as was the exchange that next occurred. Jacob asked the children in English how they were, and after they had answered and, at Milena's prompting, asked him in turn, Milena interrupted. "But you must first to eat," she said.

"It's very kind of you, but you don't have to feed me."

"But I want. Do you like it, *guláš*?"

"Very much."

She brought him a plate, still steaming, of thick beef stew, which paprika had turned burnt sienna, accompanied by small, whitish-yellow potatoes as clean and polished as bird's eggs. It was twice as much food as he would have been served in a restaurant. The children waited politely. In the tall, broad windows behind them, the day was dying. A black, ropey mantle was being unrolled and lowered, and it was lit from below, as it descended, by a faint pink wash cast by the sun. If asked about the view, Jacob would have denied that it meant anything, but it's difficult to take a thing like the sky ironically.

He pushed away his plate and made an effort. He lay the postcards face down in the middle of the table and had the children draw them one at a time, like cards from a deck, and challenge one another with the images. "Who is it?" They recognized Mickey Mouse and Albert Einstein, but Marilyn Monroe was mistaken for Madonna, and the children drew a blank on many of the faces, even when Jacob supplied the names. Jacob had to explain, and the point of the exercise was soon lost in pidgin storytelling.

Sooner than he had planned to, Jacob moved on to his second idea. He took a bag of rice and a single winter glove from his bag.

—You're still hungry? Prokop said.

"Wise guy," Jacob replied.

"Wh—, wh—," Prokop tried to mimic the words.

"Moudrý chlap," Jacob translated. " 'Wise guy.' " Now they all repeated the phrase.

Jacob set the bag of rice before Prokop and the glove before Ladislav. Then he took off his wristwatch and set it before Anežka. "Jééé," Prokop exclaimed of the watch, enviously, and Anežka, pleased that it was hers for the moment, wriggled into a kneeling position in her chair.

"What's that?" Jacob asked Prokop, pointing at the rice.

Prokop didn't know the word. "How do you say *rýže*," he asked out of the side of his mouth, with pretend furtiveness.

"Reese," his mother supplied.

"Rice," Jacob corrected.

"It is a rice," Prokop answered.

" 'It's rice,' " Jacob again corrected.

"It's rice."

"How much is it?"

"H—, h—."

"How much?"

"How much," Prokop succeeded in repeating.

Jacob took a large white-metal coin out of his pocket. "How much is it? Is it five crowns?"

"Is five crowns," Prokop agreed, as he saw the meaning of the question.

" '*It's* five crowns.' "

"No, is *ten* crowns," Prokop revised.

" '*It's* ten crowns.' "

"*It's* ten crowns," Prokop said at last.

"I'll take it," Jacob told him, and substituted for the rice a honey-colored ten-crown note, withdrawn from his wallet, from which stared a mustachioed man in an Inverness cape and a polka-dot cravat. A detective or a magician. "Thank you!"

"You are welcome."

"No, in America, you say, 'Thank you,' too."

—Truly?

"Yes, because I'm giving you money." Jacob pointed so that the meaning of his words would be clear.

"Thank you!" Prokop said. Then he repeated, as if for the mere pleasure of saying it: "How much!"

"Now you buy Ladislav's glove. Ask him what it is, first."

Ladislav stumbled, predictably, in omitting the indefinite article before "glove." If Jacob had had any foresight, he would not have brought one prop that was a mass noun and one that was a count noun. "*A* glove, *a* watch, *rice*," he interrupted, in an attempt to clarify. "*A* doll, *a* trolley."

Prokop asked to run through the exchange again, first snatching back the ten-crown note from Ladislav and restoring to him the glove. This time, when Ladislav said, "It's ten crowns," Prokop said, "Five crowns!" somewhat belligerently. Ladislav laughed once, startled but amiable.

"Say 'That's too high,'" Jacob suggested to Prokop. "'How about five crowns?'"

"How about," Prokop repeated. "How much. How about." With the new phrase he offered Ladislav five crowns for the glove. Ladislav glanced to Jacob for guidance.

"It's up to you," Jacob told him. "You can say, 'Okay, five crowns,' or 'No, it's ten crowns.'"

"No, a glove is ten crowns," Ladislav decided.

—Then no, Prokop retorted in Czech.

"'No, thank you,'" instructed Jacob.

"No thank you," Prokop repeated, with a farcical sullenness.

—Is it my turn? Anežka asked, twisting high in her chair with impatience.

Jacob asked in English about her watch.

"Jak se říká *sto*?" she asked in reply.

"A hundred," he told her.

"Hun'red crown," she mumbled shyly.

"'It's a hundred crowns,'" Jacob insisted on her saying, and once she repeated the sentence, he rewarded her with a hammy reaction: "A hundred crowns! That's *way* too high."

"No! A hundred crowns!" Prokop interjected, taking his sister's side.

"How about twenty?" Jacob offered.

—Yes, Anežka said in Czech, before Prokop could refuse on her behalf.

"'Okay,'" Jacob prompted her to say, but she understood him to be agreeing in his own person and handed him the watch. In exchange he gave her a twenty-crown note, on which a blue couple in tweed read a book by the light of the sun and an oversize atom. She fluttered it in a celebratory way, as if she were curtsying and it were a ribbon.

"How much!" Prokop said accusingly, pointing at the watch in front of Jacob. Though it felt like play money to Jacob, it was real to the children, who didn't ordinarily handle it, and it seemed to be exciting them. Jacob wondered if he had made a mistake in introducing it into the game without explaining first that he was going to take it all back at the end. "How much!"

"'How much is it.'"

"How much *is it*," Prokop repeated.

"It's a hundred crowns."

"Wise guy!" Prokop shouted. Everyone laughed. Seeing that he had scored a point, Prokop loudly repeated the exclamation until his mother had to ask him to speak normally.

"It's a hundred crowns," Jacob insisted in a level voice.

Prokop eyed his own bill and the bill in his sister's hand. "How about thirty crowns," he offered.

"Okay," Jacob agreed, because he wanted to see what Prokop would do.

Prokop grabbed the bill from his sister and, adding it to his own, threw the two notes at Jacob. "Thank you!" he said demandingly, palm outstretched.

Jacob surrendered the watch, and as soon as he did, there was screaming, because Anežka felt that it was now as much hers as Prokop's. In their greed the children lost all inhibition, and Milena had to pry the watch from their fingers. As she handed it to Jacob, she said, "Please."

She spoke sternly to her children in Czech, too quickly for Jacob to follow. Prokop, who seemed to receive the more severe reprimand, scowled and kicked the legs of his chair. Jacob wanted to signal that he was not himself upset. He slipped his watch into a pocket, and to continue the game, he placed the doll before Anežka and the trolley before Prokop, and gave the thirty crowns to Ladislav. There was a touch of danger in the air.

At Jacob's cue, Ladislav asked, "What is that?" and pointed to Prokop's trolley. Not family, Ladislav had had to suppress any wish he might have had to join the scuffle for the watch, and he had not been scolded, so the energy in his voice was now higher than that of the siblings. Jacob sensed, in a momentary intuition, that the trolley was a toy that Prokop had never before allowed Ladislav to handle, and that Ladislav foresaw a happy coincidence of the game's public reward and a private, maybe even secret wish. "What is that?" Ladislav repeated, in the spirit of one who presses a second time the button of an apparatus that is balky about starting.

Prokop touched the trolley with one finger, as if to remind himself of it, and then, as if the touch did remind him, took it up in both hands, bringing it close to his face so he could peer into its dark windows, running the rear wheels against his palm to hear the slow, razzy scratching of the inertial engine inside. "It is a tramway," he quietly said.

"A tram," Jacob amended.

"It is a tram," Prokop said, again quietly. His eyes slowly left the toy to meet those of the boy who threatened to take it from him. The possibility of a confrontation seemed to alarm Ladislav, who glanced at Jacob in the hope of a late revision to the rules of the game, which Jacob could not see a way to engineer without embarrassing Prokop—without interpreting aloud, perhaps wrongly, the change in his demeanor. The rules obliged them all to continue. "How much is it?" Ladislav asked, holding himself perfectly still.

Jacob, too, held his breath. Prokop put the trolley in his lap, under the table and out of sight, and swung his legs back and forth so that his body rocked. "How much?" Prokop repeated, as if he were registering the significance of the question. Then with a quick gesture he popped the trolley back onto the table. "Ten crowns," he announced.

"Ten crowns?" It seemed to Ladislav too good to be true.

"It's a bargain," Jacob said, with relief.

"I'll take it," Ladislav hurriedly added.

Prokop did not watch him take it but merely folded his arms and leaned forward over the table. Ladislav forgot the others in his admiration of the cleverly bent tin of the trolley's steps, benches, and pillars. Prokop waited, aware that Ladislav had twenty crowns left and that Anežka's doll remained unbought.

Anežka had seated the doll on the table before her and had brought her own body flush with the edge of the table to support its back, which was curved forward by the pull of its heavy, drooping head. It smiled its consistent smile. Anežka leaned her own head forward to speak some words of advice into its ear.

Prokop cleared his throat and looked meaningfully at the doll.

"What is it?" Ladislav dutifully asked, sensing that justice had to be done.

For the moment Anežka was pleased by Ladislav's attention. "It is Květa," she told him. She was remembering, Jacob realized, the lesson about greetings and introductions.

Ladislav paused, but Prokop, with his eyes, demanded that he continue. "How much is . . . she?" Ladislav asked.

Oh dear, a slave market, Jacob thought. Anežka was nonplussed.

"How much?"

—But I refuse! Anežka said, in Czech.

"You could set a high price," Jacob suggested. "You could say a thousand crowns, or ten thousand crowns."

—But I refuse altogether! she declared, now with a quaver in her voice.

—You have to. It's the game, Prokop said.

—I don't have to. I won't.

"How much!" Prokop said, returning to English. He saw that it was the mere possibility of sale that unnerved his sister. "How much!"

"How about selling a pen instead?" Jacob proposed, drawing attention to his own and placing it, somewhat desperately, before her.

—But I don't want to! I refuse to!

—But you don't have to, Jacob assured her, lapsing into Czech himself in order to be sure that the message got through.

—But calm yourself, little Anežka, her mother said, and held the girl's shoulders. —In fact nothing is being bought and nothing is being sold. But the girl hugged her doll and would not meet their eyes.

"How much!" Prokop said, pointing at the lonely glove in front of Ladislav, who didn't know whether he should answer. "How much!" Prokop said again, a little more violently, pointing at his lost trolley. "How much!" he asked, still more loudly, of the paper bag of rice in front of Jacob. "How much, how much, how much!" He shook himself, full of a child's pleasant, dizzy hysteria.

—That suffices, his mother said.

"How much?" he asked once more, rebelliously, of the ten-crown note that he had been left with. He thought he was asking a nonsense question.

—That already suffices, Milena warned.

"That depends on your credit rating," Jacob answered.

"Wha-a-at?"

"Nothing. *Nic*," Jacob retracted the joke. But having aroused the boy's curiosity, he had to continue. —Money costs more money, he explained in Czech. —If I give you ten crowns today, then next week you must give me eleven.

"Jo?" Prokop responded, as he took this in. Then, with a show of make-believe anxiety, he pushed his note across the table to Jacob and signaled to Ladislav to do the same with his. Ladislav hurriedly complied. Their fluster was like that of silent-movie characters. It wasn't clear they understood. It seemed more likely that Jacob's explanation was interpreted as a sort of ruse—as a polite way of asking for the return of the bills. The lesson was drawing to a close. Jacob also collected the Warhol postcards, which had been left scattered on the table where they had fallen.

Milena retreated briefly to the kitchen and returned with a sheaf of ten- and twenty-crown bills. She counted his fee out onto the table with her habitual fumbling and overcaution, bill by bill. There it was, the accumulation they had been playing with, the disruptive element, purchasing him in the colors of mud and of berries. To Milena, there was nothing shameful in money, but Jacob was afraid that Prokop might cry out "How much!" or that Anežka would find a way to ask why, if he loved them, he had to be paid to visit. Because he had lost control of the children twice, he felt unsure that he deserved his full fee, a particular doubt that resonated with a deeper and more general one, less accessible to his conscious mind. Despite his sense of vulnerability, however, the children didn't cry out. They felt the reality of the transaction and respected it, retreating into themselves. Anežka petted and consoled Květa. Prokop, still fidgety, beat Ladislav at a game that resembled Rock Paper Scissors. Jacob shoved the cash into his wallet, which the many small bills fattened.

He bid good-bye to the oblivious children. Anežka, who had forgiven him, answered softly, sucking in her breath. Prokop, who had insulated himself with a force field of excitement, barked a cheerful farewell. At the edge of the table, the trolley lay unregarded, unclaimed. Prokop had not returned to it the way Anežka had returned to her doll. The thought of it stayed with Jacob as he walked up the dark street to wait for the bus. He told himself it would be absurd to feel guilty about it. It was normal for boys to outgrow such attachments, especially straight boys. In fact, the guilty thing would have been to teach Prokop to hold on to a doll, the way Anežka was doing, and as Jacob himself had often tried to when he was a child. A spark clinked in a street light overhead. All around him the night was mild and empty.

The friends decided to revisit the yellow-walled cellar in Malá Strana where they had given Michael a farewell party in the fall. According to Henry, it had grown a bit louche. The place was set up like a speakeasy,

Jacob remembered, as Henry led him, Annie, and Thom edgewise through the ground-floor restaurant to the stairwell at the rear. They descended into stale air, which Jacob wasn't immediately reconciled to breathing. German girls with angry eye shadow were sitting below the landing, blocking the narrow staircase, and the girls swore idly at the friends as they passed.

The bar and the unevenly plastered walls were unadorned, as before. Jacob thought he remembered that they had been playing tapes of jazz music in the fall, but weak speakers now emitted American punk—a thin gray stream of sound that the mutter and talk of the rooms easily broke through. To Jacob the room seemed vaguely menacing, and he felt self-conscious and detached, as if a bully were sizing him up; he felt the need to put up a bluff.

Henry volunteered to fetch drinks. Jacob, Annie, and Thom claimed a corner table. Someone had cut into the wall beside their seats the Czech word for *gypsies* and the German word for *out*. Tourists had written their names in ballpoint pen and then dated their inscriptions.

"Ehm, so, we're off to Krakow tomorrow fortnight," Annie announced, apropos of nothing.

"Are ye, then?" Thom replied.

"Mmm. Without the likes of you."

"And a pleasant journey to you."

"Just those of us who are romantically independent, you see," she explained.

"I may soon have a right to join ye," Thom said. "In a manner of speaking."

"Have you done wrong, then?" Annie asked.

"Or too much right, perhaps," he answered.

"You're a fool if you have," Annie accused him.

"So certain that I'm to blame!"

"You're such a lad," she said, disgustedly. She was smoking her cigarette fiercely, wincing against the smoke that she herself cast up.

Thom recognized a man coming down the stairs. "Did Henry invite that wanker?"

"Who?" Annie asked, swiveling to look. "Hans? Must have done."

"They're friends, I guess," Jacob offered, because he was afraid that Thom was upset for his sake.

Just as Hans reached them, Henry arrived with four glasses, pressed against one another like cells in a honeycomb. "I should have known to buy a spare," he apologized.

"Not at all. I shall—," Hans began.

But he was interrupted by the advent of Melinda, who appeared behind him, striding across the long room eagerly, her sharp cheekbones pink from her quick transition out of the brisk night into the windowless heat of the cellar. "Darlings," she saluted them. "What a relief. I was sure I had come down the wrong rabbit hole. I had no notion it had become so ropey here. Those vixens on the stairs—bloody hell . . ." She drew from her purse with one hand her cigarettes, lighter, and wallet, her fingers splayed separately open, at all angles like the blades of a Swiss army knife. "Does anyone else need a drink?" she asked.

"Allow me," said Hans. He refused the crowns that she was unfolding and, turning unexpectedly to Jacob, said, "I heard that you . . . that a friend of yours was lost to you. I was very sorry."

"Oh, it's all right, thank you," Jacob said, awkwardly. Seated securely among his friends, he had an uncharitable impression of Hans as a pudgy child who hoped the other children on the street would let him play with them.

Hans gave a slight bow and left them for the bar.

"That was decent of him," said Melinda.

"Is Carl coming?" he asked, softly.

"I was going to ask you."

"Say, have I shown you Sarah's photos?" Henry asked, producing a blue air mail envelope.

"What are they of?" Jacob asked.

"My daughter's birthday. Mel and Rafe found me a tricycle to send her."

"Rafe heard of a shipment coming into Bílá Labuť," Melinda explained.

She let the photos slip out of the envelope and held them by the edges. The little blond girl with Henry's wide eyes was sitting in a green garden under a canopy of pink crepe paper streamers.

Henry spoke shyly. "She looks pleased in the photos."

"Oh she does," Melinda assured him.

"This is Barcelona?" Thom asked, taking the photos one by one from Annie, who was taking them from Melinda.

"It's her fourth birthday." Henry's eyes remained on the pictures.

"She's a beautiful child, isn't she," Annie admired.

"With that Czechoslovak tricycle she'll be the envy of all the Barcelona youth," said Thom.

"It's a Polish tricycle, actually."

"Will you be getting a Polish tricycle, too, then Annie?" Thom asked.

"I may do," she replied. "All sorts of good things in Poland."

Hans returned and, with his feet, pulled out a chair opposite Melinda and Jacob. As he set down the beers that he had brought, Melinda drew back with the photos she still had, as if they were cards and she were afraid of revealing her hand.

"Pictures of Henry's child," she then said to Hans, by way of explanation.

"Ah, your scattered seed," he said. When no one laughed, he added, "Cheers," hurriedly, and sipped his beer.

"Cheers," Melinda answered, since she was closest, but she didn't touch her beer.

"What a thing to say," Annie muttered.

Hans either didn't hear Annie or pretended not to.

Annie turned to Jacob. "I've been meaning to ask you, have you ever heard this notion: life is an infection of matter, and spirit is an infection of life? Is that a thing that people think?"

"I've never heard it before."

"Is that from your Thomas Mann?" Melinda asked.

"I find it rather a peculiar idea," Annie admitted. "Even to me it didn't quite sound like proper biology."

"An old poofter, wasn't he," Thom commented.

"Do you think that comes into it?" Annie asked.

"It's part of a larger idea about death, I seem to vaguely recall," said Melinda.

"A cheerful sod," said Thom. "You tell me such things from that book, I don't know why you choose to read it."

"Oh, I find I get quite *lost* in it," Annie replied, with some enthusiasm.

"Nothing whatever happens for pages and pages, and one doesn't mind somehow. It's rather like the Dům, actually." There was a sudden brightness and openness in her looks, and even Henry, who had gathered up his photos and was storing them away, looked up to admire her.

"The Dům učitelů?" Melinda asked.

"I find. With each of us in our little rooms, like. And we have balconies."

"I hope you don't slip into one another's rooms across the balconies . . . ," Melinda suggested.

"Nothing like that." Annie was brought up short by Melinda's teasing. Then, on second thought, she smiled at the suggestion, it was so unlikely. "Gah, no, not at the Dům. The balconies are rather high, for one thing. Twenty-six stories . . .

"It was a friend in Berlin gave me the Mann," she volunteered to Jacob. "When you and I were there."

"I don't remember your getting a book."

"I didn't think at the time that I was going to read it."

They were nearing the end of their first round, which they always drank more quickly than those that followed, and which they hardly felt except in the way one feels the looseness in a boat that has been untied from its mooring but has not yet left it. A silence fell over them, a part of the rhythm of their conversation, and Jacob watched Annie absentmindedly tug the long sleeves of her sweater up around her fists, leaving out only a fork of two fingers to hold her cigarette. At the bar, a couple of Czech boys were half dancing to the almost inaudible punk rock, in the convulsive, somewhat self-parodying style appropriate to the genre. The dancing boys' bangs shook and tossed, obscuring their eyes. Perhaps there *were* good things in Krakow, Jacob thought. In any case Annie was right to want to make the most of their time here, which was never going to come back.

"Carl!" Henry cried out.

On the other side of the gray-yellow room, Carl shot up one of his hands in recognition.

"I have you and you and you," Carl said, when he reached them. "I don't have you and I don't have you."

"Have us how?" asked Hans, the last person indicated by Carl.

"As photographic subjects."

"I don't much fancy pictures of myself, you know," said Annie.

"That's silly."

"It isn't *silly.*" She wouldn't allow even her self-deprecation to be dismissed.

"There may not be enough light." Carl raised his little steel rangefinder to his face and squinted shut the eye it left free. "There's not, unless you don't move. Unless you don't so much as quiver."

Annie froze cooperatively. "Well, go on."

"It won't let me take an exposure."

She held herself in place a moment longer, anyway, her back arching slightly, her mouth neutral. Then he did manage to take a picture.

"Down and out in Prague and Krakow," Carl captioned.

"Do you really think so?"

"He doesn't think so," Melinda said, raising her eyes from the table for the first time since Carl's arrival.

"I mean the *ambience.*" His eyes drifted to Melinda's, but he and she were careful not to look at the same time.

"I need Jana, too," Carl said.

"I'll see what I can do," Thom offered, "but tonight I make no promises."

"I don't want promises. I want results. Speaking of which, I also want a beer. Anyone?"

The call for another round became general. Jacob rose to offer funds and carriage, and as he walked with Carl to the bar, his feet placing themselves in a path without his conscious design, he noticed that he was no longer standing apart from the room; he was no longer holding himself separate from his experience of it. He had become a part of its pattern, together with his friends, or perhaps it was the case that he and his friends had imposed a pattern of their own upon the establishment, or at least upon the corner of it that they had taken. He wondered if this feeling was what had come to take the place of what he had once been seeking. The feeling that they were exceptional together. It was their being together that was exceptional, rather than anything any of them did or might do. It wasn't necessary for anyone outside their group to recognize it; they were in that way independent.

He knew that the feeling wasn't rational. He didn't care. He was going to believe in it anyway. He carried drinks to the table and he returned to the bar, where Carl was paying, in order to explain it to him. He knew Carl wouldn't need to be persuaded. He knew Carl also felt it. He just wanted the pleasure of trying to articulate it to him. He wanted to say that they had all become somehow permanent to one another, that Carl was right—leaving didn't matter, leaving wasn't going to change the relation that they were all in with one another. Even Rafe and Kaspar, who weren't here tonight. The connection was going to outlast the time that they were going to share, and somehow they felt the afterlife of it now, while they were still together, almost as a physical thing, casting a retrospective aura, which they felt prospectively. And it was terribly sad, as it turned out, and something else, too—exhilarating, somehow, maybe because they hadn't lost one another quite yet—and he wouldn't even be trying to talk about it if he weren't drunk. They had become the world to one another, both those who had fallen in love and those who hadn't.

"Is that what I'm feeling?" Carl interrupted.

"Is what what you're feeling?"

"The future?"

Henry unbent himself from the table and came toward them. "What are the two of you conspiring?"

"Phenomenology," Carl told him, as usual somewhere between joking and not joking.

"Of?"

"That's harder to say."

"Often the case with phenomenology."

The straight men would turn it into mere thinking if Jacob let it get away from him. "I was trying to describe the feeling that you have when you want to keep someone with you," Jacob said.

"The feeling of wanting to stay with the one story," Henry glossed.

"Yes."

"I understood the three of us to be partisans of the other story," Henry countered.

"Are we?" Jacob asked.

"We're fellow rogues," Henry said.

"Rogues!" Carl echoed, appreciating the return of the word.

"To roguery!" Henry toasted. "And rodgery."

"To rodgery, anyway," Carl repeated, clinking his glass. "That's a *terrible* pun."

In the silences that naturally punctuated their conversations, Jacob sometimes found that he noticed Carl's presence in a way that he didn't when they were exchanging words, as if Carl's presence were lying under water by the side of their boat, like a man enchanted in a fairy tale, and became easier to see when they stopped rowing and the surface of the water went still. He noticed it now, not in any single detail—not in his beard or his eyes—but in the quality of his whole person and in its reality. It embarrassed Jacob to become aware of the fact and process of his observation, and he wondered if he was staring and embarrassing Carl. He saw, however, that Henry was looking at Carl just as fondly. Melinda was right; they were all taken with him.

"But even you must feel it sometimes," Carl accused Henry, resuming their talk. "In fact I know you do."

"Feel what?" Henry asked.

"The one-story feeling."

"Maybe."

"The way you miss Frieda," Carl pressed him.

Jacob was puzzled.

"My daughter," Henry explained. "It's different," he continued.

"Of course," Carl said. "I have no idea."

"Well," said Henry, tilting his head.

"Okay, true," Carl replied to what hadn't been spoken.

Henry looked away, and when he turned back to them, he caught Jacob's eye for a second, as if he were trying to measure the distance between the two of them, or to estimate how much Jacob had understood of his near-wordless exchange with Carl. Then he hid himself by taking a deep drink from his beer.

Melinda rose from the bench in the corner. As she approached the three of them across the empty center of the room, she fell into a comic swagger, a dame in a bar, play-acting so as to channel the attention that her beauty drew to her. "Has one of you blokes got a light?"

The straight men let Jacob come up with it. "Sure."

"'Sure, podner.'"

"Are you making fun of me?"

"Taking pleasure in the sound of your voice, rather. You say it so sweetly. Like an amiable cowboy." The straight men, during this banter, withdrew into private conversation.

"I'll rustle up your dogies if you aren't careful."

"Would you. No one else bloody will."

"Is Rafe coming tonight?"

"I'm a single girl tonight, and shall remain so."

Jacob sensed that she, like Henry, was hiding. She was standing next to Jacob so as to stand close to Carl, but she didn't want to engage Carl, didn't necessarily even want to oblige him to notice her. She made no gestures, struck no poses. It was more evident than usual how delicate she was, how slender and fine.

"It is funny about Krakow," she murmured. "My mind's quite made up about America. You know, about your mate going there for good and all. But somehow Krakow . . ."

"He's coming back from Krakow."

"Yes, it seems so *unnecessary*." She held Jacob with her eyes for a moment, as if she wanted him to take care not to glance in the direction of the person they were talking about. He felt the secret that they were sharing encircle and then isolate them. "He asked again what is to be *my* project, you know," she continued. "What is to be my story."

"What did you say?"

She hesitated. It was the same hesitation that she must have given to Carl when he had asked the question. She was repeating it; her mind was running again down the paths it had taken then in search of an answer, and failing again to find one, or anyway to find one that she was willing to speak aloud. "We had a terrible row. Didn't he tell you?"

"No."

"I said he oughtn't to make it harder than it has to be." She made an effort at laughing. "And that's what we've agreed to. Not to make it harder."

"That seems civilized."

"I don't know what he does with his days now."

"I thought he was still taking walks with you."

She shook her head. "It's just as well, really." She excused herself.

Jacob watched her cross the room again and slip behind the table into a seat next to Annie, who meanwhile swanned forward her neck so that her face tilted back and her red-blond hair fell clear and she could safely touch her cigarette to Melinda's for a light. There was something Melinda had needed to realize about herself, Jacob decided, something she had had to learn from Carl, or from the attraction that drew her to him, and having learned it, she was able now to let him go. Is that what Kaspar meant? The way one becomes willing to leave behind a notebook after a class is finished, though a mild attachment may linger because of the effort that went into taking the notes. Whereas if she had gone to bed with Carl, she would never have learned this thing, according to Kaspar's theory, and would never have become willing to give him up. What a cold way of looking at it. The coldness was an objection that Jacob would have to put to Kaspar. And what was the thing that she had learned? It made Jacob selfishly happy to think that they were going to get to keep Melinda now. Melinda wouldn't get to keep Carl, of course. None of them could. And come to think of it, Melinda herself might now have to go east with Rafe, and then they wouldn't get to keep her, either. In that case, what did he mean by thinking they could "keep" her? Perhaps he meant that they would somehow be able now to keep her in memory as she had been—that there was an idea of her that they wouldn't have to give up. That was cold, too. What was this idea of her?

And what—again—was the thing she had learned? It had to be a kind of knowledge that one could come to about oneself. . . . Here his reasoning, such as it was, again broke off, because he looked up and was distracted by the observation that he had been left alone. Carl was playing pool with Thom in the next room. The women were talking to each other in the corner, guarding the men's coats and bags and ignoring Hans beside them. At the bar, to Jacob's right, Henry was saying something in demotic Czech to a burly man in a sweat-stained T-shirt, who was laughing at him. Jacob's friends were all near, but Jacob was on his own.

He fell again into the game of thinking about time. A year ago he had been in America, he recited to himself; two years ago he had been straight. Where would he be a year from now? It was a melodramatic question but he was young and he liked the way it singled him out. It froze the scene around him into a tableau, comparable with other tableaux, remembered or projected, as if he were in motion and it wasn't— or as if he were changeless while it changed.

"Do you ever think," he asked Henry, who was nearest, "a year ago I was here, and now I'm here?"

"Yes," Henry answered, turning away from the Czech man beside him.

"And will it always be like that?"

"Will you always be wandering?"

"I guess. I mean, will there always be that break?"

"That break?"

"You're free but you're cut free." Tonight the freedom excited him, like an engine that revs fiercely because it has been cut loose from what it was towing.

"Your roguery," said Henry, seeming by his look to catch the feeling that had come over Jacob.

"Mine? Maybe."

"Your American liberty."

"Is that it?"

"There's something else, isn't there, something against it. To keep us here on the eve of beauty." Henry's eyes were suddenly strange. "To keep us here on the eve of beauty," he repeated.

"What do you mean?"

"A phrase in me head. Does that happen to you ever? A phrase runs through my head, and I decide to say it aloud." Henry had gone stiff with energy, the way little Prokop had during the marketing game. He was quivering; he was holding himself in place willfully, like a hummingbird.

"Sometimes," Jacob said.

"I suppose it's how one writes," Henry said. "By abandonment."

"Really?" Jacob was cautious.

"By ecstasy." He said it as if he were tempting Jacob, who didn't know what to make of what he said, or the tone in which he said it. It wasn't how Jacob did his writing.

"I want to—," Henry began to say, but without finishing, he walked off to the pool table. It was as if they had been swimming. If one tries to talk while dog-paddling, breathing sometimes becomes more urgent than talking and the conversation is broken off, and it isn't to be understood as rudeness.

In the corner, Jacob challenged himself to sit down beside Hans. "How are you?" Jacob said, a little too loudly.

Hans appraised him. Jacob watched the movements of the blue eyes studying him. "Well, thank you," Hans answered.

"You're from . . . Denmark, aren't you?" Jacob asked.

Hans's nationality was a fact already established between them, and Jacob was surprised to hear himself speaking about it as if he didn't remember. Perhaps he wanted to pretend that he didn't remember much about his earlier conversation with Hans. Or perhaps he thought he would be safer if Hans took him for the kind of American whom it would be a waste of time to be disappointed in. "Yes," Hans answered carefully. He seemed to be afraid that he had a drunk on his hands.

"Kierkegaard was Danish, wasn't he?"

"Are you a partisan of his?"

"I've only read a little."

"Too Christian for me."

Golden hair on marble skin—Hans was like a sugar cookie, Jacob thought. "I had a friend who was very Christian," Jacob explained. "Almost mystical. So the way Kierkegaard thinks it all through. . . ." It had been a small triumph for Jacob. Daniel had wanted to hear more and in the end had taken one of Jacob's paperbacks, thereby acknowledging that it was Jacob for once who had discovered something they could share.

"Was this your friend who . . . ?"

"No, she had been Christian, kind of an extreme denomination, but she wasn't any more, when I knew her. I guess she was in what Kierkegaard would have called despair, which he considers an improvement over *not* being in despair, but still." He was trying to charm Hans as he had charmed Daniel.

"It is usually Andersen whom people ask after."

"Who?"

"The writer of fairy tales. He also was a strange one."

A strange one. A queer, he meant. "What a funny pantheon," Jacob said.

Hans grimaced, to communicate that the insult wasn't new to him. A Marxist was supposed to be superior to national heroics, but as a child, someone like Hans must have read about heroes, or he would not have grown up with the ambition to save the poor and overthrow tyrants.

"Did you ever read—I read this book as a child, a sort of fairy tale, and I've never been able to remember the title of it," Jacob said. "About two boys who die and go to another world, a beautiful valley. But there's a war in the valley, and at the end of the book they die again, and go to yet another world. I remember thinking as I read it, I can't tell my parents, or they'll take it away from me."

Hans looked at him oddly; he had gone still. "It isn't Danish," he said slowly. "It is by a Swedish author." He hesitated, as if he were afraid despite Jacob's confession that Jacob was still playing the role of drunk American and might mock him or the book. "It is called *Bröderna Lejonhjärta*," he said at last.

"*The Brothers Lionheart*," Jacob echoed.

"Yes." Love for the book lay suddenly between them, an awkward intimacy.

"What was it about?" Jacob said. "It was a strange story."

"Yes, very strange," Hans agreed.

"At the time I felt I shouldn't talk about it."

"It is perhaps, because, do you remember, in order to reach the other world, they . . ."

"Oh, that's right," Jacob said, recalling. The two boys jump together to their deaths, so as not to be parted.

The roar of talk in the bar continued for a little while without Jacob or Hans. "I suppose perhaps it is that," Hans said.

"It was a lovely book," Jacob declared, to commit himself.

Hans agreed. Their enemy was the idea that such a book shouldn't fall into the hands of children. Jacob hadn't expect to form a bond of any kind with Hans, let alone this one, but there was nothing that either of them could do about it now. They sat together silently. Annie rose to fetch another round. Together they watched her cross the room, and they watched her at the bar as several times she composed herself in preparation for addressing the barman, pressing forward on tiptoes, only to be ignored by him and sink back onto her heels. Henry left the pool players, apparently to assist her, and they watched him signal to the bartender with a practiced flip of two fingers of his right hand and then confer with Annie about the order. As the small dumb show seemed to end, Hans and Jacob looked down together at the unfinished beers between them. Jacob wondered if it was part of the charm of their circle that the name of the book had been given back to him. Or maybe it was just Hans; maybe it was Hans's nature as a missionary, as a believer, that had called up Jacob's memory of the book. And maybe that was the cause of the awkwardness that they were now sitting in. They had both loved the book, but Jacob must have loved it because he had recognized in it a story about his own nature (because Jacob had no brother, the idea of a brother was just a metaphor to him). Hans, however, didn't have that nature. Jacob had heard him boast about women the same way he boasted about his paramilitary adventures—with enthusiasm, callousness, and an indeterminable amount of fiction.

"I hope you're pleased with yourself, anyway," came abruptly Annie's voice, addressing Jacob in sharp tones. She was standing over them, though they hadn't seen her approach. "You must be quite pleased, I fancy. I might have known, is the thing. Given what you are."

"What?" Jacob asked.

"Oh, don't pretend. Not to me. Sod off. As it were."

She turned and strode away, across the room, past the bar, up the stairs.

"What was that about?" Jacob asked.

"I ought to go to her," Melinda said. She began to gather her things into her purse.

Thom and Carl, as their pool game was ending, had noticed Annie's departure and now came over. "Is something troubling Annie?" Thom asked.

"She made the most astonishing speech," Hans declared. "To Jacob, about 'what he is.'"

"I suspect it's to do with Henry, somehow," said Melinda, swinging on her coat.

"Is she on about that again," Thom replied.

"I don't see how it could be Henry," Hans said. He was enjoying his role as witness; Jacob wished he would be quiet. "She was angry quite particularly with Jacob."

"Does she think you said something to Henry?" Carl suggested.

"I didn't."

Jacob followed Melinda across the room unthinkingly. At the foot of the stairs Melinda turned and put a palm on his forearm. "I recommend you let me sound her a bit first."

He stopped halfway back, at the bar, where Henry was standing. "Annie's furious at me," he told Henry.

"Is she?" Henry didn't seem to care. "I have a question to ask you."

"Okay," Jacob agreed. He was willing to be distracted.

"Do you fancy me?"

Jacob's first thought was that he had to be careful. "What do you mean?" He looked from one of Henry's wild eyes to the other. He saw that Henry was still shivering and taut with strange energy.

"Would you fancy a shag?"

"Is that like a scrum?"

"It could be."

"I'm learning all the words," Jacob said. None of what was between any of them was going to last, he saw, and this was the way the loss was dawning on them.

"If not, I know how it is." As a gentleman, Henry was careful to leave Jacob a way to refuse him.

"Did you say anything to Annie?" it occurred to Jacob to ask.

"I may have done."

"She's upset."

"Is she? Oh, I see."

There was a reproof in Henry's casual cruelty. If he and Jacob were to be lovers, then as lovers they shouldn't reckon the consequences. The principle in his unconcern amounted almost to chivalry. Jacob, however, couldn't help knowing that if he went to bed with Henry, Annie would never speak to him again. Still, he thought he was able to meet Henry on his ground—he thought that if he refused Henry, he would not be conscious of giving anything up, of making any sacrifice. There had been no touch between him and Henry, no feeling of overture. Jacob imagined that in bed Henry would be violent, not because he would want to hurt Jacob but because violence would belong to his idea of what it was, of what the thing was that he thought that he wanted with Jacob—the idea of working against the part of his nature that wanted to feel itself brought home. Henry was straight—even straighter than Carl, in Jacob's estimation. It was the being wanted for the sake of the impossibility that Jacob objected to.

"I don't think so," Jacob said.

"No, I thought as much," Henry said. "It's like that, isn't it. Either you're interested or you're not, if you're a bloke."

Having said no, Jacob could no longer see a reason for his refusal. They were all going to lose one another.

Melinda came quickly down the stairs, and as Jacob turned to hear her news, Henry excused himself.

"I'm taking Annie to the Dům," Melinda said. "I'm so sorry about this."

"Why are *you* apologizing?"

"I said to Henry the other day I thought you'd be good for a snog. How was I to know that he would consult Annie of all people?"

"A what?"

"Jesus. 'Kissing.' How you Americans can bear to speak with such shameless clarity. . . . I should have thought of Annie but I didn't."

It was painful, as Carl, Thom, and Jacob left the building, to have to walk past Annie, who had not been able to bring herself to leave, despite Melinda's coaxing, but was twisting against a brick wall outside.

"She's in a bad way," said Thom. "I hope it's no more than a broken heart."

Not having anyone had been Jacob's way of keeping them all—it had been five months, he realized, since he had gone to bed with anyone—and now he was losing them anyway, without being ready to. As the tram pulled away, he could not help but watch Annie through the window. She was still twisting restlessly, though now in Melinda's arms.

The next morning, Jacob heard voices; someone was in Carl's room. With a sturdy knock, the person strode into Jacob's, and Jacob fumblingly armed himself with his glasses. It was Honza, the plumber. He held a bottle without a label; shot glasses thimbled his fingers. His shirt was unbuttoned, exposing a modest pot belly; beneath that, he was wearing a sagging, yellowing pair of underwear and gray socks. A disheveled elf. He must have crept in the back way, through the door that communicated between their rooms and his.

—You must toast me, the plumber said, pouring a clear liquid and approaching Jacob, who propped himself up in his makeshift bed and accepted the drink helplessly. —I am ———, Honza said. Jacob didn't recognize the verb. The root was the word for "woman"; the form was reflexive. Turning into a woman? Honza's eyes were red and rheumy; he had evidently been drinking all night. He was nodding at Jacob with a somewhat desperate smile.

—You are . . . , Jacob echoed, puzzledly.

—Today is wedding, Honza said.

—You're getting married, Jacob at last understood. He was *taking* a woman. —And what is this? Jacob asked, raising his glass.

—It is homemade.

—I already have a hangover, Jacob objected.

—So for you it is all one! Honza encouraged.

Jacob drank.

"It's Everclear," said Carl, from the doorway, wearing his blanket and holding an empty glass. "Homemade Everclear. We've been poisoned." To Honza, he added, cheerily, "It's *great!* Congratulations!"

Honza eagerly refilled Carl's glass, his own, and Jacob's. "Oh god," Carl groaned. "Not again, no, please."

Honza was chattering manically, faster than Jacob could altogether understand. He was getting married, no man should do such a thing without drinking himself blind, it was the duty of comrades to become equally drunk. The still that he had inherited from his mother was the most potent in Moravia, and it was always a treat to have a taste of such a liquor, at any hour of the day or night.

Jacob compliantly raised his glass a second time but only pretended to sip. Carl tried the same ruse.

—No, no, boys! Honza protested. —Drink it all at once, so it smashes you.

—I'm drinking, Jacob lied. He had to teach at the language school in a couple of hours.

—Honza, where'd you go? a woman's voice called from the room at the other end of the floor. Jacob hadn't realized that the plumbing there now ran well enough for a woman to spend the night, or that Mr. Stehlík had been willing to grant Honza permission to have a woman there. Of course, if Honza were marrying today, Mr. Stehlík could hardly forbid him his bride-to-be. —Honza, where are you? the woman called again.

"You're in trouble now," said Carl.

—I'm with the boys! I'm coming! caroled Honza. Then he pointed to the ceiling and grimaced, abashed and entertained by the thought that his bride's questions and his own answers might have been audible to the Stehlíks. He shrugged and padded back to his room.

"So much for today," Carl said.

Because Carl had no plans, he ceded the shower to Jacob. In the bathroom, after Jacob had stripped, he hunched over the tub, waiting for the water to warm before he plugged the drain. Because of his nakedness and his awkward posture, he was acutely aware of the jitters that Honza's liquor, coming on top of his hangover, had given him. His toes were so numb from the cold tiles that as he stepped gingerly into the tub he could not at first gauge the temperature of the water. He crouched, pointing the nozzle at his toes, which reddened in the heat. Then he held the nozzle over a shoulder so that the water fell on the nape of his neck, where, he had once read, young animals find it soothing to be seized, because their parents hold them by it in the wild. He made an effort to relax into the loss of control that the drink had forced on him. He kept his eyes closed. He didn't think Henry would want to talk about what had happened between them, but he would have to talk about it with Annie.

The rooms were still cold, and Jacob dressed quickly. Still draped in his blanket, Carl sat reading an old magazine at the kitchen table, and Jacob set out two plates, the foil of butter, and a jar of apricot preserves. Their store of *rohlíky* had staled, but they were still soft enough to be torn open. Jacob brewed tea.

"What are you going to do today?" Jacob asked.

Carl shrugged. "Be in Prague."

"What does that entail lately?"

Carl looked at Jacob apologetically. "It's so trite."

"What is?"

"I go to places we went together. Yesterday I went to Vyšehrad. Don't tell her, please."

"I won't."

"There's still snow under the trees up there. I'll forget her once I'm back in America."

Jacob didn't reply.

"I only have a few more weeks here," Carl added. "I think about that when I'm tempted to break form."

Maybe Jacob would give up Carl's bedroom after Carl left. Honza might want to rent it. As if cued by this unvoiced possibility, Honza, with a strange, silent, speed-walking gait, stole back into their rooms, darted through the kitchen, and vanished into the bathroom. Through the closed bathroom door, the friends heard him retching. Evidently the plumbing wasn't fully operational yet on Honza's side of the floor after all.

After a minute had gone by, Jacob tapped lightly on the bathroom door. Honza opened it quickly. —Silence, Honza whispered. —They're outside.

—Do you want water? Jacob asked. —Milk? Bread?

—No, no, Honza answered. Despite his haste, he had thought to bring a comb, and he now wetted it under the faucet and combed his short hair. —But water, yeah. That will doctor me perhaps. If it isn't a bother.

—Not at all, said Jacob.

Jacob brought Honza a glass of water and then packed his own satchel. He wished Honza luck. Before leaving, he mimed a warning that he was about to open the door. "See you, Carl," he then added, audibly.

In the corridor outside, the Stehlíks were grouped around Honza's door, waiting for Honza to emerge. The opening of Jacob's door startled them. Standing with the Stehlíks was a tall, buxom woman in her thirties with dyed blond hair. Since the only hair dye regularly available in former Warsaw Pact nations was an unnatural henna, a bottle blonde was a woman with connections. Her clothes were loud, and she looked as if she was enjoying an enormous joke. The Stehlíks were dressed nicely—the women in white blouses and skirts, Mr. Stehlík in a thick-braided cardigan sweater—and their smiles were nervous. The service was going to take place at the offices of the District National Committee, Běta explained.

—Have yourselves a pretty time, Jacob wished them.

—Definitely, Běta with mocking gravity replied, answering for the group, who then turned away to stare again at Honza's door.

Melinda caught Jacob on his way to the teacher's lounge and pulled him into the unused shower where they smoked. He still felt light-headed from Honza's moonshine.

"You handle your liquor so well," she assured him. "You have the makings of a great alcoholic."

"Except for that incident at the Jazz Club."

"I'd forgotten. That is a spot on your record, isn't it."

Against the rules of the Dům učitelů, Melinda had spent the night in Annie's room. The two women had been yelled at the next morning by one of the house matrons—overnight guests were not allowed unless they had been registered twenty-four hours in advance—but Melinda had seen Annie through the worst of her anguish. In the sober light of morning, Annie felt sheepish about her attack on Jacob. By way of mending fences, she had thought of showing Jacob a new foreign-language bookstore in Wenceslas Square, which had just opened in a glass-front emporium vacated by some dying socialist agency or other. The store had hundreds of brand-new paperbacks in English—the whole thing seemed to have been arranged by a British publisher. She would be there at three that afternoon, if Jacob was willing to meet her.

When Jacob arrived, he found a classic First Republic shop that didn't seem to have been altered since the 1930s. Three shop assistants in white aprons stood behind the counter, protected from visitors. The counter and the shelves behind the shop assistants were empty; the books lay flat on tables in the center of the store. There weren't enough to cover the tables completely, but Jacob hadn't seen so many English-language books for sale since Berlin. Greed made him light-headed. But the prices! In most Prague bookstores, prices were written in black ink on slips of cardboard, tucked into the books like bookmarks. There were no such bookmarks here, for some reason. Instead, when Jacob picked up a paperback *Oliver Twist*, he found a three-digit number penciled on the inside back cover. So many crowns could buy more than a dozen restaurant dinners—the cost of a single book was almost equivalent to a week of the salary that he had received when he worked full time at the language school. It was the London price, calculated at the official exchange rate with no discount. "You found it, did you," Annie said upon arrival.

"It's so expensive," Jacob complained.

"Is it? Oh, I had been thinking you might like it here, you see."

"I do like it," Jacob said. He let himself open a Henry James novel. As he handled it, he sensed the unease of one of the shop assistants, who was watching him. It's just a paperback, he thought scornfully.

"Gah, they are dear, aren't they."

They toured the room separately for a while. Jacob fell into a reverie of imaginary possession; he was visiting the books in his future library; they were prisoners he could not yet free. He settled on *Morte d'Arthur*. He could afford only the first volume, which cost half his share of a month's rent, and then only if Annie could spot him two hundred crowns. He promised to repay her tomorrow out of the stash that he kept in his Bible.

"Ehm, we don't *have* to talk about the other," Annie said. "I don't want to know, really."

"Nothing happened. I said no."

"It would be all right if you had said yes, but I wouldn't want to know is all, you see."

"Nothing happened."

"He told me he was going to ask you, as if he and I were best mates, like."

"I'm sorry."

"I'm not in love with him. Perhaps I do fancy him but what of it. I'm not in love."

"Neither am I."

"If I had thought you were, I shouldn't have minded. Quite honestly. It was the waste of it that galled me. That, and that it was in poor taste, his telling me. Don't you think it was?"

"He was going through something," Jacob answered, feeling some loyalty to Henry, after all.

"I suppose." She saw that she was still holding the Malory, which Jacob had given her to admire, and she handed it back to him. "I shouldn't have spoken to you as I did. I do know that."

"You were upset," Jacob said.

"I would be miserable if we fell out over it."

"We're going to Krakow, aren't we?"

"Are we? I didn't like to ask."

"Of course we are," Jacob said.

"And Carl, too?"

"He doesn't know about any of this."

"Not very perceptive of him."

"He was 'pissed,' as you call it. He only has a couple more weeks here, and he wants to see Krakow."

Annie's thoughts turned to the trip. "All of us with broken hearts," she said, beginning to believe again that they would go. "Or breaking ones. I wouldn't tell him, if I were you."

"I'm not going to."

"Not for my sake, mind you. It's just that I don't imagine Henry would wish for Carl to know."

Jacob agreed.

"It is a flaw in my picture, isn't it," she continued, "that the one who broke my heart wanted to go to bed with you."

"No, because it wouldn't have meant anything if it had happened."

"As men always say. But I won't believe it. That would be worse somehow."

The morning of their departure, it was warm enough to open a window, and into the heater-dried air of Jacob's bedroom fell a column of spring's breath, wet with melting snow and the rot of last year's leaf mold. Carl was not yet awake, and Jacob stood for a while at the window. The touch of the breath was ambiguous, like teeth drawn lightly over skin.

Opening his large backpack, long unused, Jacob found three of his short-sleeved shirts, which he had stored there in November because they had collars and could not be worn as undershirts. A mustard paisley, a solid navy blue, and a field of orange-and-pink flowers. They reminded him of versions of himself that he had almost forgotten, less cautious and less retiring versions. He would be able to put them on again so long as he set about it with a measure of irony. He packed them along with a couple of long-sleeved shirts.

In the kitchen, as he drank his tea, he listened to water trickling through pipes to the other side of the house, where Honza and his bride were now established. He could feel but not quite hear the muffled percussion of their footfalls on carpet. Honza's step was light, but his wife's was resonant, though she wasn't a heavy woman. Jacob was quickly getting used to hearing the slap of her slippers on the cement stairs, going to and from the Stehlíks' shower every other evening. Mr. Stehlík had determined that the plumber and his wife were to share his family's shower rather than Jacob and Carl's. Běta no longer borrowed the occasional shower from them either, and Jacob imagined that the scheduling upstairs must have become fairly martial. Běta had promised to look in on Václav while they were away, but Jacob now put down extra food and water in his cage just in case.

"Are you psyched?" Carl asked, after he had showered and dressed. He slumped his backpack on the floor next to the pantry.

"I hope Annie doesn't have unreasonable expectations."

"You patched up your little tiff, didn't you?"

"Oh yeah," Jacob said. "It's just, I don't want her to be disappointed."

"When the geographic cure doesn't take."

"Something like that."

"I think she knows it's just a weekend," Carl said. "Anyway, it's supposed to be scenic."

"Auschwitz?"

"Renowned for the charm of its architecture. I thought we weren't going there."

"I don't know. Annie really wants to."

They had agreed to meet her at the central post office on Jindřišská, a block from Wenceslas Square, where Annie wanted to check the *poste restante* once more before they left town. The building, a late Hapsburg monument, stolid and practical, sat close to the street, and its entrance was so narrow and so heavily trafficked that it was only after entering that one arrived at a sense of it. As in a fairy tale, the cavernous central hall, once one stood inside, seemed larger than the palace that contained it. Strangers who had walked in at one's side fell away; the echoing marble floor emptied. Street lamps lit the hall with yellow rays that cut into blue shadows, flattening what they exposed, reversing day for night as well as inside for outside. And far above, in obscurity, hung a dead skylight, whose dust-colored panes had been boarded over on the outside, no doubt long ago. Indented from the far wall, a wooden frame rose a few yards into the air. It held the service windows. It left undivided the bulk of the dim, unlit volume above, the way a rood screen, pointing upward, leaves the core of a cathedral intact. The room was too large to heat, and Jacob and Carl found Annie, tiny at the foot of a wall, blowing into the fingers of her knitted gloves.

"If it's any trouble, I can come back Friday week, I don't mind," Annie offered. "It's just that come the end of the month, they move the old letters into a cabinet, and I haven't stopped in for weeks now. It's miserable to have to ask the *paní* there to check the cabinet. She has a sigh that stops your heart."

"We'll all check, then," Carl suggested.

They waited together, silenced and made nervous by the hall's artificial dusk. To their surprise, both Carl and Annie had letters waiting. Annie's was from Berlin. She said she would read it later, in the car, because it was bound to be bad news. "Anyone with good news would know to write me at the Dům."

Carl's was from Boston. "Oh, this woman I went on a few dates with."

"You haven't mentioned her before," said Jacob. He felt jealous of Carl for having a social world in America to go back to. In recent letters, his own friends had let him know that they were scattering. Daniel was reported to have taken a job as an editor in Washington.

"No, well."

"You sound quite Czech when you say that," Annie commented.

"No jo," Carl clowned. The Czech phrase was a melancholy way of admitting to something.

They rode the subway north to Holešovice, a neighborhood of soot-stained brick workers' residences from the late nineteenth century, coarse and unremarkable. They walked the perimeter of the neighborhood's train station, where new tricolor billboards amalgamated the flags of Czechoslovakia, the United States, and Great Britain in order to suggest that expatriates gambled in a nearby casino. There were also several signs for massage parlors. The rental-car agency was in the corner of a bus station behind the train station; it borrowed parking space that the buses didn't use. A young woman and a young man, who seemed to be sister and brother, checked a car out to them. Unexpectedly, the paperwork was brief.

"My god, they trust us," Carl crowed, as soon as they were inside the car, a white compact Škoda with black seats.

Annie excitedly hushed him.

"Did we even give them a credit card?"

"They have the numbers of our long-stay visas," Annie said. "And the address of Jacob's and my employer."

"But this car is worth, what, as much as the two of you would make in five years? And there's no collateral. They gave *us* the collateral."

"We're driving capital," Jacob said. He was taking the first turn behind the wheel. He started the ignition and eased it into the street. "In order to jump-start capitalism, they have to give the capital away."

"For goodness' sake it's a Škoda," Annie said. She waved responsibly through the near windshield to the brother and sister. "Na shledanou!" she said brightly but no doubt too quietly for the proprietors to hear through the glass and the now-growing distance.

"What if we sell it?" Carl asked.

"We will do no such thing," said Annie.

"But we're going to *Poland.*"

"Perhaps we shall sell it, then, if you're so keen. For blue jeans and what not."

"Excellent."

Prague's one-way streets soon turned the friends around, and they had to pull over and consult their maps. Jacob had brought two: a large green one of Czechoslovakia's countryside, and a large orange-and-purple one of Poland's. Across his lap, Carl unfolded them, as well as Jacob's blue city map, which from long wear in Jacob's back pocket was now softly disintegrating into tall strips. By comparison of the unwieldy, loud-wrinkling layers, they plotted a course. With Carl navigating, they crossed a bridge, drove down the hill where Jacob and Annie's language school stood, and then turned east, along the tram tracks that Jacob and Carl rode home every evening. They passed the hospital Jacob had visited. Half a block from the Stehlíks', they reached the highway, and in a few minutes, the last *panelák* was behind them and abruptly they were among cultivated fields, methodically furrowed and just beginning to sprout pale green.

Jacob cracked his window. Annie, in the back seat, took out her letter, and Carl, without saying anything, took out his. They were getting away with driving a car to Krakow, unwatched, unregulated. Jacob had the company of Carl and Annie, his ironic friend and his earnest one, and the three of them had the solidarity of their mistreatment by the god of love. The highway was for the most part empty; between villages it was so empty that they might have been the last people still living in the world. The only challenge was not to drive so fast that the curves became unsafe; there was no one to hit or be hit by. Maybe he wanted nothing more than to be away for a little while from the burden of living in another country, to return to the insouciance of merely visiting, of mere tourism; maybe he wanted to slip away for a while from the inchoate duty he had set himself of finding the spirit of change, if that was indeed the name of the spirit he was pursuing.

A few hours outside Prague, the three climbed into a massive concrete hammer and sickle that they found beside the highway, a memorial to the Soviet Union's defeat of Hitler, and Carl took snapshots. When they took a wrong turn near the border, they were frightened by a smoggy valley, where fire spouted from black chimneys and long milky puddles lay like mirrors in a landscape of pale, clean-looking clay, free of life.

A few days later, in Krakow's main square, the afternoon was mild and Jacob offered to pay the cover at an outdoor café. He owed his friends a treat for the day before. He had started off well at Auschwitz, but at Birkenau he hadn't been willing to get out of the car.

They chose a table with a parasol, which sheltered their faces but let the sun fall on their hands. To read the menu, Annie perched her sunglasses in her hair. They were in sight of the basilica and grand stone market hall. Though the aura of Krakow was medieval, the city was full of young people—students at its university and seminary. Jacob wondered when the Communists in Poland had so relaxed as to allow a seminary. From the glimpses the friends had had, as they passed the seminary's plain yellow buildings, the solemn older gentlemen in robes and the teenage pupils with lowered eyes seemed well established in their forms, as if the seminary had been running for years, but perhaps they only seemed that way to outsiders; maybe the men had found refuge behind the walls as recently as last year. The city's university students showed no such formality, of course, in their dress and manners. Many of the clothes they wore were new to Jacob. The buses, garbage cans, and many canned goods in Krakow were identical to Prague's, but the market economy had touched young people's wardrobes. A few even wore T-shirts with English-language mottoes boasting about the city's university. In Prague, too, such T-shirts existed, but only tourists bought or wore them. For some reason Czechs never wore T-shirts as outer garments.

Carl's voice interrupted Jacob's thoughts: "I thought it would be easier in Krakow to be away from Melinda. Can I say that?"

"You can say anything," Jacob assured him.

"I can, can't I," Carl said, "because I'm going home soon. I have to take advantage of irresponsibility while I still can."

Jacob looked back out into the open square. "Have you met your quota? Have you been irresponsible enough?"

"To last a lifetime."

"I don't know. People had expectations."

"I never live up to expectations. That's my charm."

"May I ask," said Annie, "why you thought it would be easier?"

"In Prague, it takes willpower not to see her, and in Krakow it doesn't. Now I miss her *and* I miss the struggle to not go see her."

"I see, yes."

"There's nothing in the way. Nothing in me in the way."

"But if you're going home," Annie suggested.

"Oh, that's in the way."

"I don't see why," Jacob objected. He didn't want them to talk about the problem too solemnly. "According to your own theory, it shouldn't matter what comes next."

Annie frowned. "What theory is this?"

"This idea that I had," Carl replied. "That the meaning of a relationship can't come from anything but the experience of it. That it only exists in the present tense."

"Independent of consequences," Jacob contributed.

"Mmm."

"The problem is that in the present you do think about the future," Carl said. "You even care about it. For example, I want to try not to *ask*

Melinda to see me again." His tone suggested that he didn't necessarily take his pose of sacrifice at face value; he left open the possibility that he thought it was a sophisticated mistake. "Maybe what comes next wouldn't have mattered two months ago," he continued. "When I thought I had come to Europe to sow my wild oats or whatever. Before I knew her. Or any of you. Before I got to know Rafe, for god's sake."

"I see," Jacob said.

"It would be different if I could say, 'Come back with me to New York, where I work as an investment banker and live in a loft and can take you to the opera every week.'"

"That would be so violent," Jacob said.

"But I wouldn't sense that, if I were that person."

"You're a person who's open to sensing things," said Jacob.

"That's a generous way of putting it. And I'm going back to a room in Somerville and a part-time job as an English teacher."

"If you look at it that way, all of us here are nothing."

"But not *while* you're here, is the thing," Carl said.

They sipped their sour coffees. Wind beat on the canvas of the parasol above them, so that the pole and metal table trembled and the cups shivered in their saucers. Jacob wanted to believe that he was staying for some purpose other than mere postponement—for some reason other than a reluctance to face up to what his native country would allow him to be. He accepted that he was losing time. He might never catch up, but maybe the delay itself was somehow a part of who he was going to be.

"You sort of have to go to Auschwitz without thinking about it ahead of time, don't you," Carl said, thinking back to the day before. "Otherwise no one would ever go."

"I wanted to know what it was like," said Annie. "One goes to cemeteries, after all."

Sun glare was whitening the flagstones of the plaza. Carl was the first to remark on a crowd that seemed to be forming. "Is something going on?" he asked.

Young people were gathering in the square in twos and threes, not in any organized way and not in any great density. It would scarcely have been noticeable except that here and there a person was dressed a little oddly.

"Is that a—?" Jacob began but let his question falter because he couldn't think of a name for the costume he was looking at. The man he had noticed was wearing too many clothes, a few too many of which were decorative rather than practical—a scarf, a bandanna, a vest, some kind of leggings—but it was hard to say what the ensemble was intended to represent, if anything. Excess? Then Jacob saw a more identifiable outfit: "I think that man there is in drag."

With some reluctance Annie too turned in her chair to see.

"Can we go look?" Jacob asked.

They asked in German for their bill—their Czech was sometimes mistaken for Russian, and English wasn't understood—and left the café by stepping over a low rope into the square at large.

Annie lowered her sunglasses like a visor. Carl raised his rangefinder to his eye and as he walked toyed with the aperture ring to measure the light. Jacob by default led the way, though he felt himself to be more pulled than pulling—drawn into the square by discoveries he began to make there. Three young women in black, for example, had sewn gold stripes onto their blouses and had twisted in their hair wires wound with golden yarn. Bees. A man with a Roman nose, inspired perhaps by his nose, had put on a toga, combed his hair down flat like Caesar's, and then tied small-denomination zlotys, rendered nearly worthless by currency reform, to a rope that he wore for a belt, to the straps of his sandals, and to a wreath that he wore as a laurel, as if the zlotys were ribbons and he were—not Caesar—Diogenes? The man's friends came up and added zlotys to him. There were pirates. There was a sheik. Jacob's companions followed so cautiously and so slowly that Jacob from time to time found himself exposed in his admiration, smiling mutely and alone in front of a costumed Pole who seemed aware that he had put himself on display even to tourists yet by a certain disregard communicated that the display was not for any tourist's sake. Jacob felt a growing wish to establish between himself and the players before him grounds of commonality. He felt, that is, a general love, or anyway a hunger or a lust. But "Take pictures, take more pictures," his command to Carl, was all he could think to say as an expression of it. There were more than a few men in drag. One with permed hair, mascara, and freckles—the freckles were natural—glanced shyly down over his falsies when he caught Jacob watching him. Three men in ties and fedoras guarded with plastic guns a white Polish Fiat that they had painted with bullet holes and with the English words MAFIA and PROFESSIONALISTS. Most of the costumes were not so easy to unriddle. It was perhaps this vagueness of conception that left Annie unimpressed. "Rather loud," she observed, of a group of boys whose aspect suggested no particular idea. Some who were serving their compulsory military service seemed to be wearing merely their uniforms for the occasion. Others had no costumes at all but only a prop, and one such prop, carried by three men, was a large traditional Communist flag, gold hammer and sickle on a red ground, now evidently a sufficient signifier of irony in itself. Simple drunkenness signified as much for many more. It was a day of carnival, they learned from some other tourists, an annual ritual of the university.

The students began hollering. A man in a peasant's blouse and a peculiarly shapeless leather hat began to blow a slender antique clarion. No one paid attention to his call, nor did they heed the gestures of a young blond in a black robe and a cardboard miter who with mock solemnity and hauteur began to bless and to direct the crowd. The three bees grabbed hands and began to skip in a line. Other lines soon formed and began to cross through the crowd, zigging and zagging. Soon, too, there were circles, dancing around a piper or just to their own unself-conscious singing.

It was as if the friends had stumbled into a party that they hadn't been invited to.

A young man with deep-sunk eyes, his plaid flannel shirt half-unbuttoned, wildly drunk and in no disguise, began to march, fury and drunkenness cooperating in him to create a stately pace. He bellowed fiercely as he proceeded, punching first one fist into the air and then the other, sometimes both. At first, as with the trumpeter and the bishop, no one seemed to pay attention, but the rhythm of his steps, because slower, was decisive, and the bees began to trail him, shufflingly. Others in turn unseriously fell in with them. Half a dozen revelers climbed into a jeep, which had been parked on the square in anticipation, and starting its engine, they nosed it into the procession, too. On the back of the jeep was mounted a long white banner that looked at first glance like that of the workers' movement Solidarity, but instead of the word "Solidarność," the students had painted SEXUALNOŚĆ in the same iconic, bright red hand-lettering. Yet there was no trace of humor in the eyes of the young man at the head of the parade. His eyes didn't even focus. He had merely the all-hailing, impersonal belligerence of a drunk who needs to get into a fight. He trained his menace steadily outward, ahead of him, clearing a path.

He led the procession toward the north entrance of the great market hall. No clear distinction separated the parade from the crowd admiring it. One drew from the other—drew the other into it. So the friends, too, followed the leader of the parade.

"We're going inside," Jacob said as they approached the hall. It delighted him.

"Should we?" Annie asked.

As they passed under the arch of the doorway, the chants of the students began to gather and echo in the round vaults of the ceiling and the alcoves along the hall's long gallery. Having left the sunlight, they were blind for a few moments, and had for sensation only the echoes and the feel of staggering and jostling. As their eyes adjusted, the hall itself appeared: the ceilings painted with the emblems and heraldic crests of the city; gilt chandeliers, whose shape uncannily but not quite identifiably suggested an animal growth of bone or horn; and, obscured by the marchers themselves, the stalls of vendors, whose cheap goods, the usual off-brand Western cosmetics, English-language workbooks printed in China, and flimsy leather belts and purses, had disappointed the friends on a visit two days prior. They were harrowing the temple, Jacob thought. Was the word "harrowing" or "hallowing"? He couldn't remember. He turned to check on his friends and saw that Annie was slouching defensively.

"Are you all right?" he asked.

"Brilliant, thanks."

The light, as they emerged by the southern doors, washed out the sky, and the roar of the crowd, escaping the hall's confines, changed pitch, the way the roar in a whelk's shell rises and clarifies as you turn it away from your ear.

"Are you sure you're all right?"

"Would you please not ask me that so often?"

Carl trotted ahead so as to have a shot of the parade as it exited the market hall. Inside there hadn't been enough light to take pictures, but in the closeness he had caught some of the crowd's enthusiasm.

The parade left the great square by a southern street. Jacob and Annie trailed it on the sidewalk.

"I'm sorry about yesterday," Jacob said to Annie, when Carl had abandoned the two of them on one of his documentary missions.

"Yesterday?"

The parade had thinned as it stretched along the street, and in slow cycles it shouted to and was hailed by an audience lining the street.

"I wasn't ready to see it, but—"

"Gah, no," she cut him off. "It isn't that."

"You *are* angry, then."

She wouldn't meet his gaze. "Don't encourage him," she said, after a pause. "Don't encourage him to break her heart."

He heard for a moment the coarseness of the cheering around them. "But if it's what they both want," Jacob tried to answer.

"He doesn't want it for her."

"If he can't stay, he can't stay."

"That's no reason." Briefly she challenged him with her gaze but then looked away.

The parade turned west, toward the river. It passed one of the seminaries, where a couple of young men with unwashed hair were leaning out of adjacent windows in an upper story to watch. —Come down! a parader shouted, in Polish words that resembled Czech closely enough for Jacob to understand. Others echoed the call, and soon the crowd was roaring: Come down! Come with us! The two men in the window glanced at each other with guilty happiness. One retreated, but the other waved back to the crowd sheepishly, amicably. Jacob nudged Carl, but when Carl raised his camera, the remaining boy, too, ducked, and there were only the empty windows and a flapping white shade.

"We thought perhaps Thursday night," Melinda let Jacob know, when he saw her in the teacher's lounge upon their return. "In a place with the absurd name of the Love Bar, which Rafe reports is quite *sympatický*. Just south of the Charles Bridge, on the embankment itself. On the water, really."

"Which side?"

"This side. Our side."

Jacob liked being back even more than he had liked being away. He liked living in a world where the occasion didn't have to be named. He liked the sense of order according to which it fell to Mel and Rafe to make such appointments.

This world and this order Carl was due to leave in a week and a half, a few days after the new month. Henry was going to host him for those last few days, so Carl wouldn't have to spend a whole month's rent on them. Běta had confirmed that her family was willing to take back Carl's room on the first. So Carl never quite unpacked when they got back from Krakow. He lived out of his suitcase.

Was it just because of the rent? In American terms, it was a negligible sum. Was Carl, though he had come to Prague as Jacob's friend, leaving as Henry's? Maybe there had been moments when Jacob, despite his caution, had come too close. Carl was so gentle he would never have let Jacob become aware of such moments, if there had been any. The doubt was in his mind the morning he found Carl cropping off handfuls of his beard in the bathroom. "Getting ready for America?" Jacob asked.

"I hadn't thought of America," Carl confessed. "Sure, for America."

Jacob didn't try to go behind Carl's irony. Later, shaved and dressed, Carl said, as he rubbed his chin during breakfast, "It's weird. It's like that game Dead Man's Hand. The nerves feel wrong. Did you ever play that?"

His cheeks were pale from having been hidden from the sun. There was something in the alteration that collapsed the past three and a half months. The revealed face was vulnerable, unfamiliar, and handsome, and it added to the friends' unease with each other, as did their speculations about the Stehlíks' plans for Carl's room after he was gone. Between that room and Honza's quarters lay another room still uncleared of junk, so there was a chance that nothing would be done with Carl's room right away.

For the interval, what sense of home the friends had was to be found only in the arrangements of their wider circle—in the welcome that they knew they could look forward to from the others and in the intuitive way it was planned. On Thursday night, as they walked toward their appointment along the crooked familiar path through the Old Town, cutting through the alleys and *pasáže* that they now knew by instinct, past the church with broken windows, past the music store that never opened, they felt as if they were returning to something, a tradition of some kind that they had long ago been admitted to, something whose form was like a seminar or a court, where a role was defined by growing into it. A few hours before, Carl, after asking Jacob to teach him the words for "short" and "shorter," had gone and had his hair cut, and the effect of it had resolved the novelty of his beardlessness. He was suddenly again the old image of Carl that Jacob found that his mind's eye had never in fact surrendered. He was who Jacob had always known he was. Everything was going to be all right, Jacob felt, even if Carl really did leave, as it seemed he was going to.

They came out to the river at the Charles Bridge and turned left, passing under an arch and then along a hoarding, both of which blocked their view. Unable to see, they were briefly seized by the characteristic Prague anxiety of never finding the entrance—of arriving at one's goal but remaining blocked from it by a wall of stone on account of having overlooked an alley or a medieval door a few dozen yards back, which had served as the approach so immemorially that no one any longer marked or described it. They doubled back to the Charles Bridge in premature retreat; then, giving up on this retreat, proceeded once more under the arch and along the hoarding, until, at the end of the hoarding, their eyes tumbled down steps to the right, into a spit of land that angled into the river. Here they were. They descended, and as they did, left behind the blare of the city at dusk for the placidity of the water, black and quiet, which was wrinkling and smoothing itself below them at the base of the blocks of carved white stone upon which they walked.

From the end of the spit, at its corner, a weir ran out. Water passed over it so evenly and silently that it was possible to imagine walking the stone barrier all the way across the river.

"In here, I think." Carl had found the door.

The first room was shallow, crowded, and harshly lit. It was dominated by a bar with a glass top and brass trim. In a corner, in an entente that shut out the loud and busy drinkers around them, stood Melinda, Rafe, and Henry.

It was the fluster in the room, probably, that prevented Henry and the couple from responding as warmly as Carl and Jacob had expected them to. Their greetings were so quiet that Rafe at last broke out, "The boys don't get kisses? Shall I kiss them?"

"If you like," Melinda licensed him.

"I don't like," he told her, and then continued, addressing the new arrivals, "but you don't mind, do you? If you can do without *hers* . . ."

"Don't," she cautioned him.

"I don't, I don't," he answered. "I never do."

"How was Poland?" Henry asked.

"That's right," Rafe joined him. "Your expedition."

Carl abruptly excused himself to get beers for himself and Jacob. Melinda followed him to the bar with her gaze.

"It was good," Jacob answered. He wanted to delay answering in detail until his fellow travelers were at his side, so he tried to deflect the question. "I heard you might go farther east yourself."

"Poland isn't very 'east,'" Rafe pointed out.

"It's sort of farther 'west,' isn't it," Jacob admitted.

"I understood it to lie to the north," Rafe said, to finish off the joke. Then, neutrally, "No, we don't have to worry about Poland any more."

"So are you going east?" Jacob repeated his inquiry.

"It depends."

"What does it depend on?"

Rafe leaned into his girlfriend, and when she startled, he pretended to have done so by accident. "On her," he said, with a nod of his head.

"No," Melinda simply said.

"In a way," said Rafe.

"Oh, that way," Melinda agreed.

"What way is that?" Jacob asked.

"If I can't make up my mind," Melinda explained, "he'll put it off a little longer."

"An offer came through," Henry said. "For Kazakhstan. Land of the Cossacks!"

"Oh, they're the same word. I didn't realize that."

"But different people, actually. It's a Turkish word, it turns out," Rafe elaborated. "It means 'bohemian.'"

"No," it was now Jacob's turn to say.

"Well, it means 'rover.' The tribe who do not settle down."

"Your tribe, in other words."

"But Melinda's not excited for some reason."

"Do they have running hot water in Kazakhstan?" Jacob asked.

"Sometimes," Rafe replied, as if that were as often as anyone had a right to wish for. He had the excitement of a boy looking forward to a math test that has scared all the other boys, not because he's better at math but because he's better at thinking while scared.

"Why can't you save the world from an office in Paris?" asked Jacob.

"But I don't save the world. I complicate it. Paris doesn't need any help in that department."

"I tried," Jacob told Melinda.

"You tried valiantly," Melinda agreed.

"You should come, too. You'd love Almaty in the spring. The scent of acetyls and aldehydes in the air—"

"Have you heard the news?" Melinda interrupted.

"What news is that?" Jacob asked.

"Thom and Jana's."

"No."

"They're to have a sprout," Melinda revealed.

"So first you have a snog, and it leads to a scrum, and you end up with a sprout."

"That's the giniral idear, luv."

"You do a terrible Cockney accent, for an Englishwoman," Rafe told Melinda. "Do you know that?"

"It's better than my cowboy. Jacob positively shudders when I do my cowboy."

"Are they getting married?" Jacob asked.

"Provisionally," said Melinda.

"To make sure the child has dual citizenship," Henry explained. "They're here, you know."

"Where?"

"There's another room," Melinda said. "It's sort of—well, you'll see. And Annie and Kaspar as well. Shall we go in to them?"

She took Jacob's arm and pointed him to an open door at the far end of the bar, across from where they had come in. She held him tightly enough to oblige him to walk slowly, to match the rhythm of her smaller, more leisurely steps. It was a ritual of the court, Jacob thought, that Melinda was the first to proceed. Rafe naturally took up the end of the train.

They passed into a short corridor. "I wish that I had gone to Krakow," Melinda confided, leaning into Jacob, "and that you and he had stayed here."

"Why?"

"Because then I would have that look in *my* eyes. That look of having gotten away."

They emerged into the back of a small auditorium. The stage was dark and the chandeliers were dim, but from low sconces a yellow blur fell discreetly into the aisles, as if for latecomers who still had a few moments to find their way to their seats. It reminded Jacob that in the world outside, the sun had gone down for the night. Men and women leaned against the walls in conversation, or took up clusters of seats, standing or sitting crosswise on armrests so as to be able to look at one another rather than at the stage where nothing was taking place. Jacob and Melinda walked slowly down the ramp of the stage-left aisle, scanning the rows for their friends. Because the stalls obliged most people to face forward, and because of the obscure light, Jacob and Melinda had nearly reached the stage before they spotted Thom, in the front row. He had turned in his seat so as to be able to address Kaspar, who was sitting one row behind Thom, Jana, and Annie.

"Congratulations," said Jacob, as he and Melinda filed into the gap between the front row and the proscenium. "Mazel tov," he added for good measure.

"Why thank you, sir," Thom responded. He and Jana rose to accept Jacob's and Carl's embraces.

"Boy or girl?"

"He is a boy," said Jana, "and he will come in September."

They all looked at one another stupidly and happily for a few moments. Jacob had never before been in the presence of friends his age who had announced a pregnancy, and the vague but powerful geniality that the couple gave off was a novelty to him. The aura was different from that of other achievements; it was more like one of greeting than of congratulation.

"You will pardon me," a delicate voice said, "but I thought, that I heard you say, 'Mazel tov.' Is it so?"

"Kaspar, this is my friend Carl," Jacob responded.

"Ah, the poet," Kaspar said, bowing slightly.

"Poet?" Carl echoed.

"You direct what is called the poetry corner, do you not?" Kaspar asked, with a glance at Henry, his evident source.

"Oh it's Henry's poetry corner. I'm just an unindicted co-conspirator."

"Now you're in for it," Rafe murmured.

"And what is this, if you please, an unindicted co-conspirator?" Kaspar asked, carefully repeating the syllables.

Kaspar had risen to his feet when the others did, and he now swayed slightly, holding on with his stubby fingers to the back of Jana's chair for support. His clothes were so loose on him that half the collar of a polka dot shirt—another gift of Rafe's?—had slipped beneath the neck of his sweater. One of his eyes was wandering as usual, and the inward-sloping, almond shape of his eyes, Jacob saw, contributed to the expression he seemed always to wear of appealing for the answer to a question.

"It's a reference to our great leader Richard Nixon," Carl explained. "It's a way people had of referring to him during Watergate."

"Carl's a great one for the names of things," said Henry, at Carl's side. "It's he who came up with 'coddling the juggernaut.'"

"Ah yes," said Kaspar. "That was very fine." The fullness of the gratitude embarrassed Jacob on Kaspar's behalf, but Carl let it go by. "But why do you call yourself so?" Kaspar persisted.

"Because I maintained plausible deniability. I never read any poetry to the boys here. Or any prose, for that matter."

"Didn't you?" Annie queried.

"We know he wrote something," Jacob volunteered. "I heard him typing."

"He is a bit 'dissi,' perhaps," Kaspar suggested.

"Like dissident?"

"It is a style. Always joking. Always with secrets. Keeping your things in a bag, for if they come to knock in the night, and writing only for the drawer."

"There's nothing to dissent from in America," Jacob said, rehearsing his old argument with Kaspar. "There's just—other voters."

"I bet you could find something," Carl demurred.

"It alarms him, when I speak so," Kaspar told Carl, conspiratorially.

"He's not ready," Carl agreed.

The group soon broke into smaller conversations. "She let me know in March," Thom explained to Jacob and Carl. "It was her wish to have the child, a reasonable decision considering the lad's attractive father, but it's quite common here the other way. Bit of a shock to learn how common, even to a man of such a liberal mind-set as myself. Seems they're much more likely here to take care afterward than to trouble themselves in any way before."

"It's thought to be an unintended side effect of the command economy," said Henry. "No one compares costs. Sort of the way there's a dry cleaner on every street but no Laundromats."

"A weightier matter than that, I trust. It's my scattered seed we're discussing, as I believe your man Hans has called it."

"No doubt some of that has made it to a Laundromat."

"A pity that not even a father comes in for respect in the new world order. A father of his country, no less."

"And of other countries, too."

"Just the one other, to the best of my knowledge."

"And you're going to get married?" Jacob asked.

"She's quite stern. I had to promise to divorce her."

"*You* promised?" Jacob asked.

"I had to. But I tell her she's allowed to have second thoughts as she comes to a deeper appreciation of my merits."

Jana turned in her seat at this.

"How well you know your mind," Annie complimented Jana.

"But you have not said, how was your trip to Poland," Jana replied.

"They're quite jolly, the Poles, I find," Annie said. "Wouldn't you say? They want more and they give more, but it isn't *you* that they want, not quite as it is here. You know how it is, that if you open a map on a Prague street, a Czech will appear to help you find your way and to talk to you for fifteen minutes. That didn't happen in Krakow. On the other hand they were quite nice in the shops."

"Oh, in shops we Czechs are barbarians," Jana admitted.

"Not if one is a regular," Annie qualified. "They're quite fond of me in my Palmovka sweet shop, for example."

"Because they know you," Jana said. "You are theirs. But that is not yet civilization. It is only . . . family."

"But in exchange perhaps one feels that it means more, somehow."

"Still we must leave it behind," Jana said.

Thom slid down beside her. Jacob clambered over two rows to sit behind Kaspar; Melinda and Carl came down the aisle and met him there. Rafe was already sitting beside Kaspar, rolling in his long fingers the foil wrapper from inside a cigarette pack, and Jacob wondered if it cost Rafe an effort not to turn around—not to examine the way Carl and Melinda sat down beside each other, behind him, and faced as carefully forward as he did.

After they had sat for a little while in the twilight together, Carl said, as if speaking a thought in all their minds, "It's as if we're waiting for the show to begin."

"Don't say that," said Melinda. "In the next scene you leave us, you know."

"That's right, I guess."

"What was it like to leave us for Krakow?" Melinda continued. "That was your rehearsal." She said it brightly. Jacob thought he understood. If this was the last time she was going to see Carl, she had the right not to stint it.

"It was . . . ," he began, buoyantly enough, but he paused, and they waited with him, in the half dark, while he searched his memory and then his invention for something to say that was dishonest but not ungallant. "It was sort of beside the point. It was outside the story, as we say in the poetry corner." The tone of the sentence was not quite right. "It made me wonder, what if the rest of my life will be like this."

"Like what?"

"Like tourism."

"You would see the sights," she consoled him.

"I suppose I would try to."

She hesitated. "Would you miss us as much as all that?"

Without looking up, Rafe suddenly, quietly attacked her. "Do you want him? Do you want him so badly? Is *he* going to give it to you?"

"Give it to me?" She seemed shocked by the words he used.

"That thing that you're supposedly looking for. The thing that gives you permission never to know what you want."

Rafe delivered his lines without turning around, and Melinda spoke hers while staring at the back of his head and then, when he persisted in refusing her gaze, at the back of his seat. Neither voice was raised, despite the bitterness of the words.

"Should we be having this discussion here?" she asked.

"Oh, where else? You won't talk about it when we're alone." The piece of foil in his hands had been worried into strips but he continued mechanically to fold and unfold it.

"I think that's enough," she told him.

"Yes, perhaps it is," he said, rising. "I'm going, then. You, stay."

"I think perhaps I shall stay. And I shall stay with Annie tonight, later, now she's back."

"As you like," he replied. He stood still for a moment, as if he were going to add something.

"Don't," she requested of him.

"Why would I?" He walked away.

The friends traded glances apprehensively.

"I'm sorry," ventured Carl.

"Rubbish," Melinda answered. "I'm sorry that any of you had to be a party to that. Would you accompany me, Annie?"

"Ehm, let me just find my wrap and my bag. Are those they, on the next chair, Thomas?"

"Oh, only to the loo, for now," Melinda clarified.

"Just the bag, then," Annie instructed Thom.

After the two women left, Thom shook his head and said, "I've never seen him in such a state."

"It must be difficult," said Henry, "if he wants to go and she doesn't."

No one was moved to comment further. They shifted in their seats and drank for a while without talking. A trio of strangers came near in search of a place to sit and then sheepishly withdrew, sensing from the silence that they had intruded.

It was disconcerting to sit quietly in a theater not serving its purpose.

"Have you seen the bridge?" Kaspar turned and asked Jacob, with his customary sly smile. He pointed to where the Charles Bridge would be, if it were visible through the walls of the theater.

"I saw it when we came in."

"But there is a further garden."

"There is?" Jacob asked.

"I show you?" Kaspar invited.

They left the others and walked out into a blue-green darkness. There were no lights, only a glow that fell from the mist-haloed iron lamps of the bridge, which loomed over them like an ocean liner over passengers in a rowboat. Water was lapping both sides of the low, tapering strip of land. Old, thin trees were planted in the cobblestones, and from their branches new-fledged leaves drooped like limp gloves and trembled.

There were lovers, here and there, under the trees. Kaspar and Jacob walked out into the garden, taking care not to stumble on the uneven stones. They had already drunk enough not to take too much notice of the chill.

"Tell me, how is your story?"

"I haven't thought about it much," Jacob admitted.

"There is so much happening for you."

"Is there? Happening around me, maybe. Why do you ask?"

In the dark he sensed Kaspar's shrug. "I am interested in your progress," he said, again.

At the top of each of the bridge's massive, diamond-shaped piers, a black saint had turned his back to them. "When I first heard about my friend I threw flowers off the bridge."

"A pretty thing to do."

"They weren't such pretty flowers."

"Well," Kaspar said.

They found an empty bench and sat down.

"We stopped at Auschwitz during our trip to Poland," Jacob told him.

"Did you?"

"I didn't like it. I didn't like the idea of going there."

"It is a horrible place."

"I mean, I worked myself up into an argument about it. That it wasn't even right to go there, somehow. That we as tourists didn't have a moral right to. I was childish about it."

"You felt the place," Kaspar said.

"Or something."

The bridge above them was quiet, but now and then a lover in the garden murmured or laughed. "Is it not beautiful here?"

"It is," Jacob admitted. It felt imprudent to admit it. It might make it more painful to remember later—to remember that he had had to leave it. "How are you feeling? Should you be out here in this cold? You left your coat inside."

"Do not worry so. You are like Melinda."

"What do you think she'll do?"

"She is turning at last to her own garden."

"I don't want her to leave Rafe."

"It is not on you or me," Kaspar reasonably objected.

"I told her she should give Carl up, so she could find out what he meant to her. You know, your idea."

"Mine?"

"You said you don't believe in that kind of love. Where you leave someone because of an idea about yourself."

"But once they do leave . . ."

"She could still patch it up with him."

The question must not have interested Kaspar, because he let it pass without comment.

A figure approached them through the darkness and from ivory face, hands, and ankles crystallized as Melinda herself.

"La, do the rest know this is here?"

"Sit, sit," said Kaspar, making room for her between them. "It is our secret."

"Between two handsome men. I ought to have quarreled with my boyfriend sooner."

Each man felt the warmth of her thin torso beside him.

"What are you going to do?" Jacob nervously asked.

"I shall stay with Annie tonight."

"Will they make a fuss? I thought her overnight guests had to be registered in advance."

"Oh, I shall tumble her into the soup again, shan't I?"

"It's all right," Jacob assured her.

"Tell me that it will be."

"Of course it will be."

"Good," she said cheerfully. She sat upright as if to improve her posture as well as her outlook and peered into the gray sky. "Do they *have* stars in Central Europe, do you think?"

"Not in Prague," Jacob answered. "They have clouds."

"They are pretty clouds, don't get me wrong, but sometimes one does wish for a star or two. At night clouds can be rather . . . indistinct."

"Do you know the constellations?"

"Oh god, are they all different here?" She took out her cigarettes but then didn't smoke one. They were so close to the bridge that it, mist, and the river were all their view. "From here it looks less like a bridge than the wall of some great fortress," she said.

"With a moat," said Jacob.

"Yes. Defending what, exactly?" She shivered. "I think I shall go back inside. This is nearly Carl's farewell party, isn't it, and I shouldn't like for a row to be his last memory of me."

Returned to the theater, they fell into the empty stalls between their friends like pieces into a puzzle. "Another round?" suggested Henry. Annie helped him fetch it.

When the drinks arrived, Melinda proposed a toast. "Carl's restoration to capitalism," she suggested, sensing perhaps that her friends were waiting for her to grant them permission to be lighthearted again.

"Hear, hear," seconded Henry.

"Is that a fate to wish on anyone?" Carl objected.

"It's not much of a wish at all, really," said Henry, "since you'll be restored to it whether you stay or go. There's no alternative any more."

"What about the Third Way?" Carl asked.

"Oh, darling, the Third Way," said Melinda consolingly.

"It's the only way left."

"You're not meant to believe in it literally, I don't think," she explained. "Here's to eating in restaurants late," she further proposed.

"Not *too* late. I'm going home to Boston."

"As late as half-seven, say."

Carl acknowledged the toast by drinking. "You don't have to be jolly, if you aren't up to it," he told her.

"Am I doing it badly?"

"Not at all. I just mean, you don't have to do it for me."

"But that's one of the things I've come round to about you. Your wish to believe that it's for you that people do things."

"I'm the grateful type."

"I said I've come round to it."

"You can't deny that you're always doing things for other people."

"In this case, however, it is for myself." She surveyed the room, as if taking stock of the moment that she had decided to enjoy. "Why is it no one goes on the stage, I wonder."

She narrowed her eyes at Jacob, who dodged the hint by looking toward the stage.

"It's taboo," Carl answered, "unless one is performing."

"One might perform," Melinda suggested.

"If the audience wanted a performance. If they believed in you as a performer."

"And if the audience were to?" she persisted. "If the ticket holder of C-4 were to believe in you . . . ," she said, naming her own chair.

"Oh, the ticket holder of C-4 . . ."

More softly, she said, "Imagine that I'm serious."

For a moment he was at a loss. "What would you want to hear?"

"Can you sing?"

"Sing! My god."

"Well, then."

"I think I know a speech of Rosalind's."

"Did you play her?" Melinda asked.

"I wish. I played one of the fools. But she had the best lines, and she gave them every night, so I ended up learning her speeches, too."

"Give us Rosalind, then."

"Come on," nodded Thom. "Up you go."

"Wait, wait."

"Too late," Henry declared.

"I'm not backing out. I'm . . . thinking." He sidled out of his row, and in the aisle raised a hand to stroke the beard he no longer wore.

Discovering its absence, he nervously adjusted his glasses. "Okay," he said, seeing that his friends were observing him. He backed up against the proscenium and then pulled himself up to sit on it, dangling his legs like a child in a chair too tall for him.

"It is of a play by Shakespeare?" Kaspar asked.

"It is," said Carl. Continuing the conversation with his friends in the stalls protected him somewhat from the display he was beginning to make of himself. "And because it's Shakespeare, you have to imagine that I'm a man acting the part of a woman."

"Shouldn't be too much of a challenge," said Thom.

Carl folded his legs up under him and then unfolded them so that he now stood on the stage. Jacob turned in his seat to see what Carl saw; here and there in the room patrons were shifting their attention to the stage. "It's so high up here," Carl reported. "I'm so much higher than all of you."

"Awfully bold," said Thom, "for a lass like you to take the stage."

"Actually it's a little more complicated. I'm a man playing a lass dressed as a man, about to propose that you pretend I'm a lass."

"I wasn't talking to you," said Thom. "I was talking to the first lass."

"I'm not going to do the drag part of it. I hope that's okay."

"There's a great deal of prefatory matter, isn't there," Melinda said, aside.

"Okay," said Carl, taking a breath and making a show of settling himself. "Okay, I'm ready. You have to ask me, first, whether I ever cured anyone of love by mere talk."

Melinda, taking this upon herself, rose. "Did you ever cure any so?" she called out, in a voice that rang through the theater, summoning the people in it out of their separate conversations.

A quiet fell naturally over the room. "One," said Carl, taking a half step forward as he began to speak,

> and in this manner. He was to imagine
> Me his love, his mistress; and every day
> To woo me. And I to be a moonish youth,
> Grieving, changeful, longing, liking, proud,
> Fantastic, apish, shallow, full of tears
> And smiles, as boys and women mostly are.

He paused for breath. The feat of memorization held them, if nothing else. He didn't let anyone catch his eye, perhaps afraid that it would break his luck.

> He was to feel that every day his heart
> Was wounded by my eye, yet flew to me,
> Who wounded it, for succor; to feel that my heart,
> Flutter'd, fearing, turn'd about with love,
> Sought the wild alike, though I, heartless,
> For safety ventured not: And so by feigning
> That I, who loved him, loved him not, and he,
> Who loved not me, did love, we made ourselves
> A pair of doveless cotes, and coteless doves
> Too shy and too high-flown for any keeping.

He held his pose after he finished the poetry, and they waited, in case there might be more, until Melinda, in the same voice as before, answered:

> O youth, *I* would not be cured so.

Some wags at the back of the theater hallooed and applauded, and the friends joined in as the applause became polite and general.

Melinda came forward to hand Carl down from the stage. "I had no idea," she said.

"It was my secret." He held on to her hand for a moment, even after he had come to ground. The two of them, let alone by the others, leaned together against the edge of the stage, resting their drinks on it. They began to look at each other less guardedly.

"He wasn't so terrible," said Thom to the others, as they all made an effort not to pay attention. "Did you know your flatmate to be a thespian?" he asked Jacob.

"Thomas," scolded Annie.

"He hadn't come out to me as such," Jacob answered.

A gangly young Czech—a college student, probably—scrambled up onto the stage. "Být, anebo nebýt," he said, in a cracking voice. "To je otázka, že jo." To be or not to be; it's some question, isn't it.

A companion followed him to the edge of the stage. —Get down, you idiot.

Carl and Melinda remained in deep conversation. Now and then Jacob's eyes strayed to them. The freedom that they were taking frightened him. It was threatening. It was exhilarating, too. It suggested that there was no longer any reason to protect whatever it was that he had been trying to preserve. Jacob himself would be able to destroy so much, he felt, and there was so much that he was looking forward to destroying, once he himself reached the point of not having anything to lose.

"I told Melinda she could have my bed and I'll sleep on the floor," Carl told Jacob, sometime after midnight.

"Yeah?"

"So as not to get Annie in trouble again."

"You don't have to ask me for anything," Jacob said.

"We thought we should clear it with you."

"That's . . . don't worry about it."

It didn't matter whether they were lying, Jacob told himself, or whether they knew they were lying, but he found himself studying them, with eyes made unsteady by drink and with a perception loosened by it, and he noticed that their way even just of standing together had become a subtle dance, that there was one spirit in the rhythms and angles of their limbs.

"It isn't what you think," Melinda said to Jacob later, as they sat together in the back of a night tram, which rocked them noisily down the tracks. But by then he had gotten beyond caring whether they were lying, to themselves or to him. He was merely impressed by the courage of their bodies, which he sensed beside him from beneath eyelids that he kept mostly closed, resting as he gauged the tram's progress through the city by the torques and tugs that had become familiar. He was impressed by their confidence in wanting to be together. They were braving the consequences. This was how the future came into being.

At Carl's bedroom door, Melinda said, "Good night, then. You know of course that nothing is happening."

"Of course not," Jacob replied.

"Thank you," she said, and the door was shut.

While Jacob was lying in bed listening to rain, Carl and Melinda stole silently through his room, holding their shoes. He saluted them.

"Sleep, sleep," Carl urged him.

"I'm already awake." He couldn't resist keeping them company. He wanted too badly to know what they were going to do. For decency's sake he put on last night's clothes, which still had the sour smell of cigarettes.

"Perhaps I should press on," Melinda suggested, once they had assembled in the kitchen.

"Have you met Václav?" Jacob asked.

"I haven't."

"He needs some water," Jacob noticed, and took the hamster's dish to the sink to refill it.

"Why don't you eat something first?" Carl said.

"We have one kind of *rohlík* and four kinds of jam," Jacob offered. He opened the refrigerator to show off the preserves. "Land of plenty."

"Do the two of you have the stomach for breakfast?" she asked.

"I always do," Jacob answered.

"If I wait a bit, Rafe will have gone to the ministry," she thought out loud.

"Better stay."

"I'm no good at this."

Jacob insisted. "I know that French people like warm chocolate milk for breakfast, but I don't know what English people like."

"Are those eggs in that tell-tale white paper sack? Perhaps one could make an omelet."

She cracked the eggs efficiently. She flinched slightly when the butter sputtered and slid across the hot pan. Carl stood beside her as he waited for the water to boil. Jacob could tell that the two of them were willing their bodies not to speak. Jacob felt more than ever that he was living in Prague in a way that he had never lived in America. Even the commonest thing was an adventure. Nothing like this had ever happened to him in America, even if it wasn't quite to him that this, whatever it was, was happening.

"What?" Melinda asked, provoked by Jacob's observation of her. "I swear, you look at me sometimes as if you think I'm starkers."

"No."

"You're having thoughts, I can tell."

"You can stay here if you like," Jacob offered.

"You mean, if I have to. That's very kind, but I can doss down at the Dům, you know. It's my right as a teacher. Annie will set me up. She's offered to before."

"Don't they keep track of your comings and goings?"

"Oh, it's socialism. There's no mistaking it. It would be like taking to a nunnery at the end of a novel."

"After the rogue leaves," suggested Jacob.

"Hey," said Carl.

Jacob offered to take his shower, to give them time alone, but Melinda said the omelet was ready. She folded it over and cut it into thirds. They ate it fiercely. In the end, they all had jam on *rohlíky*, too.

In his room, Jacob spent a long time there pretending to choose what he was going to wear. Eventually Melinda came to find him. "Now I really must go."

"Do you remember how to get out?"

"Perhaps you could offer a hint."

Jacob padded back into the kitchen—where Melinda gave Carl a hurried embrace—and leaned out the door of their apartment. "Just out that door," Jacob said, pointing to the building's entrance, "then left around the building, and left again at the street. The tram stop is at the corner."

"Brilliant, love."

Honza was emerging from his apartment. Melinda didn't stay for introductions, and when Jacob waved good morning, Honza nodded and winked knowingly, before heading upstairs to check in for the day with his employer.

"Honza saw us," Jacob reported.

"Honza's a man of the world," Carl said, and went back to bed.

They were never to know whether Honza told or whether Mr. Stehlík found out on his own. The knock came just ten minutes later.

Mr. Stehlík seemed to have to stoop to come in through the door, his anger made him so tall. He took a position beside the kitchen table, his feet planted wide, his gray hair stiff and martial.

"Mr. Jacob, we must talk," he began.

"Okay."

"Mr. Jacob, this is not right," he said, pointing at the stovetop, where the omelet pan lay, still wet with butter.

"We were just cooking breakfast," Jacob said. "I was going to clean the pan in a minute."

"No, Mr. Jacob. This." He was pointing, Jacob now saw, not at the pan but spots of old pancake batter, sauce, and soup on the stovetop itself. Jacob had been putting off scrubbing it. "Mouses will come," Mr. Stehlík added.

"Sorry," said Jacob. "I'll clean it tonight."

"You have shoes on carpet," Mr. Stehlík continued, pointing at the path that they walked through the kitchen en route to their bedrooms. In the course of his construction work, Honza had scattered debris in the foyer, and Jacob and Carl had tracked some of it inside. It didn't look ineradicable.

"In America we don't take off our shoes indoors."

"In Czech, yes. In Czech nation, no shoes."

"I'll take them off if it's important to you. If I could borrow your vacuum cleaner . . . ," Jacob proposed, but Mr. Stehlík didn't seem to recognize the word for the device and moved impatiently to his last and gravest charge.

"And Mr. Jacob, is not hotel." He glared at Jacob after delivering the words. His face was ashen with rage.

"We were out with some friends," Jacob said as pleasantly as he could, "and one of them lives on the other side of town, so it was easier for her to stay over here."

"Is not hotel!" Mr. Stehlík shouted.

Mr. Stehlík was a powerful man, in the prime of his life. Jacob's heart thudded effortfully, thickly. What he could see of the world shrank to just Mr. Stehlík at the center. Mr. Stehlík was a man accustomed to punishing, but Jacob had come out of that box and did not want to go back into it. What's more, Jacob was innocent. He had on his side the counterposing fury of innocence.

"What's going on?" asked Carl, who had come quietly in from his room.

Mr. Stehlík ignored him. "You are my guest, Mr. Jacob. Mr. Carl is your guest and my guest. But is not hotel. No."

"Oh, I see," said Carl.

"Is *dirty*, Mr. Carl," Mr. Stehlík said, pointing to the stovetop again.

"So I heard," said Carl. "Mouses will come."

Jacob wished Carl hadn't taken the risk of being detected in mockery. "It's normal to have guests," Jacob said. "It's part of living somewhere."

"Not in my house. One, two. No more."

It occurred to Jacob that Mr. Stehlík might not know that he was supposed to be charging for wear and tear. "Maybe we're still not paying you enough," Jacob suggested. "Under capitalism the rent is supposed to be high enough that the landlord can afford to repair the damage that happens in normal use."

Mr. Stehlík stepped forward. "Is not money," he said quietly in Jacob's face, so close that Jacob winced at his stale smoker's breath. "Is *my house*."

Jacob remembered, in what did not at first seem to be a consecutive thought, the ski bags that had held Běta's grandparents. He recalled the strangeness of their presence by the driveway.

Carl was to go to Henry's the next day, anyway. Jacob himself could stay at the Dům, if he had to. But he probably wouldn't have to. There was a market for Prague apartments now. And in the interim maybe he, too, could stay with Henry.

"Fine," Jacob said, turning away from Mr. Stehlík coldly. "We will leave."

"Pardon?" Mr. Stehlík asked. "You do not need leave."

"But I don't want to stay," Jacob said. "We will leave within twenty-four hours." He felt a princely autonomy. He left Mr. Stehlík behind in the kitchen and went to his bedroom to begin packing.

Jacob opened the doubled set of windows in his bedroom. A drizzle was falling, and above the concrete barriers across the street, he could see heavy clouds traveling east, toward the Stehlíks' house, and breaking up, as they approached, to reveal ribs of blue as they passed over it.

While Jacob was fussing with the zippers and compartments of his backpack, Carl came in and sat on the sofa.

"I'm sorry," Carl offered.

Jacob shrugged and kept fussing. "I would guess it's a puritanical thing, but there are nudie pictures in the bathroom upstairs," he observed.

"But Honza had to get married, didn't he."

"It's not your fault."

"You have to find a new place," Carl insisted.

Jacob shrugged again. He cared only that he would soon be without the kindness that when he looked up he saw in Carl's face. "It's just a gorilla problem," Jacob said.

Jacob showed up with Carl on Henry's doorstep, his Olivetti and a backpack full of clothes already in tow. Henry welcomed him despite not having invited him, as Jacob had known he would. There was only one sofa in Henry's living room, Henry apologized, but there was room for a second sleeping bag on the floor. Jacob promised to move into the Dům as soon as he could and to start looking for a new apartment immediately. The next morning he went back to the Stehlíks' to clean—otherwise Běta would have to—and to fetch his posters, books, and Václav, who still fit into an emptied cigarette pack. He had hoped to see Běta. He didn't, but it was all right because he already had plans to meet her a few days later, in a café on Na příkopě, for the private English lessons that he was giving to her and her friend. In her absence he was hailed, as he left the Stehlíks' villa, by her mother, who was hanging wet laundry on the white rubberized cords strung across the family's small yard.

"Kubo," Mrs. Stehlíková said, placing a damp shirt over one shoulder so that her hands were free to mime the meaning of her words, "já mám velké srdce." With her index fingers she traced in the air before her the symmetrical outline of the large heart that she was explaining that she had, then patted her bosom. She nodded. "Rozumíš?" Do you understand?

—Thank you, Jacob said. —Until the next sighting.

As a temporary home for Václav, Henry lent Jacob a steel tureen with a lid, though he warned that he would have to borrow it back if they should decide to boil spaghetti. Improvisation seemed to be the theme of Henry's housekeeping. On their first night, Carl and Jacob had to shift piles of laundry and stacks of paperbacks in order to make room for their sleeping bags, and there was no sense that any item in the kitchen belonged in one place rather than another—flour, bowls, sardine tins, tea, frying pans, drinking glasses, salt, potatoes, and Marmite mixed in perfect democracy on the shelves and countertops. Jacob fell nonetheless a little bit in love with being Henry's guest. Henry had assembled more than a dozen different spices, whose Czech names Jacob had not seen often enough to learn, and Jacob went through them, uncapping and sniffing to educate himself. Henry also made Jacob welcome to his washing machine, and since Jacob didn't know when he might next find one, he washed everything he owned, strewing the apartment with wet clothes, laying socks across sills, draping pants over chair backs, and hooking shirts over doorknobs and window levers. Before falling asleep at night, he read at random from Henry's paperbacks. *Maumauing the Flak-Catchers. The Road to Wigan Pier.* In the shower one morning, he even tried Henry's shampoo, surreptitiously.

With Henry personally, Jacob was a little stiff, though Henry, for his part, seemed at ease. He may even have welcomed the distraction that Jacob's presence made. He had, after all, been expecting the company of Carl, but Carl didn't show up until Sunday night. Upon overhearing Melinda's news, a Czech woman who taught at the language school had lent her the key to her Prague apartment, which she didn't need because she was headed to a friend's *chata* in the country for the weekend. Not knowing she had gone home with Carl, not seeing her Friday morning or afternoon, Rafe had developed the hope that she suffered as much from the separation as he did and had convinced himself that he might be able to persuade her to accept a year or two in Kazakhstan if he promised to look for a desk in Berlin or Paris afterward. When she disillusioned him, he turned stoic, uncharacteristically businesslike, or so Melinda later described him to Carl. He wished her the best; he didn't want to hear any details. She began to cry and apologized for crying, saying she knew it was unfair for her to be the one to cry. Rafe agreed that it was unfair, but "for old times' sake," he said, he was willing to tell her that he thought she would be all right. Then he asked her to leave.

On Monday, Melinda moved to the apartment of another colleague, who was willing to let Melinda sleep on her sofa. Melinda was resisting Annie's attempts to install her at the Dům. She was spending as much time with Carl as she could manage to. After the weekend, the two passed their hours together in cafés and museums, since they had no other privacy, but it was what they were used to. Annie reported this news while signing Jacob up at the Dům, on Tuesday after work. The Dům was clean, bright, Brutalist, and very far from anything else, Jacob discovered—it was at the southern end of the longest subway line. He left without a key because one did not carry a key out of the building but rather traded it at the front desk for a card in a cellophane sleeve with one's name and room number and an official stamp. On the tedious subway ride back to Henry's, Jacob stared at his name, handwritten on the card in blue ink. He would stay at the Dům if he had to, he promised himself; he wouldn't impose on Henry past Friday, the day of Carl's departure. But he didn't think it would come to that. He had been asking his students to let him know if they heard of any apartments.

The hunt for a place to stay kept him so busy that it was only when Henry suggested that they throw a good-bye party for Carl that Jacob became aware of a dull ache in his side and wondered how long he had been pretending to himself that he didn't feel it. When Henry made the suggestion, Jacob had just come from seeing an apartment in Žižkov, behind the National Museum. It was in a large 1930s building, and the nominal tenant was a mother who had moved in with her unmarried son in another part of town. Her relocation had been kept a secret from the authorities, who might feel obliged to redistribute the property if they knew. It wasn't certain that under the new dispensation the authorities were still enforcing such redistributions, but as a matter of prudence, the son asked Jacob to say that he was a cousin from America, if any neighbors inquired, and it would be better if Jacob didn't talk to the neighbors at all, if he could manage to dodge them. The rooms themselves were worn-in and comfortable, with curtains of thin polyester lace on the windows, likable bad paintings of rural landscapes on the walls, and discordant patterns and clashing colors on the wallpaper, duvet cover, and carpet. As at the Stehlíks', there was a second bedroom crammed full of heirlooms and unused furniture, for which the son, who was showing the apartment, apologized with some embarrassment. Jacob was to have the use of a less cluttered bedroom, one of whose three chests of drawers would be emptied for him. There was also a bathroom and a kitchen. One window gave onto slopes of red clay roof tiles; another overlooked a private garden four stories below. The language school was late with Jacob's monthly pay, a recurring problem recently, but Jacob told the man that as soon as his salary arrived—as soon as Friday, he hoped—he would pay the rent and move in.

Prague was changing. There were rumors that the government was going to tighten the rules about foreign workers, which had been largely suspended in the first euphoria of revolution. Long-stay visas, it was said, would no longer be automatically renewed, and after a certain date it would no longer be legal for foreigners to work without a special visa. It was no longer going to be the Wild East. The teaching of English was falling more and more into the hands of business, which paid better but demanded more of a teacher's time. To go over to the private companies was to lose much of one's leisure and some of one's sense of exemption from the marketplace and the obligation to be ranked by it.

None of Jacob's friends had lost these things yet. When Carl relayed Melinda's wish to meet Jacob on the afternoon of Carl's good-bye party—the afternoon of Carl's last full day in Prague—Jacob recognized in the invitation the sort of grand gesture that their freedom still made possible. "You don't mind? It's your last day."

"She has something she wants to tell you," Carl said, mysteriously.

They met at the entrance of the Convent of Saint Agnes, in the elbow of a bent street in the north end of Josefov. "You'd never have come here otherwise," she said. "To see a girl and what's more a saint."

"I like girls."

"My eye."

A sandy yellow wall topped with red clay tiles hid the compound. The friends stepped through a door of metal bars, decorated with thorns, into a narrow alley. Windowless buildings hedged them in, and it wasn't until they had zigzagged through several pale rooms, climbed a staircase, and come out into a long corridor with vaulted ceilings that Jacob had a sense of where they were.

They were standing in the nuns' cloister. Along one wall, trios of windows shone sunlight into the room. Through the windows, Jacob saw a courtyard.

"Shall we sit outside for a moment?" Melinda asked.

She led him into the courtyard, where a walkway of loose white stones framed a green lawn. In one corner was the ruin of a well. In another, there stood a cherry tree. The tips of its dark branches were red with buds. Two folding chairs were angled so as to imply conversation, and Jacob and Melinda took possession of them.

"They've dumped the Czech nineteenth-century daubs in the

chapter hall yonder, where the nuns used to sleep, but it's the cloister here I wanted you to see, not the art." The sun fell angrily on her white skin, which the long winter had kept from it. "It's that kind of nineteenth-century art that every nation is so proud of having produced, but you have to be in a nostalgic mood and it has to be your nation before you can enjoy it." She sat on her hands for a moment and straightened her back, in a schoolgirl's stretch. "What's rare is this," she said, with no indicating gesture, trusting the environment to impress itself. She crossed her legs and sat up in her chair. "Thirteenth century. I imagine ladies in wimples holding hands as they walk the length of the cloister. As an aid to meditation. But I suppose that's wrong somehow. One's imaginings of history always are."

There was something diagonal about the way she was sitting in her chair, not an effect of doubt but an implication of motion—the conflict of a wish in her to walk the cloister herself and a wish just as strong to remain seated and continue talking to Jacob. High in her cheeks a flush had risen to the sun's challenge.

"The war between the simple and the pretty," said Jacob.

"Poor Carl has had to hear my lectures twice," she was reminded. "First from you, and then all over again from me, who gave them to you in the first place and can't help giving them even to you yet again."

"I bet he doesn't mind."

"He's diplomatic." The grass at their feet fluttered, like a boy's hair being smoothed. "What I wanted to tell you," she continued, "what I brought you here to tell you, is that I'm going away with him. Or rather, he's coming away with me." She glanced at Jacob and then for polite-ness's sake studied the cherry tree.

"When?" Jacob asked.

"Tomorrow," she answered. "I know," she acknowledged.

"Where are you going?"

"I told my mother a few days ago that I was leaving Rafe, and it transpires that she has a friend with an apartment in Rome. It's at our disposal for a month or so. It's terrible. We aren't being punished at all, and the car even makes it easy. That's as far as we've planned. We'll see at the end of a month whether we can still stand each other."

"I've always wanted to go to Rome."

"You should! I'm recommending wild imprudence to everyone now. There's something in it, I find."

"What will you do for money?"

"What is it Mr. Micawber says?"

"What if—"

"It's a risk, darling," she interrupted him. She waited for a moment, while he gave up on trying to think of a way to make it safer for them. She continued: "The director of the school has told me I can never come back—that they'll never even let such as me into the country again, if Klaus is given his head. But perhaps Klaus won't be given his head. It seems a trifle excessive, eternal banishment simply for having given one's *démission* to a language school two months early."

"Breaking a contract, I guess."

"Oh, don't say it," she requested. "Not you, too."

"It's only that they'd never have expected it of you. They'll survive."

"*You* don't feel that I'm abandoning you, do you? Though I suppose I am. You must write me. Send me the news from one who remains in the Czechoslovak Eden, once the gate has clanged shut behind me forever."

A wind tossed the limbs of the cherry tree and chilled them, but the sun wasn't going to let them get too cold. There was a luxury in coming to a museum and not seeing any of the art. In the middle ages they might have been a noble brother and sister whose family had given a herd of sheep and who had come to find out what the nuns had made of the gift.

"So Kaspar was wrong," he hazarded.

"Oh, maybe it's to spite him," she thought aloud.

"Maybe what is?"

She considered before answering. "It's mortifying to say, and you'll say it isn't any of your business," she began. "Still, nothing has happened."

He thought he understood.

"I don't mean absolutely nothing. You know what I mean."

"I think so," he answered carefully.

"And what's more, I'm not in love with him," she announced. "It's too soon."

He hesitated. "Are you just friends?"

"Oh god no." She seemed to feel sorry that she had confused him. "I've made a muddle of explaining."

"It doesn't have to be clear to me."

"The not having to say is what I've fallen for."

"You *have* fallen."

"But I don't have to say. It's sort of a holiday."

"I think I see." By the time this cherry tree flowered, he would have lost both of them, and by the time the flowers fell, they would probably have lost each other. "You're a pair of rogues," he said, to make light of it.

They sat together a while longer, imagining a tour of the scriptorium, in the course of which they would compliment the nuns' progress on a book of hours, commissioned long ago and years overdue.

The first to arrive at the farewell party was Annie. When the buzzer rang, Jacob set down a glass and the towel with which he had been drying it and ran to the window. "Here," he said, leaning out and dangling Henry's keys. "Catch."

"I won't do," she said from below. "You may drop them if you like, but I shan't 'catch,' thank you very much."

He lobbed them toward her anyway. She stepped back, and he heard them ping off the concrete and scuffle as they were knocked into the dusty planting beside the walkway. She was wearing her oversize, boxy glasses because spring had made her contact lenses impossible, and when she crouched to look for the keys she raised the glasses and rested them in her rust-gold hair. She gave no cry when she found the keys because it did not occur to her that Jacob would still be watching her and merely proceeded inside without a word.

Henry met her at the door in his apron and kissed her on both cheeks in greeting.

"You look quite dashing," she told him.

"Just doing a spot of washing up."

"Is all this yours, then?"

"Have you not seen it before?"

"No one ever invites me anywhere. Ehm, listen, Henry, I brought a few of me things, and I thought perhaps I might stay a few days, if it's no trouble."

"There may still be a corner left in the next room, if you hurry."

"That'll be grand," she thanked him. "And I'll be bringing half a dozen friends with me from the Dům as well."

"The more the merrier."

While Henry washed and Jacob dried, she gave herself a tour.

"And you prefer this squalor to the Dům," she resumed, upon returning.

"Say," Henry objected.

"But it is squalor."

"I found a place, actually," Jacob volunteered.

"Did you?"

"In Žižkov. The landlord doesn't live in the building this time."

She drifted away into the living room, perhaps looking for somewhere to set down her little canvas backpack. "Are you going to leave your laundry all about like this, during the party?" came her voice. "I don't mind, for myself."

"I hadn't given it any thought," said Henry.

"Quite intimate, isn't it," she said when they joined her to make an appraisal. "There isn't a closet, perhaps, where it could be stashed."

"Hang on," said Henry, checking one. "No." The closet was filled by Jacob's and Carl's luggage.

"Perhaps the shower. Have you taken your showers, the two of you?" Carl had left for a Vietnamese dinner with Melinda several hours before.

"If we take this rubbish down the tip," suggested Henry, pulling a crate out from beneath the sink, "perhaps we could put the old togs in here."

"You can't possibly put your things in there. You do mean to wear them again some day, don't you?"

"If Jacob has left us any washing powder."

"I heard that it was epic, your laundering," Annie told Jacob with admiration.

As a last resort, they piled the laundry onto the far side of Henry's bed, covered it with a blanket, and topped it with his pillows, with the intention that the ensemble should pass for a sofa, though the lumpy result instead gave the impression of an undisposed-of body, imperfectly disguised.

There was no time to improve on the arrangement, however. The buzzer was soon rung by three Czech women who taught at the language school, each bearing a white plastic shopping bag held sideways, artfully tented, with the hand clasp snapped-to and folded under. One, who in the course of the year had become friendly with Annie, exchanged kisses with her, but they were Melinda's friends for the most part, and in her absence they fussed awkwardly over Henry in his capacity as host, wishing to make themselves busy and useful. They pronounced the refrigerator that Henry and Jacob had packed full of bottled beer excellent and daunting. They knew to set an empty ashtray over the full one when they lifted it off of Henry's coffee table to dump its contents. One slid her shopping bag into the refrigerator atop the bottles that had been laid in parallel across a shelf like rollers in an assembly line, but the other two immediately extracted from their bags plates of *chlebíčky*, afterward inspecting the bags to confirm that no topping had touched the interiors and folding them in a way that did not compromise the handles.

"Peas and ham, I dare say," Annie observed.

"In mayonnaise," Jacob added quietly.

"Do you not fancy mayonnaise then?" Annie asked with dismay.

The last dish rinsed, Henry fetched a boom box from his bedroom, propped it on a pedestal of paperbacks in the living room, and plugged it in. "Now the party starts," said Henry.

"Without the guest of honor?"

"Bugger him." From a short row of cassettes Henry chose one with a handwritten label and shut it into the machine. The rotors began to turn. It was something punk, which even Jacob recognized though he couldn't have named it. Henry turned the volume up so high that they all stepped away.

"Henry," remonstrated Annie.

It was, as Henry said, the start of the party. The light inside the rooms had become more interesting than the light outside, Jacob saw, when at the next buzz he threw the keys down to Thom, who had appeared not with Jana but with Hans. Outside there were now only the evenly spaced orange glows of the street lamps, partly obscured at the height of Henry's window by the dark leaves of the street's lindens, which wavered unmeaningly, like fans loosely held in the hands of people who have become abstracted by music. Thom and Hans entered the building, but Jacob continued to lean out into the evening. Behind him the noise of the boom box was brittle. Before him the evening was rich and gentle, as it had been when he had sat with Kaspar under the shadow of the Charles Bridge. As he enjoyed its contrast with the bright, loud room that his feet, at least, were in, he heard approaching footsteps on pavement and the songlike sound of people speaking in English cadences. Carl and Melinda were walking arm in arm. They had brought Kaspar, who was limping slightly.

"Stand and unfold yourself," Jacob hailed them.

Startled, they looked up. "Nay, answer me," replied Melinda. Her face shone in the darkness.

"Thom has the keys and he hasn't got upstairs yet," Jacob explained.

They nodded. "Wild party?" asked Carl, as they waited.

"Pretty wild," Jacob answered. "Chlebíčky."

"Psych."

The distance between them was too great to have a proper conversation across it, and they fell silent. Melinda and Carl murmured to each other; Kaspar looked away down the street, in the direction that they hadn't come from. What was Jacob going to search for now, Jacob wondered of himself as he watched them. Now that this was ending. No, that wasn't the question. He knew what he was searching for, as well as he ever had. It was a feeling about the world: an answering quality. What he had lost track of was a sense of where to search for it—where he might be likely to hear it, if it could still be heard anywhere.

Behind him he recognized Thom's brogue and turned to retrieve the keys. Tossed into the darkness, they were caught by Carl overhand. "Hey," Carl said, as if inviting compliments on his catch, before unlocking the door. Jacob lingered for a few moments more, still leaning out into the empty night.

The partygoers crowded into the narrow vestibule, and Jacob saw Carl and Melinda at first only over the heads and in the interstices between his friends. The vestibule was lit by a bare light bulb, which hit the couple bluntly and made their brows shadow their eyes and their chins shadow their necks, but the revealed color of their complexions was so full of life that it had the effect of subtilizing and softening the light. Walking through the spring night had left them fresh and careless; they had brought the air of the night indoors with them. Even Kaspar, quietly fastening the bolt behind them, seemed pink and happy as he blinked against the glare.

They demanded drinks, perhaps as a pretext for shaking themselves a little free of the demanding crowd, and suddenly everyone in the room felt the need of drinks, and the press of people shifted to the kitchen. Then Henry was obliged to give Melinda a tour of the other two rooms, accompanied again by more or less everyone, though most had already seen them.

"But where are your shirts, Jacob?" Melinda wheeled on him in the living room to ask. "Henry told me the other day that it was like a meadow in bloom here, they were so brightly colored and tossed about with such abandon."

"That was only so they could dry," Jacob said.

"And now you've put them away. Shame. Is this where you sleep?" she asked, taking a seat on the sofa. She idly smoothed the Indian print that they had found under Henry's bed and spread over the sofa a few hours before. "Must we have that light, do you think?"

Kaspar, who was nearest, flipped a square plastic switch in the wall, and the bulb winked out, leaving them no more than the yellow that spilled over the lintel from the kitchen and the orange that came brokenly through the windows from the streetlamps outside.

The obscurity seemed to discontent Hans, who asked, "And what is the occasion for this party?" in a voice a little too loud and slightly petulant, as if he had been brought into this ambiguous room against his better judgment.

"Departure," Melinda told him.

"I'm leaving tomorrow," Carl explained.

"To return to the land of the Great Satan," Hans inferred.

"Gently now, gently," Thom advised.

"I'm going to the land of the Great Cannoli, actually," Carl replied.

"I'm taking him to Rome," Melinda disclosed.

"*You* are?" Thom queried.

"We're running off," she said.

"Is cannoli too North End?" said Carl. "Maybe they don't even actually have cannolis in Rome."

"They have cannoli in Rome," Henry confirmed from the doorway.

There was a silence as their other friends took in the news.

"Did you know of this, Henry?" Thom asked.

Henry shook his head.

"Did you, Annie?"

"Melinda told me this morning, as it happens."

Now Thom shook his head. "You'll be sorely missed. I know Jana will be sorry she had no chance to raise a glass to you, so I'll take care to raise twice as many meself."

"That is kind of you," Melinda said.

"Goodness," Thom added, mostly to himself, and again shook his head.

"Is Rafe aware of your plans?" Henry asked.

"Wasn't too keen on them," Melinda replied.

"Mmm."

A song ended, and in the silence that followed, a little longer than it needed to be in accordance with the casual way the tape had been mixed, the foreknowledge of what they would be to one another even after they had parted seemed to well up and become stronger in each one, perhaps because the parting was imminent, perhaps because they had been reminded of Rafe's unhappiness, perhaps because of an awareness that Carl and Melinda would carry off with them a piece of what they had all shared.

Pale Hans shifted restlessly.

"How much longer will you stay, Hans?" Melinda asked.

"I cannot bear to stay here for much longer."

"Hans is, like you, one of the last Communists in Czechoslovakia," Melinda told Kaspar, who was sitting beside her on the sofa. "As yet unrecalled by your national committees."

"Oh yes," Kaspar said. He had heard of Hans. Afraid perhaps that Melinda gave too much credit to himself and too little to Hans, Kaspar added, "I am only a new, how do you say, a new disciple."

"A convert," Jacob suggested, prompted by his habits as a teacher.

"Yes, that is the word, a convert."

"It surprised you perhaps, that your precious Havel could do such things," Hans said.

On Kaspar's face appeared in reply the mild and quizzical look that had so often irritated Jacob and now had a similar effect on Hans.

"Dollar for dollar," Hans continued, "nothing that Honecker ever did amounted to so great a crime."

From the reference to the East German leader, it was evident that Hans, on his side, had also heard of Kaspar.

"Is it in dollars," Kaspar replied, "that one should measure?"

"What other way, in *this* world?" Hans asked. One could hear from the way his words were formed that his mouth was twisted in disgust, though it was too dark to see such a detail. "These 'liberals' will give away industries made by the people, owned by the people—give them away! To sell them would be foolish enough."

"Aren't they giving them to the people?" Jacob asked.

"You *believe* that. Have you talked to the people?"

"People seem a little confused, but I haven't talked to very many about it," Jacob admitted.

"When the people are confused it is no accident," Hans said. "Someone wants them to be. Someone arranges it!"

He was shouting. Thom, who was standing beside the boom box, bent his knees so as to slide down the wall he was leaning against, and with a comic pretense of imagining himself unobserved, turned up the volume to match that of Hans's voice. Once a few people had chuckled, he scooted down the wall a second time to turn the volume down again.

"You oughtn't to attack Kaspar," Annie said. "He's likely the only one here who agrees with you."

"My chemists say they don't know what they'll do with their coupons," Jacob volunteered. "These chemists I teach. And they all have PhDs." If he was willing to concede a few points, maybe it would be harder for Hans to turn the conversation into a fight. "But the reforms have to be done quickly, after all."

"Quickly, yes," Hans replied, "before the people have a chance to give it thought. Crisis—the midwife of capitalism. The 'advisers' arrive and say, My god, they have no predatory class here. It is an emergency! We must create one immediately. Let us arrange to give everything to a few crooks. Then this country, too, will have a mess of parasites to rule it, to suck the value of the people's labor."

It was as if Hans were releasing a wasp into the room in the hope that someone would volunteer to be stung. For a few moments none of the partygoers moved or spoke, lest the wasp should land on one of them. Hans shook his head, as if giving up on them, and they sensed that the danger was passing—that the wasp was flying away and out the open window, as it were.

How tiresome that rigmarole is, thought Jacob. He drank a few times from his beer, and it occurred to him that he hated being compelled to think of ideas on a night when he wanted to think of his friends, especially when the ideas seemed to have in them nothing of the texture of what he had experienced with his friends. Jacob didn't know anything about economics; in America, a person with his ambitions, or lack of them, almost never did. In the British newsweekly he liked to read—once again the only English-language magazine available on Prague newsstands, now that the American competitor that had come with the war had gone with the peace—Jacob found the editors' confidence in their economic convictions appealing, though he hardly understood the grounds for them. "You've been reading it altogether too much," Daniel had once teased him, back in Boston; "you're starting to believe that the problems of the world all have solutions." Understanding the world's problems had been Daniel's forte; it wasn't Jacob's. For all Jacob really knew, Hans was right. After all, there was something economic about the freedom that he had experienced here, and the matter had to lie deeper than the currency exchange rate, so favorable to Western visitors, because people like Annie and him felt it even though they lived for the most part on their salaries in crowns. Jacob had never felt anything like it before. Maybe it was an aftereffect of Communism, but he preferred to think of it as an aspect of transition—of conditions changing so quickly and at so many levels that no one had yet figured out how to use them to separate people from the easy things that made them happy. What it felt like, practically speaking, was that one looked forward in the morning to the events of the day for themselves—to riding the rickety, musical tram, or to drinking a beer with friends. One did not think about getting through the day, or about winning anything with the use of it—there was no idea of losing the day as if in trade for something else. It was lost innocently, for nothing. But this quality of loss would have to be lost, in turn.

The necessity for the second loss was what Hans didn't understand. Jacob wondered if Carl and Melinda understood it.

"Where will you go, if you don't stay?" Melinda asked Hans.

"There is nowhere," he said bitterly. "To Denmark," he finished, with humorless irony. He meant that he would never return to Denmark. As a pretext for flirtation, he began to complain to a couple of the Czech women from the language school of the countries that he might have to travel to in order to carry on the struggle. The women seemed to regard his flirtation as so conscious that his politics could be overlooked; as a Westerner, moreover, he represented the end of Communism to them whether he meant to or not; and so by lust or at least a wish for company, he, too, became reconciled for the time being to the half-light of the room.

Jacob took a corner of the sofa, beside Kaspar and Melinda, and let himself sink into it. He wished that Kaspar had defended himself, because he had never quite understood how Kaspar justified his change of politics. It reminded Jacob of the way children fed animals—of the way he and his sister, in the small Massachusetts town where they had grown up, had picked tufts of grass on the near side of a wood-post fence and offered them to three llamas that a townsman had kept in a field as pets. He and Alice had always tried to feed the grass to the shyest llama, though they never got to know the llamas well enough to know whether the same one was always shy or the llamas took turns—whether the shyness was a matter of personality or of happening to be less hungry on a particular day. Sometimes a bold llama made as if to nip the shy one on the jowl, in brotherly menace, so the children feinted with their gifts, moving as if to thrust the grass over one part of the fence and at the last minute swapping the stalks to the opposite hand and thrusting them over another part, creating a game where the children's pale arms and the llamas' white necks waved and circled and nearly intertwined as if in impersonation of some monster out of Greek mythology. Whenever the game grew too challenging, the llamas drifted away, usually the shy llama first, and the children had to call them back. The animals were wary and greedy, like cats. Invariably the bolder llamas snatched most of the grass out of the children's hands despite their efforts. The children's choice wasn't any more rational than a choice to reward the most aggressive llama would have been—it would have made as much sense to feed the grass to the animal that seemed to want it most—but they always played the game so as to reward the llama that held back. Kaspar, Jacob thought, chose his politics by a similar instinct.

Jacob was drunk enough that it wasn't until he was halfway through sharing his analogy that it occurred to him that it could be considered disparaging to Kaspar—that Jacob might seem to be calling Kaspar sentimental or childish or even unprincipled—but he was too far along to stop and he stammered on to the end of his idea.

"The llama problem," Carl named it. He and the others had leaned in, to hear Jacob's explication to Kaspar.

"But can capitalism and communism be llamas?" Melinda objected. "Aren't they rather ways of feeding llamas?"

"So it's meta," Carl said. "It's postmodern."

"Oh dear," Melinda worried.

"I would say . . . ," Kaspar began. He paused to drum the fingers of one hand against his lips. He hadn't taken offense; Jacob's story seemed if anything to have pleased him. "I would say, why shouldn't how a child feels be the way to decide?"

"The llama Communism himself has a touch of mystery on his hands at the moment, it would seem," Thom alerted them. Hans, they saw, was kissing one of the women he had been talking to.

"That's a llama of another color."

"Quite a few llamas of that color of late," said Thom. "How is it you have been spared the darts of Cupid, Jacob, I have sometimes wondered?"

"I had a boyfriend for a little while," Jacob answered.

"I'm sorry? Did anyone else hear him say he had a boyfriend?" He thought Jacob was joking.

The friends waited.

"Don't be such an eejit," Annie said.

"*Is* that what he said?" Thom asked again, beginning to be confused. He looked to Jacob. "Are you gay then?" The word sounded unfamiliar in Thom's brogue, and Thom seemed unaccustomed to it.

Jacob nodded.

"Goodness." Thom took two swigs from his bottle. "And you all know. How long have you known, then?" No one answered him. "Nobody tells me fuck all, do they. And me yammering on about poofters and thespians. How could you let me?" He took another swig. "I've never been so ashamed in me life."

"As well you should be," Annie said.

"That makes me feel much better."

"I didn't care about those words," said Jacob. "They're funny words."

"You might have dropped us a hint."

"Maybe he did drop one and you were too much of an eejit to pick it up, unlike the rest of us."

"You let me say such things," Thom said. "I have no choice now but to drown my sorrows."

"I can't stand in your way."

"I wouldn't, sir, after the way you have behaved yourself. Anyone else need another?"

"You *could* perhaps have told him sooner," Annie said, after Thom had gone to fetch the next round.

"I should have," Jacob agreed happily. Now there were no more secrets, or anyway no more that Jacob could tell.

By midnight they were dancing in Henry's living room, jostling one another in the course of their movements as if by accident. The boom box had been turned up several times and was blaring as loud as it could, with a monotonous, rhythmic force. They had by this time heard the tape through twice, complained that they were bored of it, tried another, and in the end returned to it for lack of a satisfactory alternative—forced to recognize that it was their music for the night.

"I have quite nice shoulders," Annie asserted, over the din, while dancing next to Jacob.

"You do," Jacob agreed.

"Henry complimented me on them."

"Did he," Jacob acknowledged.

There was a sharpness and a greediness in her boast that Jacob took for a sign of health. They were, as a group, going to act tonight with less caution and less solicitude toward one another than usual, he thought. They were going to take risks. They were losing one another anyway, and they were healthy. They could dance with this violence all night if they wanted to, on the fuel of youth, Prazdroj, and *chlebíčky*. The Czech women wanted to prove that their zest matched any Westerner's; Thom, that for his friends he could trample down any awkwardness. Hans was sedulously giving the Czech women's energy a lascivious turn, Annie glowed with Henry's new interest in her, and Henry himself, bent at the waist, his curls sweaty, his wide eyes vacant as he concentrated on his dancing, had the vigor and wildness of a faun. Only Carl and Melinda danced in the old, tender style.

"Pardon," Jacob heard. Kaspar was touching his arm. Kaspar was too ill to share a selfish pleasure like dancing.

"Yes?" Jacob said. He cupped his ear but didn't stop his feet at first.

"I am leaving," Kaspar said. "I am curious, if we shall meet again."

Jacob felt obliged to stop dancing. "Sure, we'll see each other around," he said. He backed Kaspar up into the cold light of the vestibule, where it was a little quieter.

Kaspar looked into Jacob's face shyly but searchingly, as if he thought Jacob were keeping something there hidden from both of them. "But without Melinda . . . ," Kaspar suggested.

Tomorrow there would no longer be an apartment in Prague where Kaspar could rely on finding a bath and a plate of sausages and caraway-seed bread if he dropped in uninvited. It now seemed almost cruel of Melinda to have fostered Kaspar so generously, as if she had stocked a bird feeder with seed in November, December, and January but now it was February and moving away she had left it empty. He was an adult, but she had indulged his childishness, and he had repaid her with a readiness to believe that one could follow one's heart by the simple expedient of listening to it.

"We have to give her up," said Jacob.

"It is so," Kaspar agreed.

Jacob felt he hadn't yet been brutal enough. "We have to give up the whole idea," Jacob tried again, telling himself that his cruelty was for Kaspar's sake. "They're going to find out the hard way."

"Who?"

"Carl and Melinda," Jacob answered in a whisper, not wanting them to overhear.

"Ah, do you feel that?" Kaspar was studying Jacob with a look of concern.

Jacob tried to think of a way to explain that Carl and Melinda had chosen to break the old forms; they had chosen the new way; and therefore they had to expect that the new way would try to break them. It was a mistake to think that in the new world they would be able to care in the old way. In the new world you had to find something of value and learn not to care for it. You had to learn how to sell it.

"Are you distressed, Kuba?" Kaspar asked.

Jacob shut himself up. "No. I thought you might be."

"I am sad," Kaspar answered. "As I say, I would like to meet you again. Have you a telephone?"

"Not any more. Do you have one?"

"No." Kaspar chuckled softly at this dead end.

"We could leave notes at the language school," Jacob suggested.

"Yes, that is so," Kaspar replied, but he didn't seem to believe that Jacob would.

"I could stop by your place," Jacob offered. Jacob's new apartment was located just on the other side of the war cemeteries from Kaspar's.

"I hope that you will," Kaspar said. He took a deep breath, met Jacob's eye, and then looked past him for a moment into the party that Jacob was about to return to. He smiled finally in farewell. "So, okay," he said awkwardly, and was gone.

"I need a beer," said Carl, coming up behind Jacob.

Jacob followed him and took a beer, too. Carl's shirt, like Jacob's, was patchy with sweat from dancing. A breeze came through the open window behind Henry's refrigerator and played on them.

"This won't cost five crowns in Rome," said Carl.

"No," agreed Jacob.

"I wanted to be the one to tell you, you know," Carl confessed. "I said I'd known you longer. But Melinda said she'd known you longer in Prague and that that was what mattered."

Jacob shrugged away the implication that the case was a delicate one.

After a swig of beer, Carl continued: "We're leaving in a few minutes, you know."

"You are?" Jacob said stupidly.

"Hans invited Jitka to go home with him, so Jitka is offering us her apartment again for tonight."

Jacob nodded. The glass of the kitchen window behind Carl was dusty, and the dust caught and held a moonish glare thrown up by lights in the courtyard below. He and Carl would never live together again, not in Prague, Somerville, or anywhere else.

"I understand," said Jacob. This was as close as the two of them would ever be, so he looked at Carl carefully—at his ironic eyes and candid mouth. Carl looked the same but not the same as he always had, as if he were older or younger than he had been the last time Jacob had really looked at him. He was in the flow of time now. He was in a story.

"I'll probably blow it," Carl said, "but I'd never in a million years feel I had a right to a chance with Melinda even if I did know what I was doing with my life, so not knowing doesn't feel like a good enough reason to hold back."

"It'll work out," said Jacob, trying to match Carl's prosaic tone, and suddenly ashamed of the discouragement that he had tried to convey to Kaspar.

Blinking his eyes, Carl pulled his steel-bead chain out from under his shirt and over his head. He wiped dry the metal pendant on the front of his pants. "I was going to give you this."

Jacob let Carl place the saint in his palm. It was still warm. "But you're still traveling," Jacob protested.

"In a way."

"Italy's not traveling?"

"Do you want it or not?"

"Of course I want it," Jacob said.

"Okay, then."

He could have kissed Carl, but the point, he made himself remember, was that Carl was the one he didn't kiss. He slipped the chain over his own head.

"I don't have one to give you in return."

"That's okay."

"Do you want Václav?"

"Hamsters, Italy—doesn't seem right somehow."

Václav remained silent and hidden nearby, inside his soup tureen, which had been placed in a cabinet for safekeeping during the party.

In the event, Carl and Melinda stayed for another two hours, at which point, after a fluster of tears and hugs, they fled.

Annie cried on the sofa and accused anyone who tried to console her of not caring as much as she did. The rest returned to drinking and dancing. They seemed to grow almost angry in their revelry.

"Tonight is the last night," Jacob told Henry. "After this we can't live just for living."

"Then we're animals," suggested Henry.

"Animals who eat story."

"But we're also the meat," said Henry. Carl in leaving had taken with him their philosophy, and it was as if Henry and Jacob were casting about for a topic of conversation that Carl though absent might somehow still be taking part in. "We're meat with cinema," Henry said. Jacob's skin prickled. It was a naming like one of Carl's, the kind of understanding that they had been afraid of losing when they lost him. Henry repeated the words. Then he repeated them again and then kept repeating them, as if he were chanting. Meat with cinema. Meat with cinema. Meat with cinema. The words lost their meaning, as if he were unlocking and emptying them. The words became unfamiliar and abstract, and in this state they could have meant anything, and because of their purity, and because they were being consumed by the saying of them, they began, Jacob noticed with alarm, to seem to mean everything—to mean every aspect of the experience that Jacob was living through. He really was meat with cinema, and so was Henry. It was what they all were. Henry seized Jacob by the arms, and the two of them fell down together, Henry taking most of the blow, but one of Jacob's elbows flowering in pain, though the pain seemed to be happening to another person. As they fell, Jacob thought: *Oh, this is silly and grandiose, and I would never be so taken with it if I weren't drunk and Henry weren't my friend, but I am and he is and I understand what he means.* His meaning, which he didn't speak—Jacob intuited it as if a language teacher had acted it out instead of translating it—was that the two of them weren't in fact falling; they were merely disregarding the world; the accident and pain were incidental to the establishment of an axis between them that was, for the moment, distinct from the world's and untethered from it, drifting separately. For the moment they were taking a path of their own, and if the floor of the apartment happened to fall up and hit them while Henry was shouting his communication, while he was trying to persuade Jacob to hear it, to really hear what he was trying to say, then it was no more than a sign of the reality of their independence. The pain in Jacob's elbow seemed far away; the only sensations near him were the words, the repeated words, Henry trembling as he shouted them, Jacob crouching and wincing against them almost in Henry's arms. This was abandonment, Jacob thought, this feeling right now; this was what it felt like to be cut free.

Šárka

Oh, that valley was white with cherry blossoms everywhere. White and green, it was, with cherry blossoms and green, green grass. And through all that green and white, the river flowed like a silver ribbon. Why hadn't I ever noticed it before?

—Astrid Lindgren

In a new private bakery, a block from where Jacob's new tram let him off, he discovered cornflakes. Noticing a line in front of the bakery, he fell into it without knowing what it was for. The interior of the shop was trimmed with oak instead of the usual marbled white plastic. Wire baskets held golden loaves and batons; crumbs littered a blue tile floor. The cornflakes were on a high shelf behind the counter, facing out, ranged in a row like a boast.

The red-and-white packaging was in German, but the photograph on the box fronts was unmistakable. For camouflage—almost as a decoy—Jacob first ordered half a dozen *rohlíky*. Then, as politely as he could, he asked if the miss wouldn't mind also adding to his order one of those *krabice* there, if they were in fact for sale. They were, she conceded, and within twenty-four hours he had eaten all of one box's contents. He bought two more boxes the next day. He then rationed himself, but not very strictly, and his appetite so alarmed the shop assistants that one at last asked him, incredulously, what by god he did with so many *kornfléky*. —I eat them, he admitted giddily. It was like saying he ate gold.

He was unabashed now. It was what he had learned from Carl and Melinda, he felt, and he thought of himself as carrying the lesson with him under his shirt, in the form of Carl's pendant. He was still pursuing his original search, but he saw now that he had to go about it with a certain selfishness, which, if pursued purely enough, would turn out to be something more than selfishness in the end, he hoped. The new approach was reinforced by the knowledge that he was going to have to leave Prague by the end of the summer. He had been admitted to graduate school, and he had decided to go. Any pleasure he took, therefore, he was going to have to take with a necessary cruelty, with an implicit farewell, with the foreknowledge that it was only for the moment that he took it at all.

The Žižkov apartment restored to him a solitude like the one he had known before Carl's arrival. Though the building was much larger than the Stehlíks'—a proper apartment building rather than a villa—he never met anyone on the stairs or in the hallways. He returned to noticing such things as the sound of his own footfalls and the breath of air that cushioned a room when he first walked into it. He noticed the click of the bolt in its latch. If he wanted to, he was free to sit in the bedroom and watch a breeze toss the gauzy curtains quietly against the glass of the folded-open window. He didn't have to come up with words for any of his thoughts; there was no one to convey them to. The window faced south, and after lunch he sometimes set a chair in front of it and read in the sun, putting his feet up on the radiator, which was quiet by day though it sometimes clanked to life for an hour or two in the evening.

The apartment had a large, old wooden console radio, whose FM dial was orthodoxly limited to the Communist-approved frequencies, a few dozen megahertz lower than those on which Western Europe broadcast, or America for that matter. While Jacob cooked and ate dinner, he left it on, so as to give himself the sound of company. Sometimes, if he wasn't making any effort to pay attention, patches of the Czech state radio news tumbled comprehensibly into his mind.

He listened from the bathtub, too. On Mondays he always took a bath before dinner, because on Monday at eight p.m. the hot water stopped flowing and didn't come back on until Thursday at the same hour—a shortcoming that the landlord had disclosed during negotiations but which Jacob hadn't quite believed in at the time. The neighborhood's hot water piping was undergoing repair. On weekdays, he rose early in order to have time to boil water, pot after steaming pot of which he poured cautiously into the tub and then diluted from the tap.

As he perched on the edge of his tub one morning, combing the water with his fingers to mix the cool into the hot, and as birdsong peppered the morning air, it occurred to him that he didn't expect to remember the Žižkov apartment as clearly as the Stehlíks'. He didn't have the sense that he was memorizing it. The weakness of his attention may have had something to do with the season, late spring, when one begins to forget how rare, in the longer sweep of the year, a pleasant day actually is and then even to forget to reproach oneself for failing to bear the rarity in mind.

Thom and Henry found a new haunt for the friends, a cavernous hall set deep in the basement of a postwar white marble building, otherwise deserted, at the upper end of Wenceslas Square. The hall had been rented by a square-dancing society, which sold tickets and beer to the general public, and a hand-painted banner across the entrance declared the hall, in English, to be the Country Club. The beer was cheap, the fiddling sharp, and the dancing sweaty. Mostly the friends drank, talked, and smoked at the club's long tables, though sometimes they rose and jogged around on the sidelines. Now and then Annie was even able to persuade them into a more serious imitation of square dancing, in time to the music and in a simple four-four step. She and Henry hadn't become a couple, but she retained a hold on him sufficient to oblige him to participate in such experiments, and she had always been able to browbeat Thom and Jacob. In the aftermath of Carl and Melinda's defection, the boundaries of their circle had loosened, and they were joined on most nights by a few of the shorter-term expatriates who, in Carl's wake, seemed to be drifting into the city in greater and greater numbers. In the post office one day, Thom recognized a young woman he had known at school—Elinor, who had what the British called ginger hair. Immediately upon Thom's introduction of her at the Country Club, she was secured by Annie as an ally. Another new regular was Vincent, a young Tory with thick black curls and full lips, whom no one ever seemed to have invited but who insisted on showing up anyway, attracted by the pleasure of inserting himself into the conversation whenever it turned to intellectual matters. To Annie's disgust, Vincent's arguments contained frequent and apparently unconscious allusions to his family's wealth and to the education that had been purchased for him with it. His accent, too, dismayed her, for reasons that Jacob was too American to appreciate: his vowels were boxy and inward, his consonants mildly slurred. Henry was willing to be debated by him, but Thom found him insufferable and Hans called him the class enemy to his face. Jacob, however, quietly supported his presence, with motives he knew to be low. Vincent was a beauty, and his arrogance reminded Jacob of Daniel's, though it was clumsier—it was nature where Daniel's was artifice. Jacob's support irritated his friends, who regarded it as a lapse in judgment if not taste, but the defections had left Jacob impatient with the compromise he had struck with himself in the fall.

This impatience eventually led him into adventures. He refused to go back to T-Club, but one night, after parting from his friends at the door of the Country Club, he waited until they were out of sight and then walked to Letná, the park around Stalin's monument where Henry had once reported seeing men cruising. There, in the shadows, Jacob looked into the faces of circling men, as if in search of something. If he was trying out the role of outlaw, it would be wrong to be looking for approval, but before he could unravel this train of thought, he was nodded at by a wiry, birdlike man, who on closer approach proved to have fine hair and delicate features and to be only a few years older than Jacob himself. The man was too well dressed to be Czech, and he admitted in nearly faultless English to having come that morning from Vienna, though properly, he said, he belonged to Malta, since he was a knight of Malta.

"A knight?" Jacob asked. They were half whispering.

"It is a form of rank," he replied, putting on the sort of modesty that Jacob's Harvard classmates had used when telling outsiders that they went to school "in Boston." "And you are from the great republic. May I?" He interlaced the fingers of one of his hands with those of Jacob's and playfully pulled Jacob toward him. "I have a great desire to." They kissed for a while. "Shall we go to where I am staying? It is only a few steps from here."

It was somewhat more than a few steps, but the knight paid for the taxi. En route he caressed the underside of Jacob's forearm, invisible to the driver, and cautioned Jacob that they would have to enter the building where he was staying in absolute silence. It wasn't his apartment. He swore Jacob to secrecy ("you are now on your honor, you understand") and explained that he had come to Prague on business for the church (which? solemnly: "Rome"). There was an understanding between the church and the knights of Malta, an old alliance against atheism, socialism, and other such forces in the world. Though the Communists had forbidden monastic life, a few heroic men had persevered, even in Prague, and had taken vows and lived in secret accordance with them, unknown to the civil authorities. Did Jacob know of this? The pope himself had granted these men their dispensation; their apartments became their cells. It was to such a cell that Jacob and the knight were traveling. The church had offered the empty bed of a monk now on a pilgrimage to Rome—a monk's property, after all, was at his church's disposal—in consideration of negotiations that the knight was to make in Prague on the church's behalf. The apartment's second monk—two lived there—was also scheduled to be away, though only for the night, and to make sure that he was in fact away, it would be more prudent if the knight entered the rooms first alone. It was preferable if Jacob could omit to notice the location of the apartment, and he must promise, if he did take note in spite of himself, never to return. He must never speak to the monks. They were under orders. They were not to know that Jacob had ever visited. Their apartment was, after all, tantamount to a monastery. It was wonderful to have such a place, the knight continued after a momentary pause. He looked very much forward to Jacob's fucking him there.

"Are *you* a monk?" Jacob asked.

"I am a knight."

"That's right," said Jacob.

They stopped at a gray building across the street from a steep, wooded hill. Wordlessly they climbed to the top floor. The apartment was spare and simple. The knight declined to turn on a light, but on the mantel, a crucifix under glass glowed a delicate electric blue, and by its light and that of the streetlamps outside, Jacob saw that the mantel also held a bottle of water, labeled in Czech script as blessed by the pope; a framed postcard of an Italian painting of the Virgin Mary; a wooden rosary wrapped around a white statuette of Jesus; and a jar of earth, labeled as having come from the Holy Land. A part of Jacob may have felt a little sorry, but another part was happy to be a little brutal. There were twin beds, somewhat austere, and onto one of them the knight pulled Jacob and there unbuckled Jacob's belt. "Will you make use of this? I want it very badly. Or rather, not it, but what I would like you to use it with." The condom proved troublesome afterward, when Jacob thoughtlessly flushed it, causing the knight to worry that it might stop up the plumbing and be discovered during repair. His concern was so vivid as to suggest it might have happened to him once before. "It is not for me that I fear, but there should not be questions for the monks."

Thus ended Jacob's half year of abstinence. After breakfast, the two walked around downtown while the knight indicated buildings that the church intended to reclaim. "Do you see that rectory? In any case it will soon be a rectory again. I am speaking to a member of Parliament about it tonight." The knight's other hobby horse in conversation was the free-masonry, as it were, of nobles, which he extravagantly praised. Crossing Staroměstské náměstí, he became excited upon recognizing two tall, middle-aged German tourists, whom he identified as a count and an earl. "Now you will *see*," the knight whispered to Jacob. When hailed, the Germans, polite and cautious, spoke in English as a courtesy to Jacob, whose presence the knight left unexplained. The men showed no sign of knowing that they belonged to a secret club that ruled the world. "They didn't say anything about it," Jacob commented after the tourists had parted from them.

"Ah, but they wouldn't. They needn't, you see. We recognize one another."

"It's like being gay."

"Not at all."

"You have a society right under the noses of a society that doesn't see you."

"But it's very different. The matter is entirely different."

It occurred to Jacob that the Germans' courtesy might have been the sort extended to an acquaintance known to be harmless but delusional. By midafternoon, as the knight's supposed appointments with government officials approached, Jacob found himself exhausted, and it was a relief that the knight's instructions for a reunion in Vienna ("It will be pointless to ask for me by name at this address. Ask the housekeeper rather for the gentleman visiting in the rooms of the lawyer Detlev Bachofen; I am always to be found in his rooms on Thursdays at five o'clock. We shall have a whole evening together of delightful fucking") were too cloak-and-dagger to bother remembering, though the fiction of a future rendezvous did make the moment of farewell carefree.

Jacob's other adventure was less mysterious. The pages torn from his gay travel guide listed a café attached to a Wenceslas Square hotel, which he hadn't yet visited because the location was so public and because a coffee there cost as much as a meal elsewhere. Out of options, he steeled himself one afternoon. He took a seat in the café's second-floor balcony, which discreetly overlooked the main floor, amid waiters' knowing looks and the enveloping dull bronze and red serge of tourist's art deco. Older men sipping nearby queried him with surreptitious glances, and he felt saved from them when a skinny young man with dyed blond hair walked over and after a brief pretense of needing to borrow matches sat down to flirt in earnest. He was twenty-two; he was a pastry-cook's apprentice; he loved Americans. Not long after, he and Jacob were rolling in bed together at Jacob's apartment. They had sex and then, because there was nothing to talk about, had sex again. Idly, postcoitally, the man regretted the ugly furnishings that had come with the Žižkov apartment and began to propose colors and designs to replace the sheets and curtains. Jacob was entertained until the man said that next time he came he would bring his mother's plates, which were much prettier than Jacob's. He thought he was moving in, Jacob realized with alarm. Jacob disillusioned him; for good measure he invented dinner plans that required an immediate parting. The man looked stunned but said that he understood. He added that he hadn't expected Jacob to be such a person. Jacob shrugged.

Since his first day in Prague, Jacob had been going into bookstores. He picked books up from their tables nervously and greedily, pronouncing in his head the authors' names, which he didn't recognize, and the words in the titles, which he didn't understand, trying to gauge literary value by the quality of paper, binding, and design. He held them under false pretenses—he couldn't read; he merely wanted to—and he was afraid in early visits that a sales clerk might offer to help him choose or might try to draw him into a literary conversation. In those days, however, sales clerks in Prague rarely spoke to customers unless they had to. Jacob's disingenuousness was never exposed; it was able to ripen in time into something more ambiguous.

Now he began to go into bookstores more often. Prices were the same everywhere, but there was variation in supply, now that private publishers had begun to compete with those run by the state. Several private presses were samizdats turned moderately professional; their books were for the most part paperbacks with homemade designs. One or two seemed to have Austrian or German capital behind them, and theirs had shinier covers but even coarser paper stock, probably on Western advice. For beautiful hardcovers with sewn bindings and sophisticated illustration, there was as yet no alternative to the state-run presses, which in the last year and a half had started printing older books that had been suppressed since the "normalization" period of the 1970s, as well as a few samizdat titles. Their most beautiful books were First Republic classics whose liberalism or perversity had put them in a bad odor with the overthrown regime.

The state presses were also, at long last, printing more Czech-English dictionaries. One morning, long after he had given up looking for it, Jacob found the English equivalent of his Czech-French dictionary: a pocket-size glossy blue hardcover. He found it in a bright, new shop on Melantrichova. Cool and trim, the dictionary fit well in his hand, the way his French one did. It was really too late, though. The dictionary was for tourists and beginners; sometime during the winter he had stopped carrying the Czech-French version around with him, and he wasn't likely to consult the Czech-English one any more often.

He looked around at the other books for sale. The shop happened to be run by the state press responsible for children's books, and he noticed a small shelf devoted to the illustrator whose exhibit he had seen with Luboš in the winter. Here was the messy, oversize dog troubling a punctilious family. Here was a book of witches and princesses, tremblingly lined. Here, too, were a few books for grown-ups illustrated by the same artist, including the translation of *Tristram Shandy* with which the Národní třída exhibit had ended. The artist had drawn noses, battlefield maps, wilted flowers, lines that weren't straight, and diagrams of causality. It wasn't what Jacob was looking for and he would never "read" it, but the illustrations were in amber, pink, and chocolate, it was in his hands, and it didn't cost much more than he spent on beer on a generous night.

"Ahoj," he was startled to hear himself saluted.

Looking up, he saw a young blond man, whom he knew he knew but couldn't at first place. "Ahoj," Jacob answered. Was the man gay? He was Jacob's age. His hair was pure blond, very short, sloppily cut, as if he were a surfer who lived on a beach and had had to cut it himself. He was watching the expression on Jacob's face as if he were looking forward to whatever he was going to see there—as if he were confident that he was going to enjoy it. He had a long Roman nose. Nose, feet . . . It was the boy in Ota's circle who had hoped Jacob would turn out to be a cowboy. He was taller than Jacob remembered. An inch or two taller than Jacob, even.

"Milo," the boy said, tapping his own chest once.

"Jakub," said Jacob.

—But I remember, Milo answered. —Can I? he continued, gesturing that he'd like to examine Jacob's book, which Jacob handed to him. He leafed through the pages delicately and quickly. His fingers, Jacob saw, had the same stubby, oval nails as the construction worker who had once asked Jacob about American wages. —Well, and it's pretty, the boy said. —Are you going to buy it?

—But it's translated from English. Why would I read it in Czech?

—The drawings are Czech. Them you can read.

Several of the drawings were of bulbously lettered Czech words crowding and jostling one another. —You're right, Jacob conceded.

—Well, yes. The joke in his eyes wasn't that he knew better than Jacob. It was that the decisions Jacob faced might be better decided in a more lighthearted way than Jacob was used to. —And what further? the boy asked, imitating a sales clerk.

Jacob picked up the blue pocket dictionary again. —I was looking at this.

—You don't yet have?

—I have Czech-French.

—But you aren't French. You are from Texas.

—Once again you're right.

—Well, yes. So buy. That you may support our Czechoslovak businesses.

—Shall I really buy? Jacob doubted.

—Why not? Do you have the dough for it?

—Enough.

The boy shrugged, because of course it didn't really matter to him whether Jacob bought the books or not. Again Jacob had the impression that the boy was going to be delighted by whatever Jacob did, and the impression emboldened him.

—What are you doing right now? Jacob asked.

—Nothing.

—Nothing?

—Maybe something with you.

—I'd like that.

—Well, then, . . . I also, Mr. Cowboy. Shall we give ourselves something, somewhere?

The woman at the cashier neatly wrapped the books up for Jacob in paper printed with the name of the children's publishing house, as if the books were gifts. The pale, loose flesh of her upper arms, bare in a sundress, quivered as she folded and taped, and Jacob felt suddenly and irrationally happy, as if he had just realized there wasn't any reason not to do the things he wanted to do, if he could do them—as if he were going to get away with living a happy life whether or not he deserved one.

In the street Milo asked if Jacob liked ice cream and suggested a place in Staroměstské náměstí. They walked together up Melantrichova, along the familiar crooked route. The sun was striking hard on the street's white stones; tourists were chattering and giggling; he and Milo caught each other's eye. He felt the pleasure of walking in public next to a beautiful man. It was a pleasure that he thought even straight men must sometimes feel, though maybe they described it to themselves as pride or belonging. He and Milo weren't claiming each other, but they were going to sleep together, Jacob knew. They were going to sleep together that afternoon. No one around them had any idea, and the sense of conspiracy made the pleasure of anticipation even greater. Was it too much?

—You know, I return to America in August, Jacob cautioned Milo.

—Then let's hurry! Milo answered, and he made as if to dash ahead, but didn't.

Later, after the ice cream, on the tram to Jacob's apartment, they sat side by side, alert to everything happening in the car because for the moment nothing but attention could be made from their excitement. Milo let the back of his left hand rest against the back of Jacob's right, as if by accident. Neither glanced down at this point of contact between them; they were both too canny to need to. A bearded man with a mustard-colored shoulder bag boarded at Olšanské náměstí, and as the tram pulled ahead the man began to flash a bright medallion at passengers: he was a *revizor*, checking tickets. Two rows ahead, a grandmotherly woman rummaged nervously in her purse, unable to find her senior citizen's card. Two schoolgirls behind her, noticing her agitation, whispered, —Ma'am, here you have one of our tickets, here quickly. When the woman turned to accept their offer, her face showed surprise and a little fear. Jacob later felt that he never came any closer to the revolution.

—Do you want? Jacob asked.

—But no, Milo answered. —It damages the lungs on you.

—You're too good.

—But I'm an angel.

—Do you have wings?

—Of course. Can't you see?

The two were still in bed, and Jacob could see everything. He felt for the angled buds of bone in Milo's upper back. —Here in back, Jacob confirmed.

—I'd rather smoke something else.

—Marijuana?

—You're so innocent.

—Oh, something to smoke like for example—

—Hands off!

—And what are the parents like? Jacob asked.

—Father works. As a teacher of Czech.

—And Mother?

—She died. Years ago.

—I'm sorry. Your father knows about you?

—We leave each other in peace.

—You're going to have to tell him.

—So wise are these Americans.

—But yeah.

—Your feet.

—My feet?

—They're so beautiful.

—What?

—It's like 'worth mushrooms.'

—Do you speak Czech? Jacob asked.

—Nothing is Czecher than mushrooms. It's said of nonsense. 'Your feet.' 'Mushrooms.' 'Mushrooms with vinegar.'

—Why?

—I don't know. Just because. Mushrooms are pleasing to us.

The two of them were provoked by qualities in each other's bodies that, as young people, they didn't have much conscious awareness of: the responsiveness of their complexions, the richness, variety, and speed of the changes between hues—qualities only visible face to face, or face to the nape of the neck, too subtle to be caught on film, which has to commit to lines and static tones. They sat talking naked so often and so long perhaps because they liked to be able to read the whole opalescent page of each other at once.

There wasn't any sting to their appetites, because they were always able to satisfy them quickly; satisfaction kept their greed and lust innocent. They weren't held back by any worry about what their episodes in bed would lead to, because it was understood that before the end of the summer Jacob was going to be leaving for America and Milo for a job as a waiter in a new casino in Karlovy Vary. That limit may have been a further provocation; a modicum of malice impelled Jacob, after all. He was aware that he was taking for himself, that he had decided not to be too high-minded or too careful any more. He was consoling himself by using Milo. The good luck was that Milo didn't seem to mind and seemed in fact for his part to want to use Jacob in turn.

The city's great cemeteries lay just south of the Žižkov apartment. Jacob's tram took him past them every day; sometimes he switched to the bus at a stop with the poetic name of Mezi hřbitovy, or "Between the cemeteries."

One Saturday he decided to visit. Because his usual daily course took him past the burial grounds, turning aside felt at first like cutting short a trip rather than making one. He stepped into the shade of one of the Olšany cemeteries with the consciousness that he remained visible from the tram stop that he usually crossed to but this time hadn't.

The grass that ran between and around the heavy slabs was rich, its color deepened by an undergrowth of moss. Tall poplars lined the central lane, but among the graves themselves there grew chestnuts. A squirrel dropped an empty burr, and Jacob picked up the prickled, yawning shell and shook it in his closed fist. He was alive, and the heat made him nervously conscious of it. Conscious of wanting to fuck around with Milo again, of wanting to explore every last corner of Prague before he left. The dead didn't want anything, but on the other hand, they didn't mind anything, either. Their monuments were colorless as if to represent the absence of judgment. He felt aware of the muscles under his clothes carrying him forward.

In the recent weeks of lengthening sun, the poplars had grown a heavy green umbrage, which rocked gently overhead. The roofing green made the paths into corridors, and Jacob remembered walking empty corridors after school in Grafton, Massachusetts, on the days he had stayed late to develop pictures in the darkroom. He had repeated a sentence to himself as he walked, a kind of charm for safekeeping. It couldn't have been the sentence he thought he remembered, which now seemed absurdly unhappy, worse than could have been the case. The teacher who managed the darkroom had overheard him once, and he had had to pretend not to know what he'd been saying.

He came to a clearing. On a pedestal, a bronze soldier with a machine gun overlooked rows of white stone pillars, which marked the graves of Russian officers who had died in Czechoslovakia during World War II. The style was anonymous and menacing. Except for a heavy concrete star, emblazoned with hammer and sickle, the tableau wouldn't have looked out of place in Washington, DC.

The graves of the Victorian merchant families were more comforting, cluttered as they were with elaborated crucifixes and statues of gowned women. Jacob returned to them. Some headstones bore white porcelain ovals into which a hand-tinted photograph had been transferred. On others, there was no more decoration than spindly bronze letters, fringed with verdigris, spelling out a family name. Walking south, he reached a low wall that served as a columbarium. The ashes stored behind its gray doors must have belonged to people recently lost, because the doors were decorated with ribbons and wreaths of flowers, faded and papery from exposure.

A traditional grave slab nearby was littered with so many flowers that Jacob wondered whose it was. A margin of soiled wax disks—the stubs of burnt-down candles—rolled over the foot. The headstone was blank, but a piece of paper glued to it identified the remains as those of Jan Palach, the student who had set himself on fire and burned to death in Wenceslas Square in 1969, as a protest against the Russian invasion.

He was one of the revolution's martyrs; candles were brought to him because fire was his emblem. Jacob realized that he hated the tribute. If Palach had killed himself, he must have been fragile and unhappy, and it seemed wrong to make use of his death, even in a good cause. Where had he gotten the idea of making his death a gift? There was always a demanding voice, saying things like that, but that voice could never be pleased.

Jacob knew Kafka was buried in the New Jewish Cemetery, which was on the other side of a high wall, and he now walked half a block along a busy street to get there. The street hummed its indifference. At a tobacconist's kiosk, a sheaf of Sparty were tilted loosely against one another in a drinking glass, three crowns each. Jacob didn't want to buy a whole pack because he thought he should try to smoke less. Also, he hadn't brought his matches, and a box of matches cost five crowns. He couldn't bring himself to pay eight crowns for one smoke, and at the moment he felt too fragile to ask a stranger for a light. If he were to ask for a light and be refused, . . . He walked on, forgoing the pleasure of nicotine. After all, Milo didn't smoke.

Palach had no doubt remembered to bring his matches. He could have brought the gasoline in a thermos. When first poured on, the gasoline would have felt pleasantly cool, if the day had been as warm as today. But maybe it hadn't happened in spring—maybe it had happened in winter. Would he have taken off his coat, if he'd been wearing one? The flames would have lit up on his arms, legs, and face almost simultaneously. The fire wouldn't have hurt while it fed on the gasoline. Jacob wondered if Meredith had changed her mind after it was too late.

In the Jewish cemetery, the grass had been trimmed only in the first row of graves, those fronting the street. Jacob walked along it. Behind the irregular palisade of headstones, there were green shadows carpeted with vines. Scrub trees shot up and struggled to pierce the canopies of older trees, which kept out the sun.

At the end of the row, Jacob recognized the angular white stele of Kafka's grave from a biography he had read. A little mess of ferns had sprouted at its base. He stared absentmindedly at the cleared square of white gravel that the stele rose from. Had he expected to feel something here? He remembered the first sentence of "The Metamorphosis," but it was a strange thing to think of saying at a person's grave, from which a person would never awake and where one changed into . . . what? Kafka had been buried with his parents. Jacob wondered if it had bothered Kafka to know that he was leaving them with the burden of burying him.

Jacob took a few steps into the relative wilderness behind the grave. The disorder seemed to represent what Prague really thought of the writer—what it would have expressed if the visits of tourists didn't constrain it. Jacob had the feeling of standing behind stage, in a place where no care had been taken about lines of sight. Weeds curled up the front of gravestones whose backs, because they faced Kafka, had been kept clear. A certain protection was nonetheless afforded, even on the lee side of sightlines, by proximity to the writer's grave, and as Jacob walked farther away from it, he had the sense of wading into a sea. Bland, dark leaves hid first the footpaths and then the slabs that sealed the graves. In the deepest rows, ivy shrouded headstones as tall as Jacob was, fat leaves nodding here as everywhere with inoffensiveness and complacency. Young trees seemed to pry headstones from their bases, and older ones seemed to rummage with their roots, though the dislodging and the rifling were taking place with a peaceful, immemorial slowness. Was it upsetting, if there was no one alive to be upset by it? It wasn't accurate to call the process decay, because it was after all life. If you thought your death could be a gift, this is what you thought of, not the neatness of a tended grave but the abandon of a forgotten one, where there isn't much distinction between one grave and another, and with the passage of time less and less difference between having lived and not having lived.

He pulled himself out of the vines impatiently.

—Here the American prepares the water for his bath.

—But wait.

—That isn't a bother. Leave it. This is documentary How many pots are you boiling, Mr. American?

—Four. My hamster lives in the fifth.

—We are here witnesses of history.

—Will you be a participant?

—I'm the documentarist.

—Naked documentarist.

—So that I do not frighten the native.

—Will they print these photos?

—I'll print them.

—You know how?

—I photographed on Václavák during the revolution.

—Truly? You're a photograph?

—Photographer, Milo corrected.

—Photographer. I want to see your photographs.

—They're at Dad's. Hey, you're boiling.

—Attention, Jacob warned.

—He puts on his Czech underwear. Normally he is *furt* naked, this native. Mr. Native, why Czech underwear?

The boxers were striped red and white like peppermint candy. They held Jacob only loosely and went no lower than his crotch. He had to crumple the fabric down when he puts his pants on over them, or they would ride up too high.

—Normally these aren't to be seen. The American ones wore out.

—You lost them.

—In the Czech forest.

—The American pours the hot water into his tub. The American must be strong in order to carry his pots.

—When can I see the photos? Jacob asked.

—One or two are on exhibit at the Powder Tower. The American sweats in his labor. He reddens from the heat.

—Are you coming in with me? Jacob asked, running a little of the cold water now.

—It will be quite splendid, I think, this documentary of the American in Prague and his pots of hot water.

—Are you coming in?

—That one they certainly won't print.

—Are you coming?

—Wait, wait, said Milo, putting his camera aside.

On bright days, now, most of the streets of the Staré Město district were lively with tourists even in the early morning. Charles Bridge, however, drew so many of them away, to the far side of the river in pursuit of the castle, that in Staré Město north of the bridge one felt their absence. Along the avenues, large unimaginative administrative buildings sat mysteriously silent, their doors still, their shades drawn against the sun. Perhaps they had once been filled by government planning agencies. One morning Annie led Jacob down the neighborhood's empty walkways toward the river.

"They're this way," she said, once they came to the water. "Just a few meters on, I believe."

Below, flashing with reflection, dimples scissored themselves in and out of existence.

"Have you been in one yourself yet?" Jacob asked.

"That's just it. What if I were to fall in? Do you think the Czechs would rescue me?"

"You think I will?"

"Oh, you're the sort. Though you might be quite tiresome about it after. Come to think of it I expect you would be."

"I fell into the Charles once," he remembered.

"You *can* swim, then."

"It wasn't over my head, where I fell in. Just to my knees."

A gangway of whitewashed plywood rested on the stone wall that hemmed the river. With the swell of the river the gangway very gently seesawed, rising and falling like a sleeper's torso. Annie and Jacob walked down it to a moored barge. A second gangway led them down to a floating dock. Half a dozen skiffs were lashed to its sides.

They were welcomed somewhat skeptically. Jacob had to promise the man in charge that they knew how to row before the man was willing to take twenty crowns, untie a skiff, and hand Jacob its painter. Annie clambered into the stern. When Jacob followed, the boat swiveled dangerously until he realized he should crouch down. Seated facing her, he drew the oars up from between his legs. Once he had figured out how to hold them, he set the tip of one oar's blade against the little dock and shoved them off.

They drifted for a moment. The nose of the skiff had been pointed upriver, toward the Charles Bridge to the south, but the current soon caught the nose and the skiff yawed clockwise, into the middle of the river, until Jacob, realizing that he now had enough sea-room to swing the oars freely, pulled on them and righted the skiff so that it once more stemmed the stream.

Effortfully they climbed the river. The bright air around them was silent except for intermittent clumsy splashes that he made with the oars. The rowing took more strength than he had imagined it would. He began, however, to find a rhythm. They were far below the level of the city where they usually walked. The tall, mud-gray stone of the embankment seemed to be sheltering them.

"It's quite lovely, isn't it," said Annie. "I knew it would be." She brushed the hair from her forehead and blinked her eyes shut for a moment in the sun, appreciating its warmth.

"How'd you hear about it?"

"Your man Vincent mentioned it. In his way. 'Rather urban, compared to punting on the Cam, you know.' Or some such dreadful thing. What is it you fancy about him, anyway? His lips? He does have nice lips."

"His hair."

"His curls. I like curls on a man as well. But he's not worth it, Jacob. He's not worth putting up with the rest of him. Mind where you're taking us."

"I was going to go through."

"Through? You mean under?"

"There are boats on the other side." The plain shadow of the Mánes Bridge fell over them, cooling them.

Annie craned her neck to look between the bridge's piers. "So there are. I hadn't seen them. I suppose it's all right then."

They passed through. The sun returned to them while the broad, slow-sloping stones of the bridge's underside were still overhead. On the right bank the sun was hitting the bleached faces and orange roofs of Malá Strana's old riverside palaces.

"Anyway I'm seeing someone again," Jacob volunteered. "A Czech."

"Are you, then."

It was not as easy to tell Annie as it would have been to tell Melinda. Annie resisted hearing confessions. "We're having a good time," Jacob continued.

"Am I to congratulate you?"

"I'm just telling you about myself."

"I suppose I am to congratulate you. Do you speak Czech with him?"

"I spoke it with Luboš."

"I don't know as I realized that."

"But this isn't like with Luboš. It isn't serious."

"That is the way, now," she said, as if a little disappointed in him.

"I don't mean I don't like him. He's nicer than Luboš. What I mean is there isn't any mystery about it."

He needed to catch his breath. He shipped the oars. Annie wasn't looking at him. What he didn't say was that he was beginning to wonder if this was the way one always ought to go to bed with people: as if it weren't so meaningful, as if it were to one side of the story one was in.

"I don't know as I should mind that, if I were you."

"I don't mind it. Maybe I'm not saying it right."

"It might be quite pleasant, to be able to have that," she said, speculatively. "To be unencumbered, as it were. Though I find in my own case there's always a mystery, as you call it, if I'm soft on a person."

The current was turning the skiff again. Jacob pulled on the oars to straighten it. He watched Annie's eyes as she watched the Charles Bridge approach, and over his shoulder, every few strokes, he took a glimpse of the tall, jagged, two-story piers himself, so as to be able to aim the boat between two of them.

"Is it quite safe? With the current, I mean."

"I'll just have to row a little harder."

They passed into the black water of the shade of the bridge. Out of the corner of either eye, Jacob watched the gray, triangular battlements slide up from behind and widen, approaching them on either side, in embrace. Then the bridge itself crossed overhead with its water-blackened stones. While it covered them, hands seemed cupped over their ears; all they could hear was the water's eager lapping against the heavy walls beside them.

"Are you fair to him?" Annie asked.

The black stones lifted off, and the air was free and empty again around them. "It's not like that." He watched recede the semicircular—circular, in the water's haphazard mirroring—portal through which they had passed.

"Isn't it."

"He's going to Karlovy Vary himself, at the end of the summer."

"Not quite to the other end of the world."

"Are you going to stay past the summer?" Jacob asked.

"I might do," she answered. She glanced at him. "Don't you want to see how it comes out?"

Jacob slowed the pace of his rowing. The triangle of water that they were now drifting in had been smoothed by a weir just upriver. From a distance the river's weirs could look decorative, like narrow cuffs sewn into the fabric of the water's surface, but as their skiff came up to this one, which blocked any further headway, they were able to appreciate the mass and power of the water shoving itself over. The uniformity of the flow contributed to the impression that it gave of implacability; at every point, the same force was insistently pouring its heavy self downstream.

"It's like that between Henry and me, too, now, I suppose," Annie continued. She had to speak over the churn of the water. "Do you know, I thought I could persuade him to come boating, they give him an hour for lunch, but he wouldn't do. I think he feared I might get *ideas*—that it would be too romantic like. But I only asked for the lark."

Jacob let the current turn the skiff around. He told himself that while rowing back he would think about Annie's question, the one about seeing how things came out, but a boat travels faster with the current than against it.

Once or twice a week, Milo spent the night, after having let his father know that he would be staying over at his new American friend's place. Jacob always woke up early the next morning, eager for them to make love again in the new day. It was as if there were a contest between Jacob and the sun to see who could rise earlier. Spring was blowing into summer, and the sun was racing deeper and deeper into the mornings, but sometimes he managed to wake up into a half-light not unlike the half-light in which he had lived out so much of the winter, gray, tender, and general, though now it belonged not to dusk but dawn. The slate through the window was so even that from the bed it wasn't possible to tell whether it colored a clear sky or one that was uniformly cloudy: the ambiguous color itself seemed to be its only real quality. Milo would be lying in bed beside him at a slant, faintly radiant in his pallor and nakedness, sheets and blanket twisted almost into ropes around and sometimes between his legs. Jacob watched the rise and fall of his ribs until he couldn't watch peacefully any more and woke him.

There was never any recoil in Jacob, afterward. Because Jacob thought lovemaking was supposed to be free of such reaction, he didn't wonder much about how he had got free of it. Once, though, when he was feeling pessimistic about himself, it occurred to him that any need he might feel to withdraw from Milo might be sufficiently expressed by the foreknowledge that he was soon going to leave Milo for good, and Prague, too.

A moment later, such a speculation seemed too cynical. The truth was that there was no need to pull back from Milo, who hopped into sex like a duck into a pond—dunked his head vigorously in, swam about happily, briskly shook his feathers clean afterward. He didn't act as if the pleasure implied anything about what the two of them were going to do next, though it was clear he wasn't likely to be averse to repeating it. With regard to the future, he seemed to consider Jacob, as an American, to belong to an order of being set somewhat apart—the order of those who don't stay, who are a little comical in fact in their transience, an order in which he himself to some degree participated, in that at the end of the summer he was going to move to Karlovy Vary, a town full of tourists, and work for a casino, a cartoonishly capitalist enterprise.

Jacob wasn't returning to America for the sake of school or any career that school might lead to. He was returning for the most part because it upset him that in Prague he had written so little—just one fragmentary story about Meredith. He was impatient with his lack of progress (it was to be a long time before he was able to reason with this kind of impatience, let alone resist it), and he hoped that America would force him to prove himself, rank himself. As a measure of self-discipline he was volunteering to give up the exemption that Prague had seemed to offer. It was only on account of having given it up, of having set himself a postponed reckoning, that he was able to let himself enjoy the summer that remained.

In the summer's limit, Milo for his part seemed to see no more than a motive for bringing Jacob to experiences in Prague that Jacob had so far missed. At first he merely pointed out opportunities that Jacob was walking past unawares. Jacob was at this stage exploring Malá Strana in greater detail. He had neglected it because it lay on the far side of the river and a little too obviously in the way of the tourists who marched daily across the Charles Bridge to the castle, but he had come to feel that he ought to be bigger in spirit than to fear seeming like a tourist. Still, to distinguish himself from the tourists, he insisted on arriving in Malá Strana by a practical rather than a scenic route, rising into the district on the Malostranská subway station's long, tedious escalator, two flights of which seemed to be permanently under repair, and then walking down a crooked alley, just as long and tedious if not quite as exhausting, that ran along the rear of several palaces and was lined on both sides with faceless concrete wall for most of its length.

—There are gardens here, do you know? Milo asked, the third or fourth time Jacob led him down the charmless alley. —Take a look. He nodded at a heavy, unlabeled door the size of a horse and carriage, with a smaller door the size of a person cut into it.

—This is allowed? Jacob asked, half to himself, as he pushed open the inner, person-size door. He saw a path of blue gravel crossing green lawn. He stepped carefully over the lower edge of the larger door that framed the smaller one.

The gardens were laid out in a seventeenth-century pattern. Stiff, calf-high hedges drew squares around green lawns and within the lawns drew circles around flowerbeds. The flowers themselves had gone past; no more than a few white petals were still scattered in the leaves of the plants, which in the lateness of the season had grown from beauty into mere health, monotonously and diffusely green, washing up lazily against the woody hedges that encircled and contained them. At the corners of the sectioned lawns, bronze statues were streaked somewhat wildly with white and green verdigris. Water jetted from a statue of a woman and child into a large basin.

—Is it pleasing to you? Milo asked.

—It's excellent. We have to come back.

—But we are here now.

Maybe it was the mistaken impression that they had stumbled onto a secret that had caused Jacob to imagine that the point of the place was to come back to it later.

Two women sat gossiping on a stone bench in the shade while their children, elfishly thin, wearing nothing but underwear and sockless shoes, skipped from one hedged quadrant to another. The children had an inflatable red-and-white ball, and their game seemed to be to tag one another with it. It was so easy to dance away that in order to have any fun it was necessary for them to endanger themselves by coming needlessly close.

—They aren't shy, said Jacob.

—Why would they be shy?

—In America, even children, if they are not clothed . . .

—But you're not a Puritan, not you.

—No, Jacob admitted. —But you and I . . . , he continued, but he trailed off. He had been going to defend America's morals, or lack thereof, by pointing out that on Prague's subways and trams he and Milo allowed no more than the backs of their hands to touch, but the touch had become a habit and Jacob found that he would rather let his point go than cast a light on it in any way critical.

—Here you and I, said Milo, pointing at a bronze of two wrestling men. The figures didn't seem to be Antaeus and Hercules—their four feet were planted on earth—but merely two Enlightenment gentleman-gymnasts, thick-muscled and delicately coiffed. Rain had blanched with verdigris the rippled chest of one of them, who stood upright, pushed slightly backward, exposingly, by his partner, who was bent over and was pulling toward him the upright man's left thigh while pushing away his right shoulder. The upright man, who wore a trim moustache, looked down at the other with a look of concern, almost tender. A clean-minded viewer was supposed to understand that the statue represented the men just before the lower threw the upper off his balance, but as a statue the statue belied this interpretation, because it held them together eternally in poise, and where the lower man placed his hand on the upper one's thigh, and the upper one placed his hand over that hand, it was just as possible to imagine that the pressure of the second hand was intended to confirm and hold that of the first one.

—Like this? Jacob asked, and he abruptly bent over, grabbed Milo's thigh, and made as if to shove away Milo's opposite shoulder. Milo caught Jacob's two hands in his and under the cover of rough-housing jestingly tried to keep Jacob for a moment in the lower man's crouch, which in the statue brought the lower man's face suggestively near the upper one's fig leaf.

—But be good, Milo said.

—Good for what? When Jacob recovered, he continued to study the statue, glancing at it over his shoulder as he tried now to adopt the posture of the upright man. Was that what he and Milo looked like? he wondered. Not: Did they look muscled and naked. Not that aspect but the other: Did they look balanced. Did they look like two men touching each other. Of course they did, but it was strange to think about it. To think there might be something not unpleasant *about* it as well as for themselves *in* it. —Is this posture even possible? Jacob asked, to invite Milo to hold him again under the license of imitating the statue.

—I think, that yes, Milo said. With assumed seriousness he set his feet in the crouching man's position, one foot behind to anchor himself, the second in front and between Jacob's legs. —And then, he continued deliberately,—I give a hand here, and a second hand here, and—

He tumbled Jacob over.

"Asshole!" Jacob said happily, lying on his back in the grass.

—So trusting, these Americans.

The gardens were so extensive and so cleverly planted with boscage along the periphery that from the vantage of the ground Jacob could look up toward the castle hill and imagine that no walls separated him from its summit. A cascade of terraces and allées carried the eye all the way up. In fact the terraces belonged to other gardens—the gardens of consuls and embassies, for the most part, Milo said, when Jacob pointed to them and asked. But the illusion was almost perfect.

—But you see? Milo asked, after they returned to their feet and as they approached the central fountain. —There's no Puritanism in Bohemia.

From a young bronze matron's left breast spurted a steady stream of water. A winged boy, whose hand she held as if they were dancing, turned up his lips to catch some. He wasn't able to, but he peed uninhibitedly nonetheless from his little boy's cock, while a dolphin, which he was standing on, spat a third, lesser arc.

—The source of sources, Jacob said.

—The sources of sources, Milo corrected. —Be liberal.

From impromptu suggestions Milo progressed to outright plans. He came up with the idea of taking Jacob to Amerika, an old quarry a few kilometers southwest of Prague that had become a swimming hole, and on a Saturday morning he picked Jacob up in his father's army green Trabant, two folded towels and two bottles of Mattoni seltzer in the back seat, his Konica around his neck. They followed a highway south along the left bank of the Vltava until the highway veered west from the river and zigzagged. The city then folded itself up and away from them, and they found themselves driving through fields of yellow flowers. Sun fell generously across their laps. They rolled their windows down, and with his fingers Jacob made shapes that cut different sounds out of the warm air that they were speeding through.

—We will be able to swim, Milo explained. —But better we don't drink, you know?

—Is it dangerous?

—It's America.

They passed through a few small towns until, outside of any town, they came to a line of cars parked irregularly beside the road. Milo pulled onto the shoulder. The farmland here was planted with grasses that had grown so long and heavy that they had lain down in still-living sheaves like parted hair. Along an erratic path afforded by these parts, three middle-aged men were picking their way toward a thicket. The men had stripped to European-style swimsuits, over which their grizzled bellies hung, and they encouraged and mocked one another in voices that were no doubt amplified by beer. Milo, already wearing his swimsuit under his jeans, stood guard while a bashful Jacob changed into his more modest American-style swimming trunks in the car. Jacob was excited by the momentary peril of exposure. The fake leather of the seat felt cool under his naked ass. He wasn't able to see his own cock and balls reflected in the glass of the windshield; the angle was wrong.

They crossed the field and took a dirt path through the thicket, which gave way to meadow, which gave way to thicket again. The path was marked with white paper signs taped to trees, written in the formal Czech that Jacob had trouble deciphering.

—Does this say 'forbidden'?

—If you read it.

—To whom belongs the land here?

—It's maybe still the state's? I don't know.

The disregard was of a piece with the general liberation, not yet attenuated—the dispensation that the Czechs and Slovaks were still under to live as if no authority had more responsibility for them than they had for themselves.

Ahead, at a stand of pines, a cluster of people were admiring the artificial canyon, which they had at last reached. The irregular gorge was maybe half a mile long and as deep as a seven- or eight-story building. Toward the bottom, it was spanned by a sheet of water, so unmoving and transparent that one saw clearly the continuity of the rocks above and below it—saw the two faces of the gorge run down the opposing cliffs to meet underwater and fold knottily together, the submersion making no interruption to the eye apart from the slight compression and redirection that light is subject to when passing between water and air.

Here and there, an outcropping of yellow, rectangularly chipped lime-stone reached across the water's surface like a clumsy claw; elsewhere, a curved, grassy dais formed the shore, and people lay on it sunbathing. The exposed rock of the cliff faces was reddish tan; its parallel wrinkles ran in grand arches, like those on Auden's face in photographs.

—Like at home, isn't it? Milo asked.

—Exactly.

—Wait, I'll eternalize you.

After the photo, Milo insisted on going first down the ledge. Erosion had rendered it slightly dangerous, and he had been down it before. As they descended, he kept looking back to make sure Jacob noticed which boulders he trusted with his weight and which tree roots, laced into the face of the cliff, he used as handholds. As the cliff walls rose higher, the rim of the gorge above them began to seem to make a cutout of the blue sky, and Jacob became aware that the sun needed its full summer height in order to peep down at them, as if they were looking up at it from the bottom of a well. When, as they made their way down, small stones were dislodged by their steps and skittered over rocks in falling, the echoes ricocheted so loudly that it seemed almost redundant for Milo to call out, "Pozor! Pozor!" to those below.

They walked until they found a dais with an unoccupied patch of grass in the sun. They spread their towels. Milo stripped off his shirt and shucked off his pants. At the sight of him, Jacob's desire was loud to his own perception, but with an effort he understood that the people sitting near them on the dais couldn't hear it and that their deafness left him free, and after a while he relaxed enough to take off his shirt, too, and lay beside Milo, eyes closed, the sun warming his blindness.

In the orange darkness, he was drawn into the spirit of Milo's joke— of having brought an American to Amerika—and he let go of his certainty as to which country he was in. For clues there were only the sun, the dry touch of the air, and the bony soil that he could feel through the towel beneath him. When he opened his eyes, he noticed that colors had been bleached out of his sight by the sun; the gestures frozen into the cliff face across the water seemed gray and the hot sky almost white. Was nature nature everywhere? Or was this a different nature than the one he had been born into? This wasn't Texas heat, just a pleasant representation of it. On the other hand, the setting hardly suggested Europe. One was unsheltered here. No one seemed to be following any rules that the people present hadn't themselves made up.

—About what will you write? Milo asked, led perhaps by a similar train of association to think of the world that Jacob would before long be returning to. In late-night conversations, Jacob had confided some of his ambitions to Milo.

—I don't know.

—I think, that you will be a big writer, and I, your secret friend.

—But leave it, Jacob pleaded. —Probably I will write about America, he said. It was with something like this solemn intention, after all, that he was ending his year of travel.

—Then it was a good idea, this excursion.

—I mean, the big America.

—But we are in the Big Amerika, Milo replied. —It is this particular canyon. Over there is Little Amerika. Do you want to see Mexiko?

—And what else?

Switzerland. Milo pointed west. —You know, the business that will employ me is Australian. Perhaps sometimes they will alternate the personnel, between countries. Have you visited Australia?

—No, Jacob admitted.

Milo looked a little pensive. —There too there are cowboys.

It was frustrating not to be able to touch each other.

—Do you still see Ota? Milo continued, after a pause.

—No longer, said Jacob.

—I, too, no longer.

They sat up, and Milo drank some of his seltzer. He didn't want to go in the water, which was ice cold, but Jacob waded in, taking care not to cut his feet on the sharp rocks, the edges of which were easy to see. Once he was halfway in, he shudderingly propelled himself off an underwater ledge; because he was among strangers he held in his natural yelp at the chill. He dog-paddled out and upon turning saw that Milo was documenting his swim. By the time he reached the shore again his feet were so numb with cold that he emerged unsteadily, on all fours for caution.

Before driving home, while still wearing their swimsuits, they ate pork cutlets and dumplings in a nearby town, in a pub whose dining room was a sort of greenhouse in the middle of a farm. Through the glass walls they watched the sun set over flat farm lands, losing none of its purity of color as it descended, though the sky around it, at the moment the sun touched the horizon, deepened like a rock picked up from a river bank and dipped in the water. Afterglow still lit the sky when they began their drive back to Prague, but it was dark by the time they arrived in Strašnice, the district where Milo's father lived. They parked the Trabant on the street, and Milo ran up to his *panelák* apartment with the car keys to say good night. When he reemerged from the white building, he and Jacob walked the mile to Žižkov—not far enough to be worth waiting for a night bus—along empty streets.

Jacob had never been to Petřín, a park in the western part of the city, because it had always sounded tacky to him. But it has a replica of the Eiffel Towel, Milo pointed out. Exactly, Jacob replied. Milo pretended to be shocked by his philistinism.

They decided to go on a Tuesday. Jacob was free from teaching that afternoon; the only hitch was that they had to wait for Jacob's landlord to stop by and pick up the June rent. To pass the time, they drifted into the bedroom and lay crosswise on the red-and-black checkerboard of the duvet, and its design suggested to them another game with simple rules, often played with little strategy.

The landlord had no suspicion that he was interrupting. He was too genial. In the negotiations for the apartment, he had invited Jacob to pay in a combination of cash and English lessons; Jacob had insisted on cash, but now, in Jacob's kitchen, the man began to ask in English how Jacob found the stove, the refrigerator, the sink. He gestured for nouns he didn't know, and Jacob was too polite and by now too much by second nature a teacher to fail to supply them. The only escape that Jacob could think of was to explain that he and Milo were on their way to Petřín and to invite the man to accompany them to the tram. Jacob wanted, and knew Milo wanted, to finish what they had begun, but Jacob couldn't couldn't think of a suitable lie. By the time they had waved good-bye to the landlord, they were already on their way.

It may have been the state of yearning that reminded Jacob of Daniel; yearning was after all as far as Jacob had ever really got with him. He wondered what Daniel would think of Milo. In practice, although Daniel hadn't wanted Jacob for himself, he had never approved of anyone Jacob had shown an interest in. But in theory, at least, Daniel would have to recognize in Jacob's new indifference to consequences, in his capacity to embrace the example of Carl and Melinda, evidence that Jacob had at last reached the sort of skeptical, adult perspective that Daniel had despaired of his attaining. And it wasn't going to be possible for Jacob to be hurt. Nothing like what had happened with Luboš could happen now. He was moving too fast.

He and Milo walked up the broken escalators of the Malostranské station behind two conscripts in uniform. Each conscript's cap, neatly folded, was tucked into the buttoned-down epaulet loop on his jacket's shoulder, above where his stripes would go if he ever earned any. Jacob wondered if conscripts were instructed to carry their caps this way or whether it was a perennial innovation, which every cohort came up with by themselves. The conscripts took the steps lightly and steadily, their faces unflushed, their voices not winded. In a crowd, conscripts always looked healthier than their fellow citizens. Jacob didn't think it was only on account of their youth. Was it the effect of regular exercise? Maybe the economy had been planned so as to give them a better grade of food.

—Must you go into the service sometime? Jacob asked Milo.

—That's how Dad found out. I told him, that I didn't have to.

—Because you're gay.

—Many say it. So he can't be quite sure.

—A pity.

—It isn't.

—A pity, I mean, that you had to present yourself as . . .

—As I am.

—Well, yeah, you have the truth. But your friends from university, what with them?

—A lot are in the service, Milo admitted. They were arriving in the glass box that topped the subway station. —But I thought to myself, that at the moment there are opportunities, and I have to make use of them.

They headed down the long blank street where Milo had a week or so before shown Jacob the door to the Renaissance gardens. They walked past the door this time. They crossed Malostranské náměstí. A few minutes later, they came to the American embassy, a Prague palace that Jacob's country had somehow infused, in occupying it, with the national qualities of blandness and force.

—When my friends went off to the service, I got to know Ota.

—Downstairs? Jacob asked. The word had been one of Ota's ways of referring to T-Club.

—Downstairs, exactly.

Two American soldiers, armed but in relaxed postures, stood in a driveway that led under an arch to gardens in back of the embassy, which were forbidden to visitors. The soldiers paid no attention to Jacob and Milo, even though Jacob, made a little hungry by the sight of men who were such types of blandness and force, stared at them and at as much of the gardens as he could catch a glimpse of. On the sidewalk, a dozen or so Czechs were in a line, waiting with familiar patience to file visa applications.

—I remember, said Jacob, —that he was funny, when I met him.

—He's witty. Such friends I didn't have before. And even if . . .

—Even if?

—Nothing, Milo backpedaled. —I wasn't going to say anything. It's complete shit, what I was going to say. The street twisted sharply as it climbed a hill. —We're living through a time of changes.

They didn't need to look back at all of them. —I still have his cassette, Jacob said.

—Of what?

—Depeche Mode.

—That is fearfully typical of him.

Beyond the embassy, the street ran along the crown of an escarpment, curved left, and turned into a grassy path that led into Petřín. Nothing sheltered Jacob and Milo from the midafternoon sun, and they were conscious that they remained visible to any one on the street behind them. The castle overlooked them, far above, and anyone looking out a rear window of the American embassy could also have seen them. Out of caution, it wasn't until the path began to wind between trees, which were burgeoning with green, that Jacob took Milo's hand. Milo didn't resist. It was a weekday afternoon and the park was empty. They were once again in a version of what Czech speakers of English tended to refer to as "the nature." It seemed to be Milo's instinct to bring Jacob into it.

—Here are apple trees, Milo said, using a word different from the one for the fruit, though similar enough that Jacob was able to recognize it.

Jacob backed Milo up against one of them. He remembered the dark, clear bark from orchards in Grafton.

—It isn't a bother? Jacob asked, after he kissed him.

—It isn't a bother, Milo replied. He tugged at the hair at the back of Jacob's neck, which had grown a little long. —You need a clipping.

—Do you know how?

—Absolutely not. But maybe you want to be a longhair.

After a while Jacob noticed that they were walking among a different kind of tree, which had blossomed so recently and so abundantly that papery and translucent petals were still scattered in the grass below.

—Cherries, Milo explained. —When I was a little boy, Mother liked to come here, when the flowers for the first time open.

—It's pretty.

—Now they're gone by. You'll have to return, if you want to see them.

It wasn't a thing that could last, Jacob told himself, for the sake of discipline. Milo suggested they sit down in the sun.

—How is the school, which you will attend in the fall? Milo asked.

—It's English literature, but it's not important.

—No?

—I'm going to be a writer, he reminded Milo.

—And you won't need literature?

—I'll write my own.

Because he was going to leave, he had been keeping himself on good behavior. Since it wasn't going to last, a lifetime of effort wasn't necessary, only a couple of months—a matter of weeks, really—and he was better for this moderate exercise of willpower, he was sure, than he had ever been before. But because it wasn't going to last, it was just as feasible to get away with bad behavior—to be in some ways worse than he had ever been before—to let Milo think he was someone he wasn't, for example, or wasn't yet, in any case—to play out what was between them as if it were a daydream of getting everything he wanted. As if the story could be made to run according to his wishes, free of all checks. One day, when he was a child, he had been playing with another boy in the backyard of his parents' home in Houston, and he had made something up. There had been a sprinkler; the boys had been wearing their swimsuits. He had invented a game. Did it go back as far as that? He had put his arms around the boy. The leaves of grass in Texas lawns were paler and fatter, less mixed with the straw of what died in winter.

—Will you sell to the films?

—For millions.

—Maybe you will write me letters, between your novels.

—Maybe, but I will be very famous.

—But right now you're mine, Milo asserted.

—Yes, Jacob quietly admitted. —You see?

—An opportunity of the moment.

He was deceiving Milo for the sake of the look in his eyes.

Everyday life continues during a love affair, though it loses any power to be menacing. One sees it as if from the other side of the room. It can't issue verdicts or decide meanings and becomes for the interim no more than something to appreciate or humor, as the case may be, unless the lovers on a whim choose to bring a moment of it inside the boundary, invisible to others, that has been drawn around them.

Jacob paid no less attention to his teaching but he no longer worried about it. At the language school, whenever his students couldn't guess a word's meaning, he liked to draw a picture on the chalkboard. His drawings used to be clumsy, but suddenly he seemed to have a knack for them, which he recognized, when he studied himself a little, as no more than a new, happy indifference to whether the drawings came out so badly that his students laughed at them—as sometimes they still did.

A lover's detachment fell in conveniently with a complication of mood that had come over the city. Before Jacob's arrival, the story of the revolution had held everyone tightly, he imagined, but the season of late spring that they were now passing through was not the first to follow the revolution but the second. The revolution was receding into the past; its grip as a story was weakening. There was a general sense of unraveling, of drift, of inconsequentiality. In their thoughts people were beginning to go their separate ways. It wouldn't have been tactful to make too much of it; there was no point in throwing the fact of differentiation in anyone's face. It went largely undiscussed.

It was perceptible, though, in new patterns of life. Catercorner to the new bakery where Jacob had begun to buy cornflakes, one day a new butcher's shop appeared, where it was possible to buy fresh pork chops and beef steaks, as well as better grades of sausage than the government-run shops kept in supply. When the bakery had opened, a crowd had rushed in to try it. But no crowd gathered at the new butcher's.

There were now so many new shops that no single one was any longer a matter of general public interest. The butcher's prices were fairly high, and it was beginning to occur to people that not everyone would be able to afford every new shop that opened. Some shops were going to be for some people; others, for others. Some shops would be reserved implicitly for special occasions, which would come at different times to different people. One's pride was at stake, and as a measure of prudence, one had to begin to think a little more narrowly, keeping in mind one's personal wishes and means rather than those of the average worker—the ideal customer that the old shops, in their uniformity, had been addressed to.

It contributed to Jacob's awareness of the dispersal that the end of the school year was soon going to break up his classes at the language school. He was going to miss the regularity and sense of purpose they provided, as well as the students themselves. For a month now, the editors of the Charles University student newspaper, the ones who Rafe had introduced him to, had been putting off their sessions from week to week pleading the need to prepare for exams, and at this point Jacob no longer expected to meet with them again. Though the academic calendar didn't affect his other private students, the new restlessness did. One day after class at the chemistry institute, the well-dressed Pavel rose and with a certain deliberateness shook Jacob's hand.

"I must thank you," he said. "I have a new post, and I believe that English was of assistance."

"You spoke beautiful English long before I arrived," Jacob replied.

"I am not so sure."

"Congratulations, though. What's the job?"

"I will be a senior research designer in composite materials. It is with an Austrian firm, in Linz."

"Don't they speak German?"

"I happen to speak German also, but I believe, that they appreciate my English."

In order to listen in, the pretty Zuzana had delayed getting up from her chair. Now she observed, "He is brilliant in languages and in chemistry, Pavel."

"He is too young to know German," complained the elderly Bohumil, who had also been eavesdropping. "He is too clever for his age."

"And you, for your age," Pavel retorted. "Bohumil also speaks German, very well."

"Everyone of my generation speaks it," Bohumil said, swatting away the compliment. "One had the impression here, for a while, that it was going to be the *Weltsprache*."

Jacob wished Pavel luck. Ivan lingered; he also had news. Over the weekend he had met with a young businessman who had a new idea. He proposed to teach through television; after all, there was one in almost every home already, even in Czechoslovakia. The man would very much like to meet Jacob. He was perhaps Jacob's age. Could Ivan bring Jacob to his office?

"Are you going to work for him?" Jacob asked.

"I suspect, that I am not. But it is an opportunity for you, I think."

As Jacob walked to his bus stop, Ivan described the man's office on the northern periphery of the city, in a concrete building that the authorities had erected as a temporary structure not long after World War II but had never got around to demolishing and replacing. It didn't have many windows. A tram depot was across the street. Through the fence one could see some trams of an older design, which no longer ran, but which Ivan remembered from childhood.

"I'm going back to America pretty soon, I think," Jacob said.

"But it is an opportunity," Ivan persisted. He drew his right hand up and out, an expansive gesture not at all in keeping with his usual birdlike manner. He must have picked it up from the young businessman.

"I don't think I should," Jacob said. He felt that he was being ungrateful and slightly cruel.

That night he met his expatriate friends at the Country Club. At the back of the building's lobby, at the top of the stairs that led into the basement hall, it was possible to look over the banister and survey the rows of folding tables below. At first Jacob didn't see anyone he knew. He had arrived a little early; perhaps he was the first one. The dance floor was empty; the dedicated dancers, distinguishable by green knickers on the men and red aprons on the women, were drinking in a loose group at the bar in the far corner. A hum of talk was diffused by the hall's echoes and rose generally, like the cigarette smoke, which, as it was stirred by the hall's hot lights, dissolved into a glare that filled the volume of the room. Down into this brightness Jacob squinted until at last he spotted

Annie at a distant table. Elinor was sitting daintily across from her, and Vincent next to Annie, his large hands folded on the table in front of him. Jacob took the stairs quickly.

"Do you know if any of the fellows are coming?" Vincent asked at once.

"The fellows?" Jacob echoed.

"Vincent doesn't care to be sentenced to a night of conversation with women," said Annie.

"Not a night of *conversation*, no," replied Vincent.

"You see?" said Annie. "Elinor and I were just having a chat about Czech ice cream. I'm partial to the apricot myself."

"Have you been to the place in Staroměstkské náměstí?" Jacob asked. It was the one Milo had taken him to, on the day that Milo had picked him up in the bookstore.

"They give you a biscuit with it there, don't they. A wafer, I suppose you would call it. No, that's not right. A *cookie*. Is that the word?"

"I must try it out," Vincent said, as if Annie had urged him to go.

"You haven't heard from Melinda," Annie suggested.

"No."

"I thought by now surely one of us would have done."

"Where are these friends of yours?" Vincent asked.

Annie looked at him without answering.

"Rome, we're pretty sure," said Jacob.

"Don't misunderstand me. I quite like Rome," Vincent said.

Thom and Jana arrived. Jana was beginning to show, and the effort of walking down the stairs lightly flushed her face, which seemed to have taken on some of the translucency of an infant's complexion.

"Isn't she beautiful?" Annie whispered. Then, aloud: "And how are the two of you keeping?"

"Jana's grand, as you see, but I seem to have put on a little flesh." Thom opened his coat and swiveled. "Am I in danger of losing my girlish figure, do you think?"

"Would it be the *pivo*?" Annie wondered.

"I say, that it is a bun in *his* oven," said Jana.

"Wouldn't that be a state of affairs, if we could both have come down with one at once?"

"Like earthworms or something," said Jacob.

"Earthworms *are* hermaphrodites, aren't they?" said Vincent. "I'd forgotten that."

"What have you done to me, my dear?"

Thom and Jacob went to fetch a round: Mattoni for Jana, glasses of Staropramen for everyone else. When they returned and set the glasses down on the red-and-white gingham, the disks of the liquid's surface trembled.

"Will the poetry corner be having any more meetings?" Annie asked. "I don't suppose you will, now Carl's gone."

"What's this?" Vincent interposed.

"For a while we tried to have a writing group."

"Jana here was telling us she's going to be working as a writer," Annie said.

"As a translator," Jana amended.

"For that paper," Annie explained. "The one that's published here in English. There must be loads of Harvs on it, I should think."

"That's great," Jacob congratulated Jana.

"They pay little," she replied, "but perhaps I shall learn something, if I will be clever."

"Did *you* know that their reporters don't speak Czech?" Annie asked Jacob.

"No."

"Nor I. Should we have tried to write for it, do you think?"

"I don't know."

Vincent broke in: "I should have thought that sort of thing would be very much up your street, Jacob."

"It didn't occur to me." He thought of journalism as Daniel's turf— was that it?

"Wasn't Hemingway a journalist, before he wrote his stories?" Vincent asked.

"Are you a Hemingway fan?" Jacob asked.

"I don't know that I'd call myself a fan. There's something to him, certainly."

"Oh, certainly," Annie said and nodded with false vigor.

"Must you always be slagging me off?" Vincent complained.

"You mustn't make such claims if you're so sensitive."

Maybe journalism was too close to what Jacob wanted. Too close but not the thing itself. At a newspaper, Americans would have collected and condensed their ideas about the city. They would have passed the ideas back and forth until they had become a kind of currency, and they would expect to be able to buy him with this currency and for him to try to pay for his admission to their circle with it. It surprised him to find that he was still straining to keep himself pure. Evidently he was still on a quest.

Annie interrupted his thoughts. "Am I mad to think I can just keep on at the Jazyková škola in September? There's so much that's changing."

"They'll keep it open," said Jacob. "It's a state school."

"Everyone else seems to have a plan of some kind."

"You really are going to stay."

"I told you I might do."

A microphone whined briefly. The musicians had been unhurriedly gathering in the corner where they performed, and some began to pluck at the strings of their instruments, tuning them. There was a velvet thud as the caller touched his microphone and then a sound like someone pulling a crick out of his neck as the caller twisted it to adjust the height. —Ladies and gentlemen, the caller said in Czech, but the musicians signaled that they weren't ready yet, and he didn't continue. Dancers took last swigs of their beers and trotted out to their places on the floor.

"Milo took me swimming last weekend," Jacob told Annie, not privately.

"Did he."

"Where did you go?" Jana asked. "To the stadium at Podolí?"

"He took me to a quarry that he said was called Amerika."

"Ah, Amerika! And did you like?" Jana asked.

"It was very nice," Jacob said, nodding. "It's an old limestone quarry that's filled up with springwater," he added, still trying to interest Annie.

"They turn there all our films about the American West," Jana explained. "So we Czechs think it is literally America. Were the people, how do you say, without clothes?"

"Nudist? You know, there were a couple of people who didn't seem to be wearing much, but I didn't think I should look."

"That would rather spoil the effect, I should think, not looking," said Thom.

"I mean, I didn't know if they were supposed to be nude."

"Supposed to be?" Jana asked, amused.

"That doesn't make sense, does it," Jacob admitted.

"Who did you say took you there?" Thom asked.

"Milo," said Jacob. "This guy I've been seeing, sort of."

"There's a bit more to it than 'seeing,'" said Annie.

The caller broke into a stream of speech. The dancers on the floor before him were holding themselves tautly and self-consciously in position. The caller counted down, the fiddlers attacked their fiddles, and the dancers began to turn, the bright cloth of their costumes shifting in symmetrical arcs and swirls. They wheeled one another around in fours, the wheels tightening and relaxing as the caller issued new instructions, which came every four bars or so. He gave the calls in English, in what sounded like it was meant to be an American accent. So pronounced a curl was given to the vowels that to Jacob the accent sounded almost like a parody. It reminded him of the English spoken by the DJ at T-Club—the English in which he had announced songs, in between his muttered messages in Czech to his brothers-in-arms. It was a plastic language, a toy language. The speakers here were better than in T-Club, though, and conveyed the caller's voice distinctly over the galloping, cheery music.

"How long have you been seeing him?" Thom asked.

"Just a few weeks. Maybe almost a month."

"And here I've been dating a Czech since the dawn of time, and have I been brought to a nudist swimming hole? It hardly seems fair."

"Amerika is too dangerous for you, my dear," said Jana. "You would fall on the rocks. I will take you to Šárka, though perhaps when I am not in this state."

"Do they wear swim trunks at this Šárka?" Thom asked.

"Only those who want to."

"That's all right, then. Will you come, Annie?"

"I don't see why not," Annie answered, indifferently. "Though I don't promise that I will take my clothes off myself."

"Where my parents stay in Greece, quite a few of the beaches are nudist," Vincent volunteered.

"I suppose I'll go if Annie does," said Elinor. "Oh, look."

Henry was emerging from the foot of the stairs, followed by Hans. They had been drinking; Henry stalked toward them across the room with a somewhat comical gait. Despite the lateness of the season, he was wearing his army green coat, the seams of which were by now fraying, and he had folded his arms through the vent so as to hide both his hands inside, double-Napoleon style. His steps were bowlegged, and he was holding his shoulders stiffly.

"He's well away, isn't he," Vincent commented.

When Henry reached the table, he bent over, looked to either side conspiratorially, and then pulled out from beneath his coat two paper cups of French fries with mayonnaise.

"Hranolky!" exclaimed Jana.

From the side pockets of Henry's coat came three more cups' worth. A certain amount of mayonnaise had gotten smeared inside one of the pockets, and Henry tried to wipe it out with a scrap from a newspaper he'd been reading.

"You're champions," said Elinor, as the fries were being distributed around the table communally. There was no kitchen at the Country Club for some reason.

"You weren't challenged by the biddie at the door?" Thom asked.

"We gave her the impression that we were well and truly pissed," said Henry.

"Not quite a wrong impression," noted Hans.

"Where are they from?" Jacob asked. "Do you remember Arbát?" There had been a fast food restaurant by that name on Na příkopě when Jacob first arrived in the city. The sign outside had been in Cyrillic lettering; inside, the décor had been red and yellow, the colors of the Soviet flag. Jacob had discovered it in his first week in Prague, when everything was novel to him, and it seemed now to belong to a different city, which in a way it did. It had closed not long after—perhaps it had formally been an undertaking of the Soviet Union's and had had to be shut down on that account—and Jacob had never been able to go back to it.

"Arbát?" Hans echoed. His face took on a stubborn look. "No, that is shut now."

"These are from the stand-up place in Lucerna," Henry explained.

"But do you remember Arbát?" Jacob insisted.

"More or less," Henry answered.

Hans for his part turned away. It occurred to Jacob that Hans might think that Jacob intended to tease him—to make a remark about, say, the triumph of McDonald's, which would no doubt arrive in Prague soon and which happened to share Arbát's color scheme. He studied Hans for a little while but he couldn't think of a way to repair the misunderstanding, if in fact there was one.

"Do you think I could teach children?" Annie asked Jacob, leaning over the table to consult with him. "Very young ones, I mean. Such as you have done, with the children of that student of yours."

"Sure," answered Jacob.

"You don't find it too difficult, do you. I must ask Jana if she thinks it would be of interest to a Czech mother. To have a native speaker as an instructor."

"It's a good idea."

"Then if something *should* happen to the language school . . . I rather like to be in the company of children's voices. They're quite cheerful. Soothing, even. Like little brooks or something. I know it's what people say, but it's also true, you know. I should think a small number of them would be quite pleasant to sit and talk to, of an afternoon."

"I'm sure they would be."

"Yes," said Annie, agreeing with herself and seeming to see the picture in her mind's eye.

Jacob wondered if he was remembering places like Arbát in anticipation of leaving—if he was assembling a map of the city in his memory, so as to be able to revisit it later. It was strange to realize that one couldn't know in advance which places one was later going to wish to remember. He didn't really need to remember Arbát, for example; it hadn't turned out to be very important to him. Maybe someday he wasn't going to think that Prague itself had been very important. What was it going to represent? Especially now that he had learned to take it so casually, as if it were an interlude in a larger story, whose outlines he didn't yet know. Would he remember this room, for example? A large, white, underground room, furnished with low, flimsy card tables and filled with the smells of cigarette smoke, dancers' sweat, and spilled beer.

The smell of Milo's hair, in bed beside Jacob in the morning, was a little like the smell of butter. More delicate, maybe, if that were possible. Jacob missed it when Milo wasn't there, though when Milo was there, it embarrassed Jacob that he noticed it.

—Would you want marmalade again? Jacob asked. —Not cornflakes?

—Something a little sour is maybe pleasing to me, Milo answered. —For a change, after a night with you.

—You ox, Jacob said.

Milo got out of bed and tugged on his boxers and socks. Jacob wondered if he should buy him a pair of slippers. A spare set of slippers was probably the Czech equivalent of a toothbrush left at a lover's apartment in America.

At the Country Club Annie had mentioned that Kaspar had had a mild relapse. The news had reminded Jacob of his promise to visit, and after breakfast, he walked to Vršovice, hoping to find Kaspar at home.

The door to Kaspar's characterless white building was unlocked; maybe the key that Melinda had loaned him for his earlier visit hadn't really been necessary.

"Come, come," Kaspar said when Jacob knocked, hurrying Jacob in as if he had been expecting him.

"Annie said you weren't feeling well," Jacob began.

"The carcass still moves." Something had been exciting Kaspar; his eyes shone. His card table had been pulled to the edge of his bed, where, around the nest where he had been sitting, several dictionaries lay open. Evidently he had been translating. "I have been wanting to ask you a question. Where does God exist, do you know?"

"That's your question?"

"Isn't it a question?" For a moment Kaspar looked a little frightened and searched Jacob's eyes.

"Do you mean, is he in heaven or is he everywhere?"

"He is not everywhere, I think."

"Why do you think I know?" Jacob asked. "I don't even know *if* he exists."

"No, he does not exist everywhere," Kaspar replied, as if Jacob's attempt to evade the question contributed to answering it. "Shall we have tea?"

Jacob nodded. Kaspar shuffled in his old-bear way over to his electric pot, filled it, and clicked it on. There was nowhere to sit, unless they were both going to sit on the bed. The aluminum folding chair, like the card table, was covered in scratched-up typescripts.

"I felt it, this time," Kaspar continued. "I felt that I am not able to find him alone."

"I'm sorry, I'm not following."

"When I was in hospital."

"Oh." Jacob thought of the mystical experience that he had shared with Henry but Kaspar's forwardness filled him with so much skepticism and mistrust that he pushed his own memory away. "Do you want me to clear a place?"

"But we shall sit in my garden."

"You have a garden?"

"I have had long conversations with you in it."

"I don't think so. I had no idea you had a garden. It was winter the last time I was here."

"Was it so?" Kaspar sadly asked. "In winter a garden is less attractive," he reflected. "But they recommended the air of winter to us. To strengthen our lungs. In the time of history. How do you say, in English, 'in the time of stories'? In Czech it is quite poetic. They say, *'Bylo nebylo.'*"

" 'There was and there wasn't,' " Jacob translated.

"Do you say it also in English?"

"No. You say, 'Once upon a time.' "

"Oh yes. I had forgotten. I will make a tray of this," Kaspar said, closing a dictionary, "if you will carry. For me it is too heavy. Do you like? It is of Rafe and Melinda." He was taking pieces of a blue-and-white tea service out of a cardboard box on the floor. "For good-bye. She alone presented it, but she was at pains to name him, and so I had to find him."

It occurred to Jacob that Kaspar might be chattering because he had a fever. "Are you all right to go outside?"

"But it is summer almost. It is not so cold as this cave. The sun slays the bacilli."

"You make it sound like Sir Gawaine or something."

"It is something like. Will you pour the water? My hands . . ."

Jacob poured the hissing water into the blue-and-white teapot; the infuser rattled against the china. On the dictionary, beside the pot, Kaspar had stacked two cups and two saucers, and Jacob gingerly lifted the dictionary-as-tea-tray, careful to hold the dictionary itself shut. At the western end of his room, Kaspar opened a small door into a stairwell that ran up to a courtyard. The two men took the stairs with baby steps, the teacups clinking, Kaspar panting.

The sun fell on two wooden benches, placed where a pavement of concrete flagstones gave way to a yellowed lawn.

"It was a great trouble to find Rafe," Kaspar resumed, when they were seated.

Jacob looked in on the brewing tea, which he had set, dictionary and all, on the dry grass between them. "He wasn't at home? In Havelská?"

"He does not like to have a home, you know."

"Since Melinda?"

"Since always. It was also difficult because he is more angry with me now."

"He couldn't be angry with you."

"I am to him a disappointment. It is his job, you know, to understand people, and he mistook me. He thought I simply liked to be contrary."

"His job?"

"Oh, I do not mean to say his job. I do not mean to say more than I can. It is his métier, rather. He does not care to be wrong about a person."

The sun seemed to be calming Kaspar, as if he were an infant and it were bathing him. He closed his eyes in it and folded his arms, hugging himself in his sweater, which Jacob would have found too warm. He was catching his breath, Jacob noticed; catching it and slowing it down.

Jacob poured the tea. His grip shook as much as Kaspar's would have, and as he placed Kaspar's on the bench beside him, the cup loudly shivered in its saucer.

At the sound Kaspar opened his eyes again. "You are here," he said a little sleepily, as if he had briefly drifted off and wasn't sure upon returning that he remembered the last few minutes correctly. One ended up wanting to take care of Kaspar despite oneself.

"I am," Jacob admitted.

"Perhaps it is in talking," Kaspar said.

"What is?"

"That one is near God." He smiled as if to apologize for having reintroduced the topic. "In a special kind of talking, perhaps. Perhaps in talking with you."

"Me?"

"Yes. With you when you are here."

"Not me."

"Yes, with the you that is here."

"You mean a general you."

"No!" Kaspar seemed alarmed. "Not a general you."

"I don't know if I know what you mean."

"The you that cannot go away."

"I can always go away," Jacob said drily.

"Ah, that is so. Maybe it is *that* you, then," Kaspar said, not at all shy to assert the opposite of the idea that he had just been maintaining. "The one that can go away. You are after all a writer. You are always here and you are always not here. And I think it must also be in writing. In some kinds of writing. Will you come to shul with me?"

"Sure. Where is it?"

"Near the central train station. I will meet you outside the station on Friday, half an hour before sundown. It will make you very happy."

The windows of Kaspar's building, blinded by the glance of the sun, looked down on them.

"How is it that you know the word 'shul,' Jacob?" Kaspar continued.

"I'm American," Jacob irritably answered. "It's crazy of you to be so into Judaism."

"Is it crazy?" he asked, a little fearfully. He was sometimes aware of the fragility of his own character as well as the humor of it.

"Maybe you're interested because in Prague Judaism is something lost."

"Not altogether lost," Kaspar insisted. "One may be with them."

"Like the pity you have for Communism now."

"But it is the same with Christ," Kaspar objected. "It is only that he was lost that makes him God."

"Is that orthodox? I thought he was supposed to have been God in the first place."

"No," Kaspar disagreed. "It is that he came back. No one usually returns."

"So it's the coming back and not the being lost."

"Well, if you ask, it is the loss, I think. One needn't believe in the coming back, but it is perhaps necessary for something dear to be lost."

"Why?"

"Perhaps it is necessary to the making of a story. A story after all is a way of remembering love."

Jacob thought of the debates of the writing group. "I thought a story was something that trapped you."

"But that is how. It could not trap you if it were not about love."

"You said once that sex couldn't be put into a story."

"Oh, well, sex."

"What do you have against sex?"

There was something preposterous about introducing the topic with Kaspar. "Perhaps I have not such a wide acquaintance with it."

"I'm seeing someone," Jacob said, a little boldly.

"'Seeing,'" Kaspar echoed. "Oh yes," he added, as soon as he remembered this use of the word. "Are you happy?"

"I guess. I'm not going to stay, though."

"Why not, if you have found him?"

"I only found him because I was leaving. That was the understanding. Also I ruined it a little. I let him think I was a writer."

"But it is true."

"No it isn't."

"You will not let me say it. Perhaps I am not as beautiful as this man."

"You aren't in love with me."

"You cannot be sure. But in any case it is not that, either, that licenses him."

"What is it?"

"That you are in love with him."

"I don't think so."

"Well, it is you who will know."

Jacob had taken advantage of Milo. It was sweet to pretend to be a writer, but it was cheating; it was only by leaving that Jacob would have any chance of becoming the sort of figure that he had let Milo fall for. If, after leaving, he found that he couldn't become that figure, he could at least try to become someone responsible, someone a little more substantial.

"It's a nice day, isn't it?" Jacob suggested.

"It is only in countries where the winter is bitter that the spring is capable of this subtlety."

"Have you ever lived in a country without bitter winters?"

"In books," Kaspar admitted.

—Are they good? Milo asked. Jacob had chosen a piece of hazelnut sponge cake and a *harlekýn*. They were standing at a plastic counter in the glass-walled pastry shop in Můstek.

Jacob shrugged. —I didn't want to miss anything.

—Evidently. He borrowed Jacob's fork and sliced off a sample of the *harlekýn*. He hadn't shaved, and some vanilla cream stuck to the stubble on his upper lip. Jacob signed to him to wipe it off. —Better? Milo asked, presenting himself for inspection and glancing at two unnoticing schoolgirls beside them. The girls were solemnly, almost meditatively sharing a *věneček*, or wreath—a sort of a puff-pastry donut.

—But come with me, Jacob said. He was trying to convince Milo to go rowing on the Vltava. —Don't be wicked.

—It's so expensive. It isn't for Czechs.

—But it is. A girlfriend showed me. It's easy.

—And now you want to try it with a boy.

Jacob smashed the last bit of chocolate cake from the *harlekýn* onto his fork, unpleasantly conscious of having eaten most of two pastries by himself.

—Why won't he accept? one of the schoolgirls muttered. —The river is ours, isn't it?

—The Germans they say believe, that even our river belongs to them, her friend replied.

—Catastrophe, the first girl said.

—So let's go, Milo acquiesced.

When Jacob set his crumpled napkin on his plate, the first girl wished them "Bon voyage," her eyes flickering up only for a moment from her pastry.

—He isn't German, Milo said, in case the girl had thought Jacob was.

—He's American, she replied, as if the fact were written on Jacob's face.

Milo looked rather forlorn at first in the stern of the boat, as if he couldn't bear the foolishness of what they were doing. But as soon as they stood out from shore, too far from any other people to be recognized, his willingness to be knocked about began to collaborate almost against his will with the capering of the skiff. The wind freshened, and it ridged short, choppy waves into the river.

Jacob let the current pull them down the river, which curved to the north and then east. He touched the oars to the water only to correct the skiff's path, but even under such faint encouragement the boat was soon slicing at high speed across wave after wave, the waves cheerfully slapping themselves into nothingness against the side of it, the spray from the collisions cooling the air. Under the ponderous face of the hill that had once held Stalin's monument, beneath the municipal propriety of the Bridge of Svatopluk Čech, their speed felt rash. Surely they were going to be rebuked by someone. The river, like them, became less respectable as it turned the corner. It broadened, unpicturesquely. Along the foot of the right embankment ran a walkway of dirt and brown grass, accessible to no one. Litter from the street above had fallen down into it and seemed to have remained there for a long time uncollected. Just beyond the next bridge, they saw a yacht that had until recently been one of the state-run "botels" and was now a private night club, its new name lettered in purple on a black sign. They could make out a janitor pouring something overboard. On the left bank, the hill was punctured by a dark tunnel.

—Are you taking me to Germany? Milo asked.

—We have to turn, don't we, Jacob recognized.

Ahead of them, an island divided the river, which was blocked on one side by a weir and on the other by a range of locks. They couldn't go any farther. Jacob lowered an oar, and the skiff swirled about. The automobile tunnel and the waterborne nightclub were distasteful to Jacob, who had been hoping for an idyll like the one he had shared with Annie. It was hard work to pull the skiff back upstream, but he wanted to badly, so he laid out on the oars—he *gave way*, as they said in books about going to sea. As he pulled, he imagined that he was rescuing Milo and himself from the aesthetic threats of sleaze and automobile traffic. It was pleasant to know that the boat was powered by his own effort. Once they were above the Bridge of Svatopluk Čech again, he felt safe. Of course it was pleasant, he thought to himself, to do something simple and muscular. After long distrust of his body, it was still a surprise whenever he discovered it could be useful, even in its way reliable. Milo was now leaning back sideways in the stern, resting on one elbow. He had taken off his shoes and socks, and was twiddling his toes. Jacob was sweating freely. When he pulled, he could feel the resistance of Milo's mass in the boat, balancing him. He boasted to himself that he felt so much at ease in his body at the moment that he might even have taken off his shirt by now if they hadn't been in the downtown of an old European city. The Mánes Bridge was ahead; the Charles Bridge, just beyond it. They were returning to the company of Prague's famous sites, which it may have been vulgar to love but which Jacob did love. It was a luxury to be able to move Milo toward them with the angry strength in his hands, arms, legs, and back—to literally transport him.

—Shall we spell one another? Milo suggested.

—Yeah, good.

Jacob shipped the oars. The skiff drifted and began to rock idly with the river's swell. With indications rather than words they choreographed a change of places, matching their steps until in the center they made the mistake of holding onto each other for a moment instead of onto the gunwales and in the security of their touch unconsciously rose from their crouches. The boat seesawed; they fell apart and scrambled down into their new seats.

"Ježišmarja," Milo swore.

The boat was moseying downstream again. —You'll have to turn, Jacob advised.

The oars splashed as Milo got used to them, but he soon found a stroke that suited him. In a steady rhythm, he gathered himself forward into a hunch, then stretched out and opened his long form. Another forward hunch, another long, taut form. He was more beautiful than any man whom Jacob could have hoped to take to bed in America.

—You can do it so well, Jacob said. —Why didn't you want to row?

—I don't know. Maybe I didn't want to think, that you are like other travelers.

—I'm not.

—You are. You'll ride away, Milo said, somewhat challengingly. —But don't be sad, he added.

—I'm not, Jacob denied. —Attention.

"Jejeje," Milo exclaimed. They were passing under the Mánes Bridge so close to one of the piers that Milo had to lie on the oars quickly to swing them inside the skiff. They waited to hear if the skiff would scrape the pier; no scrape came. As they were gliding away, Jacob reached out a hand and was able to touch one of the bridge's black stones, slippery with algae. It didn't have any smell.

Milo recovered his rhythm. —Where shall we dine? he asked. —U medvídků? Jacob had taken him there a few times when they had found themselves downtown at the end of the day, and they had liked sitting quietly in a corner of the genial roar.

—I have a date, said Jacob.

—Truly?

He ought to have mentioned it sooner. —At a synagogue, he explained. —A friend wants to show it to me. We can meet later, you and I. I'm sorry.

—Perhaps I will have dinner with Father. I think, that he misses me.

They were approaching the Charles Bridge. Milo had brought them far over to one side of the river, almost to the Malá Strana bank. In fact he seemed to be steering them into Malá Strana itself.

—Where are you taking me? Jacob asked, with some concern.

—To Venice.

Most place-names in Czech were easy for a foreigner to recognize, but a few, like *Benátky*, the word for Venice, reminded one that the language was old enough to have come up with its own names for things. As the skiff approached the river's edge, several of the orange and yellow palaces seemed gently to part, allowing an inlet of the river to continue between them. It was a canal.

Where the Charles Bridge made landfall in Malá Strana, the castle drew eyes upward and few tourists walked to the edge of the bridge to peer over and consider its footings. Jacob and Milo were able to pass unobserved as the canal took them under one of the bridge's last arches. Milo let the skiff coast. It nudged a few ripples into the surface of the water, which fluttered in patterns associated with those ripples and made trickling sounds as it rose and fell against the brick bases of the canal-side palaces. They were simple palaces with tall, regular windows. A family had hung its laundry from the balcony of one of them. The canal itself had no social significance. The palaces beside it faced away. Perhaps they faced children playing soccer in a carless street nearby, because fragments of excited children's voices echoed along the chamber formed by the tall buildings and the water, though no children and no soccer could be seen. —This is beauty, Jacob said, as Milo pulled them through the green shadow of an overhanging tree. It wasn't a very manly sounding thing to say.

—I was never here before, Milo said. —Maybe I'll carry you to the synagogue like a gondolier.

He dipped the oars to carry them a little farther. The skiff passed under a stone footbridge. Jacob slid a foot forward to touch one of Milo's bare feet. It became harder, the deeper they went, for the sun to find its way into the narrowing space between the two sides of the canal. Trees heavy with greenery blocked much of what sun there still was, and it occurred to Jacob that he didn't know the exact hour when the sun was going to set. He found that he didn't want to go to the synagogue. He had liked the idea when Kaspar had proposed it, but now it was going to take him away from Milo, and he resented it. It felt willed rather than natural, like a project undertaken for self-improvement. Kaspar would forgive him if he didn't show up. Kaspar would probably even invite him to come another time.

—I have to go back, Jacob announced.

Milo held the oars suspended a few moments. —You must, mustn't you?

If Jacob were to decide to stay here, it would be impossible for anyone to find him. Hounds in movies always lose the fox's trail when they come to a river. The skiff could wobble in the green water all afternoon, into the evening, and he could make it up to Kaspar later. He could stay a little longer in Prague so as to have time to make it up to him. He could put off graduate school. He could ask Milo not to go to Karlovy Vary. They would find something to do for money. And for now they could stay in the skiff until the streetlamps clicked on and hummed and threw orange rays against the sky, the blue of which would by then have begun to darken.

They were silent as Milo pulled the skiff back down the canal and out into and across the Vltava. Though the sun was still shining, they were conscious that the day was soon to end, and the chatter of the tourists on the bridge, brought to them by gusts of wind, sounded improvident and somehow dispiriting.

On the landing just outside the main doors of the Wilson train station, two young Romany men—a fiddler and an accordionist—played to no audience. They sat on lumpy canvas bags. The accordionist, who was singing, had balanced a still-burning cigarette on the edge of the black case for his instrument; between verses he took it up and drew a breath through it. The song was sad, and there was a sweet fullness to it, as if one could rest there if one could somehow manage to get inside. The musicians didn't notice Jacob, and they didn't notice Kaspar when he came out of the train station lobby.

Jacob had arrived late, but Kaspar didn't feel well enough to walk too quickly, and he disparaged Jacob's apologetic wish to hurry. It wasn't far.

The interior was dim. After the door thumped shut behind them, they could hear words being spoken upstairs. Kaspar took from his shoulder bag a hand-knitted blue yarmulke, perfectly circular. Yellow flowers and white Hebrew letters had been stitched into it.

"Should I have one?" Jacob whispered.

"It is not necessary, I think," Kaspar answered, putting his on.

At the end of the antechamber Jacob found a basket of spare yarmulkes for guests. The fabric was dull and gray, and they were larger and floppier than Kaspar's. Jacob unfolded one and laid it on his head, patting it nervously and hoping it would stay in place. Kaspar had fixed his to a lock of his hair with a paper clip.

They mounted stairs in the corner of the building—slowly, for Kaspar's sake—and found themselves ascending into a balcony arrayed with pews. The pews were set on a mild incline, like seats in a choir or in a theater's mezzanine, so as to allow views of the central temple beyond and below the banister at the balcony's front. At the moment, the main floor of the temple was empty. Only the lights in the balcony had been lit, illuminating slightly more than a dozen men and women in their fifties and sixties. In the first row of the balcony were standing two men, presumably rabbis, though neither wore ceremonial dress, only coats and ties. Into the larger volume of the temple behind the two officiants there fell fading daylight dyed blue by the stained glass of the windows, on which the names of donor families from the First Republic were painted in Czech and, to Jacob's surprise, in German black letter. It was the first time Jacob had seen the script in Prague, outside of used-book stores.

Hearing them enter, several worshipers turned, and one of them, a short, silver-haired man with steel spectacles, nodded and smiled when he recognized Kaspar, who bowed and murmured in reply.

"He is a kind man," said Kaspar, as he filed after Jacob into a pew. "He took me to hospital."

"Does he live near you?" Jacob asked.

"I don't know. I don't believe so."

"Then how come he took you to the hospital?

"I was bleeding. It was curious. I did not notice it myself, in the beginning."

"Where?"

"It was from a cut, where they made an operation. Oh, you mean . . . It was here. In synagogue."

"Jesus."

"I suppose you may mention him here that way."

"We shouldn't be talking. We're interrupting."

"So, okay," Kaspar said. He took a book of liturgy from the pew and handed it to Jacob, who opened it to a random page and began to listen strenuously, as if to atone by attentiveness for the casual attitude that Kaspar had induced him to fall into. "But I will say," Kaspar added, "it is not possible, I do not think, to interrupt God."

It occurred to Jacob to spy out the page number that their neighbor's liturgy was opened to. Noticing Jacob's interest, the man inclined the book to him. Once secure in a page number, Jacob was able to focus on the page, and he saw that the prayers were for the most part in Hebrew, while the framing narrative was in Czech. A few of the Hebrew words sounded familiar, because when Jacob was a child, a friend studying for his bar mitzvah had taught him some. The sound, at any rate, was familiar, if not the sense, and certainly the liturgical tone was familiar, the same measured tone that Jacob had heard in the church that he had grown up in.

He was startled, however, when one of the rabbis opened his palms and his mouth and sang. The man wasn't a rabbi, Jacob realized; he was a cantor. His voice was clear and elegant. It was as sad and sweet as that of the Romany boy singing outside the train station. It had the same openness; it would have been easy to injure. The man sang alone and unaccompanied, though his manner suggested that he was a quiet, even a contained person. Jacob had the sense that the exercise of his gift required courage—that such a person would never have exercised his gift at all if he hadn't innocently believed that God had entrusted it to him for use.

What was unlike the tradition that had raised Jacob was the exposure of personal art in the cantor's voice. It seemed risky to center worship on something so delicate and unreliable. It suggested to Jacob an awareness that the conversation the worshipers were attempting could fail.

In the Žižkov apartment, in a corner of the kitchen, there was a heavy apparatus that Jacob didn't at first recognize: an unwieldy metal basin that housed two cylinders. Deep inside were black fan belts connected to a motor. A rubber hose came out of the bottom, as did an electrical cord with a plug. There was a control knob, but its face had long ago disappeared. When Jacob plugged the apparatus in, it hummed heavily. When he turned the knob, a rotor inside the larger cylinder jabbed back and forth; when he turned the knob farther, the larger cylinder stopped and the smaller one rotated, at a much higher speed. The whole thing was mounted on castors that were too gritted up to turn; it could, however, be dragged.

It had to be a washing machine, Jacob decided. He looked up *pračka,* the Czech word for "washing machine," in a large, scholarly Czech-English dictionary that he had recently bought. "Twin-tub" was listed as an English equivalent. Jacob had never heard of a twin-tub, but the two cylinders seemed to confirm that he was looking at one. The next time he went to the grocery store, he bought detergent.

He couldn't tell where it was supposed to go. More bafflingly, he couldn't see how to get water into the twin-tub. He tried slipping the end of the rubber hose over the bathtub's faucet, like a sleeve over an arm, but water pressure kept popping it off, and he realized that the hose had to be for draining. Oops. He filled a couple of pots and poured water into the large cylinder by hand. It took a while.

There were other quirks. The apparatus didn't seem to have a timer, so Jacob had to decide for himself how long to soak clothes, how long to let the large cylinder agitate them, and how many times to drain and refill when rinsing. Moreover, the agitation of clothes in the large cylinder—the "washing" aspect of the washing machine—was somewhat violent. The rotor churned despite the absence of a lid, and after the rotor tore one of his paisley shirts, he risked his fingers whenever he saw a shirt matting itself up into dangerous intimacy with the chunk-chunking blades. After one of his fingers was bruised, he found a stick of lumber and thereafter supervised the washing stick in hand, like a caveman over a cauldron.

The second cylinder, which worked as a centrifuge, also proved temperamental. It could only hold two, at most three, items of clothing at a time. Whenever Jacob tried more, it either wobbled limply or, if it reached a high speed, became unbalanced and clanked with horrifically loud clanks against the outer basin. It was a chastening sound.

Jacob was proud of his ability to figure the twin-tub out. And as the novelty subsided, he noticed that this pride was supplemented by a subtler one, a sort of boastfulness about the grotesquerie: the more backward the twin-tub was, the more authentic the difference of Jacob's experience in Czechoslovakia. Expatriate's vanity. But in the long run pride and vanity weren't sufficient compensation for tedium. The twin-tub began to irritate him. It was loud. It mauled his clothes. It took most of a day to use.

There was a public coin-operated Laundromat in Prague. It was run, rumor had it, by an American who had been flown to Prague by a fundamentalist Christian organization. The Christians had hired him to run an English-teaching program, the sooner to bring the Reds to God and capitalism, but he had defected once he had recognized the business opportunity that a nation without Laundromats represented. His prices were reasonable, but his business was located in the ambassador's district, too far away from Žižkov to be worth the trip.

A Saturday morning came when Jacob had only dirty clothes and acutely resented the expense of his life that would be required to clean them. However unfairly, to himself as well as to Czechoslovakia, he began to think about how little time he had given to writing in the past year. Was it completely wrongheaded, completely unjust, to wonder if it was because daily life in Prague was so effortful? Carl had referred to thinking along such lines as "convenience theory," the joke being that it was too self-regarding and smug, too obviously lacking the impersonality and flexibility of what counted as theory with genuine philosophers. Convenience theory didn't really amount to much more than homesickness for capitalism and the ways that capitalism made smooth, and in acknowledgment of its limits, Jacob's resentment began to take a merely personal form—to become understandable to himself as shame. The strange task of laundering his clothes in a twin-tub was one that he had chosen as a corollary of having chosen to live in an economy that had not yet gotten over the idea that everyone should be put continually to familiar trouble so that no one should ever have to be put to any new kind of trouble. Jacob could have sold himself in America for enough money to buy his way clear of such troubles, which were after all unfamiliar to him if not to Czechs and Slovaks, but he had felt that he would be soiled by such a sale. He had felt there to be something inside him too fine for compromise, so he had fled here, where no one knew how to buy that thing in him and where he had unawares thrown himself instead in the way of an existential danger new to him, the danger of wasting his energies on surmounting inconveniences. It was possible here to spend a lifetime on nothing more. What if the year that he had spent in this world had been a mistake? It had surely had an effect on him; maybe it had lowered his expectations of himself. When he returned to America, he would probably find that the people he had known in college had gotten ahead of him. They would have made some progress in the past year in passing through the nameless task that he had found so distasteful. What had he been doing instead? Someone like Kaspar could say that he had been saving his soul, but Jacob would never be able to convince himself of the materiality of any such claim in his own case. He was an American; Americans had no souls; at any rate they never pretended to be sensible of them. It was an implicit promise of the socialism dying in Czechoslovakia that money should stain no one's spirit, and the part of Jacob that wanted to hold itself pure had been taken in by that promise, even though what had first attracted him to the country was its story of revolution—that is, its story of having at last given the lie to the changelessness that was purity's complement. He had come here because he had heard that a false haven was vanishing, only to discover that in dying it still appealed even to him, a stranger, with sufficient strength that he, too, felt drawn to and then betrayed by it, so bitterly betrayed that now, although he knew it was vanishing, he felt eager for it to be stamped out of existence as cruelly and as quickly as possible.

Having thought all these thoughts, he observed that his laundry was still dirty and that he still didn't want to wash it. Milo had promised to come over, but he didn't want to see Milo, either. He put his Olivetti on the kitchen table and unzipped it from its case. The windows in the bedroom were open, as were those in the kitchen, which faced the building's inner courtyard, and a rather savage crosswind blew between them.

The wind was hot and somewhat pleasant as it beat against his face, but it kept scattering the papers that he set beside the typewriter, and he had to weigh them down with a glass of water. It didn't matter because he wasn't in the middle of anything, so he didn't really need to look at the papers; he was going to have to start something new. It occurred to him to write about the time that Běta had taken him to the hospital in the middle of the night. He liked the idea of writing about himself in a state of collapse. A collapse suggested that there was something underneath it, a foundation of some kind to collapse into, and it added a color of significance.

He typed a couple of lines.

He didn't know how he was going to explain to Milo why he hadn't showered yet and why he didn't want to spend the day with him. Milo would just have to accept it. It would be wrong for him to make too much of it. It didn't have to do with him, or with Jacob's feelings for him, except insofar as Jacob felt the apprehension, despite his decision to spend the day writing, that once Milo arrived, he would lose himself in Milo, as he usually did. When Milo was around, he wasn't able to hear himself any more. He was only able to hear what he had to say to Milo. That was the problem with other people; that was the problem with just living your life. He ought to have written a second novel during the time he'd spent in Prague. If he had, he wouldn't have had to lie when he'd wanted Milo to continue looking at him the way he'd looked at him that day on Petřín hill. What a lot of reproaches he was making of himself today. He was awfully grand, even in misery, wasn't he. He was feeling the sort of frustration whose pettiness inclines one's better self to wish to dismiss it, if it were possible to.

"Ahoj," he heard, through the huffing of the wind. The bell didn't always work, and sometimes Milo hollered up to Jacob's bedroom window. He was standing on the street below, looking up with untroubled cheerfulness. Jacob tossed the house keys down to him and then made a point of sitting at his typewriter again.

—I have your photos, Milo said a minute later, as he let himself in.

"Okay," said Jacob in English, not looking up.

—I picked them up, since they were ready.

—How much do I owe you?

—Ach, I don't know. Can we look through them?

"Okay," Jacob agreed.

—Are you writing? Milo asked, as he pulled a chair up beside Jacob.

—Maybe.

With time, the documentary function in their relationship had fallen almost entirely to Milo, but one day a few weeks ago Jacob had rebelled against the division of labor and put film in his Minolta. He had taken a roll of pictures of Milo in the Žižkov apartment and on the empty streets around it. He would have felt self-conscious taking pictures of Milo downtown, in front of other people, though Milo himself seemed to have no such shyness, perhaps because photography was his art and he had become accustomed to the kinds of indecorousness incidental to it.

Jacob had used one of the last rolls of a stock of Tri-X film that he had brought with him from America. There was a small, disorienting thrill in the discrepancy between the black-and-white images of Milo that they were leafing through and the flesh-and-blood Milo beside him. In the prints, Milo's beauty was almost classical, it seemed to be a matter of line and form, but the Milo holding the prints was pink and sweaty and his hair was a little longer, a little softer than in the photos. He hadn't cut it since the pictures were taken.

—Well, that's a magnificent man, Milo observed. —Did you sleep with him?

—Once.

—You can show him off to your friends.

—I told them about you.

—What did they say?

—I told them you took me to Amerika, and the Scot's girlfriend said, that we must to Šárka.

—I'd like to escort you to Šárka, said Milo. He flipped through a few more prints, but he had sensed Jacob's mood, and neither he nor Jacob were still looking at them carefully.

—I have to wash the laundry, Jacob said flatly.

—Do you want help?

—No. I also have to work, probably. I have to write. He didn't look at Milo as he said it. It sounded like an excuse to get rid of him. —Do you still photograph for yourself sometimes?

—How so, for myself?

—As art.

—Just the documentary about a co-laborer from the brotherly socialist republic of America.

It was unkind to throw Milo out. But it was unfair that Jacob should have to feel guilty about it. He hadn't given his life away. If he did feel guilty, he foresaw, he wouldn't be able to write anything, even if he were left alone.

—I don't know what I want to do, said Jacob. He felt awfully sorry for himself. Why shouldn't he? He couldn't be what he wanted to be, not for a long time, maybe never. It was as if over the past year or so he had taken a few steps away from a paved road. For a while longer he was still going to be able to justify his digression by pretending that he might soon retrace his steps. If things got bad enough, in fact, he might actually retrace them. For a while longer he was going to continue to be able to minimize the delay that his ever-lengthening detour involved. At some point, though, his justifications were going to start to sound like lies, and he was going to have to admit, to himself and maybe to other people, that he had gone astray. He was going to have to admit not only that he had been walking deliberately away from the road but also that for a long time he had been accomplishing little other than walking away from it. The effort might never come back to him. He might never get anything for his pains but the experience of having wandered, which as someone who actually had wandered he wouldn't be likely to idealize. He didn't know for sure that he was headed anywhere, because, to phrase it more carefully, he didn't know if he was going to live long enough to reach a place that he could learn, in retrospect, to call a destination. He didn't know how far away such a place might be; certainly he didn't seem to be progressing very rapidly toward it right now. He had to try to write something while he could. Time was running out. He was probably going to have to give up soon—he was probably going to have to double back to the paved road—but he didn't have to give up quite yet, so he should at least write a little. —Better if I'm alone today, he told Milo.

—Mushrooms and vinegar, Milo replied, and left.

"Such a spa you are!" Annie observed with amusement, in the school's tiled smoking room between classes. "To send him away like that. Poor sod."

"Who, him or me?"

"I suppose the both of yehs, but I was thinking more of him. How was he to know you had this, ehm, idea, you might call it, in your head?"

"Should I call him?"

"Well, if you can't be fagged to call him . . ."

"What do you mean?"

"Do you still fancy him?"

"I do."

"Then I think you'd do well to call him. If you still fancy him, that is. Though I wonder if he'll have you again. I don't know that I'd have you back, frankly."

"You think it's too late."

"When was it?"

"Saturday."

"Maybe if you make it up to him, like."

"How?"

"How am I to know? You're understood to be the great expert in what a bloke fancies."

"I didn't do anything wrong."

"No, not if you don't want to see him again."

"Can't I want to spend the day by myself?"

"But not sudden like. You can't surprise a person. And he offered to do your bloody washing with you, and you're an American."

"What does that mean?"

"I only mean you're sure to be very particular about your washing. The Americans in the Dům are, is why I say it. It's like chemistry for them. Science, you know. I watch how they do it. They make measurements."

"You think I fucked it up."

"I don't say that. I say you *might* have done."

Around this time a letter from Melinda arrived for Jacob care of the Libeň language school. She had managed to type it.

Milý Jacobíčku,

Has it really been a month and a half? It feels like bloody forever. Don't think that I have forgotten that <u>you</u> were to write <u>me</u> first, or that I consider you any less remiss merely because I neglected to give you our Roman address before departure. But seeing as how I did neglect to give it you, there's nothing for it, I suppose, and it must be I who writes. Herewith, then . . .

How the hell are you, darling? Do you miss us half as much as we miss you? Don't answer that. Carl by the way fully intends writing you a long letter himself, apologizes for not having written sooner, sends regards, etc., so I mustn't steal his thunder and shan't except to say that here in Rome he has grown almost unrecognizably industrious, plastering campuses with photocopied offers to give private English lessons out of purloined Czech instruction manuals. (He didn't purloin them from you, I hope? He did from someone, so perhaps it's better to keep this bit of the epistle rather close.) My contribution to our financial wellbeing is to offer to sell the car, an offer I repeat almost daily, because I am sure we are running afoul of some nuance of Italy's vehicular registration protocol and foresee the day when I shan't be able to flirt my way out of an encounter with a carabiniere. Either that or we shall turn the old Ford into a gypsy cab, so as to profit from our liability. It is widely believed here that all you need do is shout at tourists from a car for money to tumble out of them. Fancy me bawling at timid American matrons from a rolled-down window . . .

As only a few of Carl's offers and none of my threats have as yet been taken up, we are free to spend most of our days sightseeing. We have a 1909 Baedeker of Central Italy, which I bought for 75 crowns in that antikvariát in Můstek that you're so taken with, so we are a proper Mitteleuropaïsche couple, Carl and I, visiting the museums and monuments of the West with our outdated guidebook and our igelitka of homemade lunch. The Baedeker is very good on which pastilles to burn in your bedroom at night so as to fend off malaria and also on the age and authenticity of particular rocks. In fact, when confronted with a rock, Carl consults it with a fidelity that is quite touching really. But as a guidebook it does show its age. "There don't seem to be any Constables in this room any longer," I am characteristically reduced to saying. "In fact there seem to be only marbles of defeated Huns." Carl, however, perseveres. "This is where Nero put his circus," he tells me, and I answer, "Let's have a gelato, then, darling, shall we? Because I'm afraid I don't happen to see a circus."

Rome is fearfully beautiful even when one doesn't know what one is looking at. But as a Hun myself, what I like best is not the statuary but simply our apartment. If from the Campo dei Fiori, where they sell me fresh strawberries every morning, you walk north along a cobbled road, intermittently canopied with antique brick and just wide enough for a Vespa and two pedestrians to walk abreast, you find our building at the crick in the road just before the road surrenders its privacy to a vulgar corso. The building is quite narrow and tall, the apartments within stacked one atop the other like children's blocks, precariously. Our apartment is at the top—fifth floor, ten flights, no elevator. On the landing just outside the door an extraterrestrial cactus blooms in a pink and suggestive manner, under the warmth of the stairwell's skylight. The apartment proper has two floors. The lower consists of a living room mostly filled by a sofa, a bedroom mostly filled by a bed, and a bathroom perpetually damp, whose shower opens onto a balcony as if to encourage a parade of oneself, an encouragement that I suspect you will enjoy hearing that Carl has once or twice failed to resist. He stands, Baedeker in hand, purporting to identify hills in the distance, of which Rome is famously said to have a certain number—seven? nine?—I can't recall. Up a rickety spiral staircase is our second floor, such as it is, a sort of aerie: a kitchen with a tiny table, windows on three sides, and another balcony, this one generous enough that one may cart table and chairs out onto it, of an evening, evenings being always mild, and dine there, overlooking the city's makeshift rooftops of wavy red clay tiles.

I don't know where any of this is going any better than I did when we left Prague. You will no doubt be appalled to hear that we have even discussed marriage—I know my mother is appalled. Married? In Rome? I hear you say. Isn't that permanent? But I don't think it is, not any more. Modernity and all that. And it's being discussed as something tactical, mostly. The US immigration officers are going to suspect us of it anyway, Carl warns me, if we keep traveling together. Don't mention this to Annie just yet; she'll think me quite mad.

I have thought often of the conversation that you and I had in the Vietnamese restaurant, and the question of how to know whether one is choosing or whether one is giving in to something one hasn't understood. I wonder if the answer is that a choice always feels a little supplementary, a little unnatural—because it's unforced it also feels unnecessary—as if one had figured out a way to get away with something for a while. Something that usually came with a punishment of some kind and this time didn't. The loss, I suppose, is that in such a case one will never quite feel at home, one will never feel quite certain one knows where one is. What is it Freud says—as if, in the middle of a play, someone in the audience were to stand up and cry "Fire!" or "Help!"—one won't have that sensation, which is such an interesting one. Yet a play is real, in its way, even a play that never turns into an "emergency." But then there will always remain the dangerous possibility of hearing such a cry later and running off after its siren call, I suppose. One will never feel settled in—zabydlený, as the Czechs say. (I once overheard Henry nattering on to you about that word, but ask one of your lovers, if you've forgotten.)

It occurs to me upon rereading what I've so far written that you might be as likely as Annie to take alarm at the M word mentioned above, but you mustn't, you must justify my confidence in your unshockability. The word is after all love's opposite, or so I recall being told at university, with a certain asperity, when we came to read Flaubert. They're very keen on disillusioning young women at British universities, you know, I suppose to make us resigned and grateful later on.

Report everything in your reply, especially the answers to questions that you will have understood I daren't ask in case my letter should fall into the hands of the objects of my curiosity. We hope desperately that you will decide to go home to America via Rome instead of that nasty Paris you're so keen on—or simply come to Rome indefinitely. Our sofa is at your disposal, as are we, entirely. Neváhej, lásko.

And write soon.

s velkým srdcem,
Melinda

Jacob considered calling Milo. He considered walking to Milo's father's apartment and surprising him. He was afraid that Milo might reproach him. He hadn't really done anything wrong. He hadn't meant to hurt him. He had just wanted to be alone for the day. He was afraid of not being able to explain himself. The wish for solitude had sneaked up on him. It was gone now, but he had to be careful—it would come back. From hour to hour, he put off calling, because when he tried to think of what he was going to say, his explanations were so elaborate that he worried that they would sound like a justification rather than an apology. He hesitated, though, to simplify them, because if he were to give up too much of himself, he would be returning under the cover of a lie, which he wouldn't be able to prevent himself from tearing apart later. He wanted Milo to take him back, but it would be no good unless Milo understood—unless Jacob was able to stand up for himself or at any rate for the idea that he had been seized by on Saturday, which he was bound to be seized by again.

There was a new pay phone, bright orange and open to the air, on the avenue next to the new bakery near Jacob's apartment, and in order to force himself out of the mental circles that he was running in, Jacob ordered himself to leave the house and call Milo from the pay phone on his way to buying cornflakes. Twice he put his crown in to the pay phone's slot and then, unsure of what to say, pressed a lever to retrieve it. The third time, though, he dialed Milo's number. As the phone rang, he heard the coin descend into the heart of the machine.

—Please, Milo answered.

—Jacob here.

—Well, clearly.

—Are you angry?

—So it's not the end yet, Milo answered.

Jacob felt a light panic; he hadn't expected that they would come so quickly to the point. —I don't want the end, he said. In saying this, he said more than he had meant to, as one often does in a language one doesn't quite know, but he found that he wanted to be saying it. He was new to lover's quarrels and unfamiliar with the way a possibility of loss pricks appetite. —I did incorrectly, he continued. —I think maybe, that I was rehearsing for being without you.

—That's a bit romantic.

—But it's silliness. If I'm going to have to go away, it would be better if I enjoy myself prettily with you as long as I can.

—That's some sentence. Did you rehearse?

—I thought about it enough, Jacob admitted.

—Well, that's also a bit romantic. You don't have a new lover?

—No.

—You can tell me. It's normal.

—But I don't have, Jacob insisted.

—Me neither, said Milo. —Until I go to Karlovy Vary, I think, that I don't want another, he then added, as if, having obliged Jacob to make a confession, it was only fair play to make a return in kind.

—I'm a little afraid of returning to capitalism, said Jacob.

—Like everyone in Czechoslovakia.

—Will you see a movie with me tonight?

—Will we visit Václav?

Later, holding Milo's hand in the dark, Jacob felt that it was only in recovering it that he learned what he had been in danger of losing. The touch of Milo's hand seemed to remind him of parts of himself that he had already begun to forget about.

When the show let out, the streets were still light. As they crossed an avenue, Milo jumped and Jacob climbed over a set of red-and-white-striped metal railings, the kind meant to keep pedestrians from wandering across tram tracks, and in steadying himself as he stepped down, Jacob grabbed Milo's shoulder and then took his hand and kept it. Men in Prague never held hands in public. Milo looked at him and accepted it. It was as if they were issuing a challenge to the city. Jacob felt bold and happy.

—I'm liberating you, Jacob said unseriously.

—*Ježišmarja*, but you're a hooligan.

At an office that a Western airline had opened, where the Czech sales agents were already trained in the Western manner of patient, impersonal cheeriness, Jacob learned that the only planes to America that he could still afford departed from London or Paris. He had been hoping he would be able to go through Paris on his way back. Annie told him about a new private bus company, willing to carry people to France for more or less what a pre-price-liberalization, leftover-socialist train ticket had cost. He chose a departure date a few weeks away.

He tapped a reserve of crowns and dollars hidden in his Bible. There were a few hundred crowns left over, and on his way to a Staroměstská café, to meet Běta and her friend for an English lesson, he stopped in a pet supply store and bought a new glass cage for Václav, who was still living in Henry's soup tureen. He also bought a little exercise wheel. Both items had been made in China. The wheel had an aluminum frame but its tiny slats were made of light blue plastic.

The edge of the cage dug into his side as he carried it down Celetná, and people stared as if they hoped to be able to see the living thing that belonged in it, though it held only the exercise wheel. It was odd to be buying a home for Václav at the end of owning him rather than at the beginning. Maybe he had done it because he felt bad about leaving the animal behind. It would make it easier to find someone to give Václav away to. He imagined that Milo would take him if no one else would, but he hadn't asked yet.

Běta and her friend, whose name was Lucie, were sitting at their regular table. When he entered, they were speaking quietly and confidentially, their Turkish coffees already in front of them, as well as a plate of wafer cookies, most of which, he knew from experience, they would insist toward the end of the lesson that he eat.

Lucie was a sort of elf. She squirmed, her teeth were slightly crooked, and her sharp cheekbones were often flushed. She was bolder than Běta—she had been a protester, Běta had once boasted on her behalf—and it sometimes seemed that Běta learned mostly by watching Lucie learn; Běta seemed distressed whenever it was her own turn to speak, and sometimes Jacob wondered if she continued the lessons out of concern for him rather than to satisfy any wish of her own—out of a tenderhearted fear, maybe, that he felt rejected by her family and a sense that it was her duty to prove that he hadn't been. If so, then it was his duty to see to it that the lessons had a cash value. He was fairly conscientious about preparing them; he photocopied advanced drills from a newly printed textbook that he had borrowed from Thom; he clipped short articles out of newsmagazines to discuss. Because it was Běta and Lucie he sometimes let himself carry out ideas that were a little silly.

When Běta noticed the exercise wheel inside the glass cage, she covered her mouth in amusement. —That is excellent, she commented in Czech.

"Will Václav study with us today?" Lucie asked in English.

"He already knows English," said Jacob. "He hears it a lot at home." He ordered his usual soda water.

"Ah, the mouse is not there," Lucie observed, as she looked at the cage more closely.

"Není myš," Běta said, with mild indignation. "Je křeček."

"Omlouvám se," said Lucie.

"English, English," ordered Jacob.

"He is not mouse," Běta repeated herself. "Is . . ."

"Hamster," Jacob provided. "*A* hamster."

"Is not *a* mouse," said Běta. "Is *a* hamster." In Czech she softly cursed the English language's perverse encumberment with not only definite but also indefinite articles. "But Václav," she continued, resuming her tentative English, "has he not . . . *a* home . . . already?"

"He lives in a pot right now," Jacob confessed.

"A pot!" Běta exclaimed. —But you are horrible, she said, shaking her head. —Since April! It'll be dark there.

Lucie shrugged and said, "He's a mouse," taking Jacob's side.

—But he *isn't*, Běta insisted again.

—I have bought him a home at the end of ends, Jacob said in his own defense. He switched back to English: "I had to buy him one, so I can give him away."

"Mmm," Běta began. She stared at Lucie blankly for a moment as if to draw from her the words she was looking for. "You don't love Václav any more?"

"I have to go back to America."

"That is sad," Běta matter-of-factly said.

"When do you go?"

He named the date he had chosen.

"So, we have still several lessons," Lucie said. "We must learn quickly."

"We must," Běta agreed.

"Do *you* want Václav?" Jacob asked Běta.

"I?" she asked, pointing to herself, flustered as always when a question singled her out. For a few moments she made a show of considering the idea, looking first at one corner of the ceiling and then at another. She folded her hands. —No, I don't want.

"She does not want," Lucie explained, with a sly smile, "how do you say, *závazky*."

"Bindings?" Jacob guessed. "No, that's not it."

"A child is one," said Lucie. "A garden."

"Commitments," said Jacob. "She doesn't want any commitments."

—May I tell? Lucie asked Běta, who rolled her eyes for an answer. "She is going to study at the faculty of law," Lucie revealed.

"Law school? Běta?"

"I know!" said Běta, nodding her head and then shaking it, as if she thought it was a great joke. "Law school! I! Can you believe?"

"She must," said Lucie. "It is a new world."

"And I will live at the school," Běta herself said.

"In the dormitory?" Jacob asked.

She threw up her hands at the prospect of incorporating such a word into her vocabulary, but she nodded.

"And your parents?"

"Mother is very sad." She shrugged. It was the fate of mothers. "Father is nervous, as you know. They—*ale ne, ale ne,*" she broke off.

"What?"

She hesitated. "If I say, you must . . . *mlčet?*"

" 'Be silent.' 'Not tell.' I won't tell. There's no one I could tell."

"Yes?" Běta said. Despite her loyalty she was eager to communicate her secret. "They want to send him to Kuala Lumpur."

"Jesus."

"First Warsaw, now Kuala Lumpur," said Běta, as if one exile inevitably deteriorated to another. She seemed to enjoy saying the Malaysian city's name. "They say, he did well in Poland." She shrugged again; her father's equivocal success was as far beyond remedy as her mother's sorrow. —It is fearful, fearful, she said in Czech, laughing blackly.

"It could be exciting," Jacob said, for the sake of politeness.

"Could be," replied Běta, unfooled, with cool emphasis.

They turned to their lesson.

For two days Václav ran on his new wheel incessantly. Once or twice, afraid that the animal was overdoing it, Jacob took the wheel out of the cage for a spell, but the creature seemed to be at a loss without it, and Jacob put it back. When Jacob woke up the third morning, he didn't hear the wheel turning. He found the hamster bestilled, resting on its side in the curve of the toy.

The timing was convenient. Had it really exercised itself to death? A warning to Americans, said Milo. Or maybe, Jacob speculated, there had been something toxic in the glue that held the cage together. Jacob emptied a pack of cigarettes and lifted the wheel up so as to be able to tip the hamster into the pack without having to touch its body. Once the two men had dressed, Jacob took a knife and spoon from the kitchen drawer, and they walked to the foot of the street, where a row of evergreen shrubbery kept citizens from approaching a fenced-off railroad track. While Milo stood guard, Jacob crouched and dug a hole under a shrub with the knife and spoon. When the hole seemed deep enough to deter a cat, Jacob laid the cigarette pack in. He scraped the dirt back over it with his shoes and stomped it down.

—It is curious, this burying a pet, said Milo.

—It's the custom in the suburbs of America.

—It's a gentle custom.

—We buried our dog in our garden, Jacob said, as if the memory was an explanation.

Their plan for the day, a Saturday, was to see the exhibit in the Powder Tower where a couple of Milo's photos were on display. By the time they reached náměstí Republiky, they were hungry, so they bought *palačinky*, or sugared crêpes, for a few crowns from a cart on the southwest corner of the square. The corner was unshaded, and they blinked in the glare as the vendor poured two thin pools of yellow batter onto his griddle, which was still shiny and steel gray at this early hour. As they ate, a dust of sugar fell on Milo's shirt, an olive green one that Jacob liked because of a brass ring pull on its zipper. Milo fluttered the shirt to bounce the sugar off, but the oil on his fingers left a stain where he held the fabric. He swore, and in frustration he pulled the chest of the shirt up to his mouth and tried to suck the oil and sugar out of the cloth, thoughtlessly exposing the soft, pale column of his belly.

—You're crazy, said Jacob.

—I know already, said Milo.

Between the heat of the sun and the sugar in his blood, Jacob felt a little muzzy. It was just too much here, he thought to himself, looking around the square at the dark Renaissance gingerbread of the Powder Tower and at the pink Art Deco wedding cake of the Municipal House, with its muddy atlantes bent under iron-and-glass polyhedra. Were the polyhedra supposed to represent lights? Light didn't weigh anything. To decide at the last minute to stay would be melodramatic. It would seem too much like being under the spell of something, too much like not choosing. It was how a drunk or a child might make a decision.

An unmarked iron door in the side of the Powder Tower was ajar, and they climbed a narrow, winding stairway until they were the equivalent of four stories high. They stepped into a small, square chamber, the size of the tower's footprint minus the defensive width of its walls. Tall, slender windows lit all four sides of the room. At the folding table customary at all exhibitions, a shy girl with heavy glasses was sitting with a pouch of cash, a roll of tickets, and a neat stack of posters. They paid her a crown fifty each for entry, and Jacob paid another twelve crowns for the poster, which reproduced a photograph within a photograph. The inner photo, a state portrait of Masaryk, the First Republic's president, looking like Freud but without glasses, was printed in green. The photo that contained it was a crowd scene in Wenceslas Square, printed in pink. In the pink crowd scene, the green Masaryk photo was being waved like a flag. —THE PHOTOGRAPH IN REVOLUTION, read the title. Jacob rolled the poster up gently to avoid creasing it, unaware that it was going to be lost in the transatlantic mail a few weeks later.

The heavy stones of the tower and the stillness of the air kept the chamber cool. They were too high up for more than a faint echo of the street's noise to reach them. The exhibit was scheduled to close in a week, and except for the ticket seller, they had it to themselves.

Milo, as a contributor, had attended the *vernisáž* a month and a half before and he let Jacob lead the way. The images were arranged chronologically, beginning with the march on a Friday evening in mid-November that had begun the revolution. To honor a medical student mortally wounded during an anti-Nazi demonstration half a century earlier, the government had permitted marchers to climb to Vyšehrad that evening from the valley below it. After laying flowers at the national cemetery, the marchers had been emboldened by their own speeches and shouts—and no doubt by the recent sight of East Germans fleeing to the

West through Prague's West German embassy—to continue north along the river. They had turned right at Národní třída and had approached Wenceslas Square. Photographs showed Národní full of people with hectic faces—waving sparklers, shielding candles from wind, and carrying hand-lettered banners calling for freedom, democracy, and the end of the Communist Party's political monopoly. At the end of Národní, the protesters had been met by a row of riot police. The police had been wearing white helmets and had been carrying clear Plexiglas shields the shape of coffin lids. A young woman had held out a carnation to an even younger policeman, her blond hair as disorganized as the carnation's frilly petals, his features as elegant, formal, and empty as the ribbed Plexiglas balanced on his arm. In front of the police barricade some of the protesters had set up a sort of garden of candles on the cobblestone; one of Milo's snapshots had caught two young men holding four candles up to the lit cigarette of a third man, who was inhaling to kindle sparks. Soon after the shot was taken, the police had encircled a number of the protesters and forced them to exit single file through a narrow arcade, set off from the rest of the street by columns. As the protesters had passed through the arcade, a number of them had been singled out by the police for beatings.

—Were you hurt? Jacob asked.

—I wasn't encircled, Milo answered. —I'm a homo. I was *furt* watching the police, what directions they were stepping in.

—Were you afraid?

—We were so aroused. There were thousands of us.

—Were you angry?

He paused. —You're such a serious boy. He stared at one of the photos and held his breath, trying to recall what it had been like. For a moment Jacob had the impression that Milo might have stood in the street that night, at the foot of Wenceslas Square, in the pose that he was standing in now, his shoulders squared, his head a little hunched down. —Well, it was peculiar. It was rather that it was our turn.

—What do you call this? Jacob asked, pointing to a banner in a photo.

"Transparent," said Milo.

—Did you carry a *transparent*?

—I was carrying a camera.

The next few photos depicted a congeries of candles, flowers, ribbons, saints' images, and fragments of clothing—not unlike a roadside shrine in America for the victim of an automobile accident.

—This was in the arcade on Saturday night, the next night, Milo explained. —We thought, that someone had been killed.

—Who?

—Some student of mathematics. But he was in the countryside. It was a rumor.

Jacob remembered Rafe saying that a story had been planted in the heads of the college newspaper editors.

—They say some girl on drugs thought it up, Milo continued. —She had, they say, instructions. But we all thought there had been a death.

—So there was no Palach this time, said Jacob.

—Palach? No, that was the Prague Spring.

—I mean, no one had to die this time, in order for there to be a revolution. There didn't have to be a sacrifice.

—Well, that could be. I no longer remember what this one's name was, the one who wasn't dead.

Carl would appreciate the postmodern touch of a fiction in the middle of the history. Jacob would have to write to him about it. To bring themselves to the point of revolt, the Czechs and Slovaks had needed to feel sorrow and indignation, and their desire had summoned into the world a story that could focus those feelings. Of course the story would have had to come through a person whose attachment to reality was troubled—someone like an addict, whose need was more than she could stand and would tell any story to hold attention. It was better, in the end, that it had come about through a lie than through a death. Jacob wondered if the lie had been helped along, maybe by somebody Rafe knew. It would probably have been pretty easy for an American to fool the Czechs, because Americans were so trusted by them. For now they were, anyway. And for a little while longer. The question was whether one could ever use a story while seeing through it—whether one could know the truth in the moment and still do what one needed to do in order to free oneself.

Milo sidled up to one of the narrow windows and peered down at the square below, keeping himself on the near side of the stark prism of light that fell through the window, so that the light silhouetted him. He seemed to have been made bashful by something, but

Jacob didn't know whether it was by his role as the taker of some of the exhibit's photographs or by his memory of participation in the events, which even now made grand claims for themselves. There was something solemn about the numbers of people in the photographs that followed, still impressive no matter how many times Jacob had seen photographs like them before: hundreds of thousands had gathered in Wenceslas Square in the days following the police brutality, and then even more, a few days later, in the fields behind the empty pedestal of Stalin's monument, standing for hours in the cold listening to speeches by people offering to be their new leaders, offering to take them into a new world. Looking at the seas of faces, Jacob wondered if it was the emotions of so many people that caused the political changes or the other way around. Were the quantities of feeling released necessary to change, or were they a side effect of it? The people looked content to be where they were, yet "aroused," as Milo put it. Jacob's old, confused longing to take part in the lost moment in the pictures came over him again—the longing to belong to the moment, to have been alive in it. The odd thing was that he had hated to be part of any group in America. Maybe he had never been in a group large enough—a group so large that he could approach vanishing in it, which was a kind of freedom—or maybe he had never been in a group devoted to freedom itself.

—Father wanted last night, for me to tell you, that we can sleep at our house sometimes if we want. It isn't necessary always to sleep at yours.

Jacob realized that he was looking at one of Milo's photos: it showed a middle-aged man in a trilby and a tweed overcoat who had climbed a tree in Wenceslas Square for a better view. The man's hands were folded, a tricolor swatch was pinned neatly to his lapel, and he was watching and listening with a placid expression. Visible through the bare branches of his tree was a poster, affixed to a lamppost, celebrating the eighteenth congress of the Communist Party of Czechoslovakia. In the center of the poster there was a bold outline of the Party's characteristic star.
—What does that mean, your father's message? Jacob asked.
—Just that, I think, Milo said, speaking softly, but not so low that he would seem to be hiding their conversation from the ticket seller. —If ever it's more practical for us to be in Strašnice than Žižkov.
—That is kindhearted of him, said Jacob.

—He's like that. He's courteous.

—But he doesn't know.

Milo shrugged. —He invites you, as a friend of mine.

—I don't know, if I can, admitted Jacob.

—I know, said Milo. —If you were staying, maybe one day it would in fact have been more practical for some reason to stay there. Accidentally more practical.

One of the photos was awry, and Milo absentmindedly adjusted it.

—Your photos are great, Jacob said.

—But no.

—Yes. They're witty, and that isn't common in photos.

—You ox.

If Jacob had been forced to explain, he might have said that he was declining out of a sense of proportion. To accept would have started a new story that he didn't have time to finish.

—Don't you want to continue as a photographer? Jacob asked. —As for a career?

—What would I photograph? We no longer have a revolution.

—I don't know. There's a war in Bosnia.

—I'm fond of my skin.

—Then elsewhere.

—Someday I will, maybe, he said, and shrugged again. —There's an old song about the time, when Czechs had to serve in the Austrian army. 'I'll no longer fight to conquer Herzegovina.'

> *Za Císaře Pána, a jeho rodinu,*
> *Já už nechci vybojovat Hercegovinu*

Milo half whispered, half sang. The song had a waltz rhythm, and it was a little melancholy. The ticket seller looked over at them and smiled awkwardly, uncertain whether she was supposed to have taken notice.

As Kaspar had hinted, it was a little difficult to get hold of Rafe, but Jacob felt that he ought to make an effort to say good-bye to him. It was after all Jacob's idea now that the risk of a love's ending—the inevitability of it, really—was something an adult had to accept, and if Jacob were consciously to keep away from Rafe, he would be giving in to a less rigorous conception, an idea of love as a struggle that it was possible to win if one chose the right side. It wasn't possible to win; one had to side with the idea that love couldn't always be held onto.

"You want to see *me*?" Rafe asked, from the doorway of his Havelská apartment building, when on the fourth or fifth try Jacob at last found him at home one evening. "What an honor." Instead of inviting Jacob upstairs, he arranged on the spot for them to meet the next afternoon in a café on Národní třída.

The café was located in the *piano nobile* of an eighteenth-century palace that had recently been restored to the family from whom the Communists had nationalized it. The Communists must have appreciated the beauty of the rooms, because they had left intact the height of the ceilings and the generosity of the windows. The walls were now painted a delicate shade of lime, with white trim; in the windows were boxes of daisies.

The café was one of the new, fully private enterprises. The maître d' was reluctant to let Jacob wander among the tables in search of Rafe; he understood it to be within his authority to escort Jacob to a table of his—the maître d's—choosing. He trailed Jacob skeptically; only after Rafe had accepted Jacob's presence with a welcoming nod did he retreat. Moments later, a waiter brought Jacob a menu, unprompted.

"It's awfully professional here," said Jacob, admiring the menu, which wasn't a mimeograph.

"Isn't it great?" Rafe replied.

Jacob studied the menu; he was wary of meeting Rafe's eye, though Rafe seemed at ease—composed, beneath a surface animation.

"So what can I do for you?" Rafe asked, as soon as Jacob had ordered an espresso.

"I'm leaving next week."

"Back to the home front, eh."

It was the middle of the afternoon on a weekday, and only a fraction of the tables were occupied. At one of them sat three businessmen in Western suits and ties, their table cluttered with American-style memo pads and thick pens. Most of the other patrons were young people, writing postcards alone or chatting in small groups. Their cheeks were sunburnt, and they had tucked their unwashed hair under bandannas. Tall nylon backpacks sagged on the floor beside their chairs.

"They're ruining the city, aren't they," remarked Rafe. "The backpackers. Though I suppose it's hypocritical of me to regret the Americanization."

"Why?"

"Why indeed. I can't tell sometimes, Jacob—are you really naïve or do you put it on?"

"I think I really am."

"You almost convince me."

"I try to be polite," Jacob said.

"Oh, that's different. That could be quite dangerous even," he said with approval. "Have you seen Kaspar lately? Did he tell you how Goethe murdered Schiller? He's figured it out."

"He didn't mention it."

"Because, who wrote *Faust*? It couldn't have been Goethe, who never had a dramatic idea in his life. Schiller wrote it, Kaspar says, and then the devil convinced Goethe to murder him and steal his manuscript. So a *little* bit of it *is* by Goethe, actually. The part about being tempted to kill Schiller. He's made a list of parallel passages."

"He said he hadn't seen so much of you lately."

"This was about a month ago. Maybe he's moved on. Heard from Melinda? Does she write to you?"

"Not much, but she doesn't have as much reason to write to me as she does to you."

"And she doesn't have as much reason *not* to write to you as she docs to me."

"She wrote me once," Jacob admitted.

"And me once, too. She must be going down her list."

Rafe noticed that his own teacup was empty and tried to pour himself more, but he was out. He summoned a waiter and lifted the lid of his pot to ask for a refill of hot water. There was a trace of impatience in his manner, a hint that it might be considered gracious of him not to mind having to ask. No one would have dared reveal impatience to a waiter in the fall, before the latest changes. It was like Rafe to have discovered that one could now take such a liberty.

"What are you going to do in America, tell me again?" Rafe asked.

"I'm going to school."

"But what are you going to do?"

"I don't know."

"The life of the mind," Rafe conjectured.

"I guess."

"I wonder if it'll be enough for you. You've learned a lot here. Not everyone picks up Czech."

"I only picked up a little *taxikářština*. I was dating Czechs and I had to be able to get by."

"But that's something, too. I bet you learned a lot about that, and I bet it's not like it is in America. This'll interest you, I think. I had a friend, another 'Harv,' as Annie calls us, who interviewed with the 'State Department' around the time we were graduating, which is what they tell you to say when you're interviewing for one of the intelligence agencies, as you probably know. They gave him these puzzles to solve, sort of like the kind that the consulting firms give at their interviews. They told him, for instance, to imagine you're with an 'asset,' someone you hope will bring in information. Imagine you're with an asset who's gay. He's nervous. He's suspicious. What do you say to put him at ease?"

"You mean, what do you say because he's gay?" Jacob considered. "That's a tricky one."

"Isn't it? Because if you say *you're* gay, and he makes a pass at you, what then? Even if you really are gay, you might not want to go to bed with him."

"You could say you're a tolerant person."

"And that would be highly laudable in you, but a bit abstract, don't you think? Everyone likes to say they're tolerant."

"I give up."

"My friend didn't get it, either," said Rafe. His hot water had come and the old leaves were steeping; he fussed with the pot to give Jacob time for one more chance. "Come on."

"No idea."

"You say you have a gay brother," Rafe revealed, pouring himself a new cup.

"Oh, that's good," Jacob admitted. "Because then he thinks you're an ally, but there's no possibility of romantic trouble."

"Isn't it good?"

"Too bad I couldn't figure it out."

"I imagine you're usually pretty good at puzzles, though. At thinking about people. There's almost always a story that people are telling about themselves, and sometimes you can get them to tell it ever so slightly differently."

"I wouldn't know."

"Don't be bashful. I'm just saying, what if you're bored? At this school. What if you're of my party without knowing it?"

"Which party is that?"

Rafe grinned for an answer.

"Goethe's or Schiller's?" Jacob asked. "You could have told me that *you* had a gay brother," Jacob ventured.

"But I don't need to win your trust. After all we've been through. Or do I, still? Is that what you're saying? That's not very nice, if so. But then I might answer that it wouldn't be a matter of urgency for me because you don't really know anything. Not anything strategic."

"I really don't," Jacob said carefully.

"See?" Rafe met his gaze. "You say that with such conviction. That's why I say you could be dangerous."

"Dangerous to whom?"

"You tell me," Rafe challenged him. "To the Schillers of the world?"

"Wasn't it Schiller who explained the difference between naïve and conscious art?"

"To the Goethes, then. Who can be even trickier. See, I think you're more like me, and that you'd find that even what my friend went out for was too tiresome for you. You wouldn't like the having-an-allegiance part of it."

"Did your friend get in?"

"He said he didn't, but I imagine they tell them to say that, too."

"So you don't have an allegiance yourself."

"Do I seem to? I don't think I'm the sort who really has a home team."

"Kaspar said something like that about you."

Rafe sipped his tea. "I think Kaspar and I understand each other, finally."

Leaving requires work. There were a few more books that he meant to buy. He had to sort his clothes into those worth bringing home and those that it made more sense to leave behind. He decided that his fire-proof red blanket should stay but that his Russian-made windup alarm clock could come home with him. He left Václav's empty cage on the sidewalk one morning, and it was gone by the time he returned from teaching in the afternoon. Chores distracted him from such maudlin trains of thought as wondering whether he was likely to recognize in the moment the last time that he and Milo went to bed together.

In Paris, it would be convenient to have a student ID card, and he raised the subject with Henry, who worked after all at the Czechoslovak government's office for foreign students. Henry invited him to drop by his office some morning. He could issue Jacob a card, and they could have lunch afterward.

Annie helped Jacob buy a scarf for Jacob's mother one afternoon, and they ended up at the foot of Wenceslas Square, listening to the four Czech teenagers who sang early Beatles songs under the English-language name the Dogs. The Dogs were surrounded by a ring of young *trampové*, native and foreign. Cheery and dated, the songs corresponded to a popular idea of the revolution as an outburst that had been meant to happen at the end of the 1960s and had somehow been preserved from staling or souring.

"They're not bad," said Annie. They were standing at a slight remove from the Dogs' admirers.

"It's funny that people come halfway around the world to hear songs they already know."

"Everything needn't always be improving."

"I didn't say it was wrong to like it."

"But you think it's simple." The song ended; there was a clatter of applause. "It's a pity you can't stay longer," she added, before the young people began to sing again.

"I can't."

"I didn't say I thought you could. There are things you mean to do." He was silenced by her flattery, if it was flattery. He believed in his ability to turn away from things. It had served him in the past, and it had become associated in his mind with the indifference to outcome that he had decided was the best way to approach a love affair. He even felt a little sorry for Annie on account of the strength of her attachments—her inability to turn away—though he knew it was ugly of him.

To shift the topic of conversation, he told her that Henry was going to make him an ID. She wondered why none of them had thought to ask for one before, and it occurred to her that she ought to ask for one as well.

That night, at the Dům, she persuaded Thom to come along and ask for one, too.

By this chain of events, rather than through any sentimental planning, Jacob found himself having lunch in Josefov with his closest friends a few days before leaving. The meal began awkwardly, because Henry had balked when they had showed up in the lobby of his building. In a formal voice, he had asked them for documentation, and Annie had been taken aback. "But you *know* I haven't got any," she had objected. Thom had begged off, assuring Henry that he hadn't meant to put him to any trouble. Jacob, however, had brazened it out. He had brought with him a letter from the school that he was going to attend, which constituted if not proof—he was not a student there yet—then a sufficient cover. In the lobby, after Henry had vanished back upstairs to type up Jacob's card, Annie stewed. "I suppose after all *I'm* not going to poxy Paris." It took a quarter of an hour for Henry to make the laminated card.

They walked down the block to a restaurant where Henry and Carl used to eat, recognizable to Jacob from a photo that Carl had taken there. A large window opened the dining room to the street. From a stone wall, an oversize oil portrait of one of Czechoslovakia's last Communist leaders, a bland and corpulent face, ironically presided. When they chose a table—they took the corner of a communal one—Annie was still letting Henry have it.

"I had no notion of you as such an upholder of the laws," she said.

"They pay me to be."

"It's quite *responsible* of you."

"He does work for the government," Thom said. "He has to keep a clean backside."

"I wouldn't know about that." A few wisps of her peach-red hair fell across her face as she looked down to study the menu, but rather than smooth them away she merely looked steadily through them. Henry was sitting beside her, and it was easy for the two of them, facing the same direction, not to meet each other's gaze.

"He has to be something of a politician, I suspect," Thom continued. When Annie didn't reply or look up, he added, "But come the revolution, eh, Annie?"

"Oh, if it's for the revolution that you want it . . . ," Henry suggested.

"Now he sings a different tune," said Thom.

"For the revolution but not for his friends," Annie observed.

"He did make a card for Jacob."

"His papers are all nicely in order, aren't they," she replied.

No one had an answer.

"If it's very important to you . . . ," Henry began, after a pause.

"Oh no, I don't much care, really. I'm merely noticing. I had you figured as more of a free spirit, as it were. That's all. But perhaps I'm the only free spirit left—the only one who isn't fecking off to do something sensible with his life. Among the lot of you, at any rate."

"Henry and I are staying, aren't we," said Thom. "For a while more, anyway."

A waiter came and took their orders.

The rhythm of what happened in restaurants now passed without any special observation by Jacob. The strangeness had gone out of this world; he had got used to it here. If it was strangeness that he was after, he was going to have to look elsewhere, the way Rafe was going to.

"Have you got any fags?" Annie asked Thom, once the waiter had left.

"I haven't. It's against the rules now."

"What's this?" Henry asked.

"Every morning I put the crowns that I would otherwise spend on them into a bowl in the kitchen. As a fund for the young Tomáš that is to be—for his nappies and such. I've saved quite a sum. Sparty don't come free, you know."

"They're quite dear," Annie agreed.

They complimented Thom on his willpower.

"It will *all* be more difficult now, won't it," Annie generalized. "Everything will take more strength."

"Will it be as bad as all that?" Thom asked.

She nodded a few times, as if encouraging herself. "It's better to face up to it."

"It will be a shame to say good-bye, won't it," Thom admitted.

As the next to leave, Jacob didn't know what to say. Henry, too, was silent. Jacob had claimed in the writing group that stories that resisted being stories weren't to his taste, but his own search had brought him to a position not unlike Henry's, or what he imagined Henry's to be. He was playing the rogue consciously now. It was a different place in the story than he was used to looking from. He wasn't sure he could see everything—everything, at any rate, that he was used to being able to see. He wasn't sure he knew where to look in order to see it.

Their food came. "If we're free spirits," he risked, "we have to be free to leave, don't we?"

"Och, your theory again," Annie said. "Must you leave in order to prove it?"

According to his policy of insouciance, he didn't let himself think about losses, except for a vague awareness of a sort of clearing that his departure was going to make in his life.

"Are we to meet your friend ever?" she wondered.

"I don't know."

Thom broke in: "As it happens I'm under instructions from Jana to invite him and the lot of you to that immodest swimming hole this weekend. The one she was on about the other night."

"I thought you weren't to be allowed to go," said Henry.

"She's consented to take me after all, though she prefers to remain decent herself, given her condition, on the understanding that her restraint isn't to hinder the rest of us."

"I'm game," said Henry.

"I wasn't expecting anything so bold of you," Annie told Thom.

"Did you think me a shrinking violet?"

"It isn't that, exactly."

"There aren't many in Prague with ginger hair like Thom's," said Henry. "It might be said that he has a sort of duty."

"I suppose it does come with a certain responsibility."

"What does?" asked Annie.

"The magnificence of my person."

"Gah."

"There are the Czech women who use henna," Jacob suggested.

"Do you think they use it down there as well?" Thom asked. "That would be a sight."

"And you'll bring your man, if we go?" Annie asked Jacob.

"I think he'd be up for it."

"I'd like that," she said.

"Are you suggesting that the sight of myself alone would not be a sufficient draw?" Thom asked.

"You can be such a git."

Jacob's last lesson was with Milena's children. On the bus, he noticed a tickle in the back of his throat. Was he getting sick again? He didn't have time to. He sat still and closed his eyes to preserve his energy. The long, boxy bus seemed to try to curve with the hills as it mounted them. The engine whined with strain on the upward slopes, and he felt himself sway with inertia against the vehicle's turnings.

He found the lindens on the family's street heavy with dark, wavering leaves, offering themselves to the late-afternoon sun like so many opened hands. On the vine that climbed the wall in front of the family's house, the leaves were also broad and plentiful. Looking up into them, as a breeze riffled them and as he waited for an answer to his ring, he saw hidden there, as if he were looking up the leg of a man's shorts, a constellation: unripe pearls of fruit, small, pale, and tight. When the breeze dropped, the leaves covering the fruit also subsided, but having seen one cluster, he was now able to see others peeping from under drapery elsewhere in the vine.

In greeting Jacob, Prokop and Anežka were noisy with pleasure. When Jacob asked their mother for a pain reliever, he explained that his throat hurt. He didn't want her to think that he minded the children's loud cries.

—May I? she asked, and pressed the back of a hand to his forehead.
—The color isn't good, she said of his complexion. She shifted her gaze to the side and to the floor, nervous about having taken the liberties of touching him and looking at him closely.

—A Paralen will be enough for me, he said.

She hurried to fetch the medicine. He didn't like it that her worry about him was so marked. Even now, in their last session, he was still hoping to give a more professional cast to the relationship between them—to hold himself at a certain distance from her. Prokop and Anežka, hushed by the mention of illness, observed Jacob without any apparent expectation that he would speak to them before he had been ministered to. No other children from the neighborhood seemed to have come. Maybe their parents hadn't seen the point of paying for education that would have no sequel.

—I'll cook something for you, Milena said, when she returned with a box of pills and a glass of water. —I'll cook you a Jewish soup. Do you know it? Wait, wait, she said, as she moved toward the kitchen.

—I don't need, he called after her.

—Garlic, lemon, and honey. It will cure you.

—We're starting the lesson, Jacob said.

—Wait, wait, she told him again. When she saw that he wouldn't, she put her head down, continued into the kitchen, and struck a match to light a burner, as if to prove that she could be as stubborn as he could.

At his usual seat at the dining room table, Jacob began to clap his hands. Prokop studied this not-quite-adult behavior with embarrassment and admiration, but Anežka squirmed out of her chair, unconsciously covering her ears to shut out the sharp sound that he was making.

"Anežka, where are you going?" he asked in English.

She hesitated. She looked toward the kitchen.

"I can clap more softly," he offered, as he did so. "Why don't you sit down," he suggested, nodding at her seat, as he continued to clap. Here he was, prematurely using a command that he had been hoping to teach, he reproached himself. He knew Anežka couldn't understand his words, but he thought she could follow his body language and he didn't want to capitulate and speak Czech so early in the lesson.

"Moment," the girl finally replied. She darted off to find her mother.

Jacob stopped clapping while he tried to figure out how to react. Prokop meanwhile took the clapping up, as if to signal that he was willing to play Jacob's game, whatever it was, whether his sister played or not.

"Wait a minute." Jacob held up a hand, and the boy stopped. To compensate himself for his disappointment, the boy began kicking a leg of Jacob's chair.

Through the kitchen door, Jacob saw Milena bend down to accept a whispered confidence from her daughter. After a conference in lowered voices, the woman and the girl walked slowly back into the central room together, with a certain ceremoniousness, Anežka leaning shyly against her mother's side, one of Milena's arms sheltering her daughter's head and shoulders like a bird's wing.

"Please, I am sorry. Anežka make *pudink*. Do you know, *pudink*?"

"Pudding."

"For you," Milena continued. "Please, will you eat? She has fear, that you will not want." Milena paused, at the edge of her capacity in English, and watched Jacob searchingly. —It isn't necessary to eat the Jewish soup, she continued, in Czech. —But if you have a taste for pudding, it is your last day, and Anežka hoped . . .

"Of course," replied Jacob. "I'll eat the pudding right after I eat the Jewish soup."

"Thank you, thank you."

Anežka's face relaxed into smiles as Milena translated his words. It was awful that he had nearly hurt the girl's feelings because of an arbitrary wish to be more impersonal as a teacher. She was a child; children can't help but care about the people they're with. For that matter maybe it had been a little cruel of him to wish to be more impersonal with Milena.

"Five minute, soup, I bring," Milena said. "Please, teach," she added, by gesture throwing her children once more onto Jacob's hands.

It took an effort of will to clap loudly again, because Jacob now felt abashed by how cruel he had been, and a quantum of something like cruelty is needed when making a loud noise. But Anežka was merry with restored confidence and Prokop was pleased by the resumption of the game, and soon Jacob was able to fall in with their high spirits. He taught them how to command each other to clap and to stop clapping, to wave and to stop waving, to smile and to stop smiling. The soup, when Milena brought it, proved to be a sort of tisane, clear and bittersweet. Its heat soothed him. Anežka monitored him closely as he drank, and as soon as he took his last sip—at the moment he clinked his cup down into his saucer—she hopped up and ran to her mother, calling, as she ran, for the distribution of her pudding.

Milena brought three small blue bowls out on a steel tray. It was a sweet, chilled custard, the color of good butter.

—You aren't giving yourself any? Jacob asked.

—With husband, later, Milena explained, though she sat down at the table to share their enjoyment.

—It's very good, Jacob complimented Anežka after his first spoonful.

—But what's good is at the bottom, she protested. —You have to *mine* for the good part.

There was a compote under the custard.

—Gooseberry and cherry, Milena informed Jacob.

—Did you cook it yourself? Jacob asked Anežka.

—With Maminka.

—It's sublime, Jacob said. —Thank you.

—Sublime, Anežka repeated to her mother.

—He thanked you, Anežka, Milena prompted.

—You're welcome, she told Jacob, in a singsong voice.

After Milena cleared the dishes away, Jacob took from his backpack a photo of a lion, which he had cut out of a magazine advertisement. Introducing the animal as Simon, Jacob explained that the children were only to obey the commands that Simon said, not those that Jacob issued on his own authority. After a few repetitions of this rule, a few samples of commands said by Simon and commands not said by him, and at last a gloss in Czech, the children understood, and they played Simon Says with him for the next half hour, taking turns according to the rule that whoever failed to know when to obey became the next issuer of commands. From time to time Jacob introduced new vocabulary by acting out its meaning; from time to time the children asked him for vocabulary that they themselves wanted to introduce. At last, in their familiar pattern, the children began to grow a little wild, rebelling against the burden placed on their attention, and their mother, drawn by their outbursts, which she felt a responsibility to suppress, became too much the focus of the children's attention for the game to continue, and Jacob had to surrender the lesson.

"Please, if I may," Milena said. "I have for you a gift." She was holding it behind her back.

Jacob, stowing his props away in his backpack, stopped himself from saying that he didn't need one.

"It is for memory," she continued.

As she opened her fist, he knew he would leave the gift behind, unpacked, in his apartment. It was a figurine of Christ, made of ivory-colored plastic, like a chess piece. It wasn't a crucifix; the god was merely raising his hands above his head in benediction, a pose that prompted in Jacob a pagan analogy to the extended arms of a flying superhero. An American child would be tempted to zoom the figurine around the room. Prokop and Anežka, though, were observing quietly, respectful of the solemnity with which their mother had invested the object. Jacob wished that Carl was still living with him and that he could share a de-mystifying laugh with him about it when he got home. It was going to look uncanny in the Žižkov apartment. Maybe he would put it in a drawer right away rather than wait to forget it.

"Thank you," Jacob said. He was on his guard. It would only be reasonable for Milena to want to know whether he had enough faith to appreciate the gift.

"It is of church," she said. She laughed at the clumsiness of her English; she knew that it went without saying that such a figure belonged to the realm of churches. "It is of church we go," she tried again to explain, gesturing to her children and herself. She didn't indicate whether her husband went, too. Out of her there then spilled an account in Czech of her church, its location, its architecture, the saint it was named for, the priest who ministered there, and the parishioners who had returned to worship since the revolution. Jacob wasn't able to follow everything she said and retreated into nodding. He couldn't tell if the church was something new in her life or something that she was newly free to speak of. He had the sense that it stood for, or stood in the way of, a need that threatened to be overwhelming. In sympathy, maybe in hope of solidarity, he glanced at Prokop and Anežka, but there was no sign in them of resistance, unless they had taken refuge in a mild blankness.

From this blankness their mother released them by declaring that the family was going to go for a walk. Prokop groaned, then ran to get his soccer ball so that the time spent on the walk wouldn't be a total loss. He began kicking it despite his mother's insistence that he wait until they were outdoors. Anežka took up her doll Květa. Then, changing her mind, she asked if she could carry one of the rabbits from downstairs. Halfheartedly and unsuccessfully Milena argued that Prokop should leave his soccer ball behind and walk quietly and dutifully. To Anežka she pointed out that the rabbit would be frightened by the soccer ball if by nothing worse and might run off.

—But he's a good boy, Anežka said, in the rabbit's defense.

"Please," Milena asked, returning to English, "have you time? We take walk. You with us? For last time."

"To the church?"

Milena shook her head, as if embarrassed now by her earlier confession.

"I could go for a little walk," Jacob said, even though he wanted to get home to Milo.

—There is a prospect nearby, Milena said, resorting again to Czech. —It's possible from there to see far. Are you well enough? I wanted to show it to you. And I will gather herbs for you, so that you can make a tea for yourself. For your cold. She named the plants that she wanted to gather, but even in English the names would have been lost on Jacob. —It will cure your throat, she promised.

Jacob made an effort to look open to believing in the remedy. He was never going to see anyone in the family again, and it seemed important not to disillusion them—to leave them with the impression that he believed in as much as they did—that he might keep the figurine, that he might go home and brew the tea.

Outside, after they had put on their shoes at the foot of the stairs, the group paused while Anežka unhooked the door of the hutch, took one of the rabbits into her arms, petted him, introduced him to Jacob, and regretted that the walk would be too scary for him. Prokop juggled his soccer ball on a foot. When the ball went astray into the garden, where orange squash blossoms were beginning to shrink inward, sensing the removal of the sun's attention for the day, perhaps beginning the plant's greater withdrawal into maturity, Jacob said, "Whoops," and retrieved the ball for him.

Prokop giddily took up the new word as a refrain. Milena shook her head at the ebullience and glanced at Jacob to see if it was trying his patience. She scolded Prokop when he followed his ball into the street, though there were no cars, and Anežka, now rabbitless, joined in scolding him. The group followed the chaotic energy that seemed to be focused in the soccer ball, as if they were being pulled forward by something that kept slipping out of harness. Jacob was aware that he was still fighting off illness; he had the sense that there was a certain inefficacy to his idea of the world—that his idea wasn't apprehending the world as firmly as it was necessary to apprehend it—that he and the world weren't altogether real to each other.

At the end of the first block the group turned left; at the end of the next block, right. They left the neighborhood where the family lived, full of older villas, for a sort of real estate developer's fallow, a scrub wilderness of oddly shaped vacant lots on the periphery of a newish complex of *paneláky*. Children had beaten a dirt path through the fallow. Milena paused to twist a few purple twigs off of a spindly willow; in a clearing that was still sunny, she picked what looked like tiny daisies. She carried her little harvest in a pouch that she improvised by holding up the skirt of her apron.

The ground grew so uneven that Prokop gave up on his soccer drills. A white boulder ended their path with an appearance of having fallen across it. Prokop was the first to scramble up. Upon joining him, Jacob saw that they stood at the top of a tall escarpment. An eroding slurry of blond rock led downward; far below, the black Vltava wound in a gentle S. Milena warned her children to keep away from the edge, but it was not so steep as to be dangerous.

By suppressing the growth of the scrub trees, boulder and slurry had cut a sightline to the west. The vista to be had through the gap was a pastoral. On the far side of the river, in a bend of it, a green field was being mown. Horses were drawing steel rigs, under the guidance of men with dinted torsos, so distant and so far below that only the facts of horses, steel, and men were discernible. The scene was gilded by the sun, which was low but still full of power. Because no more than the presence of the men could be seen, Jacob let himself stare at them freely, his motive for staring all but invisible. Beyond the field, stretching toward the horizon, waited a forest, over which a blue haze seemed to be settling.

"What's over there?" Jacob asked.

Milena shrugged. —It's called Šárka.

"It's a park, isn't it," Jacob said.

—Yes, it's a valley, she answered.

He thanked her for having brought him to see it.

"Please I must to say something you," she said in her halting English. "You have free . . ."

"Freedom?"

"Yes. Is very dear." She seemed worried by the boldness of her words, and she looked at him as shyly as her daughter sometimes did, despite the whiteness of her hair and despite the matronly bun that she wore it in.

"You're free here now, too," Jacob said. "Here in Czechoslovakia." It felt safer to him to turn away her compliment; he wasn't sure he understood it.

"Maybe I said not right. You have free"—she paused, having remembered that Jacob had corrected her use of the word, but already having forgotten how he had corrected it; she soldiered on—"free"—she reached out and without touching pointed quickly, in a birdlike motion, at the left side of his chest, wincing as she did so at the temerity and possible rudeness of the gesture—"here. It is not America, in you. *Ne jenom.*"

"Not only," Jacob translated for her.

She bit a curled index finger as she tried to conjure up more of the words that she needed. Meanwhile, at the front of the boulder, Prokop was throwing pebbles into the vista, and Anežka was helping him by gathering ammunition. It occurred to Jacob that he wasn't going to get to see the children grow up, but there were a lot of children he wouldn't see grow up. "You have sensitive . . . ," she tried again.

"How does being sensitive make me free?" Jacob asked. He had become fairly certain that the opposite was the case.

Milena laughed and shrugged, embarrassed either because she couldn't answer or because she hadn't understood his question. "You know things," she tried again. "Of people."

Jacob nodded noncommittally.

With some agitation she pointed at his breast again. "You have sensitive sool."

She must have looked the word up. "Soul."

"Ah." She seemed remorseful at having mispronounced it. "And I, too, have sensitive soul," she continued, "that you will return to us."

"Maybe you mean 'impression'?"

"Yes. It is *osud.*"

"*Osud* is fate."

"Yes," she said, smiling, taking his translation for concurrence.

Though he hadn't quite understood, he was reluctant to ask her to explain further. It would have been immodest to ask to hear a compliment repeated, and if her interest in his soul was no more than a pretext for proselytizing, maybe he preferred not to see through it. It was possible after all that she had sensed something about him, even if only a penumbra of the sexual freedom that he had kept hidden from her. And it wasn't unreasonable to hope that he might return some day. Her mysticism fell in with an idea of himself that he wanted to keep as long as he could—of himself as a person on an errand whose nature was still unfolding. When he left, in a few days, he was probably going to have to give the idea up; in America it probably wouldn't be salutary to go on imagining that he had an exemption from a more definite, a more disillusioned story. He was willing to leave behind with Milena, or with his memory of her, like a thread left behind in a maze, the possibility that his errand could somehow persist despite his abandonment of it, in a disregarded state, incomplete unless someday he found a way to come back to it.

—What if I were to write you a letter, Milo suggested.

—Well, I'd look forward, Jacob replied.

It was Saturday, the day chosen for the swimming party at Šárka. The two of them were seated aboard a tram that was clattering steadily forward, unimpaired, in accordance with its nature as a mechanical thing, by the heat that they were passing through. Earlier passengers had opened all the windows of the car, and by the tram's motion a wet air was drawn in, which buffeted ineffectually against their faces, knees, and arms. Jacob had set his backpack on a seat, but Milo was too well mannered to make use of any more seats than the one that he was sitting in, even though they had the car nearly to themselves. Milo's towel was slung over one of his shoulders, and he had begun to sweat a shadow under it, as well as a circle in the front of his shirt.

They were traveling along the road that led to the airport. There seemed to be more placards advertising rooms than Jacob remembered having seen when he had come this way with Melinda half a year before, to pick up Carl, though he wasn't confident of the accuracy of his memory or the precision of his earlier observation. He wondered if the bus tomorrow would take him along the same route.

Though a little melancholy, he felt perfectly healthy, perhaps because he had brewed Milena's wild-herb tea the night before. Milo had
advised him to stew the twigs in one pot and the daisies in another, but
Jacob had impatiently tumbled all the debris into a single soup bowl,
over which he had poured steaming water. The flotsam had swirled up;
with a spoon he had tamped it back down; and after a few minutes the
fluid had turned a shade of sepia. It had tasted bitter. —Maybe you were
supposed to peel the twigs, Milo had belatedly suggested. Jacob had
forced himself to drink it despite its acerbity.

The tea seemed to have worked—or if the tea hadn't, a night's sleep
had—and this morning Jacob's head and mind were clear. He felt so
lucid that he seemed to perceive not only the world but also the biases
of his mind in perceiving it. He saw quite clearly, for example, that
he didn't want to leave Prague the next day, as he had planned to. He
would have to take himself in hand. For a long time, he had only been
able to enjoy himself by bearing in mind that he was leaving—that his
irresponsibility was temporary—but today he was so close to his departure that he could feel it, the way one can feel the touch of a shadow
on a hot enough day, and he saw that he had to alter the structure of his
mental compensations. He saw that now he would only be able to enjoy
the time that remained if he pretended to himself that he was going to
stay after all. He had to tell himself that it was another person who was
going to ride the bus along this highway tomorrow—an optative self,
riding a lane or two parallel to the tram that was now carrying him.
He was fond of the scuffed, painted metal of this tram's interior, its
gray bucket seats, the sleepy fullness of the air, and the warm-cool side
of Milo's right arm against his own left one. A sense of anticipation
also held him in the moment. If he were to leave tomorrow, nothing
would come of these attaching feelings. So it must be the case, he told
himself with conscious illogic and mendacity, that he wasn't going to
leave.

—How will your friends look on me? Milo asked, interrupting Jacob's thoughts.

—When you're naked?

—That, no. Nakedness lies on your heads, with you Americans.
How will they look at me as a person?

—I don't know, said Jacob.

—With their eyes, I guess, Milo joked.

—They'll look at you as a friend of mine, Jacob proposed.

—They're not buggers.

—They're not, Jacob confirmed. —So maybe they won't look at you at all.

—They're not even Czechs.

—It'll be normal, Jacob tried to assure him.

In a while the tram came to its last stop, halfway around a little rotary that it circled in order to reverse direction. The conductor shot open the doors, and before Jacob and Milo could gather their bags, he stomped heavily out of the car himself to have a cigarette and stretch his legs. To the north was parkland, thick with greenery. Milo nodded good day to the conductor, who was pacing as he smoked, and the two of them walked into the artificial wilderness.

The trees and lawns made the day's heat more temperate. After about ten minutes they came to a reservoir, long and narrow. Grass ran down to its banks. The opposite shore, where maples stooped over the water, unmirroring because shadowed, was only a stone's throw away, but to the north the clear, dark water continued until it bent rightward out of sight. Looking that way, the eye could mistake the body of water for a slow-moving river.

Annie and Elinor waved. They were sitting on an oatmeal-colored blanket, which Annie must have smuggled out of the Dům. They were wearing white blouses over their swimsuits. Annie parked her oversize, amber-tinted sunglasses in her hair, as they approached, and squinted up at them.

"Těší mě," she said to Milo, extending her hand. "That's right, isn't it, Jacob?"

"I think so."

"Ale mluviš tak pěkně česky," said Milo. You speak such pretty Czech.

"*Ale ne*, unfortunately," Annie replied. "I can hardly speak it at all, as you'll discover. But it is good to meet you at last. Jacob has kept you so to himself."

Milo smiled noncommittally, perhaps uncomprehendingly.

"I mean it's a pity we haven't met before," Annie continued. "But that's Jacob's fault, you know. *Vina je jeho*. It's his mistake."

"Muže za všecko, ovšem," Milo answered.

"What does he say, Jacob?"

"He says I'm to blame for everything."

"He is, isn't he," Annie agreed. "And most of all for leaving us. Bloody selfish of him."

"Těší mě," said Elinor, from beside Annie on the blanket.

"Oh, this is Elinor, sorry," said Annie. "Kamarádka moje."

"Těší mě taký," replied Milo, with a half bow.

"You're a right fool, you know," Annie said to Jacob, aside. "He's quite fit. *I* wouldn't give him up."

"Co říká?" Milo asked.

Before Jacob could translate, Annie interrupted with alarm: "Don't *tell* him." She made a show of looking crestfallen at Jacob's willingness to betray her confidence.

"Řeknu ti to později," said Jacob.

"No, don't tell him later, either. That's no better." Then she thought better of her tactics and addressed Milo again herself: "I said you were handsome," she confessed. She checked with Jacob: "Is it all right, to say that?"

"Říká, že jsi hezký," Jacob translated.

"No, diky," Milo thanked Annie, with some embarrassment.

"He isn't blushing, is he?" Annie asked. "I meant it in a kind way."

"I don't think anyone really ever minds being told they're handsome," Elinor reassured her.

"No, sometimes they do mind. Sometimes it isn't polite to make personal comments," Annie said, regretfully. "I'm sorry I'm all aflutter," she told Jacob. "I've never met any of your 'friends' before."

"'Friends'?"

"Whatever you call them. What does he do, by the way?"

"He's a photographer," Jacob answered.

"To sotva," Milo qualified.

"He says I'm exaggerating," Jacob translated.

"Well, it's hard, isn't it, to *be* anything," Annie said. "So I find, at any rate. I'm a teacher, for the moment," she declared to Milo. "Učitelka," she said, patting her chest.

Jacob and Milo laid their towels down beside the women's blanket.

—You, said Milo, nodding at Annie, —are Irish?

"I am, yes," said Annie, with a glance at Jacob to acknowledge him as the source of the information.

—And you, Milo continued, looking now at Elinor, —also Irish?

—English, Elinor answered in Czech.

—I, Moravian, Milo told them.

—Truly? said Jacob. He hadn't ever asked. —I thought you were a Praguer.

—Father and Mother were born in Moravia, in a little town that is called Náměšť. We have a river and a little bridge with statues, like the Charles Bridge but prettier. We have a small, square castle.

—Is there a forest? Jacob was trying to picture it.

—Around the castle. Forest and meadows. I'll show them to you. When you come back.

Jacob had never said he would come back, but the word for "when" could also mean "if." —I'm from Texas.

—And where do you keep your hat? Milo replied.

They subsided into individual enjoyment of the sun. Annie lowered her glasses. Milo stripped off his shirt and settled back on his elbows. Jacob remained sitting up, his arms around his knees. He wished he could see Milo's little town, but he would give that up, too. One had to impose a certain amount of structure on one's life.

"Are we sitting in the nudist section?" he asked.

"I believe so," said Annie. "Those two women to our right are topless, aren't they."

"Oh," said Jacob. "I hadn't noticed."

"I didn't suppose you would. Don't look at them now, Jacob."

"I don't get to see breasts very often."

"You aren't any less philistine, are you. I don't know why I thought you would have a measure of sophistication."

"Up there seems to be the clothed section," explained Elinor, pointing north. "Where those little buildings are." She indicated a few white-painted wood structures, set back a ways from the water, the sort of summer makeshifts whose little-cared-for condition suggests that they must always have existed, always as sun-faded as they are now.

Annie spotted Jana, Thom, and Henry walking toward them up the green. To counterbalance her belly, Jana was leaning back on her haunches as she walked. The men had slowed their pace to match hers.

"May I share your blanket?" Jana asked. She let Thom and Henry, each holding one of her hands, lower her into a sitting position. Like her belly, her breasts, too, were round and heavy, though they were loose, whereas her belly was taut. Thom took a folded blanket out of their bag and tucked it under her as a cushion.

"Can I slip off your shoes for you?" offered Annie.

"Pull," she said to Annie, as she raised one foot at a time.

"Still wearing all your togs, I see, Annie," Thom commented.

"I've only got on just the swimsuit, really, under this camisole."

"Just this side of decency."

"For the time being. Have you met Jacob's man?"

"Is this him?"

Milo was made slightly bashful by their attention. Jana spoke to him in Czech: —When Jacob told us, that you showed him Amerika, I told him, that I would show him Šárka.

—A good idea, Milo agreed.

"Thanks for arranging it," Jacob said in English.

"It is for myself that I arranged it. I must take every pleasure while I still can."

"*And* she came to look at the girls," said Thom.

"It is true," Jana admitted. "I wanted to see them and to remember that I will look something like one again some day."

"You're beautiful now," Annie assured her.

"Feel." She pulled the back of Annie's hand against her cheek.

"Like a baby's bottom, isn't it," Thom said.

"It's so soft," Annie agreed.

"And here's another transformation," said Thom, clapping his hands on his potbelly.

"Is it soft, too?" Henry asked.

"Feel it for yourself, why don't you," Thom offered, lifting up his T-shirt to expose it.

"That's all right, mate."

"It's like a baby's bottom. A hairy, old baby. Anyone else like a feel?"

"Jacob was telling us that Milo is a photographer," Annie said to Jana, in an effort to restore propriety.

—Only as an amateur, Milo said.

"Jana's a journalist," Annie told Milo.

—An interpreter, Jana for her part qualified. —I merely work with journalists.

Milo asked Jana the name of the newspaper. When he didn't recognize it, she excused him, on the grounds that after all it was written for expatriates like their boyfriends rather than for Czechs like themselves.

—I'm not working right now, Milo said of himself, —but next month I'm going to Karlovy Vary, where I'll be a casino employee.

—A casino, Jana replied. —They must trust you.

—I might only be some kind of barman. I don't yet know.

—You'll learn excellent English.

—Well, maybe German.

In first conversations, a gay person not in the closet sometimes has to fend off a straight's attempts to demonstrate good will. In conversation with Jana, Jacob thought, Milo might also feel obliged to show that he didn't mind that his job was less promising than hers. The difference in the nature of their jobs was likely caused, after all, in large part by the difference between his gay world and her straight one.

—What's your subject matter, when you photograph? Henry asked in Czech.

—Visitors from the West.

—Seriously?

—No. I don't have a special subject matter.

—He photographed on Vaclavák during the revolution, Jacob boasted on Milo's behalf.

—Like everyone, Milo said.

—But that's an idea, said Henry. —Visitors from the West. Do you have your apparatus with you?

He hadn't brought it.

"Because we're quite a sight, the lot of us," Henry continued in English. "Another day, perhaps."

"Though there isn't likely to be one, is there," said Annie. "Not with Jacob, I mean. It's a pity Melinda isn't here, for that matter. I imagine she's quite beautiful without her clothes on. Why do you give me that look, Thom? Don't you think she would be?"

"I'm quite sure of it."

"Did you fancy her, too?" Annie asked. "I suppose we all did."

The friends settled in. More towels and blankets were unrolled.

Books and magazines were taken out of satchels. A tube of Western suntan lotion was passed around. The possibility of nudity was mooted, but one had to be clothed to buy refreshments, and several of the friends were already hungry. A delegation walked up to one of the white clapboard stands where, under letters spelling out OBČERSTVENÍ, red letters bleached pink by the sun, it was possible to buy a *párek* on a cardboard square with the traditional daub of mustard and heel of stale rye. Some of the friends also bought bottles of Staropramen.

After eating and drinking, no one was in a rush to swim. They lay idly in the heat and light. Because it made Jacob slightly giddy to have Milo beside him among his friends, he made a series of stupid jokes that Annie pretended to disapprove of. Milo's presence was like a boast that Jacob was making—a boast that it turned out his friends liked to hear him make because they took it as a sign of trust in them. The obvious thing to say was that it was like taking off his clothes with them, at a spot where people came together to take off their clothes, and like taking off Milo's clothes, too, and discovering, once all of them were in their glory, that they were all quite beautiful.

"But I'm not sure I'm going to take my suit off," Annie said, when Jacob confusedly tried to share his idea of the comparison. "If it were just you and poxy Thom . . . ," she suggested. "But as it is, I find it a bit shy making. You don't mind, do you?"

"I don't mind," said Jacob.

"Milo's gay, you know, Annie," said Thom, who'd had a few. "He won't be looking at you."

"I know *that*," she said, exasperatedly. "It's not anyone in particular. It's just that the group is rather large, is all."

"If a fine specimen of manhood such as meself declines to be bashful before the male gaze," Thom persisted, "there's no call for you to be, is there."

"The 'male gaze,' Thom?" Henry queried.

"I believe that's what Carl used to call it, when he went on about it," Thom replied. "In his cups."

"I think I will just sit here then," Annie said, "rather than take a swim, if you don't mind."

"Allowing us quite a sight of ankle nonetheless," commented Thom.

"Perhaps it should just be the boys for now," put in Elinor, linking an arm in Annie's for solidarity. "Though we'll watch the show."

"Well, go on, then," said Annie. "If you're going to take off the rest of your kit."

"You first, Henry," said Thom.

"*Me* first?" Henry echoed. "All right, then."

"Are you serious?" Jacob asked.

"All at once, then, men," Henry declared.

"That's the spirit," agreed Thom.

The Western men unbuttoned their shorts and pulled off their briefs. A moment later, Milo followed their example, and the men walked with a studied lack of hurry toward the water. Jacob was at first careful not to look at Henry and Thom, but it seemed wrong to make a fuss of not looking, and of course it was right to look at Milo, though dangerous. It was a relief to reach the water, and though the water was cold, they waded steadily in, shivering but stoic, so as to gain the modesty afforded by its reflections and be exempted together from exposure as well as from clothing, though their limbs, once submerged, continued to glow pale and greenish beneath them, in images rippled and scattered by the shifting of the reservoir's surface.

"It's very strange to be completely naked in public," said Jacob. "It isn't something Americans ordinarily do."

"I can't say it's very English, either," replied Henry. "It's a Scottish thing, though, isn't it? With the kilts and all that."

"It is," Thom answered. "On account of our climate, I believe."

Henry spouted a little fountain up and over his head. "What does it call to mind?" he asked.

"I thought it would be sexy," said Jacob, "but it's not really sexy. Everyone's so exposed."

"Speak for yourself," retorted Thom.

"You're *not* exposed, or it *is* sexy?"

"Quite an invigorating set of sensations, I'd say."

"But for you it feels *less* animal?" Henry asked Jacob.

—What are you discussing? Milo wanted to know.

—The sense of nakedness, Jacob answered.

—Philosophically?

—More or less.

—Why it's strange, Henry interpreted for Milo. —What distinguishes it from normal social relations.

—The metaphor is, maybe, without clothes a person becomes his true I, Jacob suggested.

—You're open, Milo offered. He seemed to be describing the feeling that he was having rather than speculating about it, as Jacob and Henry were.

—Momentarily you're authentic, Henry took up the idea.

—Moment by moment.

—Especially if you're male, joked Milo.

—About certain things a naked man can't lie, agreed Henry.

—What if no one was ever ashamed, suggested Jacob.

A flurry of laughter reached them from shore. Annie and Elinor had changed their minds, and to Jana's applause, scorning to shield themselves with their arms, the women ran to the water and splashed noisily, conspiratorially in. They swam deliberately away from the men. Annie even shouted a taunt, though the men weren't able to parse it.

"I believe I'll head to shore," said Thom, "while it's safe to make a break for it."

"I'll join you," said Henry.

Left to themselves, Jacob and Milo decided to swim across the reservoir and back before leaving the water. They rested when they reached the shallows of the far shore. Milo shook his bangs out of his eyes and though he was touching the bottom swept his arms back and forth as if he were still treading water. Now that they were apart from the others, their presence together in the water changed character.

—It would be a version of utopia, your idea, said Milo.

The maple leaves above them were motionless, Jacob noticed, as if the leaves had forgotten themselves in a task. By this time of year, the leaves weren't going to change in form again, the way Jacob had imagined that he himself might still change after he returned to America. The work of the leaves now was to continue to be the selves they had become. It occurred to Jacob, rebelliously: What if he had misunderstood himself? What if he wasn't going back for the sake of his ambition? What if his ambition was just a name he gave to a kind of conformity, and he was going back because he wasn't brave enough to live a life that wasn't expected of him, a life so far from any road that there wouldn't be any signposts or milestones?

He was panicking, he told himself as a way of hushing his doubts.

He was safe here; he didn't need to panic. The water around them remained cool and quiet.

They all came to see him off the next day at the bus station.

—Don't read it now, Milo said as he handed Jacob a letter. —Read it when you're without Prague, as if I had sent it to you by post.

Jacob cried, of course, as the bus pulled away. From being people whom he had lived among, his friends became a picture of the same people, falling behind him.

Not long after the bus got on the highway, he had a moment of horror—of seeing, briefly, the mistake that he was making. He considered getting off the bus. He kept considering it, even after it would have meant having to ask to be let off in a town and having to take a train back to Prague. But he felt that he needed to move forward, a need the illusion of which he was to chase for a number of years. It was to be a long time before he accepted that it isn't necessarily foolish to change one's mind dramatically, a much longer time than the duration of a bus ride between Prague and Paris. He consoled himself meanwhile by losing himself somewhat in his feelings: *Now*, he thought, *now, now I know what it feels like to go into exile.* Quietly he watched the countryside unrolling itself by the side of the bus. He watched it, Milo's letter on his knee, until about the time the bus crossed from Germany into France. Then he opened the letter.